TALES OF THE OUTLAW MAGES SET 1

BREAKER & EFFIGEST

AMY CAMPBELL

This is a work of fiction. Names, characters, places, and incidents are the product of the author's imagination or are used fictitiously. Any resemblance to actual persons, living or dead, events, or locales is entirely coincidental.

TALES OF THE OUTLAW MAGES SET 1
Copyright © 2024 Amy Campbell

BREAKER
Copyright © 2021 Amy Campbell

EFFIGEST
Copyright © 2021 Amy Campbell

Cover design by Amy Campbell

Edited by Vicky Brewster

Author photograph by Kim Routon Photography

Map by Amy Campbell, designed in Wonderdraft

Pegasus chapter heading art © Depositphotos.com.

ISBN-13:978-1-957816-00-5

First edition: January 2024

10 9 8 7 6 5 4 3 2 1

www.amycampbell.info

v120423

AUTHOR'S NOTE

While at its heart, *Breaker* is a story of overcoming, there may be parts that are difficult for some readers. Please be aware *Breaker* has instances of animal injury, animal death, blood, bullying, death, recreational drinking, kidnapping, guns, murder, violence, and weapons.

Effigest is a tale of change, which is never an easy thing. There are portions of the story which may be difficult for some readers. Please be aware *Effigest* has instances of abuse, kidnapping, imprisonment, blood, guns, violence, and weapons.

Pronunciation Guide

Everyone who's ever learned a word by reading it has, on occasion, come across the problem of thinking, "Wait, how do I pronounce that out loud?" I hope this will help with that! However, this is just a guide so if you enjoy pronouncing one of these differently, there's no harm in that!

Argor – ARR-gor
Blaise – BLAY-z
Canen – KAY-nun
Chupacabra – CHOO-puh-cah-bruh
Desina – Dess-EE-nuh
Effigest – Eff-IH-jest
Emmaline – Em-uh-LINE
Emrys – Em-RISS
Faedra – FAY-druh
Faedran – FAY-drun
Ganland – Gan-LUND
Garus – Gair-USS
Geasa – GESH-uh
Hospitalier — Hoss-pih-TAL-yer
Hugh Fasig – Hyoo Fah-sig
Iphyria — Ih-feer-EE-uh
Itude – Ih-TOOD
Izhadell – Iz-UH-dell
Knossan – NOSS-uhn
Knossas – NOSS-us

Kur Agur – Kur Ah-GRR
Leander – LEE-ann-dur
Leonora – LEE-oh-nor-uh
Lucienne – Loo-SEE-ann
Marian – Mayr-EE-uhn
Marta – Mahr-tuh
Mella – Mell-UH
Nadine – Nay-DEEN
Nera – NEER-uh
Nexarae – Nex-UH-ray
Oberidon – Oh-BEAR-uh-don (alternate: Oby – Oh-BEE)
Oscen – Oss-KIN
Petria – Pet-RIA
Phinora – Fin-OR-uh
Ravance – Ruh-VAN-s
Reuben – Roo-ben
Seledora – Sel-uh-DOR-uh
Seward – SOO-urd
Tabris – Tab-RISS
Theilia – Thee-LEE-uh
Theilian – Thee-LEE-uhn
Theurgist – THEE-ur-jest
Tylos — TI-lohs
Vollie – Voh-LEE
Zepheus – Zeff-EE-us

Sea of Hermeia
Highhorse
Ravance
Godfury Range
Phinora
Bitter End
Izhadell
Duskgarde
Oscen
Brinewatch
Eskela
Griffin's Crest Mountains
Arbor
Umber
Salt-Iron Range
Argor
Greylight
Untamed Territory
Thorn
Cobalt Bay
Salt-Iron Lake
Lower Godspine
Fortitude
Asylum
Uncertain
Theilia
The Stormclaws
Stormwatch
Canen
Petria
The Gutter
Rainbow Flat
Burntbridge
Ironrun
Mella
Fort Courage
Bristle
Starvation
Knossas
Bigwater
Ondin
Desina
Freeport
Ganland
Sunrise Harbor
Seaside
Etla
Gulf of Stars
The Jewelled Sea
Nera
N
E
S
W

BREAKER

TALES OF THE OUTLAW MAGES BOOK ONE

CHAPTER ONE

Mavericks and Magic

Blaise

"Keep your hands where I can see them."

Blaise startled at the voice; its edge dangerous as the strike of a rattlesnake. He kept his gloved hands high as he walked into the Black Market. The speaker loomed in the pale blue glow of mage-lights that lined the long, narrow room.

"Sorry. First time." Blaise winced at the hesitation in his voice. He had every right to be here.

The man leaned his forearms along the top of the bar, dusty bottles lining the shelves at his back. His eyes were little more than slivers above a black bandanna pulled over his nose, his shoulders broad like a bull. "Who sent you?"

"Marian Hawthorne." Blaise's heart raced. Like the other man, he wore a bandanna to conceal his face. Blaise considered the bandanna helpful on the dusty road, but he chafed at the anonymity of it for this transaction. According to his mother, the proprietor was a wanted man. It was safe to assume that anyone setting foot in the building was in similar straits. Anonymity kept all involved from swinging from a tree.

All the same, the cotton bandanna tickled his nose. It was irritating. He was hard-pressed not to twitch or rub at it. Blaise reminded himself appearances mattered at the Black Market.

"Monthly delivery?" the man asked, not bothering to identify himself. Blaise didn't see anyone else in the building, so he presumed the man was Tom Slocum, proprietor of the Black Market.

"Yes." Blaise stepped closer when the silhouette of Slocum's shoulders relaxed.

"Good." Slocum's eyes glittered as he got a read on Blaise despite the bandanna. "You bring a list?"

A list. Right. His mother needed more supplies for her alchemy. The Black Market specialized in hard-to-find items. "Y-yes." He lifted a hand to the pocket at his chest.

Slocum watched him with an air of boredom. Blaise pulled the list out and laid it out on the bar. Slocum picked it up, scanning for a moment before looking back at Blaise. "Unload your wares. Set 'em on the bar."

"Right." Thankful for the guidance, Blaise turned on his heel and walked to the door. He pushed it open with his shoulder.

The blazing sun was a harsh contrast to the interior of the Black Market. Blaise tugged his hat lower to protect his eyes from the glare. The family pony, Smoky, ignored him as he walked over and opened the tailgate of the cart. Blaise adjusted the fit of his gloves and then pulled out the first of the wooden crates.

The contents of the crate sloshed with the movement. Soft linen protected the glass vials from damage. One at a time, he carried all three crates inside and set them on the bar.

Boots creaked on floorboards as Slocum moved in the back room. Blaise looked around, taking the measure of the interior while he had the chance. The bar stretched across most of the room; a few barstools butted against it. Someone had shoved broken tables and chairs into one corner. The dusty remains of a billiards table sat near a window. Blaise supposed the Black Market might have been a saloon, once upon a time. Or perhaps it still *was* a saloon. He wasn't sure.

Aside from his nervousness at dealing with Slocum, the worst part of the place was the lack of airflow. It was stifling. Between his hat, bandanna, and gloves, a steady trickle of sweat beaded his face. He mopped the sweat on his forehead with one sleeve, causing his glove to ride up.

An ominous click sounded behind him. He turned to see Slocum on the other side of the bar, rifle trained on him. "Keep the glove on. I know what you are, Breaker." His tone was low and brooked no argument.

"Sorry," Blaise squeaked, cheeks burning with shame. He tugged the glove to cover the exposed skin on his hands. *How does he know about me?* Had word of his magic traveled this far? Had one of his parents told him?

"I'd hate to put Marian's kin in the bone orchard," Slocum drawled, his tone cool as he settled the rifle beneath the bar. Blaise shivered as he realized the man meant *cemetery*. "So you get the one warning."

Blaise nodded stiffly. He hadn't expected to have a gun pulled on him. Now he knew better. Someone with the savvy and experience of Slocum would be ready for trouble. Even if it was accidental.

"Supplies are here." Slocum hefted a crate onto the bar and shoved it toward Blaise. "Coin will follow in a moment."

Blaise hesitated before pulling the crate closer and peering inside. Brown paper bags obscured the contents. He plucked them out one by one to be sure they were the correct items. Delicate purple mushrooms clustered in one bag. *Check.* Bright yellow moss in dried strips in another. *Check.*

Slocum used a crowbar to pry the lid off one of the crates. He watched as Slocum rifled through the contents, a greedy smile twisting his lips.

"Your mother's quite the alchemist. You have her talent?" Slocum resealed the crate and set it aside.

Blaise shook his head. "Not with these hands."

Slocum grunted. "True enough." He picked up a crate and carried them one at a time to what Blaise supposed must be his storeroom. The proprietor returned with a clinking leather pouch. He set it on the bar in front of Blaise.

"Normal monthly pay." Slocum settled his bulk atop a nearby barstool.

Blaise opened the pouch, spilling the coins out to count. *Trust no one to hand you the right amount the first time,* his parents had cautioned him. Alchemy was not an inexpensive profession or openly practiced. Slocum's eyes tracked him as he counted. Blaise's muscles tensed in response. He would be glad to leave this place.

"You a maverick?" Slocum asked after Blaise finished counting.

Blaise startled at the question. It was blunt and came out of nowhere. "What?"

Slocum gestured to Blaise's gloved hands. "You're the sort the Salties look for. Mage. What happens if they come calling in Desina?" He jerked his chin toward the door. "Mavericks are the ones that get away from 'em."

"Did something happen?" Blaise tried to keep the quiver from his voice.

For hundreds of years, the Salt-Iron Confederation pushed their ideology across the face of Iphyria. Their goal: to bring mages and magical creatures alike under their control. Geography and a stubborn

Consul kept Blaise's homeland from the Confederation. Had something changed?

Slocum gave a slow shrug. "I hear gossip."

Of course you do. Blaise didn't know the full story on the Black Market, but rumor had it each day of the month it moved to a new location. On the fifth, it existed in this ramshackle building near the border of Desina. Slocum's peculiar magic allowed him ample opportunity to collect news from all over.

The Black Market proprietor intimidated Blaise, and though he wanted to ask more, he didn't. "Thanks. I'll be on my way, then."

Slocum nodded. "Nice doing business. Keep your hands to yourself, Breaker."

Stress knotted Blaise's neck. He shoved the pouch of coins into his shirt pocket. Blaise grabbed the crate of supplies and balanced it against his hip as he headed for the exit. His goal was to put some distance between himself and any further uncomfortable conversations.

He loaded the supplies into the back of the pony cart, securing the crate to prevent jostling during the journey home. Blaise pulled an empty bucket from the back of the cart. He walked over to a well located a short distance from the Black Market and filled it with fresh water, then carried it over to the parched gelding.

Smoky dunked his muzzle into the bucket and drank his fill while Blaise weighed his options. He was hungry. His choices were to either picnic where he was or eat as he drove back. Smoky knew the way better than he did and would need little guidance. *The sooner I get home, the better.*

Once the gelding had his fill of water, Blaise emptied the bucket and stowed it in the cart. He untied Smoky from the hitching post, then stepped up to the driver's seat. Smoky didn't wait for him to settle into his seat and disengage the brake before starting on his way.

"I know. I want to get home, too," Blaise muttered to the pony.

Blaise pulled his lunch out from beneath the seat. Smoky had things under control. As he ate, he reflected on the outing. It had been a success. He ticked off his accomplishments. Represented his family's business at the Black Market. Sold their wares. Successfully returning home with pay. True, his parents had laid everything out for him to make failure difficult. All he had to do was follow their directions. Blaise was going to declare it a victory regardless.

Hopelessness washed over him as he looked at his gloved hands. He had endured scorn and ridicule about his magic for most of his twenty-two years. It was difficult to feel betrayed by his own flesh. *Walking disaster. The reason we can't have nice things. Ruiner. Sorcerer. Heretic.* He had heard every name in the book. Every single one of them felt true. Because of his magic, he wasn't just an example of a failure to launch—he was a burned-out boat at the bottom of a river.

But today might change things. He had a measure of success. A smile ghosted Blaise's lips. If they let him go to the Black Market again next month, he stood a chance of convincing them he could move to another town. He could seek an apprenticeship.

Blaise could start a new life.

Only if he could hide his magic. He had tried to do that before. And failed.

It was worrisome that Slocum knew of his magic. But other than treating him with caution, the man hadn't seemed upset by it. Not like the townspeople in Bristle. Anyone who knew Blaise in Bristle would turn and walk in the other direction if they saw him. No one wanted to be around to see what destruction his magic wrought.

He noticed a hole developing in the palm of his right glove, exacerbated by his nervousness. His magic was always at its worst when he was out of sorts. Blaise poked at the hole with his index finger. Before too long, his skin would be visible. He made a mental note to check and see if they had leather at home for patching.

Smoky laid back his ears and whisked his tail, nudging Blaise from his rambling thoughts. The gelding rumbled a warning nicker. Blaise cursed. *I'm an idiot.* He had forgotten one of the most important rules of the Gutter and Untamed Territory.

Always keep an eye turned to the sky.

A golden speck in the clear cerulean sky bore down on them as Blaise drew Smoky to a tentative halt. There was no sense trying to outrun them, not now. Only a fool would try to outrun an outlaw on a pegasus.

Blaise drummed a rhythm on his knees, trying to recall the old nursery rhyme about appeasing outlaws. His mind was a blur as he tried to think. *One gold coin? Two? Two sounds right.*

He pulled the coin bag out of his pocket. With luck, the outlaw wouldn't perceive him as a threat or a more valuable target than he was. Blaise shook two coins out of the pouch and pulled the laces taut. He hoped the outlaw didn't consider the crate of alchemy supplies worthwhile plunder.

The pegasus landed on the road, hooves striking the ground with a thunderous impact. A dust cloud swirled around steed and rider. As terrified as Blaise was, he had never seen a pegasus this close. It was *stunning.* The equine's coat glistened the same color as the golden coins in his palm, its mane and tail as pale and fine as gossamer. The afternoon sun glinted off the pegasus's wings as they splayed open, banded like a hawk's. Blaise inhaled a breath of admiration as the steed arched its neck.

The rider slipped down from the modified saddle, boots striking the ground with a sharp staccato. Blaise jumped, startled back to reality. The grizzled outlaw used his knuckles to tip back his hat, locks of blond sticking out like straw. He pulled up his flight goggles, snapping them into place against his forehead. The breeze tugged back the man's tan duster. In the blink of an eye, Blaise stared down the gleaming barrel of a sixgun.

Things had been going so well.

———————

Jack

THE MORNING WAS RIFE WITH FRUITLESS LEADS AND FRUSTRATION. NO ONE would blame him for hankering for trouble by spooking a random traveler. Even outlaws deserved some of the simple joys in life, Jack reasoned.

The pony cart trundling along on the road from the Black Market to the Desinan border was too much of a temptation. Jack tried to leave his antics for more deserving targets. A Salt-Iron baggage train or stagecoach was a prime target. He left the smaller merchants unharried out of common courtesy.

But not always. Outlaws weren't known for being *polite*.

His palomino pegasus snorted, prancing in place to block the pony's path. Jack cocked his head as he assessed the slack-jawed driver. Even with a bandanna covering his nose and mouth, Jack knew he was young. He didn't have the demeanor of the more experienced Untamed Territory merchants, who traveled with a rifle close at hand. *This kid is as green as a new blade of grass.*

Jack slipped down from Zepheus's back as the kid goggled at him. He pulled out his revolver in a fluid motion—he meant business. He liked the way a greenhorn's eyes went all white-ringed like a spooked colt when his sixguns came out.

Zepheus's nostrils cupped as he inhaled the unfamiliar scent. <I would leave him alone if I were you.>

Jack cast a furtive glance at the stallion, lips taut in response to the telepath's suggestion. *Another mage,* Jack mused. That was the only time Zepheus would suggest caution. The kid was young, not even worth calling a man. Jack had dealt with worse.

"You travel in the Gutter." Jack's voice was gruff and dangerous. "You got the toll?"

The young man kept his eyes averted. His terror at facing a flesh and blood outlaw froze him in place, like a rabbit in a hawk's shadow. A momentary pulse of satisfaction zinged through Jack. Yeah, he still had it. The kid stood before him, gaping. Jack cleared his throat to remind him he was waiting.

"Um," the kid mumbled as his brain caught up with the situation. He rubbed at his hands as if they itched. Then the kid looked down at them, uncurling one hand. Golden coins flashed in the sunlight. "Yes."

Jack's lips quirked. He took a step closer, but Zepheus snorted and shook his head. <I don't like whatever his magic is. I've not come across anything like it before.>

Jack scowled at Zepheus; the stallion minced backward like a spring colt. The pegasus was no coward. He flicked his eyes back at the young man. "What are you?"

The youngster fumbled over the question. "What?"

"Magic," Jack clarified, annoyance creeping into his voice. "What's your *magic*, boy?"

The boy's lips clenched into a thin line, his eyes downcast. "They call it Breaker."

Jack ignored the magical designation and clung to a single word in the sentence. "*They?* You know other mages?"

The kid blanched and shook his head. "N-no." He looked ready to throw the coins and bolt.

Jack studied him, the familiar wave of disappointment washing over him. *Another day without another damn lead.* He gave the young man a curt nod. "Get out of here then, kid."

Sparks lit the young man's eyes at the epithet. "I'm not a kid. Take your gold."

The kid was a dunderhead to think he could talk like that to an outlaw. Jack's right hand tightened against the engraved grip of his sixgun. Zepheus nickered a warning. Jack huffed out a breath and waved a hand in dismissal. He walked over to the pegasus and prepared to mount, turning to address the kid with one boot in the stirrup. "I don't take payment from greenhorn mages. Now get off my land."

"This isn't your land," the young man shot back.

Jack narrowed his eyes, moving away from his steed. "The Gutter belongs to the outlaw mages. Who do you think you're talking to?"

Zepheus snorted, fretful. <Knock it off. You're going to make things worse.>

"Then take the damn gold," the young mage ground out, jumping down from the cart and walking toward him with his hand extended. The golden coins winked in the afternoon sunshine.

Jack didn't fully register what happened next. The kid either tripped or took a bad step in a divot in the road—the cause didn't matter. His arms pinwheeled comically for balance. Gold coins arced into the air, chiming as they clattered to the dirt. The force of the fall sent the young man tumbling into Jack and they sprawled to the ground in a jumble.

A yelp of full-throated horror split the air as the young mage disentangled himself from Jack and crab-walked away, face pale. "Take it off, *take it off!*"

Jack rolled into a sitting position, staring at the young man. *Is he addle-brained?* What in Perdition was wrong with him? "What in Faedra's name are you caterwauling about?"

"I touched it. Your gun. Take it off. Throw it away. *Something!*" The young mage trembled, every muscle taut. His hat tumbled away in the breeze, knocked off by the collision.

Jack rose to his feet, glowering as he replaced the sixgun in the hip holster. No one in their right mind would demand an outlaw to disarm himself voluntarily.

<Jack—!> Zepheus never had the chance to say more.

Jack was accustomed to the sound of gunfire. But nothing prepared him for the discordant concussion of his sixgun meeting its maker. The revolver at Jack's waist exploded with a deafening crack, the cylinder and barrel ripping away from the grip. The force of the explosion shredded his holster. Faedra must have given him the grace of her protection because he wasn't hurt, but his ears rang from the force of the blast. Jack's mind raced, grappling with the unexpected event.

He howled, a feral combination of rage and fear. Zepheus moved closer, protective, ears pinned back as he pawed the ground in warning. Jack unbuckled the gun belt and dropped it like it was a hissing snake. The shattered revolver tumbled out of the ruined confines of the holster. The barrel struck the ground with a pathetic metallic clank.

Aside from the mangled mess of the gun, they were fortunate it hadn't done damage to either of them. Though Jack didn't feel charitable about the situation.

Jack pulled a small pistol from his boot, his arm quivering with rage as he pointed it at the young man's head. He said nothing. There were no words for the anger that clawed through him. Only actions.

Golden wings burst in front of him. Zepheus stood before the young mage. The stallion's ears were back, teeth bared. <No. *Your* fault. You didn't listen. You do not get to claim vengeance.>

Damn pegasus. Jack glowered. With a snarl, he holstered the pistol. Zepheus folded his wings and sidestepped.

"Get out of my sight." Jack's voice was cold and flat. It was so tempting to put a bullet right between those wide, frightened eyes. But Zepheus would interfere again. "Get away from here, before I rethink the mercy I show *kid* mages."

Swallowing, the young man staggered to his feet, scuttling to the pony cart. The stolid little pony had stayed put the whole time, indifferent to the debacle. The mage clambered into the cart, urging the pony off at a brisk trot. Two golden coins glittered on the road behind them.

Jack watched until the pony cart was only a dot on the horizon. Then he stomped his boots in the red dirt, growling as he balled his hands into angry fists to threaten the sky. After dealing with that mage, an old-fashioned hissy fit felt good. Annoyance prickled the back of his neck as Zepheus watched with mild amusement.

He felt a little better once he got it out of his system. Jack reached down and picked up the ravaged revolver. He turned it over in his hands, assessing the catastrophic damage. He needed to empty the rounds, but with the hammer missing there was nothing left to cock. Jack thumbed open the gate and discovered only pulverized shrapnel in the chambers. That half-grown colt had done *this?* It was laughable. It was *ridiculous.*

Jack turned to glare at his pegasus. "Never get between me and my target."

<I told you to leave him alone,> Zepheus pointed out, one hind hoof relaxed. The impertinent stud was calm since the threat had passed.

"Don't be a smart-ass. How was I to know he'd blow my sixgun to Perdition and back again? My *favorite* sixgun." Jack clenched his fists as he surveyed the surrounding area for the missing bits of his revolver. He wasn't foolish enough to leave anything behind that someone could later use against him.

<Maybe next time you'll listen when I say someone smells dangerous. You know, instead of going over and poking the rattlesnake in the snout.> The palomino shook his silver mane.

"Yeah, yeah," Jack grumbled. Zepheus *had* warned him. And he hadn't listened. But in his defense, the young man was about as threatening as a day-old kitten.

<Even kittens have claws.>

"Shut your trap. I don't want to hear it."

Jack should have paid more attention when the kid identified himself as a Breaker. He knew of Breakers, by historical reputation only because their line of chaotic magic was allegedly extinct. They were a breed of mage no one with any sense wanted to have on their side—or on the enemy's. They were a danger to everyone. As this encounter had proven.

The kid's presence bothered Jack. With the news he had learned earlier that day, things didn't bode well for the kid. Jack presumed Desina was his homeland, judging by the direction he had headed. He was sure to be in jeopardy soon. The Salt-Iron Confederation already knew the locations of all the mages in Desina. They were coming for them.

<You always say we could use more mages,> Zepheus observed.

"Stop spying on my thoughts," Jack grunted. He gave the stallion's shoulder a half-hearted shove. "We don't need mages like him. How in Perdition do you train *that?*"

Zepheus arched his neck, looking away with tacit disapproval. Jack picked up a chunk of shrapnel, tucking it into his shirt pocket.

"He blew up my damned gun, Zeph!"

<They will kill him if they can't use him,> the pegasus reminded him.

Jack gritted his teeth. "He's young. Believe me, they'd love to train that up. If they can." The Salt-Iron Confederation would use him. Oh, how they would use a power like that. At least until it blew up in their faces. That thought cheered him. *Would serve the damn Salties right.* "I'm not allowing magic like that in Itude. Don't even think of mentioning it to the other Ringleaders."

Zepheus lifted his tail and made a deposit on the road, a commentary of his opinion. Jack grunted and turned his back, scanning the ground for more bits of his revolver. He stowed the broken remains in his saddlebag, tucking a handkerchief around the cracked pearl handle. The corners of his eyes stung; he swiped away the wetness with one hand. *Damn dust.*

Wildfire Jack, Scourge of the Untamed Territory, *didn't* cry.

But *she* had given him that sixgun. And now it was beyond repair.

After fastening the buckle on the saddlebag, Jack swung into the saddle.

<Back to town?> Zepheus asked.

"Yeah. Need to update the other Ringleaders on the Salties' movements." Jack glanced over his shoulder. Too far away for the naked eye to see, Jack knew the Salt-Iron Confederation was coming.

CHAPTER TWO

From Shadow to Shadow

Blaise

"I'm sorry. Repeat that. The part where you did *what* to the outlaw?"

Blaise winced at his mother's incredulous tone as she stared at him from her place across the table, curly brown hair framing her face.

Everyone else at the table stared at him too, their reactions mixed. His thirteen-year-old sister, Lucienne, shook her head as if she couldn't believe how stupid he was. His five-year-old brother, Brody, thrust his hands into the air and yelled, "Boom!" at random. Their father rested his chin on one hand as if exhausted by all of them.

Blaise hadn't wanted to tell them. Upon arrival, he saw by the drawn expressions on his parents' faces that something was wrong. He pretended that everything had gone well on his trip to the Black Market to keep everyone at ease. But Blaise had found it difficult to dodge further questions at dinner. He had never been a good liar. So what else could he do but tell them?

"It was an accident." Even he wasn't convinced with that argument. *Everything* around him was an accident. He took a frustrated breath as his parents traded concerned looks. "I paid the toll. We should be fine. Right?"

His father, Daniel, steepled his fingers in front of him. "It's hard to tell with an outlaw. They're unpredictable. And dangerous."

That describes me, too, Blaise thought, glum. He pushed the food around on his plate with his fork, his appetite gone. Things had been looking up. He should have known better.

Marian glanced at her two younger children. "Luci, help Brody get ready for bed."

"Mom!" Luci wailed. "Brody can get himself ready!"

Their mother shook her head. "If by *ready* you mean neglect to brush his teeth, sure. *Go.* Help him get ready. And don't either of you skulk around listening in." She pointed emphatically toward the door.

"I don't want to!" Brody howled, fighting banishment to an early bedtime.

Luci rose from her seat, taking him by the arm. "C'mon, kid. Adults are talking and don't want us around."

"I'm not a kid!" Brody shrieked, defiant as he flopped out of his chair. Blaise winced. Had *he* sounded like that to the outlaw? Probably.

Brody's protests forced Luci to pick him up. "You owe me!" she called over her shoulder as she shut the door behind her.

Once the kitchen was quiet, Marian returned her attention to Blaise. "I'm sorry, I didn't mean to sound so harsh about the experience you had today. I know you were hoping for it to go better."

Blaise sighed. "I didn't fall and skin my knee, so don't talk to me like it's nothing. My magic got me in trouble. Again. With an outlaw."

She used a fingernail to scrape a sticky spot from the tabletop. "I'm not saying that it's of no consequence. But I am trying to do my duty as a mother to make you feel better."

Oh, he was aware. But didn't she realize that words did *nothing*? He still had to live with his magic and its repercussions. Maybe it was easier looking at it from the outside when you weren't the one with the magic. What was that even like?

"I'm sorry. I mess everything up." Blaise stared at his cold plate of food.

"Oh, son." Marian's exhaled words softened. "I know you didn't mean for it to happen. One of us should have gone with you."

The muscles in Blaise's shoulders and back tightened. That was what he had been trying to avoid. He hated the constant hand-holding required to keep his magic from ruining their lives. This had been his big chance to prove he could contribute as an adult. He had been *so* close.

"It's been a hard day for everyone," Daniel murmured.

Something in the way the words caught in his father's throat didn't sit well with Blaise. Stirred from his melancholy, he looked up at his father. Lines of stress pulled at the corners of his mouth and eyes. "What happened?"

His mother shook her head. "Do we have to talk about this now?

Daniel pushed back his chair, picking up his plate to clear the table. "It's necessary. He needs to know. We have to make preparations."

What? Blaise looked from one parent to the other. His stomach wrenched at the look of misery on his mother's face. "What's going on?"

Marian shook her head, eyes downcast. His father spoke as he picked up Luci and Brody's plates from the table. "Courier brought word that Desina has officially entered the Salt-Iron Confederation."

"What?"

"They've been courting the Consul for decades." Marian crossed her arms, her voice bitter. "And word came that Consul Stewart died. The new Consul has caved."

Blaise gulped. "What . . . what does that mean for us?" *For me?*

His mother's jaw clenched. She turned away, making a vague gesture to her husband. Daniel rested his palms against the counter. "I saw a broadside posted in town today. Next week, a company of soldiers will arrive to register all the mages in the area."

"But you won't be going," Marian said, steel in her tone.

Blaise's mind reeled. The Salt-Iron Confederation was a forbidden topic in their house. The little he understood about the Salt-Iron's stance on mages made him fearful of ducking out of the rule. Registration was a requirement for *all* mages. They hunted down those who avoided it.

"Marian . . ."

His mother's lips pulled back from her teeth, fierce as she stared her husband down. "I know what they would do with him, Daniel. Don't *Marian* me. Our child will not be a weapon."

A weapon? How could his awful magic be a weapon, when he couldn't even control it?

"Registration isn't an option. They'll send Trackers to search for any mages they miss. But we have time. We'll make a bolt-hole." She nodded as she worked through her idea aloud. "The basement—no, too obvious. The hayloft. That could work."

Blaise rubbed the back of his neck, a tension headache coming on. "Won't I have to hide all my life?"

His mother breathed out a deep sigh. Her distress made him wish he hadn't asked. She felt guilty for his birthright, too. "They can't have you. If that means we spend the rest of our days hiding you when the Confederation threatens . . . then yes."

Blaise understood, but he didn't like it. It wasn't fair. His cursed magic prevented him from having a normal life. His age-mates were getting married and having children or taking on prosperous apprenticeships. And here he was, stuck at home hiding from the Salt-Iron Confederation. He had no prospects. No future. No hope.

"I picked up more flour when I was in town," his father said, changing the subject to something more palatable. "You can take the time to bake some things to keep in the loft when you have to hunker down."

"Treats would put everyone in a good frame of mind," Marian agreed, though her heart wasn't in it.

"I can make a cobbler and some bread." Blaise humored them. He knew what they were doing. He loved to bake—it was one of the few things he was good at. The opportunity should have made him happy. But all he felt was a cold pit of despair.

He hated that his life was comprised of jumping from shadow to shadow, afraid of what he was.

———

"Can I lick the spoon?" Lucienne shot through the kitchen, heading toward the door that led to the small mudroom.

Blaise looked over his shoulder as he kneaded dough. "Right now I'm making bread, so no, that's disgusting."

"If you make a cake, I call dibs!" she shouted back.

Blaise cringed. "Raw eggs. No. Stop being gross." She cackled as she sped out the door.

He had to admit, he was in a better mood and it had everything to do with baking. It was one of the few activities he knew without a doubt would help him escape the destructive force of his magic. Blaise found freedom in the simple act of combining ingredients to create something delicious. His magic broke down and destroyed anything else he touched. It was a mystery why his magic had no impact on his baking.

Gloves were a necessity normally. It was liberating to feel the grit of flour against bare skin and the stickiness of the dough as he worked the heels of his hands into it. He kneaded the dough for several minutes, content in the simple task. It was its own sort of magic.

Blaise set aside the dough to rise. He washed his hands and moved to the cupboard to check on the sugar supply. Hard gingerbread was next on the agenda.

His mother swept into the kitchen, sniffing in appreciation. "Smells good in here. You're going to make us jealous that you get to hide away with snacks."

He smiled, shrugging. "I need some perk, right?"

Marian nodded, the corners of her dark eyes creased with worry. "Your father hauled a few jugs of water into the loft. I want you to have a go-bag packed."

Blaise put down the bag of sugar. "What?"

She moved over to the kitchen window, peering out. "When we moved to Desina, we made sure our home was as close to the border as possible. I had hoped we would never need to worry about that precaution."

Blaise frowned, tapping the counter with a clean wooden spoon. "Does . . . do they want you too, Mom?"

She bowed her head. "Probably. If they still remember me, that is. If they do, then yes—they will want me. But they can't have the both of us, Blaise."

"Why?"

Her shoulders slumped as she released a pent-up breath. "It's twofold." She clenched her jaw.

For a few minutes, Blaise thought she wouldn't say anything else. She knew more about the Salt-Iron Confederation than she had ever told him or his siblings. He wished she would just tell him. He wanted some idea of what was dropping on their heads.

She must have decided the same, for she finally spoke. "When a mage registers with the Salt-Iron Confederation, they receive a tattoo. Powerful mages receive a tattoo that has a binding—a geasa that compels subservience to the Confederation. At that point, the bound mage becomes a theurgist."

Blaise frowned. That didn't add up. "How do outlaw mages fit in? Aren't those tattooed mages who broke free?"

Marian shrugged. "Yes. Not to be confused with mavericks. Mavericks escape before receiving a tattoo." She was quiet for several heartbeats. "We can't allow them the chance to tattoo you. The alchemists work to constantly improve the formula used in the geasa and—" She clamped her mouth shut.

"Oh." Blaise looked away, unsettled. *The alchemists work to constantly improve the formula?* He wanted to ask more, but he knew she had already said too much.

"They *can't* get you. Promise me you won't let them take you. If you have to run, run to the Gutter."

The Gutter. Nothing good came from there. It was a harsh, dry region of sandstone canyons carved by the Deadwood River, inhospitable to all but the most determined survivors. Blaise had been as close to the Gutter as a Desinan could comfortably travel when he had gone to the Black Market, and that had been far enough for his taste.

The idea of fleeing to the Gutter for safety filled him with dread, but his mother's fear was palpable. She rarely spoke of her past. And she avoided mention of the Salt-Iron Confederation. If it came up in conversation, she either walked away or changed the subject. Blaise had the horrible suspicion she had fled them, but he was too afraid to ask.

What else could he say? "I promise."

Placated, she wiped glittering tears from the corners of her eyes. Blaise wasn't used to seeing her so upset. She was their rock, solid and everlasting. The one they could rely on to have a cool head in any difficult situation.

"After you finish baking, get a bag together," she said. Then she paused, frowning at the flour-covered counter. "After you've cleaned up this mess."

He smiled. There she was, her old spirit back. "Right. After I clean the kitchen."

Marian took a steadying breath, then clapped her hands together. "Good. I'll be down in the cellar. Those potions won't mix themselves."

Blaise turned back to his work, gathering the ingredients for gingerbread. His mother was off to work on her alchemy, and he could settle down to his own version—baking. Before too long, he could take out the bread to see if it was ready. That was a pleasant thought.

It was nice to have something in life that he didn't destroy with a single touch.

CHAPTER THREE

Timber

Blaise

The week of the Salt-Iron Confederation's arrival came and went. Blaise's father made several trips into town and reported that the company had arrived. One hundred soldiers, all dressed in the resplendent scarlet and gold of the Confederation. All on the lookout for mages.

The other mages in the area completed their registration. For most of them, their daily life wouldn't change even with a theurgist's tattoo. Their abilities were too weak. Blaise knew at least two other mages his age. Crispin specialized in finding lost chickens. Josephine commanded weak fire magic. The last Blaise heard, she could keep something warm, and that was the extent of her power. Neither mage boasted magic like his.

Each day, Blaise saw to his chores around the house but kept a vigil for threats. Every time hooves plodded down the road, his pulse sped, and he edged closer to the barn—just in case. He grew more paranoid by the hour. Tension knotted his muscles.

At night, his mother recommended he sleep in the hayloft. She worried the soldiers might make a surprise visit after dark. It wasn't a pleasant situation for Blaise, but he agreed with her reasoning.

The hidden compartment above the hayloft wasn't comfortable. But given the circumstances, Blaise didn't complain. The space was tight, with a low ceiling. His mother brought up quilts to cushion the rough-hewn floor. There was jerky, jugs of water, and the fresh bread and gingerbread he had baked.

Things could be worse.

Two weeks after the Salt-Iron Confederation arrived in Bristle, Blaise sat on the floor of the hayloft. He flipped through one of his cookbooks as the natural light waned. The hayloft didn't have any lighting of its own. Before long he would be alone in the darkness.

His situation gave him time to think more about his future. If he kept his magic under control, he had a chance to leave home. Maybe secure an apprenticeship in another land. One not under Salt-Iron Confederation control—perhaps Oscen. Even better, no one there would know him by reputation. And if he worked hard, someday he might have a bakery of his own. That was the dream, anyway.

To even have the slightest hope of that, he had to rein in his magic. Gloves only did so much. He flexed his fingers, looking at his hands. *Traitors*. With a sigh, he settled down on the pallet of quilts and stared into the darkness. Blaise felt detached from everyone he cared about. Was it always going to be like this? Kept at arm's-length from everyone he loved to protect himself—and them?

It was a terrible thought. True, he wished he could have independence apart from his family—but they were his *family*. He cared about them, and even in the worst of times, he never felt alone when they were around.

But in the loft, he was all alone with his thoughts. And his thoughts were terrible company. He had ample opportunity to recall all the times his magic had embarrassed or created havoc in the past. Blaise's earliest memory was that of his favorite stuffed bear coming apart in his hands, simply because he had hugged it after falling down and skinning his knee. When he was eight and the children in his class had pressed up against the windows to look at a rainbow outside, his touch had shattered the glass. And there were more. Before he had been asked not to return to school, he had been bullied for his magic. Blaise absently rubbed at his long-healed left hand. A bully had broken it "to stop your magic, sorcerer!"

Tossing and turning, Blaise growled in frustration. The warmth of the day receded, but it was still humid and intolerable. In the darkness, he pulled his gloves off. It was too warm. He usually tried to sleep with them on—otherwise, his magic ended up destroying his bedding. Blaise set the gloves aside and angled his hands so the palms faced upwards, not touching any of the quilts. He sighed. It was worth trying if he could get some respite.

It must have worked. His eyes flew open to the sound of a dog baying. The voice belonged to Chester, the family terrier. Blaise rubbed the sleep from his eyes with one hand, trying to remember where he was. Dawn's light filtered through the cracks between the walls, casting the hayloft in a surreal glow.

Chester continued to bark, insistent and frantic. Blaise imagined the little dog's ruff bristling with agitation. Something had set him off.

Hooves crunched on gravel. *Many* hooves. In the distance, the unmistakable snort of a horse punctuated the night.

Blaise untangled from the quilts and frowned as he looked down. The fabric had frayed during the night, a gentle rebuke that his hands hadn't stayed put. He shoved the quilts into a lumpy pile in the corner. If he had a chance later, he made a mental promise to mend the damaged quilt. Blaise found the indistinct pile of his fresh clothing for the day and pulled on pants and a shirt.

Smoky whinnied a query. The steady rumble of hooves came closer. Blaise fumbled around for his gloves in the dim light, pulling them on. He crept closer to the wall and peered out of a knotted hole.

Soldiers. The majority rode regular horses. But the telltale gleam of a horn proved they had at least one unicorn. The riders kept a tight formation, their uniforms dark in the haze of dawn. Blaise couldn't tell what color they were. Were they the scarlet and gold of the Salt-Iron Confederation, or some other uniform like the local militia? They drew to a stop between the barn and the house. Chickens clucked, drowsy. The few hens that had braved the outdoors hurried back into the safety of their coop with a flap of their wings. Chester darted around the riders, continuing his barking frenzy. More than one steed lifted a hoof to threaten him away.

Blaise's gut twisted.

A rider mounted on a white horse beside the unicorn dismounted. He cupped his hands to his mouth. "Hawthorne!"

They know who we are. Blaise crouched on the balls of his feet. The soldier braced his arms behind his back as he waited for a response.

Lights came on in the house. A moment later, his parents filed out of the house, still in their nightclothes. His father carried a lantern and tried to catch Chester. The little dog dodged away, still yapping. Blaise's mother had her arms crossed. She was the very picture of someone woken from her bed too soon and was none too happy about it. Pastel sunlight caught the glinting edge of a bottle carried in the crook of her elbow.

"I don't know who you think you are, but you had better have a good reason for waking us so early. I was up half the night with my child." Marian's voice was full of righteous anger.

Her mood didn't impress the soldier. He led his mount closer, waving the soldier with the unicorn after him. "I am Commander Lamar Gaitwood of the Salt-Iron Confederation. My company and I are in Desina registering mages. It's come to my attention we missed one."

A finger of ice crawled down Blaise's spine. He froze.

Daniel caught Chester and carried the little dog back toward the house. Chester flailed in his arms, whining. Lucienne poked her head out the door, eyes wide. Daniel thrust Chester at her and told her to get inside and not come out again. She took the dog without protest. In the funereal light of dawn, her face was etched with fear.

She only had to be afraid because *he* was a part of their family.

Blaise's mother addressed the Commander once Chester's yapping ceased. "That doesn't tell me why you're here interrupting my family's sleep." As she spoke, the unicorn leaned closer to the Commander, teeth bared as if to nip him.

Gaitwood didn't so much as glance at the unicorn. He reached behind him and grabbed the reins, giving them a savage jerk. The unicorn squealed, head snapping up in anguish. "As I understand it, there's a mage in your family, ma'am." In the dim light, Blaise saw a trace of malice in the man's eyes. He knew that look. Gaitwood was a bully. "Are you aware that it's a crime to harbor mavericks from the Salt-Iron Confederation?"

Blaise's father put a restraining hand on his mother's shoulder. She shrugged it off. "I'm aware." Her voice was as dry as deadwood.

Daniel leaned in close to whisper something. Blaise pulled away from the peephole and fumbled in the darkness for his boots. He rammed his feet into them, then pulled the go-bag closer. With regret, he shoved the stack of books into the corner. They would have to stay. Books were too heavy and would only slow him down if he had to run. Blaise opened the satchel and felt around inside to check on the essentials. Canteens of water. Jerky. Bread and gingerbread.

Blaise moved back to the peephole and peered out.

"—don't know what you're talking about," Daniel finished. His father had taken control of the situation while Blaise finished his preparations.

Gaitwood scowled at him. "You're lying. Five different witnesses verified a *Breaker* lives here."

There it was. Betrayed by the townspeople. Not surprising. He clenched his fists, torn between anger and the memory of his mother's words. *Promise me you won't let them take you.*

In the hayloft, he was a sitting duck. It was only a matter of time before they discovered him. Blaise eased open the hatch and slung the bag over his shoulders. As he found the top rung of the ladder with one foot, he strained to hear what they said.

"We'll find the mage if we have to tear your entire house apart," the Commander snarled.

"You will *not!*" Marian's voice rang out like the peal of a trumpet. Glass shattered. Then the soldiers coughed, gasping and cursing as they struggled to breathe. She cried out, "Blaise, *run!*"

No time to climb down the ladder with caution. Blaise pivoted on the rung and jumped down to the floor, aiming for a bale of hay. He missed and his leg crumpled beneath him. Blaise gritted his teeth. *No time to think about pain.* He bobbled to his feet, racing past Smoky's feed barrel. Blaise ducked into the gelding's stall.

"Find the mage!" Blaise recognized the strangled voice as the Commander. It sounded like he was having difficulty breathing. Blaise didn't have time to think about what that meant.

Hooves pounded a sharp staccato on gravel. Blaise bolted through Smoky's stall door and into the adjoining paddock. He slowed down long enough to slip between the wooden slats of the fence. Blaise didn't spare a moment to peek behind him. He didn't want to know anything about the pursuit. *If I don't look, they're not chasing me, right?*

Blaise knew the woods behind their home like the back of his hand. His parents had made sure they lived as close to the border as possible. That didn't mean it was without its share of perils. But if he could get through the woods, he had a chance at whatever safety the Gutter could offer. At least he hoped it could offer safety.

Whistles and shouts sliced through the air as the soldiers urged their mounts after him. Blaise headed for the densest section of the wood. Tree limbs hung low, covered with the curling green bipartate leaves of invasive krakenvine. His father had intended to burn the krakenvine out for years. That procrastination worked in Blaise's favor.

Blaise ducked under a low-slung branch, slowing as the footing became treacherous. Armadillo holes littered the ground, concealed by tall grasses, bushes, and shrubs. Blaise hoped it would hinder the soldiers.

Ahead, he saw the rusty barbed wire fence that marked the border. Blaise floundered through a tangle of krakenvine. Panic fluttered in his stomach as a curling green tentacle edged with dual-bladed leaves wrapped around his right hand. He plowed forward as fast as he could, his hand snapping back when the tendril tightened its grip on him.

"Don't have time for this." Out of the corner of his eye, a blur of dark shapes moved through the trees. There were gruff exclamations as they caught sight of him. Blaise jerked his hand back, feeling the krakenvine's barbs digging into the leather of his glove. He wrenched his hand free of the glove, bare skin brushing against the plant.

The krakenvine jolted away from him like a startled fish. His glove disappeared into its tangled depths, out of reach. The plant writhed as the tendril he had touched collapsed on itself. His magic ate through the shoot, destroying it.

"Stop right there!"

Really? I'm not stupid. Blaise didn't stop. He dodged through the worst of the krakenvine. An oak that had died years ago to a lightning strike stood near the barbed wire fence, naked branches towering high above the neighboring trees. Blaise crouched beside the massive trunk as he considered his options. Reaching the Gutter was no guarantee of safety. He rested his bare right hand against the rotting wood, catching his breath. Magic rose to his palm, the familiar itch of his power seeking something to destroy. *Oh no.*

His pursuers were almost on him. They cursed as the krakenvine snared their fellows. Sabers clattered as the soldiers drew them out to hack at the offending foliage. Blaise spun and ran for the border. He held down the lowest strand of barbed wire with his gloved hand to make enough room to wiggle through.

The middle strand of wire clawed at his clothing and bag, but he ignored it. Blaise slipped through the fence, pausing at the telltale groan of snapping wood. The ground trembled with the shuddering impact as the oak slammed into smaller trees. There was a rumble as it crashed to the ground in a tangle of deadwood and soldier. Shouts rose from the men. Blaise winced at a startled scream that cut off abruptly. *Don't think about that now.*

He had made it. He was in the Gutter! Blaise hazarded a glance behind him. The oak tree was down, a haze of dust clouding the area, the soldiers little more than haunting spectral shapes. The Commander barked an order. They were still after him. If they were mad before, now he had infuriated them.

Blaise broke into a run. The muffled throbbing of hooves rang behind him. Over his shoulder, he saw the unicorn rallying after him, this time with Gaitwood on its back. Panic flooded him. *I can't outrun a unicorn.*

The air crackled around Blaise. A glittering cage of silver magic coalesced around him. He came to a sudden stop before he crashed into its bars. Blaise gasped for breath as the Commander trotted up to him on the unicorn, one arm extended.

"Well, well, well. Aren't you full of surprises?" Gaitwood paced the unicorn around the trap, assessing him with the air of someone scrutinizing a prize-winning pig.

It was over. The hiding, his mother's attempts to stall them—all for nothing. Blaise stood in the radiance of the early morning sun, bowing his head as his hands itched with magic.

He didn't want to belong to the Salt-Iron Confederation as a theurgist. Blaise didn't want to be a weapon. Would they turn him into someone cold and cruel, like this man?

The warm breeze played over his naked right hand, a reminder that he had lost his glove. Blaise's magic was unfettered.

Gaitwood dismounted, pulling shackles from his belt. Blaise trembled, afraid of what his magic might do. He closed his eyes and slammed his bare palm against the bars of the cage.

Even with his eyes shut, the world exploded into a corona of light like a miniature sun. Gaitwood roared in pain and the unicorn squealed. Blaise's eyes flew open. With grim satisfaction, he realized his magic had ripped the ephemeral cage apart. Gaitwood doubled over, hands covering his eyes as he whimpered. The unicorn shied away, quivering near the barbed wire fence.

Heart hammering, Blaise ran as fast as he could to the north. He wouldn't stop running until he had some assurance of safety. Though Blaise didn't know if there was any such thing.

CHAPTER FOUR

Hope for the Hopeless

Blaise

Blaise's priority was finding the road that led to the Black Market. Disoriented and exhausted from his headlong run, he didn't stop until he was on the verge of collapse. He found a small stand of scrubby trees to hunker down in while he waited for signs of his pursuers.

As he fled from the border, he heard a single gunshot in his wake. Gaitwood likely fired out of sheer frustration more than the hope of finding his mark. After that, his only company was the whistling wind and birds soaring above.

It was around noon, judging by the sun's position. With the sun overhead, it was hard to know if he was going in the right direction to find the road. With only one previous trip, he didn't have a grasp for the lay of the land. In the distance, red-tinged plateaus cradled the Deadwood River. All he knew was that if he reached the canyons, he had gone too far.

Reassurance washed over Blaise when at last he found the road that led to the Black Market. He was hot and tired, his skin sticky with sweat.

Without his hat or bandanna to protect him, his face was burning to a crisp in the relentless sun.

Blaise focused on his physical misery; he didn't have the strength to think about anything else. It was too much.

Mid-afternoon, he stopped for a longer break beneath a gnarled copse of mesquite. He wasn't hungry, but he forced himself to eat a piece of jerky from his bag. Blaise had eaten nothing since the previous night. When the shock of his situation wore off, he would collapse with no food in him. But the jerky was little more than ash on his tongue.

Blaise rubbed his forehead, wincing at the latent heat on his skin. The sweltering weather sapped his strength, rendering him unable to walk any further. The tenuous shade of the mesquite provided little safety, but at least offered him some protection from the sun. There were no signs of dangerous wildlife.

Or outlaws. Although at this point, he would welcome an outlaw.

His rest gave him fitful dreams and he awoke when the sun was setting. Blaise ate another piece of jerky to keep his strength up. Go-bag slung over his shoulder, he took to the road again. He focused on putting one foot in front of the other, breaking his life down into the basic things he had control over to keep his emotions at bay. Otherwise, the enormity of his situation would become overwhelming.

The moon rose overhead, low and full, providing enough silvery light to guide his path. As he walked, he tried to make a plan, but it was a struggle. This was outside the realm of his life experiences. He didn't know what to do. *If I get to the Black Market, then what?* The Black Market itself should have traveled to another location. He hoped the abandoned saloon was still there—he needed shelter and food.

But then what? Where would he go? He thought back to Slocum's question. *You a maverick?* It seemed like it had been ages ago, not little more than a week. Such a ridiculous question.

To the Salt-Iron Confederation, he was a maverick. *Maverick.* It sounded like someone who forged their own way in life, living on the outskirts of society. A rough-and-ready scrapper. The word fit him like a small child stepping into their father's boots. Blaise was a scared young man far from home, nothing more.

But this wasn't the time to dwell on that. Ahead, he saw the silhouette of a cedar with a tattered cloth flapping from its branches in the evening breeze. An intrepid person had tied a bandanna to one of the skeletal limbs to serve as a marker— a sign that the Black Market was close. Blaise quickened his steps. *Almost there.*

He crested a hill and almost wept with relief when he saw the ramshackle saloon. The building appeared haunting and ethereal in the lambent moonlight. No surprise, the windows were dark.

Blaise walked up to the door and pushed it open. "Howdy?" His voice echoed through the emptiness.

The interior was dark, none of the mage-lights on. Blaise wished he had something to make a light.

"Mr. Slocum? Are you here?"

Nothing. Not even the skitter of a mouse. In the inky darkness, Blaise found one of the empty tables by stumbling into it. He fumbled along its edge with his gloved hand and slid his go-bag off his shoulder, then found a chair and sank into it. He didn't realize he was shaking until he heard the rattle of the chair legs against the floor.

Blaise rested his chin on his hands, shutting his eyes. He was all alone. But a building with a roof and walls provided protection, and that was a much-needed respite. Blaise exhaled a soft breath, tension receding from his shoulders.

He must have fallen asleep. When he opened his eyes, grey light streamed in through one of the Black Market's dusty windows, illuminating the cracking surface of the table his ungloved hand had rested against. Blaise rubbed the side of his face, grimacing at the scraggly growth of his beard. He rose from the table, taking in the room.

It appeared different from only days before. Dust coated the bar, a sign that the building had lacked visitors. Debris—glass shards, bits of broken wood, ripped newspaper, a discarded billiards ball—covered the floor, the tracks from Blaise's boots the only sign of recent life. A musty smell permeated the building, as if it had been closed up for ages.

"Howdy?" Blaise called. "Anyone here?"

No one answered. He ventured into the back room, into which Slocum had ducked on his visit. In the faint light, it appeared empty. A wooden countertop lined one side of the room, and bare shelves stood against the other walls.

It was as if the Black Market had never existed.

Blaise glanced around, uncertain. Was he in the right building? Exhaustion had seized him the previous night when he had stumbled upon it. He walked outside and looked around, recognizing the area where he had tied up Smoky. It was all the same, save for the aura of disuse inside the abandoned saloon.

It would be almost another month before Slocum returned with his nomadic Black Market. Blaise couldn't wait that long. He thought about his next steps. As he saw it, if he wasn't planning to stay at the Black Market, then his only option was to keep walking. There were two outlaw towns he knew of on the western side of the Untamed Territory: Asylum and Rainbow Flat. A journey on foot to Rainbow Flat would prove perilous because of the wildlife of the Untamed Territory. Asylum was his best choice. That was fitting. According to stories, Asylum was the gateway to freedom for outlaws and mavericks.

Blaise had a vague sense that it was to the northeast. If he headed for Asylum, he could skirt between the Gutter and the Untamed Territory. That route would keep him clear of the worst threats. Or so he hoped. It was his only plan since he couldn't go home.

Home. He climbed onto a barstool, slumping as he put his face in his hands. Blaise hadn't allowed himself any time to think about his home or his family. But now, in the questionable safety of the Black Market, he felt like he could—and should. It wasn't healthy to keep it bottled up forever.

What would happen to his family? No doubt Gaitwood would consider whatever his mother had unleashed on him and his men as an attack. Had they taken her, imprisoned her? A sob caught in his throat. No one could stop his mother when she had something planned. He shouldn't blame himself for her actions.

But he did. She had only acted to buy *him* time. It was *his* fault.

"I'm sorry," he whispered, a tear rolling down his cheek and dropping to the dust below.

Would they imprison his father, too? What would happen to Luci and Brody?

Blaise chewed on his bottom lip, murmuring a prayer to Faedra as he thought about his loved ones. He didn't think the goddess of magic was listening. Why would she have allowed this to happen if she cared?

After a good cry and wallow in misery, he felt a little better. He had needed to endure those raw emotions, as hard as it was. Those feelings would rise up to batter him again and again, but for now, he could lay them to rest. He needed to plan his next steps.

The Black Market had potable water and shelter; it was a suitable location to regroup. Blaise decided to stay another day or two. He had wrenched his ankle in the jump from the hayloft and needed time to heal. It was a miracle he had been able to run on it. The adrenaline had likely kept him going, but that had taken a toll. He couldn't help but cling to the hope that maybe someone would stop by the Black Market and help him.

Blaise stayed at the Black Market for another week. His ankle took longer to heal than he liked. The delay allowed him to scope out the lay of the land, though it spread his meager food supply thin.

The road from Bristle to the Black Market extended beyond the building, meandering to the northeast. It was a road merchants used between the Untamed Territory and Desina. That made sense—the well made the Black Market a prime location for a layover.

Despite that, he hadn't seen signs of anyone else. Not even an outlaw. On one hand, that gave him a sense of solace. It meant Gaitwood hadn't followed him into the Gutter. But on the other, Blaise didn't like the odds of surviving on his own.

Of his supplies, Blaise only had two strips of jerky and three small chunks of gingerbread left. He foraged around the scrubby woods and found questionable berries to add to his cache. Blaise tasted one; it had a bitter, tart flavor. He didn't have any reactions from it, so decided they were harmless enough to gather and take with him.

For the best chance at success, he needed to leave for Asylum soon or double back to Desina. He wasn't sure which had the greater risk—he might die of dehydration or exposure on the way to Asylum. Or he could face whatever the Salt-Iron Confederation planned to do with him. There would be repercussions for fleeing. Neither option was appealing.

He pulled out his go-bag and rechecked his supplies. He wrapped the berries in a linen cloth to keep them together. His canteens, full of fresh water, made a pleasant sloshing sound. Blaise scanned the interior of the Black Market for anything he might have forgotten. Once he was certain he had what he needed, he shouldered his satchel.

Blaise struck out on the northeast road. He still lacked protection from the sun, so he relied on the occasional tree for respite. By the time he made it anywhere, his face would be a permanent shade of apple red.

He had walked for more than an hour when he heard a piercing cry. It was a strange sound, a cross between a horse's whinny and a songbird's warble. The tone trilled with an edge of pain. Blaise knew in his gut that whatever creature was making the sound was calling out for help.

Blaise paused beneath a young cedar. Should he see what was making the anguished call? Indecision warred within him. Whatever it was might be dangerous. He had been fortunate to not come across any predators so far. Although the distressed creature may not be a threat to him, its cries might attract predators. As it was, an optimistic pair of buzzards circled overhead.

But Blaise knew what it was like to need help—and for it to never arrive. It wouldn't hurt to investigate. A quick look, nothing more. And if he felt the slightest bit uneasy, he could be on his way.

The cry came again, and Blaise angled his head to pinpoint the direction. *A little to the west.* He turned off the road, walking with care as the ground became furrowed and uneven. Late summer wildflowers peppered the terrain with pops of yellow, magenta, and violet. Eventually, the terrain plummeted into a ravine. Cautious, he strode to the edge and peered over.

A black pegasus stood in the middle of the gully, its glossy wings, iridescent purple in the sun, fanned out at its sides, its ebony coat lathered and soaked with sweat. The equine held one of its forelegs at an awkward angle, caught in something. It lifted its head and shrilled another plea for help. Triangular ears rotated, searching for a reply. The pegasus took an awkward step forward and stopped, lowering its head.

The pegasus had something tangled around its leg. Blaise squinted, trying to figure out what it was. The equine sank into the brown grass, the snared foreleg outstretched before it.

Where was the pegasus's flight? Aside from carrion birds keeping a hopeful vigil overhead, nothing else was visible in the sky.

The equine was trapped. It had no access to water. Unless something changed, it would die. Blaise chewed on his bottom lip, thinking back to the little he knew of pegasi from library books he had read as a child. They were supposed to be intelligent. *Will it understand me if I try to help? I hope so.*

Decision made, Blaise navigated the steep side of the gully. Midway down, he lost his footing and slid to an ignominious stop at the bottom, his back bruised and the elbows of his sleeves shredded by rocks. The pegasus snorted in alarm and pinned back its ears, but it didn't get up.

Blaise shrugged off his go-bag with a pained wince, careful of his scuffed elbows, and set it by a clump of yellow, bell-shaped wildflowers. He was going to regret that entrance later. He raised his hands to show the creature they were empty. "Howdy. I'm here to help if you'll allow it."

The pegasus gave a skeptical snort, white-rimmed eyes rolling. Blaise didn't blame it. He'd be dubious of his help, too. It wasn't like he had a pristine track record so far.

Crouching down, Blaise squinted at the pegasus's foreleg from a respectful distance. Now that he was closer, there was definitely a rope tangled around it. But it wasn't like any rope Blaise had ever seen. Dark beads glinted at intervals along its length.

Blaise frowned. "Is that salt-iron?" The equine's nostrils dilated as it snorted. Was that assent? Blaise crept closer, watching the pegasus for any signs of protest. He crouched an arm's length from the tangled foreleg, relaxing when the pegasus didn't move.

Creeping closer, he realized he was right. Polished dark metal beads twinkled within the braided rope, a pattern of sharp barbs worked into the mix. The barbs dug into the thin skin around the animal's leg, causing blood to seep from the wounds. Flies buzzed around, eager to feast.

Anger surged through Blaise as he realized someone had laid a trap—

the nefarious rope hadn't appeared from nowhere. He didn't have much experience with salt-iron, but like any mage, he knew to avoid it. It was renowned for its use against mages and magical creatures. His eyes followed the trail of rope to a stake. The trapper had concealed it in a cluster of tall grass.

"It's okay," Blaise murmured, wondering if the animal would understand him. A calming voice had always helped with Smoky when the farrier came to trim his hooves. The pegasus rolled its eyes again, flailing onto its side. Blaise rocked back out of the way in case it lashed out with its hooves. It stretched out on its side, one wing pinned beneath its bulk.

The pegasus thrashed its hind legs, frightened and in pain. Blaise paused, cautious as he thought through the best way to handle an unpredictable, injured creature with hooves the size of dinner plates. A kick from one of those would be the end of the road. He needed to earn the animal's trust.

Smoky liked treats . . . would a pegasus? Blaise inched to his satchel, trying not to startle the equine. He knelt and opened the bag, rifling through the remaining food until he found a piece of gingerbread. He clutched his prize in his gloved hand, rising to display his open palm.

"I know you're scared. You don't trust me. Consider this a peace offering."

The creature made a hesitant rumbling sound. One ear flitted forward, then backward again.

Right. The pegasus suspected poison or drugs. After being caught in a man-made snare, it would be difficult to trust a strange human. "Okay, watch. I'll have a taste." Blaise broke off a tiny chunk and popped it into his mouth. He chewed and swallowed, then held up the rest. "See? It's good."

Step by careful step, he inched closer to the trapped pegasus. He held his gloved palm out as far as he could. The creature lifted its head enough to snuffle at it, then wiggled velvety lips to snag the treat. The pegasus crunched, tongue flicking out with satisfaction. Its ears swiveled forward as it rested its head against the ground again.

"Are you thirsty?" Blaise asked. He didn't expect an answer, but the pegasus made another rumble. He pulled a canteen out of the bag, settling down beside the equine to trickle water into its mouth. It sighed in relief.

"Okay, I'm going to see if I can get that thing off of you. I promise I'm here to help."

Blaise put away the canteen, then sat down by the equine's leg. The pegasus raised its head to watch him. Blaise frowned at the tangled rope.

"I need you to stay still. I have to pull out the barbs first." Blaise counted at least two that he could see had ripped into the flesh. He shooed away the flies, annoyed when they circled back for another pass.

The pegasus snorted. Blaise decided that was consent. He reached for the rope, then remembered he had only one safe hand. With a grimace, he curled his right hand into a fist and shoved it into his pants pocket. If he didn't keep it out of the way, he risked his magic lashing out.

He worried at a barb with his thumb and index finger and pulled it free of the pegasus's flesh. The animal's shoulder spasmed with a twitch, but otherwise, the beast didn't move.

It was slow, frustrating work with only one hand. To make matters worse, the rope tangled back on itself. Blaise wished he had a knife or anything sharp. He could have cut the pegasus free. Why, oh why, had a knife not been an essential part of his go-bag?

Something to think about for the future. If he survived his predicament.

Blaise lost track of time as he worked on the snare. The sun roasted them as the day wore on. He took frequent water breaks so that neither one of them became dehydrated. The pegasus looked miserable, tongue flopping from its open mouth. Blaise suspected it might not survive, even if he freed it.

Late in the afternoon, Blaise had made very little progress. No matter what he tried, the rope tangled back on itself. He blew out a frustrated breath. What was this, some kind of magic? Maybe just bad luck. Whatever the case, it kept him from his goal. He had promised to set the pegasus free.

"I don't know what to do," Blaise admitted. "It keeps tangling. What in Faedra's name *is* this?"

The pegasus snorted. Blaise was uncertain if it was an answer to his question or the animal's own show of frustration at the situation.

Maybe working one-handed was too slow. Blaise gritted his teeth. He could untangle it much faster with two hands, but at what cost?

"I'm going to try something. I don't know if it will help. Can I try?" Blaise tried not to think about what could happen if something went horribly wrong. He took a breath to calm himself and paste on a façade that he knew what he was doing.

The pegasus lifted its head to look at him but gave no other response. It laid its head back down with a sigh.

"Here goes nothing." Blaise rubbed his hands together, magic itching beneath his skin. He laid both hands on the rope to work at it again.

Pain sizzled through his naked palm. Yelping, he snatched his hand back, rubbing at an angry red welt that arose from his brief contact with the metal. The salt-iron sapped away the magic that itched beneath the surface of his skin.

The pegasus watched him. Blaise glanced from the rope to his hand. Now he knew why magic and salt-iron didn't mix. It blistered his skin, neutralizing and leeching away his magic. He cocked his head, thinking. Blaise's magic was still there, so the brief touch hadn't drained it completely.

Blaise rubbed the welt with his gloved fingers. Salt-iron was rare. The rope's crafter had spaced the beads a hand's width apart, no doubt to save coin for whoever this trap belonged to. If he was careful, he could avoid touching the metal while he worked. Could his magic break the rope as it had broken through the krakenvine? *Worth a try. I don't have any better options.*

He grasped one of the beads with his gloved hand and touched a length of harmless rope with his right. His magic boiled up as if offended by the earlier attack. Blaise felt it jump from his hand to the rope, degrading the fibers. The bolt of magic slammed into one of the salt-iron beads and died with a hiss.

The salt-iron may have nullified his magic, but not before it had undermined the fiber of the rope. A section sloughed away, falling to the ground with a soft thump. Blaise's heart thumped a nervous beat.

"Got it," he told the pegasus as he held another of the beads with his glove and assailed the rope with his bare hand. Hemp fibers shredded and fell away.

Blaise repeated the process until he broke down all the tangles, using his glove to unwind the remaining bits of rope that clung to the animal's leg. The last piece fell away, and he tossed it as far as he could. His hands trembled with nerves, teeth chattering from the fear of blatantly trying to use his own magic. Blaise wished he had a glove for his hand.

The exhausted pegasus lay stretched on the ground, unmoving. Blaise sucked in a breath, reaching out to rub the equine's damp neck. "We did it. You're free."

The pegasus stayed down, sides heaving. Its nostrils flared in the dry grass.

Tears stung Blaise's eyes. After all that, the pegasus *had* to get up. *Had* to live. "Come on. Get up. Please?"

With great effort, it lifted its head and gathered its hind legs. Blaise scooted back to give it room to move. The pegasus remained down for a moment, unfurling its wings.

<Thank you for saving me. I would have died without you.>

Blaise blinked at the exhausted, masculine voice in his head. "Wait, what? You can talk?"

The pegasus stallion clambered to his feet, unsteady as a newborn foal, injured leg held off the ground. <Mind to mind.>

Blaise canted his head, puzzled. "Why didn't you say something sooner? Or you could have called your flight to help? I don't understand."

The stallion snorted. <My mental speech is magic, and the salt-iron suppressed the ability. So even if I had a flight, I could not have called it.>

"Oh." Blaise rubbed the back of his head. That made sense, after his experience with touching it. Nasty stuff. "Well, I guess you'll want to be going wherever your home is since you're free." As tempted as he was, he didn't ask the pegasus for a ride to civilization. He didn't want the traumatized creature to feel beholden to him.

<And where will you go?> the pegasus asked.

"Um." Blaise looked around. The sun was setting, and he didn't know if there was a safe place to bed down for the night. He gestured vaguely to the northeast. "That way."

Blaise hadn't known an equine face was capable of an incredulous expression. The stallion's ears pointed in opposite directions and his lower lip hung loose. <You have no idea where you're going, do you?>

"Not really."

The pegasus bobbed his head as if he had reached a decision. <That settles it. You have saved me. Now it's my turn to save you.>

CHAPTER FIVE

Wings and Such

The stallion's name was Emrys. He needed time to recover from the snare, but he knew of a place nearby where they could find shelter and rest. Blaise walked beside the pegasus as he favored his right hoof.

"Are you going to be okay?" Blaise cast a worried look to the west. The last crepuscular rays of the sunset fractured over the peaks of the distant mountains. Leg injuries could be life-threatening for horses. He wasn't sure if that was the case for a pegasus.

<Once I have more of my magic back, I can fly and that will serve me better.> Emrys shook his thick mane. <The salt-iron sapped my magic, and I can't fly without it.>

"I didn't realize magic makes pegasi fly. Birds don't have magic." Blaise understood the impact the salt-iron had on magic after his brief touch, but the concept of magical pegasus flight made little sense.

Emrys snorted. <When was the last time you saw a bird that weighs as much as a draft horse?>

"You make a good point."

Emrys hobbled beneath a sandstone outcropping, Blaise following in his wake. Was that true for other flying magical creatures? He had so little knowledge about anything related to magic. If he asked questions, would Emrys think he was ignorant? "So what you said earlier . . . you don't belong to a flight?"

The stallion's wings rustled against his sides, reminding Blaise of the chickens back home. <I'm a bachelor stallion. Colts are driven out of our flights once we're old enough to survive the wilds alone.>

Blaise scratched at his chin, thoughtful. "Just the colts? Not the fillies?"

Emrys blew out a derisive snort. <As if any guardian stallion is going to allow a filly or mare out of his flight. No, only colts.> He swished his tail. <But to answer your question, I don't have a flight in the traditional sense, but I do have a place I belong.>

A place to belong sounded nice to Blaise. He had to admit, he was jealous. "And that's where we're going?"

Emrys bobbed his head, turning off the trail and threading his way through red yucca plants. <Yes. I work with the outlaws of Itude. Look, here we are.> He led Blaise down an incline to a shallow cave.

Blaise followed him inside, shrugging his satchel off and peering inside at the sad remains of his supplies. His stomach rumbled. "You said you work *with* the outlaws?"

<Yes. Most often sentry duty. That's what I was doing when I was . . . distracted.> Emrys glanced away, and Blaise detected embarrassment in his mental voice.

"Pegasi get paid?" It hadn't occurred to Blaise that non-humans might receive or need a wage.

<What, I should not collect a fair wage because I'm a quadruped?> Emrys twitched an ear, head tilted askance.

"Sorry, that's not what I meant. I guess I'm not sure what use you would have for coin?" Blaise knew that sounded flimsy.

<A roof over my head and delicious food, the same as anyone else.>

Blaise winced. He was out of his depth. It was anguishing to not have any concept of life beyond the tiny world he had lived in.

<Oh, don't beat yourself up over it.> The stallion nudged him with his velvety nose. <Tell me about you. What is your magic?>

That was the last thing Blaise wanted to talk about. Tension pooled in his shoulders. Would Emrys abandon him if he knew? "How do you know I have magic?" It never hurt to stall a conversation.

The stallion snorted. <Seriously? What you did back in the ravine was obvious.>

Blaise winced. "Um, right." He rubbed the back of his head. "Breaker. That's what people call my magic."

Emrys's head swung up in surprise. <I've only heard of that magic. It's . . .> He trailed off, and Blaise suspected Emrys was trying to avoid hurting his feelings.

"Dangerous," Blaise finished for him. "It is."

The stallion swished his tail, thoughtful. <And that was what you used to free me.>

"Yes."

Emrys surprised him by stepping closer, nuzzling his shoulder. <Then perhaps your magic is merely misunderstood.>

Blaise blinked. He had never thought of it in that context. A brief memory of the magical cage exploding at his touch played through his mind. Escape would have been impossible without his magic.

Emrys bowed his head to examine the healing puncture wounds on his leg. Blaise wished he had thought to bring one of the first aid kits from home. His mother had potions that would aid the stallion's healing. "How did you get caught?"

Emrys swished his tail and made an embarrassed rumble. <Ah. Pegasi use a lot of energy to fly, and sugar is one way we recover. I should have known better. I was greedy.> He hung his head. <I was as gullible as a spindle-legged colt. A poacher set the snare with a stack of sugar cubes for bait.>

Blaise blanched. "People trap pegasi?"

<And worse,> Emrys affirmed. <It's the way of some humans. They do not care if they find their prey in time. Some want us dead because we work with outlaws. Others want to use our flesh, bones, and feathers.> His mental voice oozed with disgust.

"There are a lot of terrible humans out there," Blaise agreed, thinking of Gaitwood. "I'm glad I found you in time."

<Me, too,> Emrys said, drowsy.

Blaise smiled as the stallion's eyelids drooped. If Emrys could rest, then more power to him. Blaise adjusted his position, lower back tender from his earlier descent. He crossed his arms and listened to the relentless screech of cicadas in the distance.

THE NEXT MORNING, EVERY MUSCLE IN BLAISE'S BODY COMPLAINED ABOUT the lack of rest and comfort. Emrys looked better, at least. He could put more weight on his foreleg. He declared he was fit for a rider.

Blaise was hesitant. He had ridden Smoky sometimes, but always with saddle and bridle. Emrys had neither. Blaise wasn't confident in his horsemanship skills or how to stay out of the way of those broad wings.

But he had less confidence in his supplies lasting until he reached a town.

<I'll stay on the ground until you dare to fly with me,> Emrys told him, magnanimous.

The concept of flying on a pegasus made Blaise's empty stomach churn. He decided not to burst the stallion's bubble by telling him that would never happen. Besides, his only other option was walking, and Blaise had lost track of where he was and where to go. Emrys had a much better sense of direction.

The stallion knelt, allowing Blaise to climb on his back. His legs hung down behind Emrys's wings, which the stallion tucked to his sides as he walked. Blaise tried to not interfere with the pegasus's wings.

<It's easier with a saddle. Keeps you in place,> Emrys commented as he set off deeper into the Gutter.

As they traveled, Blaise understood why the area had the strange moniker. A network of canyons and gullies crisscrossed the land, carved into the rock by the Deadwood River. Emrys told him that in the stormy season, the gullies would be quite dangerous. But they were safe enough now—the Gutter didn't see much rain in summer.

As the landscape changed, so too did the colors all around them. Behind them, the distant hills and woodlands of Desina melted away into the parched grass and low scrub of the grasslands. The orange and crimson sandstone of the Gutter rose around them. After a life surrounded by trees and green grass, Blaise spent much of the time gawking at the scenery. Desina didn't boast landscape like this.

Emrys enjoyed his fascination and pointed out features as they traveled. He detoured down a trail, trotting up to a delicate arch hewn from the rock. He explained how wind and water carved the arch into the stone over thousands of years. In another canyon, Emrys slowed down and bade Blaise to look up. The walls of the canyon had worn into spire-like towers that Emrys called *hoodoos*. Blaise had never seen a natural feature like them. They were inspiring.

<You should see this place at sunset,> Emrys told him as he picked his way up a perilous trail that led to the upper rim. <I'll bring you back sometime when you're ready to fly.>

That wouldn't happen. *Too bad.* Blaise imagined it must be an amazing sight.

Late in the afternoon, Emrys rounded a corner and Blaise saw tiny man-made shapes atop a distant cliff. Buildings. A speck launched off the side of the cliff and flew in their direction. Another pegasus with a rider.

<We'll stop here so the sentry can clear us,> Emrys explained to Blaise, halting along the side of the canyon.

"Okay." Blaise didn't feel as certain as he sounded. He tried to distract himself by glancing over the side of the ledge. The Deadwood River roared below, capped with white foam. The muscles at the base of his neck tensed with nerves as he lifted his eyes to the approaching pegasus. After over a week without human company, he worried about what someone new might think of him.

The incoming pegasus landed and trotted over, rider bobbing in the saddle. Windswept blonde hair poked out from beneath the rider's slouch hat, though most was contained by a braid. He realized she was a teenager—she looked a year or two older than Luci. His heart ached as he thought of his sister.

"Identify yourself—oh, howdy Emrys." The girl tipped back her hat, looking from the black stallion to Blaise. Her pegasus boasted a white coat covered in dark brown spots and mottled wings that reminded Blaise of a falcon. The spotted stallion whinnied and bumped noses with Emrys.

"Who're you?" she drawled, examining Blaise as if he were a particularly interesting lizard.

Blaise supposed he made a pathetic sight, with his beet-red face, scraggly beard, and timeworn clothing. "Blaise. Blaise Hawthorne. From Desina." His voice trembled with the effort. Never had he imagined that talking to another person would be so difficult. He had underestimated the impact the last few weeks had had on him.

She tapped the pommel of her saddle with one hand, brows knitted as she looked him over. "Well, Blaise Hawthorne from Desina, I'm Emmaline Dewitt, and you're approaching Itude. Emrys vouches for you. He says you have no place else to go."

That was an understatement. Relief crashed through Blaise and his shoulders relaxed. He would have to thank Emrys later. "I . . . I don't."

"Right then. I gotta settle a few things with you first." She gave a dutiful nod. "Newcomers to town have to surrender their weapons at the saloon. You got a problem with that?"

Blaise shook his head. "I don't have any weapons."

Emmaline's eyes telegraphed teenage disbelief. "Really?"

"Really."

She frowned, eyes roving as if searching him for weapons. Emrys must have told her something in private because her eyes shifted to the stallion. She tilted her head. "Okay then. Another thing to know is the offensive use of magic is discouraged in town. That a problem?"

That was a big, big problem. His stomach sank. "What about magic I can't control?"

Emmaline's eyes widened, then she shrugged. "That's not my call. We'll let the Ringleaders sort you out." She chirped to her pegasus and the

spotted stallion turned away. "We'll fly on up to Itude and make introductions."

"Wait, wait, the who? And fly?" Panic seized him. He wasn't ready to
fly with a saddle, much less bareback.

The teen made a soft scoffing sound, and Blaise knew he'd lost any
credibility he might have with her. "You're new to this whole thing, aren't
you?" Her voice was incredulous, like she didn't think someone so ignorant could exist in the world. "The town is on a cliff. And you're not on
the right side of the canyon to take the merchant trail up. *And,* if you
didn't notice, you're on a pegasus. Wings and such." She brought her
hands together and made a little flapping motion with her fingers, in case
he wasn't clear on the concept.

Emrys shifted beneath him. <I'm sorry. I should have considered that.
But the flight won't be very long.>

Emmaline cocked her head. "Well, you coming or are you going to go
back to whatever fancy-pants place you came from?"

Blaise looked at the distant cliff. He had come too far to turn around.
He had nothing to go back to. "I'm coming." He closed his eyes and
wrapped his hands through hunks of Emrys's thick mane.

Emrys bunched his muscles and leaped into the sky. Blaise tried not to
scream.

CHAPTER SIX

Always Bet on the Jack

Laughter and music roared through the Broken Horn Saloon. Jack nursed his drink, monitoring the game of Wild Dragon in the corner. All but one of the players were regulars, a visiting merchant with more money than sense. Their rowdiness grew with each round, and Jack figured he was going to shut them down before too long.

He *hated* Wild Dragon. Why didn't they choose a different card game? Brag or Three-Card-Monte were better choices. Wild Dragon was the worst game—cheating abounded, and it was never long before a cry went up and fists flew.

Clover, the Knossan bartender, ambled over to where Jack sat by the bar. "Can I get you a refill?" She leaned one of her furry elbows against the smooth wood as she awaited his answer.

Jack pushed his mug over to her. "Maybe later. I'm done for now."

She grabbed the mug with one hand, the dark skin thick and calloused. "Are you thinking of joining the game?" Clover's brown eyes twinkled.

Jack grinned at the Knossan. At his full height, Jack's head came up to her shoulders. Clover was the tallest citizen in Itude, and she often scared newcomers shitless. She looked like an insane wizard had married the concept of a cow and a human into one creature. The hide that covered her body was the same color as the polished brown wood of the bar. Short horns crowned her head, though one had broken off years ago. A brass ring glinted in her nose. With her sheer bulk, Clover cut an imposing figure, and to be sure she could use her mass if she had a reason. She was also the kindest person Jack had ever met.

"I might," Jack agreed, "if only to save you some effort."

"Thanks. Brawls do cut into my business," Clover chuckled as she moved over to check on another client.

Jack rose from the barstool, rolling his shoulders as he paced over to the gamblers. He plucked an empty chair from a nearby table and pulled it over. "Howdy, boys. Deal me in."

"You're sassing me, Jack," flame-haired Vixen Valerie grumbled at him. She was acting as the dealer which pointed to her as the biggest cheat.

"Always, darling." Jack snickered, placing the chair next to hers. He was glad to see Vixen was wearing her smoked-lens glasses. That meant she wasn't planning to cheat with her magic, at least.

The other players paled when Jack joined them. That was fine with him. Let them squirm. Everyone was aware he was the one who took care of any *problems* in town.

"Why won't you let us have our fun?" Vixen complained as she slid cards over to him.

"If you want fun, pick a different card game." Jack watched as the others gathered their hands and started placing their bets. Vixen had spread thirteen cards face-up on the table. Once they finished, he laid his yellow chip on the Jack of Hearts.

Vixen sighed at him. "Really?"

"Always bet on the Jack," he deadpanned.

The other gamblers shifted in their seats as Vixen flipped the first card from the deck. Seven of Clubs. The ranch hand at the table hissed as he realized his bet on Seven of Hearts was a loss. Jack's eyes whipped to the others as Vixen displayed the winning card.

Jack of Clubs.

"Well, what do you know?" Jack settled back in his chair as the others glared at him. Violence telegraphed through the tightness in their shoulders and the slant of their brows. None of them would act on it. *He* was Wildfire Jack, and this was *his* town.

Vixen was about to speak but stopped. Her gaze shifted to the entrance, and Jack realized something was up. He turned and saw his daughter peering around the clusters of people in the saloon.

"Good game." Jack rose from the table. He pushed his cards and chips away, shooting a threatening smile at the remaining players. Just to make sure they remembered who they were dealing with.

Out of the corner of his eye, Clover clopped toward Emmaline. The Knossan had a soft spot for his fifteen-year-old daughter, and there was no one in town Jack trusted more. If Clover had abandoned the bar, something was up.

Then he saw the young man standing behind Emmaline, the kid's unease making him stick out in the saloon like a sore thumb. *The Breaker.*

Jack's world constricted to only his daughter beside the dangerous mage. The mage who had *broken his damn gun.* What in Perdition was *he* doing here?

As Jack flowed forward, anyone standing in his path scuttled out of the way, like birds fleeing before a storm. A roar of approval came from the dart game in the corner, ignorant of the change of atmosphere in the saloon. In the other corner, the pianist played a buoyant drinking song.

Emmaline noticed his approach, her face lighting up. It was a short-lived expression, though, as she read the thunderous look on his face. "Daddy!" she called to him. She didn't have a clue why he was angry. Jack had told no one about the incident on the road, not even his daughter. He hadn't wanted to.

The young mage gawked at the busy interior of the saloon, once again showing how out of his depth he was. He didn't see Jack coming until it was too late.

Jack pulled his arm back and slammed his fist into the Breaker's face. The kid made a satisfying squeak, and his bones crunched as the outlaw's knuckles found their mark. His head snapped backward, and he spun around, slumping to the floor. Emmaline covered her mouth with one hand, staring in horror.

Jack's hand was going to hurt like the dickens later, but he didn't care. He wanted that mage away from his daughter and out of his town, as soon as possible.

The noisy saloon grew quiet. Voices murmured and mugs clinked as nervous townsfolk set them down. The brittle clatter of Clover's hooves shattered the tableau as she clamped her tough hand on Jack's upper arm.

"*Out!*" The Knossan's melodious voice was curt as she steered him around the fallen mage. Jack snarled at her. She ignored him, dragging him out unceremoniously. Clover was strong; there was no breaking her grip. He'd more likely break his own arm if he tried.

Jack let her escort him outside, though he felt justified by the shenanigans. He would do it again if he had half a chance.

Clover shook her horned head at him. She had taken him behind the saloon where they had a modicum of privacy. "What was that? You of all people *never* throw a punch first in my saloon."

The worry in her voice grounded his anger. She knew he was acting out of character for a reason, and she was wary, wanting to understand. "That man can't be here. He's a Breaker." And he was with *Emmaline.*

Even though he hadn't said the last part, Clover understood. Her nostrils flared. "I see. And how do you know this?"

Jack glowered, rubbing the tender knuckles of his index and middle fingers. "We had an encounter."

She canted her head, a classic Knossan *tell me more* mannerism. Jack returned the look, impassive. When he didn't expound, she wiggled an ear. "And does anyone else know?"

Jack opened his mouth to tell her *no,* but boots crunched on the ground as Vixen came around the corner. "You're a hypocrite, Jack," Vixen said, her tone cutting. "Sticking your nose into my game and then you do that? Honestly?"

He crossed his arms. "Had nothing to do with your game."

"Obviously," Vixen agreed, looking at the both of them. "Thought you should know your daughter is madder than a mule chewing on bumblebees. And that kid you tried to squabash got dragged over to Nadine's clinic."

Jack set his jaw. At least that meant the Breaker would be out of the equation for the time being. He would have to deal with his angry daughter later. He turned to Vixen. "We need a meeting."

She scowled. Evening had fallen. The other Ringleaders wouldn't take kindly to a meeting so late in the day. But this was important.

Vixen shifted her weight from foot to foot, considering. "This about that greenhorn?"

Jack nodded.

She pursed her lips. "I'll send word." Vixen glanced at the Knossan. "Clover, Emmaline's hanging out in the kitchen."

Clover inclined her horns, ever gracious. She and Jack watched as Vixen spun on her heel and walked off to notify the other Ringleaders. "I'll keep Emmaline occupied," Clover assured Jack.

Jack rubbed his forehead. "Thanks, appreciate it. I don't know how long we'll be."

To Jack's annoyance, the Ringleaders refused to decide on the matter of the young mage until he spoke for himself. It didn't matter that Jack told them they were dealing with a Breaker. And that, Jack decided, was one problem with trying to have *fair* leadership. Sometimes it wasn't fair, like in a case such as this where he knew what was best for them. Personal experience proved it.

Nadine was unavailable to attend their meeting, seeing as she was tending to the downed mage. The other Ringleaders agreed they would meet the next morning. But on one condition: the Breaker must be well enough to speak.

Disgruntled, Jack headed back to the saloon and collected Emmaline. The disapproval on her face almost made him feel bad about the whole thing. Almost.

"Why did you do that?" she asked as they walked to their home on the outskirts of town, rubbing her arms in the cooling night air.

Jack didn't reply for several minutes. He collected his thoughts as he listened to the steady sound of their footsteps and shrugged off the chill of her eyes on him. "I have my reasons."

Her hair whipped around in the silver light of the moon as she shook her head. "Well, it was rude. You've never acted like that to anyone new before."

No one like that has ever set foot in this town before. Jack kept that thought to himself. He knew it sounded petty and dramatic. Mages of varying ability called Itude home. They were all dangerous in their own way. But not like *that*.

"I said I have my reasons." He heard her huff a frustrated breath. Jack didn't like getting into spats with his daughter. Emmaline was all he had, and it hurt his heart to cause her distress. But he wasn't willing to tell her more. Not now.

She said nothing else to him for the rest of the night. That was fine with him. It allowed him to avoid questions he would rather not answer. She continued the silent treatment the next morning, stomping out the door to school without so much as a glance in his direction.

Jack rubbed the short bristles on his chin. He hadn't slept well, troubled by the Breaker's presence in his town. The morning cup of coffee only did so much. He dressed and then headed out to Headquarters.

He was the last to arrive, but that was by design. Jack wasn't sure he could contain himself with minimal people around to keep him off the kid. He ambled into the back room where they held their meetings. Everyone was seated, awaiting his arrival. The injured mage sat between Nadine and Vixen, the skin around his left eye an ugly purple. His nose was crooked and swollen, a crust of blood flaked around his nostrils. When he recognized Jack, fresh panic flooded his face.

Vixen leaned over and whispered something, and the kid settled. Jack glanced around the room and found an empty seat. He slid into it, slouching.

Raven Dawson, his hair the same color as his namesake, rose from his chair as Jack seated himself. Raven was young, a handful of years older than the kid mage. The difference was that Raven was charismatic, full of savvy, and had stealthy magic that he firmly controlled.

"Now that we're all here, let's get this started." Jack didn't miss the fact that Raven's knives were sheathed at his hip. Raven was young, but he wasn't a fool. He had taken Jack's warning about the Breaker to heart. "To put everyone on even footing, we'll begin with introductions. I'll start." Raven cleared his throat. "Raven Dawson, one of Itude's Outlaw Ringleaders."

Great. Introductions. Jack was ready to ship the Breaker out of town and they wanted to introduce everyone and play tiddlywinks.

"Nine Lives Nadine, Ringleader and Healer," Nadine offered. She traced the vivid white scar that laced down her right cheek. "In case you're wondering, this would have killed anyone else." Jack noted that the young mage blanched at her words.

"Vixen Valerie, Ringleader." Vixen leaned back in her chair, smoked glasses perched jauntily on the bridge of her nose.

"Kur Agur, Ringleader." The Theilian was the second-scariest looking resident of Itude after Clover. Like the Knossan, he had the vague suggestion of a humanoid body. He stood on clawed paws, his body covered in a thick grey-yellow pelt with black guard hairs trailing down his back. His head was that of a wolf, from the upright ears to the tapered muzzle full of gleaming, pearly fangs. As a Theilian, he was supposed to be able to shift into a full lupine form, but Jack had never seen it. Rumor had it that Kur was under some sort of curse that prevented the shift.

All the same, Kur's snarly visage was frightening. It didn't escape Jack's notice that the Breaker looked at Kur with less fear than when he looked at Jack. *Good. You should be afraid.*

All eyes fell on Jack. Right. They wanted him to play nice. He could do so, within reason. "Wildfire Jack. Ringleader." He kept his voice low and gravelly. The kid's face turned another shade of pale. Jack hadn't thought it possible.

Then everyone's eyes rested on the Breaker. The kid's gaze fell away from Jack. There was a tremor in his voice as he spoke. "Blaise Hawthorne. From Desina." He looked like he was desperate to say more, but was too afraid.

Jack didn't miss the way the other Ringleaders shifted in their seats at the mention of Desina. They were all aware of the news he had brought of the Salt-Iron Confederation's advance into the nation.

Vixen leaned forward, taking off her glasses and setting them on the table. Everyone else was very, very careful not to catch her eye as she turned to look at Blaise. "It's good to meet you, Blaise. Tell us why you came to Itude."

Aside from Kur, everyone sitting in the room had magic, and Vixen was actively using hers. Jack frowned. The other Ringleaders must have agreed to the use of her magic before he arrived.

Vixen's ability was vision-based, but one would almost swear it was auditory, with the way her voice lilted and charmed as she spoke. She was so calming and welcoming that everything she said sounded like a good idea. And as long as she had her listener's undivided attention, they took the bait. Jack glanced at Blaise. She had him hook, line, and sinker.

When the young mage spoke, his voice was steady and devoid of emotion. He was in her thrall, and that spoke to the level of his exhaustion. Vixen was good, but it normally took her longer to work someone under her spell. The kid's mental defenses had to be shattered.

Blaise spoke of how the Salt-Iron Confederation had come to his home to capture him—to use him and his magic. He detailed his headlong flight and saving Emrys. To his credit, Blaise omitted his run-in with Jack.

But by the same token, Blaise painted himself as a victim. And now Jack was the asshole for punching him in the face. The kid had dropped a *tree* on his pursuers—he said so himself. He had little control over his magic. He was *dangerous*.

Once Blaise finished speaking, Vixen slipped her glasses back on. The young man blinked in a daze as the spell dissipated.

Raven rose again. "One responsibility of the Ringleaders is to ensure the safety of the town. We're charged with approving any new mages who wish to join us. We appreciate you telling us your plight, and we'll hold a vote on it in a moment." He made a tiny gesture with one hand, Vixen's cue to clear Blaise from the room.

Vixen dutifully moved Blaise elsewhere and rejoined them for the deliberation. When she had taken her seat, Jack glowered at them. "I don't know why we have to talk about it. He can't stay here."

Raven pulled out one of his knives and fidgeted with it. "I don't get it, Jack. Usually, you're eager for us to have more mages to bolster our defenses. Why not this one?"

"You got cotton stuck in your ears? He's dangerous. He has no training."

Vixen drummed her fingernails against the table. "With all due respect, you're the only one sitting here who had any formal training for your magic. All the rest of us had to teach ourselves."

Jack scowled. He didn't need a reminder of what he was or what he had lost. As far as he cared, the difference between an outlaw and maverick was splitting hairs.

"And," Raven added, "If you're thinking about it from a power level alone, he's no more a threat than you or Butch."

Jack curled his lip at mention of their resident Necromancer. That wasn't even the same thing. "The difference is *I* have training. And Butch has his damn ethics. We're safe by comparison. That kid doesn't even know which way is up."

Kur twitched an ear, thoughtful. "I will agree with Jack that the man poses a threat. The scent of his magic makes me uneasy. But by the same token, I would not be comfortable throwing him out to the elements. He looks like a lost pup."

Damn wolves. They were always protecting the ones in their pack they saw as vulnerable. Jack had hoped Kur would consider the town as the thing to protect in this case. That had been a miscalculation.

"Breakers are bad news." Jack dredged his memory. "The last one on record caused an avalanche that buried a town. There's a *reason* the Confederation ended their line."

"Spare us the history lesson," Vixen said with a roll of her eyes. "And a Stonemage having a temper tantrum could do the same."

"I'm inclined to vote in favor of the mage who got punched in the face by one of our very own Ringleaders," Nadine said wryly. She gave Jack a penetrating look meant to shame him for his behavior. *Not gonna work.*

Raven nodded. "Jack, you're the only one here who has any problem with this mage. That leads me to believe the issue is more with *you* than him. Unless anyone else has more to say, we'll take the vote."

Rage smoldering in his chest, Jack went through the motions of casting his "*nay*" vote. He couldn't believe they were voting to let the Breaker stay in their town.

That kid was going to be the end of them.

CHAPTER SEVEN

Rider

Blaise

"I'm sorry. Jack's an asshole, but he rarely greets newcomers with a fist to the face." Vixen walked companionably beside Blaise. The meeting had adjourned, and she'd brought word that the Ringleaders voted to allow him to stay in town.

After last night, he wasn't sure he *wanted* to stay in Itude. Exhausted and dismayed tears prickled his eyes, further irritated by the throbbing pain in his bruised and swollen face. Having his face smashed in by an irate outlaw was the last thing he needed.

But Blaise still grappled with the yawning emptiness of the question: where else could he go? He didn't want to ask Emrys to take him anywhere else—though the stallion hadn't seen what happened to him yet.

Blaise nodded at her words. Bullies were nothing new. He wished he could say it was the first time he had ever taken a punch. Unfortunately, it ranked up there as the most forceful and competent punch. And with his luck, it wouldn't be the last.

He wished it hadn't happened when he thought things were looking up.

"Are you okay? I can take you back to the clinic if you're not up to it," Vixen offered, scrutinizing his face.

Blaise hadn't come across a mirror yet, and he was almost afraid to. "I'll be okay. I just . . ." He trailed off, at a loss for what to say.

"That's real tough, what happened to you with the Salties," she said, guiding him down the street past the bank. "You're not the only one here who's run from them. Lots of mavericks here." When he said nothing, she continued, "But Itude is safe. And everyone here does their part to chip in. We'll get you figured out and get a job for you."

"I may be able to help with that."

Vixen steered him around, and Blaise looked *up, up, up* at a hulking, horned figure. His vision was a little blurry from the punch, but it looked an awful lot like a cow walking upright. Maybe the irate outlaw had hit him too hard.

"Oh, howdy Clover," Vixen said brightly. "Blaise, this is Clover—she's a Knossan. She runs the Broken Horn Saloon." She pointed up the street to the ill-fated saloon from the previous evening.

A Knossan? Blaise had only read about the part-bovine, part-humanoid race. And her name was *Clover?* He stared up at her. "Howdy?"

Clover gave him a patient look. "I need a dishwasher. My current staff struggle to keep up." She tipped her head. "I can offer you room, board, and a fair wage."

What? She was offering him a job? That had never happened before. Hope stirred in his chest. But first things first. "I don't know if you'd want me with my magic."

The smooth hide on her shoulders rose in a bovine shrug. "Tell me how it works, and we'll figure out a way to work around it. Don't know that you can be worse than some of my regular customers."

Blaise furrowed his brow. She seemed to have a sense of his magic, even though he hadn't told her what it was. Did she know? "Um. Wearing gloves provides a barrier from my magic." He hazarded a guilty glance at his bare right hand. How was he going to afford another glove?

He heard a swish and realized she had a tail. "Gloves? Excellent, I can get just the thing from the mercantile." Clover turned to Vixen. "He can have one of the guest rooms. If you take him to the Broken Horn, Hannah can show him where to go."

Vixen gave the Knossan a little two-fingered salute. "You got it, cowgirl." She said it fondly, and in a manner that made Blaise suspect it was something few others could get away with.

Clover looked at Blaise. "If you're up to it, start tonight. But Jack rang your bell, so it's not urgent. I'll have the gloves ready."

Blaise nodded, watching the Knossan clop down the street toward another storefront.

Vixen nudged his arm. "C'mon. I'll take you over to Hannah, and you'll be in excellent hands."

———————

BLAISE DISCOVERED THAT MOST OF THE PEOPLE IN ITUDE WERE POLAR opposites to Jack. Hannah was of a similar age to Blaise, and she had an infectious smile.

"You have no idea how excited I am by the prospect of not staying up until the wee hours of the morning washing dishes!" Hannah exclaimed as she stomped up the stairs.

It was late morning, and the saloon was empty. Blaise saw a lone figure wiping down some tables, but Hannah didn't stop to introduce them. She took Blaise to the top of the staircase where five doors lined the landing. Hannah pointed to each door. "That's Clover, Wildfire Jack's daughter Emmaline, Abe, me—"

"Wait. Hold on . . ." Blaise quailed. Wildfire Jack's daughter?

Hannah nodded, eyes widening as she realized the cause of his distress. She paused outside the room she had indicated for the teenager. "She only uses it occasionally, when Jack is out of town working."

Blaise cocked his head. "What does he do?"

Hannah blinked, surprised by his ignorance. She waved one hand in a circle. "You know. He's an *outlaw*. Goes out to find stagecoaches to rob. That can keep him away for days at a time."

"Oh." Blaise wished he could kick himself. He should have known.

She continued down the short hallway, moving to the last door and thrusting it open. "This room is for you." She beckoned for him to follow her inside. "I have to tell you that before Clover got a hold of it, this was a house of ill-repute. Sorry in advance for the decor."

Blaise tugged at his ratty shirt collar, looking around the small room. Silky red sheets covered the bed, along with a quilt. Blaise leaned over to inspect the embroidery. His face flamed when he realized the embroiderer had created tiny scenes of men and women in the throes of passion. He turned away, facing a chest of drawers with a lace doily on top. Blaise made a conscientious decision to not look at the doily.

Hannah coughed, glancing at the quilt. "We, um, never come in here. I forgot about that, and I'm sure Clover did, too. Knossans don't see things the same way we do . . ."

Blaise rubbed the back of his neck. At least he wasn't alone in his embarrassment. "It's fine. It'll beat the cave I had to sleep in the other night."

His words cheered her, and she grinned. "I guess so! Well, I'm sure Clover won't mind if you redecorate. She's not attached to any of the stuff in these rooms, far as I know."

Blaise glanced around. "Did you redecorate your room?"

Hannah rolled her eyes. "Oh, sweet Faedra, yes. It was awful. I won't ever tell another soul what painting was in *my* room. I dropped it off the side of the cliff."

He hadn't even looked at the painting over the dresser. Blaise hazarded a glance and then regretted it. A gilded plaque beneath it that read "*Orgy of Pleasure*" spoke volumes. "I like that option. That would be an uncomfortable number of people staring at me while I sleep."

Hannah giggled, and for the first time since he had arrived in Itude, Blaise felt like things might not be so bad. Out of principle, he took the painting down from the wall and turned it around.

"Do you have any belongings?" Hannah asked once the awkward artwork was no longer a source of distraction.

Oh. Right. Blaise pursed his lips. "I did. I don't know what happened to them." He had lost track after Jack's fist had been introduced to his face.

"Stop by the clinic—Nadine may have it. It's two doors down from us." She pulled a key out of her pocket and handed it to him. "Here—key for this door. You should stop by the mercantile to pick up whatever you need."

Blaise sighed. "Thanks, but I can't afford anything right now."

She flapped her hands at him. "Don't worry about that. Go on. Get." Hannah turned and hurried off, heels tapping on the floorboards.

Blaise took Hannah's advice, and after locking up his room, he checked to see if his go-bag was at the clinic. He caught Nadine packing a black medical bag. She glanced up as he tapped on the door.

"You have good timing. I was about to leave to check on a poor sod who got chewed on by a chupacabra at one of the outlying ranches last night." Nadine tipped her chin to indicate his go-bag, resting beside a clean white cot. "Let me check on you before I go. How are you feeling?"

Blaise shrugged, wondering how much she wanted to know. Hopeless. Fatigued. Heartbroken. And that didn't even touch the physical pain.

Nadine pressed her lips together and made a humming sound. "Sit on the cot." He followed her direction, and she snagged the leg of a short stool with her foot, pulling it over. Nadine's nimble fingers probed his tender nose. "I need to straighten this while I can. I should have done it last night, but you were bleeding like a stuck pig."

Nadine wasn't exaggerating. Blaise's nose had bled and bled, ruining his clothing. Some thoughtful citizen had donated a second-hand shirt to him. Blaise's pants had traces of blood, but they weren't the same spattered horror as his shirt had been.

Her practiced hands settled over the bridge of his nose. Blaise bit his tongue as the pressure of her fingers flushed out a fresh wave of intense pain. Then warmth flooded the abused cartilage, and he heard a soft crunch as Nadine used her magic to realign it.

"That should help. Let me see that shiner now."

Blaise fought the urge to cower as she examined the bruised flesh around his left eye. Nadine paused, pulling back to look at him. "Something wrong?"

"No." His racing heart exposed the lie.

The Healer assessed him with cool eyes, moving in to continue the examination. This time, she moved with caution, as if she were trying to calm a frightened animal.

"Here's some advice. Don't lie to a Healer. We can feel the tension in your muscles and the fear in your pulse." Nadine drew her hands away. "Am I right in thinking you didn't like my hands near your face?"

He nodded.

The Healer sighed, settling back on the stool. "That's normal after what Jack did to you." Nadine studied him, thoughtful. "You're not a fighter by nature. Yet you have old, healed injuries. Cracked ribs. A broken hand."

She could tell all that about him with her magic? The injuries were testaments to how much his age-mates had despised him for what he was. After those experiences, he was shy of touch or anyone getting too close. He didn't know how to explain, so he shrugged.

Nadine crossed her arms, angling her head to get him to look her in the eye. "Anything you want to talk about?"

"Not really."

She ran a hand through her short hair. "I respect that. Oh, and you should know I took the edge off that blistering sunburn. Be sure you wear a hat from now on."

Blaise blinked. He had forgotten about the sunburn. He rubbed his left cheek and found that it didn't have the roasted sensation from two days ago. "Oh. Thank you. For everything."

Nadine waved it off. "It's my job. I'd better get to that ranch."

Blaise collected his go-bag and headed out. Nadine followed along, stowing her medical bag on the back of a strawberry roan pegasus. The roan gave Blaise a curious look, ears pricked forward.

<There you are.>

Emrys swooped down from above, dirt billowing as he back-winged and landed nearby. The stallion folded his wings and trotted over. <Your face didn't have spots before. Why do you have spots?>

"Bruises." Blaise gingerly touched the skin below his eye and winced. "Wildfire Jack punched me."

The pegasus swished his tail, agitated. <What? Why would he do that to my rider?>

Blaise shook his head. He didn't want to go into it. "Don't worry about it." Then Emrys's words gave him pause. "Wait. What do you mean your *rider?*"

<I picked you, obviously.>

Had the outlaw hit him harder than he thought? Blaise rubbed his tender cheek. "I don't understand."

Emrys flipped his velvety nose in Nadine's direction as she set off with her pegasus. <Many stallions without a flight of their own pick a rider, usually a mage. It's always been that way, ever since the first outlaw mage set foot in the Untamed Territory. At least, that's the story passed down from mare to foal.>

Blaise blinked. "Oh."

<We're a good team.> Emrys stomped a forehoof, as if declaring something made it so. The pegasus prodded Blaise with his muzzle, his next words uncertain. <We are, aren't we?>

Maybe Blaise wasn't the only one in need of a friend. He reached up and gave Emrys's cheek a pat. True enough, he and Emrys may have perished in the Gutter without each other. "We are. Let me put this bag in my room at the saloon. Then can you show me around?"

<Of course.> Emrys followed him over to the Broken Horn, his mental voice radiating contentment.

With his meager possessions stored, Blaise came back out and walked beside Emrys. Itude was smaller than Bristle. Blaise noticed it still had many of the same amenities. Every building had an outhouse a suitable distance behind it so that people could take care of their necessaries. Emrys told him a bathhouse and a laundry were located on the northeastern side of town, in the shade of the massive wind-pump.

Blaise shaded his eyes, peering up at the spinning blades. Exhaustion had kept him from noticing it sooner. It was larger than any Blaise had seen before, the bulk of the structure made from whitewashed stone.

"What's it do?"

<Pumps water from below to the cistern and livestock trough. I don't know how it works. It's the oldest building in town.>

Blaise nodded. He couldn't imagine how long it had taken to build the wind-pump. It looked like a true feat of engineering and—he presumed—magic.

Emrys took him to the mercantile. Blaise gave an appreciative sniff with his newly healed nose. The diner next door had amazing smells wafting from the open door. Down the same street, he saw a bakery, hardware store, greengrocer, and dry goods store.

"How long has Itude been around? I didn't even know it existed."

The stallion snorted. <Hmm. I'm not sure. That would be a better question for a human.> He nudged Blaise with his nose. <Go into the mercantile and get what you need. Ellie and Gus run it—they're good people.>

Blaise trotted up the steps to the mercantile. A smattering of customers browsed the wide assortment of goods. A little girl begged for candy from one of the colorful jars beside a window. Blaise looked around, overwhelmed by the amount of merchandise.

"Hello! You look like someone in need of assistance." A short, sturdy woman with brown hair pinned up in a messy bun hurried over to him. "You must be our newcomer who has Jack's tail tied up in knots!"

Blaise blinked in surprise, then nodded. "Er, yes?" Word traveled fast in Itude.

The woman introduced herself as Ellie Pembroke. She pointed to a white-haired man ringing up another customer. "That's Gus, the love of my life." Gus offered Blaise a nod before returning to his work. That done, Ellie looked him up and down, clucking her tongue.

"Child, I'm guessing you came to us with little more than the clothes on your back, is that right?"

Not even that. The clothes on his back had been too bloody to save. "Um . . . that's the gist of it. I have a bag of a few things but . . . not a lot."

Ellie tapped her fingertips together. "As I thought. That won't do, not at all." She ducked behind the counter, returning with a pad of paper and pencil. "Let's brainstorm. Tell me what you think you need, and I'll give you my suggested additions."

This was not what Blaise had expected. He rattled off the few things he knew he needed (clothes, new gloves, a razor, comb and brush, maybe a new hat). Before he knew it, Ellie had filled the page with her florid handwriting.

She gave him a kind smile. "No offense, but you look a little out of your depth." She tore the paper out of the notebook and handed it to him.

"We have some items here. I made a note of where you can go to get the ones we don't have."

Blaise looked over the long list, his heart sinking. "I don't have any way to pay."

Ellie waved a dismissive hand. "Here in Itude, we take care of each other. Don't worry yourself about that. We'll open a line of credit for you. Once you have some funds, you can pay it down as you're able."

Here in Itude, we take care of each other. Blaise felt an unexpected prickle in his eyes again. Someone cared. Someone was *kind.*

"What happens if someone skips town without paying?" Blaise blurted out, curious.

The laugh-lines around her mouth puckered as she grew serious. "Oh child, you are new as a day-old calf, aren't you? No one would dare skip out on their debts from any folk in Itude. No one wants one of our Ringleaders hunting them down."

The skin around his eye throbbed a painful reminder. Point taken. Blaise nodded. "Makes sense. I appreciate the help."

Pleased, Ellie nodded and hummed a contented tune as she helped him gather the items on the list. Before Blaise knew it, she had a wooden crate full of items.

Ellie peered out the window and noticed the pegasus waiting outside. "Oh! Is that Emrys? Can't let him wait out there without a treat." Ellie hurried over to a colorful jar of candy and pulled out a striped peppermint. She excused herself and spryly skipped down the stairs to the stallion, holding the candy in her extended palm. Blaise watched as Emrys's delicate lips plucked it from her hand. No wonder the pegasus had called her *good people.*

She came back inside and set up an account in his name and listed the items and their prices. Blaise watched as she pulled a yellow piece of paper out from beneath the one she had written on. "This is your copy."

Blaise took the paper from her and regarded it with curiosity. "Never seen anything like that before. Is that magic?"

"Oh." Ellie's smile was gentle. "Ditto paper. Nothing magic about it. It's imported here from Thorn. Not sure where it comes from before that."

He folded the copy down into a square and tucked it into his pocket. Ellie passed the list of items he still needed back to him, then directed him to see Jasper Strop, the knocker who ran the dry goods store.

When the afternoon drew to a close, Blaise was the proud owner of almost everything on the list. He had a new hat to keep the worst of the sun at bay, a smart new dark blue duster, and several matching bandannas. He had a few changes of clothes, a hairbrush and comb, pomade, and most importantly a replacement pair of leather gloves.

Blaise was uncomfortable about the amount of money that he owed the Pembrokes and Jasper Strop. But they didn't seem at all bothered by it, so he let the concern slide. He stowed his new purchases in his strange little room. Happy that his nose was feeling better, and that he had some possessions to call his own, he went downstairs to see if Clover wanted him to start work.

CHAPTER EIGHT

Breakfast, Interrupted

Clover's ears flicked in surprise at Blaise when he made his way down to the ground floor of the saloon. She was buffing the wood on the bar to a soft luster, and she set aside her cloth at his approach.

"I didn't think you would be up to starting today." She moved out from behind the bar. "Are you sure you're well enough?"

Blaise shrugged. "I may as well start now. It'll take my mind off . . . things."

The Knossan gave him a considering look, then led him into the small kitchen in the back. Blaise felt more at ease. The man he had spied earlier was at work in the kitchen, tending to something that smelled like a stew.

"Abraham, this is our new dishwasher, Blaise. Abe is the cook." Clover clopped past the older man to the washstand.

Blaise nodded to the cook. Abe glanced over his shoulder and gave a salute with a wooden spoon. "Howdy."

Clover picked up a pair of gloves and slapped them against the rough palms of her hands. "Rubber gloves from the mercantile." She held them out to Blaise.

He accepted them, pulling off one of his new leather gloves. The rubber was a strange barrier against his skin. A weird, squeaky sensation. He tugged it on, twisting his wrist and flexing his fingers. His magic prodded the new material, but that wasn't anything new.

"Will those work?" Clover asked, watching him with interest.

"For a while," Blaise replied, replacing his right leather glove with the other rubber one. "The test will be to see how long they last."

Clover seemed content with that answer. "Let me know when you need more. The evening rush will be here soon."

She wasn't kidding. Hannah came down for work, tying an apron around her waist as she blew into the kitchen. When Blaise looked out the door a few minutes later the saloon had a full house. Cheerful music emanated from the floor as the pianist came in to play, and a steady flow of dishes circulated into the kitchen for Blaise to wash.

The evening was a blur, which was a relief to Blaise. It left him with little time to think about all that he'd lost, which was his inclination anytime he had a quiet moment. Abraham cooked, Hannah took orders and delivered food, Clover kept the brew flowing, and Blaise washed the dishes. The rubber gloves felt odd on his hands, but as the night wore on, Blaise grew used to them. He was so caught up in his task that Abraham nudged him partway through their shift, pointing with meaning at a plate of food he had left nearby. Blaise smiled his thanks and took a quick break to eat before going back to work.

"Wouldn't reflect well on me if you collapsed your first night on the job," the cook commented.

Blaise knew he looked haggard. His time on the run hadn't been kind. He made a note to do something about his unkempt hair and beard tomorrow.

It was well after midnight by the time Clover shooed the last customer out of the Broken Horn. Hannah carried back the last dishes, blowing out a weary breath.

"My dogs are barking." She set the dishes down for Blaise and wiggled her left foot with a groan. "Survived your first night working here, I see."

"It's not over yet." Blaise picked up one of the plates.

"I'll dry," Hannah volunteered, picking up a towel as he washed.

The sound of hooves on the wood floor announced Clover's arrival as she came in from the bar. She surveyed the kitchen. "Where's Abe?"

"Snuck up to bed already, as usual." Hannah used her wrist to swipe a lock of damp hair from her eyes.

Clover sighed. "Should have known." She watched them work for a moment, then scrutinized the dishes Blaise had washed. The Knossan nodded her head. "You did well, Blaise. Not a speck of dirt on them."

Blaise winced. "I should hope not."

Hannah laughed. "What Clover means is we're not used to a dish-washer doing a good job."

That seemed terrible to Blaise. Clean dishes, pots and pans, and uten-sils were important. Clover helped put away the remaining dishes. When they finished, they stumbled up the stairs to their rooms. Blaise was so tired that he had no difficulty falling asleep in the uncomfortably deco-rated room.

When he awoke the next morning, light filtered in through a tiny window above the bed. Blaise sat up, disoriented. The last comfortable place he had slept in had been his own bed at home. His face throbbed, reminding him of his situation in a strange counterpoint to the soft sheets.

Blaise sank back onto the cotton-stuffed mattress and pulled the covers over his head. His face hurt. He was still tired, and he had aches in muscles he hadn't known existed. He wanted to go home. But he couldn't go home. The knowledge settled on his chest like a weight, and for a moment he almost couldn't breathe. Anxiety and the yawning expanse of his unknown future clawed at him. The warmth of his magic flowed over his palms, and out of reflex, he clenched them into fists to try to call back the power. It was of no use, though, and his magic threaded its way into the sheets.

"*No*," Blaise hissed, panic rising. He didn't want to ruin the sheets so soon, hideous as they were. He sat up and folded his hands into his lap before too much damage was done. The fabric looked worn but didn't have any holes. Yet.

He rubbed the side of his face, cringing as his fingers ran across the untamed beard growth. Blaise took deep breaths to calm himself. As tempting as it was to hide in bed all day, he had vowed to make himself presentable. Reluctantly, he dragged himself out of the tangle of obscene bedsheets. He turned on the mage-light perched atop the dresser.

He pulled out a set of fresh clothes and changed. The simple, familiar task was an anchor to normality. Blaise found a hand mirror in the top drawer of the dresser and pulled it out.

"Sakes alive," Blaise murmured, angling the mirror from left to right to see both sides of his face. He'd known he looked bad, but he wasn't prepared for the reality. The lid of his left eye was an impressive shade of purple. The bruise extended down his cheek and into the scruffy beard that had sprouted during his time on the road. His nose was puffy, but at least it was straight. He didn't recognize the face in the mirror. It couldn't belong to him.

But it did. He tucked the mirror back into the drawer. He needed to do something about that. Tame his beard, comb his hair, and maybe he would feel more like himself.

A sharp knock on the door interrupted his thoughts. "Morning, Blaise! Me 'n' Clover are going to the diner for breakfast, if you want to join us," Hannah called.

The mention of food made his stomach rumble. That was tempting. It was a good idea to eat first and then take care of everything else.

He cracked the door open. "I'll come."

Hannah beamed at him, looking like she hadn't been ready to drop only hours ago. "We're going now if you're ready."

Blaise ran the new comb through his hair, then headed down the stairs. Hannah and Clover waited for him by the door, and a sense of camaraderie filled Blaise. It was a foreign sensation after everything he had been through—people waiting for the simple act of sharing a meal with him.

And neither Hannah nor Clover cared about what he was.

HANNAH'S OLDER SISTER, CELESTE, AND HER WIFE, MINDY, WERE THE proprietors of the Jitterbug Diner. Hannah admitted to Blaise in a low voice that as much as she loved her sister, she couldn't bear to work for her. She had opted to take her talents to Clover at the Broken Horn. Blaise felt a stab of jealousy that she lived so close to her sibling. He squelched the thought as Mindy handed him a menu.

"If you don't know what to pick, I can pick for you." The young woman's yellow eyes danced with amusement. "My magic is never wrong." She bustled away to give them a few minutes alone with the menu.

Blaise glanced at Hannah. "What sort of magic is that?"

She set her menu down on the white tablecloth. "We call it Hospitality. Mindy can pick the best dish for any customer to enjoy just by looking at them. Without fail."

"And it can change from day to day. If you come see me tomorrow, it may be something different, hon." Mindy swept back over to their table. "Did you make your choices?"

Clover and Hannah placed their orders. Blaise glanced at the menu, then handed it back to Mindy. "Surprise me."

She saluted him with the menus. "Challenge accepted."

It wasn't long before Mindy came back bearing a tray laden with griddlecakes, sausages, bacon, and eggs. She made a return trip with a variety of syrups, jellies, butter, coffee, sugar, and creamers. Blaise's stomach growled eagerly when he saw the spread. Maybe there was something to her magic.

Clover and Hannah tucked into their food. Blaise's face was sore, so he took his time. He was certain one of his teeth was loose. Despite the pain, the food was excellent. He thought it was odd there weren't any fresh-baked items, though. He asked Clover and Hannah why that was.

"Oh, the town baker had black fever about a month ago and up and died," Hannah explained with a grimace. "Bakery's been empty ever since. Celeste will whip up the occasional cake or loaf of bread, but she doesn't like it as much as making other things."

"And Abe tried to make a loaf of bread once. It was a brick." Clover shook her head.

Blaise tapped a finger against the table. Should he tell them? After everything he had been through, he didn't think he could handle disappointment or scorn. Baking was the one skill in which he had any confidence. He didn't want to risk it. Safer to say nothing at all.

Hannah carried most of the conversation at the table, at ease as they talked about a wide range of topics. Blaise decided she'd had a lot of practice from her work as a waitress. She had a way of keeping the conversation flowing without delving too deeply into uncomfortable topics. She asked him a few things about his past that he could answer without too much angst or embarrassment.

They had almost finished their meal when the bell over the door jingled, Wildfire Jack striding through cloaked in determination. He surveyed the occupants of the Jitterbug Diner until his eyes settled on Blaise.

"Oh no." Blaise debated hiding under the table. He didn't think the table would stop a resolute outlaw, though.

Hannah gave him a confused look, then her eyes widened when she saw Jack. "Um, Clover?"

The Knossan didn't so much as twitch. Blaise figured she had no reason to worry since she outweighed the outlaw two or three times over. She also hadn't been the recent recipient of a punch in the face from him.

"Howdy, Jack." Clover was serene and unruffled as Jack approached their table. She took a sip of her coffee.

"Ladies." Jack nodded to Hannah and Clover. "Pardon my interruption." He turned, stabbing a finger at Blaise. "You. Out at the stables in five minutes. We're going to have a *talk.*" His ice blue eyes pinned Blaise to his seat.

Blaise stared at him, pulse racing. Things had been going so well. *Of course* Jack wanted to talk to him. Probably with fists or guns or whatever his horrible magic was.

The corners of Jack's lips twitched, an acknowledgment of Blaise's terror. But instead of saying anything to lower the tension like a compassionate person might, he pivoted and stalked to the door.

Hannah waited until he left, then squeaked, "Um, Clover, is he going to kill Blaise?"

Blaise wished he could curl into a ball and hide. "Did you have to say that out loud?"

Clover laughed, a deep sound like rolling thunder. "Jack may wish you dead, but he wouldn't have you go to the stables if that were the case."

Blaise lifted his head, frowning. "Why?"

"I know Jack. Anytime he goes to the stables, it's to be held accountable. His pegasus and yours will not tolerate reckless behavior again."

CHAPTER NINE

A Little Sugar

Jack leaned against the top rail of the paddock, watching a pair of donkeys snacking on the flakes of hay a stable hand tossed over the fence. Zepheus was nearby, pretending to browse the dry vegetation on the outskirts of town. It was a ruse. The stallion had cleaned out his bucket of oats and sweet feed, chased down by sugar water. The pegasus was like a blasted hummingbird.

When Zepheus raised his head with ears pricked, Jack knew that the Breaker was approaching. He didn't budge from his place. Out of the corner of his eye, Jack noticed the Breaker's black stallion stride up beside Zepheus. Jack turned to frown at the stud. So what if the kid had freed him from a snare? Didn't mean the pegasus owed him any allegiance. Didn't change the threat he posed.

But for whatever misguided reason, the young stallion liked the kid and had picked him as his rider. And Zepheus had relayed to him that Emrys wasn't happy about the punching incident. *Too bad.*

It didn't matter, though. Jack had decided that since no one else saw things his way, he was going to feed the young mage enough rope to hang himself. Then matters would be out of Jack's hands.

Boots scraped the dirt. Jack looked back and saw the kid walk up, head bowed. Jack had to admit, part of him thought he wouldn't come. No doubt Clover had told him it wasn't optional.

The young man said nothing as he approached. He leaned against the fence, one of the fuzzy donkeys ambling over, curious about the newcomer. Jack pursed his lips when he saw the young mage offer the donkey a sugar cube.

"Your pegasus will be jealous." Jack tilted his head toward the two stallions. They were pretending to graze again, tails twitching to shoo away flies, wings fluttering with the motion.

"I have some in my pocket for him, too." Blaise kept his focus on the donkey. He scratched the little equine behind one of its long, shaggy ears. It leaned into the motion with a blissful sigh.

Jack blew out a breath through his nose. He shifted to face the Breaker, one hand braced against the fence. "I don't like that the other Ringleaders agreed you could stay, but it's something I have to live with now. I wanted to make some things clear."

Blaise kept his eyes averted, shoulders hunched. He gave a tiny nod, the only sign that he'd heard Jack's words.

Damn, but it felt like he was haranguing a day-old kitten that didn't know any better. But Zepheus had said it himself—even kittens had claws. "Itude is *my* town. I've worked hard to make it a safe place for the people who call it home. I'm watching you."

Blaise turned to him, and for a moment Jack anticipated a fight. But the kid's bruised face crumpled, eyes watery with the tears he was holding back. "Do you think I *want* any of this?" He held up his gloved hands. "I *never* wanted this. Never wanted magic, *especially* this magic. It's taken *everything* from me. I don't have a home anymore. Family. I have *nothing*."

Jack narrowed his eyes. Somewhere deep in his iron-clad heart, sympathy stirred for the kid. He knew how it felt for everything he loved to be stripped away. But that was different. He wasn't the same as this mage. Not at all.

"You have a home. Clover gave you a room at the saloon."

The Breaker shook his head. "That's a roof over my head. Not a home."

He didn't clarify, but Jack understood what he meant. Home wasn't where you bunked. It was having a place where you belonged, surrounded by people you cared about—and who cared about you. Blaise needed to find that somewhere else. Not in Itude.

"I'm sorry about the thing with your gun." Blaise's voice was so soft that Jack almost didn't hear. "I'm sorry if that's why you hate me."

Jack snorted. "Don't think I'll ever forgive you for that, but the gun itself is not why I have a problem with you."

Blaise wiped a tear from one eye. "Then why?"

"You're dangerous. You have no control. A mage with no control gets other people killed. Especially with magic like that." Zepheus raised his head, paying close attention to their exchange.

"Then teach me," Blaise said, almost begging. "I've never even met another mage like me. No one has shown me how any of this works."

Jack turned away, shaking his head. "I can't teach you. You'd piss me off, and I'd kill you, and that would be the end." *But that's not why. Can't let you or anyone else discover why.*

"Then . . . then I'll find someone here who will." Blaise swallowed, an edge of determination in his voice.

Jack pushed his hat up, thoughtful. So the Breaker wanted to learn to control his magic. Jack liked to consider himself a fair man, as far as outlaws went. He could hate this kid but still be fair. At least until he had reason to drive the Breaker from town. "Try Vixen. Her magic isn't the same as yours—gods, no one else breathing today has magic like yours. But she probably has some concepts that will work for you." Yeah, the more he thought about it, the more Vixen seemed like the best match.

Blaise raised his eyebrows like he hadn't expected Jack to offer him the slightest bit of help. *Yeah, look at me. I can make nice sometimes, too.*

"Oh. Thanks." The kid shifted, uncomfortable.

Jack was about to tell the Breaker to get out of his sight, but then he remembered the other reason he had summoned him. "One more thing." Blaise's eyes shifted to him, full of trepidation. "When you told us about the Salties chasing you from Desina, you mentioned they had a commander with a unicorn. What was the man's name?"

Blaise chewed his lip, considering. "Gaitwood, I think."

"Shit." Jack slammed his open palm against the fence rail.

Blaise turned in surprise, his fear lost for a moment. "You know him?"

Jack bared his teeth. "Yeah. We have a history." He would not go into that history. Not here, and not with the Breaker.

The younger man shifted his weight from one foot to the other, indecisive. It took him time to gather his courage to speak. "My mother attacked them. The soldiers."

Jack whistled, impressed. That took gumption. "Did she, now?" The kid hadn't mentioned that in his little speech with the other Ringleaders. It hadn't been relevant.

"I think . . . they wanted her, too. She told me I couldn't let them capture me. But they have her. Or . . ." He trailed off.

Or they killed her. Jack knew the unspoken words. He didn't think

Blaise wanted his thoughts echoed aloud. "She's gone, at any rate." Jack kept his tone neutral, not meaning any harm by the words. It was a reality. A reality he was well aware of.

Blaise splayed his arms across the fence rail, resting his chin against the wood. "Why did you want to know about Gaitwood?"

"Needed to verify some information from one of my sources." Jack wasn't going to tell the kid that it was bad news to have Gaitwood so close to the Gutter. That wasn't his concern. If Jack had his way, Blaise would be long gone before Gaitwood was any threat. Jack glanced at the kid's ramshackle countenance. "You look like the south side of a northbound mule. Barber's up the street." He hitched his thumb over his shoulder.

Blaise nodded, stepping down from the fence. He looked relieved by the dismissal. Jack stayed put as his footsteps receded. Zepheus ambled over. <You should carry sugar in your pockets for me,> the stallion suggested.

"You heard, huh?"

<Oh yes. All of it,> the palomino confirmed. <You should be nicer to him.>

Jack grunted. "I was nice. I told him to see Vixen about his magic. And I didn't punch him again, even though it's tempting."

<We have got to work on your people skills.> Zepheus sighed.

"My people skills are fine. Everyone else just needs to work on their me skills."

———

"WILDFIRE JACK!"

Jack paused, one foot on the bottom step leading up to the Ringleader Headquarters. In the space of a week since his chat with Blaise, he hadn't seen anything to call the kid on—yet. Clover kept him apprised of everything related to the saloon. According to Vixen, Blaise took his suggestion to heart, and he had asked her to help with his magic. She agreed, and they met regularly. Every time someone stopped him on the streets, Jack hoped for some minor bit of news he could leverage against the Breaker.

Jack kept his expression neutral as he turned to face Hank Walker, Itude's postmaster and a part of Jack's spy network. To be sure, he trusted the man about as far as he could throw him. But Walker's magical talents made him a valuable asset. Not just anyone could travel across great distances in a short time using the natural network of plants.

"Howdy, Walker." Jack crossed his arms as he addressed the postmaster. "News for me?"

Walker fidgeted, nervous. "From Desina."

Desina. Jack motioned for Walker to wait. He hurried up the stairs and poked his head into HQ. It was empty. "Come on up."

The postmaster followed him inside. Jack led him to the meeting room, shutting the door behind them.

"What did you find?"

Walker's forehead puckered. "First, confirmation of what you already know—Desina has joined the Confederation. They're rounding up all the mages they consider worth a damn and taking them to the capital. From there, they're going to pack them onto steamers to Izhadell."

Jack scowled. Depending on the flavors of mages they found, putting them on steamers was a poor choice. Did they have enough salt-iron to keep their magic at bay for a long trip? No new salt-iron veins had been struck, as far as he knew.

Jack already knew most of the information Walker provided, except for the bit about transportation. "What else? Do you know how many mages they took in?"

"Ah, the last count was two dozen. But I know there's a small group of mavericks evading them. The Salties are pissed, from what I heard."

Jack perked up. "You made contact with the mavericks?"

Walker shook his head. "Not yet. Last I found out they were in Morton, but then the Salties plowed through."

Striding over to the window, Jack leaned against the frame, thinking. With the tides turning in Desina, he needed to proceed with caution. "Are you familiar with the name Gaitwood?"

The postmaster straightened. "The politician or the soldier?"

"Both. Either. Doesn't matter."

Walker scratched his head, thrown by the question. "I know *of* them."

Jack scuffed the floor with the heel of one boot. "I need you to do what you can to intercept any missives between them. Bring any information you find to me."

The postmaster's eyes widened. Out of respect to his profession, Jack generally avoided having Walker tamper with the mail. Especially mail that wouldn't normally route through Itude, one way or another. But now that Jack knew Lamar was close, he needed to tread carefully.

"That may be a tall order," Walker admitted with reluctance.

"Why?"

Walker spread his hands. "Couriers handle military correspondence, rather than the normal means."

Damn. Jack grumbled to himself. As far as he knew, no one in his network had any ins with the couriers. The Black Market was due back in less than two weeks. He might have to wait that long to pick Slocum's brain. If anyone knew a courier or a way into their confidence, it would be him.

"Fine, scratch that," Jack relented. "I want you to keep your eye on those mavericks and let me know if they reach an extraction point."

Walker considered it. "I'll try. But it will take some time. Can't use all my magic hunting for them if the town still wants me to do my day job."

It was tempting to tell him that the postal service could go to Perdition as far as he cared. But businesses and townspeople relied on the mail. Itude was cut off from everything else—as much as Jack could keep it, and mail was one of the few means of communication they had. It was a lifeline.

"Mail still needs to flow," Jack agreed. "But keep searching."

"Understood." Walker turned and headed for the door.

CHAPTER TEN

Practical Magic

Blaise

month had passed since Blaise's chat with Jack. Their paths crossed—it couldn't be helped in the small town—but at least Jack didn't punch him again. But anytime he was near, the outlaw watched Blaise. Waiting for him to screw up so Jack could throw him out of town.

"You can't let him play mind games with you," Vixen told Blaise one afternoon as they sat at a table in the saloon. Blaise stared uneasily through the plate-glass window as Jack spoke with someone outside the bank.

Blaise fell into a routine, and part of that included magic lessons with Vixen several times a week. It was a slow start—Vixen had her own duties to attend to. Blaise was thankful for the time she spared. Clover allowed them the use of her saloon as their practice area. Each time they practiced at the saloon, the Knossan found an excuse to tidy things up around their vicinity.

Blaise scratched at his close-cropped beard. "I can't help it."

Vixen removed a shot glass from a serving tray stationed on a nearby table. Grinning, she set it down in front of him. Then she picked up a mug and took a long drink. Not for the first time, Blaise wondered if she'd agreed to work with him at the saloon as long as the free booze kept flowing.

She wiped a drop of foam from her lips. "If there's one thing to know about Wildfire Jack, it's that his favorite thing in the world is to scare the piss out of someone. Am I right, Clover?"

The Knossan looked up from the pitcher she was drying. "That is the highlight of his day."

Blaise sighed. Every time he sat down to practice with Vixen, if he caught sight of Jack, things went wrong. And the blasted outlaw had a penchant for appearing outside every time he practiced. It was like he knew what Blaise was doing and wanted to sabotage him.

The thing was, Blaise was no stranger to bullies. But Jack was a league above any provincial bully from Bristle. Something about the man terrified him to his very core. It was hard to shake.

"Hey Clover, you're sure we're good to use this set of shot glasses?" Vixen asked, gesturing to the grouping on the serving tray.

"Yes. They're chipped, and I have new ones on the way."

Vixen motioned to Blaise with a flourish. "Have at it."

Blaise picked up the shot glass. His gloves were off, and the smooth glass was cool to his touch. It was strange to not feel the glass through rubber gloves.

Vixen wanted him to focus on gaining a level of control over his magic. She said once he had that figured out, they could do more. But they had to start with the basics.

Blaise gritted his teeth, concentrating on the glass. His aim was to *not* break it. That was so much harder than it sounded. Shot glasses stood up to heavy use, but they were still glass. Glass was fragile. His magic didn't do well with fragile things. Blaise didn't know why they couldn't start with a sturdier target. Like a horseshoe. Or a boulder.

But Vixen insisted on glass. She reasoned that it would benefit him in the long run to go from hardest to easiest. So far, all Blaise had to show for it was a trail of a half dozen broken shot glasses, courtesy of Clover.

His hands itched. Sweat trickled down his forehead. A crack split the side of the glass. "I can't do this." Blaise's shoulders sagged with defeat.

Vixen took the glass from him before it could shatter, tucking it into a burlap bag. They both knew from experience that the glass wouldn't stay in one piece much longer. "Right, let me think." She pushed her glasses up the bridge of her nose. "When you're nervous or upset, your magic grabs the bit and runs. Is there ever a time when you *can* control it? Where it doesn't . . . do what it does?"

Blaise rubbed the back of his neck. "Yes." But after all he had been through, would it still work? It had been so long since he had done anything besides wash dishes in a kitchen.

"Well?" Vixen leaned forward, expectant.

"I . . . I used to bake. That was the only time I never had to wear gloves at home." Blaise's voice was soft and reluctant, expecting Vixen to laugh at him.

Vixen cocked her head, looking intrigued. "Really? Are you any good?"

Am I? Blaise asked himself. He wasn't sure what to say, so he shrugged.

Vixen traded a look with Clover. "Can we use the kitchen?"

The Knossan flicked an ear as if listening for something. "I don't see why not."

Blaise didn't know what Vixen had in mind, but he rose from the table and followed her into the kitchen. Abe was already preparing the evening menu. He gave them a curious look when they entered.

"Let's clarify some things." Vixen looked around the kitchen, getting her bearings. "Is it just baking, or cooking too?"

Blaise thought about that. The kitchen was his domain—relaxation flowed over him as soon as they walked in. His father had done most of the cooking at home, but Blaise had helped. And he hadn't worn his gloves then, either. He didn't lose himself in the joy of it the same way as with baking, but he didn't destroy anything, either.

"Cooking should be safe, too," Blaise told her. "Baking is the sure thing."

Abe grunted, pulling out a bowl and a bag of cornmeal. "Was planning on making cornbread tonight. Have at it."

Blaise's eyes lit up, but he glanced at Vixen to see if that was something she had in mind. She waved him on. "Go ahead. I'm curious to see if you can do it with gloves off. If you can, we'll try something while that bakes. And it'll be a bonus if you can make it taste less like rocks."

"That happened one time. *One*," Abe muttered.

Blaise ignored their exchange, getting to work. The tension oozed out of his muscles as soon as he had the bag of cornmeal in hand. He sifted it and made dough after combining it with boiling water. Abe watched for a moment, then shoved the other ingredients to his side of the countertop. Lard, salt, brown sugar, and a cake of yeast. The familiar pleasure of working with his hands in the kitchen consumed him. Blaise was disappointed when he had to stop to allow it time to rise.

Vixen gave a low whistle when he set the bowl aside. She moseyed over to inspect his work area. Not a single bowl or utensil had any signs of wear outside normal use. "You weren't kidding."

Blaise rubbed his hands together. They were gritty from the cornmeal, but it was like a balm for his soul. "I've missed this."

Vixen lifted her chin, studying him for a moment. Then an impish grin crossed her face. "Catch!" She flung open her hand, a shot glass arcing through the air.

He didn't even think about it; he reacted. Blaise saw the projectile flying toward him and he reached out and caught it with both hands, cradling it against his chest. He stared at Vixen with wide eyes.

"Think about what you just did." Vixen pointed at the countertop where the batter was resting. "Not on the thing in your hand."

Blaise shifted his weight from foot to foot, the small glass feeling heavier in his hand with each passing moment. Then a thought occurred to him that made him forget about the glass. "I didn't grease the pan and get it in the oven to warm."

Vixen raised her eyebrows, then laughed, amused by his priorities. "Do that. Then I want you holding that glass until you're ready to put your cornbread in the oven."

Blaise sighed, setting down the shot glass on the counter as he found a cast iron pan. He prepared it and put the pan in the oven. When he picked up the shot glass, he realized it was still in one piece. He had expected it to shatter into a thousand tiny pieces.

But it was pristine, aside from the wear of Clover's customers.

"Huh." Blaise turned it over in his hands. He didn't feel itchy, either. He looked up at Vixen. "How am I not breaking this?"

She shrugged. "I'm not an expert, but I think you just lack practice and confidence. That means a lot of your problem is in here." She tapped the side of her head. "When you do what makes you happy, you expect your magic won't mess up. You don't have that expectation for the rest of your day-to-day, though. You become a self-fulfilling prophecy."

Blaise winced. That sounded accurate. And a lot simpler than reality. He fervently wanted his magic to not destroy his life. But he had always had a low level of confidence in that actually happening.

Vixen rubbed her hands together with glee. "So this is what we're gonna do. Every practice from now on, we're going to meet in this kitchen. You'll bake something first, and we'll go from there."

Blaise nodded, setting the unbroken glass down beside the dough. "It's worth a try." Even if it didn't help his magic, at least he would get to do something he loved.

AFTER THAT, BLAISE DIDN'T MIND PRACTICING WITH VIXEN. THE KITCHEN'S windows faced away from the town square, so Blaise never saw Jack. That alone was a boon, but the opportunity to bake as a calming outlet was the biggest help.

During the second week of their practice in the kitchen, Blaise discovered that Clover had started to stock more items for baking. Abe ceded half of the workspace as well. However, the cook was overall lazy and enjoyed having someone else do his work so it didn't mean much. Blaise still worked every evening washing dishes, so his days were full.

As much as he loved baking, it was his newfound control over his magic that thrilled him. It was tenuous at first, and Vixen started him small. Initially, they focused on holding something and not breaking it. After he had success with the shot glass, she and Clover brought in a wider array of items: porcelain figurines, ceramic beer steins, mirrors—every session something new.

The effort paid off. Clover challenged him to wash dishes one evening without the rubber gloves. Blaise wasn't sure about it, and he told Clover as much.

"Try it. I'll not take anything you break out of your pay," the Knossan said with a swish of her tail.

How could he tell her *no* after that? Blaise tried and surprised himself, ending the night without a single broken dish. His hands were pruney from the dishwater, but otherwise, nothing was the worse for wear.

His successes restored his sense of self. Blaise hadn't realized how low he felt since fleeing his family, but looking back, he saw he hadn't been in a good place. He had been adrift and heartsick. But now he had a routine and purpose. He enjoyed practicing with Vixen and working with Clover. Some days, Emmaline hung out with Clover while Blaise practiced. He didn't particularly like that, though Emmaline was harmless compared to her father. She liked to sit and talk with the Knossan while Blaise mixed dry ingredients or convinced his magic to not break whatever random object he was holding.

One afternoon, Emmaline watched him put a pan of bread into the oven, and she frowned. "Vixen, why don't y'all just use the bakery for this?"

The Knossan twitched with surprise, and Vixen made a soft sound.

"Out of the mouths of babes," Clover murmured. But she was nodding, and Blaise straightened up, paying close attention. Itude's bakery had sat empty for months. Blaise thought about it whenever he passed by.

Vixen rocked on her heels. "We'd have to ask Jack. He owns that building."

Blaise winced. *Of course, Wildfire Jack would own that building.*

Emmaline bounced to her feet. "No one's using it. We'd have a town baker again." Her eyes gleamed mischievously.

Blaise frowned. Was she trying to annoy her father on purpose? He knew the antics his own sister pulled back home were meant to aggravate without causing damage. He wanted to tell Emmaline *no*, but the words didn't come. Working in the bakery in any capacity was too tempting. It had always seemed so far out of reach. Now Emmaline placed it in front of him on a platter.

"Clover better be the one to do the asking. She has the best odds out of any of us to convince him," Vixen reasoned. "Your stuff is good, Blaise. If Jack agrees, we could have the rest of the Ringleaders and the Business Association hold a vote to see if you could lease the bakery. What do you think?"

Blaise almost collapsed in shock from her words. That was beyond anything he could have hoped for. "Okay." *Okay? Just okay?* He knew he was capable of more words than that.

Clover chuckled. "In that case, I'll ask. I think you're right that I'm the best one to broach this topic. As it is, he won't be thrilled with me."

CHAPTER ELEVEN

Outmaneuvered

Jack

"Not just *no*, Clover. *No way in Perdition.*" Jack glared at the Knossan, not caring that she towered over him. She'd tricked him, and he wasn't at all happy about it. And to make matters worse, this was the third time she had asked him. *Ridiculous.*

When she invited him to see her at the Broken Horn, he was suspicious. Vixen was nowhere in sight, and Jack had the vague idea that this was the usual time the Breaker practiced with her at the saloon. Emmaline confirmed as much. But it wasn't unusual for Clover to request a word with him, so he agreed.

Clover leaned against the bar, flicking an ear back at the voices coming from the kitchen. She gave him a disapproving look. Jack knew they could hear him in the kitchen. He didn't care.

"You're not being reasonable." Clover pulled a bottle from beneath the bar and poured Tanglefoot into a mug, pushing it over to him. "The bakery is not making you any coin sitting there empty."

I'd rather have it sit there empty than have that mage squatting in it. Jack took a swig of Tanglefoot, savoring the burn in his throat. "I said *no*. I thought I made myself clear."

She lowered herself, bringing her head down to look him in the eye. "Why won't you give him a chance? You gave *me* a chance."

Jack set down the glass, meeting her gaze. "That's different. You were little more than a calf. And you . . ." He faltered, annoyed she had him thinking about that.

Clover couldn't smile—her lips didn't work the same way as a human's. Her equivalent expression was a slight tilt of her head, ears pitched forward—as she was doing now. "You're the big tough outlaw with a soft spot for the broken." Clover's voice was quiet, not carrying beyond Jack's ears.

Damn her. The mage wasn't a broken thing—he was a *Breaker*. Jack knew he was being stubborn, but that didn't matter. He was trying to keep everyone who mattered safe. It infuriated him that none of them saw that. It was like trying to keep a gaggle of chicks from the side of a cliff.

When he said nothing, Clover lowered her muzzle. "He's worked at the saloon for two months now. Guess how many things he's broken in his shift during that time?"

Jack frowned. "I don't know."

"Two glasses," Clover said, her dark eyes serious. "And those weren't even his fault. That happened a night you weren't around, and a brawl made it as far as the kitchen."

Jack grunted. "So you're saying it's *my* fault he broke those glasses?"

Clover snorted at him. "That's not what I said at all. *Hannah* has broken more things over that span. Blaise is vigilant, even before he practiced. He's had to learn to be that way. You should give him a chance. Let him try to get that bakery up and running. Faedra knows, this town could use decent fresh bread."

Jack drummed his fingers on the bar. He didn't understand their fascination with Blaise. Clover and Vixen had fallen for his woe-is-me ploy far too easily. But they were right. The bakery served no purpose as an empty building.

And Jack would be Blaise's landlord, which would add a layer of discomfort to the young mage.

"Fine, Clover. You win. If the Ringleaders and Business Association agree, he can lease the bakery on a trial basis."

Cheers erupted from the kitchen. They *had* been listening. Jack scowled. Clover inclined her horned head, an innocent twinkle in her eyes.

Blaise

THE NEXT MORNING, BLAISE FOUND HIMSELF BACK AT THE HEADQUARTERS —under different circumstances than his last visit. This time, the Ringleaders weren't the only ones in attendance. Most of the town's business owners were there, seated in wooden chairs that creaked as they settled down. Clover sat atop a stump designed to accommodate her bulk. She lowered her horns to Blaise in a greeting. Celeste and Mindy from the Jitterbug sat nearby and grinned at Blaise. Ellie Pembroke gave a friendly wave and gushed about how excited she was for him.

Jack was there too, lower lip curled as if he'd eaten something sour. From what Blaise had seen, *disgruntled* seemed to be the standard mood for the outlaw. He was pretty sure Jack didn't know how to smile.

"Thank y'all for coming!" Vixen Valerie bobbed her head as she took her seat. The Ringleaders sat in a row at the front of the room. Blaise sat with the rest of the Business Association, the chairs laid out in neat rows.

"My kingdom for fresh bread on the regular," Celeste mumbled, earning an elbow in the ribs from Mindy. Monty Fromhold, the ice mage who ran the icehouse, chuckled.

Raven Dawson rose from his seat, his gaze sweeping over the gathering. "Clover has raised the proposal to allow the use of the bakery to Blaise Hawthorne on a trial basis. Jack has generously agreed." Blaise saw a few gazes wander to Jack, and the indistinct murmur in the room proved that most noticed how *generous* Jack felt about it. "The town charter dictates that the Ringleaders and Business Association hold a vote to agree on the addition of any new business or lessee. Blaise, if you're still wanting to go forward with it, we'll hold the vote on that now."

Blaise nodded, still not quite believing that if the vote went his way, he would have a bakery to work out of. He felt a tingle in his hands, an early warning that anxiety was tugging at his magic. *Breathe.* He curled his hands into fists, focusing on the rough leather of his gloves.

"All right, Ringleaders, all in favor?" Raven raised his brows as he looked at his cohort. He raised his own hand, as did Vixen, Nadine, and Kur.

Jack glowered. "Abstain."

Raven cocked his head, a lock of black hair falling into his eyes. "Unusual, but . . . moving right along. Members of the Business Association, all in favor?"

An enthusiastic chorus of "*aye*" and raised hands rumbled through the room. Blaise had the full support of the Business Association. His heart hammered in his chest. It was almost hard to breathe, he was so surprised.

"You have a bakery!" Vixen crowed when the meeting ended, running over to Blaise and swooping him into a hug.

He blinked, going rigid in her arms. No one outside of his family had ever hugged him before. Vixen didn't seem to notice and gave him a sound thump on the back. Clover plodded over and patted him on the shoulder when Vixen peeled away.

"I guess so," Blaise mumbled.

"Lease. It's a lease," Jack growled, glaring at them from his chair.

Vixen put out her hand. "Not talking to you right now, Mr. Abstain. That was lower than a snake's belly."

Jack rose, reaching into his pocket. "I could have voted nay and scuttled the whole thing." He fished a key out, then held it out to Blaise. "I'm still watching you."

Blaise took the key, lifting his chin in defiance. He would not let Jack steal his joy. "I'd be surprised if you weren't."

THE BAKERY'S INTERIOR WAS PAINTED A PALE YELLOW THAT REMINDED Blaise of melting butter. He liked it immediately. The hue made him feel optimistic, as if his life had turned a corner. He mentioned it to Hannah and Emmaline, who were helping him organize the bakery.

"Yellow is Daddy's favorite color." Emmaline sat on a multi-colored rag rug spread across the hardwood floor painted in a motif of alternating black and white squares. She sorted through a box of gadgets. "What's this? And this? And this?" She held up three items for his inspection.

Blaise grimaced. Figured that Jack would paint the bakery his favorite color. The exterior boasted the same color, though with white trim that reminded him of the outlaw's palomino. He cast a glance at the items Emmaline showed him. "Pastry jigger, hand mixer, and—I think that's garbage." Whatever the last gadget was, the metal was so warped from its original shape, the damage rendered it useless.

"Right." Emmaline dutifully tossed the unknown item into a sack set aside for trash and moved the other two to a counter. More utensils and dishes lined the counter, all in need of a thorough wash before use.

The interior of the bakery was more of a challenge than Blaise had expected. He didn't know if the last baker had been careless or if it was because of the disuse, but it was a mess. Blaise needed to inventory everything, if only to know what he had on hand. Then he would make a detailed list of replacement items needed.

Someone had left the flour unsealed, and weevils had gotten into it. Blaise scrunched up his nose, putting the flour aside. The sugar was in better shape, sealed in an air-tight container. He discovered a tin of salt hidden behind the sugar, along with lard. Blaise made a face when he realized mice had gotten into the lard container. He chucked it into the trash. It was rancid, even without the mice. *Might have to get a cat.*

The oven was in excellent condition. Blaise bent down to get a better look at it, whistling with appreciation. The words *Argor Metalworks* and the outline of a mountain peak were embossed near the bottom. Argor boasted some of the best metalworkers on the continent. Whoever purchased the oven had bought the best that was available. And then would have had to transport it a long distance at a considerable cost. Had Jack done that?

"I hope someone looks at me someday the way you're looking at that range." Hannah grinned as she looked back at him from where she nested a set of bowls.

Blaise shook his head, chuckling. "Sorry. I just . . . wow, this is something I never thought would be possible."

Emmaline moved a container of wooden spoons to the *'to be washed'* pile. "You can make eyes at that oven all you want if it means you'll make cinnamon buns."

"And cake," Hannah agreed.

"And cookies," Clover said, ducking down to get through the doorway. She carried a sheaf of paper in her hand and offered it to Blaise.

He wiped his hands on a towel, taking the paper from her. "What's this?"

"Something I remembered from my past." Clover watched as Blaise read over the paper. It was a recipe. "When I was a calf, they tasked me with helping in the kitchens at—" She shook her head, tail swishing with sudden agitation. "That part doesn't matter. But it didn't occur to me the recipe was unusual. Not until I came here and realized it was uncommon. I wrote down what I remembered."

Blaise hadn't seen her handwriting before. Her strokes were severe and sharp, with few curves. But it was easy to read, and he admitted he hadn't seen a recipe like it before. He thought it would work, though—if he had all the ingredients on hand. Blaise tapped the last item in the list. "Is that the same as baker's chocolate?"

Clover leaned over to see what he was pointing at. "Semi-sweet chocolate? No. But if you want to make this, I will have the Pembrokes special order some." Her tongue stuck out as if savoring the taste of an old memory. "This is the one thing I miss from . . . my old life."

As curious as he was, Blaise didn't ask. Emmaline and Hannah clammed up, feigning absorption in their tasks. Blaise nodded. "I'd be honored to try your recipe, Clover. Thank you."

She dipped her horns. "I will leave you to your work. I'll stop by the mercantile and see about the chocolate."

They waved goodbye to the Knossan. Hannah opened the small utility closet, peering inside. She used an old rag to whisk away a cobweb and then pulled out a broom. "Are you going to run this place all on your lonesome once it's in shape?"

Blaise looked around. He hadn't thought that far ahead. Jack was only allowing him to use the building on a trial basis. But there was no doubt the bakery would be popular—curious townspeople were already peering inside, asking when he would open for business. Blaise wondered if Jack had any inkling how eager the townsfolk were for the bakery to open.

The outlaw must know. From what Blaise saw, there was very little Jack didn't know about what was afoot in *"his"* town.

"Maybe. I'm not sure. Never done anything like this before." Blaise sat back on his heels. If the bakery was busy, it might turn into more than he could manage on his own. That would be a problem.

"Well, even if you don't get someone right away, you might want to consider bringing on an apprentice or something," Hannah advised as she swept the floor. "That's what got us into this mess in the first place. The last baker refused to let anyone learn from him and then he up and died."

"Which is a shame, because his cinnamon buns were amazing," Emmaline lamented.

Blaise chuckled. "I'll keep that in mind. Thanks, Hannah."

"If you think you need help, I wouldn't mind working here." Emmaline's voice was soft, tentative.

What? Blaise winced. Wildfire Jack's young daughter working *here* with him? That sounded like a recipe for disaster. Hannah's broom came to an abrupt stop, her eyebrows raised as she glanced from Blaise to Emmaline and back again.

"Please consider it." Emmaline closed the cabinet she was looking through and got to her feet, dusting off her knees. "I don't get to do much but sentry duty, and not even that often. There's so much I don't get to do."

Blaise cringed. She didn't say it, but he could hear it in her voice: *There's so much I don't get to do because I'm Wildfire Jack's daughter.* Blaise had been shackled with limitations by his magic. She was hobbled because she was her father's daughter.

But that didn't mean he liked the idea of her working with him. It meant he could sympathize.

"I don't know . . . don't you have school?"

"Only three days a week," Emmaline shot back, eager. "And those days I could come by before school. And after. If you needed me."

Blaise studied her for a moment, then looked at Hannah. She shrugged as if to say, *your funeral.* Blaise pursed his lips. He asked himself the dangerous question: would Wildfire Jack be more likely to kill him if he let his daughter work at the bakery, or if he upset her by telling her *no*? Both options were terrible. "I'll consider it on one condition," Blaise relented with a sigh.

Emmaline grinned, pressing her hands together. "Thank you! You won't regret it! What's the condition?"

"Your father has to agree."

Her face fell. "That's just topping."

Blaise grunted agreement. That about covered it.

CHAPTER TWELVE

Fragility

Jack

Jack stared at his daughter, hardly believing the absolute bosh coming from her mouth. Did she think he had fallen off Zepheus and hit his head?

"And I'll make sure all my chores are—"

"No."

Emmaline stopped in surprise, green eyes wide. "But Daddy, I—"

Jack held up his hand. "No. I said *no*. I will not allow my *daughter* to be a part of that Breaker's cockamamie scheme. Bad enough he's bamboozled the rest of the town."

Maybe it was time to clean the young mage's plow again, to remind him not to trifle with Jack's family.

Zepheus was out on patrol, so his pegasus wouldn't be around to interfere. Jack angled past his daughter, pushing open the front door and trotting down the steps. He would check the bakery first. Hopefully, the Breaker was there and not at the saloon. Clover wouldn't be too happy at what he had planned, but he would deal with the Knossan later.

He heard a muffled exclamation as Emmaline figured out what was afoot. He heard the sharp staccato of her boots. "Daddy! Stop! Please *don't*." She came running up alongside him, tugging at his right arm.

Jack shook her off. "It's for your own good, Emmaline." She clawed at his arm again, but he was moving faster. She broke into a jog to keep up with his ground-eating strides. The bakery wasn't far, but he had to get by the stables, which could pose a problem.

"Oby!" Emmaline called, and the beating of massive wings heralded the arrival of her spotted stallion. With a grumble, Jack checked over his shoulder. At least the black stud wasn't anywhere in sight.

Emmaline pulled herself onto the stallion's bare back as Oberidon trotted in front of Jack. The stallion squared up and spread his wings, blocking Jack's path.

"Out of the way, Oby."

"Daddy, I'm tired of you treating me like I'm a little kid," Emmaline said, her voice low and full of righteous anger. A distant part of Jack's brain registered that she was channeling his attitude. "Have a row with me, I don't care. But don't take it out on Blaise."

Jack's fists clenched at his side. "He needs to know his place." A few citizens had stopped what they were doing to stare at the spectacle. Jack shifted his glare to them. "Shoo! Go on, get!"

The gawkers hurried off. Over the edge of Oberidon's wing, Jack saw the door to the bakery was open. Jack set his jaw as the Breaker strode into view.

"Emmaline, everything okay?" Blaise asked.

Jack growled to himself as Emmaline looked over her shoulder and shook her head. Blaise walked to the edge of the boardwalk in front of the bakery, leaning against the wooden support of the awning. His ungloved hands were in his pants pockets.

"Emmaline will not be working with you," Jack snarled.

Blaise's mouth pressed into a thin line, but he nodded. "All right, then."

"It's *not* all right." Emmaline slid off Oberidon, pivoting to look between them. The spotted pegasus maintained his position, keeping Jack clear of the bakery. "It was *my* idea, Daddy. Not Blaise's. So if you're going to be mad at someone, be mad at me."

Jack scowled. Didn't she understand he *didn't* want to be mad at her? He wanted to protect her.

Emmaline wasn't finished. "And I'm not a little girl anymore. You keep treating me like . . . like I'm a fragile doll! But I'm not. And I want a chance to learn new things away from *you*." She waved her arms in a descriptive circle.

He winced. Was he doing more harm than good, trying to keep her safe? She didn't know what the world was like beyond the Gutter. She had been so little the last time she had been anywhere else. Damnation, Emmaline was so much like her mother. He had to be careful. If he didn't give her some rein, eventually she would break free, and he might never see her again.

Jack bowed his head, thinking. She was growing up before his eyes, and he had to acknowledge that. The next words pained him to say. "Give me a few minutes to talk about the arrangement with the Br—with Blaise."

Emmaline raised a brow, and Jack's heart jumped. *She has my hair, but I'll be damned—everything else about her is Kittie.*

"You mean *talking* like normal people, or *talking* like punching him in the face? 'Cause there is a difference, and I'm strongly opposed to the second one," Emmaline drawled.

Jack snorted. "You have my word. I won't punch him in the face without good reason."

Blaise rested his head against the wooden support. "I'm doomed."

Emmaline glowered. "Daddy!"

Jack sighed. What did she want from him, a miracle? "I promise I won't punch him in the face for the next five minutes."

She gave a sharp nod. "Get talking." Emmaline nudged Oberidon with her knees, and the pegasus headed back to the stables.

Jack watched her go, then turned his focus back to the Breaker. "I don't know why she wants to be involved with your baking nonsense."

"With all due respect, sir, it isn't nonsense," Blaise replied, still leaning against the support.

Jack walked closer, annoyed that the young man didn't cower in the slightest. "Be that as it may, Emmaline has other things she needs to keep her mind on. And *you* are a distraction."

"I'll remind you, *she's* the one who had the idea. She was the one who asked if she could help organize the bakery." Jack heard a tremor in Blaise's voice. *Good.* He wasn't actually as confident as he was pretending.

"You don't understand—"

"But I do," Blaise cut in, and Jack was just as surprised as Blaise looked by the interruption. The Breaker plowed on, like a horse with the bit clenched between its teeth. "I know how it feels to be in her place. Told that she can't do certain things because of who and what she is. Do I really want her working with me? No, because I know it'll bring your wrath down on me like a hammer if the slightest thing goes wrong. But I'm at least willing to give her a chance because everyone deserves a shot at happiness."

Jack crossed his arms. The *nerve* of this kid to lecture him. By the same token, Blaise had a point. And that really got up Jack's dander. He wanted to stick to his firm *no*. But he also wanted Emmaline to be happy. *Damnation*. Jack let his arms hang loosely at his sides, stepping onto the boardwalk. He was so close to the Breaker now, it would be a simple thing to attack. He had made a promise, though. And Blaise had done nothing to warrant it unless Jack counted the fact that he was still breathing. "Emmaline's all I have left in this world."

Blaise nodded. "I figured as much. You can't protect her forever. You can try. But eventually, she'll end up like me."

"A maverick opening a bakery?" Jack asked dryly.

Blaise chuckled, a sound that surprised Jack under the circumstances. "Hopefully not exactly like me."

Jack turned, peering through the plate-glass window at the interior of the bakery. It had been in rough shape after Bart's untimely death. Jack hadn't wanted to bother setting it to rights. He grudgingly realized that the place was in better shape than the last time he had looked inside—better than he could have done for it himself. Items clustered together in neat piles, the floor freshly swept. It looked like someone competent had been at work.

"Emmaline has a target on her back because she's my daughter," Jack said after a moment of assessing the bakery. "Whether she has magic or not, that will be the case until my dying day. All the young-uns in our town train to defend themselves. But she's pushed harder than the rest—because she's mine, and she must." Jack didn't know if the Breaker understood, but the young man nodded as if he did.

"It's good you're letting her learn to take care of herself. I wish I had that chance," Blaise remarked.

Remorse seeped through the kid's tone. Jack frowned. *Don't trick me into thinking you're a broken thing. You're still dangerous.* "I'll let Emmaline work with you. Two days a week to start." Jack rocked on his heels. "But if you do anything to harm her, I'll make that punch in the face seem like a love tap."

Blaise rubbed his jaw, and Jack felt a grim satisfaction at the sight of a bead of sweat on the kid's forehead. "Understood."

In a flurry of wings, Oberidon touched down on the road in front of the bakery. Emmaline looked at them expectantly. "Time's up. Did y'all behave?"

"I stuck to my promise, if that's what you're asking," Jack told her. "Two days a week, Emmaline. That's what you get."

She crowed as she jumped off Oby's back, punching the air with her fists. The sheer joy of it made Jack's face crack into a brief smile. He liked to see Emmaline happy. She raced over and plowed into him, wrapping her arms around him so fiercely he staggered under her enthusiasm.

"Thank you!" She rested her head against his shoulder, and for a moment his irritation melted away.

Then he remembered Blaise's presence. He pulled back from his daughter. "I'll be watching. And if I see anything I don't like, this tomfoolery ends."

Emmaline's face fell, and Jack almost wanted to take back his words. *Almost.* But he didn't. She nodded to him, then stepped over to her pegasus.

Jack sighed. Why did he feel like he was still pushing her away? Figuring out how to interact with his daughter was becoming harder and harder. And he hated to admit it, but he couldn't blame *that* on Blaise.

CHAPTER THIRTEEN

Free Market Pegasi

Blaise

Blaise learned many things while getting the bakery up and running. First, running a business was a lot harder than it looked from the outside. It took two weeks to get the building ready to open from its original state of disarray. Second, he discovered that he—much to his dismay—had to become one of the dreaded *"morning people"*. Gone were the days of lingering in his bed until the sun's glare woke him. It made working his shift at the Broken Horn difficult. But he didn't want to leave Clover short-handed.

With the bakery, his days began before the sun was even a suggestion on the horizon. He moved his belongings from the uncomfortably decorated room at the saloon (he had never found time to redecorate) to a loft room situated over the bakery. On the plus side, the new living arrangements meant he didn't have to go very far after stumbling out of bed each morning.

Every day began the same. He pulled on clean clothes, then covered them with a white smock and cap. For the agreed-upon two mornings each week, Emmaline joined him at the outrageous hour, and despite her wide yawns, she never complained. She rubbed the sleep from her eyes and listened as Blaise explained how to build the fire to heat the oven.

Blaise had to relearn how to build the fire himself—he was rusty from months out of practice. He had thought getting firewood would be problematic. It pleased Blaise to discover that, although Itude was in an arid area, the town had steady access to firewood thanks to the local Greenmage, Uriah Jackson. Jackson lived on one of the area farms, and Emmaline helped Blaise make his acquaintance and work out the details of a steady firewood delivery. Jackson, a pleasant older man boasting a halo of frizzy grey hair and the grit of permanent dirt beneath his fingernails, was much obliged.

While the fire blazed to life in the oven, Blaise demonstrated how to mix the dough for bread, knead, and shape it into loaves on a sturdy wooden table. When that job was complete, they set them near the oven's warmth to rise.

Emmaline was a quick study. Her attention never flagged as they moved from one task to the next. Once the bread was in the oven, Blaise showed her how to prepare the other items he planned to bake. Through trial and error, he found it worked best to bake cakes or pies after the loaves of bread were removed from the oven.

The final recipe of the day was Clover's cookies. He had to admit that Clover was right about how delicious they were. They were chock full of melty deliciousness with the addition of the semi-sweet chocolate.

When Blaise officially opened the bakery on a crisp autumn morning, he underestimated the popularity of his business. The response gobsmacked him. As far as he could tell, everyone in Itude was in line at the door. Even Jack.

Blaise blew out a nervous breath. Emmaline was beside him, and she fidgeted with the end of her ponytail as she peered out. "Ready to open?"

Blaise licked his lips. He glanced at his bare hands, afraid they would betray him. His magic lay quiescent below the skin, calmed by the morning's baking. "May as well."

Soon the murmur of customers filled the bakery, accompanied by the sweet, yeasty aroma of fresh-baked bread that fell over the building like a warm blanket. Blaise stayed busy as Emmaline gathered up orders and took payment. He tried not to glance up as the line wove through the bakery. The hum of voices was constant and worry seized him.

These people were here for *his* bakery. What if they liked nothing he made? What if something went wrong? Panic smoldered, causing his stomach to clench. His palms itched.

No. He closed his eyes and took a calming breath. Focused on the dust of flour coating his skin. Vixen said he was getting *good.* He could control the magic. It belonged to him. He was the master. Not the other way around.

"Blaise? You okay?" He heard Emmaline's boots tap on the floor as she shifted in his direction. Blaise nodded, eyes flitting open as he shot a glance over his shoulder.

Wildfire Jack stood at the counter, cold eyes moving from the display case full of fresh-baked goods to Blaise and back again. Watching. Judging.

Blaise swallowed. The magic settled down in his hands, going dormant. He lifted his chin. "I'm good. Was just thinking about something."

Emmaline handed her father his order. Blaise had half a mind to wish Jack would choke on it but banished the thought. That wasn't kind. He decided that taking the high road was the better option when dealing with Jack. Besides, Jack *would* blame him if he choked on his food.

By the end of the morning, he and Emmaline were bushed. Almost everything they had prepared sold. Emmaline dragged a chair over, sitting down and pulling off her boots. "If every day is like that, you're gonna need more help."

"That's the truth." Blaise slouched in a chair. Besides his feet hurting, he had a headache from worry.

"I might know someone," Emmaline said, cocking her head. "Nadine's son, Reuben. A few years older than me."

Blaise tipped his head back and groaned. "I don't need the town Healer wanting me dead."

Emmaline laughed. "Nadine likes you. I think."

Blaise tapped his fingers against the countertop, considering. It couldn't be any worse than Jack. "I suppose it wouldn't hurt to ask."

The next thing he knew he had a second employee. Reuben was gangly, taller than Blaise and still growing into his body. He didn't have any magic, and it pleased him to help at the bakery. Anything was better than learning medicine from his mother, he said. Turned out, Reuben was squeamish. Blaise didn't blame him.

They settled into a routine. Emmaline cast a spell only a daughter could get away with—she convinced Jack to let her work at the bakery daily. She reported to Blaise that her father said the food was *"decent"*, which she translated as *"pretty darn good"*. Blaise couldn't decide if Jack liked their baked goods or if he was just adamant about keeping tabs on them. He stopped by the bakery every morning for bread or a donut.

As far as Blaise could tell, everyone in town enjoyed the items from the bakery. But the pegasi were their biggest fans, because of their famous sweet tooth. Every morning, Emrys and Oberidon stood outside the window at the back of the bakery. Blaise discovered the stallions were taking orders from the other pegasi. Emmaline or Reuben would fill a bag with their order and hand it to them through the window. Most mornings, both stallions ended up with a bag to carry back to the stables.

"They're paying for that, right?" Blaise asked, rubbing at his forehead as he watched Emrys trot off.

"Yup," Emmaline said with a grin. "Your Emrys has the banker move the amount from his or Oby's account to yours each day. And the banker moves the funds from the other pegasi accounts to Emrys's and Oby's."

Blaise furrowed his brow. He still thought it odd the pegasi were interested in money, but they seemed invested in the idea. "Wait. Are Emrys and Oby making *money* off us?"

<We charge a delivery fee,> Emrys said, indignant. His voice was distant—likely almost back at the stables.

Blaise shook his head. Would wonders never cease?

THE BAKERY HAD BEEN OPEN FOR A MONTH WHEN CLOVER INVITED BLAISE to sit with her at the bar before the start of his shift. "I am letting you go." She rested her arms atop the expanse of wood, her thick fingers threaded together.

Blaise's eyes widened, and his stomach clenched with worry. Had he done something wrong? Clover straightened, laying one of her enormous hands on his shoulder, a reassuring gesture. "Not because you do a poor job, but the opposite." Clover gestured to the pristine kitchen counters. "Between your work at the bakery, practice with Vixen, and your shift here, you are running yourself ragged."

Blaise's shoulders slumped. He didn't want to admit it, but she was right. His last few sessions with Vixen had been abysmal. Whatever progress he had made slid backwards as he stumbled through each day fighting off exhaustion. "I don't want to leave you short."

Clover lowered her horns, an acknowledgment. "We'll be fine. It's your turn to take care of yourself and your fledgling business."

He stared at the woodgrain of the bar as he tried to come up with excuses to stay. Excuses that hid the truth of the matter. "I enjoy working with you." And he *needed* to fill his days and evenings. It meant less time to be alone with his thoughts. Was he exhausted by his schedule? Yes. But he preferred that to the alternative.

Clover laid a hand on his shoulder. "You are one of the kindest humans I've met—and you do not know what a compliment that is, coming from me. If it makes you feel any better, you can help a few times a week. But you've dropped weight from when you first came into town, and that is odd since you work at a bakery."

Blaise glanced down at his slender belly. His arms had gained muscle tone from all of his work, but he kept so busy he didn't eat much. When he ate alone, dark memories burdened him. Things in his life that he couldn't do anything about; couldn't change.

"Okay, Clover," Blaise agreed, his voice soft. Conflicting emotions warred within him. Rest in between his obligations would help. But it would also allow too much time to think. Clover's unwavering brown eyes watched as he slid from the stool and gave her a half-hearted wave.

Blaise slipped out of the saloon at the time he would have normally started his shift. Vixen waylaid him, lurking just outside the door.

"Howdy, Blaise. Let's go." She jerked her head, encouraging him to walk with her.

He took a step back, surprised by her sudden presence. "Where are we going?"

The red-haired outlaw grinned. "Practice. I heard you have time on your hands."

Blaise shook his head. "That's not a good idea."

Vixen tilted her head to one side, hands on her hips. "It's the best idea. Let's go break something."

"Wait. What?" He scowled. This was contrary to the normal focus of his lessons: preventing his magic from doing any harm.

"It's the natural progression of things." Vixen steered him toward the bakery, his safe place. It was quiet in the afternoons—Blaise closed up shop after lunch since he worked early mornings. "You've spent too much time not using your magic. Time to focus on *using* it."

"But I don't want to," he protested as Vixen shouldered open the door.

She tut-tutted as she covered his preparation table with a cloth he hadn't even noticed she had tucked beneath her arm. "You said you wanted to learn control. This is part of that. Hang on." Vixen slipped out the door, boot heels tapping as she jogged around to the back, reappearing a moment later with a crate filled with different objects. The sly fox had come prepared.

Wrapping paper crinkled as Vixen pulled a cracked blue and white porcelain teapot from the top. "You've spent so long pulling the magic back in, you gotta learn how to push it out when you need to." She rested the teapot on the table between them.

Blaise eyed the teapot like it was a rattlesnake. "I don't know when I'd ever need to."

She leaned forward, ginger hair brushing the top of the teapot. "Oh?

How 'bout the time you ran from those soldiers? Seemed mighty helpful then."

Blaise's gut clenched, and he dropped his gaze. Pinpricks of stress knotted the back of his neck. *Not that.* Nightmares of that day still haunted his dreams. "It was an accident."

Her silver eyes twinkled, fierce. "Confederation *soldiers* were after you. They weren't planning to invite you for afternoon tea, ninny."

Blaise put his elbows on the table, resting his chin in his hands. "I know. I know that. But it doesn't make what happened *right*. Those soldiers—they were someone's son. Maybe a husband or father. Who am I to take that away?"

Vixen shook her head, sorrowful. "You can't be so nice. That's going to end up getting you hurt. Or worse."

He appreciated what she was trying to do. He understood. But that didn't mean he liked it. His desire to not hurt others set him apart from those soldiers. Vixen was an outlaw, and he couldn't expect her to understand. "My magic has hurt enough people. Does yours hurt people?"

She gave him a considering look. "It can, depending on how I use it. It's all in the intent, Blaise. Did you intend to kill anyone?"

No. "I just wanted them to stop chasing me. To leave me and my family alone." *And I failed at even doing that.*

Vixen tapped her index finger against the teapot. "Right. And what happened because you couldn't control it?"

He gritted his teeth, tightness growing in his shoulders and back. Blaise could almost hear the sickening sound of the massive oak crashing down. "I probably killed someone."

She snapped her fingers. "Exactly. If you'd practice, you coulda done it without squabashing anyone."

What? Blaise blinked, shaken out of the conversation by the unfamiliar word.

Vixen laughed. "Means killing."

Blaise made a face. *That's colorful.* Then he refocused on what she'd said. "Wait. You're saying if I practice breaking things *on purpose,* I can use this curse of mine with more forethought?"

"You got it." She grinned. "It's like learning to shoot a gun. At first, your aim's gonna be off, and anyone near you is in danger. But afore long, you can hit your mark."

"Terrible example, since I've never shot a gun."

Vixen rolled her eyes. "Surprised Jack doesn't give you grief over that alone."

"He's not aware yet. And I'm better off if you don't tell him."

She canted her head. "I won't tell him so long as you break the things I brought here. On purpose."

Resigned, Blaise ran one thumb against the edge of his trim beard. "Hope you realize how ridiculous that sounds."

Unabashed, she shoved the teapot closer to his side. Just to be difficult, he was tempted to give the teapot a hard knock against the edge of the table. But Vixen wouldn't let him get away with such a childish move. Besides, she made a good point. It would be nice to have options beyond dropping unexpected trees on people. "Okay, but give me an idea of what to expect. How does it work for you with your magic?"

Vixen settled back in her chair. She wore her signature glasses, but pulled them off briefly before settling them back on the bridge of her nose. "My glasses serve the same purpose as your gloves. It dampens the effect of any magic I don't keep under wraps." She pursed her lips, thoughtful as she puzzled out how to explain it to him. "Being a Persuader differs from being a Breaker. I'm trying to work on minds, not physical things. For me, it's eye contact."

"Oh. So for me, it's skin contact." Blaise drummed his fingers against the table.

Vixen nodded. "Right. And magic has rules. I can't control anyone's mind, even though that's what most people think I do. I don't. What I *can* do is push my ideas and perceptions onto them. Suggest things. Make them think we're best friends. I can get people to relax and talk about things they may not otherwise say. But I can't make anyone put a gun to their head and pull the trigger, unless they already had some notion of that floating around in their head."

Blaise gaped. Her magic was daunting. She didn't mean to spook him; she was just laying out the ground rules of her magic. His magic had rules, too. "Okay."

"Far as I know, all mages share one rule: you can only hold so much magic at one time, and when you use it, it can take a while to replenish. Use too much too fast, and you run dry." She slanted her keen gaze at him. "Your magic ever run low?"

Blaise snorted, shaking his head. "Not even sure what that would feel like. You?"

Vixen chewed on her bottom lip. "Once. When I escaped. Had to use so much, I ran out. Makes you feel exhausted, like a nap and a good meal are the best idea." She picked up the teapot and thrust it over to him, punctuating the end of her sentence. "Enough of that. Let's try this."

He took the teapot from her, holding it gingerly. He had questions. From who—or what—had she escaped? Judging by the jut of her jaw, he wouldn't discover more on that topic today. Was it possible he wasn't the only one in Itude plagued by dark thoughts?

"Well? What are you waiting for, moss to grow over us?" Vixen asked.

Blaise's forehead wrinkled, focusing on the cool smoothness of the teapot. His magic swam beneath his skin, like fish beneath the glassy surface of a pond. Blaise sat there for a moment, marveling at the sensation of magic pooled, waiting for his command. No longer leaking from him with abandon. It stayed put, obedient as a hunting hound, ready to let fly. Blaise hadn't thought it possible.

Vixen cleared her throat, reminding him she was waiting.

He called on his magic, and it rose to the surface. Too much. More than necessary. And it was *fast* as a striking rattlesnake—too quick to call back. Blaise felt it flow from his fingers and into the porcelain, washing over the teapot. His fingers scrabbled, trying in vain to call some of it back.

The teapot imploded into a fine powder, crumbling through his hands like sand. Blaise pulled his hands apart, shaking off the grit. His heart pounded a furious rhythm in his chest.

Vixen's jaw hung open. "You didn't break it. You *squabashed* it."

Blaise winced. "Is that good?"

She eyed the remains of the teapot, skeptical. "Mmm. Looks like another aspect of your control needs work."

Blaise sighed.

CHAPTER FOURTEEN

Second Chance

Jack

"Wildfire Jack, sir! A moment, please."

<Ignore him or stop?> Zepheus flitted an ear backward at the sound of Hank Walker's voice. The stallion arched his neck as he awaited Jack's answer.

Jack gritted his teeth, biting back a curse. He had spent the morning making preparations for the run he and Zepheus were about to take—a stagecoach loaded down with Confederation gold was in striking range. Jack and Kur had moved a transport wagon into position, and the Theilian was waiting for him to make his move. The stagecoach wasn't going to rob itself.

"May as well stop," Jack groused, hoping this wouldn't take too much of his time. At his command, the palomino pivoted, stirring up a whirl of dust that blew into the postmaster's face, spurring a coughing fit.

"What is it, Walker?" Jack crossed his wrists over the pommel of his saddle, the reins loose in his hands.

Walker jogged up, eyes squinting against the dust. He huffed and wheezed from the exertion. By Jack's guess, the postmaster had at least ten years on him, which put him at roughly a half-century old. It must have been a ghastly time. Wrinkles lined his pudgy face. Walker wasn't wearing a hat, and the late morning sun beat down on his bald pate, the breeze whipping his wisps of grey hair about.

Walker held up a bundle of rolled papers in one hand and offered them to Jack. "Got some new bulletins for you. And . . . you told me to keep an ear out. See what I could find out about the Confederates."

That captured Jack's attention. He slid out of the saddle, patting Zepheus's neck in a *pay close attention* signal. Walker was the only mage in town the pegasi didn't like. As useful as he was for a spy, Jack wasn't foolish enough to dismiss the pegasi's misgivings about him. Zepheus's head dipped into a relaxed position, but he kept one ear swiveled in the postmaster's direction.

Jack scanned the street for anyone who might eavesdrop. Itude was full of nosy gossips. One of the ranch hands from the neighboring farms swaggered out of the barbershop, heading across the street to the stables. Gus Pembroke opened the door to the bank, pausing long enough to give Jack and Walker a polite nod before going inside. Once the immediate area was clear, Jack turned back to the postmaster, holding out his hand. "Learn something about the situation we spoke of before?"

Walker offered the bulletins to him. "I did. I found them. They're near the border of Desina and the Tombstone River. Going to get hemmed in by the Salties before too long."

Jack narrowed his eyes, thinking. At times like this, he wished he had a clearer idea of how the postmaster's magic worked. Jack knew he could transfer inanimate objects between points—that was how the bulk of their mail got to its destinations. "Can you bring them here?"

Walker shook his head. "No."

Zepheus's head jerked up as if annoyed by a fly. <That may not be true.>

Jack stroked the stallion's mane. As much as he'd like to call Walker on his bullshit, it was difficult to do so. No two mages were the same, even if they shared the same magic. Jack had no hope of knowing all the rules that bound Hank. There was the possibility that Hank had tried that move before, and it hadn't gone well. Might not be worth the risk.

That made rescue more challenging. But it was still on the table. "Who're the mages?"

"Two women and a half-grown boy."

Jack's pulse quickened. *Two women.* Could one of them be her? He wanted to ask what they looked like, but that would seem like a ridiculous question. What did it matter, in the grand scheme of things? *It matters to me.* Even so, he held back the question.

Instead, he gave a firm nod. "Right. Once I'm ready to make my move, I'll need you to rendezvous with them, to get them to stay put, and then place a marker. Can you do that?"

"Shouldn't be a problem," Walker agreed.

Jack studied him. Something in the way the postmaster acquiesced with calm assurance jarred him. Walker was one of his more reluctant operatives, and Jack often had to follow up with him for updates and information. "Not a problem?"

Walker shifted his weight but stood his ground. "I have my own reasons to want this to work out."

"That so?" Jack glowered, suspicious.

The postmaster cleared his throat, eyes wide in alarm. "You misunderstand. My brother. I'm doing this for my brother."

Jack's shoulders eased. "What's he look like? You think he's in Desina?"

"Desina or Mella," Walker clarified. "Joshua looks like me, but five years younger."

Jack inclined his head in acknowledgment. "I'll keep an eye out."

The postmaster blinked in surprise. "Appreciate it."

Jack nodded, and Walker took it as a dismissal and stepped away. That was fine by Jack. He watched the postmaster walk back to the post office, then shook his head as he considered his next steps.

Zepheus arched his neck. <That man makes me twitchy.>

"You 'n' me both." Jack hated that his most reliable informant was one who he didn't fully trust. So far, Walker hadn't fed him any worthless information. And if the postmaster knew what was good for him, he never would.

With Walker gone, Jack unrolled the bulletins and paged through them. They were bits of mail intended for other recipients but pilfered by Walker at Jack's direction. Technically, as a postmaster, doing so would get Walker into a heap of trouble. But as long as no one else knew, Jack didn't care. Information was vital.

It was the usual stuff. The bulletins sent through the mail to the field commanders were generally ripe with inconsequential information, and when Walker could scrounge them up, Jack mined them for what little he could. There was one in this batch, carrying news of disturbing weaponry advancements that the Salt-Iron Confederation's engineers were developing. Rapidfire guns? Flying vessels called *warbirds*? He grimaced.

A sheaf of updated Wanted posters fell away from the back of the bundle. "Wonder how much I'm worth now." Jack skimmed through them, disappointed. Nothing new for him. Some faces were familiar—outlaw mages he had tried to recruit, but who had eventually set out for other towns. The last poster was a *very* familiar face, however.

A poor sketch of Blaise stared back at him. The words *Wanted Dead or Alive* framed the top of the kid's portrait. Below it read: *For the Murders of Two of The Confederation's Finest.*

"Huh," Jack murmured, scratching the bristles on his chin. "So the kid really killed somebody." He was always pleased to read about the Salties losing any of their number, but this news conflicted him. He still didn't trust the Breaker's magic, even if he was training with Vixen.

<Should I head back to the stable and get untacked?> Zepheus interrupted his train of thought.

Jack pulled out his pocket watch, flipping it open. It was nearly noon. Tempting as it was to lay the groundwork immediately to look for the mavericks, Jack also needed to do his part to keep Itude financially stable.

"Nah. It would take time for Kur to bring the wagon back anyway, and he'll need to attend the meeting I'm calling." Jack felt around in his pocket and found his yellow bandanna, taking it out and tying it around his face. His fingers fumbled with the knot as he thought about the mavericks.

Zepheus nudged Jack with his nose. <Don't set yourself up for disappointment. You know the odds are good Kittie won't be one of them.>

Jack scowled. "Don't care. I'm going to keep trying until I find something. Until I find her," he corrected himself.

The palomino bobbed his head. <And I will be by your side until you do.>

Jack couldn't help but think that most of the time, he didn't deserve Zepheus. He rolled the bulletins up and tucked them into the saddlebag for safe keeping. Then he put his foot in the stirrup and swung into the saddle.

"ARE YOU OUT OF YOUR ALL-FIRED MINDS?" JACK SHOULD HAVE KNOWN that the easy agreement of the other Ringleaders to his plan was a bad sign. Nothing was ever simple. It was a miracle that Jack even managed to convene a meeting the next morning without argument.

Despite serving as the informal spymaster for Itude, the other Ringleaders always analyzed any information he brought to them. Jack didn't mind that part—it was shrewd, to be sure. Keeping Itude safe was Jack's priority and the way he saw it, the more eyes on that goal, the better. However, he preferred that they agree with him when he had strong opinions on the matter at hand.

Everyone was receptive to his idea to rendezvous with the fleeing mavericks in Desina and bring them to Itude. If the Salt-Iron Confederation was coming, they could use every bit of magic in their arsenal. But with Confederation soldiers in Desina, they were hesitant to send anyone into the nation. Every single qualified mage in town had a bounty on their heads. The price of failure was high.

And the other Ringleaders, to Jack's utter amazement, thought it was a good idea to send the *Breaker* along with him on a mission.

"He's from Desina," Raven reasoned, rubbing his fingers over a golden coin. Before the meeting started, they had divvied up the haul that Jack and Kur had brought in the previous day. "He may know things we don't."

Jack ground his teeth. "Then consult with him. Don't send a greenhorn along with me." Sure, he saw the logic in sending along someone familiar with the country. But why did that someone have to be Blaise?

"It's a good chance to see what he is made of," Kur Agur said, his tone infuriatingly reasonable. "It's a common practice among the Theilians to send new pack members on an easy hunt. Builds their confidence and fosters working relationships." He bared his fangs in the semblance of a smile for emphasis. "And if the Salt-Iron Confederation is truly as close as you have heard, this may be the last easy hunt."

"We're not hunting a sick antelope—which I doubt Blaise could do. Sending him with me will only slow me down and put us both in danger." Jack crossed his arms.

Vixen drummed her nails against the table, drawing everyone's attention. "Do you even know what he can do? 'Cause *I* do."

"I do, too." He pulled the *Wanted* poster out of his pocket and unfolded it, tossing it across the table to her.

Vixen picked it up and smoothed it flat, scanning the words before looking up at him. "Everyone in this room has blood on their hands. You could choke a river with yours."

That was the truth. But Jack wasn't the one on trial here. He had proven his dedication to Itude many times over. "I don't want him dropping a damn tree at the wrong time."

Vixen scoffed. "Here I thought you knew everything—but it seems you don't. That maverick has *control* now. Leastwise, more than he did when he first got here."

Jack snorted. That didn't take much.

Raven studied the map of Desina on the wall, hands clasped behind his back. "Jack. What if we made a deal?"

Now that was interesting. Jack lifted his chin, considering. "Depends on the deal."

Nadine, who had kept her opinions to herself, hissed. Jack glanced at her—she had some idea of what Raven was all about. "I told you that's hardly fair."

Jack bit back a growl. Damn the lot of them. They must have discussed this and left him out of the loop. But if Nadine didn't like it.... He smiled. It was something that would give Jack an edge.

Raven ignored Nadine, turning to Jack. "It's no secret you hate Blaise. You've been trying to run him out of town from the start, and to be honest, it's irritating the rest of us because you're itchy as a shaved cat." He stalked closer, laying his hands flat against the table. "Take Blaise along with you. If it doesn't go well and you still want him gone, then we'll arrange for him to travel to Asylum."

Jack's brows flew up. That was . . . well, he hadn't expected that. There must be a catch. "I'm listening."

"If it goes well, then you have to stop harassing him. It doesn't make the rest of the Ring look good when you're baiting him and no one else can see why. His magic has caused no problems. His bakery is popular."

My bakery, Jack groused, but kept it to himself. Blaise was just using his building. But that was beside the point. "And if I don't?"

Nadine took over for Raven. "Then I hate to say it, but we'd have to ask *you* to leave town."

He flew up from his seat, slamming his palms against the table so hard they stung. "You can't do that. I brought this town back from *nothing*."

The other four Ringleaders met him with calm expressions. Raven shook his head. "It's in the charter. The one *you* agreed to years ago."

He growled, frustrated. But then he had a thought. It was a gamble, but the odds were weighted in *his* favor, not Blaise's. Jack had a lot more savvy than Blaise.

Jack settled down in his chair. "Fine. I agree." He paused, looking at Vixen. "If his magic gets me killed, I'm telling Butch to raise me just so I can haunt you for a few years."

She met his words with a mischievous grin. "Don't worry your pretty head about that. He's gonna be solid."

Jack canted his head, doubtful. That remained to be seen. "Then you should probably tell the kid what we're doing, Vix. He's like to piss his pants if I tell him."

CHAPTER FIFTEEN

Just Outlaw Things

Blaise

Blaise stared at Vixen, jaw gaping. "You can't be serious."

The fire-haired outlaw had stopped by the bakery before the normal practice session, and Blaise, Emmaline, and Reuben were cleaning up after a busy morning. Reuben pretended not to eavesdrop and continued to work, but Emmaline stopped sweeping and set the broom aside when she heard her father's name mentioned.

Vixen took a bite of the cookie she had bought before dropping the news, savoring the flavor before speaking. "You're a mage, Blaise. And you have considerable magic. This will be an excellent test. It doesn't get much easier."

"That's not . . ." Blaise wasn't sure how to explain it to her. The mission she proposed was far outside the realm of things he was comfortable trying. "I didn't come here to use my magic and do . . . outlaw things. Can't I just bake in peace?" He kept the whine out of his voice. Mostly.

Vixen nibbled on her cookie. "Mmm, this is good. And this isn't an outlaw thing. We're not asking you to rob a stagecoach, though I guess we could arrange that if you'd rather."

"*No!*"

She grinned, pleased to have tugged his tail. "This is to help people. Maverick mages. People just like *you*, from Desina. They're probably scared out of their minds. You know a thing or two about that, I reckon."

Blaise frowned. Blasted Vixen, playing on his empathy. Of *course*, he knew what that was like. He tried to forget, but he never would. It was too raw, too personal.

The potential to help others in the same predicament appealed to a tiny sliver of his persona. But not if it meant going with Wildfire Jack.

"I don't see how I'd be any help if things got ugly," Blaise reasoned. "I can't shoot a gun."

"First off, if Jack plays his cards right, this won't get ugly. Only Raven is better at sneaking around, and that's 'cause of Raven's shadow-hopping magic. And if things turn sour . . . well, Jack's seen more than his share of fights. He's a hard one to bring down."

Blaise glanced at Emmaline, who was paying close attention. She grimaced at the mention of her father in fights, her eyes troubled. It was probably difficult, having a father who always flirted with danger.

"And if that happens, someone with more experience should be along." Blaise didn't want to be responsible for anything happening to Emmaline's father.

Vixen waved a hand. "It won't. They'll be close to the border, so it should be easy." Her expression sobered. "Everyone who lives here learns to defend Itude, Blaise. *Everyone*. This is a simple way to start."

Judging by her tone, Blaise assumed the decision was made, regardless of his feelings. He didn't like that, but there was no way around it—aside from flat-out refusing. He wasn't sure what the repercussions for that might be. It would be easy for them to force him to leave. And that would be heartbreaking, after he had worked so hard to carve his little niche with the bakery.

No, he couldn't let his dream go so easily. There was no telling what else lay out there for him if he left Itude.

"I'll do it," Blaise relented. "Does Wildfire Jack know, or am I going to end up with another black eye for my troubles?"

"He knows," Vixen confirmed. She didn't say it, but by the slash of her brows, Blaise surmised Jack wasn't happy with the arrangement, either. Curiouser and curiouser.

"I wish he wouldn't go." Emmaline's lips puffed out with concern.

Vixen gave her an encouraging look. "It's going to be easy-peasy, Em. It'll be no more than two days—they'll have the pegasi. And you know Zeph won't let anything happen to your daddy, either."

Blaise groaned. He had forgotten about the pegasi. Flying was not one of his favorite things, despite Emrys's best efforts. Then he thought about what she had just said—two days. "The townspeople won't be happy if the bakery is closed for two days."

Vixen gestured to Reuben and Emmaline. "You sure? You seem to have two very capable folks working with you."

Blaise frowned. She had a point—both teenagers were quick studies, and even though Reuben wasn't as confident as Emmaline, he wasn't bad. Their inexperience wasn't an excuse. The criticism would tear them down, and he appreciated the hard work they contributed. Vixen had backed him into a corner he couldn't get out of without making them look incompetent. That was not only unfair; it was untrue.

And then he realized something else. Vixen was clever. Emmaline had latched onto her words, too, and she bounced on her feet, distracted from her father's mission.

"We can do it, Blaise! Might have to ask for an excuse from school for those two days—but it shouldn't be a bother. Right, Reuben?" Emmaline elbowed the older teen.

Reuben blinked, head bobbing with uncertainty. "Um, right?"

Blaise scowled at Vixen, who returned it with a wide-toothed smile. She looked like she had won a game of Wild Dragon. "I'm fine with it if Jack and Nadine agree."

"They'll agree," Vixen said sweetly.

He rubbed his forehead. "When do we leave?"

"Tomorrow morning."

Damn.

"Don't forget to—"

"Sweep out the embers after I take out the last loaves of bread. I know, I know." Emmaline flung a flour-covered hand over her shoulder, a shushing motion if Blaise ever saw one.

"We got this. Go be a hero." Reuben grinned as he ran a fresh cleaning cloth across the top of the display case.

Blaise shook his head, feeling anything but heroic. He would rather stay and hide in the bakery. This business of taking part in a rescue—risky or not—wasn't for a baker like Blaise. Strange enough to think someone like *Wildfire Jack* would go to anyone's rescue.

To be fair, Blaise suspected that in some ways, the outlaw was softer than he let on. Not that Blaise would ever tell him so. Offhanded things Clover had said in the past made Blaise think he had rescued her from an unpleasant situation. She didn't speak of it often, but she was steadfastly loyal to the man. Even if she had to knock sense into him on occasion.

If that were the case, Wildfire Jack would keep his eyes on the outcome and not give Blaise as much grief as he might otherwise. At least that was what Blaise hoped. He turned to gather his bag, but a tiny form on the windowsill caught his attention. He leaned over, curious. It was a doll, no longer than his thumb.

"What's that?"

Emmaline pursed her lips, ducking her head with embarrassment as she dusted her flour-covered hands on her apron. "Daddy gave me that when I was small. I keep it with me whenever he leaves. Makes me feel better."

Further proof that Wildfire Jack wasn't as hard-boiled as he pretended to be. Blaise was glad for that. Emmaline deserved kindness from her father. She didn't speak about him often, but from what Blaise could discern, her relationship with her father was strained. He imagined it was difficult to be Wildfire Jack's daughter. Maybe even harder than being Wildfire Jack's hated enemy.

"Shake a leg, before Daddy comes looking for you. Not a good idea to start the day on his nasty side." Emmaline flourished a rolling pin in his direction, a mocking threat.

Blaise grimaced. She was right. He strode across the checkered floor and picked up his travel bag from the base of the steep stairs that led to his loft. He paused, checking to make sure he had everything. Blaise wore a long-sleeved shirt, denim jeans, and sturdy boots. His dark blue duster was slung over one arm, his hat on his head, and a bandanna in his pocket. Earlier that morning, he had tucked a canvas sack with leftovers from the previous day into the travel bag. A full canteen sloshed in the same sack.

With his check complete, he headed out to the stables. Blaise discovered Emrys and Zepheus waiting for their riders in the stable yard, both tacked and ready to go. It was normal to see Zepheus saddled. Emrys was a different issue. Blaise didn't own a saddle or bridle.

Blaise walked over, noting the fine tooling on the rich mahogany leather of the saddle. He ran a hand over it, admiring the star-shaped basket-weave pattern that a talented artisan had embossed on the leather. Blaise hadn't seen an outlaw saddle up close before, and he noticed how the design differed from a normal saddle to allow the pegasus to have full range of motion for their wings. The skirt at the front of the saddle slanted back at an angle, and a breast collar complete with wither strap to prevent the equipment from fouling the wings secured everything in place.

A pair of flight goggles hung from the saddlehorn, the brass fittings winking in the early morning sunshine. "Where did this come from, Emrys?"

Emrys craned his neck to look at him, the metal pieces of the matching hackamore that graced his head jingling with the movement. <I bought it. Figured we needed a proper kit.>

"*You* bought it?" Blaise asked, bewildered.

<I bought it.> The stallion sounded smug. In the morning light, tiny starbursts of silver gleamed on the bridle.

He didn't have time for further questions. Zepheus shifted his posture as Wildfire Jack came around the corner, saddlebags perched on his shoulders. The outlaw's eyes settled on Blaise, and he saw a brief sign of chagrin.

"Surprised you showed up," the outlaw said, giving voice to his thoughts. "There's room in your saddlebags for anything you might need to add." He dumped one saddlebag into Blaise's arms.

"Good morning to you, too. And I'm here because this town gave me a second chance, so I figure I'll help however I can." Blaise took the leather bag, not hazarding a look at Wildfire Jack's face. Judging by the weight, one side of the pack was already full. Curious, Blaise peered inside and saw a pair of first aid kits. He heard the gentle slosh of alchemical potions and pulled them out, checking the labels.

"Why do I have two?" Blaise asked, holding up the kits.

The corners of Wildfire Jack's lips pulled back in irritation. "Put those back. We may need them for the mavericks if they're injured. And you have two because my bags are already full. Extra cartridges."

That drew Blaise's attention to the outlaw's new gun belt, the cartridge loops full all the way around his waist. The sight made him uneasy, but he tamped down his nerves. No doubt Jack was trying subtle intimidation. "My mother was an alchemist, specializing in medicinal potions. I was checking to see what we had."

Jack gave him a considering look. "And what do you think?"

The question surprised Blaise, and he almost dropped a vial—which would *not* have inspired any confidence. "Um." He wrapped the vial in its protective cotton wrapping and tucked it into the kit, surveying the array of potions as he did so. Pleased, he noted that he was familiar with everything in the kit. There were potions to treat injuries from burns to cuts or breaks. But there was something missing. "It looks good. I would add Faedra's Embrace. Mom always kept it on hand in case we needed it."

Wildfire Jack canted his head, and Blaise realized the outlaw was unfamiliar with the potion. "What's it do?"

"Helps stabilize patients with critical injuries." Blaise relished feeling competent about a topic other than baking. "One of our neighbors had a horrendous accident with his thresher last year." Blaise shuddered at the memory of Jethro Whitt's arm entrapped in the thresher. He could almost hear Jethro's wail and the drip of his blood on the sheaves of wheat. "Anyway, Faedra's Embrace was the only thing that kept him around long enough to get freed and taken to the doctor in town."

Wildfire Jack raised his brows. If he was wondering about the wisdom of letting a Breaker anywhere near an accident of that magnitude, he didn't mention it. Blaise couldn't help but wonder—if he could have controlled his magic then, could he have freed the man sooner? Something worth thinking about.

"Might be worthwhile to have around. Side effects?" the outlaw asked.

Blaise chewed his bottom lip, thinking. He knew the benefits of most of the potions, and their contents. Side effects were another matter—and every potion had something. The miracle of alchemy balanced out in that it wasn't always pleasant. He thought back to Jethro's accident. After they had loaded him onto a wagon and stabilized him, he wouldn't stop talking. Blaise didn't know a lot about Jethro, but he recalled that the older man was usually quiet. That was out of character enough to be an effect from the potion.

"I don't remember all of them, but I think compulsive talking is one."

Wildfire Jack wrinkled his nose in distaste. "I'll see if the mercantile has it and then pray we don't need to use it on anyone. Wait here."

Blaise repacked his saddle bags, adding his items. The outlaw had packed a canteen of water and a bag of food that included hard biscuits, dried strips of meat, and fruits. Blaise thought the fruit might be emergency rations for the pegasi.

Jack returned a few minutes later, handing the red vial of Faedra's Embrace to Blaise. He packed it in the first aid kit with the others, nestling it into the protective cotton wrappings. That done, he looked up, up, up at Emrys's tall back. His stomach lurched.

"Hold up." Blaise glanced back as Wildfire Jack strode over. He scrutinized the saddle and tugged at the girth. "Some pegasi are jokers. They suck in air when you tighten the girth. Then when you mount, the saddle slips and you go face down in the dirt. Sometimes that doesn't happen until you're airborne."

<I wouldn't do that!> Emrys snorted, stamping a rear hoof in offense.

The outlaw shrugged, and Blaise didn't know if Emrys had broadcast to him as well or if he understood the stallion's body language. "Don't want anyone accusing me of foul play before we leave town. You're welcome."

Blaise winced.

Jack made the same check of Zepheus's saddle, though Blaise suspected he only did it for show. He swung into the saddle but didn't ask the palomino to go anywhere. "I've arranged for a couple of colts to come along. We'll make better time if everyone is mounted. They were getting saddled with loaner tack last I saw."

Blaise nodded. That made sense. The sooner their rescue party got back to Itude, the better.

A few moments later, two new pegasi trotted up. The first colt, Rhoxio, reminded Blaise of a magpie with his black and white coloring. The other colt, Icoron, was a beautiful sorrel with a flaxen mane and tail, and a large white star between his eyes. They whinnied at Blaise with recognition.

<Cookies?> Rhoxio asked, nostrils flared as he drank in Blaise's scent.

<Greedy colt,> Emrys snorted, pinning back his ears.

Blaise chuckled. "I'll make sure you get some when we come back to town. Stop by the bakery the next time I'm there and I'll get some just for you."

The two colts bobbed their heads, delighted at the prospect. Jack shook his head at their antics. "I'm the lead on this mission. If I give an order, you follow it. Understand?"

At first, Blaise thought Wildfire Jack was speaking only to him, but Emrys and the two colts dipped their muzzles in agreement. Blaise winced at his oversight. He needed to remember that the pegasi were equals in Itude.

Zepheus minced forward as Wildfire Jack continued. "When we get close to the rendezvous point, I'll go first. Zeph and I will come back to you when it's all clear. Any sign of trouble and you get somewhere safe. We can handle ourselves. Can't do that and babysit y'all, though."

Blaise frowned, but said nothing. What was the point of him going along, then? Blaise wasn't spoiling for a fight—quite the opposite—but he didn't want to be useless baggage.

Wildfire Jack studied them, and Blaise realized the outlaw would much rather do this all on his lonesome than with a mage he hated and two half-grown colts. But that option was off the table. Jack shook his head, Zepheus spinning beneath him. "Let's ride."

CHAPTER SIXTEEN

Unhappy Reunion

Jack

<*I'm flying low,*> Zepheus warned Jack as they dropped down into a canyon.

Jack scowled. Between the bandanna protecting his mouth and the fierce wind whipping his grumbled words away, there was little chance the stallion heard his annoyance. But Zepheus could read his mood and detect his displeasure without hearing anything.

It wasn't a point worth arguing. For the sake of their strategy, it was sensible to stay low. Potential enemy look-outs kept their eyes upward for outlaw threats. Standard operating procedure for Zepheus and Jack was to either stay so low that they could pass for a horse and rider, or so high that they were mistaken for a bird of prey. Jack preferred height, though that presented its own set of challenges. It was exhilarating to swoop down on his prey like a falcon.

For this trip, they had too many unknowns. Emrys could handle the height, but his rider was another matter. And Rhoxio and Icoron would have a harder time with high altitudes. Zepheus didn't tell him much about the life of a wild pegasus, but Jack was an astute observer. He had seen pegasus flights out in the Untamed Territory, and the youngsters seldom flew at the high altitudes the adults weathered. They had some growing into their gangly bodies to do before they were proficient enough.

And Blaise . . . well, he definitely wasn't ready. The way he clutched the saddle horn, knuckles white as lilies, when Emrys took to the sky was deplorable. If he ended up staying in Itude, Jack had to make sure he dropped such behavior. It was downright embarrassing.

Zepheus kept the lead, though he slowed so the colts could keep up. They were still adjusting to the drag caused by their tack. It was harder to fly with saddles but no rider, Jack reasoned. A rider, at least, could help minimize the blow of the wind against leather. He had tied up the stirrups on their saddles as much as possible, but it was still a lot for them to get used to. They were stalwart little colts, though. He liked them.

Once Zepheus reached the rim of the canyons that gave the Gutter its name, he turned to the east. It would have been more direct to keep a southeastern path, but Jack didn't trust the simplicity of it. If something was simple, it was predictable. He hadn't made it this long by being predictable.

The other pegasi followed as they hooked to the east. This path would take them to the area where the Gutter transitioned to the Untamed Territory. Zepheus turned again, the Tombstone River a dancing ribbon off to Jack's left. Their destination wasn't too much further. The Tombstone arced into a lazy bend where it intersected the Desinan border. That was where Jack expected to find the first of the waypoint markers.

The palomino dropped altitude and touched down on a bluff overlooking the river. The other pegasi circled overhead like massive buzzards, awaiting instructions from Zepheus. Jack scanned the nearby tree line as his pegasus trotted up to it, searching for a telltale pop of color.

There it was. Anyone else might have thought it just an unfortunate scrap of cloth lost from its owner, but Jack had worked out a color code with Hank Walker. The cheerful blue strip of calico fluttered in the breeze.

"West." Jack nudged Zepheus with his knee, and the stallion took to the sky again. A short distance later, Jack spied the next marker. Orange. They shifted and headed south. Jack lost the trail of markers and called a break for lunch on a bluff overlooking the river. Blaise's face was tinged with green from the flight and he didn't say a peep during the quick meal. That suited Jack just fine.

After lunch, Jack was re-energized and had no trouble finding the next marker, though the color was cause for concern. Red. Jack bared his teeth.

Red meant they were close—and *proceed with caution*. Salt-Iron Confederation soldiers were in the area.

"Tell 'em to come down but keep quiet and low," Jack murmured to Zepheus.

The other three pegasi came to the ground, clustering around Jack and Zepheus so they formed a square. Blaise's face was green, and he still held onto the saddle horn for dear life, but he didn't look like he had vomited. *Yet.* He was thinking about it. Jack smirked.

"I want y'all to go back and wait at the orange marker. Zeph and I will check things out, make sure everything is right before calling you to come get the mages." Jack shifted in his saddle. He debated telling them what the red flag meant but discarded the idea. Much as the Breaker annoyed him, Jack didn't need him losing his mind with worry right now. "We're in hostile territory, and we don't need any undue suspicion. You know what that means."

By Blaise's puzzled expression, he didn't know what it meant. But the pegasi did, and that was what mattered. All pegasi had the ability to hide their wings when a situation demanded it—a crucial adaptation for their survival. Jack watched as their wings faded from existence, making them look like four normal horses. It was a discomfiting sensation, knowing that Zepheus should have wings, but he couldn't see them. The best part of their trick was that they weren't just invisible—they vanished completely. If Jack ran his hand over Zepheus's shoulder where his wings sprouted, it felt like the shoulder of a normal horse.

Blaise made a little gasp when the pegasi did their trick. "What?"

Jack grinned. Emrys must have told the kid something because his expression cleared.

Time to get down to business. Jack laid a reassuring hand on the revolver strapped to his pommel holster. It was one of many weapons around or on his person. "If you hear any sounds of trouble—gunshots, shouts, anything—or if I don't come back at all, go back to Itude. Don't come after me."

Blaise frowned. "With all due respect, I'm here to help."

Jack spat on the ground. "And I'm here playing schoolmarm making sure nothing happens to any of your fool heads." He wouldn't tell the kid, but he had a grudging respect that he wanted to help. It was more than Jack thought him capable of—unless his brand of help was baking a cake. Truth be told, Jack wasn't sure if he would want even a seasoned outlaw beside him on this scouting mission. The more people involved, the higher the risk. With knowledge of the soldiers in the vicinity, Jack almost had a mind to call off the rescue mission.

But he couldn't. Not if it meant a chance to find Kittie.

Blaise pulled a silver pocket watch out, checking the time. "Thirty minutes."

Jack's train of thought derailed at the Breaker's words. "Thirty minutes what?"

The younger mage patted Emrys's neck. "That's how long we'll wait before we follow you in. As I said, I'm here to help."

Jack ground his teeth at the impertinence. How dare this—

<Thirty minutes.> Zepheus twisted his head to look back at him. <Or I don't lift a hoof.>

Infuriating, that's what the lot of them were. Jack glared at Blaise and gave a stiff nod of agreement. "Thirty minutes." He whistled to Zepheus, and the stallion spun, whisking into the copse of trees before Blaise said another word.

Jack kept his head on a swivel, surveying their surroundings. Autumn had the region in her grasp, the forest floor carpeted in flame gold leaves. The skies overhead were clear, and the temperature was crisp. Everything worked in their favor so far. Jack was determined to keep it so.

A black strip of cloth hung from a tree branch on the deer trail ahead. Zepheus slowed, sniffing the cloth. <Walker.>

Jack pursed his lips. *Black.* It meant they were close. He pulled down his bandanna, then removed his flight goggles and hung them from the saddle horn. Normal folk wore bandannas, but not flight goggles. If he ran into anyone, he wanted to project the illusion of normalcy.

But just in case, he pulled out a sixgun and tucked it into his belt for a quick draw.

He clucked his tongue, and Zepheus ambled forward, ears pricked and attentive. Ahead, Jack saw motion as the underbrush parted, a grey shape moving through it.

Zepheus paused, ears flicking back and forth with indecision. <Something isn't right.>

Jack froze in the saddle, straining his senses. Silence descended over the surrounding woods.

That was *wrong.* The utter absence of sound stood out in sudden stark contrast to the birdsong and chittering of squirrels from moments earlier. It was as if someone had wrapped a heavy blanket around the area, muffling everything. Gooseflesh shivered across Jack's skin. He was familiar with that magic. *A Dampener.*

Jack opened his mouth to yell at Zepheus, but nothing came out. He tugged at the reins and nudged the palomino with his knees, but Zepheus was already backing up in alarm. Trees and low-slung brambles hemmed in the stallion on either side, making it difficult to turn.

Instinct and years of training had a sixgun in Jack's hand in an instant.

But the lack of sound was utterly disorienting—Jack hadn't realized how much he depended on his ears for information until silence cloaked him. Dark shapes moved through the underbrush and Jack targeted one.

He felt helpless, torn. Should he shoot? What if it was a maverick, thinking he was a threat to confuse and defend against? He kept the form in his sights, vacillating. Damn, he didn't want to shoot a friendly.

Pain lanced through his right shoulder. Without the benefit of his ears, he didn't realize immediately that they had shot him. But Zepheus smelled fresh blood, and the pegasus telegraphed his outrage and fear with his quivering body. Jack aimed at the grey figure, but his right arm wouldn't obey his command. Clumsy and slow, he switched hands and fired with his left, but the shot went wide.

<Hold on.> Zepheus surged forward, head snaking. He locked his course on the person in grey, and Jack knew the stallion intended to trample them. That was fine. Best option since his gun was useless.

The stallion never made it. Jack's stomach lurched as Zepheus staggered—*what, why?*—and pitched forward violently. A normal horse would have gone down, crushing its rider beneath its bulk, but pegasi were made of sterner stuff. Zepheus's wings fluttered back into existence, correcting his precarious balance. But wounded as he was, Jack couldn't compensate for the hard bobble. He flew over the stallion's shoulder.

The world spun around him; the air whooshed out of his lungs as he hit the ground rolling. Agony bit at his shoulder like a terrier shaking a rat. Jack struggled to gather his wits. He was face-down in detritus, dirt in his mouth, lungs burning for air. His useless right arm crumpled beneath him, and his left hand was empty of the sixgun, which he'd lost during the fall. His fingers scrabbled, searching for one of the other revolvers he had squirreled away.

Something ground against his spine, keeping him down. Jack might have screamed at the pain, but there was no way to know with the dampening field surrounding them. Fingers twined around the hair at his crown, tugging his face out of the dirt. His vision swam with the sudden movement.

The cool muzzle of a revolver pressed against his temple. Jack spat out dirt, vision sharpening as the haze caused by his fall fled, banished by his seething outrage. All he saw were boots. *Right. Who do I need to kill?*

The boot pressed against his back lifted and then surprised him by kicking him in the ribs, just under his gunshot wound. Jack's vision exploded into stars of agony and he tried to scream, tried to curl into a ball to escape the torment.

When the anguish settled and his eyes focused again, he saw the face of his attacker. A Salt-Iron-issued revolver pointed at his head. Jack knew the hawk-nosed features of the blond man holding the gun on him well.

Lamar Gaitwood.

Gaitwood made a gesture with his hand, and suddenly the disconcerting hush fled. Jack heard birds chirp and the sound of Zepheus snorting with barely contained fury.

"If you attack my soldiers, your outlaw gets a bullet in his head," Lamar told the stallion. "I've been told your kind are smart, so if you give a shit about this man you *will* behave."

Jack groaned. *Gaitwood.* Gaitwood was here. He should have turned back at the sight of the red calico. Walker had warned him. But Jack hadn't thought they would be so close. And he hadn't thought it would be Lamar Gaitwood, of all the damned Salties.

Zepheus lowered his head, his ears pointed forward to show he would keep his peace. Distantly, Jack thought it strange the stallion wasn't trying to communicate with him.

"Get up, Jack. You don't have a choice." Lamar kept the revolver trained on him, but jutted his chin to the side, indicating the pile of Jack's sixguns. They must have disarmed him while he was on the ground, disoriented.

Jack panted for breath, withholding the anguished whimper he wanted to make. It wasn't the first time he'd been shot, but this one was bad. His shirt was slick with blood and bits of dirt and shredded leaves. If only his right arm would obey. *Damn Lamar.* Jack dragged himself into a sitting position, blood dripping to the forest floor with his effort.

"I said *get up,*" Lamar repeated.

"The last time I saw you I told you to go to Perdition, yet here we are," Jack wheezed, his voice sounding foreign to his ears.

Lamar laughed, a bitter sound. "Oh, Jack. I missed you. We had such good times tearing up the countryside, hunting down mavericks and outlaws."

The muscles in Jack's jaw tightened. He wanted desperately to get up, to fight off Lamar and his soldiers and get out of there. His eyes slid to Zepheus, noting the coil of salt-iron rope looped over the stallion's neck. Small wonder the stallion hadn't spoken to him. He couldn't even fly with that rope on him. There would be no help from him, though Jack knew the stallion would fight by his side if it came down to it.

The odds weren't in their favor. Five more soldiers strode through the woods to back Lamar. Their number included a woman who Jack pegged as the Dampener. She moved with the calm assurance of someone who enjoyed messing with people. Jack knew the type because *he* was the same.

"What do you want with me, Lamar?"

Lamar spat at the ground. "You should know. We worked together long enough." He stalked in a tight circle around Jack. "Oh, but that's right. You're worthless after our last encounter, *traitor*."

Jack bared his teeth. That was low, even for Lamar. But then, he never did like to fight fair. "I've been called worse things by better people. Let's settle this like men. Twenty paces."

Lamar scoffed. "I'm not stupid. I know even with a bum arm, the legendary Wildfire Jack could still outgun me in a fair fight." He gestured to a pair of soldiers, and they stepped closer. They reached down and jerked Jack to his feet. "No, we're—"

He stopped when the Dampener's eyes widened. "Commander. Someone's coming!"

Lamar aimed an inquisitive look at Jack. "Did you bring friends? You should have told me. I like company."

Jack coughed, the coppery tang of blood thick on his tongue. Pain radiated through his body, and it became more difficult to focus with each passing second. But he couldn't stop, not now. Had to bluff his way out of this. "Be afraid, Lamar."

Lamar's eyes flicked to him with interest. "Do tell."

"The Breaker's coming, and he's going to grind you under his boot."

Avarice lit Lamar's eyes. "*Breaker*? Oh, Jack." He laughed, the sound resonating and chilling Jack to the core. He had miscalculated. "Maybe I'll let you live after all. All these years later, and here you are—still doing the work for me."

"Go lick salt-iron."

Lamar Gaitwood, former friend and now bitter enemy, addressed his small force with asperity. "Williams, bring up the dampening field again. Screen the pegasus from view if you can."

"Aye, Commander."

Two soldiers dragged Jack behind a bush. The world around him rocked with the quick movement. He tried to shout a warning, but no sound came out.

He squeezed his eyes shut, trying to fight off the pain. Black tentacles of unconsciousness threatened to pull him under. He had to stay awake. Had to fight back. Couldn't let Lamar get Blaise.

The Breaker had escaped him once. He wouldn't be so lucky a second time.

CHAPTER SEVENTEEN

He Had It Coming

Blaise

Blaise walked in a circle around Emrys, relieved to stretch his legs after the time he'd spent tense in the saddle. Only luck had kept the contents of his stomach in place until Jack and Zepheus trotted off. Emrys had politely looked away as Blaise found a convenient shrub to vomit behind.

The curious colts hadn't been so sanguine. They approached with nostrils wide, ears pricked with questions until Emrys warned them off.

Blaise took a sip from his canteen and swished it around in his mouth before spitting it out to clear the sour taste. Then he drank deeply, chasing the water down with a piece of bread to settle his stomach. Blaise leaned against the bough of an oak, enjoying the shade and the pleasant weather. He took a calming breath, listening to the sounds of calling birds and the distant murmur of the river.

He was back in Desina. Miles from home, but still in his homeland. Blaise thought he would feel *something* when he came back. Longing. Or sadness. But cool detachment washed over him, like it had been a part of someone else's life. He missed his family, and he always would. Perhaps he had come to grips with their loss and had sealed the pain away, like a surgeon cauterizing a wound.

Blaise vowed that someday he would find out what happened to them. And if he had the chance, apologize for what he was. What he had unleashed on them.

Emrys nudged his shoulder, interrupting his thoughts. <Something's wrong.>

Blaise screwed down the lid on his canteen, moving around to the stallion's side, securing it back in the saddlebag. "What is it?"

The pegasus shook his mane. <Hard to explain. It's more of . . . an absence.>

Blaise's brow furrowed with concern. He pulled his pocket watch out. "It's been forty-five minutes. We should check it out."

<Wildfire Jack didn't seem inclined for us to follow,> Icoron reminded them, lifting his head from grazing. Wisps of grass poked out from his lips.

Oh, Blaise knew. Risking Wildfire Jack's wrath wasn't at the top of his list. He thought about Emmaline, humming as she worked at the bakery with a tiny doll sitting nearby. Emmaline, whom Blaise would have to face if her father didn't make it back home. The outlaw was a bastard, but Emmaline didn't deserve that.

<Well? > Emrys faced the woods, ears pricked.

"We'll go a short distance." They didn't have to go far. Just far enough for Emrys to know that Jack and Zepheus were okay. No problem.

Rhoxio snorted, a half-eaten clump of grass falling from his mouth. <We'll come, too.>

Blaise rubbed the side of his face, not bothering to dissuade the colts. He doubted they would listen to him. He put his left foot into the stirrup and swung into the saddle, his thighs and calves outraged that he had the audacity to mount up again so soon.

Mockingbirds darted from tree to tree. Emrys followed the trail Zepheus had taken. The underbrush scraped against the stallion's sides and Blaise's legs as they delved deeper. Blaise thought they must not be close to any towns or farms. Some trees were pecan, their branches heavy with this year's crop. If they were closer to a town or farm, he would expect industrious harvesters to keep the ground passable.

Blaise scanned the area ahead, searching for any sign of Jack or Zepheus. His shoulders were rigid. How far had they gone? He hoped Emrys would hear them soon.

Emrys kept to a cautious walk, brambles grasping at his mane and tail. Blaise had to duck below branches, and others he had to lift overhead with his gloved hands. He had considered not wearing his gloves but was glad he had. They were sturdy protection.

Both colts had their ears pinned back with unease and shied at the slightest provocation. Blaise asked Emrys to stop, and he turned to the young pegasi. "If you're scared, follow the trail back and wait for us at the marker."

Rhoxio shook his mane. <We're sorry. We'll try to be brave like you.>

Blaise gave a tight-lipped smile. *Brave?* That didn't describe him. Terrified. Worried. Those were more accurate. He turned back around in the saddle so that Emrys could continue onward.

His magic rose, startled by a sudden, strange sensation that swept over him, like cotton stuffed in his ears. Emrys's head rocked back in alarm. The world shifted into muted chaos. Emrys lunged forward. <Look out!>

The stallion's mental command was deafening in the silence. Blaise was too slow to heed it. He never saw the tree branch that swept him from the saddle. One moment he was astride Emrys, and the next he was flat on his back, the wind knocked out of him. He gasped like a fish out of water, hoping he didn't end up trampled by the colts.

<Blaise, you have to—> Emrys cut off abruptly.

Blaise's eyes widened. He rolled to his side, thorns scratching his face. What would interrupt a pegasus's mental speech? Was Emrys dead? He tried to get up, but something came down hard on his chest, his breath whooshing out again. A dark-clad foot pinned him down. *What?*

In a sudden rush, the world came alive with sound. The colts squealed, Emrys screaming a challenge. An unfamiliar voice cursed.

"Get him up!"

Oh, no. No, no, no.

He knew that voice. It haunted his nightmares. Lamar Gaitwood grinned down at him as one of his men grabbed Blaise, twisting his arms behind him as he hauled him to his feet. Bruised muscles protested, and Blaise huffed in pain. He tried to ignore the agony—it could be handled later when he understood the situation.

Zepheus's flaxen tail was visible through a cluster of saplings. Emrys, Rhoxio, and Icoron froze in place, ears pinned back as they stared at something. Blaise followed their gaze.

Lamar Gaitwood had his revolver out, Wildfire Jack in his sights.

Blaise almost didn't recognize the crumpled man at first. The hale and hearty outlaw who had left them behind to scout was motionless on the forest floor, dark blood spreading across the autumn leaves. His skin was ashen, eyes closed. Blaise had thought the surly outlaw was larger than life; indomitable. Wildfire Jack would never be so vulnerable.

"This is what we're going to do." Gaitwood's tone was matter-of-fact as he kept the muzzle trained on Jack. "My men are going to tie you up, and then we're going to have a pleasant walk through the forest. If you do anything I don't like, your friend dies."

Blaise clenched his jaw. "*Friend* is a stretch, but fine." He grunted as a soldier wrenched his arms behind his back, using a rope to bind his wrists. Blaise's heart thudded like a drum at the unfamiliar touch, and he wished he could squirm away. He kept his eyes on Jack, willing the outlaw to get up. To fight. *You can't seriously leave this up to* me.

But he didn't move. If not for the uneven rise and fall of his chest, Blaise would have thought the man dead. One of Gaitwood's men led Zepheus over, and Blaise narrowed his eyes at the familiar glittering rope looped around the stallion's neck. The same sort that had snared Emrys before. Now Blaise knew what had interrupted Emrys's warning. The salt-iron ropes hobbled the pegasus's magic.

Two soldiers draped Jack's limp body over Zepheus's saddle, securing him with mundane rope. Zepheus stood as still as a child's pony, twitching ears and furtive glances belying his worry. Gaitwood moved behind Blaise, revolver still out. Blaise stared straight ahead. He didn't particularly want to see a gun aimed at him.

"Start walking. Follow the horses. We'd prefer to bring you back in one piece."

Blaise plodded along in the wake of the colts. He kept his head down, turmoil eating at him. This wasn't supposed to happen. How had things gone so wrong? The mission was supposed to be simple. Easy. Not this.

He had come so far, done so much. And yet, it had resulted in his capture. Frustrated tears pricked the corners of his eyes.

Gaitwood kept pace behind him. He was quiet for the first ten minutes of travel, but eventually, he spoke. "You've probably missed your mother. Won't it be nice to have a family reunion?"

Panic gripping him, Blaise froze, and then regretted it as the muzzle of the Commander's revolver prodded his back. He didn't turn around. "Where is she?"

Gaitwood chuckled. "Back where she belongs. On a train to Izhadell by now, I imagine."

Blaise's stomach clenched as Gaitwood prodded him forward. Izhadell was half a continent away. Was that where they would take him, too? He wanted to ask about his father and siblings, but doubted Gaitwood would freely offer the information. Blaise kept his mouth shut.

He thought they would walk for longer, but after about an hour they came upon the remains of a camp. Near the ashes of a fire, a single tent was visible. Tethered horses grazed nearby, only looking up at the approach of the pegasi. No other soldiers were in sight, aside from the ones who had made the walk back to the camp.

This couldn't be all of Gaitwood's soldiers. Six was a small number, an intimate number. Gaitwood had gambled at taking them by stealth, and it had worked.

The soldiers pulled Jack from Zepheus's saddle, depositing him on the ground at the outskirts of their camp. The outlaw still didn't move, his face slack. Gaitwood stalked over, prodding him with the toe of his boot. When Jack didn't respond, he gestured with one hand, and a silver cage hummed into existence around the injured man.

"He's hurt. He needs help." Blaise gritted his teeth.

Gaitwood strode over, coming so close that Blaise flinched. "Oh no, I hurt the poor outlaw." Gaitwood clutched a hand over his heart. "There's no mercy here, boy. The Dollmaker's a washed-up outlaw. The only kindness that awaits him is a noose."

A chill crept down Blaise's spine. Zepheus angled a hind hoof, ready to kick anyone who came close. The stallion had heard, and he was angry. But he was helpless, just as Jack was.

Gaitwood stepped away, lifting a hand to gesture at Blaise. A similar silver cage coalesced around him. "That was a pretty trick you pulled the last time we met. I'll admit, I've never seen anyone hit the bars of my trap and live to tell the tale, much less break through." He canted his head, thoughtful. "I wouldn't try it again if I were you, though. Salt-iron bindings are nasty."

The Commander joined the other soldiers, who had secured the pegasi to a picket line with the salt-iron rope. A soldier came over and stood watch while the others prepared the evening meal and gathered wood to start the fire. Blaise closed his eyes, the familiar scent of smoke a balm for his tattered nerves.

Head bowed, Blaise watched them from the corner of his eye. His stomach rumbled. He was thirsty, but they didn't bring him anything. He should have listened to Rhoxio—should have gone back to Itude for help. Even better, someone more proficient should have come along with Wildfire Jack. Vixen would have been an excellent choice.

Blaise chewed on his bottom lip. *Vixen's not here. I am.* Even with his hands tied behind his back, he was the only one capable of getting them out of there.

Because he was a *Breaker*.

He thought back to his conversation with Vixen, about using his magic for a purpose. If ever there was a time, this was it. But how?

He listened as Gaitwood instructed a soldier to serve as a messenger.

"Bring the jail wagon. We'll reinforce it with salt-iron when it arrives. I don't want to take any chances."

Blaise's eyes widened. The soldier rode off, leaving Gaitwood with five, including the man himself. Jaw set, he realized there was limited time to act. The soldiers laid out their bedrolls for later, planning to spend the night there.

His shoulders throbbed from the way his arms were wrenched behind his back. Long sleeves and gloves protected him from the worst of the salt-iron, but small patches of skin above his wrists were growing raw and irritated. Blaise exhaled a frustrated breath. The metal leeched his magic away, bit by bit. How long until the salt-iron rendered him useless? He had no idea.

He summoned his magic, welcoming the familiar itch as it rose to his palms. Blaise angled his hands until he could grasp a strand of rope with his fingers. He had no way to wrest his gloves off, so he planned to let his magic eat through the leather.

Blaise stayed still as he allowed his magic to break down the leather, and as time wore on, the guard on watch grew bored. Wildfire Jack was still unconscious—Blaise refused to think he was any worse off than that. He kept his focus on his magic, struggling to ignore the bite of salt-iron against his skin.

Silently, he thanked Vixen for all of their practice sessions. He hoped to make her proud.

By the time the soldiers sat down to eat, Blaise had a big enough hole to touch the rope with his bare skin. He worked his thumb against the braid, biting back a hiss when he touched metal by accident. His magic rose in agitation. It was almost sentient in its own way, angered by the salt-iron. He let it work through a few strands of the rope, then reined it back when the soldiers moved around the camp.

As the sun set, Gaitwood retired to the tent. The lone female soldier took the first night shift, and she settled against a nearby tree, her glittering eyes intent on her caged prey. The hungry look in her eyes bothered Blaise. She reminded him of someone with something to prove. She would not be a lax guard. That was unfortunate. Blaise needed someone sloppy.

The lambent moon rose overhead, casting the clearing in silvery shadows. Nearby, the fire crackled and snapped as it grew low. The woman fed the fire, and it hissed back to life, adding its golden light to the night. Blaise waited for the woman to settle back down into her place, watchful. He kept still as he sent his magic against the rope again. If she suspected anything of him, she would have to get closer to see what he was doing.

Eventually, she swapped with another man, who yawned, unenthusiastic about being roused from his slumber. He grumbled about caged outlaws not going anywhere. A wisp of hope unfurled within Blaise.

The soldier's head lolled against his chest as he relaxed against a nearby pecan tree. Blaise observed him for a few more minutes, then let his magic eat through the last strand. The rope fell away, and Blaise grabbed it with one hand before it could clatter to the ground. He stifled a relieved gasp and gently discarded the rope. Sure that the guard was asleep, Blaise brought his hands around to the front and massaged his wrists, wincing at the skin blistered by the salt-iron.

The pegasi pricked their ears, attentive. Blaise lifted an index finger to his lips, hoping they understood to stay quiet. Emrys bobbed his head. Blaise scooted closer to the silvery bars. The last time he had broken Gaitwood's cage, it had shattered in a dazzling light show. That would draw too much attention.

This was a time for subtlety and control. Blaise swallowed, quailing. It terrified him that he might not have what it took. But his friends were counting on him. Vixen thought he could do it. *I can do this.*

With a calming breath, he peeled off his ruined gloves. The corner of his mouth quirked as he realized this was the first time he had tried to destroy his gloves on purpose. He shook his head at the thought, then reached out and wrapped his right hand around a single bar.

The last time he had come across Gaitwood's trap, he had plowed through it like a bull. The contact was brief but fierce, like breaking an egg. This time was different. He held the construct of Gaitwood's magic in his hand, and he could *feel* the malevolence in it. Blaise didn't understand the magic of the trap, but he knew it was cruel. And if his magic wasn't as powerful as Gaitwood's was, he would succumb to it.

Blaise's hair stood on end as he sent his magic into the bars of the cage. It flooded the construct, learning every facet. Blaise saw the essence of the magic that made up the cage. It hung suspended around him like twinkling stars. It was almost beautiful. Blaise clenched his jaw. Wicked magic didn't deserve to be beautiful.

He sent his own magic against it, small amounts dripping from his hand. Blaise ate away at the construct, like the persistent tug of water eroding a riverbank. He released a little more magic, and it flowed out, consuming the trap until it winked out of existence. No great blast of light or sound. It simply ceased to exist. Nothing stood between Blaise and freedom.

He rose from the ground, listening for any hint of movement or awareness from the soldiers. Nothing. Icoron stamped a hoof, impatient. Blaise slipped over to the pegasi, moving as quietly as his bruised and sore body would allow.

He sidled in front of the four equines, pitching his voice low. "It's not much of a plan, but here we go: I'm going to free all of you first, but it's important you don't move from here until I get Jack. Can you do that?"

The four heads bowed.

"Good. Once I get him loose, if you can come over and help me get him out of here, that would be appreciated."

Zepheus bumped him with his muzzle. Blaise decided the palomino was volunteering.

Blaise slipped in between Emrys and Zepheus. The sheer size of the stallions would make it difficult for the soldiers to spy him if they realized he was missing. He freed Emrys first, since the black stallion knew what to expect. Blaise wished the colts weren't there. They were skittish and scared out of their minds, and that wasn't a good combination.

Blaise gripped the rope the soldiers had laced tightly around the stallion's neck. They had secured it to the horn of the saddle which annoyed Blaise, but he left it alone for the time being. He could take care of that later. A thrill of satisfaction coursed through him when the last strand tore free.

<I'm going to give that rope a good stomping later. Thanks,> Emrys said, the muscles of his neck quivering. <I'll help keep the colts in line when you free them.>

Blaise nodded his thanks. One less thing he had to worry about. He turned to Zepheus and repeated the same magic.

The palomino sighed as the rope fell away. He craned his neck down, his broad forehead close to Blaise's head. <You have my gratitude. When Jack is free, get him on my back. If you need us to provide cover while you free him, we'll do so.> Zepheus eyed the two colts, including them in the mission. They shifted nervously.

Blaise nodded to the golden stallion, feeling a little better that he wasn't going it alone. He freed the two colts, their hides twitching as the salt-iron ropes fell away. Blaise was afraid they would flee. But even in their terror, they held their ground.

<Listen to me,> Zepheus said. Blaise stood still, deciding that anything Jack's pegasus had to say was worth listening to. He had a lot more experience with these situations. <We'll stand here *quietly* while the Breaker frees Jack. No snorting. Do not so much as lift a hoof. If the Salties raise the alarm, that is when we move. Fight them like you would battle a murder of chupacabras.>

Three other heads bobbed in agreement. Blaise decided not to ask about the logistics of that last statement.

Blaise crouched down and eased, slow and silent, toward Wildfire Jack's cage. The campfire was dying down to embers; the full moon overhead lit his path. The soldiers were dark lumps in their bedrolls, the nasal sounds of snoring the only sign of life. The sentry dozed by the tree, a rifle propped beside him.

In the cage, Wildfire Jack turned onto his side with a soft moan. Blaise froze. It was the first movement he had seen from the outlaw in hours. His face was ashen, his chest dark with blood. His glazed eyes locked onto Blaise's in the moonlight. The injured outlaw's lips twitched as if he wanted to say something.

Blaise settled beside the cage. Wildfire Jack's chilly eyes stayed on him as he wrapped both hands around the bars. Blaise kept his focus on the cage, feeling the slide of Gaitwood's magic against him. He had used more magic tonight than he had ever used before, some of it siphoned away by the salt-iron. Vixen had warned him about the repercussions of draining his magic. He didn't know his limits.

Gaitwood's magic pushed against him, every nerve in Blaise's body on fire as he braced against the power. He made a soft grunt, pausing when he heard a soldier yawn behind him.

Blaise halted, hands still on the bars. He felt like he was trying to prop up a wall that would otherwise collapse and crush him. Out of the corner of his eye, he saw a dark outline untangle from a bedroll and get up, walking groggily toward a tree. The soft rustle of clothing followed, and then the splash of the man urinating. Blaise's heart pounded as he made a silent supplication to Faedra to send the drowsy soldier promptly back to sleep.

Dry leaves crunched beneath boots. The man was back at his bedroll. Blaise saw him kneel, but then he paused.

"Huh?" the man muttered, lethargic. "Thought there were two."

His voice woke the sentry who cursed softly. Apparently, he hadn't been planning to fall asleep.

"Commander!" the sentry squawked.

The pegasi whistled a challenge, the night descending into confusion as they unfurled their shrouded wings. Zepheus charged to Blaise, wings extended. Emrys and the two colts barreled toward the soldiers who were grabbing guns as they disentangled themselves from their bedrolls.

<Free him. NOW!> Zepheus commanded.

If only it were that simple. Blaise ducked his head, sweat beading his brow. He felt the shock of Gaitwood's magic butting against his own. *I don't have time for this.*

"Close your eyes!" Blaise said, hoping that the pegasi with their sharp ears would listen and obey.

He gathered all the magic he could and slammed it into the bars.

The cage exploded in a corona of light. The soldiers' horses squealed in terror. Jack groaned; the soldiers cursed and howled. Gaitwood was one of those voices, but Blaise didn't know what he said because he was focused on the outlaw.

Zepheus knelt. Blaise studied Wildfire Jack, trying to figure out the best way to get him onto the pegasus's back. There was no gentle way to do it. He put his hands under Jack's arms and dragged him into the saddle, blood smearing against Blaise's shirt. Zepheus flinched as an agonized squeal answered the retort of nearby gunfire. Blaise wished he could see how Emrys and the colts were doing, but there was no time.

<I'm going due north.> Zepheus spun and bolted. Blaise didn't know how, but Jack somehow kept his seat, slouched over the pommel like a rag doll.

<Go, go, go!> Emrys came up behind him fast. Blaise turned and ran, staggering as a bullet whizzed past him. He heard another devastating whinny but didn't look back.

Emrys raced by his side and slowed. Blaise didn't stop to think as he shoved a foot in the stirrup and lunged into the saddle. The stallion dashed off before he even had his seat, surging through the forest. Blaise glanced back, thinking he saw one of the colts behind them. He hoped it was the colts, and not the soldiers.

"Can you fly?" Blaise gasped for breath once Emrys slowed to a trot.

<Not yet. Still drained from the rope.> Emrys's sides heaved like a bellows.

"Are they going to come after us?"

<Without a doubt.> The pegasus sighed. <But it will take them a while to regroup. Rhoxio broke their horses free and scattered them. And with any luck, I broke Gaitwood's arm. And maybe some ribs. I can only hope.>

"Wait, you did?"

<He had it coming.> Emrys snorted.

Blaise couldn't agree more.

CHAPTER EIGHTEEN

Faedra's Embrace

Blaise

The eastern sky blushed with the pastel pinks and yellows of dawn when Blaise and Emrys finally found Jack and Zepheus. Rhoxio trotted along behind them, his gait uneven and eyes ringed with white. Icoron hadn't survived the fight. Blaise didn't ask Emrys for details. Not yet. He couldn't stomach any more grief.

It took them longer to find the outlaw than Blaise liked, because Zepheus hadn't traveled true north as he'd said. They had made it across the border to the fringe of land between the Gutter and the Untamed Territory. Jack sprawled beneath the scraggly limbs of a mesquite, the slight rise and fall of his chest the only hint that he lived. Zepheus stood over him, the palomino's saddle and sides splashed with dried blood. The stallion's wings were ragged with feathers missing, and a deep gash seeped blood on his flank.

<Sorry. Chupacabras.> Zepheus's mental voice was faint with exhaustion.

Rhoxio shied away and Emrys flung up his head. <Here?>

<A mated pair. I fought them off. But Jack dismounted, and he can't get back up.> The golden stallion nuzzled the fallen outlaw.

Blaise swung out of the saddle and knelt down beside him. "Jack?"

The outlaw's eyes fluttered open. But he said nothing, and that worried Blaise.

<He should be dead. He's bled out so much. How is he not dead?> Emrys asked Blaise.

Blaise figured the man was too stubborn to die. But he didn't want to jinx them. Blaise had never seen a wound like Jack's before, and he hoped to never see it again. The outlaw's clothing was black with dried blood, and fresh red gore oozed from the wound at his shoulder. Blaise brushed a hand against Jack's forehead. He was feverish, and Blaise didn't know if that was good or bad.

<Try the first aid kits?> Zepheus nosed at the saddlebags behind Emrys's saddle.

"Oh. Right." Blaise rose and went to Emrys's side, hoping that the soldiers hadn't removed them. They had taken all Jack's weapons and ammunition. He breathed a sigh of relief as he tugged a kit from the saddlebag, along with a canteen. Blaise was light-headed and exhausted from using his magic, not sleeping, and not having eaten since the previous day. He took a sip of the water, his parched tongue savoring the taste. Food would have to wait until after Jack was stabilized.

Blaise pulled out the kit. Despite their headlong flight, everything seemed whole and accounted for. Blaise opened the metal box and found gauze, adhesive plasters, dressing, bandages, sutures, and the cotton-wrapped alchemical vials. He wasn't sure where to start.

<Clean the wound first,> Zepheus directed him.

He spread a spare bandanna on the ground beside Jack and laid out the kit's contents. There was so much blood and blood-caked debris it was challenging to see what was what. Blaise followed Zepheus's direction, peeling back the clothing to reveal Jack's injury. His clothes had twisted during the scuffle, tattered bits digging into the wound. Blaise found a small pair of shears in the kit and cut off Jack's sleeve and as much of the shirt around the wound on his shoulder as he could.

Zepheus was a competent instructor. It made Blaise wonder how often the stallion had observed moments like this—not only with Jack, but others. Zepheus had him make a dressing for the wound and then secure it with surgical tape. With that task complete, Blaise did his best to clean up the area around the injury. Mostly he succeeded at smearing blood to new locations.

He found the outlaw's theurgist tattoo, arcane sigils inked onto his bicep in a dusky blue. Blaise didn't mean to stare, but he couldn't help but look as he cleaned away the crusted blood. He worried at his lower lip. If he hadn't escaped, he would have borne one of those tattoos, too.

"Can't . . . stay here."

Blaise winced, pulling his gaze away from the tattoo at the sound of Jack's faint voice. "What?" He studied the outlaw's face, eyes shut and lips still. "We should send Emrys back to get Nadine. Or someone who can help. I don't think—" *I don't think you'll survive being moved.* He didn't like Jack, but he didn't want to say the words out loud. They were horrific.

<The chupacabras will come back with the rest of their murder. And Gaitwood will not give up so easily. He'll come.> Zepheus arched his neck, stamping the ground with a hoof.

Blaise sighed, mopping at his face with one hand. He was tired and scared. Managing a crisis like this wasn't part of his skill set. He wished another functional adult would wander up and take control of the situation. The pegasi watched him, expectant.

Jack was no longer bleeding, but he wasn't out of the woods. Blaise sorted through the potions in the kit and pulled out the red vial of Faedra's Embrace. He didn't want to give the potion to Wildfire Jack. Blaise recalled his lack of enthusiasm for the side effects.

But then again, side effects didn't matter too much if you were dead.

<Jack would rather die in the saddle than in a hangman's noose.> Zepheus lowered his muzzle, sniffing at the vial.

"I'd rather no one die, but I get your point." Blaise held up the potion, swirling the vial as he checked the color and consistency. Wouldn't do any good to administer the wrong potion. It was true to the colors he recalled —a deep violet at the base, shifting to a sparkling crimson above. He uncorked it, and the rosy scent met his nostrils.

Blaise glanced up at the palomino. "If he gets mad at me later—"

<I swear he will not harm you ever again. Give him the potion.>

He raised his brows at the hefty promise. What would Jack think of that? The fact of the matter was, for the outlaw to have an opinion, he had to survive. Blaise raised the wounded man's head so he wouldn't choke on the potion and gently pried open his mouth and poured it down.

"It'll take a few minutes. If it even works." Blaise sat down criss-cross as he waited. The pegasi kept vigil, monitoring their surroundings for danger.

A half-hour passed before Jack's eyes fluttered open, his gaze locking onto Blaise. The outlaw coughed, flecks of blood on his lips. "Did you just pour shit into my mouth? Because my tongue tastes like shit."

"And he's back," Blaise muttered.

Zepheus nickered, lowering his head to inspect his rider. Jack scowled, trying to sit up. He groaned with the effort and only got as far as prop-ping one elbow beneath him. Lips pulled back from his teeth in a rictus of pain, his eyes slitted in frustration.

"Do you need help?" Blaise asked.

Jack's lips closed into a thin, angry line.

Blaise ran a hand through his hair, belatedly realizing he had lost his hat somewhere along the way. Most likely yesterday in his fall. *Great.* "I know you hate me. But you said yourself we can't stay here. Let me help." Did the outlaw resent him so much that he would rather die than have his aid? That stung. Or was it simply foolish pride? He didn't understand what went on in Wildfire Jack's crazy head.

The outlaw said nothing. Zepheus rumbled, and Jack lifted his left hand into the air. Blaise clasped it and gently wrapped an arm around Jack, helping him up. The injured man trembled with the effort. He wouldn't get very far under his own power. Zepheus and Blaise worked together to get the outlaw into the saddle.

"Can you fly yet?" Blaise asked the pegasi.

<Not yet. And even if we could, Zeph shouldn't fly with Jack.> Emrys's ears flicked back as a haunting cry echoed in the distance. <We need to go. The chupacabras will be here soon.>

Blaise glanced at Jack, then climbed into the saddle. Every muscle in his body hurt, but he was thankful he was in better condition than Jack. The outlaw was pale, the reins slack around Zepheus's neck as he clutched the pommel with his left hand.

The pegasi broke into a trot, holding an easy pace that even limping Rhoxio could maintain. Zepheus changed his gait to a rolling stride that protected the outlaw from the jarring of a regular trot.

After an hour, Jack seemed more alert, though his wound was still grievous. Faedra's Embrace kept his pain checked.

"Do you know what it means?" Jack asked suddenly.

Blaise didn't think Wildfire Jack was speaking to him at first. He assumed he was talking to Zepheus. Then the outlaw cleared his throat, and Blaise realized his eyes were on him. "Sorry, what?" He wanted Jack to be okay, but he didn't want to talk to the outlaw. That only led to trouble.

But he had taken Faedra's Embrace. *Oh, no. Wildfire Jack's going to chat, and he's going to kill me later when he tells me something he shouldn't.*

"The tattoo on my arm. You saw it."

Blaise swallowed. "Oh. Um, no, I'm not sure what you're—"

Jack laughed, the cackle reminding Blaise of the times at the saloon when some poor sod had one too many drinks and found everything hilarious. That was a sound Wildfire Jack never made. "You're a terrible liar, Breaker. I'm drugged on whatever swill you gave me, and I can still see that."

Blaise shook his head. "I gave you Faedra's Embrace so you would stabilize enough to ride. One goal I have for this trip with you is to not die, so please stop talking. It hurts when you punch me in the face, and I'm scared of what you may do when you get your hands on a gun."

Jack spat out a bloody glob of phlegm. "Guns. Bastard got my guns." He sounded more baffled by it than angry—which Blaise found strange. Another side effect. Jack frowned as he struggled to recall his train of thought. "The tattoo."

Blaise rubbed his face with his hand. "Zepheus, can you stop him?"

<Sorry, his mind is hazy, and I can't get through.> The pegasus was apologetic.

Wonderful. Just wonderful.

"I was a theurgist."

Blaise pinched the bridge of his nose. After his narrow escape from Gaitwood, he really didn't want to hear any more about the Salt-Iron Confederation at the moment.

Heedless of Blaise's opinion, the drugged outlaw blundered on with an unstable grin. "That's the mark of a theurgist. All of 'em have it, but they're supposed to be red, not blue. If Lamar got you, you'd be getting inked with one." He coughed, and Blaise winced in sympathy at the grating sound. "Mine's special, though. The last time I tangled with Lamar, he did a little something to me. You wanna know what?"

Blaise shook his head. He didn't want to know. Not at all.

Jack's pale visage warped, becoming savage. "Bastard burned out my magic. *My friend burned out my magic.*"

Blaise felt like a hammer struck him between the eyes. Jack didn't have magic? And Lamar Gaitwood was his *friend*?

"You . . . you don't have magic?" Blaise couldn't take back the question once he'd uttered it, but he wished he could.

"No." Jack's voice was small and defeated.

They rode in silence for a few more minutes. Blaise picked apart what the outlaw had said, boggled. He was an outlaw *mage*. Everyone said as much. Even Jack. Had the potion scrambled his brain and caused him to think he didn't have magic? Jack was terrifying. He *had* to have magic.

<He doesn't. Not anymore,> Zepheus confirmed.

Blaise thought about that. The outlaw put on a bold front, projecting a larger-than-life image. Tough. Indomitable. And to be sure, he was. And he did all that without the trademark magic the outlaw mages were renowned for. No wonder he was perpetually in a foul mood.

"Wildfire Jack?"

"Just call me Jack."

Blaise blinked, surprised. "I'm sorry they took your magic from you. I didn't know that could happen."

Jack stared into the distance between Zepheus's ears. "I thought it was the worst feeling in the world. But it wasn't. Not compared to my biggest loss."

Blaise's eyes widened. "I don't want to know."

"Tough luck. That shit you gave me has me gabbing, and you're going to listen. If I don't make it, I need you to tell Emmaline. Promise me."

Blaise's heart sank.

"*Promise me.*" Jack's voice was dangerous. With the potion dulling his pain and clouding his judgment, he was unpredictable. But there was also an edge of fear, as if Jack worried he might not make it.

"I promise."

Jack calmed and exhaled softly. "Give me a few minutes to catch my breath. Talking is hard. But I'll tell you."

CHAPTER NINETEEN

The Gift of Gab

Jack felt a pleasant disconnection from his body, like nothing below his head existed. He figured his legs clung to Zepheus's sides out of sheer stubbornness. The reins dangled in his hands, which seemed to move and twitch of their own accord. He had only pin-prickles of sensation from his neck down, but it was probably a blessing. Jack remembered enough to know Gaitwood had shot him, and it had been ugly. Really bad. Buried with your boots on *bad*.

Zepheus was trying to speak to him, but the words were muffled and made little sense. But his ears worked—he heard the pegasi's hoofbeats and Blaise's words fine. A tiny part of his mind was alarmed and angry, but the blissful sensation of talking outweighed it. Yeah, talking was good. It was cleansing. It was the best.

His mouth felt like it was full of cotton, and his tongue tasted like death, but that didn't fetter the need to speak. "I'm not from these parts," Jack began once he felt rested enough to speak. "To be sure, most of the folks in Itude aren't from here, either. Anyone with magic is an outlaw or maverick. Those without are outcasts."

"But we're called outlaws as a group." Blaise sounded tentative, like he was expecting the gift of a punch in the face.

Jack smirked. "Makes us sound scary. The bad guys." Yeah, Jack knew without a doubt that *he* was one of the bad guys. He had the blood on his hands to back it up. Blaise gave him a puzzled look. The kid was too scared to ask questions. Wasn't he lucky that Jack was in a chatty mood? "You think everyone in Itude is bad?"

Blaise shook his head. "Not now. But before . . . well, we're told that outlaws are scary. So a town full of outlaws sounds like an undesirable place." The Breaker ran a hand down Emrys's silky neck. "I was wrong."

Jack snorted. "I still don't regret punching you in the face on your first day." Zepheus twisted his head to look back, a move Jack assumed was a warning. It was convenient that he couldn't hear the stallion. "Aren't you going to ask where I'm from?"

"Do I have to?"

"Humor me. I'm the one who bled out."

Blaise sighed. Jack felt a warm fuzzy feeling at needling the kid. "Where are you from?"

"Izhadell."

At the word, Blaise straightened in the saddle, as if on alert. "Isn't that the capital of Phinora?"

"It's where this whole damned Salt-Iron Confederation business started." Jack leaned to the side and spat on the ground. He tasted blood on his tongue. *Should I worry about that? Nah. I'm good.* "Never met my father. I—"

"Wait, you're telling me everything from the very beginning?" Blaise interrupted, dismayed.

Jack glared at him. "Shut your piehole and listen."

"As I was saying, I was raised in Izhadell by my mother—never knew my father." Maybe it was a side effect of the potion—a hallucination, perhaps. As Jack spoke, the scenes came to life before him like he was in the audience at the theater. Maybe his entire life was flashing before his eyes because he was dying. *Whatever.* He went with it.

The white clapboard house rose from the ground before him, surrounded by a picket fence. A tow-headed boy tussled with a playmate in the front yard, shoving handfuls of leaves down the other's shirt.

"In Phinora, Trackers are sent out regularly to hunt for new mages. I'd just turned ten when the Trackers came through our part of town, leading a unicorn." The scene unfolded before him. His younger self still played with his friend—Robbie, that had been the other kid's name. They dove into a pile of leaves and tossed them up into the air, watching them rain down as they laughed. Both boys froze as the moon-white unicorn approached, horn shining like a beacon. "My mother screamed when she saw the unicorn come up to me and dip its head."

In his vision, Robbie looked at young Jack like he was a demon straight out of Perdition and bolted away, crying for his mother. That had been Jack's first sampling of the fear magic could impose on another. And he had liked the power it gave him.

Blaise stared at him. "You didn't know you had magic until then?"

That was an interesting question. Jack had thought about it before and always came to the same conclusion. "I didn't know what magic was like, to know it was any different from . . . just being me. There was a strange tingling in my fingers whenever I played with some of my toys, but I thought that was normal. Thought it happened to everyone."

The Breaker nodded.

"That was the day everything changed. My mother was furious—and I was excited. She didn't want to give me up." Jack's mother wept before him, her tears shining diamonds. Jack hadn't understood her sense of loss, not back then. But he did now.

"Kids in my neighborhood used to play theurgist and outlaw." Jack chuckled at the memory, then regretted it. The metallic taste of blood was thick in his tongue. Should he worry about that? That was for later. "I thought I was top shelf for being the first of my age-mates to get pegged as a mage. They took me to the Golden Citadel, and I thought life couldn't get any better."

Blaise frowned at the unfamiliar term. "What's the Golden Citadel?"

"The Golden Citadel—" Jack coughed, and then shook his head, touching his throat with one hand.

Blaise called a halt. Jack heard Zepheus in the distance again, but he still didn't make sense. Blaise pulled out a canteen and helped him drink. The water was sweet and refreshing as it went down, and he wanted more.

"Sorry," Blaise winced. "Zepheus says I shouldn't give you too much. It might make you worse."

"Zepheus is an asshole."

The stallion stomped a rear hoof, tail flinging from side to side with annoyance. Blaise wiped his forehead. "This is the weirdest day ever, which is kind of depressing in the grand scheme of things." He gave Jack a scrutinizing look, his lips tense as he scanned the dressed wound. "You were saying about the Golden Citadel?"

Right. The pegasi started forward again, and Jack fell back into the tale. "It's a big place outside Izhadell. Former fortress, maybe. Somebody with more money than common sense had it painted gold. Gaudy as all get-out." In his vision, a soldier accompanied young Jack up the well-maintained road that led there. It was sunset, and the building reflected the light so it glowed as if it were magic. And to a young boy, it was.

"The Cit—that's what we called it—became my home. They didn't allow my mother to visit. It bothered me at first, but there was so much to see and learn that it soon seemed like a small thing." Jack clenched his teeth. Stupid young Jack.

"The geasa?" Blaise asked.

Jack frowned. That was a word he hadn't heard in a very long time, and even in his drugged state it was odd to hear it from the Breaker's lips. "How do you know that word?" The geasa wasn't widely known. Few theurgists knew the proper name for the specialized binding that tied them to their handler.

"Um . . ." Blaise backpedaled. "The tattoos are magic, right? But most Phinorans don't like magic because it's against their morals?"

Jack snorted. "Most of the tattoos aren't infused with the geasa. They're simply a way to mark someone as a mage. As a *tool*." Old outrage rose to the surface. "And even then, someone with the most mundane of magics must enter an indenture to earn their freedom." That was a farce. How many mages attained that goal? So few it was laughable. "But mages with powerful magic, or *interesting* magic . . ." The outlaw paused, casting a glance at Blaise, who fit both of those categories as surely as Jack had. "Those poor sods have a tattoo applied with special ink to bind them to a handler. *That's* the geasa."

Blaise blinked, his mouth forming a small *o*. "I see." He fiddled with the reins. "What's your magic, if you don't mind my asking, since you're so chatty?"

"Not my magic anymore," Jack reminded him, the bitterness of his words a sharp slap in the face. "Ritualist. Effigest, to be exact."

Blaise blinked at him. "Huh?"

Of course, the kid didn't know what that meant. Jack snorted. Time to use his favorite explanation that caught people off guard. "I make dolls."

"Um, what?" Blaise looked at him like he was unhinged. Maybe he was. Jack wasn't sure. For all he knew, he was unconscious in the dirt somewhere and this was a fever dream.

"Effigests specialize in making figures to represent someone—we call them poppets or effigies. I could make one out of whatever I had on hand —dry grass, fruit, clay, almost anything. They're more potent if I had a personal item from whoever I intended to cast on, but I could still be successful without." That was more than the angry Jack in the corner of his mind wanted to tell Blaise, but he reasoned this was all information the Breaker would need to tell Emmaline if he died. It was important.

"What kind of spells?" Blaise asked.

"Whatever I intended. I was strongest with spells meant to help someone. I could heal people. Give them more strength or endurance. But I could hurt people with it, too. That was the real power they wanted from me." Jack gritted his teeth, his face stony as he remembered the first time he had used his magic to take a life. "I could make people sick or wounded. Even die."

Blaise stared at him nervously.

"Once they found out I was an Effigest, they assigned me to a mentor —this crazy old one-eyed woman named Nora. She was creepy and strange, would talk to her poppets. But she was smart and knew what she was about, so I learned from her because I didn't have any other choice. Nora taught me how to make poppets and effigies, and it was the craziest thing—but I found out I loved to make them." Jack saw an image of Nora hunched over his younger self, guiding him as he pieced together a poppet from a corn husk and rags.

"When I finished learning with her for the day, I took scraps to my room so I could make more. But I wasn't just making poppets for practice. I was making dolls, and I gave them to all the new children that came into the Cit. Most of them were younger than me. Scared. So I breathed magical words of peace and hope into dolls I gave to those kids." Jack closed his eyes, shutting out the image of himself handing out the dolls.

"Awful nice of you," Blaise hazarded.

"In the Cit, they don't train up their theurgists to be *nice*," Jack growled. "They took every doll they could find from those kids. Tore them to shreds before their eyes to make them cry."

Blaise sucked in a breath. "That's cruel."

Jack allowed himself a satisfied smile. "I found out later they did it for good reason. My magic *worked* on those kids. And they didn't like that. Not one bit." He stared through the twin arcs of Zepheus's ears.

"What happened?"

Jack glanced overhead at a circle of carrion birds. *I'm not dead yet, boys.* "What you'd expect. They beat me for my insolence after Nora found me making more tiny dolls to give away. Then they threw me in a cell with salt-iron shackles for a week." His stomach wrenched at the ghost-memory of the metal blistering his skin as it sapped his magic. "They made the message crystal clear: we tell you when you get to use your magic."

Blaise shook his head. "You couldn't fight back?"

Fight back? The Breaker had no idea how laughable that concept was. "I was bound to my asshole handler Reynolds by the geasa at the time. Factor in the salt-iron shackles and it's impossible."

The Breaker made an uncomfortable sound of acknowledgement.

"After that, I was a model student." Jack listened to the comforting rhythm of hooves for a moment. "Once a theurgist has gone through their training at the Cit, we're sent out to work on behalf of the Confederation. They paired me and my handler with another kid about my age, but he was from a rich family. His name was Lamar Gaitwood."

Blaise's eyes widened, but he said nothing.

"Lamar had a complex about being a mage—his family followed Garus's teachings, so that put a bee in his bonnet. He became something of a fanatic, thinking if he used his magic for the glory of the Salt-Iron Confederation, Garus might forgive his impurity. But even with that baggage, we were friends." Jack looked askance. The word *friends* seemed wrong in his mouth, but it had been accurate enough. "They assigned us to bring in mavericks. Especially those who were dangerous. The dissidents. Sometimes we were assigned the occasional assassination to help with politics. An illness here, a death there." He waved his good hand, nonchalant. "I hate politicians."

The Breaker's face paled.

"I was good at it," Jack's voice was soft as he recalled the memory. The thrill of bringing down another outlaw or maverick. The heady rush of taking a life—the knowledge he had that power over someone. "Lamar and I made a devastating team. We kept at it, but all that time, I didn't realize that because of my earlier rebellion, the Salties had collected a surety for my good behavior: my mother."

Blaise watched him, eyes full of concern.

"One day, we received the orders to kill a child. She was the daughter of a family causing trouble for the Luminary, and they wanted the parents to fall back into line."

"You didn't." Blaise's tone was sick.

Jack thought back to that day, shaking his head. "I didn't. But I wasn't the one who suffered for my refusal. Lamar was furious and reported how I had botched the mission. It was then my handler showed me they had my mother." Jack trembled with momentary rage. "Reynolds made me watch as they scourged her for my misdeeds." He would never forget the flesh stripped from her back, blood oozing to puddle on the stone floor.

"Jack..." Blaise's eyes grew wide, horrified.

"They proved their point. Again. I behaved and did their bidding." Jack bowed his head. "Then, one day, they sent us on the trail of a female maverick. She was causing the Salties grief in Umber, speaking out against the Salt-Iron Confederation. She was wily and had avoided everyone sent on her trail." A smile ghosted his lips. "I knew she wouldn't be so lucky with us." He had been wrong. He was so glad he had been wrong.

"Lamar found the inn she was staying in and pilfered a mug she had drunk from. I had a little poppet ready and activated it by touching it to the rim where her lips had made contact."

Blaise muttered something that sounded suspiciously like, "Your magic is so much creepier than mine." Jack let it be since it was true.

"That night, we broke into the room she was staying in." He made a long, low whistle. "She was fast. And powerful. And ready for us. She burned Lamar's casting arm before he could trap her. Her entire body was aflame, a walking bonfire. I tried to bind her with my poppet, but her fire was a shield my magic couldn't pierce. I could have shot her, but . . ." Jack grinned. She had been glorious, even more so than when he'd caught sight of her earlier in the evening, giving a rousing speech against the oppressive abuse of mages. "I couldn't. I saw her, and I saw freedom." *And love. And hope.*

Blaise looked confused. "So you let her go?"

Jack canted his head, which was a bad idea because that made him dizzy. "No. She set my poppet on fire, which pissed me off. Lamar and I had backup, and the soldiers came up to see what the ruckus was. She burned those men to a crisp, but didn't harm a hair on my head. Kittie was a sight to behold in her fury. She was absolutely the most dangerous and awful thing I ever laid eyes on."

"And you had a crush on her?" Blaise guessed.

Yes. Stupid, young Jack had a crush on her. "There's something alluring about seeing a woman destroy your oppressors. Kittie saw me gaping at her, and I still don't know why she didn't kill me where I stood. Instead, she asked if I wanted to be free." Jack took a ragged breath. "I told her I did, and with a snap of her fingers she reduced Reynolds to a flaming husk. Killing my handler shattered the geasa, and for the first time in my adult life I was free."

Blaise ran his fingers through his hair. "And now I no longer wonder why the Salt-Iron Confederation hates you so much."

Jack nodded. "And that's how I met my wife." He grinned at the Breaker's surprised expression.

CHAPTER TWENTY

Born of Despair

Blaise

Blaise had a tough time reconciling Jack as the marrying type. He would never tell Jack, but he assumed Emmaline was the product of an indiscretion, and he somehow ended up saddled with the results. The mental image of Jack giving his icy heart to anyone was at odds with Blaise's perception of the man.

Blaise hid those thoughts. Jack's eyes glazed while he spoke, and Blaise wasn't optimistic about what that meant for them. He wasn't sure how long Faedra's Embrace would last. As long as Jack kept talking, the outlaw seemed determined to plow onward.

As much as he hated to do it, he needed to keep Jack speaking. "Didn't realize you had a wife."

For a heartbeat, an angry Wildfire Jack glared at him through fierce eyes. "I did. I hope I still do." Then the faraway look returned. "We had a good thing, Kittie and me. She was the fire of my heart. We did what stupid, young people do. We ran off and got married, and then hid because she was a known outlaw and I was . . . well, I was not only an outlaw but a traitor. Eventually, we had Emmaline."

Jack stared off at the horizon, shaking his head. "Around the time Em turned three, I regretted that the Salties still had my mother. I hated myself for it. Kittie saw it was eating me up from the inside, so we made a plan. It was a good plan, one I assumed would work.

"Kittie stayed behind with Emmaline. We had moved to Petria to be closer to Phinora. I got to Izhadell, and I used my poppets to evade the Trackers and hunters who might be on to me. It was looking good. Until I discovered that—that my mother was dead." He stroked Zepheus's mane, his voice catching.

"I'm sorry," Blaise murmured. He mused about his own mother. What would happen to her?

Jack waved his good hand, then grabbed the saddle horn when he nearly toppled over. "What's done is done. I was furious, but all I could do was go home. But when I got back to the little cabin we were renting . . ." His lower lip quivered.

The outlaw's shoulders convulsed. Blaise studied him, sobering as he realized that Jack was crying.

<He's never allowed himself to release his feelings over this before.> Zepheus's voice was solemn.

Jack's chin dipped against his chest. "I found Emmaline hiding under the bed, blankets and things pushed around her to keep her hidden. Kittie was . . . she was gone, the grass outside scorched. She . . . she hadn't left without a fight. Em was so little, and she said her mother told her to play hide and seek and to be quiet as a mouse. I don't know how long my child hid until I arrived." A tear rolled down Jack's cheek, splattering against the saddle.

A lump formed in Blaise's throat, uncertain what to say. What could he say to something like that? There were no words to serve as a balm. Jack wasn't looking for a balm, anyway. Jack wanted him to understand his past so that he could present it to Emmaline if necessary.

"I took Em, and we fled to Asylum. I had to get somewhere safe. Somewhere the Salties couldn't go easily. We came across Zeph, and we found our way to Itude. I won't give you the long story about taking over the town and my times working the roads as an outlaw. We cleaned Itude up. But I still wanted Kittie back. I had already failed my mother. I couldn't fail my wife." The glaze cleared from his eyes, replaced with determination.

Blaise nodded. He understood that.

"I had saved—I found Clover by that time, so I knew Emmaline would be safe with her. Zeph and I went to Petria to take up Kittie's trail. I thought my experience working with Lamar and my time as an outlaw made me so slick and crafty. But with that came a self-assurance that I should have checked at the border. I was high and mighty. Because I had the best intentions and my magic, I would save the day."

Blaise glanced away. "Did you find her?"

"I was certain I had her trail. Maybe I did, I'll never know. But Lamar found me first."

Zepheus gave a mournful nicker, glancing back at his rider. Not for the first time, Blaise wished he didn't have to hear this. He didn't like tragedies.

"Zeph got away by some minor miracle. But he couldn't help, not without risking himself. Lamar was furious at my betrayal. I thought I would talk him down. But then they strapped me down with the salt-iron ropes and poured a potion down my throat that stole my magic." Jack's left shoulder slumped.

"I won't soon forget that potion. It felt like every vein in my body was on fire. I thought it might kill me." He looked away. "For a short time, I wished it had. I lost my magic and any hope of finding my wife. But . . . *Emmaline*. Lamar planned to take me back to Izhadell for trial and execution. I refused to allow that. I needed to get back to my daughter."

<And that was the moment Wildfire Jack was born from despair,> Zepheus told Blaise privately.

"To this day, I'm not even sure how I escaped. I saw an opening, and I fought without magic. Wrestled a gun from a soldier, and Zepheus was close enough to come to my aid."

Blaise considered escaping from Lamar with life and limb a win. He thought about what Jack had said, and about their original reason for going to Desina. "Were you hoping your wife would be one of the mages we were looking for?"

Jack bowed his head, the tears glinting in his eyes all the answer Blaise needed. Instead, Jack asked, "Do you know why I hated you?"

Blaise blinked, surprised. That had been the last thing he expected to hear from Jack. "No."

"I can't protect against your magic. Once upon a time, I could have. The only way I can stop you now is with a well-placed bullet." Jack wasn't looking in his direction, so missed Blaise's wince. "And that scares the shit out of me. Your magic is dangerous. I thought you would tear my town apart." The outlaw opened his mouth to say more, but instead, let out a low groan. He sank forward, his good arm wrapped around Zepheus's neck as the only means to keep him from falling.

Faedra's Embrace had worn off.

"WHAT THE BLAZES HAPPENED IN DESINA?" KUR AGUR SNARLED, EYES aglow.

Blaise scrubbed at his face, fatigue dogging him all the way down to his bones. He didn't want to be here, sitting in the Ringleaders' HQ. He wanted a soothing soak in the bathhouse, a meal, and then the gentle oblivion of sleep for a few days.

That wasn't in the cards.

Not long after Jack had collapsed atop Zepheus, a sentry pegasus spied them and flew down to investigate. It was Alekon, Vixen's mount, and he sped back to town for help. Blaise assumed help would come in the form of more pegasi. Never had he imagined the fearsome sight of Clover charging toward them, her long legs covering more ground than Blaise thought possible, horned head stretched out before her. She said nothing when she slid to a dust-scattering halt; she only shook her head and snorted in distress. Clover reached up and gently pulled Jack down from Zepheus's back, cradling the unconscious outlaw against her like he was nothing more than a sleeping child exhausted from a day of play. Jack had looked fragile and vulnerable in Clover's arms, and that bothered Blaise a lot.

The Knossan sprinted back to town, taking the long trail up the east side. Blaise and the pegasi kept pace with her on the ground. Once they reached Itude, Clover high-tailed it to Nadine's clinic. The pegasi took Blaise to Headquarters at some unbidden command.

Now Kur Agur, Vixen Valerie, and Raven Dawson were asking too many questions, and Blaise was tired of it.

He told them everything, though they kept stopping him and back-tracking, asking for clarification. He tripped over his own words, his head muddled from lack of sleep, lack of food, and stress. At one point, Blaise dozed off in front of them. A threatening growl from Kur woke him.

The only thing Blaise left out from his repeated recitations was Jack's long discourse with him. His brain felt like mush, but he had enough self-preservation to remember that Jack had said it was a story for Emmaline's ears. Jack had a secret to keep, and Blaise didn't want to be the one to spill it.

A knock at the door interrupted the questioning. Raven pulled it open, and Hannah poked her head in. "Hey, y'all. Sorry to interrupt, but Nadine needs to see Blaise to ask some stuff about Jack."

Blaise sighed. Not again. He wasn't ever going to get to sleep.

The three remaining Ringleaders traded looks. "Go." Raven clenched his jaw.

Blaise followed Hannah out. She kept her head bowed and stayed quiet, which was unusual for her. Her behavior set Blaise's nerves on edge. "Hannah, is Jack . . . ? Did he . . . ?" He couldn't bring himself to finish the question.

She glanced at him. "Oh. No, I don't think so. But Nadine's got her tail in a knot, and she has Reuben helping, so things aren't good."

Poor Reuben. But at least Jack was alive. For now, anyway.

He followed Hannah into the white clapboard clinic. She didn't bother to knock, just pushed open the door with purpose. Nadine leaned over a prone form covered in a white sheet, her eyes flicking to the door the only sign of acknowledgment. Reuben stood beside her, squeamish and miserable.

Hannah clapped Blaise on the shoulder and turned to leave. He stayed near the door, shifting his weight from foot to foot.

"I think I know his injuries, but you were there. How did you treat him?" Nadine's voice was crisp, matter-of-fact.

"He was wounded before I got to him. Zepheus told me they shot him, so that's what I treated," Blaise said. "If he has other injuries, I don't know."

"How long ago did it happen?"

Blaise sighed. A dull throb pounded at the base of his skull. He was bleary-eyed, and barely had any concept of what time it was. Reuben pulled out his pocket watch and showed him. *Right. I should have checked my watch.* "It's been at least twenty-four hours. Maybe a little more?" Time was a confusing concept. Everything was a blur.

Nadine released a hissing breath. "Too long, too long. How did you treat him?"

Blaise told her about the first aid kit and Zepheus's instructions (so he wouldn't take all the blame if he had done something wrong). He had done his best in a terrible situation. Nadine didn't criticize, just nodded as she listened. When he mentioned Faedra's Embrace, her eyes narrowed. "That wasn't a good idea."

You have no appreciation for how terrible an idea it was. "I didn't know what choice I had. He was in so much pain I don't think he would have stayed upright in the saddle as long as he did without it."

Nadine pursed her lips, unhappy but not arguing. "The problem with that potion is idiots never realize how hurt they are, and then they do stupid things like riding a pegasus for the better part of a day." She held out her hand, and Reuben gave her a wad of gauze.

"I'm aware." Blaise's voice was tight. "My mother's an alchemist."

She gave him an assessing look. "Well, you got Jack home alive, which is impressive."

"Is he . . . will he live?"

Nadine busied herself with a set of steel instruments arrayed on a silver tray. "He's closer to needing a Necromancer than a Healer. I'll do all I can. The one good thing that damned potion did is convince his body to not start shutting organs down." She was thoughtful as she spoke. "Actually, that may have saved his life."

Blaise released a pent-up breath he hadn't realized he was holding.

The Healer looked up at him for a moment, then stepped away from Jack. Nadine lifted a hand more quickly than Blaise's tired mind could process, brushing her palm against his forehead.

"Blazes, boy. How are you still standing? Go eat something and rest. Healer's orders." Nadine strode back over to Jack, all business. "I need to cajole Jack's brain to keep everything working and convince the gangrene to stay clear. It's going to be a long day."

Blaise nodded, stumbling out the door. Jack was someone else's concern now, and that was good. His eyelids felt like they were being pulled down by weights. He wasn't sure that eating first was a good idea. He would likely fall asleep and choke on his food.

Mindy and Celeste saw him stagger by the Jitterbug. Celeste slipped out, grabbed his arm, and steered him inside. Blaise didn't have the will to protest.

"You look like you were ridden hard and put up wet," Mindy pointed out, bringing a bowl of soup and setting it in front of him. "Eat."

Blaise blinked at the soup. The aroma of salt and chicken broth tickled his nostrils, and his salivary glands awoke. He tried to pick up the spoon, but the utensil was clumsy and foreign in his grip, so he sipped from the bowl. Despite his best efforts, soup dripped onto his shirt.

"You okay, Blaise?" Mindy asked, her voice sounding distant even though she stood at the other end of the table.

"Ugh." Blaise put the bowl down after draining its contents. He was wearing less of it than he first thought, so that was a victory. "I don't think I'm any version of okay right now."

The two women wore concerned looks, but they didn't press him for details, which he appreciated. He offered to pay, but Celeste waved him off and watched him totter out the door and head to the bakery.

Blaise hadn't expected to find Emmaline there. If he had a firmer grasp on time, he would have realized that it made sense that she would be there, cleaning up on her own since Reuben had been summoned away. She stood in the kitchen sweeping, tears streaming down her face as Blaise walked in.

"What happened?" Emmaline asked when she saw him. She clutched the little doll between one hand and the broom handle.

Blaise opened his mouth to speak, but his brain declared itself done with his antics of pretending to be awake. The familiar sights and smells of the bakery wrapped around his exhausted body like a blanket, and the next thing he knew he slumped to the floor and descended into blissful darkness.

CHAPTER TWENTY-ONE

The Apple Doesn't Fall Far from The Tree

Blaise

The floor of the bakery wasn't a contender in Blaise's mind for top places to fall asleep, but when he awoke later, he noted that his body didn't care. Someone had gone upstairs and brought down his pillow and blanket. At least his head wasn't flat against the floor.

Emmaline sat across from him, arms hugging her knees. Blaise groaned as he sat up. Hardwood floors weren't comfortable mattresses. "How long have I been out?"

She shrugged, eyes red from crying. "I'm not sure. More than a day." It was dark outside, the kitchen lit by a single mage-light.

Blaise scrubbed at his face with one hand. He wasn't sure that he felt much better after sleeping. "How's your father?"

Emmaline kept her head bowed, studying her nails. "Bad. Real bad."

Blaise shut his eyes. "I'm sorry." He hoped she didn't blame him. Would she understand he had done what he could, or would she hate him for what he represented?

"What happened?" Her voice trembled with fear. Confusion. Worry.

He told her what he knew. How Jack had made him stay behind as he scouted ahead. How it must have been a trap—and that same trap had sprung on Blaise when he had gone to see what was taking so long. Her lips pressed together in a thin line when he recounted how Gaitwood threatened her father's life. He hated to tell her those things, but sugar-coating it wouldn't help matters. She deserved the truth.

When he finished, tears streaked her cheeks. Blaise wished he could help her, but he was at a loss. Then she surprised him by surging toward him, almost knocking him over as she tangled him in a hug, burying her head against his shoulder.

"Thank you for bringing him back to me," Emmaline whispered into his shirt. Belatedly, he realized Jack's blood stained it.

"You're welcome." He patted her back, awkward and tense from her sudden closeness.

She pulled away from him after a moment, rubbing at her eyes. "Sorry. It's just . . ." Emmaline chewed her bottom lip, as if debating if she wanted to continue. "I was afraid if he went alone, he wouldn't make it back."

Blaise tilted his head. Had she learned her father's secret? Jack said that no one else in Itude knew. "What makes you say that?"

Emmaline glanced away, embarrassed. "I just . . . nothing." She twisted a lock of hair around one finger. "Can I ask you something on a completely different topic?"

Blaise raised his eyebrows. "Sure."

"When did you come into your magic?" She sat back, watching him.

Completely different topic? Hardly. This was a conversation she should be having with her father, or anyone other than him. But perhaps she was comfortable talking to him after all the time they had spent together in the bakery.

He respected that. Even if it meant delaying a soak in the tub that would ease his strained muscles.

"Well." He paused, stomach rumbling a reminder to eat. Blaise got up and sought the previous day's leftover cookies. "My magic is weird, so it's hard to say. I think I came into it early, but how much of it was just a kid being a kid and my magic doing its thing is anyone's guess. Definitely before I was ten." He found the coveted cookies and pulled the tin open, grabbing two. Chocolate chip, exactly what he needed. He held one between his lips for safe keeping and offered her one from the open container.

Emmaline plucked a cookie out. "Oh." She placed a mountain of weight on the single word.

Blaise savored the sweet rush of chocolate over his tongue. Tempting as it was to eat the whole tin, he needed to get proper food into his stomach before long. "Any particular reason you're asking?"

Emmaline nibbled at her cookie, then pulled something small out of her pocket. She opened her fist and showed him the tiny doll. "This is why."

After his hours with Jack, Blaise had a better understanding of the doll's importance. He scratched his chin, considering. What a very Jack-like thing to do—create a poppet and give it to his daughter.

"It's . . . special. And I . . ." She shook her head, cheeks blushing with a mix of frustration and embarrassment. "You're going to think this is ridiculous."

Blaise shrugged. "I break things by touching them. Try me."

Emmaline's voice was so soft it was almost difficult to hear. "I felt something when y'all were gone. From the doll."

"What was it like?" Blaise cocked his head, curious.

Tears welled in her eyes. She brushed them away with a fist. "It's hard to explain. I thought something was wrong with *me* at first. Then I realized the little doll was hurting. It hurt so bad, Blaise, and it scared me. I felt it—all of it. I kept it in my pocket, so I could take it out, and I kept whispering to it. That it would be okay. To . . . to . . ." She chewed on her bottom lip. "*Live.*"

The hairs on Blaise's arms prickled at the supplication, filled with the unmistakable whisper of magic. The scent of ozone after a thunderstorm filled the bakery.

Blaise thought back to the sight of Jack in Gaitwood's silver cage. He had looked bad—so bad that Blaise feared he was already dead, or close to it. But he hadn't died, even when they made their escape, and Jack had looked so much worse.

Had Emmaline somehow given him a touch of healing through the poppet? It sounded reminiscent of the magic Jack had described to him. There was no mistaking that Blaise had experienced the thrum of her magic just a moment ago.

"Sorry. It sounds ridiculous," Emmaline whispered, shamefaced.

Blaise shook his head. "No, it doesn't sound ridiculous at all. Do you . . . know anything about your father's magic?"

Emmaline hunched her shoulders. "I know some of it. But he doesn't talk about it too much around me."

Discussion of magic would be a sore spot for Jack. Blaise winced. Emmaline needed to be informed. He hoped that Jack survived so *he* could be the one to tell her, not Blaise.

"I think you have your father's type of magic," Blaise said after a moment. There was no other thing he *could* say. Emmaline needed to know she wasn't crazy. She had, in fact, saved her father's life. Blaise would not tell her that, though. He couldn't prove it; he just had a hunch.

She blinked at him, owlish. "I guess that makes sense." Emmaline cupped the poppet in her hands. "What if he doesn't make it?" She sounded like a scared, heartbroken child.

Blaise pointed to the doll. "If you keep on doing whatever you're doing, I think he stands a good chance."

The smile that turned the corners of her lips was all the reward Blaise needed. But an excellent second place prize would be a good meal in his belly—and a bath.

<hr>

Blaise closed the bakery for a few days, just so he had time to recover from the rigors of his misadventure with Jack. It galled him to do it, but Emmaline and Reuben were scarce, and he was so exhausted he couldn't tackle the task alone.

Blaise spent most of the first day sleeping. Nadine checked on him at midday, to "make sure you're still alive," as she put it. She told him his body was likely needing time to recover after the drain of the salt-iron and the quick, successive expenses of magic—not to mention the exhausting ride back to town.

On the fourth day, when he was up and shuffling about, Clover ambled up to the bakery. Blaise hadn't seen her since she had carried Jack back to Itude. She was calmer now—Jack was out of danger. The Knossan eyed the *Closed* sign on the door, knocking gently with one of her gnarled hands.

Blaise let her in and stepped back as she ducked through the doorway. "Howdy, Clover."

She glanced at the empty display case, then fixed her attention on Blaise. "I wanted to thank you for saving Jack."

He bowed his head in awkwardness. It seemed like something that should have been done, regardless. "It was the right thing to do."

She snorted. "The right thing is often the hardest thing. But I appreciate it." Clover tipped her horns to the side. "You should stop by and see him."

Blaise straightened up, setting a bag of flour on the counter and opening it. "He's awake?" The last report he had received, the outlaw had been unconscious still.

"Awake and in a foul mood," Clover confirmed.

"Does he have any other?" Blaise muttered.

The Knossan flicked an ear. She didn't dispute it. "He was asking for you."

Blaise sighed. Jack was probably mad as a wet hen about the secrets he had spilled. Blaise would have been happy to coexist in Itude without seeing the grumpy outlaw face to face again.

"*Today*," Clover clarified. By the tone she used, Blaise supposed she meant *now*.

Grimacing, he reluctantly closed up the sack of flour. "Guess I'll go pay him a visit."

"You do that," the Knossan agreed.

He put the flour back and followed Clover out. She trotted to the Broken Horn after instructing Blaise to head to Jack's house. Nadine had either released him from her clinic or gotten fed up with his presence there. Either was just as likely.

Emmaline met him at the door to the house, a wan smile on her lips. "Howdy, Blaise."

Blaise noticed her red-rimmed eyes, lower lip jutting out. "How's he doing?"

She shrugged. "Complaining and giving everyone who pokes their head into his room grief. The usual." Emmaline leaned closer to him, her voice softer as she added, "He's like to bite off the hand of anyone who gets too near his wound. It's been rough."

He could only imagine. "I'm sorry."

"Me, too." Emmaline rubbed at her cheek, her face pale. "He was asking after you when he woke up."

"Clover told me." Blaise rubbed his forehead. Emmaline moved aside and pivoted so he could follow her inside.

She led him to a door off the parlor where she paused before knocking. They heard a grunt, and she pushed the door open. "Daddy, Blaise is here."

Jack said nothing as they entered. The outlaw reclined on a bed, pillows placed under him to prop him up. A book with a tasseled bookmark rested on a bedside table. Funny, Blaise hadn't considered Jack the literary sort.

"Need anything?" Emmaline kept her voice neutral.

"Some privacy."

Emmaline's face crumpled, and Blaise understood what she meant about Jack's mood. He was as prickly as a spiny basilisk. Emmaline wiped a tear from her cheek and shut the door. Blaise sat down in the chair beside the bed, judging that Jack looked ill enough that if he took a swing, he would have time to get out of the way.

The room was sparsely furnished. A chest of drawers loomed in one corner and was the only other piece of furniture aside from the bed, bedside table, and chair. Atop the chest stood a doll as tall as his forearm was long, its pale porcelain finish marking it as more a work of art than a plaything. Fragile and beautiful. Dark brown hair framed the doll's face.

Jack stayed quiet, so Blaise pointed at the doll. "One of yours?"

The outlaw's gaze flitted from Blaise to the doll and back again. Was it a figment of Blaise's imagination, or did Jack's eyes soften? "Why'd you do it?"

Blaise frowned. Jack was incapable of holding a conversation like a normal person. "I don't know what you mean."

"You could have left me to Gaitwood. Not even the pegasi would have faulted you. I had one foot in the grave. But you didn't. You rescued me." Jack sounded baffled. "Why?"

Blaise wasn't sure why that was such a puzzling thing. "Because . . . " Why had he? Jack had been nothing but cruel to him. Blaise hated bullies, and *Jack* was a bully. But that didn't mean he deserved to die and leave Emmaline alone. "It was the kind thing to do."

Jack looked at him as if he had been expecting something more profound. "There are those who view kindness as a weakness."

He didn't say it, but Blaise supposed Jack might be counted in that number. "I prefer to consider it a strength."

The outlaw studied him for a moment, considering. He gestured to the porcelain doll, wincing as the movement bothered his injuries. "Kittie."

Blaise blinked, thrown off his train of thought again. "What?"

"You asked if it's one of mine. It is. That's Kittie."

"Oh," Blaise said, then gaped when his brain made the connection. "*Oh.* Your wife—wait, you remember us talking?" He swallowed and scooted his chair the tiniest bit away from the bed.

Jack's eyes crinkled with something like amusement. "I knew what I was saying, even if I was delirious and wouldn't shut my trap."

Blaise blanched. "I won't tell anyone what you told me."

"I know." Jack's voice was matter-of-fact.

"Wait. You do?"

"Yeah." Jack sighed. "I've treated you like a cow patty from the start, and I shouldn't have. You've been nothing but discreet about our first meeting, and I've held it against you."

"I'm really sorry I made your gun explode. I didn't . . ." Blaise felt his pulse race as he thought about it. "I didn't mean to."

The outlaw's gaze roved to the porcelain doll, his lips pressed together in a thin line. He still looked pale and drawn. "Can't say I'll ever forgive you for that. Kittie gave me that revolver." Blaise sank back into his chair, dropping his gaze. "But you proved me wrong. You got control over your magic. If you hadn't, there's no way we'd be alive to have this conversation now."

Blaise realized that, in his cantankerous way, Jack was praising him. It was an unfamiliar sensation to receive praise for his magic—especially from Jack. Maybe he was dreaming. That would make more sense.

"What I'm trying to say is you're welcome in Itude. You saved my life. Back when we were best of friends, I don't think *Lamar* would have saved me." Jack's eyebrows drew together, two angry slashes.

"Oh. Thanks." Blaise wasn't sure which was more awkward: being on Jack's good side, or being hated by him. A change of subject might help. He pointed to the porcelain doll again. "Is . . . is that how you know she's still alive?" He thought about how Emmaline had told him of her connection to the tiny doll that represented Jack.

Jack looked thoughtful. "Something like that. Before I . . ." His voice faltered, and he looked like he was about to shift into a foul mood again. He took a breath and started over. "Not anymore, for obvious reasons. But before that day, I used to cast on that doll all the time. Gave her strength. Perseverance. Love." His eyes softened. "And now it's all I have left of her."

Blaise rose, inspecting the doll. Jack pined for his wife. Blaise looked at the glossy hair—it looked so real. "Wait. Is that your wife's hair on this doll?"

For just a moment, a feral grin lit Jack's face. "I told you how my magic works. Gives me a better connection."

Blaise made a face. "That's creepy, Jack."

The outlaw snorted a laugh, then grunted in pain. Laughing was off the table, apparently. Blaise had to admit, it was nice to hear Jack laugh when he wasn't out of his mind on an alchemical potion.

"But that's how I knew I could always help her. Believe it or not, her magic was the stronger in our relationship."

Blaise massaged his cheek. "That's terrifying." He moved back to the chair and sat. "I understand why you would keep the creepy doll with you, though."

"It's not creepy; it's art. And a hobby," Jack grumbled.

Blaise chuckled, then had a sobering thought. "Have you talked much to Emmaline?"

Jack looked uncharacteristically guilty. "I just woke up a few hours ago, and everything hurts."

Blaise grunted. He suspected Jack had been short with her. Blaise didn't blame him—the outlaw had nearly died, so he was allowed some level of boorish behavior. But not to his daughter.

He took a chance and leaned closer to Jack so he could get his point across. "You need to talk to her. I think she's the reason you're alive today."

Jack's eyes widened as he took his meaning. "What did she tell you?"

Blaise shook his head. "That's a conversation for you to have with her."

The muscles in Jack's jaw clenched. "At least tell me this much: is she an Effigest?"

Blaise glanced at the porcelain doll again, then back at Jack. "She doesn't play with fire, I'll tell you that much."

CHAPTER TWENTY-TWO

The Talk

Jack

Jack wasn't a stranger to being shot. That was a fact of life as an outlaw. He had been grazed several times, shot in the arm twice, and the leg once. Those had been inconveniences more than anything. He sought out Nadine or another similarly gifted Healer not long after suffering the injuries. He hadn't been so fortunate this time.

Nadine had done her best. She had focused on keeping his organs from giving up the ghost, and he was appreciative. She had to keep some magic in reserve for others, so couldn't completely heal him. Nadine told him the rest of his recovery would be up to him. He understood, but that didn't mean he liked it.

She estimated it would take him at least two months to recover, which he grumbled about until she pointed out that without her healing, it would take a year or more. He had been at death's door, and Nadine said more than once she didn't know how he hadn't crossed over the threshold. Jack knew but didn't tell her.

Nadine instructed him to keep to light duties. No Salt-Iron merchant heists. No intelligence gathering. No leaving town at all, for that matter. That rankled him.

Jack defied Nadine in one area. He was furious about the misleading intelligence from Hank Walker, and he made an excuse to go to the post office. The postmaster was there, and he visibly quailed when Jack strode in. Walker was lucky he wasn't up to his usual hijinks. Jack wanted to throw him up against the wall and demand answers. He settled for glowering.

Walker swore he had known nothing about the ambush. He was aware the soldiers were around, but not that they were so close. He claimed they'd fed him deceptive information. Jack couldn't prove otherwise, so he let it go. That didn't mean he trusted Walker anymore.

Nadine caught wind of his transgression and gave him a piece of her mind. After that, she had him under house arrest until she gave her leave.

Blaise reopened the bakery, and Emmaline went to help him every morning. Jack still hadn't talked to her about her magic. He wasn't sure how.

Jack was a damn good outlaw. But he considered himself a piss-poor father.

Faedra knows I bungled the birds and the bees talk with her, Jack thought wryly. That had been a disaster.

He decided to talk to her about it today. He had put it off for too long. It was unusual for him to procrastinate. Jack generally preferred to take the bull by the horns. But magic was a sore spot.

The door reverberated with a booming knock. Jack frowned and rose to answer. It was about time for Emmaline to get home, but she wouldn't knock.

He discovered Clover at the door, shifting from hoof to hoof. "Clover? You all right?"

She glanced over her shoulder, her hide twitching as if irritated by an invisible fly. "May I come in?"

Jack nodded. "'Course. You're always welcome here. You know that." He shuffled aside and allowed her to duck inside. She carefully lowered her bulk onto a sturdy chaise Jack had purchased years ago. "What's worrying you?" It took something considerable to worry a Knossan like Clover.

"An outrider came to notify the town that someone with ties to the Salt-Iron Confederation is coming to Itude."

That surprised Jack on several fronts. First, he wouldn't have expected any of the Salties to give the courtesy of advance notice—not to a town full of outlaws. Second, it was akin to asking permission. The outrider could be told *no* and sent on his way. The Salt-Iron Confederation wasn't known for asking permission; they trampled and took what they wanted. Many of their entitled merchants displayed the same behavior. Was it a trap of some sort?

"Who?" Jack asked after he'd considered those angles. He had been out of Confederation lands for many years, but thanks to his network of spies, he was aware of more than the average outlaw.

"An entrepreneur from Ganland. Jefferson Cole."

Ganland. Now Jack understood why Clover was nervous. She had a grim history with the Gannish. Jack had stolen her away from one of the Gannish elite who thought it was cute to collect children of varying races.

There was something about the name that tickled the far recesses of Jack's brain. He would need to go through his sheet of references later to see if it was listed there. "Did the Ringleaders meet to discuss it yet?"

"That is why I came. Raven sent the outrider to cool his heels in the Broken Horn. Hannah and Abe are there, monitoring things, so I could come tell you. The Ringleaders are meeting without you."

Of course they were. *Get shot, and everybody acts like you're made of glass.* Jack eased out of his seat. "I'll just make my way to HQ and invite myself in."

Clover swished her tail, distressed. "Will they be upset I told you? I know Nadine doesn't want you too active."

Jack shook his head. Clover had serious abandonment issues. She didn't show it often, but she was afraid they might cast her from Itude for what she was. The Knossans hadn't allowed her back on their lands, calling her *domesticated.* "Don't you worry your horns about it. They'll be too irate at me showing my mug there to worry about who told me."

That mollified her. Her furry shoulders relaxed. "Be gentle to your body, Jack. You're still healing."

Oh, he was well aware. In fact, as he picked up his hat and put it on, a rush of pain served as a fresh reminder. Jack made a good show of hiding it from Clover, but Knossans had a sharp eye for body language. He couldn't fool her.

"I'll do my best," Jack allowed. She would have to be content with that.

Zepheus waited for him as he made his way out the door. The palomino tossed his head, giving him an innocent look.

<What? I know you too well, Jack.>

"I'm going to have to work on being less predictable," Jack groused.

<I just know what gets you all in a dander.>

"That's unfair. That's most things."

Zepheus snorted, amused. He knelt down, and Jack clambered onto his back. He hissed when his shoulder complained at the movement.

Nadine was going to be mad as a hornet if she saw him riding. It was not on her list of *light* activities.

Clover watched him with concern until he straightened and waved her off. She nodded to him, brass nose ring flipping with the movement, then trotted back to the saloon. Zepheus turned toward town, shifting to a floating, smooth pace that didn't jar Jack in the slightest.

The savvy stallion stopped before they reached HQ to allow Jack a chance to dismount out of sight of any wag-tongues. Two townsfolk saw him, but he pinned them with one of his trademark glowers until they stopped gawking and hurried on their way.

Jack patted Zepheus's neck, then slowly walked up the steps to Headquarters. He shoved open the door, a spirited discussion resonating from the meeting room.

"Got started without me, I see."

The other four Ringleaders turned in surprise. Nadine's face colored scarlet with fury and she looked like she was ready to get up and throw him all the way back to his bed. Vixen, bless her, laid a hand on Nadine's arm and murmured something Jack couldn't hear. That didn't stop Nadine from glaring at him like she was ready to kill him if his wound didn't get him first. Jack was pretty sure he heard her mutter, "Pure cussedness."

"We assumed you were still recovering," Raven said, his voice bland, then gestured to Jack's customary chair.

"That's where he's supposed to be," Nadine grumbled.

"But you're welcome to join us since you're here," Vixen added brightly. Kur shrugged, not caring either way.

Jack gingerly sat in his seat. "I heard there's a matter for discussion." He made it a point to ignore Nadine's intense stare. Yeah, he was going to get an earful from her later.

Raven nodded, pushing an envelope across the table to him. "Yes. Information that has us regretting you're out of commission or we'd likely have known about this in advance."

Jack picked up the envelope and drew out a letter written on expensive paper, judging by the thickness and woven finish. The author used precise, ornate writing, with no misspelled words or strange punctuation. Someone educated had written this.

He scanned the words on the page. Jefferson Cole, Gannish businessman extraordinaire, humbly asked to stay in Itude for a period of up to a month, to observe the area and seek investment opportunities. Jack scowled. A month was a long time.

"No." Jack folded the letter and nested it in the envelope. He slid it across the table to Raven. "That's my vote. No damned Salties in my town."

"Are you sure?" Vixen asked. "We were thinking I might get some information from this Mr. Cole or his men."

That hadn't occurred to Jack. He was off his game—that should have been one of his thoughts, too. But that didn't mean it was a good idea or one that he even liked. "I stand by my vote. No Salties."

"I am with Jack on this. No." Kur Agur hunched in his chair, hackles raised. He was looking bitey, which was never a good sign.

Raven tapped the letter with his index finger, thoughtful. "I understand your reasoning. It's not a comfortable thing. But it would be good to learn more. We've been cut off. And I would rather us be asked for hospitality like reasonable people than have them march on us."

"We're not *reasonable people*, according to the Confederation. We're outlaws." Jack thought that shouldn't be something he needed to remind them of. Yet here he was, doing it.

"You've also brought us enough intelligence to know not everyone in the Salt-Iron Confederation sees eye to eye, Jack," Nadine pointed out.

And damn, she was right. To an extent. The nations of the Salt-Iron Confederation bickered among themselves like jealous siblings. Phinora, the eldest and grandest, thought she was better than the rest. The others sniped at her however they could. Ganland was one of the more recent additions—though not as recent as Desina—and many of the people there felt differently about magic than those in Phinora. They were much more sympathetic to it, and open to mages using their abilities to better the world (and make a profit) in new and creative ways.

Jack grunted. Damn Nadine and her logic.

"I think it's worth the risk." Uncertainty lit Raven's eyes as he spoke, though. That was good—it was healthy to be cautious around the Salt-Iron Confederation. "We'll outnumber and outgun them, at least for now. And who knows? This could give us a measure of safety if this Mr. Cole wants to do business with us."

Jack snorted. "Look at us, gettin' into bed with the Salties. Deplorable. You lay down with dogs, and you get fleas." Kur twitched an ear and snarled at him. Jack raised his hands in supplication.

Raven ignored him. "I believe the vote is three to two in favor of allowing Mr. Cole one month in our town."

Kur growled softly. *Yeah, I know what you mean,* Jack thought.

"Y'all have some faith in me." Vixen's gaze swung from Jack to Kur. "I'll have it all under control, just you wait and see."

Jack nodded stiffly. Not that he didn't believe in Vixen and her potent form of magic. He was just violently opposed to a Saltie setting foot in Itude. It was *wrong*.

But he had opposed Blaise's presence in Itude, and that had turned out differently than he had expected. Maybe he would be wrong about this, too. For the sake of his town, he hoped so.

The meeting adjourned, and Jack escaped while Vixen caught Nadine and spoke with her about something. The flame-haired outlaw gave him a sly wink. He owed her.

Jack sighed. He would thank Vixen for sparing him Nadine's wrath later. He had to focus on getting home and having The Talk with Emmaline.

Nadine's wrath was almost preferable.

"Daddy? Where were you?"

Emmaline pushed her schoolwork aside when Jack walked in. He did his best to hide his discomfort. The walk back had winded him, and his shoulder burned. Damned inconvenient, this business of being an invalid.

"Ringleader business." Jack hooked his foot around the leg of a chair to pull it out and sat down. He glanced at the discarded homework. Arithmetic, something she had a good head for. Jack knew his numbers and how to figure, but he felt about math the way he felt about politicians: something overall useless to him, but must be tolerated.

Emmaline raised her brows, disapproving. She had been around when Nadine gave her orders.

He didn't want to hear her sniping, and he didn't want to think about the impending arrival of a blasted Salt-Iron Confederation businessman. So he did the only other thing he could. He charged headlong.

"Blaise said I should talk to you. About magic." It was strange to say the Breaker's name. He couldn't remember if he'd said it aloud before. It made him sound more familiar, like a friend. Jack wasn't sure what he thought about that, even if the kid had saved his life.

Emmaline set her pencil down, wary. "He did?"

Jack nodded. "You . . . ah . . . do you have the poppet I gave you years ago?" It was a stupid question. A stalling question.

She plucked the doll out of her pocket, dropping it on the table. Emmaline looked from him to the tiny figure, hesitant.

"Em, what do you know about my magic?"

"You use poppets like this one. They represent people, and you have a better connection if we attach something personal to the doll."

She had paid attention and gleaned bits and pieces from him. Jack made a note to be careful around her, for she had somehow connected things he was certain he'd kept hidden. He had made it a point to not talk about his magic in front of her. Mostly because it stung to talk about something he no longer possessed. Same reason he hadn't spoken about Kittie much in front of her.

Kittie. She would have been better at this talk. Gods, how unfair that she was the one who had been taken. "Good, good." Jack leaned forward, picking up the poppet. He had primed this one by tucking a few strands of his hair beneath the doll's makeshift rag clothing. It didn't take magic to prepare a poppet, but it was required to do just about anything beyond that. He used his index finger to wiggle the doll's shirt down enough to expose the hairs. "Did you know this represents me?"

Emmaline swallowed, studying her hands before giving a tentative nod. "When you gave it to me when I was small, I pretended like it was. And then the last couple of years, whenever you left town, I kept it with me." The corners of her mouth twitched.

Jack sighed inwardly. He was a poor excuse for a father. He should have been paying more attention to see if she was coming into magic. Once upon a time, he prayed she might be normal. If she were normal, then one day she might be spared the outlaw life, the constant danger of capture. He had worked to prepare her to protect herself every other way but magically, and that was an oversight brought about by his own hubris. It was time to correct that.

"You're probably an Effigest like me." Jack's voice was soft. "I think . . ."

"Blaise said I'm the one who kept you alive."

He met her eyes and nodded. "He told me something similar. Can you tell me about it?"

Emmaline picked up the poppet and cupped it in her hands. "I kept it with me when you were gone. I thought I was going crazy, but I could feel the poppet hurting. It was so bad."

Pain haunted her voice, and Jack's heart ached. She had a deep connection to that doll, forged by years of carrying it with her. Poppets were difficult, but not impossible, to use if the target had no connection to them. That was a lesson for later.

"What did you do?"

"I was so scared. It felt like . . . it was like having you in the room with me. You were hurt, and what could I do? I whispered to it and cradled it and just . . ." Tears rolled down her cheek, and she scrubbed them away with one hand. "I didn't want you to leave me all alone. I wanted you to live. To come back to me and be healthy."

She was still holding the poppet. Warmth blossomed in Jack's shoulder, like skin bared to the sun. The pressure of magic built in the room like a summer thunderstorm. It was subtle; a normal person would have written both off as nothing to be concerned about. But Jack noticed. Emmaline had magic, was actively using it, and wasn't aware of it. The outlaw's jaw clenched in chagrin as he thought back to Blaise's uncontrolled magic. *I'm a damn hypocrite.*

He placed his hand over hers, the movement enough to distract her. The magic released, the pressure whooshing away. "You definitely have my magic. And you kept me alive." Jack rubbed the back of his head, trying to figure out where to go from here.

Emmaline pulled her hand from beneath his and released the poppet. "Will you teach me?"

What else could he say? He had taught her how to shoot a gun and survive the rugged life outside the Salt-Iron Confederation. There was no way he would deny her this. "It won't be easy, but I will."

Relief flooded her face. She feared it, he realized. Good. A mage needed a healthy respect for their magic.

"Thank you, Daddy."

She pushed her chair from the table and came around to hug him. He let her, ignoring the burst of pain from the gesture because for a moment his turbulent life calmed. His daughter had magic, but he would figure it out with her. And he was pretty sure she had just healed his shoulder a little more, which was a pleasant bonus.

CHAPTER TWENTY-THREE

A Piece of the Action

Jtude buzzed with the impending arrival of someone from the Salt-Iron Confederation. Blaise heard the gossip that afternoon from Ellie Pembroke when he stopped by the mercantile to pick up a few items. She was a bustling mix of curiosity and anxiety, which Blaise soon realized was the overwhelming feeling of most of the town.

He thought to ask Vixen about it, since she was the most forthcoming of the Ringleaders. He was on better terms with Jack after everything that happened, but he wasn't sure they were friends. Jack wasn't going around trying to punch him in the face, but Blaise figured he was only hampered by his injury.

Vixen was nowhere to be found. Blaise stopped by the stables to look for Emrys. It could be hit or miss finding the stallion—sometimes he was out working sentry duty or in areas that Blaise couldn't access, grazing. But this time he found most of the pegasi stabled, and the barn had an unsettled air to it.

"What's going on?" Blaise let himself into Emrys's stall. The pegasi stalls were so large the equines could unfurl the full length of their wings if needed.

<No one is happy about this Jefferson Cole coming,> Emrys answered. <Raven told us to not go out on sentry duty until he and his party have arrived.> The sound of a donkey braying reached them from outside. The stallion's ears swiveled. <Peanut says they're approaching.>

Blaise gave Emrys a conciliatory pat on the shoulder, then slipped out of the stall. Other townspeople had gathered outside, though he didn't miss the fact that it was only the humans. The pegasi were the largest population of non-humans, though Itude boasted others: Clover, Kur, a family of harpies, a knocker.

Everyone present watched the road that led into town from the east—the only side of the town accessible by horseback or wagon. It wasn't long before a lead rider trotted into town, wearing the forest green and white of Ganland. Blaise hissed out a breath. He had been afraid to see the red and gold of the Salt-Iron Confederation.

Two others followed the outrider, one of them a man who sat tall and straight in his saddle, a wide-brimmed hat shading his eyes. He wore a black duster, and he looked so much like any other rider that it took Blaise a moment to realize that nearby whispers identified him as Jefferson Cole. A woman so short Blaise nearly mistook her for a child rode beside him, strands of bright pink hair wisped loose beneath her hat.

Raven, Vixen, and Nadine stepped out to greet them. Blaise was too far off to hear the exchange of words, but he saw Vixen gesture to the stables for their mounts and then toward the boarding house. There were nodding and animated gestures all around, and Jefferson Cole even shook their hands in a show of good faith. The tiny pink-haired woman stayed on her horse and surveyed the situation, her critical eyes reminding Blaise of Jack—who wasn't in attendance.

It all looked mundane from Blaise's vantage point, and he relaxed as he saw there was nothing out of the ordinary about these visitors. He had expected Cole to come with a platoon of guards to protect him and the pennants of the Confederation flying overhead. Maybe this wasn't anything to worry about. Just a regular merchant.

He went back into the stables and told Emrys as much. It didn't escape Blaise's notice that the other pegasi had their heads over their partitions, listening in.

<You may be right, but we will still be vigilant.> Emrys shifted his weight from one side to the other. <You should be wary, too.>

"I will," Blaise promised.

For the most part, life returned to normal after the Salt-Iron Confederation businessman's first day in Itude. The humans settled back into their routines, though the non-humans were ill at ease. Kur Agur prowled the streets, hackles up and fangs bared. Clover hardly left the dark interior of the saloon.

Late in the morning, the bell over the bakery's door jingled. Emmaline had already left to practice her magic with her father, so only Reuben remained to help Blaise finish up for the day. Blaise kept his attention on mixing strained honey, sugar, and melted butter into a bowl of sifted flour, content that Reuben would handle the new customer.

"Oh, this is the charming bakery I've heard so much about."

Blaise froze, then pivoted at the unfamiliar voice. He knew everyone in town—if he forgot their names, he at least recognized who was a regular by their voice. And this speaker was new, with an accent that set him apart.

"Are you the one who owns this place?" The man leaned against the glass display case, eyes on Reuben. He owned the room with his presence, standing tall in a dark grey frock coat that cloaked his form, a burgundy vest with silver accents peeking out from beneath. His head was bare, a black felt derby hat held in one hand.

"Not me." Reuben shook his head, jerking his thumb back to indicate Blaise. "I work here. Wildfire Jack owns the building, but the business is all Blaise."

The newcomer cocked his head, tendrils of hair shifting with the movement. Intense green eyes settled on Blaise. "I see. Jefferson Cole, pleasure to meet you."

"Howdy." Blaise shrank under the power of Cole's gaze. From the gossip circulating town, Blaise gleaned that Cole was rich. Which made it exceedingly suspicious that he'd come to a tiny town like Itude. Blaise had hoped to avoid Cole's attention during his stay. So much for that.

Reuben quirked an eyebrow, then took Cole's order. Blaise tried to tune out the whole transaction, but his hands were twitchy with nerves. He still practiced his magic regularly, as Vixen advised, but just thinking of the Salt-Iron Confederation renewed his panic.

"Blaise?" It was Reuben.

Blaise blinked, turning. "Oh. Sorry. What is it?" Jefferson Cole stood on the other side of the counter, a half-eaten chocolate chip cookie in his well-manicured hand.

"I wanted to extend my compliments. This cookie is phenomenal." His eyes flitted from the cookie to Blaise. "It's amazing. Almost magical. So I have to ask: is it?" Cole bit off another chunk. He licked a morsel of chocolate from his lips and sighed with contentment.

"What?" Talking with this man was as frustrating as speaking with Jack.

Cole raised the remains of his cookie. "Magical. Is the food here magical?"

No one had ever asked him that before. Was magical baking even a possibility? And if so, why couldn't that have been his magic? "I don't think so. I just know what I'm doing."

Cole regarded the cookie with a small measure of disappointment. "That's unfortunate. But all the same, it's delicious by itself. Best thing I've had in my mouth since I was home in Nera." His forehead puckered, thoughtful. "Do you sell to any outside vendors?"

Blaise's pulse raced. These rapid-fire questions were disorienting. Why wouldn't Cole just leave? He took a moment to puzzle out what the entrepreneur meant before answering. "Oh. Um, I sell bread every day to the Jitterbug next door."

Cole nodded, making a small sound of assent. "I see." His eyes scanned the case of baked goods, a covetous look flitting across his handsome features. "I'm always seeking out new investments and profitable ventures. I see—or should I say, taste—a lot of potential here." His gaze settled unerringly on Blaise, posing an unspoken question.

Blaise wasn't sure what he was getting at. "Well, thanks."

"If you ever think to expand this operation, keep me in mind." Cole picked up a box of cookies that Reuben had put together for him. "I wouldn't mind getting a piece of the action." He gave them a friendly nod, then pushed open the door and strode out.

Reuben rubbed his forehead. "What was that all about?"

Blaise released a long, pent-up breath. "Your guess is as good as mine, but no way would I work with that guy." He finally finished mixing the ingredients, but the pit of his stomach roiled with nerves and not even baking calmed it.

"Those Gannish know how to bring in the money, though, from what I've heard," Reuben reasoned.

"There's more to this life than money."

"Maybe. But it doesn't hurt."

"I HEAR COLE STOPPED BY THE BAKERY." JACK'S VOICE WAS NEUTRAL, though his stiff-legged stance and crossed arms belied the casualness of the statement.

Blaise glanced from Jack to the line of teenagers standing in a row, taking practice shots at targets placed on the little-used north side of the plateau. Jack had taken over training the younger outlaws while he convalesced, and he had demanded Blaise take part in that training. After escaping Lamar Gaitwood for a second time, Blaise wasn't inclined to tell him *no*.

"He stopped by," Blaise agreed, deciding not to offer Jack any more information than necessary. That seemed like the most prudent way to stay on the outlaw's good side. There were way too many revolvers around right now for Blaise's comfort.

"What'd he want?" Jack kept his eyes on the teens. "Stop slouching, Reuben!" Reuben yelped and straightened with a guilty glance over his shoulder.

"He bought cookies, so that'll help me pay this month's lease," Blaise said dryly. "He asked if my baking was magical. Is there such a thing?"

The outlaw rubbed his chin, contemplating. "Huh. Hadn't thought about that. I don't know of anyone with such magic, but that doesn't mean much."

Blaise sighed. "I wish that *was* my magic."

"Anything else?" Jack pressed.

"He asked if I sold to any outside vendors, so I told him I sold to Celeste and Mindy."

Jack's lips pressed into a taut line. "Hmm." Then he cast whatever he was thinking aside in favor of the trainees. "Keep a proper grasp, Cordelia! You've got the grip slipping around in your hand like a slick basilisk. Tuck those thumbs!" The raven-haired teen winced and addressed the issue.

"What's he doing in Itude?" Blaise asked once Jack finished haranguing Cordelia.

Jack shook his head. "That's what I've been trying to figure out. He told Vixen he's here looking for investment opportunities and to see the sights. I don't trust him. He's too full of himself, and he's a businessman, and I hate both."

"I'm going to split hairs here, but you could be considered both, too."

The outlaw snorted. "Shut your piehole."

Blaise clamped his mouth shut, the corners of his mouth twisting with amusement.

"He's also a Saltie which means I trust him about as far as I can throw him. Maybe not even that far." Jack angled his right foot and dug the heel of his boot into the ground.

"Seems like a lot of strikes against him. Why is he even allowed to stay in town?"

Jack grimaced. "I'm not the only one who gets to decide. Which is unfortunate."

Blaise nodded, though he knew very well the outlaw had felt the same about his presence. Before he could say anything else, Jack had the current group of five step back so that Blaise and four others could replace them taking practice shots.

Blaise sighed and unholstered the revolver at his side. He didn't like the feel of the weapon in his hands at all, and after his first nervous touch of the metal, he had quickly taken out his gloves and slipped them back on. Jack frowned but didn't argue. No one wanted a gun blowing up in their midst.

A row of tin cans perched atop the remains of a fence served as their targets. Each student had to take down five cans—or wait until Jack called their group back, whichever happened first. It was no surprise that Blaise hadn't hit a single target yet.

Emmaline was in Blaise's group, and she gave him an encouraging smile as she lined up her shot. She squeezed the trigger, her grip on the sixgun steady and flawless. An instant later, she was rewarded by the ping of a bullet connecting, the can clattering to the red dirt. She made a flourishing gesture, encouraging him to take his turn.

"Yeah, yeah," Blaise grumbled, his gloved right hand wrapped around the grip. Sweat trickled down his forehead and seeped into his eye. He shook his head to flick it away, then took aim again and pulled the trigger. The revolver recoiled, surprising him when the bullet winged the tin can he had aimed at and sent it tumbling to the ground.

"There you go!" Emmaline whooped.

"You're still winning."

She aimed at the next can in her set. "Been doing this for years. You'll get there." Her shot sent the can flying.

Jack called for a change, and Blaise was more than happy to retreat. "Wasn't completely awful. Just mostly awful," Jack acknowledged.

Blaise gave an ironic salute. "High praise. Thanks."

Jack snickered. "Next time keep your thumb against the recoil shield. Then you can put pressure against the back of the sixgun, and it'll keep it from bouncing up. Acts like a counterweight."

Blaise blinked at the constructive feedback. "Oh, thanks." He sat down cross-legged next to the outlaw. "So, do you think Cole is here after investments? He's not . . . a spy or something?"

"Everyone's a spy until I find out otherwise." Jack said it so deadpan that Blaise figured he spoke the truth.

"Did you think I was one?"

Jack snorted. "No. I thought you were a green as grass kid who couldn't wield his own magic. And I was right."

That wasn't fair. "There were no complaints when that green as grass kid broke you out of Gaitwood's trap."

"You asked, and I answered honestly." The outlaw scratched his chin. "Cole could be a spy. He came to town on day one with that itty-bitty, pink-haired woman, and then she took off, and no one's seen hide nor hair of her since. But his story checks out in that the Gannish are always looking for a profit, which makes them . . . less antagonistic toward magic than some other Salties. But in my mind, once you throw in your lot with them, you're not to be trusted."

That made sense to Blaise.

"Some other Ringleaders see his presence here as protection. If we work with them, it would make Gaitwood and his ilk look bad if they attacked. And it may even tie their hands." He said the last with reluctance, as if he also saw the wisdom of that.

Blaise rubbed his chin. He had to agree, that sounded like a compelling reason. "That would protect Itude. So that's good, right?"

Jack snorted. "Only if you take it at face value. What if it's a plot? A double-cross?"

"You have serious trust issues," Blaise observed.

"You think?" Jack grunted. "I just don't want to take foolish chances. We have too much to lose." His gaze rested on his daughter as he spoke, the afternoon breeze whipping her long blonde hair behind her. "Cole also spoke to Vixen about permission to bring a survey team here to look for something. I didn't find out what. Maybe salt-iron. Before I was . . . a few months ago I heard there were some miners striking veins in Argor."

"Wouldn't it be a problem if salt-iron got discovered around here?" The thought gave Blaise chills. He didn't know much about mining, but a lode of salt-iron near magic users was a disconcerting idea. And with how highly the Salt-Iron Confederation treasured the ore, it could quickly become a bone of contention.

Jack's mouth tugged down into a frown. "It would be a problem. But I've got my ears open, and our knocker has been putting feelers out for me."

Blaise cocked his head, perplexed. "Jasper Strop? What do knockers do?"

"They have an affinity for precious stones and metals." Jack looked like he might say more, but he left it at that. "If the Confederation sends people here and they find something like that, no one on the outside will get word of it." His voice took on the brutal, no-nonsense tone that Blaise associated with Wildfire Jack, the outlaw who tolerated no bullshit.

Right. Jack would murder them. Blaise rubbed the side of his face.

"Anyway, you're up again." Jack jerked his chin toward the line of practicing teens. Blaise groaned.

CHAPTER TWENTY-FOUR
Every Man Has a Price

Jack

"Mr. Dewitt! A moment of your time."

Jack stopped mid-stride, hackles raised at the voice. *The entrepreneur. How does he know my name?* He pivoted, schooling his face into a cool, stony expression. "The name is Wildfire Jack."

Jefferson Cole flashed a charming yet apologetic smile. "Of course, of course. My sincere apologies. If you could spare a moment of your time, I'd like to buy you a drink and discuss a business proposition with you."

I'll bet you would. Jack fixed him with an impassive look for a beat, then shrugged. "Sure." It wouldn't hurt to keep his ears open and get an idea of what the Saltie was playing at.

Oblivious to Jack's machinations, Cole made a welcoming gesture and started walking to the Broken Horn. Jack followed. It was midafternoon, and the saloon would be empty. When Cole pushed open the door, Clover was wiping down the bar. That was good. She had sensitive hearing, so would keep an ear out for signs of trouble.

Cole selected a table in the corner. Clover didn't bother coming over; she eyed them from across the bar. "What'll it be?"

"The usual." Jack scratched at his right ear as he spoke, a sign the Knossan would understand from previous dealings.

"I'll have the same." Cole nodded.

Jack concealed his smirk. He hoped Cole had a solid constitution. The greenhorn was about to be in for a surprise.

Clover ambled over with two tin mugs. The stuff inside reeked like fetid old boots and the contents of an outhouse. Prior experience proved the vile concoction was harsh enough to take paint off a building. All the same, he took a long, steady gulp. It tasted as awful as it smelled, but Jack tolerated the occasional rotgut, even though it truly wasn't his preferred drink.

Cole followed his example, and Jack chuckled inwardly—the other man didn't outright gag or spit it out. He'd seen that before, and it amused him every time. Cole took a sip, his perfect complexion taking on an interesting shade of green. He swallowed it and then politely scooted the mug aside.

"What'd you want to discuss?" Jack took another disgusting dreg, purely for the amount of discomfort it would cause his counterpart.

The businessman coughed, and for one sweet moment, Jack thought he was going to lean over and retch. Clover snorted with concern. Fortunately, for the sake of her hardwood floors, Cole regained his composure and straightened with a great deal of effort.

"I've come to your fine town in search of some investment opportunities." Clover, showing more kindness than was strictly necessary, brought over a glass of water which Cole drank with a grateful sigh. "And it's come to my attention that you own the bakery building."

Jack noted by the way Cole settled in his chair that the businessman expected him to make some affirmative reply. Instead, he took another drink of rotgut, meeting Cole's eyes as it burned all the way down.

Cole looked away first, then started again. "Do you own the bakery, and if so, would you be willing to sell it?"

"It's not for sale."

Cole frowned. Here was a man who wasn't told *no*, Jack decided. That gave Jack even more incentive to deny him. "I understand if it has sentimental value to you. I can be generous with my offer."

"As I said, not for sale."

To his credit, Cole didn't show any outward signs of frustration. Instead, he pulled a small rectangle of paper and a pen from a pocket hidden inside his pinstriped waistcoat. He wrote something down on the back of the card, then pushed it across the table.

Jack scowled, then used his index finger to draw the card closer. He flipped it over. One side was a business card, listing Jefferson Cole's address in Ganland along with a secondary office in Rainbow Flat. On the back, he had written a number. Ten thousand golden eagles. Far and away more than the bakery was worth, at least in little Itude.

That didn't matter. It was the principle. No Saltie was going to own so much as a blade of grass or speck of Itude's dust. He shrugged and slipped the card back across the table. "I don't think so."

Cole drew the card back over and gave Jack an assessing look. The businessman tapped the card with his pen, contemplative. He wasn't done with their charade, so he wrote a new number and slid it across the table.

Jack picked up the card. This time, he was the one who was surprised. Five hundred thousand golden eagles. Who *was* this Jefferson Cole, to throw around these kinds of sums as if they were naught but crumbs? Jack needed to dig into his research as soon as he could.

But damn him, that figure was tempting. Cole's strategy of throwing money at him almost worked. Jack could buy Itude ten times over—maybe more. Bribe and pay off officials in the Salt-Iron Confederation to stop looking for him. Move around the continent with the freedom bought by gold. He could use it to find Kittie.

Every man has a price, Jack cautioned himself. Cole had just found his. He kept his cool—he couldn't let the businessman perceive how much he *wanted* that, for the sheer amount of magic that wealth could make happen. As an outlaw, Jack never hurt for money; he took what he wanted. But this was on a different level.

He made a show of thinking about the offer, but in actuality, he was trying to analyze why Cole wanted the bakery so badly. He didn't like any of the reasons he came up with. First, if he knew what Blaise *was*, that would give him direct access to the Breaker. The kid loved that bakery and that would be a binding leash for him. Even if Cole had no idea what Blaise was, there was still the fact that this would give someone with ties to the Salt-Iron Confederation a foothold in Itude, no matter how small.

Jack had worked hard to make Itude appear insignificant to the Salt-Iron Confederation. It bothered Jack that this had changed, just as it bothered him Cole knew his last name.

Jack allowed himself a whistle of appreciation, then shook his head with regret that was easy to feign. "I'm sorry. And you are a man of your word—that is *most* generous. But I won't sell the bakery."

Cole stared at him, dumbfounded. "I can do better."

Damn him. "And I'll still turn it down."

The entrepreneur concluded that he had met his match. He nodded and rose from the table. "I see. I appreciate you taking the time, regardless. It's been a pleasure."

Yeah, right. "Likewise."

Cole made a dignified retreat for the exit. Jack watched him go, then thoughtfully picked the business card up from the table. Clover plodded over and peered at the figures on the card, ears pinned back in shock and her eyes white-rimmed.

"I don't like the Gannish and even *I* think you've lost your mind."

Jack chuckled, shaking his head. "It's not about the money." He paused. "Well, I'm lying. It is, but that's why this rubs me the wrong way."

Clover considered, then made a soft sound of understanding. "You think he's trying to buy his way into making you complacent?"

"Something like that," Jack agreed. He didn't want to give voice to all his ideas. He needed time to mull over them. And he had research to do. He got up but paused as he had a thought. "He eats here sometimes?"

Clover nodded. "Most evenings."

"He talk with anyone here?"

The Knossan nodded. "He is friendly with our citizens."

Of course. He was working to curry good favor. "Anything I might find of interest?"

Clover thought for a moment. "He mentions Rainbow Flat frequently. He said that is his next stop, after Itude."

That tracked with the information on his card. "Thanks for keeping an ear open. I'm heading home."

Clover gave him a gentle thump on the back as he headed out. Jack made sure Cole was nowhere in sight, then quick-stepped toward home.

Emmaline wasn't there when he arrived, which suited his purposes. He didn't want anyone seeing what he was about to do. Jack shouldered his dresser away from the wall, revealing a panel that opened with the press of his fingers. He pulled out a leather messenger bag, opening it and spreading the contents over the bed. Then he opened the top drawer on the dresser and pulled out a notebook. It listed names and numbers, but he had devised a system that made them appear meaningless to most.

He flipped through the notebook, comparing notations to some of the folded missives. Jack went through them for several hours, long enough that the natural light faded and he had to turn on mage-lights to continue his research. He heard Emmaline come in, but he called to her that he was busy and not to be disturbed. She wouldn't be happy, but he wanted to solve this puzzle.

It took some doing, but eventually he found the reference he was looking for regarding one Mr. Jefferson Cole. The handwriting sample was a match for the writing on the back of the business card.

"Gotcha, you bastard," Jack murmured, glancing from one missive to the chart in his meticulous notebook.

> *Malcolm Wells*
> *Salt-Iron Council Doyen Representative: Ganland*
> *Occupation: Investor*
> *May use pseudonym Jefferson Cole to conduct business in Untamed Territory*
> <u>*Assets in Rainbow Flat???*</u>

Sometime in the past, Jack had underscored the last sentence several times. The significance panned out with the business card. Rainbow Flat. That town was downright civilized compared to Itude, and from there Cole would have no trouble going back to Confederation territory. And he would take everything he had learned about Itude with him.

With this additional information, he felt validated in his conviction that Cole was a threat to Itude. "Ace in the hole," he murmured, closing the notebook and placing it back in the drawer. Now he would lie in wait to see when he could exploit that information. Cole would not get the best of *his* town.

CHAPTER TWENTY-FIVE

Good Luck and Have Fun

Jack

Jack watched as the thirteen outlaw trainees—including Blaise —assembled. He tugged his hat down to shade his eyes from the sun. His revelation of Jefferson Cole's identity had him on edge, though the Gannish man had been nothing but a model visitor, much to Jack's consternation. To keep his annoyance at bay, Jack focused on training the younger outlaws, and it was high time for one of the more entertaining training activities he had devised.

Today they would blend magic and the mundane. Most of the trainees were excellent shots, but they weren't used to aiming *at* someone. Which, to be fair, was an overall good practice while learning. Aside from Blaise, none of the youngsters had seen a true fight of any kind. If trouble found Itude, Jack wanted everyone prepared.

The other Ringleaders thought him daft when he placed the order for first-generation hexguns from Ravance. Hexguns were relatively new, the invention of a talented gunsmith attempting to blend magic and bullets. They were still in development and had limited success, but they intrigued Jack, and he thought they might be fun to tinker with.

The set that had shipped to Itude came with a trial batch of ammunition. Hexguns loaded the same way as a standard revolver, but the
cartridges were different. Instead of a lead or copper casing, the hexgun's
round bullets were cased in flexible gelatin. Enchanted water filled the
ball's interior, designed to hold a spell. From what Jack had gleaned, only
two spells worked with the hexguns so far: a sleep spell and a nullification
spell. Jack preloaded the hexguns with nullification spells, but also added
an injection of food coloring to show when someone was struck.

Jack was pleased with the idea. He liked the opportunity to try out
new technology and see how his trainees would fare in simulated combat.
The other Ringleaders had reservations, but he had successfully argued it
was better than letting the trainees wing each other. Nadine didn't have
the time or magic for that much carnage.

The trainees eyed the crate next to Jack with interest. He drew the
cover off, pulling out a bundle covered in wrapping paper. Jack peeled
away the paper, revealing the hexguns. Rather than steel, they were
crafted from brass, which gave them a different heft from a standard
sixgun.

"Today's training is going to differ from any in the past," Jack said to
the assembled group. "You'll be pitted against one another, using anything
at your disposal to come out on top—including magic."

A few of the non-mage trainees quailed. Reuben raised his hand. "Um,
I thought it was against the rules to use magic in town?"

Jack glared at the teen. *Give me patience with these kids.* "This is practice.
My goal is for this training to be as close to an actual fight as you can get.
But don't worry, no one will get hurt." To prove his point, he targeted
Reuben's left leg and squeezed the trigger. Reuben yelped as a bright
purple splotch appeared. Maybe that did sting a little. "No one will get
hurt too much," Jack amended.

The kids traded anxious looks. Jack wouldn't let that bother him. In an
actual battle, they wouldn't have time for misgivings. He pointed to the
crate. "Everyone gets a hexgun. You have six shots. Make them count. If
you're a mage, you can use your magic to your advantage. If you don't
have magic, you had better pray that you can get a shot off before
someone else gets a spell or shot on you." He paused, gesturing to the
hexgun in his hand. "These are loaded with nullification shot. If you're a
mage and you're hit, you won't be able to use magic for a while." Eyes
widened in surprise. "This exercise will take place in the box canyon."

Jack whistled, and a moment later, thirteen pegasi answered his
summons. The trainees who hadn't ridden a pegasus before looked on
with expressions of excitement and wonder.

The trainees came and picked up their hexguns. Blaise was the last in line, chewing his lower lip. "Can I not do this?"

Jack quirked an eyebrow. "You know the dangers that await us outside of the Gutter."

The Breaker dropped his gaze. "I'd rather not be reminded of that."

That was too bad. "You don't get to make that choice. Not in Itude." Jack picked up the last hexgun and handed it to him. "Keep your gloves off, unless you don't want to use your magic."

Blaise heaved a sigh and removed his gloves, sticking them in his back pocket. He accepted the hexgun, tucking it into his waistband before walking over to Emrys. Zepheus trotted up to Jack and paused long enough for him to swing into the saddle.

"Let's go," Jack ordered. Everyone mounted, and the pegasi bolted into the sky, following Zepheus the short distance to a box canyon nestled to the north.

The box canyon held the tumbledown remains of the original town of Itude. Thick vegetation choked the remnants, obscuring the streets. Several of the buildings had fallen in on themselves, though at least three were still in a condition to serve as hiding places.

Jack called for everyone to cluster around Zepheus in a circle. "Your pegasi will drop you off at predetermined locations. I'll whistle twice when it's time to start. You can form alliances if you want—that's up to you. But the game doesn't end until there's only one person standing."

Cordelia cleared her throat to get his attention. "Um, can I ask why we're doing this?"

Jack stared at her until she dropped her gaze. "Survival. The world is unfair. It's past time y'all learned how to get the upper hand." He jutted his chin toward Blaise. "Of all of you, *he* knows how to do that. No one escapes the Salt-Iron Confederation twice without learning from the experience."

Blaise looked away, embarrassed.

Jack didn't care. It was true. Blaise was, against the odds, a survivor. Whether he used his skills in this practice didn't matter. But Jack wanted the others to have a chance to use theirs.

"Pegasi, take the riders to their positions. Good luck and have fun."

CHAPTER TWENTY-SIX
Man Down

"Jack and I have very different ideas of fun," Blaise muttered as he slid down from Emrys's back. The stallion flew to the north side of the ghost town, near what appeared to be the dilapidated remains of stores built side-by-side along a boardwalk.

The pegasus snorted. <No one has real bullets. This is a simple way to gain practice in a combat situation.>

"Doesn't mean I'll have *fun*, though." Blaise patted the stallion's neck. "Thanks for the ride."

<Good luck.> Emrys bobbed his head and trotted off before lurching into the air to join the other pegasi on a cliff overlooking the canyon.

Blaise stood on the main drag of the ghost town and turned in a slow circle, taking in his surroundings. A building with a steeple crouched at the end of the defunct, dusty road. Scrub grew up around the remains of the buildings, obscuring their facades. Blaise walked closer to one, peering through the window. The structure's roof had collapsed into the interior, sunbeams illuminating the wreckage.

Jack's piercing whistle sliced the air. Blaise rolled his shoulders, drawing a deep breath. He exhaled, forcing out his annoyance at the situation. None of the other trainees were in his view yet, but it would only be a matter of time. Blaise was reluctant to take part in this exercise, but he didn't want to be the first out. Jack wouldn't let him live it down.

Blaise slipped into the building with the ruined roof. Once inside, slanted pieces of timber proved some optimistic person had tried to shore up the roof before it fell in, but time and the elements rendered their attempts useless. Blaise skirted the worst of the debris and found a questionably safe place to wait and consider his options.

Six shots. Each trainee had six, so no one person could take out everyone. That meant they would have to rely on crossfire or allies taking out their opponents. If he teamed up with one other person, they would have twelve shots between them.

He expected the teens without magic would group up, bolstering their lack of magic with numbers. Would the other mages feel the same way, or would they prefer to keep apart?

Blaise thought about that. He would prefer to work with someone else. Maybe he could find Reuben and join forces. Reuben had no magic and wasn't a better shot than Blaise, but at least they could be hopeless together. And maybe he could find Emmaline. They would have a chance with her on their side.

That was a solid idea. The hardest part was going to be finding them and not getting shot by anyone else first.

He crept closer to the window, peering out. Skunkbush and stunted cat-claw trees provided cover, obscuring his position. Two teens scurried down the street, crouching as they ran to keep a low profile. The shrubs hindered his view, so Blaise couldn't tell exactly who they were, but he didn't think they were mages.

A pop split the air, followed by the ping of a pellet hitting a target. One teen yelped, a bright yellow splash blooming across their back.

"Damn it!" the struck girl shrieked, spinning around to see who had fired on her. Her companion dove away, scarcely avoiding another pellet that struck the ground where he had been a second earlier.

Two shots. Whoever had just fired only had four remaining. Blaise followed the gaze of the girl to the bell tower of the church. Blaise blinked, not believing his eyes. Someone stood on the side of the steeple, as easily as anyone else would stand on flat land. Another pop sounded, and the teen on the tower skated around the side, keeping their feet in contact with the surface as they moved.

Blaise squinted, trying to figure out who it was. The figure moved, and he recognized the profile as one of the young mages, Austin. What sort of magic was that? Blaise hadn't bothered to find out the abilities of the other mages in town. He considered changing that.

The trainee firing on Austin missed, but now everyone knew his position. He had the advantage of high ground, but if enough came after him, he wouldn't have the ammunition to hold them off.

Boots crunched on the ground, a shadow flickering as someone else approached Blaise's location. He held his hexgun at the ready, keeping his position close to the door. From this distance, he had a chance to strike an opponent. It wouldn't be fair, but it occurred to him that Jack wasn't trying to teach them about playing fairly today. He wanted them to think about how to survive. And Blaise had learned how to survive.

The door opened slowly. Blaise's index finger flitted against the trigger as he waited. He recognized Emmaline's blonde hair, illuminated by the bright light, a golden halo. Blaise kept the hexgun aimed in her direction, and when she noticed the glint of its muzzle, she pointed hers at him, but didn't fire.

"It's me," Blaise hissed. "Want to team up?"

Emmaline eyed him, then lowered her hexgun. "Austin's up on the steeple. Not a terrible place. I considered joining him, but I think he'd shoot me first."

Blaise chuckled. "I saw that, too. And he probably would."

"There's already three out." Emmaline settled down by the other window. "Cordelia was the first to go. Too slow to use her magic. Then two norms, Tilla and Ambrose."

Blaise nodded. Tilla must have been the girl he saw sniped by Austin. "What's Cordelia's magic? Did you see it?"

"Briefly. The shot disrupted it," Emmaline murmured. "She's a Phase Shifter—she can shift herself out of our reality to avoid damage. She looked all wavy, but then Ambrose saw her. I got Ambrose."

Blaise blinked as the explanation went over his head. *Right.* "So you only have five shots left?"

"Right."

Three mages and five norms left. Four teens were excellent shots, if Blaise remembered right. "Think we should join Austin?"

"No." Emmaline shook her head. "We'd be exposed. I—"

The door at the rear of the building slammed open. There was no more time to discuss strategy. Two silhouettes appeared in the glare of sunlight. Blaise scrambled away as a pellet spattered nearby. Wood clattered as Emmaline dashed to a better position, startling Blaise with how fast she moved. She vaulted over a broken table and fired a shot at the intruders, hitting one squarely in the chest. The boy yelped.

The other teen trained his hexgun on Emmaline, who had lost her momentum and was cornered. She dove behind a chair, running out of options. Blaise glanced at the floorboards, an idea springing into his mind. He slammed his palm down against them, willing for them to shatter beneath Emmaline's attacker. His magic responded, surging into the planks. The wood was easily suggestible, creaking and disintegrating to dust beneath the boy's feet.

He staggered as he lost his footing, barely catching himself as he came down. But he was agile, and as soon as he landed, he pointed his hexgun at Blaise. The muzzle made a muted pop, and Blaise felt the sting of a pellet against his chest. Yellow paint splattered across his shirt, accompanied by a dull sensation that forced his magic to recede.

Then the boy groaned as Emmaline returned fire, turning the side of his shirt bright yellow, too.

"Gotcha, Desmond!" Emmaline crowed, shooting Blaise a guilty look. "Sorry. But thanks for the save."

Blaise waved a hand at her, getting up. "Don't mention it. Go out there and kick some butt."

Victor, Emmaline's original target, wiped dye off his shirt before walking out the door with his hands raised, showing he was out. Desmond got up, holstering his hexgun and wincing at the demolished floorboards. "Wasn't expecting that. Nice move—I hadn't seen your magic with my own eyes before."

Blaise smiled at the compliment. "You weren't so bad yourself. I don't know how you made that shot while falling."

Desmond grinned. "Mostly luck. Come on, let's go watch and see how this shakes out."

Emmaline skulked out the back door as Blaise and Desmond exited through the front. Austin was still perched on the side of the steeple, but he didn't fire on them. Blaise glanced at the bright yellow spot on his shirt.

"Everyone who's out went that way." Desmond pointed in the overlook's direction. The two-legged shapes of trainees stood by the pegasi.

"How many are left?"

Desmond squinted, counting the tiny forms. "Just four or five."

Blaise nodded. Once they reached the outskirts of the ghost town, a small game trail wound up the side of the canyon to the overlook. Outside of the town, the vegetation obstructed more of the canyon. Young ironwoods and mesquite forced them to duck under low-slung branches. Blaise skirted around them, though he still had to navigate tangles of greasebush and purple sage.

He froze at the unmistakable report of a revolver. It was close—too close. Blaise turned, pain lacing through him as scarlet blood blossomed from his left arm.

Jack

"WHAT IN PERDITION WAS THAT?" JACK SHIFTED HIS ATTENTION FROM THE remaining active trainees, scanning the area. That was a real gunshot, and it was close. Too close for his liking. No one in the box canyon carried anything beyond a hexgun.

Blaise's black stallion screamed, leaping off the ledge. Zepheus turned to Jack, ears flicking with alarm. <It's Blaise. Someone shot Blaise.>

Jack cursed, turning to the trainees and the waiting pegasi. "Game's over. Oberidon, you and the other pegasi go down and get them to stop." The spotted stallion bobbed his head, popping open his wings as he dropped over the side to glide down to the canyon.

He swung into Zepheus's saddle, ignoring the hitch in his shoulder. The palomino coasted down to the scene, where Desmond was crouching over Blaise. Zepheus paid no mind to the scrub, simply folded his wings and plowed through. Emrys had already torn through the worst of it in his haste to get to his mage.

"What happened?" Jack demanded, staying in the saddle.

Desmond looked up, face pale. "Someone shot him, sir."

"Who?"

"Didn't see anyone. I'm sorry."

Jack clenched his jaw. He didn't like this. Not one bit. Blood oozed from Blaise's upper arm—probably nothing life-threatening unless an artery had been nicked. The kid probably felt like shit, but Jack wouldn't do him any good playing nursemaid when there were more important things to do.

"I'm gonna search for the shooter in case they're still nearby looking to finish the job. Desmond, help get him onto Emrys. Kralix is coming over and when he does, accompany Blaise to Nadine's clinic."

Desmond nodded. Zepheus spun, and Jack scanned the area for anything out of place. The brush was thick and would have made a shot from further away challenging. The shooter had to be close.

"Smell anything?" Jack asked Zepheus. It was a pity Kur Agur wasn't here. His nose would be handy. But Jack would lose precious time waiting for him.

The stallion fluttered his nostrils, sucking in a deep breath. <The usual. Gunpowder, as you would expect.>

"Any people?"

Zepheus snorted. <I'm not a bloodhound.>

"I'm not sorry for asking."

Jack slipped out of the saddle. If Zepheus detected gunpowder, then the shooter would have fired from nearby. Zepheus moved aside as Jack eyeballed the area from where he was standing to where Blaise had stood. Desmond was helping him get into Emrys's saddle. Jack cocked his head. Sage blocked the shot. He wished he had been watching Blaise at the time to know the path he had taken. Then Jack would have a clue about the trajectory.

A few minutes later, Jack's search was interrupted by heavy wings as Oberidon landed nearby. Emmaline jumped off, scrambling over. "Daddy, who shot Blaise?"

Jack continued to study the ground carefully. "Don't know. Trying to find something helpful, like shell casings."

Emmaline joined him in the search. The two pegasi did their best, trying to filter for any strange scent. Though as Zepheus pointed out, they weren't the best choice for the task.

Jack asked Emmaline to look for footprints coming into the box canyon. The canyon wasn't easy to access. Someone should have seen whoever it was, and that bothered him. Itude had two citizens who traveled using unusual means. Hank Walker with his succulents, and the town knocker, Jasper Strop. Knockers were a mystic race capable of travel via mineral deposits or precious stone veins. But Jasper was so near-sighted he was virtually blind. And he didn't own a weapon, as far as Jack knew.

Hank Walker didn't own a gun, either. But he was a postmaster, with a lot more access to supplies than a knocker.

Jack knelt down by a prickly pear. He thought he saw faint impressions of boots in the surrounding dirt, but it was impossible to verify. His hunch wasn't enough proof for anyone.

"Let's wrap it up, Em," Jack told his daughter at last, dissatisfied.

She came back over, unhappy. "I wish we found a shell casing. I could use it, right?"

"Use it?"

Her eyes were fierce. "With the magic. If I had a shell casing, I could find out who did it?"

Jack's forehead furrowed. That honestly hadn't occurred to him, but . . . he didn't see why not. At the very least, if she had found a casing but couldn't deduce who had shot it, she might be able to make their mystery shooter extremely uncomfortable.

He didn't tell her that, though. He wanted her to hold on to what was left of her innocence. It would slip through her fingers like water soon enough.

"You could," he said at last. *And so much more.*

CHAPTER TWENTY-SEVEN

Allies

Blaise

Blaise flinched at the creak of Nadine's office door opening. The quick movement jarred his injured arm, and he groaned. He was better off than prior to Nadine's attentions to it, but there was still healing to be done.

A partition blocked his view of the door, but he heard familiar voices: Jack and Emmaline.

"How bad is it?" Jack asked the Healer.

"Could have been a lot worse. If whoever shot him had aimed a little to the right, Butch would be dressing him for a pine box right about now."

Blaise used his right hand to fiddle with the grey blanket covering his legs. He didn't enjoy considering any other scenario. Being shot was bad enough. Full stop.

"His recovery won't take near as long as yours, though. I got to heal it right away. And Blaise is more likely to listen when I tell him to baby it."

Jack grumbled in reply to Nadine's criticism then asked, "Is he up to talking?"

Nadine peered around the partition. "Are you?"

"Sure." Blaise figured it was better than sitting there pondering all the might-have-beens.

Jack stalked around the partition like a hunting cat. Emmaline trailed in his wake, her mouth a small, thin line of worry. She brightened a little upon seeing Blaise.

"Hey, did you win?" Blaise couldn't help but ask her.

Emmaline stared at him, as if that was the last thing she expected him to say. Then she laughed, shaking her head. "You're ridiculous."

Jack settled down on the edge of the cot opposite Blaise's. "I called it as soon as we saw you go down. From a *real gods-damned bullet*." His voice held a raw edge of frustration.

Blaise watched Jack for a moment and realized he was seeing the outlaw's version of guilt. He had set up his exercise so that no one would get hurt. Maybe painted a new color, but not hurt.

"Can you tell me what happened?" Jack asked. There was a silent *I'm sorry* attached to the way his voice cracked on the last word.

Blaise sighed, using his good arm to sit up. "I was just walking back with Desmond. Then I heard a shot. I knew it wasn't one of the hexguns —they sound different. It sounded close, and when I turned I realized it had hit me." He looked down at his arm, a panicky lump forming in his throat as he recounted it. He should have been paying more attention. His guard had been down.

"You didn't see or hear anything strange?"

Blaise shook his head. "No. I just took a different trail than Desmond, since he was going under the trees more than I liked. I ended up going around the brush, but I didn't notice anything unusual."

Jack sat back, rubbing his chin. "They shot you from behind. I found an area where the brush had been broken by someone, and it wasn't any of our people. I don't understand it, though. If they stood where I think they did, then someone should have seen them coming or going."

He knew Jack was right. The canyon had sheer walls, except for the trail leading to the overlook. "Any tunnels?"

The outlaw paused, as if he had considered something similar. "Not any the average person could use."

Blaise wasn't sure what Jack meant by that, but he wasn't feeling well enough to request clarification. He was ready to go home and burrow in his bed and hope that when he woke up, this was an elaborate nightmare.

"Is there any reason someone would want to hurt you?" Jack paced between the cots, the tapping of his heels accentuating his words.

Blaise bit his lip, glancing away. He had thought he was accepted in Itude, perhaps even well-liked. The citizens certainly enjoyed the bakery. "I don't think so."

The outlaw paused in his pacing, eyes meeting Emmaline's as he asked her some silent question. Emmaline shook her head in response. "If anything changes, you let me know immediately," Jack said, pointing a finger at Blaise.

Jack's words held an intensity Blaise hadn't expected. He had moved from regret to righteous fury. "I'll let you know."

"You do that," the outlaw agreed. "I'm going to make some inquiries." He pivoted and prowled out the door.

Nadine stopped Emmaline before she could follow, hooking a thumb in Blaise's direction. "Don't expect him to do *anything* at the bakery for the next couple of weeks, got it?"

Emmaline paused, shooting Blaise a sympathetic look before giving a firm nod. "Understood, Nadine."

Blaise sighed, beginning to understand exactly why Jack had been so grumpy with Nadine's restrictions.

CHAPTER TWENTY-EIGHT
A Little Light Mail Theft

Jack

The business with the shooter bothered Jack more than he let on. The Gutter and Untamed Territories were wild places with hot tempers and flying bullets, but that wasn't how things were in the towns unless something shady was afoot. The exercise in the box canyon should have been safe enough. He didn't like this, not one bit.

He had two suspects, though he doubted their likelihood. First, he stopped by the dry goods store, run by the town knocker, Jasper Strop.

There were a few reasons Jasper was on his list. As a knocker, he had the innate ability to travel from place to place via mineral deposits or veins in the land. In theory, he could have appeared in the box canyon and vanished moments later without a trace. The other reason was his family connections. As a part of his intelligence, Jack kept copious notes on his fellow citizens. Over time, he'd learned Jasper had a niece who lived in Ganland.

That was odd. The Salt-Iron Confederation wouldn't be hospitable to a knocker. Oh, they looked humanoid, but they were different enough to stick out like a gangrenous thumb. Earning their racial name from their penchant of warning miners by knocking on walls just before cave-ins, knockers were grey-skinned and shorter than most humans—Jasper only reached to the middle of Jack's chest, and he was considered tall. Their heads were larger and more bulbous than a human's, with prominent noses. Their legs were short, their arms gangly.

He found Jasper manning his store, which was quiet this time of day. The knocker smiled at Jack, an expression that reached his dark eyes. "Afternoon, Jack. What can I do for you?"

Jack liked most of the non-humans in town more than the humans, and he chafed at suspecting Jasper of the attack. But he had to be thorough. "I need to ask you a few questions. This a good time?"

Jasper's eyes widened with fear. No one was at ease when Jack came sniffing around. Many of them knew bits and pieces of his past in the Salt-Iron Confederation. Jack had never told them, but the truth had a way of getting out. He wasn't the only one with connections.

"Sure," Jasper agreed, easing against the counter. His long fingers tapped the polished wood in a nervous beat.

"When was the last time you were in the box canyon?"

The knocker blinked, owlish. "I couldn't tell you. Not recently. Nothing good there."

"Hmm." Jack browsed a display of leather gloves, picking up a pair to examine. "No good veins that way?"

Jasper shook his head. "Nothing I like. Found a phoenixeye deposit north of here." His eyes gleamed with momentary longing. Knockers collected gems and baubles, and had some they favored more than others. Jasper dabbled with jewel-crafting when he wasn't busy running the dry goods store. The fingers on his left hand twinkled with rings, the latest fruits of his efforts.

"Good to know." Jack moved to a row of hats hanging on pegs. It had been a while since he'd gotten a new hat. Might have to check into that later. But it would wait. "How's your niece?"

The knocker swallowed, and his voice was strained. "My niece?"

"Yeah. She lives in Ganland?"

Jasper stared at him in shock. "How did you know?"

Jack ignored the question, taking down a dapper little bowler and spinning it on his index finger. "You have contracts with excellent merchants. She help with that?"

He almost felt sorry for the knocker. He didn't pale as a human would when frightened. Instead, his skin turned a shade of violet, so he looked something like a purple potato. "N-no, sir. That is all my own hard work."

Jack studied the knocker. "How are you with a sixgun?" He glanced to a display of revolvers locked behind a glass case reinforced with strips of metal. He whistled with appreciation. Winking jewels and precious metals adorned two of the sixguns.

Jasper lifted his gnarled hands. "No good." He pointed his glitzy left hand to the display. "I'd rather do other things with them."

Jack nodded, looking at a little number that glimmered with a phoenixeye-inset muzzle. He wondered if that impacted the balance. Or did Jasper take that into account when he worked? "I see that. How long have you been embellishing the guns? Didn't know you'd started doing that."

The knocker's eyelids drooped with contentment, pleased with the change of subject. "I'm just learning. Started a month ago. Only completed three so far."

"Three? There's two in the case. Did you sell one?"

Jasper nodded. "Yes, but I shipped it by request of the buyer."

Jack narrowed his eyes. "Who's the buyer?"

"Jefferson Cole."

Cole. *Interesting.* Jack hadn't considered Cole as a suspect because there was no way that the Gannish man could have been in the box canyon undetected. But perhaps he had to consider other angles of the puzzle. "I wasn't aware you shipped guns out of here. How do you secure them?"

"It was the first time, so I wasn't comfortable doing it myself. I had it wrapped in linen, but I took it to the post office so Hank could help. It was a rush job, so he planned to transport it personally."

"Is that so?" If it was a rush order, it should have a receipt at the post office. "Thanks for your time, Jasper."

The knocker relaxed as Jack turned for the door. Jack cast a parting glance at him but noticed nothing more unusual than Jasper's skin returning to its normal stony color. His boots tapped as he took the steps down to the dusty road and headed to the post office.

Hank Walker was helping Celeste when Jack pushed open the door. "Hello, Jack. I'll be with you in a moment." A vein in Hank's forehead ticked with visible tension.

"No rush." Jack crossed his arms and leaned against the wall by the door. He nodded a greeting to Celeste. He noticed the postmaster's hands tremble as he set her parcel on the counter.

"Anything else I can help you with?" Walker asked with more fervor than usual.

"No, that's all. Thank you!" Celeste tucked the box under her arm and strode past Jack, waving as she exited.

Jack waited for the door to swing closed before stalking over to the counter. Hank gestured to the sorted mail behind him. "I saw nothing for you, and I think I went through everything."

"Good to know, but I'm here on town business." Jack cocked his head. "You seem nervous, Hank. Everything all right?"

"I got back from Thorn about an hour ago. You know the farther I travel, the harder the recovery can be," Hank said, faltering.

"I see." Jack made a show of looking behind the counter. The outgoing mailbox was empty, so Hank may have just finished his rounds. "Heard Jasper had you help him mail a revolver to Jefferson Cole's residence. A special piece, as I hear it."

The postmaster nodded. "That's right."

"When was that?"

Hank shifted his weight against the countertop. "Shipped out today."

"I need to see the receipt."

Hank paled. "I can't show you that unless you're one of the parties—"

Jack leaned across the counter. Didn't say a word; just pinned Hank with a chilling gaze that promised a world of pain if he didn't comply.

The postmaster broke eye contact, upset. He shifted, then pulled a pad of carbon paper from a drawer. He paged through, turning it for Jack to inspect.

Jack peered at the scrawled date and time, which was in fact that very afternoon. He pursed his lips, thinking. The time stamp would have given a brief span for Hank to act with that weapon, but it was possible.

"Jefferson Cole, eh?" Jack pushed the book back over to Walker.

Hank nodded, then came around the counter to look out the window. "But you didn't hear that from me."

"No, of course not." Jack gave the counter a hard smack with his hand, causing Hank to wince. The outlaw pivoted and headed for the door. "Thanks for the help."

CHAPTER TWENTY-NINE
Feast of Flight

"*R*euben, that's *amazing*."

The young man grinned, ducking his head at Blaise's compliment. Blaise sat nearby, overseeing as Reuben and Emmaline assembled and decorated a quintet of massive, three-tiered cakes for the Feast of Flight celebration. Just days after he'd been wounded, Vixen had come to the bakery to place an order for desserts for the upcoming festivities. Blaise discovered from her that the Feast of Flight was a true holiday for the outlaws, celebrating the bond of friendship forged by the first outlaw mage and pegasus. Though Nadine was adamant Blaise take it easy, Emmaline and Reuben had been eager to tackle the job.

Reuben had revealed, with a little embarrassment, that a few years ago he had spent a summer with an aunt who specialized in sugar sculpture, and he had helped with her work. Blaise set him to the task of creating decorations for the cakes, and he didn't disappoint. Brightly colored sugar pegasi rested on parchment paper, ready to be added to the cakes. Their coats were whimsical, reminiscent of a rainbow; their delicate wings, manes, and tails sculpted from spun sugar. They were breathtaking.

"Don't break them getting them onto the cake," Reuben fretted, eyeing Emmaline as she piped frosting onto a layer.

"You're worse than a mother hen," she grumbled, finishing the last flourish. "I was thinking we'd wait and put them on the cakes once we got them to the town square."

Blaise watched as they put the final touches on the cakes, though he couldn't help a pang of envy. He rubbed at the bandage wrapped around his upper arm. A week had passed since the shooting, and thanks to Nadine's masterful healing the injury didn't bother him much. Even so, she stopped by the bakery more than normal and would fix him with an assessing gaze, a silent warning to take it easy.

"It's too bad you can't ride in the parade tonight," Emmaline remarked to Blaise as she carefully packed a set of sugar pegasi in a box for transport.

"Yeah, *such* a shame," Blaise said, eliciting an amused snort from Emmaline. She knew quite well that flying didn't agree with him.

"You should still go to the stables for the preparations, though." Emmaline paused as Austin and Desmond arrived to move the cakes to the town square. She tasked Reuben with overseeing the process, then turned back to Blaise. "It's tradition for all the riders to gussy up the pegasi before the parade."

Blaise raised his brows. "I'd like to stay on Nadine's good side."

Emmaline waved a hand. "I don't mean you have to do anything. I can get Oby and Emrys ready. Just be there for Emrys. It's his first Feast of Flight with a rider."

A rider who wasn't allowed to ride him at the moment. Blaise sighed. He hadn't realized that the Feast of Flight was as important as it was. Emrys was disappointed with Blaise's restrictions and did a terrible job of hiding it. Blaise nodded. "I'll let you run interference with Nadine in that case."

"Deal." Emmaline grinned as she packed the last decoration.

Reuben pushed open the door to the bakery, a stricken look on his face when he saw Emmaline holding the packed boxes. "I'll take those, thanks." He pulled them from Emmaline's hands, nestling the boxes against his chest.

"They were fine," Emmaline shot back.

Reuben gave an unabashed grin. "I spent a lot of time on these! And besides, you need to go see to the real thing."

Emmaline rolled her eyes. "Fair enough."

Blaise followed her to the stables, and he was surprised to see others already there, braiding colorful ribbons into the manes and tails of each pegasus. Even Jack was in attendance, plaiting Zepheus's mane with cerulean. Blaise had never seen the pegasi decorated before—their manes and tails usually hung loose. He watched Emmaline select a purple ribbon from the basket and then deftly start to work on her stallion's mane.

<Blue, I think,> Emrys commented, bumping Blaise with his muzzle.

"What?" Blaise blinked.

The pegasus gestured at the basket with his nose. <Get out the blue for Emmaline to use for my braids. Or . . .> Emrys paused, shaking his head so his mane went flying. <Do you have a waistcoat?>

What was Emrys going on about? "No."

<That's unfortunate. I suppose your blue duster will do in a pinch. Yes, the blue ribbon.>

Blaise rubbed his forehead. "Why are you worried about my duster?"

Emmaline glanced over at them, catching his half of the conversation. "Emrys probably wants to match you. The pegasi aren't the only ones dressing up for the occasion."

Oh. That made sense. Blaise's cheeks warmed with a flush of embarrassment. To cover it, he bent over and pretended to sort through the basket until he found a blue ribbon buried at the bottom.

Emrys detected his discomfiture and craned his head around. <I want to match you because you are my rider. Even if you can't ride me tonight. We'll figure something out.>

Blaise nodded, stroking Emrys's neck. He needed a change of topic. "How's your magic going?" He glanced at Emmaline, watching as she artfully braided Oberidon's mane.

She paused, making a face. "Some of it's easier than others. I thought learning would be simple. Instinctive, you know?"

He understood. Some elements of magic were instinctive, but others required practice. He was glad he was over that hump. "You'll get it."

She nodded, but her lips puffed out with dissatisfaction. "It's hard. I already have to learn to shoot as good as him. Now I have the same magic. I don't know how I can live up to that." Her voice was low, so it didn't carry far.

"Do you have to live up to it?"

Emmaline tied the purple ribbon into an obnoxiously enormous bow. Oberidon looked over his shoulder, huffing with pleasure. "I'm *his* daughter. I live in his shadow. I have to live up to that."

Somehow, Blaise didn't think those were Jack's expectations. "Just do the best you can, Em."

She nodded, and their conversation stalled. In silence, Emmaline picked up the blue ribbon Blaise had selected and started to work on

Emrys. She made quick work of it, and before long the pegasi were saddled for the parade.

Emmaline shoved blond hair from her eyes as she finished adjusting the last strap. "Now it's our turn to get cleaned up so we can look as good as this lot."

Blaise parted ways from Emmaline, walking back to the bakery. Emrys tagged along, declaring that he would oversee the wardrobe matters from outside.

Shaking his head with amusement, Blaise carefully climbed up to the loft and pawed through his limited selection of clothing. He found a white dress shirt with a high collar and paired it with dark blue canvas trousers, his duster, and hat. To appease Emrys, he held the items to the window to meet the stallion's approval. With Emrys's blessing, he changed and decided the pegasus was right—a waistcoat would complete the look. Something to pick up in the future. Blaise consulted his small mirror and decided he looked presentable, all things considered.

Emrys bobbed his head with approval when he returned. <You'll do.>

Together, they set off to the town square where the other riders were already astride their mounts. Emrys rested his head against Blaise's chest for a long moment before trotting to join the group of saddleless pegasi. Blaise wondered if Emrys was disappointed to be stuck with the younger colts who hadn't bonded with a rider yet.

"Must be frustrating," a familiar voice said.

Just what he needed. Blaise angled to Jefferson Cole, who stood behind his left shoulder. The entrepreneur hadn't stopped by the bakery since the ill-fated training session, and Blaise had thought perhaps he'd left town. So much for that idea. "What?"

Cole jutted his chin to indicate Emrys. "You can't ride your pegasus at the Feast of Flight." Was it just Blaise's imagination, or did he sound envious?

Blaise shrugged. "I'd rather keep my feet on the ground."

Cole tilted his head. "To each his own, I suppose." He paused. "I was sorry to hear of your injury. I hope you're feeling better."

Self-conscious, Blaise rubbed the fabric of the duster over his wound. He didn't want to be reminded of it, not here in this crowd of people. The very thought that his attacker was likely out there somewhere made him want to turn tail and flee to his loft. "I'm fine."

The other man gave him a speculative look. "Good. That's good."

Blaise nodded, keeping his gaze fixed on the column of pegasi and riders as they made their final preparations. He hoped Cole would take the hint and stop talking. He felt the other man's eyes on him for a moment, but when Blaise glanced back, he had drifted away.

Raven and Vixen led the top of the column on their pegasi, Naureus and Alekon. Jack was positioned behind them on Zepheus, with Emmaline and Oberidon at his side. Blaise almost didn't recognize Jack. The rough-and-ready outlaw had exchanged his usual clothing for a more refined fashion. He wore a long black coat over a striped gold vest. The white shirt beneath boasted a high collar like Blaise's, but Jack tastefully accented it with a black puff tie. Jack completed the look with a black top hat perched atop his head.

Emmaline had dressed up too, which made Blaise glad he had changed. She wore tan twill riding pants that fanned around her legs, a cream-colored camisole covered by a brown corset, and a brown derby. A thick gold necklace hung around her neck; golden bracelets clung to her wrists. Blaise wondered if those were spoils from Jack's outlawing.

Raven and Vixen's steeds surged into the air. It reminded Blaise of watching a flock of geese rise up from a pond, the way all the pegasi burst forward into the air together. The crowd around him murmured in appreciation at the spectacle of pegasi circling overhead. Blaise kept track of Emrys, alternately proud and feeling more left out than he thought he would. He had to remind himself of the way his stomach lurched during flight.

The column of pegasi landed in pairs, trotting down the street to a cacophony of cheers, applause, and whistles. The wild fanfare would have spooked normal horses, but the pegasi reveled in the attention. Tails flagged behind the stallions like banners, ears pricked forward and eyes bright as they pranced. Blaise admitted they made a stunning sight.

Everyone ended up at the town square. Planks of wood laid out atop barrels created long tables laden with a buffet, pennants and streamers fluttering in the breeze. Blaise's cakes were at the end of the line, ready to be enjoyed. The pegasi even had their own special tables set up at the festivity.

"There'll be fireworks later," Hannah chirped as she waved a greeting to Blaise. "After the music."

"I've never seen anything like this before."

"I figured when I saw you gawking. But now it's time to eat." Hannah pointed to the line forming at the buffet. "Go enjoy. I can't wait to dig into one of those glorious cakes you made."

He thanked her for the information as Emrys sidled up next to Oberidon at a table that was covered in an array of sweet treats. Blaise joined the serving line, impressed by the spread that Celeste, Mindy, and Abe had assembled. There was boiled mutton, roast beef, fried apples and bacon, goose with olives, chicken stuffed with truffles, oysters, baked apples, asparagus, green peas, hot oatmeal mush, and the cakes. Blaise filled his plate and found a place to sit.

The food was delicious, and as he ate, he reflected he had never seen so many joyful people together all at once. It was magical. It was something he had never expected to be a part of. The sense of belonging warmed him.

After everyone was sated, they moved the makeshift tables into a new arrangement to create a stage. A handful of people climbed onto it, some of the Ringleaders among their number.

Kur Agur and Vixen took their places near the front. Raven carried a fiddle and stood behind them, resting the instrument atop his shoulder. Butch the undertaker joined them with a harmonica and Nadine with a zither. Hannah and a few other young women took to the stage, dressed in short skirts with riding breeches beneath and corsets that allowed freedom of movement.

Jefferson Cole sat a few seats down, alone since most of his dinner companions were now onstage. He noticed Blaise's sideways glance and offered a friendly smile, then slid down the bench until he was closer.

Blaise still didn't know what he thought about the businessman, but it would be in poor taste to ignore him. He tipped his head to indicate the stage. "What's next?"

"Music." Cole cocked his head as the performers tuned their instruments, angling his body toward Blaise. "The dessert cakes . . . were those your creations?"

Blaise glanced at the table where the last cake still stood, only the lowest tier remaining. The revelers had demolished the four others. "It's my recipe and it was made under my direction, but Nadine's not letting me do much right now. The sugar sculptures were all Reuben."

Cole's eyebrows rose, intrigued. "Is that so? You and your employees are exceedingly talented. You should be proud." He leaned forward conspiratorially. "Those cakes would stack up against the best of the best in Ganland."

Blaise blinked in surprise. "You think so?"

"I know so," Cole replied, his gaze sliding from the cakes back to Blaise. "You're looking rather delicious tonight yourself."

Blaise's face flamed at the odd compliment. He rubbed the back of his neck, uncertain about the attention.

"Is this your first Feast of Flight?" The businessman's acute eyes stayed on Blaise even as he changed the topic.

"Yes."

Cole's face lit up. "You're in for a treat. Every outlaw town celebrates, though this is my first time seeing Itude's. I try not to miss this holiday."

He clasped his hands in front of him. "We don't have this where I come from."

Ganland. That served as a reminder that Cole was an outsider. Blaise made a mental note to remain aloof.

But the entrepreneur was right—it was a spectacle unlike any Blaise had seen before. He didn't know if the group had practiced together beforehand—if they had, he hadn't seen or heard them. The musicians played a spirited song, Vixen and Kur providing vocals. Vixen's voice was sultry, and Kur's was beautiful but haunting. Hannah and the other women danced along to the music, short skirts flapping and whirling about with their energetic movement.

The audience clapped and cheered along, and Blaise found himself swept up with the crowd, doing the same. His arms pebbled with goose-flesh at the harmonic magic created by the performers. He recognized it wasn't true magic, not like his. But there was an ethereal beauty to the music that made every listener feel as if they had cast a spell over the town. The entire town was filled with a warmth and revelry that made him feel more secure and welcome than he had in his life.

The group played several more songs, and before long everyone was dancing along. The dancers hopped off the stage and selected partners. Hannah made a beeline for Blaise, grabbing his hand.

"C'mon!"

His eyes widened, and he sputtered, jerking away his trembling hand. "I—no, I've never danced before. There's no way I can dance like you just did." The dancers had been so *close*. Blaise shook his head, his pulse racing. "And I just . . . can't."

"I wouldn't expect you to. I know you're hurt and have to take it easy." Hannah's face clouded at his panic, but she gave him a circumspect look and nodded. "If you change your mind, I'm around."

His shoulders relaxed at her words, and he settled back onto the bench away from Cole, aware that he had witnessed the whole spectacle. Blaise sat and sipped his punch, his nerves slowly calming as he listened to the music.

After the song ended and the musicians prepared their next tune, Cole slid down the long bench until he was near Blaise. "Are you okay? Is your injury bothering you?"

The concern in the other man's voice caught Blaise off guard. He looked into Cole's face and discovered the crinkle of his brow matched his words. "No. I . . ." Did he really want to go into that here? Not really. But it had been an awkward scene, and Blaise feared more questions. "I don't like to be touched."

"Ah, I see," Cole said, tone light. He leaned back, quiet for a few minutes as he watched the festivities. "I've known others with similar issues."

Blaise blinked. "You have?" As soon as the words left his mouth, he regretted them. He shouldn't be talking to Jefferson Cole.

The entrepreneur nodded. "Yes. I've teamed up with a politician in Ganland to try to end trafficking." He picked up his cup, swirling the contents as he spoke. "I'm friends with several trafficking victims, and I know of at least one who won't let anyone touch her. Even those she trusts."

Blaise hadn't expected that. The way Jack spoke of the Confederation painted everyone with a broad brush—no redeeming values whatsoever. Deep down, he knew that couldn't be true of everyone. "Oh." He tried to think of something else to say but failed. Blaise was too focused on the fact that here was someone who had some understanding of his peculiarity.

Cole waved a hand. "But that's an unpleasant topic. Not one to dwell on tonight." He smiled. "Have you had any further thoughts on our discussion the other day?"

Blaise was suddenly very glad for the riot of noise all around them. It made the question less daunting. "I . . . I'm afraid I must decline. I'm happy here."

"That's too bad." Cole sighed. Blaise feared the answer might upset him, but he continued to watch the dancers, tapping a foot to the downbeat. "Have you been in Itude long?"

"Only since summer." Blaise glanced away, chewing on his lower lip as he tried to think of a way to excuse himself without appearing rude.

"Who taught you to bake like that?"

Blaise frowned, puzzled by the question. "You really want to know?"

Cole smiled at him. "I do. I enjoy learning about other people. That's part of why I travel. The world is full of people with interesting pursuits. And I take it baking is yours."

"It's a better pursuit than magic," Blaise muttered.

"I'm sorry, what was that? Couldn't hear you over the music."

Blaise cleared his throat. "Um, I taught myself to bake. I've been doing it for years since—" He broke off, not wanting to get into his past. "It's calming. I enjoy it."

Cole tilted his head but thankfully didn't ask about Blaise's omission. "Impressive that you taught yourself."

"It was a lot of trial and error. And a lot of mistakes. The recipes in the cookbooks I had made it sound easier than it was at first."

Cole chuckled. "That sounds like an accurate description of life."

The musicians played several more songs, and Blaise continued his conversation with Jefferson Cole until the last notes of music faded into the night. The festivities concluded with a stunning firework show, and once the last sparks fell harmlessly to the ground, the crowd dispersed. Blaise excused himself and followed the other pegasus riders as they took their charges back to the stables, painstakingly removing the ribbons and braids so they wouldn't tangle through the night. He hovered near Emmaline, wishing that he could do more than offer moral support.

<What did you think of Feast of Flight?> Emrys asked as the last ribbon unraveled from his mane.

Blaise yawned. "It was . . . nice. I haven't felt like I belonged somewhere for a long time. But I did tonight."

Emrys sighed, content. <It's good to belong.>

Blaise agreed. It was.

CHAPTER THIRTY

Cheap Thrill

Blaise pushed open the door to the Broken Horn, the boisterous sounds of drinking and gambling rolling over him. He wove through the crowd and grabbed a stool at the end of the bar. Clover ambled over to him, puzzled. "You don't drink."

Blaise managed a small smile. She knew him well. "Still don't. I wanted a change of pace from the diner, though. Can I have a plate of whatever Abe is making for the special tonight? And do you have any of the raspberry vinegar switchel to drink?"

She studied him for a long moment, one of her ears flicking back and forth in thought. "I do." Clover tapped the bar before turning to call the order back to Abe.

"This seat taken?"

Blaise turned, startled to find Jefferson Cole pointing to the neighboring barstool. "Yours for the taking." He decided this wasn't the time to be choosy with his friends, and he couldn't help but recall the companionable conversation they had shared at the Feast of Flight.

Cole's mouth parted in pleasure, and he bellied up to the bar. Clover came back over and regarded him courteously, but lacking the usual warmth she showed her customers. "Will you be having the usual tonight?"

"Please," Cole replied. Clover called another order to Abe, then surprised Blaise by producing a wineglass from beneath the counter. They were used so infrequently at the Broken Horn that Blaise recalled only washing a single one in his time there. The Knossan uncorked a bottle of wine and poured it.

"I'm going to miss this." Cole sighed, picking up the glass and swirling the contents. "Knossan dandelion wine is a rare delicacy."

Blaise raised a brow. He didn't know much about wines, much less that Clover even stocked Knossan wines. Cole took a blissful sip.

"I wanted to tell you I'm leaving in the morning. But the offer still stands."

In the days after the Feast of Flight, Blaise had thought more on Cole's offer. It was a definite temptation, and if he hadn't found a place to belong in Itude, he would have accepted in a heartbeat. "Thank you, but I'll be staying here. I'm happy here."

Cole pursed his lips, forehead furrowing. He looked as if he wanted to say something, but Clover's arrival was heralded by the sound of her hooves. She slid two plates of the daily special in front of them.

Cole cut into his beefsteak and took a bite, pointing his fork at Blaise. He spoke when he finished chewing. "I understand. But I'm very serious about going into business with you. The cookies alone would be excellent sellers."

Blaise took a swig from his drink. "Why's that? I don't understand why anyone would buy cookies made by a maverick."

Cole's lips slid into an indulgent grin, the corners of his eyes crinkling. "They would sell better *because* they're made by a maverick. Although, perhaps for branding we'd call you an outlaw. It sounds more roguish." Blaise's confusion must have been obvious on his face because the other man pressed on. "Call it what you will—romance, prestige, a cheap thrill. There are those who will be titillated by the thought of eating something made by an outlaw. They're the same people who will only buy wines from certain vineyards or from a 'good year'. Also, the ones with the deepest pockets." He snapped his fingers as if having a revelation. "If you don't want to bake for me, maybe we could work out a licensing deal. We could market something made by another baker, but under your name—"

"No." Blaise didn't understand half of what Cole was blathering about, but he understood that much. He didn't want his name attached to anyone else's inferior baked goods.

Cole chuckled, the sound melodious and warm. "Fair enough. Is there anything I could offer that would pique your interest?"

Blaise pursed his lips, considering. Was there? He had what he wanted now, and that was enough. "I don't think so."

The entrepreneur sighed. "If you change your mind, let me know. You'd never want for a thing."

It wasn't about the money. Blaise made enough to get by—he paid his monthly lease to Jack, paid his employees, and bought more supplies for himself and the bakery. Beyond that, he didn't need a lot. But Blaise appreciated having options. "If I change my mind, you'll be the first to know."

Cole gave him a dashing smile. "Excellent. I'll be in Rainbow Flat for the next few weeks, and then after that, I'll be traveling. But your postmaster can always send a letter to my residence in Nera. The message will reach me, eventually."

Blaise nodded. It was strange to have someone take such an avid interest in his baking. Flattering, but strange.

Cole finished his meal and excused himself, saying he had to get back to his room to pack. Once the other man had left, Clover plodded back and leaned over the bar.

"He's very interested in you," the Knossan said, her tone neutral.

Blaise glanced up the stairs as Cole retreated. "He wants to go into business with me."

Clover snorted. "The Gannish always do. They dangle coins before humans like a carrot before a donkey." She regarded him curiously. "What will you do?"

"Stay here." Blaise looked over the busy saloon. He liked the people of Itude. He *belonged* somewhere, finally.

She nodded, as if he had said the right thing. "That is good. I think Itude needs you, just as you need Itude."

Her reassuring words gave him pause. Blaise wanted to ask her what she meant, but another customer flagged Clover for a refill. He watched her clop over, taking another sip of his drink. Maybe it was going to be okay.

CHAPTER THIRTY-ONE

Accusations

Blaise

The only downside of having friends, Blaise decided, was that sometimes they persuaded him into questionable life choices. Last night, for example. Emmaline and Reuben convinced him to attend the weekly dance at the town square, which extended into the wee hours of the morning. And though he didn't do more than talk to people and watch the dancers, he had enjoyed himself and stayed the whole time.

Fortunately, he wasn't alone in his exhaustion. Emmaline dragged herself in as the oven was warming. She looked just as tired, so he decided they would be a good pair. Neither one of them said much as they set about their usual tasks. It was too early, and they'd had too little sleep to even consider making coherent conversation. Maybe after coffee.

Once the first loaves of bread were in the oven, Blaise took a breather and stumbled over to the diner to grab two cups of coffee. Emmaline normally didn't drink coffee, but Mindy added sugar and cream to make it enticing. Emmaline was so tired she didn't scoff at the cup when he pressed it into her hands. She tipped it back and took a sip.

"Mmm," she murmured, appreciating the sweetness. "Doesn't taste like dirt."

"I'd never hand it to you black." His brain felt a little more willing to string together thoughts. That was an improvement.

Emmaline took another sip, then sighed as if it had made all the difference in the world. She quirked an eyebrow at him, mischievous. "Are you sweet on Jefferson Cole? I would have expected you might have an interest in someone like Hannah, but you kept to yourself last night."

Blaise froze. "What?"

She gave him a pointed look. "I saw him talking to you at the Feast of Flight. What did he call you? *Delicious*, if I remember right?"

Blaise almost dropped his cup of coffee. "He was talking about our cakes. Were you spying?"

She fluttered her eyelashes, all innocence. "I was just walking by. And he was definitely not talking about our cakes at that point." Blaise turned away, setting down his coffee and pulling out the bag of sugar. Emmaline made an exasperated sound. "What's wrong? It was nice. He *likes* you."

Blaise shook his head. He didn't want to get into his confused thoughts on the subject, not now. Emmaline couldn't understand what it was like to be scorned by everyone during his youth. He'd missed out on the formative years of flirting and relationship-building, and he had no idea how to even respond—or if he wanted to. Sex didn't appeal to him as it apparently did to others. And while Jefferson Cole was easy on the eyes, he was also the enemy.

"I can't talk about this right now," Blaise finally said, picking up the empty water bucket sitting beside the door. "I'll refill the wash water."

She gave him a puzzled look, then shrugged. "Okay. Sorry, didn't know it was a sensitive subject. Since you don't show an interest in anyone else, I thought it was nice."

Blaise shook his head as he headed to the cistern, the bucket swinging beside him. Truth be told, he hadn't minded talking to Cole at the Feast of Flight. The man had gone from intimidating entrepreneur to companionable conversationalist in such a short time that he wasn't sure what to think about it. It was like Cole was two different people.

He placed his empty bucket beneath the spigot and turned it on, mulling over his feelings as water splashed against metal. Emmaline thought Cole *liked* him? As in, was *attracted* to him? Blaise couldn't possibly see why. He just wanted to go into business together. That was all.

Once the bucket was full, Blaise turned and started back toward the bakery. He was stepping inside the door when suddenly the air around him seemed to ripple and the floorboards shimmied beneath his feet, bucking like a cavorting pegasus. Blaise lurched forward, nearly spilling the bucket's contents.

Emmaline yelped, a falling pot almost hitting her on the head. Blaise set the bucket down beside the washstand and they traded startled looks.

"What was that?" Emmaline's voice was small and unnerved.

Blaise shook his head, a rush of frightened adrenaline in his veins as he hurried to the bakery windows. One of them had cracked from the concussive force of whatever had happened. That was a concern for later. Shouts echoed outside, people rushing up the street past the bakery.

"Bloody buggering basilisks!" Emmaline exclaimed softly, peering out behind him.

A cloud of dust rose in a plume over the town to the east, tinged red with dirt. It was close—so close that when Blaise opened the door, dust billowed into the bakery, choking them. He slammed the door shut again and scrambled up the stairs to the loft, grabbing a pair of bandannas. He tossed one to Emmaline, and she tied it over her nose in silence.

The dust cleared a little when they poked their heads outside again, though the morning light filtered through the haze. Emmaline gasped as they both realized that Itude's skyline was missing its most prominent feature: the wind-pump that towered four stories over the rest of the town.

Blaise stared, a chill racing down his spine. He had been mere yards from the wind-pump only minutes ago. *I could have been crushed.*

"We should help," Emmaline murmured, her words prodding him out of his frightening revelation.

"Let's gather up the leftovers into baskets." Blaise withdrew into the bakery, coughing at the remnants of dust in his throat. Emmaline didn't respond, eyes downcast with worry as she found clean linen while Blaise pulled out a pair of wicker baskets to pack loaves of bread and cookies. He stalked over to the oven and opened it, removing a pair of pies destined to never finish baking. Blaise didn't want to risk leaving them unattended in the oven. That done, he extinguished the fire.

They each slung a basket over their shoulders and raced out the door to join other responders surging to the site of the wind-pump. Pegasi milled around, some of them using their bulk to form a perimeter around the disaster. Parents tugged away curious children, taking them back to their homes on the outskirts.

Blaise set his basket down in the shade of the barber shop awning, taking in the heartrending sight. Itude's wind-pump had been unlike any windmill he had seen before. Not only tall, it was broad-based, constructed of stone blocks cemented together. Blaise had never been inside, but he had heard in passing that there were gears and things that made the whole thing work to pump water up from the river below to fill the town's large cistern. It was sturdy and built to last, meant to sustain the town for decades.

Now the wind-pump was in ruins. It had collapsed, tumbling like a tower of blocks kicked down by a child. The heavy stone facade had smashed through the icehouse, though it had somehow fallen clear of the town laundry. One of the steel blades—its length greater than two pegasi standing nose to rump—pierced the side of the nearby boarding house.

The Ringleaders were already on site. Clover was there, too, bracing her leathery hands against the stone, straining to tug them off the icehouse.

"Monty!" A woman wailed, running over from the houses outside the town proper. Blaise swallowed when he recognized the ice mage's wife, Eleanor.

The rest of the day was a sobering blur. Yesterday's celebration was all but forgotten. Vixen steered anyone away that she deemed unnecessary. Jack was there, though Nadine tried to send him off. He ignored her and did what he could to help. When Emmaline saw her father, she hurried over and stayed near him.

Blaise helped however he could, though Nadine kept her eagle eye on him as well. Vixen bade him come around to the back of the icehouse to use his magic to break some of the larger chunks of rubble. Donkeys and mules in harnesses appeared, and they hauled debris out of the way.

Late in the afternoon, Blaise watched Jack approach Butch, the town undertaker. He had a talent for necromancy, according to Emmaline.

"Any news?" Jack jutted his chin toward the crumpled icehouse. They were still struggling to move the larger pieces of the wind-pump off the icehouse without causing further collapse.

"Monty's not mine yet." Butch's voice was strained.

Jack's eyes slid to Emmaline, who was staring at the icehouse with determination, clutching something in her hand.

"You okay?" Blaise walked over to her, concerned about the intensity in her eyes.

She bit her lip. He realized she was holding a hastily made doll—no, a poppet—in her hand, wrapped in a light blue bandanna. "Maybe."

Blaise suddenly understood. "Your magic?"

Emmaline nodded the tiniest bit. "Doing what I can. I have him, but it was easier when it was Daddy."

Blaise blinked in surprise. "Do you know where Monty is?"

She shook her head. "No. Just . . . under there. He's bleeding and unconscious."

That was impressive. And she was bolstering him as she had her father.

"I see him!" Kur Agur howled. He and Clover led the vanguard of rescuers and moved with renewed purpose as they shifted more rubble.

Before long, a blood-covered arm poked through the wreckage. Clover pulled Monty out gently, his head lolling as she tried to support his neck. One of his legs was bent at an unnatural angle. They loaded him onto a stretcher and hauled him off to Nadine's clinic for treatment. Eleanor followed along, thankful tears streaming down her face.

Blaise felt mentally and physically exhausted. He looked up and realized it was almost sundown. They had been at their frantic rescue for hours.

Vixen spoke the words everyone had been holding back. "How did this happen?"

Jack's eyes glittered, dangerous. "I don't know. But I intend to find out."

"How will we get water now?" a woman wailed.

Everyone was quiet as they contemplated the disturbing question. The wind-pump provided the lifeblood of Itude. Water was one of the most necessary resources.

Raven glanced at the large cistern standing behind the laundry, both of which had been relatively unaffected by the disaster. "We should have enough for the next few days, but we'll have to supplement by hauling water up from the river."

"We can probably do it with donkey trains and help from the pegasi," Vixen agreed.

"Gotta prioritize rebuilding the wind-pump." This from Jack, who scowled as he surveyed the ruins, his face unreadable. "I'll send word to Charlie Creagen in Thorn and get supplies ordered." He sighed, taking off his hat to run a hand through his sweaty hair. "Won't be cheap."

The Ringleaders moved away, engrossed in discussion. Emmaline walked over to Blaise, toting an empty basket on her shoulder. "Need some help to clean up the bakery?"

He considered it, then shook his head. It would be peaceful to clean up by himself. His nerves were rattled after the long hours of rescue work. "I should be fine. I'll take the basket back and see you in the morning."

"Will do," Emmaline replied, handing over the basket to him.

He headed down the street toward the bakery, trying not to glance at the skyline that was now empty of the massive wind-pump that had so seamlessly provided Itude with all of their water needs. He hoped that it could be rebuilt soon.

Footsteps heavy from exhaustion, he almost didn't notice the folded bit of paper tucked into the door frame. He slowed, pulling it free and opening it.

We know what you did, Breaker.

Blaise stared at the words and reread it. His mouth went dry as bitter memories reared up. Not again. He wasn't responsible for this disaster.

No. No, he wasn't. He controlled his magic now—he had done *nothing* to the wind-pump. Blaise gritted his teeth, wadding the note into a ball. He shouldered open the door and slammed it behind him, the glass rattling from the force. He set down the basket and braced his hands against the table, ignoring the dusting of flour from earlier in the day.

Blaise inhaled slowly to calm himself, but it was no use. Accusations like these were supposed to be behind him. He thought they had accepted him in Itude.

<Blaise?> Emrys's mental voice called out from nearby.

He looked up and saw the stallion outside the back window of the bakery. Blaise didn't feel like talking to anyone at the moment, whether they had two or four legs. But he didn't want to push the pegasus away, so he straightened and opened the window. He said nothing, though.

The pegasus craned his head inside, snorting. <What's wrong? Are you hurt? Are you upset you never got to finish baking those pies? I'd be happy to eat them for you as-is.> His muzzle quested toward the unfinished pies.

Blaise slid a pie tin over to the stallion. "It's nothing."

Emrys nibbled straight from the tin, velvety lips smacking. <Here's a tip: don't lie to a telepath. Also, this is delicious, so thanks.>

Blaise scrubbed at his face with one hand. "Someone thinks I'm responsible for the wind-pump."

The pegasus licked the tin clean of crumbs, savoring the puddles of oozing apple filling that seeped out. <Is it true?>

"Of course not!" Blaise couldn't conceal the hurt in his voice.

Emrys bobbed his head. <So what are you worried about? And can I have that other pie?>

Blaise scooted the second pie over. "It's just the way humans work. If one person thinks I did it, others will think the same. Even if it's not true." He shook his head. "It's what happened when I lived in Bristle—why I couldn't go to school anymore. Or into town. Even if something wasn't my fault, I took the blame."

<That's stupid,> Emrys pointed out.

"It's the way it is." Blaise picked up a pot that had fallen from the wall hours ago. He glanced around at the messy kitchen. Right, he was supposed to be cleaning.

<Vixen and Jack are familiar with your magic. They'll know this is baseless.> Emrys had more confidence than Blaise felt.

Emrys didn't realize it, but that was exactly the problem. They were familiar with his magic. And in Blaise's experience, all it took was someone knowing about his magic for it to become a problem.

CHAPTER THIRTY-TWO
On the Hunt

Jack

The next morning dawned with a sunrise of fuchsia and gold reflections on wispy clouds, Itude's skyline forever changed. The wind-pump missing from the horizon made Jack even more irritable. After Emmaline left for the bakery, he headed out to the site of destruction with fresh eyes. He wasn't the only one with that idea. Kur Agur raised a clawed hand in greeting as Jack approached.

"Find anything yet?" Jack watched as the Theilian cast around the area, nose low to the ground.

Kur straightened, lips curled in distaste. "As you would expect, there are too many mixed scents. If I had a chance to cast for a scent trail before everyone arrived, I might have had more luck."

Jack nodded. It was unfortunate, but they couldn't go back and change that. He stepped over a pile of rubble, examining the base of the wind-pump that still stood.

"It makes little sense. The wind-pump was just inspected a month ago, and we found nothing. It's withstood gale-force winds. There was nothing unusual about yesterday. What changed?"

Kur twitched an ear. "An earthquake? I've never experienced one."

Jack had. He shook his head. "No. The entire town would have felt it. Damnation, the entire town would've gotten dumped into the canyon in that case." That was a nightmare to even consider.

"Hmm." Kur cocked his head, stalking around the circular base of the wind-pump widdershins.

Jack crouched down, scanning the debris trail for any clues that might tell him what caused the failure. He picked up a tiny green plant that seemed out of place among the rubble and turned it over in his hand. He had seen these before around the post office. "Do you scent anything like powder or fire? Dynamite?"

Kur tensed, the fur on his ruff rising. "You think someone would blow up the wind-pump?"

Jack narrowed his eyes.

"But Jefferson Cole is long gone," Kur argued.

Jack studied Kur's shaggy visage. "All the more reason to suspect him. Damn Salt-Iron dandy." *And more. So much more. Should I tell Kur?*

Kur ducked his head in acknowledgment. "But why would he do it? What's the motive? And furthermore, *how?*"

Jack snorted. "The *why* is not a far reach. If there's no water, it's hard to live here. If we can't live in Itude, we must go elsewhere. And a bunch of families traveling out of here would be child's play to capture." Not to mention that if anyone from the Confederation wanted to mine salt-iron in the Gutter in earnest, it would be easy to do so if Itude no longer existed. As Jack thought about it, that sounded right. With the Salt-Iron Confederation in Desina, it would be easy to move into the Gutter next. And as a bonus, they could snap up any of the families forced to leave town.

"As for the *how,*" Jack continued, tilting his head as he studied the scene, "that remains to be figured out."

Kur sneezed, then shook his head violently as if to rid his nose of whatever scent had agitated him. "I detect nothing that a normal human could have used to take down the wind-pump." He scratched behind one ear.

Jack frowned. "What do you smell?"

Kur barked a laugh. "Too many people. Grease. Blood. Something else that makes my nose tingle, but I can't place it."

"Is it magic?"

The Theilian considered. "I'm not sure what it is. Possibly magic, but if so, not one I have scented before."

Breaker, perhaps? Jack glanced over his shoulder at one of the large chunks Blaise had used his magic on the previous day to help the effort. It looked like the rest of the rubble. He kept his troubling thoughts private. Jack couldn't imagine the kid doing something like that. Even Jack would admit it was out of character. But Clover reported that Cole had met with Blaise before leaving town.

"I see the wheels turning in your head," Kur commented, leaning against a stabilized chunk of fallen wall.

Jack shook his head. "Just thinking is all."

"Will you share the trail you're stalking?"

"No."

Kur looked disappointed. "Fair enough. But remember that you must, if it will help the town."

Jack bristled. "I know what I'm about, wolf."

Kur gave him a toothy grin. "In that case, good hunting, Jack."

CHAPTER THIRTY-THREE

Parlor Tricks

Lamar

*Y*our instructions were simple. What is the delay?

Lamar Gaitwood glared at the offending dispatch in his hands. It was only two days old, courtesy of the amazing telegraph line recently completed to Ondin, the capital of Mella. Ondin was the closest city to Fort Courage, and express couriers hustled it across the remaining distance as quickly as possible. No one delayed a message from a Doyen of the Salt-Iron Council to a Commander.

Lamar prepared a thousand barb-tongued retorts, but he would never send them as much as he wished to. His elder brother was a righteous asshole, but he held the leash in the family. Lamar had magic, but Gregor . . . Gregor possessed *power*.

If only Gregor had been born with magic. Lamar reflected on it often. *He* was more cunning than Gregor. He had to be, to survive in a world where he wasn't an equal because of his magic. Theurgists were useful but inferior. Real men didn't rely on pretty parlor tricks.

Parlor tricks. As if imprisoning someone in a cage sizzling with magic strong enough to lock them inside their own bodies was a mere *trick*. The only thing that soothed his pride was the knowledge of how many of the elite *normals* suffered to his *parlor trick* before they handed him his command position.

And that brought him back to his current set of instructions. Gregor wanted the Breaker alive. Lamar preferred him dead. He was troublesome, a hassle. And he had made Lamar look like a novice. And beyond that, history supported Lamar's notion. Breakers were extinct for a reason—the Confederation had exterminated the lines that spawned them. Their magic was dangerously unpredictable.

It was all because of that wretched woman in Bristle. The Breaker's mother. *Marian Hawthorne.* Lamar knew the name as soon as he had heard it. The runaway alchemist was found after all this time.

Lamar had shipped her off to Izhadell, with Gregor pleased by the alchemist's recovery. Alchemist Hawthorne thought she had been so slick, passing herself off as a simple apothecary in the little podunk town. But now she was back in Confederation hands, where she belonged. Lamar liked when everyone was in their proper place. It made things right in the world.

That made him think of Jack, who had somehow found himself in league with the Breaker. Jack, the formerly loyal Confederation theurgist turned traitor. After everything Phinora had done for him—trained him in the ways of his foul magic, fed him, sheltered him—and he turned his back on the harmony of the Confederation that they had stood for. Lamar had even given Jack a chance to come back into the fold when he had captured him years before, but the outlaw had refused.

Lamar tilted his head, considering the dispatch in his hands. Gregor wanted the Breaker. Lamar wanted Jack to be punished. Perhaps the two were not mutually exclusive.

An idea began to take shape as he rifled through a sheaf of old informational dispatches. It would require a favor from Gregor, but the end goal would be one that his brother couldn't refuse. Getting his forces to Jack's little town would be problematic by foot. Not so from the air.

He found the page, eyes alight with avarice at the illustration with the label *Warbird.* The latest technological marvel from Cole Productions. A fast, efficient way to move troops across any terrain.

The warbird looked very much like a ship out of water, and perhaps it was. Its industrious designer had included an elaborate diagram of the vessel, and Lamar gave it a cursory look. He expected the leviathan of an airship to require magic, but that didn't seem to be the case. The article declared it to be steam-powered, taking advantage of groups of spinning blades—five on each side of the ship, encased in protective steel cylinders

—to stay airborne. The hull was reinforced with magic to ward against attack.

Lamar considered it. A working prototype was in testing for use. The military hoped to create another version that would serve as a gunship eventually, but first, they wanted to see how this vessel fared.

He smiled. Lamar knew exactly what he was going to ask for. And as soon as his operative notified him that the plan to separate the Breaker from the Dollmaker had succeeded, Lamar hoped everything would be in place to make his move.

CHAPTER THIRTY-FOUR

Sorcerer

Blaise

ornings in the bakery became uncharacteristically quiet. Mindy made a point to come over each morning and order the usual amount of fresh bread to use in the diner, but aside from that, there was a marked decrease in the number of regulars stopping by.

Blaise packed the bread for the diner in a basket, spreading linen over it to retain the warmth. Emmaline was in the midst of preparing a pie, and Reuben was helping one of their now-rare customers, so Blaise hitched the basket onto his shoulder. "Be right back. Going to take this next door."

Emmaline lifted a flour-covered hand in acknowledgement. "Maybe stop by the mercantile afterward. We're running low on strawberry preserves."

Blaise nodded, pushing through the door. He paused, lips pursed as he looked up and down the street at the townspeople going about their daily lives. A line of pack mules waited outside the stables, waterskins filled to almost bursting from the river below attached to the harnesses on their backs as they waited their turn to have the contents emptied into the cistern. Wagons rattled down the street, dogs barked, and the sound of voices rang out. Everyone had adapted to their harsh new reality while they waited for the promised wind-pump repairs. Life had returned to a tentative, nervous new version of normal. Except not for Blaise.

He had been hopeful that business would pick up again at the bakery, but the townspeople were spooked. Jack and Kur had been unable to uncover the cause of the collapse—the only conclusion they drew was that it wasn't natural. And aside from the accusatory note, no one said a word to Blaise about the matter, but he could read the writing on the wall. The bakery's former regulars dwindled to only a handful. People outright avoided him.

Blaise had one hand on the doorknob to the diner when a booming voice froze him in place.

"—you can guarantee we'll stop eating here if you continue to buy from that *sorcerer* next door!"

Swallowing, Blaise dropped his hand and took a sideways step to one of the windows. He leaned over just enough to peek inside. Mindy and Celeste stood, arms crossed in defiance, in the middle of a ring of men dressed in the dusty outfits of wranglers and farmhands. A stocky, bearded man had taken point on the mob, shaking his finger in Mindy's face.

"I'll remind you, Silas, to not use such language in public. If any children were around, I would wash your mouth out with lye soap," Mindy snapped, eyes narrowed.

Silas didn't cower from her threat, but he did lose a little of his bluster. One of his fellows spoke up. "Pardon his language, Miss Mindy, but he has the right of it. Sure as the sun rises, the Breaker had to be the one to tear down the wind-pump. That, or Faedra herself did the deed, and that ain't likely."

Blaise trembled at the anonymous man's words, almost dropping the basket of bread. Heart pounding, he retreated from the window, fighting back tears as he headed back to the bakery. But he didn't go in immediately—Emmaline and Reuben were there, and he didn't think he could face them. Instead, he went around the back, to the lean-to that sheltered his firewood. He sat under the overhang, legs curled up against his chest and his face in his hands.

It was Bristle all over again, and this time he had no one to shield him from the growing tide of public disdain. Blaise rubbed his eyes with the heels of his hands, racking his brain for what to do. His life had already been endangered, and now this.

"Blaise?"

He wiped away his tears, trying in vain to compose himself as he lifted his head to look at Emmaline. "What?" Gods, why did she have to see him like this? A flush of embarrassment reddened his cheeks.

She stared down at him, her head tilted. "What's wrong?"

Blaise shook his head, unwilling to repeat the hurtful words he had heard. That would only make them more real, enhance how deeply they cut, and he couldn't bear that. "I don't want to talk about it right now. We can close the bakery early. In fact, you and Reuben can head out, and I'll clean up." He straightened, his hands braced against a bundle of firewood.

Emmaline scowled, her braid rocking gently in the chill wind. "Whatever's wrong, you can tell me. We're friends, and that's what friends *do.*"

Friends. She tossed the word at him like a rescuer throwing a rope to a drowning man. Blaise desperately wanted to grab at it, wanted to be pulled from the nightmare of his life, but he was afraid if he did so, he would pull her down with him. And that wasn't fair. So instead, he looked away. "I need time alone."

"Blaise!" she protested.

His magic swarmed beneath his palms, agitated and unstable. Unbidden, it flowed from his hands and into the firewood, splintering the kindling with a piercing crack. Hissing, Blaise pulled his hands away, tucking them beneath his armpits. "*Please*, Em. I–I can't right now."

She took a step backward, the skin on her chin puckering with concern. But she didn't argue. Instead, she nodded. "If . . . if that's what you want."

"It is." Blaise stared at his feet, quivering at his loss of control.

The crunch and soft slap of boot heels on the ground heralded her exit. Blaise stayed where he was for another half hour, just to give them ample time to leave before he entered. After checking the time on his pocket watch, he rose and slowly approached the back door of the bakery. He opened it cautiously, listening for any hint that Emmaline or Reuben had stayed behind to confront him. But the bakery was quiet, and though he had told Emmaline he would clean up, they had done the job already. The kitchen area was freshly swept, not even so much as a dusting of flour visible. At least it still held the comforting scents of yeast and sugar.

Blaise sank down to the floor, his back flat against one of the cabinets. His gaze drifted from the black and white checked floor to the cast-iron pots and pans hanging on pegs to the washbasin across the room. He had thought he'd found what his life had been missing—acceptance, friends, a place to belong. But like all things in his life, it didn't last. His magic fractured everything eventually.

What could he do? Blaise swallowed, thinking back to Jefferson Cole's parting words. "*If you change your mind, let me know.*" He straightened up as he reached a painful conclusion. Rising from the floor, Blaise wobbled over to grab the calendar atop the sales counter. Checking the date, he realized Jefferson Cole would still be in Rainbow Flat.

He took a shaky breath, sliding the calendar back to its proper place. *Running away again.* Blaise shook his head. No. Not running away. He was running *toward* another chance. And maybe this time the shadows of his past wouldn't haunt him. With his decision made, Blaise climbed up to the loft to pull out his old go-bag.

<YOU DIDN'T HAVE TO BRIBE ME WITH COOKIES, YOU KNOW,> EMRYS pointed out as Blaise hoisted the outlaw saddle onto his back. The stallion crunched on one of the bakery's unsold treats, tail swishing with contentment.

Blaise said nothing. His lips pressed into a firm line as he focused on the task at hand. He knew he was doing the best thing for the town by leaving, but that knowledge offered him little comfort. He had thought Itude was different, and it hurt that he was wrong.

<Will you talk to me?> Emrys asked, craning his head around to look at Blaise. <You've been silent since fetching me from the stables, and all I can read from you is sadness. I want to help.>

Blaise pressed his forehead against Emrys's neck, centering himself with the stallion's warmth. He'd waited until nightfall to coax the pegasus from the stables, bringing Emrys behind the bakery so he could prepare to leave town in relative peace. "I need you to take me to Rainbow Flat."

<Oh.> Emrys's ears drooped with understanding. <Now? Why not wait until the morning?>

The moon hung overhead, low and full. Blaise glanced skyward, then back to the cinch as he finished the final adjustments. "I don't want to explain." The thought of it made him queasy. He wasn't sure if Emmaline and Reuben would try to talk him out of it or—his worst fear—be relieved that he was leaving them. Blaise rubbed at his face, pulse racing as he thought of Jack. He would be out of the outlaw's hair, too.

"Explain what?" Clover came around the corner of the bakery, hooves crunching against the dirt. She cast an assessing look at the saddle on Emrys's back and the readied saddlebags. The Knossan tilted her head as she connected the dots. "You're leaving?"

Blaise sighed. This was exactly what he had hoped to avoid. "Yes."

She nodded. "I won't stop you."

That was unexpected. He frowned, leaning against Emrys's side. "You won't?"

"No," the Knossan replied, taking a step closer and hunching over so that she met his eyes on the same level. "I understand the path of the exile. More so than others."

Her words gave Blaise pause. Clover had never revealed her story to him, but he knew she grappled with being different. "But everyone here likes you. Respects you." *They don't blame you for destroying the town's lifeline.*

"But my life has not always been so. I know how it is to be treated with suspicion when they see you as something *other*," Clover said quietly. "There was a time when . . ." She faltered, as if trying to gather the words. "I understand how it is to be called *monster*. To be feared for what you are." Clover tipped her head to look at the stars as she gathered her thoughts, her nose ring catching the moonlight. "Do not let their words— their thoughts of who they believe you to be—define you." She lowered her head, so her rich brown eyes bore into his, insistent. "*You* define who you are by your actions."

Blaise swallowed the lump in his throat. "Does it matter if others think I'm responsible for things that I wasn't?"

Clover blew a warm breath through her nostrils. "It would be a lie to tell you it doesn't matter. It does." Her eyes held shadows of past pain. "You are the sum of many things. You are a son, a brother. A baker."

"A Breaker."

"I was going to say friend next, but yes, that as well." Clover glanced at Emrys, then back to Blaise. "This is a difficult thing. An ugly thing. But you are resilient, and like land recovering from a wildfire, you can sprout new life. Hope persists."

Funny, it didn't seem like that now. Everything was raw and painful. He knew she was trying to be kind. "Thank you, Clover. For being good to me when you didn't have to be."

She offered him an encouraging nod. "I would do it again in a hoof-beat. Even if it annoyed Jack." Clover thought for a moment, and she flicked her ears mischievously. "Perhaps especially if it annoyed Jack."

Blaise managed a tiny smile at that. "I appreciate everything you've done for me, Clover." Blaise picked up the saddlebags and fastened them in place. "I should get going." *Before this gets any harder.* "Are you going to tell Jack that we talked?"

"Do you wish me to?"

"No."

Clover squared her shoulders. "Then I will not." She pressed a rough hand against her chest, a salute. "Remember that every storm runs out of rain." Then she turned and plodded around the corner, the sound of her hooves soon lost to the night.

Blaise swallowed, then made a final check of the tack. Every strap was secure, each buckle fastened tight. He slipped his gloves out of his pocket and pulled them on, then added a thick wool coat before shrugging into his duster. Icy winds blowing in from the north promised the flight wouldn't be pleasant. He shoved his left foot into the stirrup and swung into the saddle.

Emrys's hooves rang as he clopped away from the bakery. Blaise shivered, not from the chill that brushed against his face but from the uncertain future that yawned before him. He settled his flight goggles over his eyes, then pulled the stampede strings tight under his chin so his hat wouldn't blow off.

<You really want to do this?>

"You called for Clover to come talk to me, didn't you?"

Emrys angled a hurt look at him. <You wouldn't speak to me.>

Blaise winced. He had been unfair to not consider Emrys's feelings in this. "I'm sorry. I can't stay here anymore. You . . . you don't have to stay in Rainbow Flat with me." His teeth chattered on the last words, and not from the cold.

The pegasus went rigid, neck arching. He nearly vibrated with intensity. <That is *not* how this works. You do *not* get rid of me so easily.> Emrys fidgeted in place. <You are *my* rider and *my* friend. I'd follow you to Perdition and back.>

Blaise nodded, reaching down to pat Emrys's neck. Warmth curled around his heart at the prospect that he had Emrys by his side. "Thank you." At the nudge of his knee, Emrys turned and broke into a trot and then a lope before his wings snapped opened and the stallion hurtled into the overcast sky.

CHAPTER THIRTY-FIVE

Gone

Jack

"What do you mean, he's gone?" Jack squinted at Emmaline in the murky darkness. She was backlit by a mage-light, standing at the foot of his bed. He was an early riser, but because of her work at the bakery, Emmaline generally arose even earlier these days. She had given him an unceremonious wake-up call, barging in and caterwauling that Blaise was *gone*.

"*Gone*," she snapped, and though he only saw her silhouette, he heard the sorrow in the single word. There was a metallic clank, and Jack sat up, flicking on the mage-light beside the bed. She had dropped Blaise's key on the bedside table.

He picked up the key, turning it over in his hand as his foggy mind put together her words. "Blaise skipped town?" Jack frowned, thinking. "You sure he's not at the stables?"

Emmaline swallowed, shaking her head. "He was acting funny yesterday. And the oven is *cold*." At his blank look, she clarified. "He would have lit it by this time to get it to the right temperature. The key was left in the middle of the counter. And Oby says Emrys left in the middle of the night."

That got Jack's attention. He rose, digging out fresh clothes. "I'll get to the bottom of this." He paused, struggling to think of some way to offer her solace and reassurance. Emmaline was a lot like him, and keeping her busy might be the best thing. "You can go work at the bakery in the meantime, if you want."

Emmaline blinked, and for a moment, Jack thought she would protest. Instead, she nodded. "I think I will."

With that settled, they parted ways. Jack stalked to the stables. "Zeph!"

<You don't have to yell,> the palomino chided, popping his head over the stall door. <And if you're planning to ask about Emrys, we don't know where he went.>

Jack glared at the pegasus, hands on his hips. "You head up the sentries. Who patrolled last night?"

Two stalls down, the dust-colored head of a buckskin stallion appeared. <Oby and I were on patrol,> Naureus replied.

The outlaw frowned at Raven's mount. "And neither of you thought to ask Emrys or Blaise where they were going? What they were doing?"

<Sentry protocol is to *not* question those leaving town,> Zepheus reminded him tartly. <And Blaise is an adult, not a child running away from home.>

Jack growled to himself. That was true enough. But the Breaker leaving town so suddenly raised a slew of questions. Had he truly been responsible for the fall of the wind-pump? Was it possible Jack had been right all along? For once in his life, Jack didn't want to be right.

Itude was small, and news of such import flitted through the town like hummingbirds moving from flower to flower. By mid-morning Raven called for a Ringleader meeting, which was not unexpected. Jack was grumpy and unnerved by the Breaker's departure, and he wished a meeting could be delayed so he had more time to puzzle through things.

The other Ringleaders were deep in conversation when Jack arrived. As soon as he took his seat, Raven called them to order and didn't waste any time. He looked right at Jack. "Why did Blaise Hawthorne leave?"

Jack crossed his arms. "Are you accusing me or asking me?"

Raven snorted. "Both."

The outlaw spread his hands. "Your guess is as good as mine at this point. Guilty or scared." Jack's gut leaned toward the latter option, but his brain was another matter. Everyone knew Blaise had been at the cistern shortly before the wind-pump fell. It was difficult to discount that, even if there was no clear motive for *why*. Had he lost control of his magic, and that was the result? Or was something more sinister afoot?

"He's not guilty." Vixen's lower lip jutted out. "Blaise wouldn't do that. I've worked with him enough to know."

Kur's ears were flat against his pelt. "Innocent people do not leave without so much as a goodbye."

Jack wasn't so certain of that. The kid was awkward and didn't have the best grasp on social niceties when his nerves got the best of him. He drummed his fingers against the table, thinking. With a sinking feeling, he realized where Blaise was likely going. Clover had told him about the last conversation Jefferson Cole had before he left town.

"Shit," he growled. The other Ringleaders turned to look at him. He hadn't realized he'd interrupted Nadine speaking. Jack shrugged an insincere apology.

"Have something you want to tell us?" Nadine asked dryly.

"Rainbow Flat. He went to Rainbow Flat." Jack rubbed the stubble on his cheeks. As the pieces fell into place, he wished he could kick himself. Jack had been a fool, snookered into believing Blaise's woe-is-me plight. He had been right from the start. And Jack should have told the other Ringleaders about Cole's identity sooner rather than playing his damned wait-and-see game. "Because that's where Jefferson Cole is. And Jefferson Cole is a Doyen for the Salt-Iron Council."

He thought they might respond to the news with exclamations of shock and outrage, but instead, they stared at him, puzzled. Vixen shook her head. "That doesn't make a lick of sense. I would have been able to persuade him to tell me that."

"And there are no Doyens named Jefferson Cole," Raven added, though judging by the way he tugged at his short beard, he was bothered by the potential for trouble.

"That's because he's Doyen Malcolm Wells." Jack stabbed his index finger into the grain of the table, emphatic. "Somehow he maintains the front of this Cole man as well."

"How did you discover this?" Kur inquired, his eyes glowing golden with interest.

Jack shifted in his chair, uncomfortable. He recounted Cole's hefty financial proposition and the business card Jack still had in his possession. "I have dossiers on most of the eastern Confederation Doyens and anyone who dabbles financially in the Untamed Territory. My records indicate they're the same person."

Nadine crossed her arms. "Jack, we put a lot of stock in your skills, but we also know your inclinations. How sure are you?"

Jack straightened, shoulders rigid at her calling him into question like that. He narrowed his eyes. "Certain enough to worry about my town."

Raven nodded, his head bobbing from side to side as he mulled over the information. "So Blaise has gone to this Doyen in Rainbow Flat—and we have already agreed to allow his survey team to come here. The question is, how do we proceed now?"

"Refuse the team." Jack didn't even spare a second to think about it. It was the most sensible answer.

"Not so fast," Nadine said with a shake of her head. "Or have you forgotten the Gannish and their damned contracts? We have a contract—"

"With Jefferson Cole, not Malcolm Wells," Jack shot back.

Nadine held up her hand, her face lined with ferocity at his interruption. "I'm *speaking*." Magic hummed to life around her, a wispy aura of green sparks.

Jack glanced away, knowing full well he shouldn't piss off a Healer. Especially one as strong as Nadine. "Go ahead."

She gave a small nod. "As I was saying, I'm *from* Ganland. I reviewed that contract, and it's ironclad. Doesn't matter the name he used. It's valid, and if we break it at this point for anything less than an act of the gods, then we owe restitution."

Jack snorted. "*Restitution*. The Gannish would bleed a rock dry." But that was interesting. Nadine had never before revealed where she hailed from. Jack filed that away for later.

"They would," Nadine agreed, turning her gaze to the other Ringleaders. "And that would put us even more on the Confederation's map than we already are. So my suggestion is we allow the survey team to come and do their thing. Treat them with the same courtesy and caution that we showed Cole." She gestured to Vixen. "And you can pick their brains."

The red-haired outlaw grinned. "I can do that."

"And what do we do about Blaise?" Kur asked.

Jack levered his elbows onto the table, crossing his arms in front of him as he leaned forward. "Nothing."

Kur flicked an ear. "Why?"

"Because he won't come back here. If he does, I'll put a bullet in his brain." And Jack meant every word.

CHAPTER THIRTY-SIX

The Armor of Bureaucracy

Blaise

The flight from Itude to Rainbow Flat buffeted Blaise and Emrys with brutal cold. Flurries of snow threatened their progress, and several times Emrys had to land and continue on foot to prevent his wings from icing over. Blaise welcomed the chill—the weather echoed his bleak thoughts. When Emrys flew, Blaise was so bitterly cold that all he could do was focus on staying upright in the saddle, goggles and bandanna in place to protect his vulnerable face from the elements.

Due to the inclement weather, it took three days to travel to Rainbow Flat. Emrys guided them to a shanty each night, and together they curled up against the blustering wind. The shanties were little more than a roof and four walls to keep the worst of the weather at bay, but they provided the respite they desperately needed.

Rainbow Flat was a balm for Blaise's battered soul. It was two or three times larger than Itude, and it was pretty as a picture with the rooftops covered in a light dusting of snow, the Tombstone River running beside it sparkling like it ran with sapphires and diamonds rather than water. The buildings in the town were all smartly painted, with care taken in their construction. The townspeople investing in Rainbow Flat intended it to last.

Blaise found accommodations for Emrys at the local stable, content when they saw other pegasi used it as a base. Emrys was happy to bury his head in a bucket brimming with sweet feed while Blaise headed to the local saloon to ask after Jefferson Cole.

His arrival in Rainbow Flat was uneventful compared to his departure from Itude. In this town, Blaise was just another face, another traveler. At first, he was on edge, afraid that somehow his reputation had preceded him. But when he walked up to the bartender to make his inquiry, the man didn't so much as bat an eye. At mention of Cole's name the bartender gestured up the street to one of Rainbow Flat's two hotels. Blaise thanked him and walked to the hotel. After the minor matter of asking the desk clerk to hand off a note to Cole, the deed was done.

Cole invited Blaise to his elegantly appointed suite to relax after his long journey. He was too tired and bone-chilled to turn down the hospitality, and Blaise gawked at his surroundings as Cole asked the staff to deliver a meal to the lavish room.

They were in a sitting room, which boasted a pair of rich brown velvet-covered armchairs, a chaise with a floral design, and a desk pushed into a corner. The sitting room connected to a dining alcove large enough to hold an ornately carved oak table and four matching chairs. A closed door led to what Blaise assumed must be the sleeping quarters. The suite was larger than his bakery and loft combined.

Blaise told Cole he had thought more on the offer and decided to seek him out. He disliked the dishonesty but hoped to keep any information about his magic to himself. He wanted to be Blaise the Baker. *Not* Blaise the Breaker.

"So here I am," Blaise said with a shrug as he finished. It was a struggle to pretend to be nonchalant after the whole ugly situation. He eyed the glass of liquor that Cole had poured out for him, froth boiling around the top. He had never been one to drink, but his stress warranted it. Blaise picked up the glass and took a sip, then nearly hacked it out as the strength of the liquor kicked him in the mouth.

Cole bit back a laugh, covering his mouth with one hand. "Sorry. I didn't realize you may not have a constitution for alcohol after living in Itude. Some of the brews served at the saloon were . . . unusual."

Blaise wrinkled his nose. He knew about some of them firsthand after working there. "I'm not one to drink, but it's tempting to start."

"Is it, now?" Cole asked good-naturedly. He leaned forward, eager. "So, what made you reconsider?"

Blaise coughed. Now that he was here, he felt self-conscious as he recalled Emmaline's assertion that Cole was interested in him for more than his desserts. Maybe coming here was a mistake, but what other option did he have? "I thought it might be a good time for a change." The words felt hollow and he hoped that Cole didn't see through them.

Cole, however, seemed oblivious. His eyes shone. "Let me be certain: you're accepting the offer to be my business partner?"

It was now or never. Blaise met his gaze. "Yes."

A muscle in Cole's jaw twitched, and Blaise thought he was holding in a celebration. A smile spread across his face. "Outstanding! I can't wait! There will be so much paperwork and forms to fill out, but that's the best part."

A blissful look crossed Cole's face, reminding Blaise of the awe-filled looks on the faces of the children in Itude as they looked at the dessert table at the Feast of Flight. The Gannish were a strange lot.

The businessman took another sip, then set his glass aside. "We have a lot to think about before we even get that far, though. We'll need to locate a bakery to serve as a base of operations." He rubbed his chin. "Damn. You won't like my suggestion."

Blaise lifted his chin. "I'm not in a position to be choosy at the moment Mr. Cole."

The other man waved a hand. "Mr. Cole? No, call me Jefferson if we're to be partners." He rose from his chair and moved to the desk, pulling a rolled-up map off of it. He brought the map over to the low table centered between the couch and two armchairs, then gestured for Blaise to come closer.

It was a map of Iphyria. Jefferson tapped a finger on Ganland, in the southwestern portion of the map. "We'll do our best business if we're close to distribution lines. Ganland is a prime contender for several reasons. Number one, I'm kind of a big deal there." He flashed an indulgent grin. "Number two, it will position us closer to our potential vendors and investors. And three, as far as Salt-Iron Confederation nations go, we're geographically one of the furthest from the elite in Phinora. Especially if we work out of Nera." He pointed to the capital of Ganland, which clung to a peninsula. "I know that may be a concern considering your . . . status." His voice rose with a curious inflection, as if he wanted to ask more but restrained himself.

Blaise grimaced. "You're right. I don't like that suggestion. You didn't forget that I'm a maverick by chance, did you?"

Jefferson laughed. "No, I'm aware. And there are mages in Ganland. In the other countries, too. It's not as if you'd be the only one."

Blaise chewed on his bottom lip. Jefferson didn't know what his magic was. If he knew, Blaise doubted he would suggest Ganland. Though the way Blaise saw it if Jefferson knew then this entire plan would fall apart. "From what I've heard, I'd be the only one not tattooed and indentured and if a Tracker came across me, I would have problems."

Jefferson see-sawed one hand back and forth. "That's not fully accurate."

Blaise stared at him. "What?"

"Mmm," Jefferson gave him a speculative look. "My wealth can provide certain protections if you work for me." He roughed a hand against the velvet of the couch, making the fibers stand on end before smoothing it down again.

"I'm no one's servant." Blaise's heart pounded frantically in his chest. What if he was blowing his only chance? If Jefferson turned him down, he had no alternatives that kept him free.

Jefferson shook his head, appalled. "You misunderstand, I'm not speaking of indenture. I don't agree with that. In fact, I—" He cut himself off with a sour look. "I'd like to see it changed. What I'm saying is I have a fair hand at writing contracts. And I intend to honor what I said earlier and *partner* with you. You wouldn't be the first mage I've worked *with*. None serve me." His mouth quirked with distaste.

Blaise wanted to believe him. He really did. But this was Salt-Iron Confederation business, and that worried him. "How do you do that? I was led to believe mages aren't considered equals."

Jefferson cocked his head. "That is true. But people have to know you're a mage for that. You said you don't have a tattoo?"

"No tattoo."

"Can you keep your magic hidden? No bursting into flame or whatever it is you do?"

Oh, thank goodness he had a modicum of control now. "I can keep it hidden." It would drive him crazy, and he would have to find some way to release it at times. But he could do that now. A year ago, he would have answered *no*.

Jefferson gave him a sly smile and shrugged. "Then no one would know you're a mage. I can draft the contract as such."

"Would you be in trouble later if the truth comes out?"

Jefferson shrugged, unconcerned. "Plausible deniability."

Blaise wet his cold-chapped lips, uncertainty gnawing at him, but nodded. "Okay. But if the truth does come out later, could they force me into other service?"

Jefferson looked pleased that he was thinking this through. "Good question. If we have the proper paperwork signed and filed, no one could force you into the military or into any other servitude, unless we broke our contract. That's the wonderful thing about bureaucracy in Ganland. As annoying as it is, it's also a kind of armor."

Blaise hadn't considered that. No wonder Jefferson didn't mind the possibility of paperwork. "I think I'm going to need a little time to think on it and then ask some more questions once I've rested. Is that going to be a problem?"

"Take your time. I was planning to head back to Nera tomorrow after I finished my business dealings, but I'll gladly extend my time here. I'm not needed back home just yet." Jefferson rolled the map back up into a neat cylinder. "You look fatigued. Do you have a room yet?"

Blaise shook his head. "No. I was trying to make sure I could find you first."

Jefferson rose from his seat. "From what I understand, the suite next door is empty. I'll see if it's available, and if so, we'll put you up there."

Blaise's eyes widened. A suite? He didn't know how much that might cost, but he could only assume it would chew through the coins he had brought quicker than he would like. "That's unnecessary. I can get a different room."

"I insist. I'll cover the cost," Jefferson said with a dismissive wave of his hand. "It's the least I can do for my new business partner."

Blaise stared at him in surprise.

CHAPTER THIRTY-SEVEN

Partners

Blaise

The massive wheel of the paddle steamer propelled the boat down the dark waters of the Tombstone, yellow and green pennants waving riotously in the breeze. Blaise watched as it slipped into the distance, headed for far-off ports. Muleshoe and then Freeport, according to Jefferson. Places Blaise had only seen on maps but which the entrepreneur seemed quite familiar with.

"Haven't seen a steamer before, hmm?" Jefferson asked as they leaned against the fence overlooking the docks.

"No." Blaise rubbed the back of his neck. "Nothing more than creeks or ponds around where I grew up, and . . ." He trailed off with a shrug. "You travel on them often?"

"Paddle steamers are the safest way to travel any part of the Untamed Territory." Jefferson said with a nod, then reconsidered. "Well, aside from a pegasus, but they're not as good for moving merchandise."

"You know a lot about the Untamed Territory for someone who doesn't live here," Blaise observed.

A wistful expression flitted across Jefferson's face. "If I had the chance, I would."

That was interesting. Not what Blaise would expect. "So why don't you?"

Jefferson's eyes shifted away briefly. "Obligations, mostly." He cleared his throat and changed the subject. "Have you had time to consider our agreement?"

Jefferson had displayed remarkable restraint in keeping the topic at bay for the past few days while Blaise considered his options. He hadn't attempted any further flirtations, which was a great relief. But Jefferson had made it a point to spend time with Blaise each day, which had felt awkward at first but soon became almost a comfort. The entrepreneur seemed determined to keep Blaise's attention and took him to see the sights in and around Rainbow Flat. Jefferson had treated him to a night at a dinner theater and had taken him (and Emrys, who wouldn't let Blaise leave the town's boundaries without him) to see a herd of unicorns that called the prairie outside town home. Today the steamer docks were on their agenda. Blaise had to admit that the distractions were pleasant, and Jefferson made for good company, all things considered.

"I have, actually." Blaise shifted, draping his arms over the top of the fence as birds called overhead. He had thought about it so much that his brain felt like little more than mush. As it stood, he was going to run out of money within a month if he didn't figure out a solid plan. And Jefferson, with his eagerness, seemed like his best bet. "I'm willing to go to Ganland and go into business with you." Jefferson looked ready to jump with joy, but Blaise held up a finger to qualify his words. "But I want it to be an equal partnership. Whatever you get from it, I want the same amount."

Jefferson settled, lips twitching with an impressed smile. "I see you *have* been thinking about it." He considered the proposal, then shook his head. "I'm investing up front to get us started. With overheads, I'll be out a considerable amount. What about seventy percent for me, thirty for you?"

"Forgive me if I'm wrong, but I suspect you wouldn't be out living on the streets at fifty-fifty," Blaise responded as he watched a new steamer powering upstream to the town.

Jefferson gave him a sly look, then grinned. "I need to dress down." He stepped back from the fence, hands behind his back as he paced in a circle, thinking.

Blaise took a breath, schooling himself into a serious expression. He wasn't going to back down from this. "Baking is one of the few things I *know* I do well. I'm not settling for less than an equal partnership."

"I think you sell yourself short." Jefferson halted his pacing, giving

Blaise a sharp look. "But I can respect that. I've tasted your cookies, and I know what we can reap from them." He walked back to rejoin Blaise at the fence, so close their shoulders nearly brushed. "I can get us a location in Nera. It will take time to get it ready. Two, three months perhaps—but that doesn't take into account the time to get a message to my associates there. You would need to wait here. Would that be a problem?"

Blaise shook his head. "There's a boarding house, so I can get a room that I can afford while I wait. And I can see if the local bakery is hiring."

Jefferson raised his eyebrows, giving Blaise an amused look. "That won't be possible."

"What? Why?" Blaise scowled. Was he going to have to rethink things?

"You're new to Gannish contracts." Jefferson sighed. "When we sign the paperwork, you'll effectively be an asset—"

"No," Blaise said so quickly he almost hadn't realized he spoke. His heart pounded. "I'm not." *I don't belong to anyone. I'm not property.*

"It's a legal term, Blaise," Jefferson said, his tone gentle. "Nothing more. And for our purposes, it means I would rather not have you working for someone else. It could allow them a chance to learn from you, which could impact our future profit."

"Oh." Blaise glanced away, cheeks warming with embarrassment. But the problem remained that he would need to find a way to survive until he could work with Jefferson. He chewed his bottom lip.

Jefferson bumped his shoulder against Blaise's. "What's bothering you?"

Blaise shook his head, rubbing his hands together to ease the magic that responded to his tension. "It would be simpler to ask what's not bothering me."

"Yes, but that won't help matters," Jefferson pointed out. "Is it the contract?"

"No." Oddly enough, the idea of the contract gave Blaise a strange sense of security. He pulled away from the fence, gesturing to the town. "I'm not going to be able to afford to stay here if I can't work."

"Oh, is that all?" Jefferson blinked in confusion as if it were a minor problem. And perhaps to him, it was. He waved a hand, dismissive. "You'll have a stipend while you're here, of course."

"I will?"

"It will be in the contract." Jefferson allowed himself an amused smile. "So if you're still in agreement, I'll work on getting the paperwork drawn up. We can get it formalized in the next few days. I can stay another two weeks before I need to catch a paddle steamer back home."

Home. Jefferson's use of the word sent an unsettled shock through Blaise. Once again, he was without a true home. If Jefferson followed through, then Ganland might become Blaise's home. A touch of Jack's suspicion clouded Blaise's mind, and he wondered if Jefferson might somehow take advantage of him. Or lure him into a trap. Was Jefferson luring him to Ganland where he would meet his doom?

Did it even matter? Blaise was so tired of struggling.

"Blaise?" Jefferson was scowling at him with concern.

Blaise banished his worries. "I'm fine. Sorry. I . . . I was thinking of something. You can start on the paperwork."

Jefferson smiled, the expression lighting his face with passion. "Excellent! Tonight at dinner we should toast our new endeavor!"

"Raspberry vinegar switchel," Blaise said.

Jefferson's tongue poked out in disgust. "Ugh. Raspberry vinegar switchel for you. Wine for me."

"Deal."

CHAPTER THIRTY-EIGHT

The Battle of Itude

Clover

Clover had her shotgun in hand as she trod out of the saloon's dim interior, Hannah and Abe in her wake. She twitched an ear, unsettled by the dull vibration rumbling through the ground beneath her.

"Thunder?" Abe asked, puzzled. He looked at the sky. There were clouds, but nothing that heralded a storm.

The Knossan shook her head, scanning the area. A light breeze blew from the west, carrying the acrid bouquet of machine oil.

Hannah gasped, pointing with a trembling finger. "Sweet Faedra, what is that?"

Clover pivoted to look where Hannah pointed, and she flattened her ears back at the behemoth vessel in the sky, tiny dots clustered protectively around it. "*Go*. Both of you. Run, run away as fast as you can." Clover prodded Abe in the shoulder to get him to stop gawking. The man had frozen in disbelief.

Hannah gulped. "But . . . we're supposed to fight."

Clover bowed her head. "You are outmatched by whatever that is. You do not possess magic. You are a fair shot, but war is coming. Gather anyone who can't—" And then her words were devoured by a void of silence. Startled, Clover tried to speak again and shook her head with frustration, making a shooing motion.

Hannah swallowed, then broke into a sprint after Abe, who was a sensible coward and had already started to flee. Clover didn't fault her cook. He was old, and his knees were bad. She hoped he would get to safety.

It was mid-afternoon, almost time for school to let out for the day. The children would make vulnerable targets. Clover slung her shotgun against her shoulder and trotted up the street, past townspeople who stopped to stare at the terrifying vessel that was already casting a shadow over the town square. Mouths opened in mute whimpers and sobs. A few regained their senses, running off to arm themselves. Good. Itude needed her defenders.

The schoolmarm, Julia Lincoln, had her head out the door. Small faces pressed up against windows, a mixture of curious and fearful. It was a strange thing, to not even detect so much as a titter from their mouths. But, Clover supposed, even if not for the oppressive silence forced on them, the children would still be quiet. They raised the children of Itude knowing that theirs was a dangerous existence.

Miss Lincoln opened her mouth to ask Clover something, her face pinched with worry. A little girl clung to her leg. Behind her, Clover realized that any child old enough to fight had left. Only the smallest huddled around Miss Lincoln, terrified and defenseless.

The children needed to get to safety. Clover could take some, but it was too late to flee. Their legs were too short. They could not run fast enough. Across the street, small Jasper Strop waved his arms to get her attention. He pointed at the children, then back to the dry goods store. The knocker pointed at the ground. Clover's nostrils flared in understanding. Jasper was offering to shelter some of the children in the hidden tunnel beneath his store.

Together Clover and Miss Lincoln herded the children over to Jasper. The knocker's tunnel that led to his travel-vein was short, but after he opened the hatch, he fit Miss Lincoln and ten of the children inside before hopping down and closing the trapdoor. Clover turned, left with five of the smallest children as the airship drew overhead.

No time left. Clover hunched over, hands braced against the dirt as she tossed her head to encourage the children aboard. They climbed onto her back as quickly as they were able, their frightened tears dampening her hide. Tiny hands bit into her skin, but she ignored the pain. She had to get them to safety. Picking up the shotgun, Clover lurched forward as the first bullets flew. She couldn't hear them, but she felt the concussive force as they peppered the ground nearby.

Clover surged to her feet, her bulk angled awkwardly forward so the children wouldn't lose their tenuous grips on her back. And then she ran as fast as she could to the northeast, to the trail that led away from Itude and, she hoped, to safety.

She ran and didn't look back.

———————

Jack

ZEPHEUS TROTTED BESIDE THE MULE TEAM PULLING THE STURDY WAGON loaded down with a pair of heavy, locked safes filled with gold. Jefferson Cole's survey team had arrived in town mere days ago, and Jack's annoyance grew every time he saw one of the foreigners wandering around. This heist with Kur had been just the thing he needed to burn off his agitation.

The job he and Kur Agur had completed would easily pay for the wind-pump reconstruction, and the outing gave him a chance to get away from town and clear his head. No doubt it would also increase the bounty on both their heads, but that was a minor matter. Jack had yet to meet a bounty hunter ballsy enough to come after anyone in the Gutter.

Besides, Jack and Kur had let the crew manning the Paragon Bank Coach off easy, even after the audacity of trying to murder the pair. They'd left the men tied to the spokes of their armored wagon, bleeding and naked, their flesh pebbling in the chill air. In the distance, the cries of chupacabras echoed. Jack wasn't heartless. Although he and Kur had disarmed the men, he left the driver's belt knife six inches out of their reach. The proximity of the chupacabras provided a strong incentive for the men to get to the knife once Jack and Kur cleared out.

They would be fine. Probably.

Fifty thousand in gold eagle coins clanked in the twin safes. It took considerable maneuvering and cunning to complete a heist with a wagon and mule team, but Jack and Kur had figured it out. The mollies Candy and Rosie were the canniest and most dependable of the mules to call Itude home. If not for Zepheus, the lady mules would be Jack's favorite creatures on four legs.

Atop the wagon, Kur stretched out his neck, scenting the wind blowing in from the west. "Machine oil. Why is the wind carrying machine oil? And gunpowder?"

"What?" Jack's gaze snapped on the Theilian. "Zeph?"

<I smell it, too.>

Jack pulled down his flight goggles and tightened the stampede string on his hat. "We're gonna take a look. Guard this windfall with your life."

Kur lifted his upper lip, displaying yellowed fangs. "I know what I'm about, human."

Jack ignored the impertinence as Zepheus broke into a lope to gain momentum to go airborne. His hooves left the ground, tucked neatly below the stallion as his wings pumped against the wind, defying gravity. Jack's vision was a blur of silvery mane and puffy clouds as he waited for Zepheus to level out.

The pegasus spotted the threat first. <Sweet Mare of Mercy, what is that thing?>

Jack tore his gaze from the ground as Zepheus angled to allow him a better view. In the distance, a massive thing that looked ridiculously like a flying ship hovered over Itude.

A flying ship hovered over Itude.

Jack's heart thundered at the sight. His daughter. His town. Tiny dots circled the ship. Griffins with riders. Itude was under attack.

Through the years, Jack had prepared for this day. Itude had moved from a susceptible town in the canyon to a stronghold overlooking the gorge, only accessible by a narrow road from the east. He made sure that everyone in town who was old enough to stand in a fight could do so. Jack had brought in all the mages he could for additional defense. But he had only planned for an attack from the ground, not from the sky.

<Jack?>

He shook his head, returning to the present. No sense dwelling on his failure now. "Let's circle back to tell Kur. We'll have him notify the ranches. Maybe some of the outlying mages can come in." *If it's not too late.*

The palomino banked and dove to the wagon where Kur waited, furry arms crossed. Jack told him the news, and his lupine face changed from annoyed to furious. He argued that he needed to get to the fight, but Jack and Zepheus would reach the town sooner. With a reluctant growl, Kur turned the mollies and sent them to the nearby Smith farmstead to give them the news.

That task complete, Zepheus bolted back into the air, not wasting a moment to ask Jack. They were both possessed with the single-minded drive to get back to town, to do what they could to fight the enemy at the door.

As they flew, Jack checked his sixguns, reloading. He had three, plus knives tucked in each boot. Eighteen shots he needed to make count because this was war and not one of his heists or gunfights. One shot, one kill.

A mile out of town, Jack thought it peculiar he couldn't hear any sounds from the airship. It hovered overhead, silent. As Zepheus drew nearer, Jack spotted a slender form at the front of the vessel, arms outstretched in concentration. *The Dampener.* Jack admired her range—it took a considerable amount of skill to exert her magic as far as she had. Not a single scream or gunshot escaped the oppressive bubble she forced over the area. He knew firsthand how disruptive the lack of auditory cues were in a fight.

"Take her out!" Jack bellowed to Zepheus.

The palomino set his course for the airship. Jack felt the palpable silence as they passed through the bounds of the Dampener's field, the hair on the back of his neck rising at the eerie tableau beneath him. The fighting must have started recently. The streets below were a mix of soldiers and armed townspeople, surreal with the utter lack of noise. There should have been peals of gunshots. Screams. Shouts.

Zepheus checked his course hard, nearly unseating Jack with the motion as a griffin swooped inches overhead, the beast's talons raking against his hat. Jack strangled for an instant as the stampede strings garroted him, but on instinct, he loosened them and his hat ripped away. Gagging, Jack touched his tender throat with one hand as he pulled out his revolver with the other. He took aim and pulled the trigger. The griffin's beak gaped in muted agony as the bullet ripped through its side, fouling its flight. It wasn't dead, but it would think twice before coming after Jack again. And its flight was so uneven its rider had difficulty lining up a shot.

With the griffin out of the way, Zepheus swooped around to put them on a new attack path. The Dampener stayed where she was, eyes closed in concentration as she kept her spell going. The more noise and people within, the more difficult the upkeep would be. Jack smirked. Courtesy of her own spell, she would never hear him coming.

<The deck is empty. Touch and go behind her, so you have a clear shot.>

Jack patted Zepheus's neck to let him know he agreed. Touch and go landings were no easy feat, but they were something Jack had all the Itude pegasi learn. It was difficult on their flight muscles, and it wasn't something he asked them to do lightly.

Zepheus's hooves touched down on the polished wood of the deck, lowering his neck and wings for a heartbeat to allow Jack a clear shot. Jack already had his revolver up, silver muzzle gleaming as he pulled the trigger, and a silent bullet sped into the theurgist's brain. The Dampener's body hadn't even hit the deck before Zepheus shoved off with his hooves, his wings creating a sound like thunder as the bubble of silence popped.

Screams and gunfire shredded the air.

<What now?>

Jack's heart was torn. He wanted to tell Zepheus that their priority was to find Emmaline. But the town was a war zone. There was no time to waste. His daughter might already be dead in the streets below.

Fury blazed through his veins. "It's time to introduce those soldiers to Wildfire Jack."

JACK AND ZEPHEUS SEPARATED AS SOON AS HIS BOOTS HIT THE GROUND behind the bakery. The griffins and their riders harried the pegasi defenders from the air, with several of the equines already downed. The other stallions needed all the help they could get.

Jack flattened himself against the bakery's yellow wall, a red spatter marring the paint at chest level. He glanced around the corner and saw a dead soldier on the porch, a sticky crimson pool spread beneath him.

The outlaw caught his breath, peering out in time to catch the shadow of a griffin overhead. With the Dampener down, the din of battle echoed through the town. Sixguns and rifles roared. Men and women screamed or cried. Griffins shrieked as pegasi stallions whistled their defiant challenges.

Jack stayed hidden, taking the measure of the enemy. The soldiers had the old Saltie penchant for firing high. They were far less likely to connect with their target—though those times they did, it would be ugly. The soldiers outnumbered the townspeople who had rushed out to Itude's defense. They were going to die in a battle of fire and fury, without a single chance to coordinate their efforts.

Somewhere nearby, Jack heard a baby wail and a mother shushing the infant, frantic. A soldier turned to locate the sound. Jack stepped out and shot the man in the head, then withdrew before anyone else saw him.

Sixteen shots left.

Jack leaned against the bakery's exterior, head back. He had beaten the odds before, but nothing like this. Overhead, a pegasus and griffin thrashed together, a tangle of feathers, claws, and hooves. Glass shattered, and wood screeched under pressure as they crashed into the second story of the boarding house. Jack cringed, thankful that the pegasus was a bay and not Zepheus's gold.

How could they win this?

We can't win this.

Jack's jaw clenched in grim determination. If this was the end of the trail, he was going to drag as many of them to Perdition with him as he could. The Salt-Iron Confederation wouldn't sack Itude and take light casualties. Not if Jack had a say.

He pulled out a knife, slipping it between his teeth for quick access. Jack ducked into the melee, dodging through the confused combatants. He paused, heart catching in his throat at the distant blur of long blonde hair in the hayloft above the stables. *Emmaline.* It took every ounce of willpower to not run to her. The enemy was a thick knot between his position and the stables. It would have been suicide.

Jack snaked past the saloon, ducking into the post office for a brief respite. He was behind most of the enemy forces, and he picked off a few as he moved, forever mindful of his dwindling supply of bullets. His boots were painfully loud on the wooden floor as he shut the door behind him. Jack paused and slipped the knife back into his boot, scowling at the pool of blood spreading across the floor behind the counter.

He crouched down and crept forward to investigate the legs sticking out from the other side of the mail counter. Hank Walker? Jack's revolver stayed out as he eased around for a closer look. The dead man was dressed in foreign garb, too formal for the Gutter. One of the Gannish survey team. What in Perdition was he doing on the floor of the post office with his throat slashed?

"You weren't supposed to see that."

Jack spun, muzzle pointed at Hank Walker, who loomed in the doorway with a pistol in his hand, blocking the exit.

"What are you playing at, Hank?"

"Of all things, I thought you'd approve of that." Walker snorted. "You've been walking around town itchy as a shaved cat over Jefferson Cole."

True enough, but still. "Doesn't give you leave to kill a man."

Walker shrugged. "You're one to talk. They'll die today anyway."

A chill raced down Jack's spine, rage consuming him at Walker's implication. "You *knew* about this. You son of a bitch!"

Jack moved with a speed born of betrayal and outrage, and the postmaster didn't stand a chance. He barreled into Walker, his left hand against the man's throat as Jack pinned him against the wall, right hand pressing the muzzle of his sixgun against the postmaster's temple.

"*Did you sell us out?*" Jack growled, eyes blazing.

Walker trembled, gagging. Jack loosened his grip enough for the man to speak. "P-please. I had to. Those . . . those bastards have my *brother.*" The heartbreaking sob at the end gave credence to his claim. That, or he was a talented actor in a high-stress moment.

"You *lied* to me." Jack's voice was a deadly whisper among the symphony of destruction outside.

Jack intended to kill Walker where he stood, but the chance never came. The door exploded inward from a forceful kick, and with a bellow, Jack hurled Walker into the trio of soldiers pushing into the building. The havoc of the postmaster spinning into the men gave Jack all the time he needed to break open the nearest window and run.

He had more people to kill. Jack bit back a curse when he found himself at the funeral parlor.

"Damn irony," Jack grumbled, noticing Butch hiding behind a pine box, taking pot shots at soldiers out the window. "You can do better than that, Butch."

The undertaker's face was pale, eyes owlish with fear. He was also a Necromancer, a terrifying force if only he would use his magic. Jack didn't know his story, but Butch had vowed to only use his unholy power in very specific situations. And this was one of them.

"I don't know if I can, Jack." Butch quivered.

Jack bit back a frustrated howl. "We've got folks dying out there. And you might be next." He flicked his eyes to his revolver. Not that he was threatening Butch. Well, maybe a little. Sometimes motivation was necessary.

Butch's eyes widened, taking his meaning. He blew out a breath, then scuttled over to a desk and pulled a small velvet pouch out of a drawer. "I need to get to the cemetery. Can you cover me?"

Jack sighed. Damn it. That was a long way and a lot of open ground to cover. "You can't use the dead already outside your door?"

"That's not how it works," Butch said with regret.

"Damned picky magic," Jack groused.

Butch made a noise of agreement. "Least you can use your magic and your sixgun as we go."

That's a no on the magic, Jack thought bitterly. He tipped his chin toward the door. "Let's go."

Jack led the way, slinking behind buildings to provide them with cover. Most of the soldiers had convened around the town square. Jack paused—they were too close to the stables for his liking. Butch stumbled against his heels, and with a soft curse Jack crept forward again. Smoke rolled across the town, and a glance to the north confirmed that flames engulfed several of the buildings. That was going to be a big problem later. If there was a later.

A tussle of gold and brown streaked overhead, Zepheus locked in battle with a griffin. Jack held up a hand to keep Butch from trampling him, scowling at the deep slashes of scarlet on the stallion's flanks. He lifted his revolver and took aim. They were a respectful distance away, and they were moving targets, but he didn't take kindly to that beast trying to kill his pegasus. He squeezed the trigger.

The griffin screeched, releasing its talons from Zepheus's neck. The pegasus spiraled away in a burst of loose feathers that fell like leaves from an autumn tree. Jack whispered encouragement skyward, then continued onward to the cemetery.

"Jack." Butch tugged his sleeve, gesturing to a dark form off their path.

Another pegasus hadn't been as lucky as Zepheus. Jack sucked in a breath as he recognized the mortal wound on the stallion. The pegasus made pained, rasping noises. His wings were shredded to tatters, feathers loose on the surrounding ground. Blanchydas staggered to his feet, but a griffin had tangled with him and slit his belly open. His intestines were ugly ribbons spread on the gore-splattered dirt beneath him.

Blanchydas fixed his white-ringed eyes on them. <Please. It *hurts*.>

Jack cursed. Damn the Salties. There was no saving the stallion, and they both knew it. He raised his revolver.

"Wait," Butch cautioned, and rushed over to the stallion, avoiding an enemy bullet with a startled yelp. Jack waited impatiently as the Necromancer murmured to the stallion. The pegasus bobbed his head, eyes rolling in agony. Butch picked up one of the fallen feathers and tucked it into his pouch. "Do it."

Jack came closer to the stallion. "Thank you for protecting our town. May your spirit fly up to the stars singing of your heroism." He should save his bullets, but this fallen defender deserved a quick, merciful end. A lump in his throat, he lifted the revolver, placed the muzzle against the pegasus's head, and pulled the trigger.

The stallion slumped with a soft exhalation. Jack swiped at his eyes as he turned away from the scene. "Come on."

The cemetery wasn't far. Butch raced ahead and settled down among the tombstones, pulling items from his pouch and arraying them on the ground. Jack kept watch, noting only a handful of griffins remained in the air. One griffin was on the ground, snapping at two injured pegasi who had cornered it. Jack smiled with grim satisfaction as the pegasi worked together to outmaneuver the beast and take it down.

"This gonna take much longer?" Jack asked, scanning the area. The town was on fire. He coughed as the wind blew smoke into his face.

Butch didn't answer. The temperature chilled, and Jack whirled to see the Necromancer standing in the middle of the cemetery with his arms spread wide, a look of ecstasy on his face.

"Vengeful dead, come forth and defend your town!" Butch threw something into the air—dust?—and magic pulsed.

Jack had never met another Necromancer aside from Butch, and he had never seen necromancy in action. He was pretty sure if Blaise was there, he would never call Jack's magic creepy again. The ground above the graves shattered as their skeletal occupants broke through caskets and topsoil, released to the world again. They were in various states of decay as they clawed their way out of the dirt. Their empty eye sockets blazed with an infernal light. Most of them were armed. Itude had a tradition of burying its outlaws with their weapons. And ammunition, just in case.

The dead pegasus trotted over to Butch, innards and wings dragging behind like a ghoulish wedding train. The Necromancer climbed onto Blanchydas's back, moving with a renewed grace and energy that Jack hadn't thought him capable of.

Necromancy was some freaky, scary shit.

"The dead stand with us," Butch intoned.

Jack nodded, his skin crawling as he turned his back on Butch's small force. "Then let's go take our vengeance."

CHAPTER THIRTY-NINE

The Dollmaker

Emmaline

She thought this would be easier.

Emmaline crouched in the hay hood above the stables, using the partially opened roll-away door as cover. Her heart raced in her chest like a runaway horse, her hands trembling as she took in the chaos below. She felt like a failure, hiding up in the hayloft. She was Wildfire Jack's daughter. He had trained her to fight, and here she was trying to hide like a little girl behind her mother's skirts.

But the practices and training hadn't prepared her for this. The screams of agony, the acrid smoke in the air, the shouts and impact as griffins and pegasi tore into one another. The hexgun training in the canyon had been child's play by comparison. Tears stung her eyes as she saw Gus Pembroke fall, blood spurting from the back of his head as the light left his eyes.

The breath caught in her throat, and she clutched a hand to her face. This couldn't be. This was her town. The people wounded and dying out there were friends. Emmaline didn't know if she stood the chance of a candle in a downpour, but she had to try.

The chill of rage and adrenaline flooded her body, and time seemed to slow as she slipped a trio of poppets from her pocket. She hadn't had time to run home and grab her sixgun, but she wasn't defenseless. Brow furrowed with determination, she cast around for things she could use. She pulled a thick stalk of hay from one of the nearby bales, then scooted over to the door so she could peer out.

Emmaline took a calming breath to center herself, just as her father had taught her. "Until effigy work becomes second nature to you, always do it from a place of calm," he had reminded her time and time again. An Effigest working from a state of upset was more likely to have their magic fail—or even worse, snap back and impact the caster rather than the target.

She spread out the three poppets, glancing from them to the melee below. Her range was limited, so Emmaline selected three nearby enemies. She had to be careful—Itude's defenders wove in and out of the tide of soldiers. Chewing her lip, she targeted the soldier closest to the hayloft as he lifted his rifle to fire. She jabbed the poppet she bound to him in the back with the thick hay stalk. Below her, the soldier contorted in sudden discomfort, his shot going wide and sparing Vixen what might have been a mortal wound. The redhead kicked the man to the ground, drawing her knife.

A thrill rushed through Emmaline at her success. *I can do this.* She scanned the masses and went to work. Some of her attempts failed, but none of them backfired. She tripped a soldier who had Nadine in his sights, sending him tumbling to the dusty street where Raven appeared from nowhere and ended him with a wicked slash across the throat. Emmaline lost track of the flow of time, focused on the fighting below her. Out of the corner of her eye, she saw a scarlet-clad form trot down the steps from the Ringleader HQ, but it was too far away for her to wonder about.

The battle raged on, vicious. Once, she saw a flash of gold and realized Zepheus had joined the battle. Which meant her father had, too. In between casts, she searched for any sign of him but found nothing. What if he was dead?

No, she couldn't consider that now. She worked her magic with fervor, unrelenting even as Emmaline knew she was doing too much, too fast. Despite the chilly afternoon, sweat dripped down her face. Emmaline watched as Nadine fought a soldier like a wildcat, but the older woman was tiring. She was slow, and when the soldier closed in and punched a dragonfang knife into her gut, she writhed in agony.

Emmaline screamed at the sight, then clapped a hand over her mouth. She couldn't give away her position. Hands damp with perspiration, she frantically tried to bind a poppet to Nadine, to grant her strength and healing.

Nadine pulled herself deeper onto the knife, wrapping her arms around the soldier in a macabre embrace. The soldier screeched, floundering to get away. Somehow, Nadine reached down and dug the knife from her gut and flung it away. The soldier sagged in her arms, his skin and raw red muscle sloughing away over bones that clattered out of his uniform.

Nearby soldiers, witness to Nadine's act of horror, disengaged from their combat to circle the Healer, guns aimed at her.

"Well, well, well. What have we here?"

The wooden boards of the hayloft creaked behind her. Eyes wide, Emmaline slowly scooted around on the floor to face the tall, blond-haired man wearing a pristine scarlet and gold Confederation uniform. It wasn't mussed or bloodied from the fighting, not like the others below. Shiny gold medals pinned to his left breast likely meant he was someone of rank.

"Aren't you a little old to be playing with *dolls?*" the man leered, sinking more meaning into the last word than Emmaline liked. She had the strong suspicion he knew what she was doing.

"Just . . . just hiding from the fight." Emmaline kept her eyes wide and afraid, which wasn't a stretch by any means. *You have an advantage I don't, Em,* her father had told her. *You can look like a young, innocent girl. You don't have to like it, but there're times that will come in handy. Don't forget.*

The soldier took a step closer, head cocked as if he were trying to decide if he should believe her. She prayed that he did.

"I'm so scared," Emmaline whispered. Another truth. She squeezed her eyes shut, a move she disliked because it was difficult to track him, but it lent credence to her words.

The wood grated again with his movement. Then fingers closed around her chin, jerking her face up, her eyes flying open as the soldier stared at her.

"Please," Emmaline implored, her voice a whimper. "Please don't hurt me." Her pulse raced at the very real threat of the soldier looming over her.

His clean-shaven face would have been considered charming, even handsome, at any other time. Now it was terrifying. Emmaline heard a soft click, and with sickening realization, she saw the brass muzzle of a hexgun in the man's hand. Pointed at her.

"I'll admit, you're good. But you don't fool me." He prodded a poppet with his toe. "I'd recognize those anywhere. You must be the Dollmaker's daughter."

Trembling, Emmaline held his gaze as she covertly snagged a single poppet with one hand and slipped it into her boot. She'd never heard her father called that name before, and she suspected it wasn't a compliment. She wanted to say something, anything, to defend her father. But her tongue sat heavy in her mouth, and she had never felt so helpless as his fingers tightened on her chin, the hexgun nuzzling her side.

"Your father was careless to leave these just lying around where anyone might find them." The soldier chuckled. Emmaline knew it for the lie it was. The hexguns had been stowed away in a safe at HQ.

Someone in town had tipped this man off. Someone in town had betrayed everyone. She trembled, fury flooding through her as her mind connected the dots. Her father's near-death at the hands of the Salt-Iron Confederation. The collapse of the wind-pump. Blaise had been there for both. Blaise knew about the hexguns. Were the rumors true? Was Blaise the traitor?

"Why are you doing this?" Emmaline whispered.

The man leered, a feral grin. "Too many reasons to list. But right now? This is personal. I'm going to enjoy seeing your father suffer." The hexgun nudged her again. "What do you say we find out which sort of ammo this is loaded with, hmm?" Before Emmaline could react, he pulled the trigger, and she slumped to the ground.

Jack

With Butch and his undead legion, Jack had become hopeful. And that was a mistake. Hope was a fragile thing, meant to be shattered.

The undead were unkillable, for obvious reasons, and their appearance in the battle as they preceded Jack and Butch in a wedge formation sowed momentary confusion and chaos as the soldiers fought an implacable force that wouldn't die. But unkillable was not the same as invulnerable. The enemy assailed the undead (who, Jack noted, were piss-poor shots unless they were close to their foe) with blades and blunt weapons when bullets did nothing. That was fine with Jack. It allowed him the opportunity to take out a few more unsuspecting soldiers with well-timed bullets. But his supply was dwindling, and the two Confederation weapons he had come across were empty.

A screech ripped the air overhead, and Jack dove to avoid the reaching talons of a griffin. The undead outlaw in front of him wasn't so fortunate, and with a sorrowful moan, the beast lifted her into the air, skeletal legs flailing. Jack cursed as the griffin launched her over the side of the cliff.

Jack lost sight of Butch as he wove through the thinning throng of undead defenders to visit death and destruction on the enemy. Somewhere along the way, a bullet grazed his right leg—a minor annoyance, all things considered—and a knife sank into his left arm. Jack lost himself in the frenzy of battle, shrugging off the wounds for later. He fought like Butch's undead, an implacable force that nothing short of death would stop.

Or so he thought until a familiar voice rang out above the cacophony of battle. "Jack! I know you're here somewhere. Come out, unless you're a coward."

That damned taunting voice. Jack followed it through the writhing knot of soldiers, casually shooting a man here, stabbing one there. Blood caked his hands, slashes of red lacing his arms. Some of the blood was his, but most of it belonged to the enemy.

Around him, the sounds of fighting died off as the last of the defenders were defeated or surrendered. Panting, Jack stepped into a ring of Salt-Iron soldiers, weapons trained on him. Jack made a quick mental count of his bullets. One. He should have one left unless he had lost count in the heat of battle. One was all he needed.

"I'm here, Lamar, you frothy, sheep-biting pignut." Jack tightened his grip on the sixgun, eyes glittering as he searched the surrounding faces for Lamar. *C'mon. Where are you?*

A soldier tittered nervously at his insult, then cleared their throat as they realized the error. One side of the ring of soldiers shifted, and Jack tensed, prepared for action. He froze as Lamar stepped into the circle, Emmaline limp in his arms, her head lolled back.

Jack's blood ran cold, heart leaping in his chest. His mouth was dry, gaping.

Then rage slammed through him like the Wildfire of his nickname. He lifted his gun, a blur that the soldiers recognized too late. He sighted just over Emmaline's slender shoulders, aimed for Lamar's head. Pulled the trigger.

Nothing.

Lamar should have crumpled to the ground with a hole in his head. Why was he still standing?

Jack had failed. He had lost track of his bullets, the worst thing he could do in this situation. His brain froze, refusing to process what had happened.

With a taunting smile, Lamar handed Emmaline to a nearby soldier, gesturing as a silver cage coalesced around Jack, beautiful and deadly. The Commander put his hands behind his back, ambling over.

"Oh, Jack." Lamar shook his head, projecting false pity. "What happened? It's not like you to miscalculate something so basic." He slid his gaze to Emmaline's form. "Something distract you?"

Jack wobbled on his feet as the exertion of fighting, his wounds, and the psychological trauma of his daughter in Lamar's custody rocked him. He had a knife in his boot. He could throw it—but no, that wouldn't work. Nothing could get out of the trap.

"Let . . . let her go, Lamar. You have me. Take me in for the bounty." Jack's head pounded as the fight ebbed out of him. He was so tired. All he wanted was for his daughter to be safe. Then he could die knowing he hadn't failed everyone he cared about.

Lamar smirked. "As tempting as that is, I have other plans." He cast a glance around, the smoke from the fire ravaging the bakery and diner blowing over him. Lamar smiled, as black as his heart. "I'll be kind, traitor. I know you treasure this hole-in-the-wall town. So you get to stay here and watch it burn down while I leave with the mavericks."

Jack stepped as close as he dared to the bars, scanning the crowd. Heart sinking, he spotted familiar faces interspersed among the soldiers. The shock of Vixen's red hair. Raven, his handsome face purple with bruises and spattered with blood, in salt-iron shackles. Cordelia with a gun to her head. The soldiers herded the surviving magicless defenders across the square, held in a tight knot in front of HQ.

Jack closed his eyes. This was a nightmare. "Lamar. *Please.* Take me. Leave everyone else alone."

"As much as your begging is music to my ears, that doesn't work for me." Lamar shrugged, then turned away to address his surviving forces. "Get the new recruits loaded up and prepare the *Retribution* for travel." He paused, looking back at Jack. "One thing: I will commend you on the ferocity of your fighters. I thought we would waltz in, but they put up a fight despite our surprise." Lamar plucked a piece of lint from one sleeve. "Lucky for me, I made sure your Breaker wasn't here. You might have stood a chance otherwise."

Blaise? Jack's blood ran cold. Shit on a shingle. The Breaker was innocent after all.

Lamar noticed his expression and canted his head. "Do you know which way he went, by the way? He's next on my list."

"You leave him *alone,* Lamar," Jack snarled.

His old friend made a sour face. "I wish I could, but you know how these assignments go." He waved a hand, dismissive. "It is what it is." Lamar pivoted to trail behind his departing soldiers, pausing beside the man who still held Emmaline. He gave her a covetous look. "It's been years since we've had an Effigest worth a damn, Jack. Will she be as good as you, do you think?"

Jack knew better. Damned, dirty Lamar was goading him, the same as he did anyone in one of his blasted traps. Always poking at them, hoping they would slip. Jack realized his mistake too late as he slammed a hand against the bars of the cage with a ferocious roar.

The last thing he saw was Lamar's stupid grin as every muscle in his body pulsed with fire. And then everything was dark.

Clover

Veruc, the Great Bull, smiled on Clover with favor. She considered it a stroke of fortune that she and her load of children came across Kur Agur as she trotted down the road that meandered away from Itude. The Theilian hunched atop the driver's seat of a loaded wagon, furry arms crossed and shoulders rigid with agitation, as Clover gently lifted the children from her back and to the bed of the wagon. Clover didn't chide him for his behavior. She felt much the same way, frustrated to be away from the fighting.

Kur, to his credit, had gathered a small force from the outlying farms and ranches and led a column of loaded wagons heading to the town. Men and women who routinely traded goods with Itude came to support it however they could, armed with rifles, pitchforks, magic, and healing ministrations.

As the sun set, their group camped at the Collins place, the closest farmstead to Itude. It was a necessity, but Clover agonized at the delay. Winter's dark descended early, and it was ill-advised to travel in the consuming veil of night. This irritated Kur, too, and he paced their camp-site, snapping and growling like he had an infestation of ear mites.

As soon as dawn touched the horizon, they broke camp. The wagon train lumbered toward Itude, slow and steady. The airship had long departed, but Clover supposed that might be for the best. The people responding were not fighters, but they had big hearts. They wanted to help.

As the molly mules crested the final rise, Clover hopped down to the wintry ground from her seat beside Kur. The Theilian's lips curled back, eyes glowing gold. Clover sucked in a breath, flattening her ears.

Death. So much death on the wind. The humans couldn't smell it yet, not with their weak senses. But soon they would.

She traded a look with Kur. He said nothing, only lowered his head, the fur on his ruff erect. "I will scout ahead," she told him, pulling her shotgun down from where she had stashed it beneath the seat.

Clover loped ahead of the vanguard, scanning the area as she travelled. Only a few human bodies, and those dressed in the scarlet of the Salt-Iron Confederation. Viscera and broken feathers from pegasi and griffins littered the outskirts along with their corpses. The humans were griffin riders, she supposed.

The homes outside town still stood, though a few suffered broken windows or roof damage from falling aerial combatants. Curtains twitched in a window, and a moment later a gaggle of trembling women streamed out, surrounding Clover.

"Our babies! Where are our babies?" Tears and blood streaked their faces. They were dirty, terrified, and heartsick. Clover wanted nothing more than to reassure them, but the empty words died on her tongue.

"Five children came with me, and they will arrive soon in the wagon with Kur Agur. The others . . ." She looked toward town, squinting. So much smoke. "Jasper took them to his bolt-hole beneath his store."

Choking back sobs, the women fled toward town. Clover lowered her head and whispered a prayer to Veruc. *Please let the children be safe. Please.*

Head down, Clover trailed behind them, the biting wind coiling the stench of death around her. She paused, noting a skeletal corpse clutching a rifle. Clover snorted, head cocked in alarm until she caught a familiar scent wafting from the bones. *Butch.* The Necromancer had wielded his terrifying craft.

Bodies of friend and foe littered the streets of Itude. Blood pooled in the dirt, congealing in the chill temperature. Near the edge of the mesa, carrion birds croaked and danced around the bloating corpse of a pegasus.

Clover surveyed the gutted town. Most of the buildings on the northwest side of the square were smoldering husks—bakery, diner, mercantile, hardware store, greengrocer. The windows in her beloved Broken Horn Saloon were shot out, and part of the roof caved in. Some miracle had spared the dry goods store, and Clover watched as the mothers led a shivering line of children from the depths of Jasper's bolt-hole.

She sighed, closing her eyes as she thanked Veruc. Trembling, she opened them again and resolved to search for any wounded defenders clinging to life. More survivors joined Clover, including Hannah, who silently wept as she went from body to body.

They found Nadine amid a circle of slain soldiers, though Clover saw no wounds on their bodies. Against the odds, the Healer somehow lived and breathed, though bullets riddled her body and a rust-colored stain on her abdomen hinted at a grievous wound. The farmers and ranchers arrived, and a pair brought a stretcher and took Nadine to her clinic.

Clover straightened, gazing across the carnage spread out before her.

Her breath caught at a limp, too-familiar form face down in the dirt. *Jack.* With a bellow of despair, she tore over to him, kneeling beside him.

"Jack, no." Clover dipped her head in sorrow, turning him over gently. With a gasp, she realized that his chest rose and fell. Shallow, but there. She placed a furry ear to his chest. Sluggish heartbeat.

He lives. Barely.

Clover called for help, and moments later, Jack lay on a stretcher, face slack and eyes closed. The men carried him to Nadine's clinic. Clover rubbed the side of her muzzle, overwhelmed.

"Clover?"

Tiny hands tugged at her elbow. Clover glanced to the side and saw Jasper Strop staring up at her, imploring. She dwarfed the knocker which normally intimidated him. "Jasper, thank you for saving the children."

He waved his hand, a *think-nothing-of-it* gesture. "The man. The leader of the enemy." Jasper pointed to the nearest soldier in Salt-Iron crimson and gold, to clarify. "They are going after Blaise next."

"What?" Clover blinked, trying to decipher how Blaise fit into this horror.

Jasper tugged at one of his ears. "Excellent hearing. I heard him talking to Jack. It was a set-up, Clover. They tricked Blaise to leave so they could attack." His face fell. "And now they plan to go after him."

Clover sucked in a breath, eyes wide as his words struck her like a hammer to the head. Blaise was innocent. And he was in danger.

Jasper waited as she put the pieces together, his lips pressed together with determination. His eyes glittered. "It does not have to be that way, Clover."

"What do you mean?"

The little knocker smiled, a feral grin of bared teeth. "If he is in Jefferson Cole's company, I can find my niece. I can tell her. Warn him."

Clover jabbed her horns at him. Under any other circumstances, she might have thought to consult the Ringleaders first. But aside from Kur, who patrolled the town with barely restrained fury, they were all missing or near-dead.

"Do it," she ordered.

Jasper gave her a determined nod, scuttling off to the dry goods store.

CHAPTER FORTY

A Matter of Appearances

<I want to go with you,> Emrys insisted for the thousandth time, pressing his forehead against Blaise's shoulder.

Blaise shook his head. He was having an impossible time convincing the stallion that accompanying him to Ganland—to a new life—was a terrible idea. And to be honest, he hadn't made a convincing argument against Emrys's desire. The stallion was emphatic that he would be fine hiding his wings. But Blaise feared what might happen if anyone discovered the pegasus. As much as he craved a familiar friend along on his journey, he didn't want anything bad to happen to the loyal stallion.

"I know," Blaise murmured, and together they watched a paddle steamer trundle down the river. When they made the journey to Ganland, it would be by ship. If Emrys went, Jefferson explained, he would have to stay in the hold for an extended time, unable to move around. Definitely unable to spread his wings.

Emrys declared that a stupid idea, countering that he saw no problem with flying to a better location before getting on a boat. Blaise admitted the pegasus raised a good point—flying would be preferable to spending a long, long time on a steamer.

"There's nothing stopping you from going back to Itude, though," Blaise said. He had told Emrys that before.

<And I've told you before: you're my rider.> Emrys snorted, flicking his ears back. <Company's coming.>

Blaise glanced behind them, lips slipping into a smile as he saw Jefferson striding in their direction. The businessman looked pleased with himself as he joined them, arms resting on the top rail of the scenic overlook.

"We're all official now." Jefferson grinned, eyes alight. "My local attorney checked over the documents and said everything appears to be in order. She's sending them by courier to Nera. We're officially business partners."

Emrys rolled his eyes. <I'll leave the two of you to your boring business talk.> He ambled off, tail swishing.

Blaise returned the grin. It had taken longer than expected for all the paperwork to get together once he and Jefferson had agreed on the terms. He had no idea it took so much effort to open a business. When he said as much to Jefferson, the other man had shrugged and said that it varied by country. Ganland loved paperwork so it was more arduous than others.

Jefferson sent messages to his associates to put out feelers for a bakery location that could be snapped up for a cheap price and improved. Blaise was giddy at the thought of having his own bakery. Again.

It had taken time, but he had adjusted to life in Rainbow Flat. He didn't mind staying there another few months until Jefferson gave him the go-ahead to make his way to Nera.

"I leave in three days," Jefferson reminded him, watching a flatbed ferry convey a stagecoach from one side of the river to the other. "I don't like leaving you here alone to your own devices, so I have an associate coming out here to keep you company."

Blaise eyed him. "What's wrong? Do you think I'm going to skip town now that we have a contract?"

Jefferson shook his head. "Not that. It's a matter of . . . appearances." When Blaise raised an eyebrow, he continued. "Until we're a known quantity in Ganland, if I were to send you a message here in Rainbow Flat, it may appear suspicious. Do you follow my meaning?"

Blaise glanced down at the water lapping below, trying to keep his face impassive. "You're concerned to be seen as a traitor."

Jefferson gave him a fond look, chucking Blaise's shoulder with a gentle fist. "You catch on quickly. But yes, I already get enough flack for my Untamed Territory business ventures. I have some rivals who would love to throw me to the wolves for the slightest reason."

Blaise cocked his head. "That's the first time you've mentioned that. So why take the risk of working with me at all?"

Jefferson paused, rubbing the back of his neck as if he wished to take back his earlier words. "Sometimes the risk is worth the reward." He straightened, clearing his throat as he gestured to the surrounding town. "And I enjoy taking risks. It's the reason I go out to these exotic locations and make my own deals."

Blaise tilted his head, suspecting that Jefferson was keeping something from him. He thought about pressing but decided not to. He hadn't told Jefferson what his magic was, so who was he to judge? He wished he could talk to someone other than Emrys about it. As much as Blaise loved Emrys—and he did, the pegasus was like family to him—he craved someone else not fearing his magic, but accepting it as part of who he was.

"Blaise?" Jefferson was giving him an expectant look.

He blinked. "Oh. Um, sorry. I was thinking about something."

Jefferson smiled. "As I was saying, tomorrow Flora Strop will arrive. I'll introduce you, then I'll leave you in her tender care."

Strop? That was a familiar last name, but it could be a coincidence. Blaise shook away the thought. "I'm changing hotels when you leave. We'll have to let her know." He couldn't afford the place Jefferson had him in now.

"You will not," Jefferson said, straightening as if he had taken offense. When Blaise opened his mouth to protest, the other man stepped closer, his face serious. "I have good reason for you to stay in the hotel I chose."

Blaise's forehead wrinkled. "Why?"

"Protection, among other reasons." Jefferson studied him with concern. "It's one of my properties, so I know the staff will keep you safe and well-tended."

Blaise's jaw dropped. "Wait. This entire time . . . we've been staying at *your* hotel?"

Jefferson had the good grace to look slightly embarrassed. "Obviously."

Blaise rubbed his face with one hand. "Okay. That's fine. I assume you won't charge me for the stay."

Jefferson grinned. "Oh, I will—but steeply discounted. You're welcome."

Blaise rolled his eyes. "You mentioned other reasons. What are the other reasons?"

Jefferson studied him, as if trying to decide what to say. He seemed uncharacteristically nervous and gave a small shake of his head. "It's nothing. Come on. We should go celebrate with wine. Well, that blasted switchel for you, I suppose."

"I might give the wine a try tonight."

THE RESTAURANT BUSTLED WITH ACTIVITY, AND WITH A SINKING HEART, Blaise realized it was the most expensive that Rainbow Flat offered. He gave an imperceptible shake of his head as he studied the menu. It was difficult to adjust to Jefferson's casual flaunting of wealth.

"What?" Jefferson peered across the table at him. "Don't see anything to your liking?"

Blaise folded the menu and set it down. "It's not that. I just don't fit in here." He gestured to the plush, velvet-upholstered chair in which he sat.

Jefferson rested his chin on his hand, frowning. "Don't belittle yourself. You're my business partner. Of course you fit in."

Blaise shook his head. "I've signed a very large stack of papers. I don't think that qualifies me for much of anything yet."

"It does. And we need some of that wine to toast it." Jefferson flagged the server over. "Two glasses of the Umber Dolce." The server bowed his head gracefully, then strode off.

"What, I don't get to pick?" Blaise asked.

Jefferson gave him an exasperated look. "I'm not about to let you ruin this by picking some cheap wine that tastes like vinegar."

Blaise chuckled. "If I didn't know better, I'd say you're insulting my raspberry switchel."

"I would never do that," Jefferson intoned solemnly, though his mouth twitched with humor.

Blaise relaxed in the opulent chair, running his thumb over the velvet. The last several weeks in Rainbow Flat with Jefferson had been . . . nice. He had discovered that Jefferson was more than an entrepreneur—he was a comfortable conversationalist, and he never seemed to consider Blaise as anything less than an equal. And best of all, he never asked about his magic. It rarely came up in conversation. "You're right. I'd have no idea how to pick wine. So why that one?"

Jefferson leaned back in his chair. "Umber Dolce is one of the livelier wines on this menu. It will be a good starter wine for you. It has a fresh, fruity flavor."

Blaise tapped the exorbitant number beside the menu item. "And it's the most expensive."

Jefferson grinned. "You have a lot to learn. The finest bottles of wine are the most expensive."

The server returned with the wine and made a flourishing show of uncorking it and then pouring into a pair of crystal goblets. Jefferson's eyes gleamed as he watched, savoring the show. After the server finished and retreated, Jefferson lifted his glass and swirled the golden contents. Blaise took his cue and followed suit.

"And now a toast. To bright futures." Jefferson hoisted his cup toward him. Blaise let his goblet ring against Jefferson's.

"To bright futures," Blaise echoed. Jefferson took a sip, so Blaise did as well. It wasn't bad, though he had been expecting a little more on the fruity side. He could still taste the aggressive headiness of alcohol. Blaise was polite and took another sip.

Jefferson watched him, intent. "What's your opinion?"

"Um. It's different," Blaise stalled, setting down his glass.

"You don't like it." Jefferson's shoulders drooped with disappointment.

"It's not bad," Blaise amended. "Just not what I was expecting."

Jefferson rested his arms against the white tablecloth and leaned forward. "I could say the same for you."

Blaise froze. "What do you mean?"

"You're not what I was expecting." Jefferson glanced away, and Blaise realized he was discomfited, which was unusual. Jefferson drummed his fingers on the table, then looked up at him again. "We've spent a lot of time together and I . . . I care about you." He licked his lips as if they had suddenly gone dry. "In more than a professional manner."

Blaise stared at him as he wrapped his mind around Jefferson's words. He didn't know what to say to such a direct statement. His mind whirred and came up blank, his heart racing in response.

"Forget I said that. It was improper." Jefferson rubbed the back of his neck, ill at ease. His eyes darted around the restaurant like a man looking for rescue. "Where's that server? I'm ready to order. Are you ready?" His voice rose, almost feverish.

Blaise leaned forward, his brain finally catching up to the situation. "Jefferson. Stop."

Jefferson gave him a pained look, his mouth a down-turned slash.

"I'm flattered. You're . . ." Blaise pursed his lips, trying to grasp how to describe it. The best he could do was to gesture at Jefferson, then the restaurant. "You're like this. I'm not. And I've never had anyone interested in me, so I don't know how to feel about that."

Jefferson blinked. "Ever? You're kidding, right?"

Blaise rubbed the edge of the tablecloth between his index finger and thumb, self-conscious. It was a hard thing to admit that he had resigned himself to a life alone. He liked the idea of a companion, but it seemed out of his grasp. "I wish I were."

Jefferson shook his head, puzzled. "Then you've been surrounded by short-sighted fools."

Blaise's breath suspended for a split second at Jefferson's words. "What?"

"I'm serious. Look at that strong jaw beneath the rugged beard. That long bit of hair above your brow that sometimes falls into your eyes." Jefferson grinned as he added, "The way your eyes narrow when you think I'm being ridiculous."

"I'm doing that right now, aren't I?"

"Yes," Jefferson deadpanned.

Blaise shook his head, hoping his cheeks weren't aflame with embarrassment. "I've enjoyed my time with you. I don't know if I share your feelings. This is new to me." His stomach writhed with indecision. This was uncharted territory. No one—man or woman—in Bristle would have him after the disasters of his youth. And now the opportunity stared him in the face in the guise of a golden-haired, green-eyed man who saw none of Blaise's faults.

Jefferson reached across the table, laying his hand atop Blaise's. Not claiming or grabbing, but reassuring. It took all of Blaise's willpower not to startle away from the touch. "Take all the time you need." Jefferson drew his hand back.

Blaise swallowed, caught off guard by the enormity of the situation. Jefferson could have anyone. "Why me?"

"Why not you?"

"I'm serious."

"As am I." Jefferson's green eyes sparked. He relented, glancing around. His voice was low when he spoke. "Because you're kind. You talk to me like . . . like a normal person. Not like you're trying to groom a prized racehorse to make you rich. You're not chasing after me for my money or . . ." He trailed off, shaking his head.

"To be fair, I chased you for the chance at a bakery."

Jefferson blinked, then chuckled as he waved a hand, dismissive. "That's different. That's business, and you'll do your part." He smiled, and it was a content expression. "And you have this single-minded determination to open a bakery, of all things. You have magic, and I'm sure could do other things. But you chose that." He tucked his chin. "It's cute."

Blaise leaned back. "Let me assure you that baked goods are a serious business."

Jefferson's smile widened into a grin that reflected in his eyes. "That's what I'm counting on. Businessman, remember?" He pointed to himself.

Blaise relaxed. This differed from anything he had ever imagined, this comfortable banter with someone who found him attractive. The server circled around and took their orders, and when she hurried off, Jefferson picked up the conversation as if he hadn't moments earlier rocked the foundations of Blaise's world.

"I know you're from Desina. You told me that much. Which town?" Jefferson asked as he picked up a slice of bread and buttered it.

Blaise cringed. He hoped Jefferson didn't plan to delve too deeply into his past. "Bristle." When Jefferson nodded, he asked, "Do you know it? It's not a large town."

"I've never been to Bristle, but yes, I know it. If I travel by boat, we usually stop at the ports in Sable Point and Gulfton before making the longer trek across the Gulf of Stars to Nera." Jefferson sank his teeth into the bread.

Blaise seized the opportunity to learn more about Jefferson, especially since he couldn't pose another question without being rude while chewing. "You speak of Nera often. Is that where you're from originally?"

Jefferson shook his head, swallowing the bit of bread before answering. "I was born in Seaside, and most of my family is still there. Do you know anything about the Fortune of Majority? It's particular to Ganland."

Blaise's forehead puckered, quizzical. "No."

Jefferson settled back in his chair. "They prize business acumen where I'm from. The Fortune of Majority is a tradition that most families take part in. When a child turns eighteen, they're gifted a hundred golden eagles to spend as they choose." His eyes glittered with the fervor of a distant memory. "The new adult can spend it however they choose. Save it, invest it . . . or spend it on frivolous things."

Blaise cocked his head. "It's a test?"

"Exactly." Jefferson nodded.

"So what did you do?"

Jefferson coughed and glanced away, embarrassed. "I, ah . . ."

Blaise smiled. He thought he had Jefferson figured out. "You spent it on frivolous things, didn't you?"

Jefferson swung his head back around, meeting his gaze with sudden intensity. "Not exactly *frivolous*." He brought his right hand up from beneath the table and pointed to the ring he wore on his index finger, holding it out so Blaise could see.

The ring featured a large cabochon-cut dark red stone; a garnet, Blaise guessed. The precious stone was set in a golden enamel bezel accented with tiny diamonds that winked in the light. He was no jewelry appraiser, but Blaise knew he was looking at top-of-the-line craftsmanship.

"I made some investments and then cashed them all in to buy this— and yes, I'm well aware that seems frivolous. But I assure you, it's not. Did I spend the investment money on new ventures like any sensible young

Gannish man would do? Absolutely not." Jefferson shook his head, rueful. "But this opened doors for me. Would you believe a year after I bought this ring, I quit my job working for my father, traveled to Rainbow Flat, and invested in my first hotel?"

The server brought out their meals, and Blaise waited to reply until she had left. "If anyone else said that, I wouldn't believe them. But it's you so I do."

Jefferson smiled, and this time it was the satisfied expression of a hunter reminiscing on a fine hunt. "That was eleven years ago. I like to think I've done well for myself since then."

Blaise opened his mouth to respond when the front door to the restaurant blew open in a great gust of wind, a petite form hustling inside. The doorman yelped at the sudden intrusion.

"You need a *reservation!*" the hostess hissed urgently as the invader ignored her, shucking off a rain-dampened oilskin greatcoat and tossing it over the hostess's extended arm.

A courier? Blaise wondered, tensing as he watched. The stranger scanned the restaurant before their eyes settled on Jefferson, moving with speed and purpose in their direction. Blaise clenched his fists, alarmed. His palms itched as his magic rose up, ready.

"Relax, I know her," Jefferson murmured. He waited as the small woman claimed an empty chair from a nearby table without so much as asking, butting it up beside their table. "Flora, good to see you. Wasn't expecting you until tomorrow."

Blaise blinked. So this was Flora Strop. She was nothing like he expected. Flora was short, the tip of the cheerful pink bun of hair atop her head coming no higher than the middle of Blaise's chest. She wore scarlet-framed glasses that reminded him of Vixen, giving him a brief pang of homesickness. Blaise thought she wasn't fully human—if he had to guess, he would say she might be half-knocker, which made sense if his guess about her last name was correct. But that wasn't something he was prepared to ask.

"Something came up, and I had to rush," Flora replied, then clapped her hands. "What's a girl gotta do to get some service around here?"

A harried server came over, offering Flora a wine goblet and pouring out a sampling of Umber Dolce. She lifted the glass in a salute of thanks and sipped, releasing a pent-up sigh as she closed her eyes in bliss. As she enjoyed her refreshment, Blaise realized he had seen her before—for a brief time on Jefferson's first day in Itude. Afterward, she had vanished, never seen in town again.

"Mmm. Good vintage. That hits the spot." Flora's eyes shot open, reinvigorated. "So which do you want first? The bad news, or the worse news? Also, is this the place that has the oysters in that creamy sauce? I could go for oysters."

Blaise's mouth ran dry, and he traded a worried glance with Jefferson. Somehow retaining an air of calm, Jefferson flagged another of the staff down and ordered oysters for Flora before answering. "I'm assuming the news should wait until we're no longer in polite company?" He gestured with his fork to encompass the restaurant.

Flora tilted her head, considering. "Hmm. After oysters, then."

Dinner didn't sit well in Blaise's stomach after Flora's arrival. Jefferson attempted to eat, but Blaise noticed the developments bothered him, too. Only Flora attacked her food with vigor, eating like she had been starved for days. She asked Jefferson if he was going to finish his trihorn fillet and promptly claimed it when he pushed it over to her.

Afterward, they retired to Jefferson's suite. As soon as they entered, Jefferson hightailed over to the bar and poured out a finger of whiskey for himself and Flora.

Blaise sat in an armchair, perched near the edge with his hands clasped, consumed by alert apprehension. With a sigh, Jefferson eased onto the side of the chaise nearest Blaise, setting his whiskey on a coaster on the low table. They waited as Flora peeled off her boots with a groan, flexing her stockinged feet as if they ached. Then she produced an oilskin-wrapped envelope from a carrier Blaise hadn't noticed strapped to her back.

She pulled a smaller white envelope out but didn't offer it to Jefferson. Instead, she pointed it at Blaise, her eyes narrowed to dangerous slits. "I have questions for you. First of all, how dare you?"

He blinked, unbalanced by her query. "What?"

Jefferson uttered a frustrated sound. "Flora, don't. Please." He cast a furtive glance at Blaise before settling his pleading look on the pink-haired woman.

Flora frowned, turning her pique on Jefferson. "Of all the mages in the world, you had to find a *Breaker*?"

The blood rushed from Blaise's head. No. No, no, no. He closed his eyes, pained. *Not again.* Why did this always happen when he found some place he might belong, someone who didn't hate him?

A firm hand latched onto his, warm fingers twining together. *Reassuring.* Jefferson. Blaise trembled. "It doesn't matter." Jefferson's breath warmed Blaise's ear, voice gentle. But he was wrong. It *did* matter. It always ended up mattering.

Flora sighed. "Ignoring all the history—"

Blaise's eyes flashed open, indignation overcoming his panic. "History doesn't define who *I* am." Flora gave him a side-eyed, skeptical look. "I'm more than just a Breaker." He squeezed Jefferson's hand, warmth blooming when the gesture was returned.

Jefferson reluctantly released Blaise's hand. "I agree with that, and as far as I'm concerned it has no bearing on this conversation." He refocused on Flora. "Tell me your news. And try to do it in a way that won't insult my new business partner."

Flora blew out a huffing breath. "Fine, but I think you'll find he *does* have bearing on this conversation. I have three news items, and they range from bad to horrible to awful. Which do you want?"

Jefferson raked a hand through his hair. "I don't even know where to begin."

With a shrug, Flora offered him the envelope. "Then start here."

He took the proffered envelope, pulling a small pocket knife out to slit it open. Jefferson drew out the letter, eyes scanning the page before he fully unfolded it. His jaw tightened as his teeth ground together. Without a word, he passed the letter to Blaise and took a long gulp of whiskey.

Full of misgivings, Blaise opened the page and read. By the second sentence, he understood why Jefferson required a stiff drink. The author of the letter claimed that Jefferson's Gannish survey team in Itude was slain by *"the bloodthirsty outlaws"*. In retaliation, they sent a force from Fort Courage out to *"bring the guilty to justice"*.

The letter was dated several days ago. Maybe the attackers hadn't arrived yet. "They . . . they wouldn't have killed your survey team, Jefferson. We have to warn them."

Flora gave a tiny shake of her head. "The letter is misleading in more ways than one. It was penned the same day as the attack."

Jefferson drained his glass and rose for a refill. "How did you discover this?"

The pink-haired woman's eyes went steely. "First-hand information." She lifted her glass, a silent request for more. Blaise hoped her metabolism could keep up with it.

"Your uncle?" Jefferson poured out golden liquid for her. He paused, glancing at Blaise. "Can I get you something? Water?" Blaise shook his head.

"My uncle," Flora confirmed. For Blaise's benefit, she added, "Jasper Strop."

Ah-ha. He pressed his lips together. "I thought your last name was familiar."

Flora waved a hand, warding away distraction. "This is important.

Uncle Jas survived by hiding in his bolt-hole. He heard things, Jefferson." She crooked a finger at Blaise. "Gaitwood's next target is your boy here."

Gaitwood. Blaise shuddered involuntarily.

Jefferson pinched the bridge of his nose. "First off, he's not my boy. *Business partner.* I know it doesn't roll off the tongue as well, but there it is. Second, why would he want Blaise? They were fed the same history lessons we were. The Salt-Iron Confederation line dictates Breakers are bad news. The normal response to a Breaker is . . ." He trailed off, eyes studying his whiskey as he swirled it in the glass. Flora helpfully completed the thought by slashing her index finger across her throat.

Blaise blanched.

"Not helping," Jefferson growled.

"*Lamar* Gaitwood doesn't care for him, far as I can tell," Flora clarified. "*Gregor* Gaitwood is a different story."

For the first time since the world-shaking conversation began, Jefferson was thunderstruck, as if Flora had punched him in the gut. "Why does *Gregor* Gaitwood want a Breaker?"

Flora smiled, devoid of mirth. "That's the question of the day. The one I can't figure out." Her eyes slid to Blaise. "Why would someone like that want you?"

He leaned back in the chaise, scratching at his beard with one hand. "For starters, I don't even know who you're talking about. If it's not obvious, I'm unaccustomed to people wanting me for anything." *Except Jefferson.* Strange as it was, that thought offered a moment of comfort. An oasis in a desert of despair.

Jefferson and Flora traded glances and came to a silent decision. Jefferson rubbed his chin, thoughtful. "Have you heard of the Salt-Iron Council?"

Blaise winced. "The Confederation wasn't discussed in my home. My mother . . ." He shook his head, closing his eyes as he took a breath.

Jefferson set his whisky on the table and then sat down beside Blaise on the chaise lounge, leaning forward so his forearms braced against his knees. "It's fine. Short answer: every nation in the Confederation places members called Doyens on the Council. The number of positions vary by country. Phinora, Ganland, Canen, and Petria have three district representatives, while Mella and Umber only have two. Desina and Argor don't have representatives yet, as the Council won't be in session to admit them for another few weeks." Jefferson watched Blaise to make sure he was following along. "Gregor Gaitwood is a Doyen for Phinora. Does that make sense?"

Blaise chewed on his lower lip. "Yes, but I don't know why he'd want me." He paused, thinking. "Except . . ."

"Spill it," Flora growled.

"Be nice." Jefferson gave Blaise a reassuring look. "Will you please tell us? It may be important."

He didn't want to tell them, didn't want to relive that day. Blaise bowed his head. Jefferson was right—it might be important. In a whisper, he told them of his first encounter with Lamar Gaitwood and his mother's gambit. And then he spoke of his second brush with the Commander, when he found out his mother's fate.

Flora scratched at the arm of her chair. "Something to do with her then. She a mage?"

Blaise shook his head. "Alchemist."

Jefferson's eyes widened, and Flora groaned. "That's almost worse. What's her name?"

"Marian Hawthorne."

She tipped her head, considering. "Not familiar with that name. But I'll do some digging, see what I can find out." Flora swallowed, her eyes hooded with regret. "And now the last bit of news, which I don't think either of you really registered because the human brain can only process so much dragonshit at once." She sucked in a breath. "Lamar Gaitwood *already* attacked Itude. He sacked the place and took the surviving mages back to Fort Courage."

Blaise stared at her, his mouth so dry he wished he had taken Jefferson up on the offer for water. He clutched the padded arm of the chair, so focused on Flora's words that he didn't notice the telltale itch in his palm as his magic responded to his distress. The wood beneath the velvet made a thunderous crack as his magic assaulted it, and an instant later Blaise held the sagging arm onto the chaise. He closed his eyes, hating himself for his failure to control it.

"Leave it," Jefferson murmured, shaking his head. "It's just furniture."

Flora muttered something Blaise couldn't quite make out, but he suspected it wasn't flattering.

"I should have been there," Blaise whispered.

Flora snapped her fingers. "That's the thing. Lamar specified he *didn't* want you there." A wicked smile played on her lips. "Something about your presence made his odds of winning unfavorable."

The hairs on the back of Blaise's neck stood on end, chilled. He had thwarted Gaitwood twice. From what Jack said, Lamar Gaitwood wasn't a stupid man. He was canny. Which meant he was crafty enough to force Blaise out of Itude before he went on the attack. Blaise shook his head as white-hot rage coursed through him. But the sensation only lasted a moment. It didn't serve him to be angry around Jefferson and Flora. Anger could wait.

Flora watched him, head cocked to one side. "I see all these emotions crossing your face, and I don't know if I'm more concerned that you're not collapsing the building around us or that you're just sitting there like a fly landed in your soup."

"I can control my magic," Blaise muttered. "Getting mad right now won't solve any problems." He took a shaky breath. "I . . . I should go to Itude. There must be survivors. They'll need help." His stomach lurched as he connected what had befallen Itude with the people he cared about. Jack. Emmaline. Reuben. Clover. Hannah. Vixen. So many more. It was easier to think of Itude as a unit—it was less personal. But as he thought of the individuals, he felt sick.

"There are survivors," Flora confirmed. "But I don't know that you should go there." She glanced at Jefferson, imploring. "He can't go there, not if Gregor wants him. It's too close to Courage. He needs to go far, far away. Thorn or Arbor. Even Highhorse if they'll allow it."

Jefferson's smile was sad. "Blaise has my support to do whatever he thinks is best." He touched Blaise's arm. "You didn't leave under the best conditions. I'm assuming this changes things?"

Blaise exhaled. "I suspect Gaitwood set me up."

Jefferson nodded, grim. "I agree with that assessment." He reached for his glass, draining the last dregs of whiskey. "Allow me to recap what we know. Flora, correct me if I miss anything. One, Gaitwood has made sure my survey team is out of the picture. Two, Gaitwood wants Blaise, but we're not sure why. Three, they attacked Itude. Did I miss something?"

"Lamar took the surviving mages with him, back to Courage."

Blaise's heart raced. So many of them had fled to Itude to escape that fate. He clenched his fists. This couldn't stand.

"I'm going back to Itude," Blaise said, voice soft. "I'm going to help the survivors, and then I'm going to get back the mages that were stolen."

Flora gave him a speculative look. "Don't get me wrong, I like where you're going with this, but you and what army?"

Blaise was done running away. "I may not have an army, but I don't need one." He refused to meet Jefferson's worried eyes. "I'm a Breaker."

CHAPTER FORTY-ONE
It's Complicated

Blaise

Emrys tried to ignore Blaise at first when he came to the stable, but the stallion didn't hold out long when he sensed the palpable anger rolling from him. The raspberry tart Blaise had snagged from the hotel room service as a peace offering didn't hurt, either.

Once Blaise explained the news, the pegasus was full of righteous fury. <We should go now,> Emrys demanded, his neck curled in a tight arch and every muscle in his body tense. <There's no time to lose.>

Blaise shook his head, laying a hand on the stallion's shoulder to quell him. He felt much the same way, but it would be dangerous to leave now. It was dark and cold; the moon was hidden by clouds heavy with the promise of snow. "We have to wait until morning, if the weather holds."

The stallion hung his head. <We should have been there.>

Blaise nodded, threading his fingers through Emrys's warm mane. "We can't change the past. We can only respond."

They stood in companionable silence for a few minutes. The stable was quiet but for the soft sounds of some of the other occupants snoring or shifting around their box stalls. It was a safe place in a world that was anything but.

<What will Jefferson do?>

Blaise leaned against Emrys, brushing dust from his glossy neck. "He . . . ah, he has his own obligations. Jefferson leaves for Izhadell tomorrow." Izhadell, where Blaise's mother might be. "But he's sending his associate with me, Flora Strop."

<Strop? I know that name.>

"Jasper's niece."

Emrys snorted. <Jack's going to have kittens when he finds out.>

Blaise chuckled, then stopped as his blood ran cold. He didn't know Jack's fate. The surly outlaw was a survivor. Surely he had survived with wits and raw cussedness.

<Don't count someone out too soon,> Emrys cautioned, following Blaise's trail of thought.

He nodded. No sense worrying about Jack or anyone else until he had a better grasp of their fate. If the weather held, in two days, he might know more. Blaise sighed, releasing those worries for his future self.

"I need to get back to my room to rest. See you in the morning." He filled Emrys's bucket with a late-night snack of sweet feed before letting himself out. Blaise left the stable with Emrys's contented crunching in his wake.

He trudged down the hotel hall, tired but consumed with the manic energy of anticipation. As Blaise turned down the hallway to his suite, he saw Jefferson carrying a burlap sack into his room. He paused, dropping the bag just inside the door before closing it as Blaise approached.

"I thought you'd be asleep by now."

Blaise shook his head. "I was with Emrys. It's going to be hard to sleep tonight."

Jefferson's green eyes intensified. "Do you want to talk?"

Did he? Blaise wasn't sure how to bleed off the nervous energy—not even using his magic would take the edge off. He was angry and distressed, determined and ready to take action. Blaise had hoped time with Emrys would help, but it only stoked the fire.

"I'm sorry I grabbed your hand earlier," Jefferson murmured, his own hands threaded together over his middle. "That was thoughtless of me."

The unexpected apology shook Blaise out of his worries. "Oh. I didn't mind it, actually." If anything, it had been the thing he had needed in the moment—someone stalwart beside him, unshaken by the news of what he was.

Jefferson stepped closer, tentative. "All the same, I should have known better." He sighed, running a hand through his hair. "And we don't have to if you don't want to. But this path you're going down will not be an easy one for us to reconcile." Was it Blaise's imagination, or did Jefferson sound hurt?

Blaise bit his lip. He liked Jefferson and didn't want to leave him on a sour note. He unlocked the door to his room and tipped his head toward it. Jefferson blinked in surprise but didn't hesitate to follow him in.

"I can't allow what Lamar Gaitwood did to go unanswered." Blaise dreaded the words coming out of his mouth. They sounded like they belonged to someone else.

"I understand." Jefferson met his eyes. "And as I said earlier, I support you." He sat down on the edge of the bed, sighing. "Do you want me to cancel the contract?"

Blaise blinked, startled. All thoughts of business ventures with Jefferson had fled his mind long ago. "What?"

Jefferson pursed his lips. "Do you want me to cancel the contract? Our partnership. I can do that." The way he said it made Blaise think Jefferson desperately wanted him to say *no*. But that was madness.

Blaise paced the short distance to the dresser, staring at his reflection in the mirror that hung on the wall. "I just want to be a baker. But I don't think I get that choice."

A smile ghosted Jefferson's lips. "You always get a choice." He exhaled a pent-up breath. "I can leave it as-is?"

Blaise swallowed. "I saw the clause about death breaking the contract."

Jefferson's eyes frosted over. "Don't you die on me." His voice grated with unexpected ferocity.

Blaise sat down on the bed beside him. "I just don't know what's ahead of me."

Jefferson's eyes softened. "Isn't that the thing about life, though? None of us know that. We can only go forth and choose to live with courage."

"I don't feel very courageous," Blaise admitted, glancing away. He wasn't dauntless or quick-witted like Jack.

"You don't know it, but you already live with courage." Jefferson tilted his head, smiling. "Look at you. You're a *Breaker*, and you've made it this far. Your life is extraordinary."

Blaise raised his eyebrows, dubious. "I don't know that I'd call it *extraordinary*." But the simple act of speaking with Jefferson was so calming that the next thing he knew, they talked into the darkest hours of night, voices soft and companionable.

Blaise grumbled as the first rays of sunlight pierced the lace curtains. He burrowed into the warmth of the bed, freezing when his left hand brushed another solid form. His eyes shot open, and he looked into Jefferson's emerald eyes.

"You slept," Jefferson murmured, content. He used one hand to adjust his pillow, aiming a sleepy smile at Blaise.

"I guess so." A blush raced through his skin. They were both fully clothed. Nothing had happened aside from talking. He had discovered that Jefferson wasn't afraid of him, even after he coaxed out a litany of the path of destruction of Blaise's youth.

"I think we overslept. Is Emrys going to be annoyed?" Jefferson yawned, stretching out his arms to loosen his muscles.

"Not if I bring him breakfast pastries from room service."

"Mmm. That sounds like a good idea for everyone." Jefferson rose from the bed, languid. Mussed hair and rumpled clothing added to his appeal, and Blaise turned away to keep from staring. Jefferson filled out an order card on the corner desk and hung the placard on the door. "Give it fifteen minutes, and we'll have a feast."

Blaise shook his head, still adjusting to the way that Jefferson made things happen with his wealth and influence. But money couldn't solve all their problems. It wouldn't bring back the dead or lost.

Jefferson studied his unkempt reflection. "Hmm. Let me go do something about this while the food comes." He walked to the door, then paused, uncertain. "You, ah, don't mind if I have breakfast with you?"

His hesitance was endearing. He really was attempting to not impose. Blaise cocked his head. "I didn't see how much food you ordered, but I suspect even with taking some to Emrys I couldn't eat it all myself." He rose from the bed, closing the distance between them. "I would be happy if you had breakfast with me." And wonder of wonders, it was true.

Jefferson's eyes widened in delight. "Then I won't be long. We'll make every moment count."

He hurried off to his suite, allowing Blaise a moment to decompress. What was he doing? Blaise raked a hand through his hair. Who was he turning into, this person spending time with a romantic interest? This audacious mage preparing to butt heads with a Commander of the Salt-Iron Confederation? He was becoming a Breaker.

He closed his eyes for a moment, then set to dressing for travel. Blaise traded out his rumpled clothes for a pair of fresh dark blue cotton trousers, a white button-up shirt, and a blue vest for warmth. His duster and gloves were slung over a chair back. Flight goggles, bandanna, and hat awaited him on the dresser. Packed saddlebags rested on the floor by the door.

A tap at the door announced breakfast, followed by Jefferson's return. After the waitstaff left, Jefferson eyed Blaise with appreciation.

"Everyone who turned their back on you before doesn't know what they're missing," Jefferson said as he sat down at the table, loading a plate with sausages, toast, and eggs. He gestured with his fork. "And I'm not saying that just because you look good—and make no mistake, you look *good.*"

Blaise ducked his head. "They had reason to. I told you last night."

Jefferson set down his fork, lifting a hand to tick off his fingers. "Yes. Let's see. There was the chifferobe incident. The Spinning Wheel Disaster. The shelves you broke at the library. The rain collection barrel and the hitching post outside the general goods store at the same time—that's impressive, mind you." He grinned. "Should I go on?"

Blaise's cheeks flamed with shame, pin-prickles of doubt sharp on his skin. "Please don't."

Jefferson winced as he realized his misstep. "I'm sorry. I was trying to be flippant, not hurtful." He offered Blaise a cinnamon roll in apology. "What I mean to say is I don't care what your magic has done or may do. I care about *you.*"

Blaise added the cinnamon roll to his plate, relaxing. *Jefferson doesn't care about my past. Doesn't care that I can cause disaster.* It was a strange sensation—one that Blaise could get used to.

Jefferson ate, prodding Blaise to do the same when he noticed him picking at his food. "I know you were hurt in the past. I promise to never do that, if I can help it."

Blaise blinked back tears. He wanted to believe it, he really did. He just wasn't willing to gamble on it—not with the track record of his life so far.

They finished their breakfast, making small talk. But it couldn't last forever, as much as Blaise wished they could linger. With regret, he packed a chocolate muffin, glazed donut, and strawberry tart into a linen cloth for Emrys. Jefferson watched with appreciation as he shrugged on his duster, tied the bandanna around his neck, slipped on his gloves, and settled his flight goggles on his forehead beneath his hat.

Jefferson chuckled. "Can't believe I'm letting you walk away from me looking like that."

"Like what?"

Jefferson rose from his seat. "Like an outlaw who just stole my heart."

"You're being melodramatic."

Jefferson stepped closer, eyes intense. "Hardly. But I could be, if you like."

Blaise met his gaze, something that he avoided with most people, but he couldn't help with Jefferson. His breath hitched for a moment, surprised by the importance of the permission the other man was asking. There was no telling what his future held. And here was Jefferson, offering a piece of a puzzle Blaise hadn't realized he was missing. "I'll allow some melodrama."

Jefferson closed the gap between them, leaning in, his lips questing against Blaise's. Blaise lifted his chin in response as Jefferson wrapped him in an embrace. And then he gave in to the tide of passion, returning the kiss with the ferocity of someone facing the gallows.

After a hundred years—or just moments, for Blaise had lost all concept of time—Jefferson drew back. "Ah, sorry. That was rather presumptuous of me. I didn't want to have any regrets."

Blaise's shoulders relaxed. "Neither did I."

FLORA HIRED THE SERVICES OF A STURDY, NEARLY WHITE PEGASUS STALLION by the name of Tylos. Emrys dwarfed Tylos, who measured only twelve hands tall at the withers. The little stallion boasted colorful wings with alternating bands of magenta and violet.

"Hope your big beast can keep up," Flora said with a smirk as she patted Tylos's shoulder.

Blaise glanced from Tylos to Emrys. He expected that small Tylos might be the one to have trouble. "Why is that?"

"Because this handsome fellow is an Eskelan pegasus." Flora adjusted the girth, making sure no feathers had been trapped beneath the leather. At Blaise's blank expression, she added, "Imagine a hummingbird's wings on a pegasus. That's what you get with an Eskelan. Their wings beat forty times a second."

<And we must stop every hour so he can eat,> Emrys advised Blaise privately, ears pinned with annoyance.

Blaise saddled Emrys, tightening the girth and buckling his breast-plate. With their path laid out before them, he wasn't in the mood for banter. He wanted to get ready and focus on the grim task ahead.

They completed a last round of checks. Every buckle fastened and secure. Everything accounted for. Jefferson waited beneath the stable's overhang as they walked out, hooves and boots ringing on hard-packed dirt.

"You're going to miss your boat," Flora chided him.

He chuckled. "I paid them to wait." Because of course he had. Jefferson wore a warm, charcoal grey cutaway morning coat over his grey paisley vest. "I would tell you to be careful, but . . ." He shrugged.

"We'll be fine." Flora waved a hand. "As long as the airship's not at Itude we'll—"

"Airship?" Blaise and Jefferson squeaked in unison.

Flora blanched. "Uh, did I fail to mention that Gaitwood attacked the town using an airship?"

Jefferson massaged his forehead. "Gods. Gregor had the balls to send the *Retribution* out there? It's meant to be a prototype." He clenched his fists, a vein ticking in his jaw. "Blaise, a moment?"

Tilting his head, Blaise came over to Jefferson.

Jefferson pitched his voice low, so low that any passersby would have difficulty hearing it over the ambient noise of the river. "I have . . . insider information about that airship. Remember the Council we spoke of last night?" Blaise nodded. "Some members are strong proponents of air travel to tame the Untamed Territory. To loosen the grip outlaws with pegasi have over the area."

Blaise swallowed. "But the Untamed Territory doesn't belong to the outlaws. They're just allowed to stay there."

Jefferson made a helpless gesture. "I'm aware of that. But try arguing that with people who have more greed and hatred than common sense." He glanced over his shoulder, hands on his hips as indecision warred on his face. "I'm going to the gallows or firing squad if word of this gets out."

Blaise scowled, alarmed. "Word of what?"

Jefferson shoved his hands into the pockets of his coat. "My treason."

"Wait, what?"

Jefferson's face was serious, his voice urgent. "The airship. Destroy it. Use your magic. Break it."

Blaise stared at him, heart racing. He stepped back, horrified that Jefferson would ask him to do such a thing. "Why?"

Jefferson's eyes were fierce. "It's my fault the thing even exists." Before Blaise could sputter a question, he plowed on. "Originally, it was meant to transport goods across the Untamed Territory. Not soldiers. I made that clear in the contract. But the Confederation Safety Act was invoked after the prototype was completed." A muscle twitched in his jaw.

Blaise glanced back to where Flora awaited him. "What happened?"

"The military seized the airship and dubbed it a warbird." Jefferson shook his head. "I shuttered my manufacturing plant in response. But now it's too late. This won't end with Itude. Don't you see, Blaise?" He rubbed his forehead. "It will bolster their confidence as a success. They'll attack the other towns. Asylum." He gestured around them. "Rainbow Flat. More innocent people will die."

And not only that, but the accord forged by the pegasi and outlaws would shatter. The other sentient magical creatures would retaliate.

Blaise felt sickened as the inevitable timeline of death and destruction stretched out before him, painting the Untamed Territory and the Gutter in rivers of blood.

Blaise closed his eyes. "I wish you were telling this to anyone but me."

Jefferson chucked him under the chin. "You're the only one I would trust to do this." He stepped back, turning in a restless circle before facing Blaise again. Worry lines crinkled the corners of his eyes. "I hate to ask you to do that. I know it's not who you are."

Blaise bowed his head. "Sometimes it's not about who I am, but what I can do."

"It's *always* about who you are," Jefferson shot back. "And you're *more* than a Breaker. You have a good heart. And I'm proud to call you a friend."

Jefferson's words fortified Blaise in a way he hadn't expected. He allowed himself a tentative smile, basking in the other man's acceptance. "Thank you."

"I should head out before the captain loses his patience with my dalliance," Jefferson said with regret. He shifted, as if he were contemplating another moment of melodrama before giving Blaise a wink and striding off to the docks.

Blaise watched him go before walking back over to Emrys. Flora swung into Tylos's saddle, the small stallion fluttering his wings as she settled. Blaise mounted Emrys, and Flora stayed quiet until they trotted to the outskirts of town.

"What was that about?"

"I have to break the airship."

Flora blinked at him, stony-faced. Then she shrugged. "Okay."

CHAPTER FORTY-TWO

Tenacious Cuss

Blaise

The weather held, though the skies were frosted with clouds and the constant threat of flurries. True to Emrys's prediction, Tylos spent so much energy flying that he required hourly stops to keep his stamina up. Their progress slowed, so it wasn't until early afternoon on their third day of travel that the dead-grass prairie of the Untamed Territory shifted to the rocky sandstone outcrops leading to the Gutter.

Flora pulled a map out of her saddlebag as Tylos hungrily grazed nearby and Emrys rested with one hoof cocked. "I think if we continue the same, we can get to Itude by mid-afternoon." She peered at Blaise over the rims of her glasses. "The problem is we don't know if there will be hostiles there when we arrive."

Blaise shook his head. "The townspeople won't hurt us."

Flora gave him a pitying look. "It's not them I'm concerned about. I mean a military presence."

He winced. He had forgotten about that. "Right."

Flora pursed her lips. "When we get closer, Tylos and I should go first.

If Gaitwood has men there, I have reason to be there—looking into the deaths of the survey team."

"They could try to silence you."

She bared her teeth in a smile, and the feral look was chilling. "They can try."

"Okay, then." Blaise decided not to push the issue anymore with Jefferson's tiny scary lady.

Once Tylos was reinvigorated, Blaise and Flora got back into the saddle and continued the journey. Blaise's legs were like jelly from the days of travel—he wasn't used to being in the saddle for so long. But he pushed away the discomfort. He might fall over with barely functioning legs later, but that was a problem for future Blaise.

The pegasi kept up their steady pace, and Flora was right—they would make it there in the afternoon. Emrys promised to signal Tylos once they were close to the town. Blaise felt a thrill rush through him as he recognized the canyons and hoodoos blurring below them. He was almost home.

Emrys slowed and landed on a canyon rim. Tylos flew ahead, Flora's hair a cheerful twinkle in the afternoon sun. Blaise took a break to stretch his legs while they waited for Flora's return. If he was going to fall over, he would rather it not be the first thing anyone else saw when he returned to town.

The white pegasus flew over a nearby ridge a short time later, hovering near Emrys. "It's clear," Flora called. She wasn't close enough for Blaise to get a good read on her facial expression, and her tone was neutral.

Emrys snorted, and Blaise climbed back into the saddle. The stallion took a running leap off the side of the cliff, wings snapping out as Blaise's heart jumped into his throat. Moments later, Itude spread out before them.

Blaise peered over the stallion's side, gripping the brim of his hat as the wind threatened to knock him around. Emrys swept over the town in a wide circle, allowing time for any sentries to come out and investigate. Blaise's gut clenched as he took in the destruction below. His bakery was a burned-out shell, only the ash-covered bulk of the oven standing sentinel. The Jitterbug and mercantile shared the same fate. Other structures had suffered roof damage. Three massive dark piles huddled at the outskirts of the town—one north, one south, and one to the northeast. As Emrys descended, he realized they were piles of bodies.

A clarion call shattered the crisp air. A familiar golden stallion launched into the sky. <Blaise? Emrys? You may land.>

Still-healing slashes crisscrossed Zepheus's body. Primary and secondary feathers were missing from his wings. He likely shouldn't have been flying in such a condition. They landed, and Emrys touched noses with the palomino.

The town was painfully quiet. The normal hum of voices, the squeak of the wind-pump working, the braying of the donkeys, and the laughter of playing children were all absent. No one walked the streets. Faces peered out of windows, like rabbits afraid of a stooping hawk. Bullet holes riddled the storefronts that weren't damaged by fire. The only sounds were the drumming of pegasi hooves and the whistle of the wind.

Oberidon trotted out of the stable, ears flicking as he joined them. <You came back.>

Blaise nodded. "I . . . I did."

<I wish you had come sooner.> Oberidon hung his head so low his muzzle almost touched the ground.

The spotted stallion's dejection set Blaise on edge. "Where's Emmaline?"

<She's gone. I failed her.>

Blaise's heart hurt for Oberidon. He knew the feeling. "We'll get her back. Where's Jack?"

Zepheus flattened his ears, and the palomino's agitation filled Blaise with apprehension. Renewed hope filled Oberidon's brown eyes. Zepheus's only held desolation.

<Follow me.> Zepheus turned, leading them out of town to the rows of homes.

ITUDE WAS BROKEN.

That much was clear to Blaise as they followed Zepheus. Flora and Tylos joined them after a brief introduction. The faces peering out of the broken windows wore mixtures of resignation and exhaustion, fraught people pushed to the edge of their existence. No one came out to greet him. They were scared. He wasn't sure if they were afraid of Blaise the Breaker or reliving the trauma of the enemy in their streets.

Zepheus led them past Jack's house, continuing on to Nadine's. The palomino provided no explanation, only stopped outside the house, rustling his wings like a sparrow coming to nest.

Movement flickered in one window, and then Nadine darkened the doorway. Blaise gaped when he saw her, recognizing her only because it was her house and who else would come out the door? Divots pocked her face, one eye swollen shut. The scalp above her right ear was bare, the skin pale and smooth, like it was newly regrown. Her left hand was a wizened mess. Despite the trauma, her undamaged eye was sharp. "You should have seen the other guy. Guys," she corrected, her voice raspy.

"What . . . what happened?" Blaise asked. Nearby, Flora pretended to not be too interested, but she kept sneaking glances at Nadine.

Nadine grunted. "Taught some boys why you don't attack Healers." She rolled her shoulders, wincing. "After they stabbed me and shot me a dozen times, I had to drain their life to sustain myself. Lucky for me, they thought I was dead."

Drain their life to . . . Blaise blinked. *And* I'm *the one people are terrified of?*

Nadine waved her good hand, inviting him in. "You can come in, but your friend has to stay out there. I've got my most critical patients here, and I don't trust anyone else right now."

Flora held up her hands, placating. "I'm not coming in, trust me. But I am going to go check on someone else." Blaise was mildly impressed that Nadine intimidated her.

Nadine moved at a slow pace, negotiating her way between tables and chairs. Some of the tables had bloodstains on them, as if they had served as last-resort operating tables. Perhaps they had.

"You shouldn't have run away." Nadine paused, bracing her good hand against the back of a chair.

Blaise bowed his head, blinking rapidly as he noticed a trail of dried blood beneath his feet. "I couldn't bear people thinking . . ."

"What? That you destroyed the wind-pump?" Her words had a bite to them, and her tension reminded him of an agitated rattlesnake. "Did you?"

He lifted his head, meeting her good eye. "*No.* But people were starting to say I did." The very thought made Blaise light-headed with panic. "And when the rumors start, no one has ever believed me in the past."

"This is a small town. There's always going to be rumormongers and backbiting." She leveled a finger at him. "And when you run like that, it makes *you* look guilty."

"But I didn't—"

"We know that *now,*" Nadine cut in. Her eye glittered, dangerous. "Someone is a traitor, and it's not you."

Blaise nearly trembled with relief. He had feared he would have an uphill battle vindicating himself with the survivors.

"Zepheus said you wanted to see Jack. He's . . ." She shook her head, then gave him a long look. "He's not doing well."

A chill slithered down Blaise's spine. "How bad is it?"

Nadine didn't respond. She pushed open a door, and Blaise followed her inside. The room might have been Reuben's, judging by the possessions tucked away on the dresser. He didn't dare ask Nadine about her son. He wasn't sure if he wanted to know.

Jack lay on the bed and appeared to be asleep. His skin was ashen, with no signs of visible wounds. His face was almost skeletal, and the arm that rested outside of the blanket was gaunt. Jack's tattooed shoulder was bare, the arcane symbols vivid against his skin.

The man in the bed wasn't the tenacious cuss who had punched Blaise in the face his first day in town. He was a shell. If the hard look in Nadine's good eye meant anything, he was dying.

"What happened to him?"

Nadine scratched at the smooth skin over her ear. "One survivor said Gaitwood had him in a trap and Jack made the mistake of touching the bars." She pursed her lips. "He knew better, but still he did it. Gaitwood baited him with . . . with . . ." Nadine cleared her throat, unwilling to complete her sentence. "They found him collapsed in the middle of the street. Clover thought he was dead, but then she saw he was breathing." She shook her head. "He hasn't woken up or moved in . . . I don't know how long. I don't know what day it is. My magic is too drained to do anything for him. All I know is that he's barely alive, and he's trapped in his own body." She closed her eyes, pained.

Blaise stared at Jack. "Has he eaten?"

Nadine nodded. "Celeste comes by daily and brings broth or whatever she thinks he'll keep down. But it's not much. He won't last much longer at this rate."

Blaise pulled a chair closer to the bed. Only the gentle rise and fall of the outlaw's chest gave proof to the shred of life left in his body. "Jack?" He studied the outlaw's face, looking for some sign of movement or comprehension. When nothing happened, he laid a hand on Jack's arm.

Magic surged across the outlaw's skin, thin as a hair. But it was there. Blaise felt it. Or rather, his magic did. Sucking in a surprised breath, he let his magic quest against the hostile power. He recognized the magic. He had encountered it twice. Blaise had *broken* it before.

Nadine watched him like a hawk, hyperaware. "What is it?"

For Jack's sake, Blaise hoped he was right. "I recognize the magic on him. The trap is still active, it's just *on* him now instead of acting like a physical cage. His skin is a cage."

Nadine made a *tch*-ing sound. "Damn, that's sadistic enough to be something Gaitwood would do."

Blaise nodded. He thought so, too. "I . . . I might be able to break it."

Her eye cut to him like a dagger. "*Might?*"

He swallowed. Once, when he was ten, his worst bully had cornered him before school. The son of Bristle's mayor was an insufferable tormenter who considered himself untouchable. He enjoyed harassing Blaise every way he could. Charles tried to snatch Blaise's lunch away and throw it into the nearby pond so that he would have to choose between wading in after his soggy food or going hungry. Blaise couldn't take anymore. He had grabbed Charles's arm with his ungloved hand. He would never forget the sound of the bully's bones snapping as his magic roared to life. Blaise hadn't been allowed back at school after that. He was still so ashamed of the event that he hadn't breathed a word of it to Jefferson.

I have control now. He rubbed his forehead. "I broke Gaitwood's traps before, but not when they were acting as a second skin. It may behave differently." It might hurt Jack. He feared speaking it would make it so.

Nadine gestured to the prone outlaw with her mangled hand. "Do it. It can't be worse than this. He's dying."

Blaise leaned over Jack, wrapping his right hand around the outlaw's left arm. He closed his eyes to concentrate, shuddering as the sinister magic assaulted him like a thousand wriggling maggots. His own Breaker magic rallied to the surface at his call, and he opened his eyes to survey the nefarious Trapper magic. With his magic engaged, he recognized the remnants of the trap overlaying Jack like a ghost. It made him a prisoner in his own body.

Gods, Jack was alive and awake in there. He was living in a personal abyss. But not for much longer, if Blaise had a say.

He studied the magical overlay, hunting for the weakest links. As much as he wanted to slam his magic through the trap, he didn't want to risk harming Jack. With surgical precision, he found a weak strand of magic and sheared through it. It snapped as it broke, blowing loose like unanchored spider's silk. Blaise found his next assault point and sent another pulse of magic, satisfied when it came unfettered.

A moment later, the trap dissipated entirely, and the outlaw's chest rose as he took his first deep, conscious breath. Still clutching Jack's arm, Blaise's magic prodded at something buried deep in the outlaw's brain. Something foreign; out of place. Harmful. Afraid that it might be a lingering effect from the trap, Blaise let his magic shred it before pulling his power back under control. Blaise let go of Jack's arm and scooted the chair back.

Jack took another ragged breath and then coughed, a dry sound from his parched throat. His ice-blue eyes snapped opened, locking on to Blaise. "It's about damn time you got here."

CHAPTER FORTY-THREE

Secrets and Traitors

Jack

Jack didn't fear death. After days trapped in his own skin, with only his own regrets and failures for company, he longed for the respite of eternal darkness. It was preferable to the knowledge that he had failed everyone he'd ever cared about. For all his hoarding of information, he should have seen the attack coming. But he hadn't.

Jack wasn't a religious man. But he was wondering if someone with a plan bigger than his had kept him in play for a reason.

At the present moment, all that mattered was that Blaise had broken him from his waking prison, the enemy had stolen Emmaline away, his town was in ruins, and he was weak as a newborn kitten.

"Let me up, Clover," Jack growled, staring down the Knossan. Nadine had summoned her after Blaise had freed him, muttering she didn't have the strength to hold him at bay.

"No." Clover's ears swept back, upset. "You are not well. You need rest and food, and perhaps in a few days—"

"We don't have a few days. There's an ass I need to kick before then."

Jack sat up, ignoring the wave of dizziness and nausea that threatened his ability to remain upright. He didn't have time for this. His body was just going to have to get its shit together.

She placed a hand on his shoulder and prodded him back down. "I understand. Truly, I do."

Jack shrugged out from under her hand, struggling to sit again. In the same motion, he swung his legs over the side of the bed. His stomach churned, and he was in genuine danger of losing whatever they had fed him while he was out of commission. He closed his eyes, ignoring the Knossan's grumbles.

He wanted to get up. *Needed* to get up. But he was quickly realizing that, while his body and mind were free, Lamar's damned trap had sapped every last reserve of his strength. He would look about as graceful as a newborn colt if he tried to stand. And he would get an up-close-and-personal view of Nadine's floor if he tried. Defeated by his own body, he shifted back onto the bed. "You win."

"I don't want to *win*," Clover said with a snort. "I just want you well. But perhaps we can talk and plan? Strategize?"

Jack closed his eyes. Yeah, that might help. "Aside from me and Nadine, any other Ringleaders still here?" He almost didn't want the answer.

"Only Kur, and he's as grumpy as a freshly shorn grasscat. He's still mad you left him at the farms."

That sounded like Kur. The attack distressed the Theilian, and his instincts would be working overtime to make things right. That was a losing battle.

"Fine, leave Kur out for the moment. If Nadine's up to it, have her come. And Blaise." Jack relaxed into the soft pillows. Maybe laying down wasn't so bad.

Clover shifted. "Blaise isn't a Ringleader."

"No, but he's the only other mage we've got. And I think we *need* him." He stared at the ceiling, Lamar's words haunting him. *Lucky for me, I made sure your Breaker wasn't there. You might have stood a chance otherwise.* Damn it.

Clover nodded, ducking out. A short while later, Nadine arrived. She still looked like shit, but Jack imagined that was going to be her look for quite a while. He hadn't seen his own face in a mirror yet, but he assumed he shouldn't be one to talk.

She dragged a chair over and sat down, glancing at the door for any signs of others joining them. When she saw no one else, she said in a low voice, "Jack, what in tarnation?"

His eyes were thin slits watching her. Sleep dragged at his brain, telling him that maybe a meeting right now wasn't the best idea. "What?"

Her lower lip stuck out. "Kur and I put the pieces together. You haven't used your magic on any of the missions you've taken with him."

The muscles in Jack's jaw twitched. "Not sporting to use magic against those men. Hardly fair."

"And you didn't use magic in the battle. Even *Butch* used magic." Her voice was soft and dangerous. An accusation accompanied her unspoken question: why would Wildfire Jack, Effigest, self-proclaimed Scourge of the Untamed Territory, not use his magic?

Jack realized he was on the knife's edge with an angry, life-leeching Healer beside him. Nadine had a sharp mind, and he could guess the two scenarios running through it. Scenario one: Jack was a turncoat which made about as much sense as a one-legged donkey in an ass-kicking contest. But stranger things had happened. Scenario two: Jack didn't have magic. The simplest explanations were the most sensible. And correct.

Jack cursed. "It wasn't any of your damn business."

She arched the eyebrow over her good eye. The one over her swollen eye tried to keep up but failed. "You didn't think that was something the rest of the Ringleaders should be aware of?"

He was quiet, thinking. Jack was tired, and his heart ached. This was the last thing he wanted to deal with right now. But as so often happened in life, the worst shit appeared when the outhouse was occupied.

"You don't know how it feels, Nadine. To have the magic stolen away from your flesh. The alchemical potion burning through your veins, making you wish your body would burst into flames and call the deed done." He turned to stare at the wall. "The shame of knowing what you could do, and now can't. If I told you, you would have thought less of me."

"Pretty sure they wouldn't revoke your badass card," Blaise commented, startling Jack as he pushed through the door. The Breaker pulled a chair up next to Nadine's.

Jack glared at Blaise. Damn it. At least his secret wasn't news to the kid.

"You're an infuriating cuss," Nadine grumbled, glaring at him. "But that's neither here nor there. I reserve the right to be pissed at you for a while." She shifted in her chair. "I've got other patients to attend to. What do you want? I can't be lollygagging around all day with you."

She should be taking it easy, too. Her body was just as poor as his. Maybe worse. He hadn't been shot enough to look like a patch of ground full of prairie dog holes. He didn't tell her that, though. "They set us up. All of us. Even you, Blaise."

"I know."

Jack had expected a quiet hush and shocked breaths. "What do you mean, *you know?*"

Blaise rubbed the back of his neck. "Jasper Strop overheard Gaitwood talking to you. Jasper's niece, Flora, brought the information to me in Rainbow Flat."

Jack narrowed his eyes. "Tell me more about *Flora.*"

The Breaker glanced around the room, seeking a distraction. Jack wouldn't let him get away so easily. Blaise wised up and sighed. "She works with Jefferson Cole."

Jefferson Cole. Malcolm Wells. Son of a bat-eared harpy. Jack tried to sit up fast, wincing when he recalled what a terrible idea that was. Nadine cleared her throat in warning. So they knew about Gaitwood's treachery. That was less for him to explain, at least.

"Who did Gaitwood have working on the inside?" Nadine asked.

Jack smiled, an expression that promised future violence. Blaise looked up, meeting his gaze. The Breaker's eyes held a spark of anger and burned with questions. The young man needed answers like plants needed water. "Who?"

Exhaustion swept over Jack, and for a moment he regretted summoning them. He should've listened to Clover. But this was *important,* damn it. "Walker. Hank Walker is working with Gaitwood. Where is he? Is he still here, Nadine?"

The Healer's eyes widened. "He's recovering from the attack at his home. His leg got blown clean off."

"We got any salt-iron? Shackle him. He could still bolt, missing leg or not." Something occurred to Jack. "Has Walker heard that I'm awake?"

Nadine shrugged. "Don't know. And you know as well as I do we don't have any salt-iron. We're not monsters."

Jack snorted. "Speak for yourself."

"Is . . . is Walker the one who shot me?" Hope and dread warred in Blaise's voice. "Is he responsible for the wind-pump?"

"I don't have all the answers yet, but I want to rip them from his flesh." Yes, Jack thought, that would help relieve some stress. "I know for a fact he killed at least one of the Gannish surveyors, though." Walker had killed *Cole's* Confederation man, which didn't sit well with Jack. Something was off with that. He still didn't like Cole. Needed to tell Blaise about his duplicity.

Nadine crossed her arms. "Let me see if I have this right. Walker— who, by the way, is *your* asset, Jack—works for Lamar Gaitwood. Walker killed the survey team on the day of the attack." She cocked her head. "Safe to assume Walker led you to the earlier ambush, tried to kill Blaise, and somehow made the wind-pump fall?"

Jack gritted his teeth. No use explaining to her he hadn't trusted Walker from the start. Sometimes a man had to work with the hand life dealt him. *Always bet on the Jack.* "That's about right. But Walker is *Gaitwood's*, not mine at this point. He admitted as much in the post office during the attack."

Nadine frowned. "He's a maverick. Why would he cross us?"

Jack shook his head, not wanting to mention Hank's brother. He didn't want any sympathy for the man. Not after all he had wrought. "Every man has a price. I need to interrogate him." Jack bared his teeth in anticipation. Walker would never cross them again.

"You'll do no such thing," Nadine contradicted, waspish.

"I will." Steel gleamed in Blaise's eyes, forcing Jack to pause his protest. The Breaker lifted his chin, daring them to deny him.

Jack grunted, deciding to leave it be. It would be difficult to terrify Walker in his current state. "Fine. But if he finds out I'm awake, mark my words, he's going to make a break for it."

Nadine tilted her head, smirking. "I wish him luck with that. Had to give him a mix of laudanum and krakenvine to get his pain manageable. He's high as a mountaintop right now."

"I think we should keep word of Jack's recovery quiet," Blaise said.

Nadine frowned. "For what purpose?"

"We need time to come up with a plan."

Hope lit a small fire in Jack's heart. "We?"

"No offense, but I don't think you could do it alone." Blaise's shoulders went rigid, as if he expected an angry retort from Jack. When none came, he continued. "I know you'll want to go after Emmaline and the others."

"And prigging kill *Lamar*," Jack growled emphatically. *Priorities.*

Nadine shook her head. "I don't see how we can. They destroyed the town. They wounded or killed everyone who can fight worth a damn. Families are already leaving for the farms or Asylum with whatever they can carry on their back."

Jack closed his eyes, pained by the news. He had worked so hard to build Itude up. The battle would be the last straw for many. And he didn't blame them.

"I'm not going to back down and let the bully win this time." Blaise's voice was soft, tinged with the promise of danger, like the strobe of lightning and rumble of thunder in a distant storm. Jack opened his eyes and really *looked* at the kid. He was tired and grungy, but he had the poise of someone who had found purpose and clarity.

"You're not a fighter," Nadine shook her head.

"He is," Jack murmured. Blaise twitched at his words, as if he hadn't expected Jack to contradict Nadine. "He fights for what's important."

"I fight for the ones I care about," Blaise agreed, resolute. "It's something I should have done sooner but lacked the courage."

And now, somehow, he had found it. Jack studied the Breaker with an approving eye.

Nadine looked from Blaise to Jack and sighed. "I'm in. Just don't expect me to pick up the pieces and put either of you back together when it's all said and done."

CHAPTER FORTY-FOUR

Absolution

Blaise

When Hannah saw Blaise, she ran up to him and enveloped him in a hug, burying her face against his shoulder. With the conversation with Jack and Nadine at the forefront of his mind, her sudden appearance startled him. She quivered, sobbing into his shoulder. Blaise reined in his inclination to dodge away, instead wrapping his arms around her in consolation.

"I'm so glad to see you," Hannah whispered, her voice cracking with emotion once she mastered her tears. "We lost so many."

Blaise patted her back, and as she rested against him, he realized how devastating the attack had been. He only saw the aftereffects—the destroyed buildings, the wounded, the bloated dead. But Hannah and the others had witnessed it with their own eyes. Some of them had lived and fought it. And none of them would ever be the same.

"I'm here," Blaise murmured.

"Abe's dead. And Monty. Ellie. Victor." Hannah continued a litany of more names, honoring the dead. Blaise held her and listened as she dampened his shoulder with her tears and her choked words. He let her pain stir the coals of resolve in his chest. Blaise stowed each name she whispered into his heart, promising that their deaths were not in vain.

He didn't know how long they stood together, but eventually, she pulled back, her face red and eyes watery. "I'm sorry."

"Don't be. I wish I had been here to help."

She shook her head. "I'm glad you weren't. Or . . ." She wiped her runny nose on her sleeve. "What are we going to do, Blaise?"

"We're going to get them back."

Hannah stared at him like he'd spoken another language. Her lower lip trembled. "How?"

That was the question. "I'm going to figure something out." Since he wasn't sure how to approach that problem yet, he thought it was a good time to change the subject. "My friend, Flora, and I need a place to stay. Nadine told me you could direct us to some houses that are available."

"Oh." Hannah turned as Flora walked up. "Um, you want one bedroom or . . ."

"Two different accommodations would be best," Flora said, saving Blaise from embarrassment. "I'm here on business."

Hannah fixed bleary eyes on Flora, then gave Blaise a quizzical look. He shrugged. He wasn't about to explain Flora's business. Hannah gestured to a clapboard house close to Nadine's. "That one's open right now. It was . . ." She laughed humorlessly, the sound of someone who had seen horrors. "You know what? Never mind. There's some clothing in there. Might be some food. We haven't gone through every house yet. It took us long enough to—" Her gaze drifted in the graveyard's direction.

"It's fine," Blaise reassured her. "I'll take that one. It'll keep me near Jack and Nadine." With that decision made, Hannah showed Flora the house next to Blaise's temporary quarters.

"I'm going to get settled. Is there a place I can grab dinner later, or do I need to go out and hunt my own?" Flora asked.

Hannah's eyes widened, and Blaise supposed his eyes did, too. "Um. Most things are rationed right now since we depend on whatever the farms can bring up, but we have enough to fill bellies most nights. We've been holding communal meals at the town square." She looked at the ground. "Gives us a sense that we're not alone in this."

Flora nodded primly and strolled to her house. Blaise watched Hannah, concerned. She seemed on the verge of shattering. "Are you going to be okay?"

Her eyes were desolate. "I don't know. I've never been so scared."

Blaise set his jaw. Hannah didn't deserve to live in fear. She deserved happiness. Hannah was meant to be full of ready smiles and cheer. Not this frightened ghost of herself.

He placed his hands on her shoulders, looking her in the eye. "You don't have to be scared. I'm going to make sure they can't do anything like this ever again."

Tears streamed down her cheeks, but this time hope kindled in her eyes.

———

BLAISE AMBLED TOWARD THE TOWN SQUARE, TAKING IN THE MULTITUDE OF damage inflicted on Itude as he walked to the communal dinner. He spotted a man ahead of him, hobbling along with a crutch. His right leg was missing below the knee. Blaise swallowed, the brisk wind enhancing the chill that raced across his skin at the sight of Hank Walker. The traitor.

Rage coursed through his body as Blaise quickened his steps to catch up, but he quickly mastered it. It was senseless for Blaise to be angry with the wounded man. He wasn't Jack, to wear his wrath like a duster. Blaise only wanted to understand.

Walker heard the crunch of Blaise's boots. He looked over his shoulder, eyes widening in terror as he realized who his pursuer was. He shifted his crutch and tried to sidestep, but lost his balance and tumbled into the dirt, sending up a spurt of frigid red dust. Walker rolled onto his back, moaning.

Blaise stared at the fallen man in dismay. Fear. Walker feared *him*. Blaise didn't like that; the role of a bully was the last thing he desired. Did he have reason to be upset with Walker? Yes. Did he wish him ill? Absolutely not. He took a deep breath to compose himself.

"Do you need help?" Blaise asked, approaching at an angle to appear less threatening.

Walker laid on his back, pain etched on his face. "What?"

"I said, do you need help? I'm sorry if I startled you. Didn't mean to," Blaise replied, crouching down.

Those offerings of simple kindness disarmed Walker. He blinked. "I . . . yes, I need help. Still getting used to that damn crutch."

"Must be difficult," Blaise agreed, offering his hand to help Walker up.

The fallen man trembled, staring at Blaise's hand with mistrust. Blaise kept his hand extended, face neutral as he waited. Walker's face was grey with fear and doubt, but after an uncomfortable beat he took Blaise's hand.

"I'm sorry you fell," Blaise said as he helped Walker up, picking up the man's crutch and handing it to him.

Walker's eyes were wide, spooked. Blaise wondered if perhaps he was handling the situation wrong. But then Walker nodded, acknowledging the apology. "No matter." He shifted, uncomfortable for reasons that went beyond his crippling injury, eyes darting to the town square.

"Do you need help to get to dinner?"

Walker stared at him as if he had offered to throw him over the cliff. "I can get there just fine. I have to take it slow."

Blaise nodded. "Okay. Let me know if you need help with anything." While he needed to talk to Walker, Blaise decided it was best to take his time. Nadine was right—he couldn't run. Hank's leg was gone. He would never be whole again.

He felt Walker's eyes on his back as he strode to the town square. Makeshift tables reminiscent of the Feast of Flight were spread across the lawn. Mismatched chairs had been pulled from any building with furniture that survived the battle. Celeste and Mindy served food to a line of hungry, frightened faces. Murmurs swept through the line as the survivors noticed his presence.

Mindy had a bandage over one side of her face, but she smiled, handing him a plate of food. "Blaise, we missed you. It's good to have you back. Sorry, there's no bread."

Blaise took the proffered plate. "I'll remedy that for you if I get a chance."

"That would be welcome!" Mindy said almost too quickly, and several people nearby chuckled.

Someone seconded it with a rowdy "Hear, hear!"

The laughter popped the tension like a soap bubble, and Blaise found more townspeople murmuring greetings to him. He had thought he might be treated as a pariah, but word of his innocence must have already spread. There was a general air of apology, and a handful of people clapped him on the shoulder, welcoming him back. Blaise steeled himself and accepted their brief touches. Many of the adults were wounded, and those who weren't bore the trauma on their worry-lined faces. Even the normally raucous children were subdued beside their parents.

Blaise found a table and sat, surprised when Walker hobbled over to him. "Mind if I join you?"

Curious. Blaise nodded to the empty seat. "You're welcome to it. Would you like me to get you a plate?"

Walker smiled, a real, genuine smile that reflected in the depths of his eyes. Blaise hadn't noticed it before, but Walker's eyes had always radiated sadness. "If you don't mind. It's hard with the . . ." He gestured to his missing limb.

Blaise nodded and rose to get the additional plate. As he headed back to the table, he caught sight of Nadine. Her eyes slid from him to Walker, a silent query. Blaise shrugged. He would see where the conversation led.

"Here you go. I'll get some water for us, too," Blaise said, sliding the laden plate to Walker. The postmaster watched him like he was a puzzle to decipher but seemed content.

"Can I ask you a question?" Walker asked a few minutes later, after they had each eaten some of their meal. When Blaise nodded, Walker put down his fork. "Why are you doing this? Being nice to me, I mean. Is it because I'm hurt?"

Blaise studied him for a moment. "No. It's because I don't want to be the sort of person who hurts others just because I can. There's strength in kindness."

Walker picked up his fork again, poking food around his plate. "Why did you come back? I know what people were saying about you."

I'll bet you do. Blaise somehow kept a neutral expression. "Because I'm through with letting other people's perceptions rule my life." He pushed his plate aside. "I'm not going to be manipulated anymore. And you shouldn't allow others to manipulate you."

The postmaster froze, releasing his fork so it clattered to the table. "You know. You knew as soon as you saw me."

Blaise said nothing. He crossed his arms, inclining is head.

Panic flitted across Walker's face. "What are you going to do to me?"

Blaise shook his head, thinking that perhaps he wasn't so different from Walker. Bullies came in many forms. "Nothing. We're going to talk like reasonable people. And as long as you're honest with me, you'll have no fear of reprisal."

The postmaster regarded him in silence for a moment. "Once you hear what I've done, you'll regret that."

Blaise kept his steady gaze on Walker. "I'm already aware of most of what you've done. I just want answers at this point."

Renewed fear registered on Walker's face. Blaise pulled his plate closer and took another bite of his food to prove he didn't have any ill intentions.

"How can you break bread with me and act so civilized?"

"I'm going to remind you we're lacking in the bread department," Blaise quipped to keep the conversation light. "And I can do this because I do things my own way. I want answers." He pointed his fork at Walker. "I expect answers."

The postmaster bowed his head. "Ask away."

A thrill zinged through Blaise. His gambit was working. "Tell me why you worked for Gaitwood. What would compel you to sell out all these nice people sitting around us?" He kept his voice low so it didn't carry to the surrounding tables.

Walker's eyes were tinged with sorrow. "My reason won't be worth a hill of beans to anyone else."

"Try me."

Walker glanced around, self-conscious. His voice was so soft it was difficult to hear over the ambient noise. "Gaitwood has my brother, Joshua. He's all I have in this world for family."

Blaise's breath caught, recalling his mother begging him not to get captured. He remembered Jack's mother being used to keep him in line. He kept his thoughts to himself as Walker plowed on.

"Joshua was . . . born with problems, and our parents wanted to leave him to die of exposure from the start. But I was his big brother, and I swore to help him. Protect him." A tear trailed down Walker's cheek, and he swiped at it. "He grew, but he was never right."

His voice broke as he continued, "Our parents sold us to the child slavers when he was five. I was ten. Too many mouths to feed, or so they said." Walker rubbed his hand over his face. "We were passed between buyers like damaged goods and eventually ended up in Umber. More shit happened, but the long story short is we ended up under Lamar Gaitwood. He thought I'd make a good spy and kept my brother as a surety for my behavior."

Blaise stared at him, aghast. His palms tingled at his slumbering anger, and he quelled his magic. "That's horrible. I'm so sorry. I had no idea."

Walker shrugged. "No one here does. I never speak about it because no one ever cares what happens to someone like Joshua."

"That ends now," Blaise vowed. "I care. Does Gaitwood still have him?"

"As far as I know. I . . . Gaitwood was supposed to take me with him after the attack. He said he would. My reward was supposed to be that I could be with my brother. But when I went to him, the bastard shot out my knee and laughed." His face clouded at the bitter memory. Small wonder Walker had betrayed the people of Itude. Betrayal had been a common theme in his life.

Blaise hadn't arrived in Itude with a plan, only the desire to right wrongs. But the seed of an idea was forming. And it gave him hope. He would nurture that plan, but first he needed more information. "Next question. Did you shoot me?"

Walker stared at his plate, guilt etched on his face. "Yes."

Blaise took a shallow breath, trying to stay detached, though he wanted to run and tell Jack he had solved that mystery. He had to sit across from the man who tried to kill him and pretend like it didn't bother him. "How?"

To his credit, Walker seemed miserable as he answered. "My last name comes from my magic—Walker. Technically, I'm a Succulent Walker. I specialize in them." Blaise nodded, feigning that he knew what he meant. "It was a simple matter to snag the revolver that was being shipped to Jefferson Cole, pop into the canyon via a prickly pear, and take a shot at you." He grimaced. "I'm not a very good shot."

Lucky for me. Blaise gritted his teeth. "Did you cause the collapse of the wind-pump?"

"Yes."

"How?"

Hank Walker rubbed his face with one hand, and at that single question seemed to age another ten years. He wasn't a young man. If Blaise had to guess, he thought he might be in his fifties. "Potion. Alchemy potion Gaitwood gave to me."

Blaise's mind whirled as he thought back to everything he had seen his mother work on through the years. She specialized in medicinal potions, but he knew she dabbled in other areas. Potions that Blaise suspected a normal alchemist would have stayed away from. Since he was stuck home for so many years, he had pored through her notes and alchemical recipes when boredom struck. He couldn't replicate her craft, but he had intimate knowledge. "What's the potion called? And what does it do?"

"Breaker's Touch." The older man stared down at his plate. "Slow-acting corrosive potion."

Goosebumps pebbled Blaise's arms. *That's my mother's recipe.* He felt ill with the new knowledge, but he had to keep his stoic act together. He drummed his fingers on the table to stall as he thought. Inside, he was shaking. *The plan. Back to the plan.*

"Are you familiar with the layout of Fort Courage?"

Walker stared at him, thrown by the change in questioning. "Um. Sort of. I know certain parts of it."

Blaise latched onto that, setting aside the painful suspicions about his mother. Walker had inside information on Fort Courage. This was a promising start. "Do you know where Gaitwood has your brother?"

Walker nodded. "They give him busywork, usually around the stables. He's good with horses. Why?"

Blaise leaned in closer to the postmaster, conspiratorial. "What if I told you we're going to get him out of there? Him and our people that Gaitwood kidnapped? Would you help me?"

Hope shone in Walker's eyes. "Without hesitation."

CHAPTER FORTY-FIVE

Necessary Deceptions

Jack

"No."

"But—"

Jack slammed a fist against the table in raw frustration, cutting Blaise off with a menacing glare. It was infuriating enough the Breaker vowed Jack wouldn't deliver his particular brand of punishment against the traitor. It didn't matter if Blaise's manner of gentle interrogation produced results. Walker needed to be held accountable for many wrongs, and including him as a lynchpin in a delicate operation was ill-advised at best and foolhardy at worst.

Nadine's good eye was closed, as if their argument gave her a headache. Kur Agur refused to sit, instead stalking from one end of HQ's meeting room to the other like a caged animal, hackles raised. The Theilian, at least, seemed to side with Jack on the matter.

"The man *sold us out.*" Jack's voice was calm, reasonable. See? He could play nice, too. "What's stopping him from handing us over to Gaitwood, pretty as you please?"

"Gaitwood has his brother as a surety."

Jack snorted. "If anything, that gives him *more* incentive."

Blaise spread his hands. "Look at him. Gaitwood *crippled* him."

Jack crossed his arms. "I don't give a shit. Lamar's shot missed as far as I'm concerned." *That asshole was always a terrible shot.*

Nadine sighed. "To be honest, it's not the worst idea in the world to include him. Let him draw a map."

Jack wouldn't trust a map drawn by Walker. Nope. He glowered.

Blaise shook his head. "A map is helpful, but won't be enough." He spread his hands, imploring as he addressed Jack. "You have every reason to be furious with Hank Walker. I won't lie. Talking to him and not getting angry was one of the hardest things I've ever done." Blaise blew out a breath. "But he didn't have to talk to me. Didn't have to come clean. And you're right, Jack. He could've skipped town. I didn't know about his magic."

Jack gave a small nod of acknowledgment. Now if only they would listen to him about *this*.

Blaise continued, tenacious. "His magic is what we need for this to work, though. He can get us *inside* Fort Courage."

What? Jack scowled, reviewing his knowledge of Hank Walker's magic. Walkers attuned to different plant life—in Hank's case, cacti. He moved himself and objects from one point to another, tethered by corresponding vegetation. Hank had outright denied it was possible to take other people with him.

Jack uncrossed his arms and leaned forward. "Enlighten me."

Blaise smiled a *gotcha* smile that Jack wished he could erase. "Hank can take us, one at a time, to Fort Courage. He told me he can move people with his magic."

"That damned liar!" Jack shoved back his chair, wincing as the brisk movement made the room swirl before his eyes. He was sick and tired of feeling sick and tired.

Blaise cocked his head, wisely not taking offense at the outburst. He waited, tapping a finger against the table. Nadine shook her head. Kur continued his pacing.

Jack mastered his temper as the room settled into place, though he wove on his feet, unsteady. Jack decided he wouldn't make a very good argument if he fell over in front of them. He sat again. "I asked him about that before. He told me he couldn't. What makes you think we can believe this?"

"Because all his life, he's been used and manipulated." Blaise's face was shadowed, as if something about his conversation with Walker troubled him. One of the truths that had unfurled.

"And isn't this more of the same?" Jack asked. He knew a thing or two about being used, and how it chafed.

"Maybe. I hope he doesn't see it that way. I think we need to take the chance unless you know of another way into the fort." Blaise rubbed his forehead, and Jack saw the mental toll this was taking on the young man. This wasn't his forte. Put him in a bakery and cover him with flour and he was in his element. He didn't want to be the one planning an assault on a stronghold crawling with the enemy. But he was doing everything possible to help, to right a wrong that was not his fault.

The least Jack could do was hear him out. He sighed. "I won't lie. I don't like your idea, not one bit."

He lifted his eyes, studying the map pinned to the wall. If Jack was the one making the plan, he would use the pegasi to fly their team in. But then the enemy would see them coming, and they lost all hope of stealth. He needed more information about how Walker could get them inside, but it was worth considering. Jack wasn't a fool. Even at the top of his game, he wouldn't last five seconds against a company of soldiers who saw them coming from a mile away.

"But I'll entertain it as a part of the plan." Jack tipped his chin. "However, because this is important, I'm asking again: what's stopping him from delivering us to Gaitwood? Surety or not, if he takes us there and betrays us again, it's over."

"A fair question," Kur agreed with a growl.

Blaise held up two fingers. "One: Gaitwood has lost Walker's trust. Gaitwood left him behind and shot out his knee."

Jack snorted. "I'm going to be the terrible person who says he had it coming."

"You *are* a terrible person," Blaise confirmed, then sobered. "And here's the second reason. Something is wrong with his brother, so no one thinks much of him. Hank was his protector. He's worried about his brother's safety, with no one to look out for his well-being."

Kur Agur paused, his furry head canted. "You offered to rescue his brother?"

Blaise inclined his head, a casual move that spoke of a poise he didn't possess under normal circumstances. Not for the first time, Jack wondered at the mantle of confidence the Breaker wore. Where had *that* come from?

All eyes were on Jack. He scratched at his forehead as he took Blaise's words into consideration. "For the record, I don't like this. I'll allow it on one condition."

"And that is?" Nadine asked.

"If I get wind of Walker betraying us, I get to shoot him."

Blaise winced. "Jack—"

"I *won't* go after him for his past transgressions," Jack cut in. "But that man has a long road to travel before I'll trust him. If he's a turncoat, I'm taking him down with me."

Blaise met Jack's eyes, unflinching. Tough for the Breaker, but Jack was unwilling to concede this point. Someone with common sense had to be ready to put a rabid animal down.

"Fine," Blaise relented, breaking their staring contest.

They discussed other parts of the plan, debating the best strategies to use. After an hour, Nadine declared that both she and Jack needed rest, and they would adjourn but resume after dinner.

Blaise trailed Nadine to the door, but Jack whistled, catching the young mage's attention. He glanced back, quizzical. Jack nodded to the chair the Breaker had vacated.

"What?" Blaise asked once they were alone.

Tired as he was, Jack had fresh concerns about Jefferson Cole's ties to their troubles. Blaise thought the man was innocent. But there was much he was unaware of. "Tell me about the woman you traveled with. Flora Strop."

Blaise pursed his lips, suspicious. "Cut from the same cloth as you in a lot of ways."

"Gonna assume you're complimenting her, then."

A small smile twisted the Breaker's lips. "Actually, yes. She's scary. Tough. Loyal." He stopped there. Jack let things simmer and just watched him. "And I already told you she's Jasper Strop's niece."

"That how Cole knew Itude was more than a two-bit town?" Jack's voice was knife-edge sharp.

Blaise shrugged. "You'd have to ask Flora."

Jack nodded. He would when he didn't feel so damned tired. Not that he would tell anyone that he wasn't fit as a fiddle. "You go into business with Cole?"

"I did." Blaise met his eyes, a dare to chastise him for the move. "What else could I do?"

Jack wanted to say *anything but that,* but that was a lie. "You could have stayed. You could have not *run off* with your tail tucked between your legs."

Blaise chewed on his bottom lip, his veneer of confidence eroding. "I can't change the past. But I'm here now."

And that would have to be enough. Jack didn't want to pull the rug out from under Blaise with his information, but he hoped it would guard him against future pain. "There's something you need to know about Cole."

"I know you hate him."

Jack made a frustrated sound. "This isn't about my likes or dislikes. Believe it or not, this is *me* looking out for *you*."

That got Blaise's attention. He fidgeted with his fingers, rubbing his hands together, unsettled. "What?"

"He's not who he claims to be."

The Breaker's face paled, hurt in his eyes. "How do you know this?"

Jack paused. He expected Blaise to say *that's not true!* Or anything else to refute it. But he didn't. The Breaker suspected Cole had hidden something from him, and he had steeled himself.

"You're aware I deal in information. When Cole was here, he offered to buy the bakery—"

"What?"

Jack sighed. "He offered to buy the bakery. I refused to sell. He gave me his business card, and it jogged my memory. It took me a while, but I did my research. Jefferson Cole is a front."

Blaise closed his eyes, pained. "Who . . . who is he?"

Damn, Jack didn't want to tell him. He didn't want to stomp all over Blaise's hopes and dreams. But he would do him a disservice to leave him ignorant. It was dangerous to not know. "Salt-Iron Council Representative for Ganland by the name of Malcolm Wells."

Blaise's eyes flashed open, and he jerked like a ghost had poked him. "How certain are you?"

Jack lifted his chin. "Certain enough to tell you."

Blaise sighed, seeming to collapse in on himself before shaking it off. "Malcolm Wells," he murmured, as if tasting the name. Jack saw the wheels turning in his head, piecing things together and coming to some disastrous conclusions. "Oh biscuits."

"That's about the long and short of it," Jack agreed.

Blaise rose from his chair. "I have to go."

Jack disliked the tension framing the young man's eyes and the slash of his mouth. "Where are you going?"

"I have to talk to Flora."

Blaise

"Flora."

The petite woman turned at Blaise's voice, frowning at his firm tone. "What's wrong? Got a bee in your bonnet?"

She was on the porch of her borrowed house, sitting in a rocking chair across from Jasper Strop. The shopkeeper regarded Blaise with wide eyes.

"I should go. Shop won't clean itself." Jasper slid from the rocker, giving Blaise a respectful nod before slinking away.

Blaise watched him go, then climbed up on the porch. He jerked his chin to the rocker Jasper had vacated. "Mind if I sit down?"

Flora kept rocking. Her feet didn't touch the ground, so she shifted her weight back and forth. "I can't stop you."

She could. Blaise was keenly aware that with Jack still recovering, the pink-haired woman was the most dangerous person in town. More dangerous than Kur or Clover, which said something.

But that wouldn't stop him from this necessary conversation.

"Why did Jefferson lie to me?"

She blinked at him in confusion, her standoffishness evaporating. "Wait. What?"

"Why didn't he tell me who he is?" It took every bit of Blaise's resolve to keep his voice from breaking. Anxiety and tension roiled through him. He was tightly wound from all he had done since his return to Itude. Jefferson's duplicity chipped away at the last of his determination. Blaise bowed his head to hide the hurt.

"Oh. *Oh*." Flora drew the word out with extra emphasis, eyes round. "Jefferson didn't lie to you. At least not the way you're thinking."

Blaise lifted his chin just enough to glance at her. "Is he or is he not Malcolm Wells?" The name was strange on his tongue. Difficult to reconcile with the man he knew.

"He is Malcolm Wells. But he's *also* Jefferson Cole."

Blaise mopped at his face with one hand, feeling the itch of his magic. He took a breath to steady it, sending it back to slumber. Blaise wished he had the time to sit down and have a good cry. He deserved it. But that would have to wait. "That doesn't make sense."

"Sure, it does." Flora slipped out of her chair and dragged the rocker closer, climbing back up. "In this very town, you have Wildfire Jack and Jack Dewitt. Same person."

"Jack never lied to me about who he is." In fact, Blaise thought with derision, Jack had made it very clear from the start.

"Neither did Jefferson. Neglected to tell you? Sure. But he can't just go around blabbing to everyone. Defeats the purpose."

Blaise frowned. "I'm not following."

Flora sighed, bobbing her head from side to side as she considered her explanation. "Okay, first off, I need to know how many people know this information. Because I may need to do some damage control."

Any other day, those words would have unsettled Blaise. As tired as he was, he refused to allow casual promises of violence to shake him. "As far as I know, only me and Jack. And if you're suggesting you'll try to kill us, we're about to have a big problem."

She held up her hands, quelling. "I'll never hear the end of it from Jefferson if I harm a hair on your pretty head." Blaise didn't miss the fact that she failed to mention Jack.

"Jack will keep the secret. If there's one thing he can do well, it's keep secrets."

Flora gave him a speculative look. "You realize you're staking *your* life on this, too?"

Because Blaise signed contracts with Jefferson Cole, they were forever intertwined—along with Malcolm Wells. "Yes. Jack will keep the secret. Now explain."

Mollified, Flora nodded. "Right. So the first thing you have to understand is that Jeff—Malcolm is the Doyen for Ganland." She swallowed. "We discussed the Salt-Iron Council with Jefferson the other day. I trust you remember the gist of it?"

Blaise gave a stiff nod. He remembered, and the knowledge made him nauseous. Did Jefferson secretly support the atrocities Gaitwood and his men committed? Stealing mages from their homes, their families? Blaise closed his eyes, remembering discussions with Jefferson about those very points. He opposed them. But could Blaise believe that now?

"You're terrible at hiding your emotions. You should work on that," Flora pointed out.

Blaise rubbed his face. "Forgive me for having feelings. I'm listening."

"Anyway, that's what *Malcolm* does. He politics and invests. And he has to do all the political hobnobbing with snobs that comes with his position. Fancy parties and whatnot. Dreadful things. Makes me want to stab my eyes out for a change of pace."

Blaise raised his eyebrows.

"Okay, yeah, that's off topic. Sorry. All those things I just mentioned? Those aren't his passion. Well, he likes the political stuff—he *really* is trying to create change. But he enjoys travel and seeing interesting things, meeting new people. And stumbling across the occasional investment as Jefferson is icing on the cake."

"Oh." Blaise cocked his head. "But can't he do all that as Malcolm Wells?"

Flora snorted. "He could, but not the way he wants to. Doyen Wells is required to travel with a security detail." Her voice softened. "Malcolm can't do that—not while navigating the towns in the Untamed Territory without suspicion or outright battles. Don't get me wrong, I'm all for a brawl, but even I know it's unnecessary. He doesn't want to come here and be cosseted like a prized pony. His words, not mine."

Blaise frowned. "Isn't it dangerous for him to do that?"

Flora shook her head. "Not as dangerous as under his actual name. And I usually travel with him. As long as he's Jefferson Cole, playboy investor with more money than he knows what to do with, he's safe."

Blaise didn't see the logic in that. "Wouldn't that make it more likely for him to come to harm?"

She smirked. "There are some well-paid outlaws around Rainbow Flat who will do their best to make sure Jefferson Cole doesn't so much as have a mosquito look at him cross-eyed."

Blaise thought back to Rainbow Flat. Everyone in the town who crossed paths with Jefferson treated him with a mix of reverence and charitable protectiveness. Jefferson had his own outlaw protection. That made sense in a strange way. Blaise wondered how much of Rainbow Flat Jefferson owned. All of it? "How does he keep up his front? Jack figured it out."

Flora scowled. "I need to ask that cuss how he connected the dots so I can correct the oversight." She rocked her chair, thoughtful. "And I'm sorry, but I won't tell you how he does it. That's not my secret to share." Her expression bordered on sympathetic. "I doubt he wanted to mislead you. He seems to like you for some reason. But outside of Salt-Iron borders, he *must* be Jefferson Cole. Any other name and . . ." She trailed off, gritting her teeth.

Blaise nodded, relaxing now that he understood. It didn't absolve Jefferson. He still had to answer for the deception, as necessary as it was. But Jefferson hadn't done it with malice, so Blaise allowed himself a moment of contentment. He respected the need for protection.

"Thank you for telling me what you did. I appreciate it."

She gave a stiff nod. "Sure. What's next on your agenda? This place is kind of boring."

Blaise sighed. "Interested in helping with a brazen assault on Fort Courage?"

Flora grinned. "I'm always up for a little treachery."

CHAPTER FORTY-SIX
The Importance of Succulents

Blaise

*P*eople would die today. There was a good chance people he cared about would be in that number.

An emptiness had filled Blaise yesterday as he watched the remnants of the townspeople mill about, voices soft as they spoke in clusters in the town square. So many devastated citizens threw in their lot with the plan, despite the losses they had already taken. It seemed surreal watching the support team ride out of Itude, flatbed wagons loaded with medical supplies, food, and weapons.

Nadine led the support team, assisted by Clover and Kur. The Knossan and Theilian disliked the plan; they wanted inclusion in the assault. But the plan relied on subtlety.

Now Blaise stood in the bakery's husk, his boots crunching the grit of charred wood. The loft had collapsed into the lower level, creating a tumbledown maze which he threaded through as he identified the wreckage. Anything made of cast iron had survived, and he made busywork of rescuing pots and pans, setting them in the dusty street to be reclaimed later.

The scuff of boots in the street drew his attention. Jack strode up, his movements stiff from recovery. He stayed outside the walls of the bakery, arms crossed.

"It's probably not safe to be in there," Jack said.

Blaise used his booted foot to nudge the remains of a cabinet out of his way. Ash flaked against his toe. "Bold statement considering where we're going today."

Amusement played on Jack's lips. "Need you in one piece for that." He glanced through the remains of the bakery's scorched walls at Emrys grazing a short distance away. "Alekon just returned and reported the support team and our ringers are in place." Jack studied him, as if the outlaw was afraid that Blaise would be their weak link.

He wasn't wrong. For all the show Blaise had put on in the last few days, he feared faltering when they needed him most. But Jefferson believed in him. His heart flip-flopped in his chest, and he shoved away thoughts of the handsome entrepreneur.

"Thanks for telling me." Blaise picked his way out of the scorched bakery, then whistled to Emrys. The pegasus lifted his head and trotted over, sweeping out his wings as he drew to a stop.

<Is it time?>

Blaise scratched the stallion's cheek. "Let's get you saddled up." While he wouldn't be riding Emrys to the fort, he was optimistic that he would have need of the saddle later.

As they approached the stable, Blaise realized Jack had been busy doing things he should have left for others. The other pegasi involved in the rescue operation waited, saddled and ready, their breath frosting the air in anticipation.

"You should have gotten me sooner," Blaise murmured.

Jack shook his head. Blaise understood. The outlaw *needed* to stay busy, as much as Blaise needed to find peace before their mission.

Blaise saddled Emrys, finding comfort in the squeak of leather and the warm scent of equine. After checking to make sure he'd fastened every buckle and the cinch was snug, he rested his forehead against Emrys's. The stallion's breath tickled his chest.

<I will not leave you behind.>

Blaise smiled, gratified by the pegasus's sincerity. "I know. Thank you."

Emrys stepped back, hooves ringing on the hard-packed dirt. He pivoted and joined the other pegasi. Zepheus shared a private moment with Jack, then broke into a lope before leading the flight of stallions into the sky.

It was hard to watch them go. Blaise released a pent-up breath. Aside from the group making the foray into the Fort, the pegasi were the second most vulnerable group. They planned to take turns conducting periodic fly-bys over the fortress, waiting for their chance to wing the prisoners to safety.

"C'mon." Jack whacked Blaise on the arm with his elbow. "Time to get *dressed*." He spat in the dust, his distaste clear.

Blaise trailed along. "How do you do it?"

Jack glanced over his shoulder. "Do what?"

"Not panic."

The outlaw was silent as they walked, and Blaise thought he wouldn't get an answer. After a moment, Jack said, "Tell me how you had those hard conversations the last few days."

Blaise shrugged. "I faked it."

Jack gave a mirthless grin. "Exactly."

Blaise blinked, puzzled. And then he understood. Gaitwood had Emmaline. Jack was still recovering, not at the top of his game. He had to rely on others—something he hated to do. Jack was terrified.

<hr>

BLAISE STARED AT HIS REFLECTION IN THE CRACKED, FLOOR-LENGTH MIRROR. Ever the pragmatist, Flora reclaimed a pair of Salt-Iron Confederation uniforms from dead soldiers when she was doing *"intelligence gathering,"* which resembled rifling through the pile of corpses for anything she found useful. A kind soul had cleaned the worst of the gore from the uniforms and mended the damage inflicted during the battle as best they could. Wearing a dead man's clothing did nothing to bolster Blaise's confidence.

Macabre as it was, Flora's casual perusal of the dead had its uses. Her search was so thorough she discovered five of the dead were enemy theurgists, information which pleased Jack. Flora identified one of them as an Inker, based on tools the dead soldier had in his kit.

Jack's face split into a smile when Flora shared that tidbit. No one offered to tell Blaise why that was important. Instead, they moved on to another discussion topic. Their conversation ground to a halt when Blaise fractured the tabletop they were sitting at in a rare fit of pique. "Why is that important?" Blaise demanded. "The Inker?"

Jack fixed him with an expression that would have wilted him months ago but had little effect at present. "They can't move the mave-ricks until they're branded—not this many, at any rate. There's lots of Inkers, but most are going to be in Phinora. Gaitwood will send for the closest. Ondin, probably. It means we have time to get our people out unscathed."

The hope flaring in Jack's eyes allowed Blaise to forgive him for the oversight. Everything was on the line for him. Failure wasn't an option.

With that in mind, Blaise adjusted the collar of his scarlet overcoat, tipping his chin to inspect the shaving job Jack had forced on him earlier. It seemed like a small detail, but Flora impressed upon him the importance of a clean look. The Salt-Iron Confederation didn't allow their soldiers to have facial hair.

The cool blue eyes staring back at him felt like they belonged to someone else, an enemy. He rubbed his bare chin. *Weird.*

Flora tilted her head in appreciation when he trotted down the steps of his borrowed home. She muttered something that sounded suspiciously like "*I love a man in uniform.*" Blaise's face flamed.

Jack waited beside Flora, arms crossed, disgust etched on his face. He wore the same uniform, though the outlaw squirmed in it like he was trying to shed a second skin.

"The asshole who died in this had fleas," Jack grumbled as an explanation.

Blaise heard the lie in his voice. Jack detested wearing the Salt-Iron Confederation uniform because of what it represented to him. Everything he had escaped. And everything he stood to lose.

Flora scrutinized them, adjusting bits of their uniforms and peppering them with reminders. They both had a single revolver—another thing that galled Jack, who expected to walk into the fort armed to the teeth. Flora pointed out that this was a stealth run (until it wasn't, which they hoped was when they found their missing mages). They would lose the element of surprise if Jack's solution was to shoot everyone he came across in the face.

"All right, you'll do," Flora declared at last. "Let's go."

The trio walked to the post office. Hank Walker sat on a bench outside the damaged building, the awning overhead shredded during the attack. His crutch butted up against the bench, and a small brown satchel was nestled on his lap.

"What's that?" Jack's voice was throaty with suspicion. His hand twitched beside his holstered sixgun.

Blaise sighed. "Will you calm down?" Hank stared at them with terror, beads of sweat on his temple.

"What do you have there, Walker?" Jack repeated, insistent, ignoring Blaise. Blaise had the sudden worry an unhinged outlaw might become the biggest hitch in their plan.

Hank didn't answer, frozen in place by the menace. Jack snatched the bag and opened it, dumping the contents into his palm. Tiny plants shaped like clusters of miniature crescents, the edges of their leaves a vibrant purple, rolled into his palm. "What in Faedra's name are these?"

"M-mother of thousands," Hank stammered. "Plantlets. They'll help me move around the fort more easily. I swear, I brought them to help."

"Jack," Blaise warned, pulling a growl of authority into the word. Hank Walker was a crucial part of their plan. If he backed out, they were going to be in serious trouble.

Jack's eyes whipped up to him, acknowledging him at last. "Fine." He poured the tiny succulents into the bag and handed it back to the postmaster.

"I want a sample of one of those if we survive this," Flora said, as cheerful as if she were asking after produce at a farmer's market. "Do they have any medicinal properties?"

Hank blinked at her. "Um. I think so?"

Jack cleared his throat.

Flora waved a hand, dismissive. "We'll figure that out later."

Blaise groaned. He was a ball of stress, and they hadn't left Itude yet. "We should go." Before he lost his nerve.

Walker shook three plantlets out of the bag. "Need you each to hang on to these. If you have them, I can locate you."

Jack cocked his head, distrust in his eyes. He opened his mouth to say something, but in a rare moment of clarity, bit back his comment. Or maybe it was the fact that Blaise leaned in close and whispered, "Emmaline."

Jack plucked one of the tiny plants from Walker's hand, tucking it into a pocket. "I promise, if you pop up next to us with Gaitwood, I'll put a bullet in your skull."

Blaise selected a plantlet and slipped it into the pocket on the underside of his coat. "Please stop threatening our ride."

"No." Jack's lower lip stuck out, reminding Blaise of the times his younger brother had been on the verge of a tantrum. He decided not to point that out.

"I hate Gaitwood as much as you, you know," Hank muttered. "I want to get our friends back. And my brother."

Jack's eyes narrowed into speculative slits. Blaise assumed he was thinking no one could hate Gaitwood as much as he did. Blaise had to admit, he was probably right.

Flora tucked her plantlet away. They were ready. Blaise drew on his fake mantle of authority, hoping that one day this would be more comfortable. "Hank, review where you're going to drop us."

The postmaster took a breath. "Supply room. Located between my jump point and Gaitwood's office. Not used much, from what I saw. Plan is, I jump to my cactus at the fort, and when the coast is clear, I drop one of my babies in the supply room." He patted his satchel.

Blaise nodded and spoke up before Jack could issue any new threats. "Good luck."

Walker's wrinkled face parted in a tremulous smile, then he vanished with a soft pop.

Flora stared at the space he had occupied. "Huh. His magic works like a knocker's, but with plants."

They waited in silence, Jack shifting his weight from one booted foot to the other. Blaise spent the time with his eyes closed, practicing his calm. His hands were itching. He couldn't afford to leak any of his magic. But thinking of control made him think of Vixen, and she was among the captured, too. They were depending on him.

"Snap out of it," Jack growled.

Blaise cracked one eye open. "Need to work on your people skills."

Jack's mouth quirked, and for an instant he allowed himself levity. "Maybe people need to work on their me skills."

Blaise snorted. Hank reappeared with a pop, his sudden return startling Jack so he had his sixgun aimed at the postmaster's head before Blaise could even blink. Jack corrected himself when he realized it was Walker, lowering the muzzle and slipping the weapon into its holster. He ducked his head, which was as good as an apology as anyone would get from him.

"It's clear," Walker confirmed once Jack had his gun put away. His eyes were wide, though he seemed resigned to the fact that if he so much as sneezed, Jack might shoot him. "I'll take you one at a time."

"Me first!" Flora volunteered, excited.

"No," Jack growled.

Flora wheeled on him, her eyes twin daggers of ferocity. "Where are your manners, Mr. Dewitt? Ladies first."

Blaise feared it might come to blows between the tiny, vicious woman and the gruff outlaw. Jack stared at her, unblinking.

Flora tut-tutted. "If this is a trap, who has the better likelihood of squeaking out of it?"

Jack ground his teeth. "But it could be dangerous."

Her eyes lit up. "*Will* be dangerous. And I'll be fine." She spoke with such self-assurance that Flora left no room for doubt. Blaise worried for her sake. He imagined Lamar Gaitwood wouldn't be happy to discover a subordinate of his brother's political rival skulking around. If that crossed her mind, she didn't show it. Flora grinned at Hank. "How do we do this?"

"Link your arm in mine," Hank instructed. She did, and a moment later, they were both gone.

"Faedra's tits," Jack grumbled. "I have to be arm-in-arm with that man?"

Hank reappeared at the end of Jack's complaint. Blaise stepped beside the postmaster and linked arms before Jack could say anything. Hank activated his magic, and Blaise's stomach churned. It felt like the ground opened up beneath them, and Blaise's magic rose like a watchdog. He tamped it down, afraid to find out what might happen if Hank's magic shattered in the middle of transport.

Hank's method of travel didn't take long. Blaise blinked, and then found himself in a dim room. Flora busied herself reading labels on jars lined up on a shelf.

"If I don't make it back, Jack got pissed and killed me," Hank grumbled.

"He won't," Blaise promised. If he said it, maybe it would be true.

Hank vanished and then reappeared with Jack, the outlaw stumbling away from Walker as soon as he was able. He turned in a quick circle, assessing their surroundings with a sixgun in his hand.

"Hello. We're not dead yet." Flora waved at him. "Wow. They shouldn't just leave this stuff here for anyone wandering around to take." She pulled a small vial off a rack and pocketed it.

Hank stared at them like he couldn't believe Blaise had talked him into this. Blaise sighed. He wondered about that, too.

"You still want me to . . . do the thing?" Hank asked, gesturing to the door.

"Yes." Blaise nodded, then glanced at Flora. "Hey. Stop stealing their stuff. You were going to go scout for us."

"It's not stealing. I'm reallocating resources," Flora said, indignant. "I'm on their side, remember?"

"Uh . . ." Blaise stared at her, half-expecting Jack to have his revolver aimed at her head.

"That's what they'll think, anyway," Flora clarified, chipper. "I'll do more shopping later if I get a chance. Be right back."

Walker waited a beat, then slipped out in her wake. Blaise sat on a crate, elbows on his knees.

Jack pulled another crate over to sit opposite him. "You hanging in there?"

Sighing, Blaise shook his head. "No. I don't think I can do this." The enormity of the task before them was daunting. The chance of success seemed laughable.

"Why did you *really* come back to Itude?" Jack murmured.

Blaise closed his eyes. "Because I found a new family. You, Emmaline,

Reuben, Vixen, Clover. Even if I thought you hated me, I couldn't allow this."

Jack was quiet for a while. Blaise opened his eyes to watch him, noticing the pensive expression on the outlaw's face. "You've changed, kid."

"Not a kid."

"No, you're not." Jack agreed quickly, leaning forward. He pointed his index finger at Blaise's nose. "You're a damn good outlaw mage."

Blaise rubbed the back of his neck. "Doesn't feel like it. I should be sitting here calm and collected like you."

Jack rolled his shoulders, the golden braiding atop his uniform glinting in the low light. "Jack Dewitt is not calm and collected right now." For the barest moment, he dropped his façade, and Blaise saw the worry lines around his eyes. Then, as if donning a mask, his face hardened. "Wildfire Jack, on the other hand, is."

Blaise nodded. Jack had endured so much trauma in his life. It made sense he compartmentalized what he could when necessary. It made as much sense as Jefferson's need for an alter ego. Lost in thought, he didn't notice Jack reach out to pluck hairs from his head until he felt a sharp tug and yelped.

"Hey! What was that for?"

Jack clapped a hand over Blaise's mouth. "Shh, you're going to get us caught. And I have my reasons." He tucked the three hairs into the same pocket as his plantlet, buttoning it closed to keep the contents safe.

Blaise opened his mouth to ask, but the door opened. Jack had his revolver out. Flora poked her head in. "All clear. Let's go!"

CHAPTER FORTY-SEVEN

Fire in Her Eyes

"Your father is dead. Your town is destroyed. Everything and everyone you ever loved is gone. *You are worthless.*" Lamar repeated the words over and over, a mantra of suffering, as he walked in slow, steady circles around Jack's daughter. She refused to give her name, spitting in his face when he asked and yowling that she would never submit.

Stubborn. So much like her father. That only appealed all the more to Lamar. Jack would pay for his betrayal with his daughter's servitude. Everything had come full circle.

He continued the relentless chant, watching her closely for any signs of cracking. She bowed her head, flexing her arms against the salt-iron restraints that pinned her to the ladder-back chair. Her eyes watered, either from the sting of the metal or from his words, but she refused to allow her tears to fall.

A knock sounded on the door. Lamar scowled. He had left instructions not to be disturbed. He ignored it, but it came again, this time more insistent. Biting back a growl of annoyance, he stalked to the door and opened it a crack. "What is it?"

Lieutenant Smithson stood outside, clenching the arm of a man Lamar hadn't thought he'd ever see again. "Apologies, Commander. This man says he has urgent news."

Lamar gave Hank Walker a cool once-over. The maverick leaned heavily on a crutch, the empty bottom of his right pants leg pinned up over the stump of his knee. "I made it clear I'm through with you."

Walker's face contorted, a mix of fear and supplication. "Please. I have important news—news you need to know. Wildfire Jack and the Breaker are coming."

Impossible. Lamar stared at the old man, dumbfounded. No one touched one of his traps and survived. Anyone stupid enough to do so withered away, a slow and horrific death. He had seen Jack make the fatal mistake with his own eyes. But then a thought occurred to him: that damned Breaker. He'd found a way when no one else could. Gods, if only Gregor would let him kill the man.

Lamar glanced over his shoulder at Jack's daughter. Her head was up, ears straining. No doubt she had heard her father's name. Hope kindled in her eyes, undoing all of Lamar's hard work to extinguish her fire. He couldn't risk her hearing anything more that could jeopardize his progress. Lamar stepped into the hallway, closing the door behind him.

"Wildfire Jack should be dead," Lamar said, his tone low and dangerous.

"He's not. He's coming here, and he's mad as a demon straight from Perdition." Walker gulped and added, "Sir."

Bit by bit, Hank told him what he wanted to know. Lamar reined in his annoyance until his former spy finished recounting his information.

"Lock him up with the others." Lamar waved a hand, ignoring the devastation that shone in Walker's eyes.

"But . . . but I thought if I told you—"

"That I'd take pity on you? Let you have your brother?" Lamar asked as a soldier walked over and slipped a braided salt-iron rope around the mage's arms. Walker flinched as a bead of salt-iron burned against his skin. "I'm *done* with you. I thought I had made that abundantly clear. With the shooting out your knee and all." Lamar's lips curled into an amused smile.

Walker's anguished howl echoed through his office as a pair of soldiers escorted him to the holding cells. It would have been a kindness to end the man's miserable life. Lamar didn't do kindness.

He threw open the door and crossed the distance to where Jack's daughter sat in three long strides. "There's been a change of plans. We'll have to continue your education later."

The girl fixed a baleful look on him. She wasn't broken, not yet. Lamar and his cohorts had more to do to destroy the spirit that burned so brightly in her. Her young, pliable mind had to be shattered to its core, until her fierce independence was nothing more than tatters. Lamar enjoyed a hands-on approach. She said nothing, only lifted her chin in defiance.

Lieutenant Smithson had followed him inside and scowled. "I'd be happy to teach her *respect*, Commander."

Lamar waved a hand. While Smithson's methods could be effective, the lecherous man would be a poor choice in this situation. He had broken one of the Desinan mavericks beyond saving, the poor wretch. Jack's young daughter could serve the Confederation for decades to come if Lamar took the right approach. She would make amends for her father's betrayal.

"Thank you, but no," Lamar murmured. "This one is mine. You may take her back to the cell, however. I have preparations to make."

Smithson jumped over to her. "Yes, Commander." He dragged the girl to her feet. Lamar didn't miss the way he grabbed her bottom in the process. Jack's daughter stomped on the soldier's instep, causing him to howl and stagger away.

"You bitch—" Smithson thundered, raising a hand.

Lamar grabbed his arm. "Have a care, Smithson. She is *mine* to break. Forget that and I'll have you on latrine duty." He turned to the girl. "I'll bend your will into a theurgist yet." It was both promise and threat. She spat at him, though the glob of spittle went wide. Jack's daughter was going to be entertaining.

Smithson hauled the unruly teenager away, allowing Lamar to refocus on the matter at hand. Walker's trust in him had been misguided. Lamar smiled. A pity he had already sent out a squadron, headed for Rainbow Flat. Lamar planned to ride after them once the replacement Inker arrived. He couldn't send that many outlaw mages to Phinora without first knowing they were contained. Couldn't afford any more missteps.

He hadn't counted on the Breaker coming back to help Itude. Lamar studied the map on the wall. Hank had reported the pair were riding in from the east, coming across the Deadwood River. He supposed Jack would plan some sort of ambush. His old friend was wily and hadn't escaped justice for so long by being stupid. That he was in the Breaker's company made them an extremely dangerous pair.

"Gallagher. Prepare three squadrons," Lamar barked.

Gallagher, dozing nearby, snapped to attention. "Yes sir." Rubbing sleep from his eyes, he hurried out of the room. Lamar hoped he remembered the damn instructions.

Lamar checked the guns at his side, then pulled his rifle from its place behind his desk. He settled it on his back, then headed out to the stables.

A glimpse of pink gave him pause. He knew that hair. A growl of annoyance rumbled in his throat. "*Flora Strop.*"

Cole's little shadow turned to greet him, peering at him over her glasses. "Lamar."

Damn her, not even giving him the benefit of his hard-won title. "Commander."

She dimpled. "Oh, I don't have a rank."

His fingers twitched. Blessed Garus, if only killing her wouldn't start an *incident*. "Why are you here?"

Flora's eyes widened, playing at innocence. "Mr. Cole received word of the awful killings of his people. He sent me to investigate."

Of course he had. Lamar gritted his teeth. "We retaliated against the ones who took their lives."

She squinted at him. "You did? That's too kind of you. However, since they were Gannish citizens, you won't mind if I'm thorough. I have forms to fill out in triplicate about this incident after all! I'll stop by your office later so you can sign them. But don't mind me—you'll hardly know I'm here."

Gods, the Gannish and their damned paperwork. "My lieutenant can sign them. I'm busy."

"I'm sure you are," Flora agreed, waving him off and walking away with purpose, as if she were in command of the whole damned fort.

Lamar shook his head to clear it. Later. He would deal with Cole's little crone later, if he could find a way to do so without causing a ruckus. Lamar continued on to the stables, pleased to see that the word had gone out and the horses were being readied. He found his stolid bay gelding saddled and awaiting him. Things were looking up.

CHAPTER FORTY-EIGHT

Deal Me In

Jack

Jack and Blaise studied the rough map that Flora had scratched on a sheet of paper using a charcoal pencil. Her perusal of the fort allowed her the opportunity to locate their sentry postings, and she helpfully marked them with little smiley faces. Besides sentries, the fort still had the usual complement of soldiers going about their tasks. Flora reported that some of them were preparing to ride out with the Commander. That would help, but there were still more soldiers between their location and the prisoners than Jack liked. He folded the map and tucked it into his pocket.

"Splitting up is a bad idea," Blaise said, giving voice to Jack's own concern.

"Not fond of it myself," Jack agreed. "But it's our best shot."

As far as strategy, what they had to work with was less of a plan and more of a rough outline glued together with unfounded optimism. Hank hadn't returned. Flora hadn't seen him, and the only thing that kept Jack from believing Hank sold them out was no one came to the supply closet looking for them.

Regardless of Hank's status, Blaise had promised to free Joshua Walker. Time was of the essence, so Jack proposed they split up. Blaise would search the stables for Joshua while Jack located the prisoners. It was too soon for the wheels to come off the plan, but Jack supposed he should be pleased they had gotten as far as they had.

"I'll follow after the count of twenty," Jack reminded Blaise as the younger man got up, his uniform whispering with the movement. After Blaise closed the door, Jack reached into his pocket and pulled out a tiny poppet he'd brought along. Keeping a mental count in his head, he wrapped Blaise's hairs around the doll.

At the count of twenty, he tucked the poppet back into the safety of his pocket and shouldered the door open. He stepped out into the lantern-light of the hallway, glancing around for any witnesses he might need to silence. It was empty, though voices echoed in the distance.

Out of reflex, Jack touched the holster at his side, reassured by the steady presence of his sixgun. Six shots. He had a knife in his boot, but he wanted access to more guns. He never carried less than two. Flora had told him he would look suspicious if he were armed to the teeth.

"I'm coming, Em," Jack murmured, following the hallway to a wide corridor that opened onto a courtyard.

Overhead, engines rumbled like an ever-present distant thunder. The warbird loomed over the fort, docked against a rampart that had been built to serve the purpose. Jack studied the area, committing it to memory. He wished he could take a potshot at the airship out of spite, but that would draw unwanted attention. He settled for a middle finger.

"Later you get your reckoning with the Breaker," Jack muttered to the warbird.

He got himself back on track, heading to the wing that housed the holding cells. Flora, bless her vicious little heart, received confirmation that the prisoners from Itude were still there. Jack wasn't sure what he would have done if he'd found out they were shipped off to Phinora already. Razing the fort was high on the list, though.

A nearby soldier called out a question, but Jack pretended to not hear and plowed forward. His fingers twitched, ready to pull his sixgun at a moment's notice. If any of the soldiers inspected his weapon, the gig would be up. His revolver was not their standard issue.

Jack paused as a hiss and a pop reverberated across the fort, followed by shouts. A plume of violet smoke wafted into the air. He smiled. Something was working in their favor. As much as he detested Jefferson Cole, he liked his woman, Flora. She was a proper scoundrel.

He turned another corner and slowed, listening. The telltale sounds of a card game echoed ahead—the scrape of coins on the table as money changed hands and the swish of reshuffled cards. Someone wasn't doing their job. *Now isn't that a shame?*

A puddle of light spilled from the cardsharks' room. Jack paused, studying the visible area. The hallway ahead was poorly lit. They had little care if their prisoners could see. Jack knew from personal experience it was psychologically horrifying to be imprisoned in near-dark. He bit back a growl.

Jack's well-broken boots were silent as he ghosted down the hallway. Nothing on his person rattled or chafed to betray his presence. The shadow work of an assassin was more Raven's wheelhouse, but the guards ahead were lax. They would never hear him coming.

Twenty feet. Ten feet. Then Jack was right outside the door, back flat against the wall. He listened to their banter for several heartbeats, getting a peg on how many were in the room. Three, maybe four. He had enough ammunition to take them out.

Jack stepped into the doorway, sixgun in hand. "Deal me in."

Four soldiers turned to look at him in surprise. They were slow to react, confused by his sudden appearance. *Bang, bang, bang!* Two of his shots ripped into the eyes of his targets, taking out a pair sitting side by side before they could flinch. His third target was on the move, and the bullet grazed the top of the man's head as he ducked.

The fourth soldier, the dealer, overcame his surprise and lunged to a nearby table arrayed with weapons. Jack fired a shot at him before the man could reach it, grunting in satisfaction as blood and brain matter spurted from the back of the soldier's head as he sank to the floor.

The last surviving soldier scrambled for a weapon. He found a knife and hurled it, the pommel glancing against Jack's shoulder. The knife clattered to the ground as Jack finished his opponent with a shot to the forehead.

Jack holstered his sixgun. *Two shots left.* He needed to restock and to pick up anything else that might be helpful. Keys to the holding cells, for one. He searched each of the dead men, scowling. No keys, damn them.

He turned his attention to the table of weapons. His eyebrows flew up in recognition, the breath catching in his throat. Hexguns. *His* hexguns. Shit, in all the chaos he had forgotten about them. Hadn't checked to make sure they were still there. Didn't matter. They were here now.

One hexgun lay disassembled, as if someone had either taken it apart to clean it or had been trying to figure out what made it tick so they could reproduce it. Damn. His contact in Ravance would be pissed if she found out these beauties had fallen into Confederation hands. Jack counted them. Of the original thirteen, only six were on the table.

Jack would deal with that later. He checked to see which ammunition was loaded. Four were loaded with sleep, the fifth with null. Jack picked up a sleep hexgun and shoved it into his waistband. Now wasn't the time to be choosy.

He pulled the rough map from his pocket, studying it. Although it wasn't to scale, he wasn't far from the holding area. Jack cocked his head, straining as he caught the timbre of a voice he recognized. It was Raven, though his words were indistinct.

If Raven was close by, then so was Emmaline. Sixgun drawn, Jack left the cooling corpses behind him in pools of congealing blood. Dim lantern-light revealed the T-intersection in the hallway ahead. Cells lined the end of the hallway, the dark bars looking rough and uneven. Jack would bet his sixgun those were salt-iron bars. Raven's pale face was visible in the distance, the captured outlaw shaking his head at Jack. Jack slowed, cocking his head as he listened.

"I know someone's there," an unfamiliar voice echoed in the quiet. There was the soft click of something being engaged. A rifle, perhaps. Or one of the missing hexguns. "Who's there?"

Raven shot Jack another pleading look. "I've already taken out four of your men. I'm much obliged to make it five," Jack said.

There was a grating laugh, and a mocking voice rang out. "So you *are* an outlaw. I have one of your people lined up in my sights. Pretty little thing. Blonde hair."

Jack bit back a growl. Emmaline. He couldn't see her from where he stood, or the man who threatened her. Jack wanted nothing more than to storm around the corner and take out the threat. But he couldn't—not at the risk of her life.

Raven's gaze flicked to the neighboring cell, then back to Jack. Something he saw made him reconsider the situation. He gave Jack the tiniest of go-ahead nods.

Jack smiled. He may have had his share of disagreements with Raven, but he knew he could count on him in a pinch. He tossed the revolver to the floor, wincing at the clatter of metal on stone as it slid forward. Jack hated giving up his favorite weapon, but he had to make this seem legitimate.

"Fine, do it your way. Don't hurt the girl."

A satisfied chuckle preceded the clomp of heavily booted feet. The guard yelped as he tripped and went down hard, his balding head sliding into Jack's line of sight as he hit the ground. Jack lunged, skidding along the dirt floor as he scooped up his sixgun. A bright flash illuminated the dim holding area as he fired. The guard went still as his body tumbled to a stop, blood oozing from a hole in his temple.

"Daddy?"

"Emmaline!" Jack stepped over the corpse, heart pounding. Her eyes were watery, face grimy and tear-stained. She looked like a lost little girl, and he wanted nothing more than to crush her against him and protect her from the world.

He scowled as he laid a hand against the bars, hissing as he drew his fingers back. *What in Perdition?* They were salt-iron, but he hadn't reacted to salt-iron in *years.*

"Jack? Is that really you?" Vixen interrupted his thoughts, walking up behind Emmaline. Her eyes were glassy, red hair mussed, and her clothing torn and bloodied from battle. Her trademark glasses were missing.

He nodded. "I'm here to get you out." He glanced at Emmaline, gesturing to the dead guard. "Was that you?"

She released a shaky breath, coming as close to the bars as she dared. Emmaline cupped a poppet in her hand.

"Good girl," Jack whispered, pride warming his heart. His brave, unyielding daughter had somehow cast a spell through salt-iron. Not impossible, but damn difficult. Then he addressed the rest of his captured friends. "Anyone know if this asshole had a key?"

Raven shook his head. "If it's not on him, it may be around the desk in there." He pointed into the guardroom.

Jack was tired of searching corpses. He cast a hopeful look at Butch, who was in the same cell as Raven. Along with Austin and Hank—well, that answered his earlier question about what happened to the Cactus Walker. "Butch, can you do your thing and reanimate him just to give me the key?"

Butch winced, his face battered. "I . . . I can't. Even if I wanted to." He turned away, shaking his head.

"They stripped our magic," Vixen whispered, her voice shaky.

Jack's tongue dried, and for a moment buried memories threatened to overwhelm him. "Well, shit."

"That about sums it up, yes," Raven agreed wryly.

"Everyone?" Jack scowled. Emmaline had her magic . . . .

"Not the kids," Vixen answered, rubbing her face. "They think they can still break them. And Hank is a recent arrival."

Jack sighed and continued searching for the damned key. The guard ended up face-down after Jack shot him. Jack checked his back pockets first. With distaste, he turned the man over. "You better have a damn key, or I'll shoot you again on principle," Jack muttered to the dead man. As he searched, the internal timer in his head kept track of how long he had been at his mission. Every second counted. *Where is Blaise?*

He discovered the lump of keys in the guard's front pocket. Jack rose with his prize and freed the men first. Raven hobbled out with difficulty, followed by Butch. Austin helped Hank up and out of the cell.

Raven claimed the guard's rifle. Jack nodded. That was wise. And it reminded him . . . . "They got my hexguns. Need y'all to grab them from the room up ahead to the left." He tapped the grip of the hexgun poking from his waistband.

"Shit. All of them?" Raven asked.

Jack scowled. "I'm guessing so. You'll find five in the room, but only four are usable."

Once Jack unlocked the women's cell, Raven, Cordelia, and Vixen hurried to reclaim the hexguns and commandeer any other weapons they could find. Jack intended to go with them, but Emmaline rushed out and wrapped him in a hug so fierce he didn't want it to end. She buried her head against his secondhand uniform. Jack nestled his face against her hair. He wanted to hold her in his arms forever, but the cold outlaw within reminded him that time was of the essence.

Jack drew back from her and looked at Hank. "How's your magic?"

The postmaster took a pained breath. "Not good. They had me bound with salt-iron until they got me here, and the cells are just as bad. Drained a lot of it. I may have enough to jump myself and Joshua." He swallowed. "If I can find him."

"Blaise went after him," Jack said, trying to keep the accusation out of his voice and failing. *That was your job, Hank.* The postmaster hung his head, wrung out and miserable.

"What's the plan?" Raven asked as he returned with the hexguns. "There is a plan, yes?"

"Eh." Jack waggled his fingers. "More or less." The new plan was for Blaise to rendezvous with Jack at the holding cells. They couldn't delay any longer. Five men were dead. Discovery was inevitable.

Jack pulled the poppet he had made earlier out of his pocket, pressing it into Emmaline's hand. "Hang on to this. We'll need it."

She blinked with confusion. "Who is it?"

"Blaise."

Her expression frosted, her fingers tightening over the doll. "Did he betray us?"

Jack stared at her, confused. He shook his head, realizing that her harrowing experience had brought her to some startling conclusions. He couldn't blame her. Gaitwood had set up the chain of misdirection masterfully. "No. *No,*" Jack emphasized, closing his hand over hers before she cast something she would regret. "He came back. Blaise is here to help."

Emmaline's eyes were bleary with unshed tears. "Okay."

Gods, she sounded hollow, as if her very soul hurt. Jack wanted nothing more than to lash out at the ones who hurt her, but he settled himself with the knowledge that retribution was coming. *Soon.* He looked her in the eye. "We need your magic. Understand?"

Emmaline nodded.

"Are we just going to stand around and wait for them to recapture us or what?" Raven asked.

Jack snarled in frustration. Raven had a point. "Let's go."

Their group inched down the hall, slowed by the need for Austin to support Hank and Raven's limp. Jack led the way, revolver out. He held up a hand, calling for a silent halt when he heard the shuffle of heavy feet coming toward them.

"Don't shoot," Hank called weakly. "I feel one of my plantlets getting close."

Jack glanced at him, brows raised. Walker had better be right. Jack kept his revolver readied. He would not be caught unawares. The footsteps came closer, the uneven cadence a hint it was not a trained soldier. Jack remained frozen at the head of their group, ready. The silhouette of a man rounded the corner.

"Hank? Hank, I'm here!"

"Joshua!" Hank's voice was raspy with relief. "Oh, thank Faedra you made it."

Jack pursed his lips, watching as Joshua Walker hurried over and gave his big brother a desolate look. "They hurt you. Oh, who hurt you?" Joshua wailed.

Hank shook his head. "Doesn't matter. I'll be okay. We need to go, Joshua." He held out his hand.

"Wait." Jack stepped closer. "Where's Blaise? Did someone bring you here?"

"Oh." Joshua nodded, turning to Jack with enormous eyes. "Yes. He said to tell you the soldiers were coming back already."

Jack stared at him, chilled by the news. The fort was about to be overrun with the enemy. "Shit." He turned to Hank. "Get your brother out of here." To everyone else, he said, "Follow me. We don't have much time. Keep your weapons at the ready." He reconsidered, and added for the three younger outlaws, "And your magic, if it will be useful." He led their small group down the corridor after Hank vanished with his brother.

Vixen came up on his right. "Where's Blaise?"

Jack ducked his head. "If I had to guess, making his way to the airship."

Everyone stared at him. "The airship?" Raven asked.

Jack nodded. "The plan is to break it."

CHAPTER FORTY-NINE
What Friends Are For

Blaise

By the time Blaise had located Joshua Walker, Gaitwood's forces were returning to the fort and he knew every moment counted. He'd lost too much precious time on his search. And then on convincing the frightened, mistreated man that Blaise was there to *help*.

Hank's tiny plantlet had been the key to convincing Joshua that he had good intentions. Clutching the succulent in his palm, Joshua was eager to reunite with his brother. With Blaise's instructions, he hurried off to find Hank and the others.

But now Blaise was alone. A fort teeming with enemy soldiers stood between him and his friends. And the airship still hovered above, a looming reminder of everything the Confederation was capable of.

Blaise marched out of the stables as soldiers filed in with their mounts. He kept his strides purposeful, trying to fit in. Like he belonged there. Despite the chill wind, a nervous drop of sweat trailed down from his hairline.

A distraction on the other side of the fort had many of the soldiers engaged, fighting against a plume of violet smoke. Blaise prayed that between the smoke and the need for the returning soldiers to care for their mounts, he would be unharried.

"Psst!"

Blaise jumped, whirling at the voice. He put a hand to his chest when he realized it was Flora. "What?"

She frowned at him. "Why aren't you with Jack?"

Blaise shook his head. "Hank didn't come back. I found his brother and sent him to Jack."

Flora's eyes widened. "*Oh.* Um, not to be a wet blanket, but Gaitwood's already back."

Blaise raked a hand through his hair. "I saw. I'm going to the airship."

She winced. "Alone? It's under guard." Flora pursed her lips, thoughtful. "I'll try to distract Gaitwood and his lieutenants. I can't do much for the rest. Can't have everyone sign my forms in triplicate."

Blaise swallowed. He had already scoped out the pair of guards standing atop the platform leading to the warbird's deck. The guards were Jack's purview. Fighting was his forte. But Jack wasn't there, and they were running out of time.

Flora followed his gaze, her eyes hardening. "You don't have to do it, you know. You could rejoin your friends and leave."

He could. And it was tempting. But it wouldn't end the threat posed by the warbird. The Confederation had shown they had no qualms with attacking a town of innocent people. Well, *mostly* innocent people. "Jefferson asked me to," Blaise whispered.

The half-knocker shook her head. "He would understand if you didn't."

Would he? Blaise shivered, remembering the destruction of Itude. To allow anything like that to happen again was unconscionable. More death. More heartache. "It only delays the inevitable."

She surprised him, reaching up and grabbing his smooth chin in her hand. "Do what you have to do. No wonder Jefferson saw something special in you."

When Flora released her grip, he rubbed his chin gingerly. She was stronger than she looked. "Thanks."

She humored him with an impish grin before she turned and trotted off. Blaise watched her go, then looked at the rampart leading to the airship. Red and gold pennants fluttered in the breeze. He clenched his jaw and mounted the stairs. Blaise flexed his fingers, shucking off the standard-issue Confederation gloves and discarding them over the side railing.

I hope I can do this. He ascended to the first landing, pausing to summon his magic. Blaise traced a finger along the well-worn wood at the top of the stairs, power spiking into it. The wood crunched as it shredded under the magical assault, flaking and curling as if impacted with instant dry-rot. Breaker magic slithered down each step, fragmenting the wood until all that remained was a flight of stairs too treacherous to climb. Chunks of wood sloughed off to the ground below.

Getting down would be difficult. Taking a shaky breath, he decided to worry about that problem later. He had made it impossible for Jack to join him, and that was the more pressing matter.

Keeping his magic checked, he put a hand on the railing and continued up. Blaise heard a loud exclamation as someone discovered the damage he had wrought, followed by more querulous voices. He took the stairs two at a time to put more distance between himself and the soldiers below.

Blaise still didn't know how to handle the pair guarding the top. He discarded the notion of breaking the platform—doing so would cut off any chance he had of getting to the ship. He paused on the landing below, crouching to keep a low profile. What would Jack or Flora do?

He shook his head. He wasn't either of them; Blaise couldn't replicate their level of intensity in a situation like this. He had a revolver, but he had little confidence in using it in a high stakes situation.

This was why he wasn't supposed to be doing this alone. He had no chance.

On the platform above, a guard made a sharp exclamation. Blaise missed the words, but he glanced up at the familiar thunder of wings. The pegasi had arrived. He scooted closer to the side and peered down, his breath catching at the knot of outlaws in the courtyard.

Jack was at the forefront, sowing confusion by virtue of the uniform he wore. Blaise cursed softly when he realized why Jack had started the assault. The soldiers were bringing ladders and barrels over, constructing their own makeshift means to reach the undamaged section of stairs.

Jack must have found a weapons cache somewhere. He waded through the soldiers like a dragon ransacking a town, magnificent and terrible in his fury. Every move the outlaw made was deliberate, calculated. Every pull of the trigger was prioritized for the greatest impact.

A shout overhead drew Blaise's attention. "Breaker!" A bullet pelted into the wood beside him. Blaise dove as another bullet whistled by. Heart pounding, he kept a low profile. They would come for him, and then it would be over.

I can't do this.

A challenging scream sliced the air. Blaise looked up in time to see Emrys drop from the sky like an obsidian boulder. Blaise feared the stallion would collide with the platform, his wings mantled close to his sides and his neck outstretched, legs tucked neatly beneath him to cut the wind resistance. The soldiers stared at the sight, realizing too late they were the targets.

A pistol glinted as Emrys's wings snapped open to complete his stoop. His body ratcheted as he extended his hind hooves like an osprey stretching out talons to take a fish. The soldier took aim at the stallion.

"No!" Blaise screamed, racing up the stairs.

The muzzle flashed. The soldier turned toward Blaise's voice as Emrys slammed into him and his companion with the force of an avalanche. Massive hooves crunched against fragile bone. Crimson blood and viscera peppered the air as Emrys slammed them over the side of the platform to fall on their fellows below, raining down a cloud of gore.

Uncontested and panting for breath, Blaise gained the top of the platform. Emrys was already a blur in the distance, his speed and mass carrying him away. The stallion circled around, threading through the pennants atop the fortress to land on the platform, the wood groaning beneath his weight. Blood dribbled from a wound on his right foreleg.

A bullet whistled nearby, a reminder of their dire circumstances. "Emrys, you need to get out of here. You're too big a target!"

The black pegasus's nostrils flared as he sucked in deep breaths from his exertion. <I couldn't let you do this alone.>

Blaise swallowed, hot tears threatening his eyes. He had thought he was alone, but he wasn't. "You're the best." Blaise wrapped his arms around Emrys's neck, and the stallion arched his neck, lipping at Blaise's back. Blaise touched the bullet wound. "You need to get out of here before you get shot again. Can you fly?"

<I am not leaving you to do this alone.>

Blaise shook his head. "I'm not alone. You cleared the path for me." He glanced over the side of the platform, down at the fighters below. Blaise pulled away from Emrys, unable to delay the inevitable. "Can you tell the other pegasi to get them to safety? This warbird won't be in the air much longer if I have a say in it."

Emrys backed up a step, flicking his ears. <I will tell them. And I'll come back for you.> He shoved his head against Blaise's chest. <And we'll celebrate with apple pie.>

Blaise smiled, scratching Emrys's throatlatch. "Whatever you want."

Emrys turned and bolted off the strained platform, wings snapping out as he swooped over the courtyard. Screams heralded his descent as he buzzed over the heads of the combatants.

With a shaky breath, Blaise crossed from the platform to the airship's gangway. No one challenged him, thanks to Emrys. Bullets tore through the platform behind him, but it was too late. They wouldn't be able to get a line of sight on him now with the ship's bulk protecting him.

The wooden deck of the airship vibrated beneath his feet. He grimaced at the sensation but walked the length of the deck to get his bearings and decide the best location to start his work. Massive blades housed in metal spun along the sides of the ship. Was that what allowed it to fly? If he had the luxury, Blaise would like to know more about how the behemoth took to the air. But that wasn't meant to be.

The dull pressure of a tension headache pounded in the base of his skull. Blaise frowned. Had the stress gotten to him? Maybe. He felt strange, as if his magic were being leeched away, like the time Gaitwood had him in salt-iron shackles.

With a sinking feeling, Blaise realized that parts of the airship were forged from salt-iron. That was an added difficulty he hadn't accounted for. The salt-iron would make his task more difficult, but not impossible. The Confederation wouldn't want to render their own theurgists useless after a flight on the ship. How did they manage?

Blaise sat down on the polished wood of the deck. The added drain on his magic made his work urgent. When he touched the ship with his palms, his magic bloomed to life.

He nibbled his lower lip, puzzled at what he discovered. Against all odds, the airship had magic, too. Magic and salt-iron coexisting in one terrifying leviathan. Blaise was no expert, but that seemed impossible. How had they done it? And how was he going to break it?

The magic sluiced over the warbird like a second skin. Blaise sent out tendrils of his own magic, feeling it trace along the lines of the ship, following the grid of the enemy's enchantment. Not attacking—not yet. Simply questing, gathering information. The magic armor didn't extend to the metal propeller blades. He had found the salt-iron.

Blaise wondered if there was a way to avoid the blades. There were so many of them. Their proximity tugged at his magic, and he already felt the drain. He shrugged away the sensation, flattening his palm against the wood once more.

His magic painted a clear picture of how the airship's protective sorcery functioned. He couldn't see the details—he could never replicate whatever the spell was. But his Breaker magic identified multiple spells layered over the vessel, woven together like a failsafe. If one failed, another would kick in to keep the ship from harm. As far as he could tell, they were purely defensive. Smart, Blaise decided. Nobody wanted a massive airship falling out of the sky. Normally, anyway.

A single spell overlaid the others, and it was more aggressive than the rest. It actively probed Blaise's magic. He frowned as he felt the ghost of a tickle against his shoulder. His shoulder? He startled as he realized the magic was searching for a theurgist's tattoo. That was how the Confederation kept their mages from being drained by the airship. It identified friendlies by their tattoo.

He shook his head. Blaise didn't know how someone convinced the salt-iron to play nice with the identification spell. But that wasn't his concern. He needed to crack through the magic armor. Fast.

From what Blaise could decipher, the spells kept hostile magic from destroying the ship. It made it resistant to mundane weapons like cannonballs, too. The identification spell kept the workings below it from being breached. Whoever had designed this had been meticulous.

"Hmm." Blaise cocked his head, still probing. The theurgists intended to make the ship impervious to magic. That didn't mean they had succeeded. He was a Breaker, and this was his specialty.

I can do this.

Blaise's only concern was the sheer size of the spells. And once he had made it through those, he still needed to crack the ship like an egg. That was going to take a lot of strength and a lot of power. And it was being leeched.

"For hating magic, they sure packed a lot into this monster," Blaise grumbled. He settled down to work, hoping his friends below were either still holding the line or winging their way to safety.

He laid both hands against the deck and closed his eyes, concentrating. The identification spell was child's play for his magic, ripped apart with the ease of punching through a spider's web. There was an audible pop as it broke. One down, too many more to go.

The protection spell was the real challenge, as he'd suspected. Blaise strained his magic against it, like a mouse struggling to break a boulder. The wind carried the acrid stench of gunpowder and the sounds of fighting. He didn't have time to dally with that spell. Blaise hammered his magic against it, relentless. His head throbbed, and his hands were raw as if he were physically scrabbling against the enchantment. His magic told him he was making progress, but it was so infinitesimal Blaise quailed that he had met his match.

Shoulders hunched, breathing hard, he threw everything he could at the protective working. His muscles ached with the effort, and he understood how Nadine's body had held up to such abuse—her power had converted her own flesh and blood to magic, to restore her. Blaise felt his body doing the same, only it wasn't to heal his body. It was to destroy the airship.

The protective sorcery shattered with a resounding boom. The wood shuddered beneath him. Blaise's eyes shot open. Now he only needed to slice through the other spells. *Right. No problem.*

With a hiss, a silver cage slid into existence around him. Confusion clouded Blaise's mind. *How?* He didn't see Gaitwood—oh. Heart pounding, Blaise saw the Commander standing on the rampart across the courtyard, arm extended.

He couldn't break the trap *and* the spells on the airship. It would be a challenge for his ebbing magic to complete even one of them.

Blaise didn't think twice. He slammed his palms down against the deck, spiraling the last dregs of his magic into the thrumming wood.

CHAPTER FIFTY

Vengeance Incarnate

Jack

Jack was in his element. Blood coated the front of his uniform, though he appreciated the fact that the scarlet fabric made it difficult to tell. He could respect a practical color choice.

The rescued outlaws fought around him, creating a unified front of bullets, flying fists, and bladed weapons. Courtesy of Flora's map, Jack had led his group to the armory first, where they laid claim to more weapons. And then, to further sow chaos, Jack had Cordelia torch the armory. Her phase-shifting ability proved handy—she set the fire and skulked out without so much as a worry.

Smoke billowed behind them as fresh cries of dismay met the new development. The smoke would hinder the pegasi's vision, but the benefit of destroying the enemy's access to weapons outweighed the risk. Determined, Jack wove through the courtyard toward the stairs to the rampart. He ground to a stop, dismayed.

Blaise had already come through, and he had made sure no one could follow him. *Stupid kid. How are you going to get past the guards, bake them a cake?*

A pegasus screamed overhead. Jack cursed, shoving Emmaline out of the way as a pair of pulped corpses splattered to the ground. He swiped gore from his cheek, his lip curling in disgust. *Damn Emrys.*

"Where's Blaise?" Emmaline asked, eyes wide, her face tinged green at the sight of the mangled soldiers.

Jack pointed up. He narrowed his eyes as a soldier leveled his rifle at them, casually shooting the man with one of his newly acquired revolvers. "Time for the extraction," he called to the group. It was just as well; they would be overrun soon if they didn't get out

Heads bobbed in acknowledgment, though everyone was still locked in combat. Jack ducked under a swinging saber, Emmaline kicking out his attacker's knee and driving the man down to the ground with a ferocity that made Jack's heart pound. *She's the spitting image of her mother.*

He hoped Zepheus was close. Gold flitted in the sky above, and Jack filled his mind with thoughts of *get us outta here.*

<On it.> Zepheus's mental voice was a whisper, proof the pegasus was at his broadcast limit.

The courtyard was a riot of activity. The soldiers not engaged with Jack and his group gained a foothold on the rampart stairs. Jack growled as soldiers swarmed up the structure.

"Send Austin!" Emmaline yelled over the din. Jack frowned, not following her train of thought in the heat of battle. "He's a *Skater*. He can just run up there!" Emmaline pointed to the rope and wood gangway that led from the platform to the airship.

Damn. She had a good idea. But doing so would trap Blaise.

Emrys circled above the airship, his challenging cries echoing through the courtyard, answered by the whinnies of the other approaching pegasi. The stubborn black stud had the Breaker's back.

Jack pulled his knife from his boot, ducking over to Austin and shooting the teen's newest opponent in the face. Austin blinked at him in surprise as Jack shoved a blade into his hand and pointed. "Get rid of that gangway, then get out of here."

Austin's eyes widened, then he nodded and ran to the side of the rampart. He made an incredible sideways leap, his boots clamping down to the brick as he skated his way up the facade, dodging bullets as he went.

Jack turned his attention from the Skater as the first pegasus landed in the courtyard, Vixen's Alekon. The bay stallion screamed, strafing over a group of soldiers, knocking several over. His hooves kissed the dirt for a heartbeat as Vixen vaulted into the saddle in a perfect touch-and-go. Alekon's wings created a wind so fierce it blew a soldier back.

One by one, the other pegasi came in for pick up. Jack worried that Raven and Butch would have difficulty, but the Necromancer could hustle when the situation warranted it. Despite his wounds, the battle invigorated Raven, and he mounted his pegasus quick as a wink. Cordelia followed, and then Austin, who had left the gangway a drooping, useless tangle.

And then only Jack and Emmaline remained. The surrounding soldiers kept a respectful distance, many of them out of ammunition and humbled by the unforgiving hooves of the pegasi raining down on their fellows. Jack and his daughter had a healthy supply of weapons. Jack wasn't afraid to menace anyone who looked at them the wrong way. Most of the soldiers focused on attempts to get to the Breaker, alone and vulnerable atop the airship. Soft targets were always more appealing for cowards.

Oberidon lined up for the maneuver, speckled wings steady as he descended. "If it's safe, circle until you know—" Jack started, then paused when he heard a familiar voice.

Emmaline was already hurtling onto her stallion's back when Jack turned and fixated on Lamar Gaitwood. The Commander stood atop the undamaged rampart opposite the warbird, arm outstretched.

"Daddy, no!" The wind of Oberidon's departure blew away her protest.

Rage consumed Jack, spurring him on as he stalked across the courtyard, inevitable as the chill of winter. Emmaline must have worked magic on him because the exhaustion from his recovery had faded, replaced with a swiftness and agility the men who tried to get in his way couldn't match. Jack was a living wildfire, racing from one man to the next, snuffing out lives with cold indifference before his enemies had the opportunity to react.

A solitary soldier, no older than a boy, stood at the bottom of the stairs, knees knocking together in terror, eyes wide at the trail of death in the outlaw's wake.

Wildfire Jack stared. He smiled. A wet stain spread across the front of the kid's pants. He ran.

Jack shot up the stairs like a bullet, intent on his target, unerring. He didn't think twice about what he was doing. Jack only saw the man who threatened everything he loved, everyone he cared about.

<Jack!> Zepheus was frantic. <Jack! We have to go. Jack!>

The outlaw shook his head as he reached the final landing before the top. He was almost there. Lamar would pay for his treachery. Across the courtyard, metal and wood groaned like an abused accordion.

<Jack, STOP!>

He couldn't stop. He wouldn't stop until Lamar was *dead*, damn him thrice to Perdition.

Zepheus slammed into the railing ahead of him, a shower of wood splintering from the impact of his hind hooves. Jack slowed, growling as the stallion's left wing brushed against his chest for a beat before the pegasus swept by, circling around.

The airship wailed again, and out of the corner of his eye, Jack saw the entire vessel shudder, the midsection beginning to buckle as if it were being squeezed by a giant hand.

Lamar screamed something unintelligible. *Lamar.*

<If you kill Lamar now *you will die*, crushed by that airship!>

Jack blinked at Zepheus's cold assessment. The damn stud was right. Already the airship was listing, and before long it would slam bow-first into the rampart where Lamar stood.

<Touch-and-go,> Zepheus advised him, swooping around.

Jack stepped back and crouched to give the pegasus room to maneuver. It was all up to Blaise.

CHAPTER FIFTY-ONE

Together

Blaise

ands braced against the wood, Blaise poured everything he could against the warbird. He ignored the pulsing hum of the magic trap surrounding him, keeping the knife's edge of his focus on breaking through the spells woven around the vessel.

Blaise hoped he was close. He was so tired. As he sank down against the deck, his mind drifted as his forehead rested against the grain of the wood. *Maybe I could just take a quick nap . . . .*

The echo of gunfire nearby reminded him he didn't have the luxury of rest. His body was being consumed from the inside out by his magic. And the ship was still leeching away the little he had to give.

Speckled wings zipped in the periphery of his vision. Blaise frowned, struggling into a sitting position as Oberidon banked overhead. He lifted his head, the wind tousling his hair as power seeped into him. It was like the first cup of coffee in the quiet peace of the bakery, waking him up to the possibilities of the day. Blaise closed his eyes as another wave of strength flowed through him. It was a ghost of the joy of togetherness from the night of the Feast of Flight, before his world had cascaded into disaster.

His eyes flashed open as magic suffused him, granting him renewed resolve. *We take care of each other.*

He was alone and vulnerable on the deck, trapped in a silver cage. Blaise smiled. He wasn't truly alone. Overhead, two pegasi circled, waiting as Emmaline poured her magic down on him. Her spell spoke of the belief the townspeople had in him, and it was like they stood on the deck beside him. Solid, reliable Clover, who could carry Jack like a baby. Hannah, with her ready smile and unerring positivity. Growly Kur Agur, who would stand and fight for the weak. Wildfire Jack, who had become an unlikely friend.

"We'll do this together," Blaise murmured.

Bolstered, he sank his magic into the hull, but this time with the seed of an idea. He thinned his magic into long tendrils, wrapping them around the airship like krakenvine claiming a tree. Emmaline continued to feed strength to him, and Blaise pushed more into his vines. He had seen vines break through wood and stone before. Not everything required force.

Unlike in nature, his vines didn't take time to grow. They writhed around the warbird, tightening his magical grasp. He pushed his magic, forming barbs like on a living krakenvine, hooking them into the enchantment. The protective spell reacted to the threat, recoiling. The barbs of Breaker magic snagged and shredded the working.

The airship keened as its protections were ripped asunder, leaving it vulnerable. Breathing hard, Blaise grinned.

<Blaise! You have to get free,> Emrys warned, coming to ground on the deck. His glossy hide twitched as he was sapped by the salt-iron, and he took off again quickly before it could do more damage.

Blaise bowed his head. The last of the power from Emmaline was fading, and he still needed to break the airship. Taking out the spells wasn't enough. Emrys swooped overhead, hanging stationary for an instant as he pumped his wings backwards.

"Thank you for being my friend." *For believing in me.*

Blaise poured the last of his magic into his vines, crushing them around the hull as Emrys winged away, whinnying in frantic denial. Emrys battered at his mind, desperate. But Blaise pushed him out as the deck started to buckle beneath him.

His muscles trembled with the effort of sitting up. The ship lurched, and Blaise's hands scrabbled for purchase against the wood. The airship listed to the port side, then shimmied starboard. Metal squealed, and lumber splintered as his magic ripped the ship apart, sending it spiraling toward the opposite rampart where Gaitwood stood, gaping.

And then the deck dropped sideways. Blaise struggled to stay away from the bars of the cage, but the force of gravity was inevitable. He slid against the deck, flailing as he struck the perilous trap.

His magic spent, there was nothing to protect Blaise. Darkness washed over him as the wreckage of the airship ripped through the fort.

⸻

Jack

EMRYS'S HEARTBREAKING WHINNIES SPLIT THE FRIGID AIR. JACK SAT IN Zepheus's saddle, shoulders hunched. Emmaline, astride Oberidon, brushed tears from her eyes. They stood on a ridge due west of Fort Courage, far enough inside the boundaries of the country of Mella to be problematic if anyone cared to come after them. But the mangled airship, that destroyed a good portion of the fort as it went down, distracted the enemy.

Jack was silent as smoke rose from the fort in the distance, mingling with dust motes stirred by the impact of the airship. He squinted as he watched Emrys fly over the fort, the stallion searching for his rider with single-minded determination. Emmaline clutched the poppet with Blaise's hair in her cupped hand. She was pale and exhausted after pouring everything she had left into the effigy.

"Feel anything?" Jack asked.

She swallowed, biting her bottom lip. "No. It's like . . . he's not there."

Neither of them wanted to say aloud what that likely meant. Jack balled his fists. *Damn it, the kid wasn't supposed to die.* The outlaw hung his head, comforting himself, knowing that at least Blaise knew they had succeeded. His friends were safe. Emmaline was safe. And he had guaranteed the cursed airship wouldn't bother them. Victory had never tasted so bitter.

"Let's head home," Jack said, nudging Zepheus with his knee. He cast a final look over his shoulder, knowing he should be satisfied by the defeat of his enemy. Instead, the piercing stab of loss suffused him.

Oberidon followed Zepheus into the sky. Together, the palomino and the spotted stallions convinced the black pegasus to join them, and they flew homeward to Itude.

CHAPTER FIFTY-TWO

A Minor Setback

Darkness enveloped him.

Blaise assumed he was dead. But being dead shouldn't have so much pain attached to it. Dull aches and sharp pains washed through his body, unrelenting. He tried to move an arm, confused when the request didn't register with his limb. Where was he? Why was it so dark?

Then he *remembered*. Panic seized him, and if he had command of his body, he would have been sick at the memory of the airship shattering beneath him, the deck twisting and lurching as he fell into the wicked silver bars—

No. He forced the memory down, trying to master the horror as he had mastered his magic. *My magic.* Blaise recalled the utter emptiness, nothing left to give; feeling his body convert his own flesh into power to continue the fight. Was he, like Jack, trapped in a living prison after hitting the cage? That was the only explanation he could devise.

Blaise relaxed into the darkness. He had no other option. This was a battle he couldn't fight. Even if he could, he was so tired. He slipped in and out of wakefulness, his dreams filled with angry voices talking over him. They sounded distant, and he didn't bother to decipher their words. A corner of his mind recognized one voice, but he was so deep in the darkness it wasn't worthwhile to figure out who it belonged to.

He felt a jarring sensation when he was alert—as if he were being moved somewhere. That was a positive sign; with luck, he wasn't buried under a pile of broken airship. Idly, Blaise wondered if his magic would come back. Would it shatter the barrier of Lamar's magic? Or was he trapped in the depths for the rest of whatever time he had left?

His aches and pains receded. How much time had passed outside of his prison? He remembered how Jack looked, wasting away from the days of his imprisonment. Blaise tried not to think about how certain Nadine had been that the outlaw would succumb to the nefarious trap. There was no one to free Blaise.

Words and voices surrounded him again, most of them unfamiliar. But one voice remained, the same one he had tried to place before. His groggy mind grasped at the voice like a drowning man reaching for a rope. The timbre belonged to Jefferson Cole.

Blaise clung to Jefferson's voice, trying to understand his words, but failing. Jefferson spoke to him, relentless but soothing. Sometimes Jefferson spoke with others, but then he was terse, stressed. Jefferson's presence gave him hope. *I'm not alone.*

His magic came back, a slow, painful trickle. Blaise had never spent all of it before, didn't have a concept of how long it would take to replenish. Though as his magic returned, it didn't come to his call. Instead, it had a mind all its own, assaulting the spell layered over him. His weak magic attacked the trap like ants swarming a wolf.

Little by little, painstakingly slow, his magic ate away the spell. The effort was exhausting. He regained control of his body a bit at a time; first his fingers, then hands and wrists. Encouraged by that victory, he wiggled his fingers.

"Blaise!" Jefferson gasped. "Can you hear me?"

I didn't think that through. Blaise twitched his fingers again in reply. Communication by finger wiggling wouldn't work out so well. He didn't know how to say, "Help, I'm stuck in a spell that's trapped me within my own skin."

Hope kindled in his heart as his magic continued its battle. Relief flooded him. *I'm not alone.* Once Blaise won free of the trap, there were questions he needed Jefferson to answer. But first, he had to get that far.

His awareness grew as feeling returned to his body. Someone dribbled broth and water into his mouth to sustain him. Someone kept him clean and saw to his bodily needs. His eyes still refused to open, and it frustrated him not knowing where he was.

Jefferson spoke to him often. So much that Blaise might have been annoyed by it any other time, but as he drifted in and out of wakefulness, he rested in the security of Jefferson's presence.

Finally, his magic roared back with full force, lifting the veil of shadow from his eyes as it shredded the fleeing remnants of the trap. His eyes flew open as he took a great, gasping breath.

Jefferson stared at him like he was a ghost, then dropped the book he was holding onto the floor with a resounding thump. He sat in a chair beside Blaise's bed. Clean white sheets covered Blaise's prone form.

"Blaise?" Jefferson's voice quivered, as if fearing disappointment and heartbreak.

"Howdy," Blaise rasped. *Ugh.* His throat was raw like he had breathed in a dust storm.

Jefferson leaned closer, running a hand through his unruly hair. His face was pale, cheeks and chin covered in shaggy bristles. He looked nothing like the put-together, dapper man Blaise remembered. "I was afraid you would never come back."

Blaise swallowed. He had been afraid of that, too.

Jefferson staggered to his feet, wobbling like he hadn't stood for days and his legs were unfamiliar with the idea. "I need to tell the doctors. They need to check you—"

"Wait. Please," Blaise whispered. His heart pounded. "Where am I?"

Jefferson glanced away. "Izhadell." He licked his lips, voice edged with steel. "We'll speak after I have the physicians check on you. They were certain you were going to die."

Izhadell. Blaise squeezed his eyes shut as Jefferson crossed the room and pushed open the door, flagging someone down outside. He was deep in Salt-Iron Confederation territory. *This is bad.*

Blaise opened his eyes as footsteps cascaded into the room. A flurry of activity swirled around him, men and women dressed in white poking and prodding him, looking into his eyes and mouth, taking his temperature, and asking him rapid-fire questions.

Blaise realized he was a curiosity to them. The doctors had never encountered a Breaker. And, judging by their studious murmurs, they had never come across anyone who had broken free of a Trapper's cage on their own. And survived an airship crash (on top of him, according to one nurse who read a passage from a report detailing the effort to extract him from the wreckage).

The specialists bickered about their theories. Blaise dozed as they talked, picking up bits and pieces. They argued over the strength of a Trapper's cage and the load the magic could bear versus the weight of a broken airship. They seemed to think Lamar's cage had saved Blaise's life.

Maybe it had. Blaise didn't care. All that mattered was that he was alive. And he was in *Izhadell*.

Eventually, the doctors concluded poking and prodding him, and filed out, leaving strict instructions that he was to stay in bed. The concept of walking was hilarious for someone just regaining control of his body. His muscles were mush.

Jefferson reclaimed his chair after they shut the door. "How do you feel?"

"I just fielded that question from eight different people. Did you miss that?"

Jefferson reached out and put his hand on Blaise's. "I'm the only one who *cares*."

Blaise blinked. He hadn't meant to snap. "I'm sorry. I'm scared and . . ." He wasn't sure what else to say. There were no words to describe the overwhelming mishmash of emotions.

A bitter smile played on Jefferson's lips. "You don't have to apologize." He sobered. "You're right to be scared. You broke a big, shiny airship and a very expensive fort."

A lump formed in Blaise's throat. "How many died?"

Jefferson shook his head, a tendril of hair covering one eye. He flicked it away with a finger. "Don't count the dead. Count the living. Your friends made it out."

Blaise closed his eyes. He counted the living, but that didn't absolve him of his guilt. He knew attacking the fort would end in the loss of life. Crashing an airship would, too. He had blood on his hands, blood on his soul.

"What's going to happen to me?"

"I . . . I'm handling it. Don't worry." Jefferson answered so quickly, Blaise popped one eye open to look at him.

"You're handling it? Or Malcolm Wells is?"

Jefferson sucked in a breath. He cast a furtive glance over his shoulder and leaned in so close that an onlooker might assume it was an intimate moment. "We *cannot* discuss that here. *Please.* I'm Jefferson here and now. I *have* to be."

The desperation in his voice was so raw that Blaise could do nothing but agree. Jefferson had stayed by his side for . . . he didn't know how long. He owed him that much. "I'll honor it."

Jefferson rubbed his cheek, relief slacking his muscles. "Thank you. It's complicated. I promise to explain when I can."

Blaise nodded. He was exhausted and wanted to rest again, but he was loath to succumb to the darkness so soon after clawing his way back into the world of the living. "Why am I in Izhadell?" They had every reason to kill him at the scene of the crime.

"That's complicated, too," Jefferson breathed. "There are those who want to put you on trial for your crimes. And still others want to take you apart piece by piece to discover what makes a Breaker different from other mages." His voice rose with anger at the last. "We're in the hospital at the Golden Citadel. It was the best accommodations that Doyen Wells could argue for you to be placed in that would also keep you safe and allow you to recover."

The Golden Citadel. Why was that name familiar? *Jack.* This was where the young theurgists trained. Wonderful, Blaise was deep in enemy territory, in a place frothing with opposing mages. But he also understood from Jefferson's words that the location provided a manner of safety for him, too.

"Visitors to the Cit go through a stringent approval process. They lock this place down tighter than a nun's habit. Unfortunately, the hospital wing we're in is of salt-iron construction." Jefferson jerked a thumb to the wall. Once Blaise was up to it he would have a tough time breaking free.

"Understood." Blaise thought for a moment. "Ah . . . are *you* in trouble for associating with me?"

Jefferson raised his brows. "Well . . ."

"Are you?"

Jefferson held up his thumb and index finger, pinching them together. "A tiny bit of trouble. Nothing much. Just a minor setback, really."

Blaise's heart sank. "You're a terrible liar."

Jefferson offered a brief smile, then cleared his throat. "In this case, I am. Phinora recognizes all the paperwork we signed back in Rainbow Flat differently than in Ganland. In Ganland, we were partners. Phinora . . ." He see-sawed one hand from side to side. "They consider you my charge so I may be the teensy-tiniest bit culpable."

Blaise scowled. "What happened to plausible deniability?"

Jefferson coughed. "The funny thing about that is it's less plausible and more difficult to deny when you drop an airship on a fort."

Blaise groaned.

"We'll get through this." Jefferson reached out and took his hand again. "So what if I have a few new lawsuits? That's an average day in Ganland. It's what I pay my lawyers for." He shrugged, as if it wasn't a bother at all.

It bothered Blaise a lot. "I'm sorry."

Jefferson shook his head. "Don't be."

If only it were that simple. Blaise studied the lines of Jefferson's face. "I still don't understand what you see in me."

Jefferson sat back, giving him an exasperated look. "Do you wish me gone?"

Blaise shook his head, terror gripping him at the thought of being alone. "No, no. I just . . . you deserve better."

"You're being ridiculous," Jefferson returned, leaning closer once more. "You've been around me long enough. You're aware I'm a man who knows what I want." He moved in, brushing his lips against Blaise's. Gentle, merely a reminder of his feelings on the issue. "I'll fight the entire Salt-Iron Confederation for you if I must."

Blaise stared, heart thudding. No one had ever spoken to him like that before. He swallowed, closing his eyes. He may be in enemy lands, but he wasn't alone.

CHAPTER FIFTY-THREE

A Minor Setback

Jack

"Hold up," Jack ordered as Zepheus swooped over Itude. The palomino slowed and turned when Jack pointed to the town signpost. Zepheus landed and trotted over to the bullet-riddled sign.

Some joker had painted the word *Fort* in front of *Itude*. Jack frowned. *Fort Itude.*

"Hope you don't mind, but it seemed right. And I enjoyed the irony."

Jack turned in the saddle. Vixen stood outside the Broken Horn, shading her eyes against the bright spring sunshine. She no longer wore her smoke-tinted glasses. Vixen had no need, with her magic stripped away.

"What?" he asked, not following her logic. *Fort* made him think of the Confederation, and that made him want to shoot somebody.

"Fortitude. Strength in adversity." She strode over, the breeze tugging at her long brown coat.

Jack raised his brows as understanding dawned. *Fortitude.* He tilted his head, considering it. Yeah, he had to admit he sort of liked it. "I'll allow it," Jack told her, gruff.

She smiled, brushing her long, red hair over her shoulder. "It also seemed like a good poke in the eye to the Salties."

Jack grinned. "When you put it like that, it does."

Zepheus dropped him off at his home. Jack ducked inside, shucking off his duster and removing his hat, hanging them on pegs near the door. Emmaline was elsewhere with her few friends who remained. He slipped into her room, removing the tiny poppet that sat on her bedside table, turning it over in his hands. Yesterday, something changed. Emmaline *sensed* him. Alive.

He planned to have her check the poppet again when she returned home. Just to confirm her findings. Jack was about to slip it into his pocket as a reminder when something happened that stopped him in his tracks. *Magic.* In his fingers.

Frozen, he stared down at his hands. He lifted his right up for closer inspection. Foolish—he wouldn't be able to see magic like a squashed bug or a clod of dirt. But he felt the unmistakable promise, like a rain-tempered breeze blowing through a parched land.

Shaking, Jack staggered to the table, pulling out a chair to sit. He dropped the poppet on the table, and the sensation subsided. Cautious, he picked up the effigy again, and magic prickled through his skin.

"How?"

It was nothing short of a miracle. Jack had exhausted his resources searching for a way to reverse the alchemical process that had stolen his magic. He'd reached the grudging conclusion that once it was gone, that was the end.

He had been wrong. His magic was returning. It was sluggish, coming back at a trickle, as if he had overextended and emptied his reserves. But it was there.

He closed his eyes, shaking his head. Jack had come to terms with not having magic, had finally admitted it to the other Ringleaders. And now, like a bolt of lightning in a clear sky, it was coming back.

Jack thought about testing it to make sure he wasn't mistaken. But he held off. He needed to allow more time for it to pool, to refill his empty reservoir. Jack almost reached out and pushed his magic against Blaise's poppet, so tempted. But no, he needed to leave that for Emmaline.

He took a shaky breath as he came to terms with what this meant. Jack stared at the poppet. "How in Perdition did you do that, Blaise?"

EFFIGEST

TALES OF THE OUTLAW MAGES BOOK 2

CHAPTER ONE

Biggest Toad in the Puddle

Jack

Outnumbered again. Jack wasn't about to let a little detail like that stop him, though, as he peered through the spyglass at the distant campsite.

It was a jumble of tents and canvas huts arrayed like discarded toys, men and women outfitted for hard labor in a mine, trundling back and forth like worker ants. They were burdened with tools, laughing and calling to one another. He wondered how many of them were there of their own free will and how many were criminals or wrongfully accused, working off indentures.

He scowled, shifting his view to observe the guards along the mining camp's perimeter. Guards to keep the laborers in line and to protect them from the threats of the Gutter. *Threats like me.*

A year ago, Jack would have had little trouble running off squatters like the feckless son-of-a-guns that had staked a claim on the northern ridge of the Gutter. He had a posse of outlaw mages ready to scare them off. But that was before the devastating attack on the town of Itude. Before their world changed forever.

But what he lacked in manpower, he made up for with magic. Jack limbered up his fingers in anticipation. He had been without it for so long, he was still becoming reacquainted with that long-lost part of himself. It was a strange thing, having to retrain himself to pull out his old bag of tricks. It was insignificant when he reflected on all that had been lost.

"Don't think about that," the outlaw grumbled to himself. The more he thought about the avalanche of events that had led to the destruction of his town, almost losing his daughter, and losing...well, it was an outright lie to call Blaise Hawthorne anything less than a *friend*...the angrier at the world he became. There was a time for anger, but this wasn't it. *Later.*

A warm breath huffed against the back of his neck as Zepheus peered behind him. <There are so many. Will this work?>

Jack glanced back at the pegasus stallion. Would it? He didn't know, but he wasn't about to admit it. Jack survived on the notion that if he believed something was true, it would simply be so. "'Course it's going to work."

The palomino tilted his head so that his long, silvery forelock fell over one eye. <Is this the sort of working where if the spell fails, it rebounds on the caster?>

Jack snorted. "Do I look like a wet behind the ears greenhorn to you?"

<You're out of practice and this is a large spell.> Sometimes Zepheus was too damned practical.

The stallion was right, of course. Even in his days as a theurgist, Jack would have approached a spell of this magnitude with caution. It was the sort of working that a coven of Ritualists would cast together, each adding their own specialty. But Jack didn't know any other Ritualists in the area, and even if he did, he wouldn't want to work with them. Too much room for error, the way he saw it.

"It'll be slick as a whistle," Jack said, terse. Anyway, it wasn't as if he were unfurling the working willy-nilly. The moment he caught wind of the incursion in the Gutter, he had begun designing the spell. It annoyed him that his previous run-ins with Confederation filth had done nothing to deter others from playing the same game.

Jack laid the blame for that at the Confederation's feet because of the decimation of Itude. Before the attack, they would have thought twice about setting foot on this land, as the outlaws of Itude had a reputation for running off Salt-Iron Confederation intruders. As word of the town's assault spread, the emboldened vultures of the Confederation decided the time was ripe to swoop down on the Gutter as if it were a bloated carcass to be squabbled over.

He and Zepheus waited in their position until the sun sank low on the horizon. It gave him time to study the canvas tents dotting the ridge, nestled beside more permanent fixtures. Someone had hauled in fresh lumber to assemble a rudimentary stable yard for horses, mules, and donkeys. Skeletal frames for future buildings dotted the area, though they didn't have enough sturdy coverage to be called habitable. If Jack had his way, the place would never *be* habitable.

Once nightfall claimed the last gold-tinged rays of sunlight, Jack and Zepheus made their way down to the mining camp. The pegasus magicked his wings away in case they were spotted. Much easier to explain a man arriving on horseback. But Jack's goal was to remain undetected. The moon was a crescent slash on the horizon, and it wasn't long before he had to rely on Zepheus's superior night vision and the distant lanterns of the camp to orient him.

The stallion stopped a half-mile away from the nearest sentry, and Jack slipped down from the saddle. He unbuckled the saddlebags and drew out a canvas sack, pulling a single feather and bit of leather thong out before tying it to his gun belt. Aside from his belt, he had dressed as simply as he could, donning a cotton button-down shirt and heavy trousers just in case of discovery. At a glance, he would fit in. But his sixguns would give him away, and there was no chance he was leaving those behind, magic or not.

The outlaw drew a tiny figure from his front pocket, a doll wrapped with a lock of his own hair. He used the bit of leather thong to secure the feather to the poppet's midsection. He cupped it in his hand, his flesh prickling as he awoke his power. Every mage worked a little differently. Some had to speak for their spells to work, some needed specific reagents, and others had to draw symbols or work with a coven. And then there were those like Jack, who exerted his will through sympathetic magic to invoke a spell.

An invisible spark of magic danced over the poppet as he activated his first spell, Owlsight, to allow him to navigate more easily in the dark. But he needed more than to *see* in the inky darkness. The next one was an old favorite, and he was so adept at it he didn't need a reagent: Obfuscation. It was the closest he got to invisibility. People could see him, but if their eyes drifted over him, they wouldn't be inclined to challenge his presence or remember that he was there after the fact. Proper spell warding would disrupt it, as could certain other magics, but Jack didn't think either of those scenarios were likely in this situation. If the camp ahead of him boasted any mages, they were more likely to be indentured workers than anything more treacherous. He had seen no signs of theurgists among the guards.

<Be careful,> Zepheus advised.

"Stop fussing at me like a mother hen," Jack grumbled, patting the stallion's neck. He took a calming breath to focus on the job ahead. "You'll keep tabs on me?"

<Of course. Someone has to be ready to pull your tail from the fire.>

"My fat's not in the fire yet," Jack said dryly. Zepheus gave a soft nicker of amusement.

Jack ambled into the camp unchallenged, striding right past the closest sentry as a preliminary test for his Obfuscation. The man on duty stared at him for a moment in confusion, scratching his forehead before scanning the area. Jack smirked. *I'm the biggest toad in this puddle.*

He took his time once inside the perimeter, getting his bearings as he studied the camp proper. He listened in on sleepy conversations and heated dice games, hoping to glean bits of useful intelligence. One such conversation confirmed that the mining company's purpose was to prospect for gold and, to Jack's disgust, salt-iron. He bared his teeth, revolted by the mention of salt-iron. *Not if I can help it.*

Jack discovered that the mining company boasted a small contingent of indentured mages. That gave him an idea. He started with their section of tents first.

He tugged the canvas bag from his belt, opening it and pulling out an effigy. It differed from his standard poppets, which were humanoid in design. Constructed of supple willow sticks woven together with a leather thong and beads, it looked like a square decoration that might hang over a hearth. Jack had prepared his spell on the effigies beforehand but hadn't accounted for the presence of mages. He pursed his lips. *This'll require a few modifications.* When he was done, he hung it atop the framing at the back of the tent before moving through the camp and stringing up his other effigies throughout.

Once he completed his round, Jack slipped to the outskirts of the camp, mindful of range to activate the working. He was rather proud of this spell, something he had developed himself. The effigies were linked to one another like a daisy chain, and once triggered, his magic would pulse down the line. It reminded him of the new-fangled electric circuits he had read about in Confederation dispatches.

Jack pulled the keystone effigy from his pouch, the one used to trigger the others. He settled down on the ground, legs crossed and hoping that no blasted scorpions or rattlesnakes were in the area. Wouldn't do to get stung or bit in the middle of this. He'd never tested his Obfuscation spell against critters, but he hoped it made him uninteresting to them, too.

He cradled the effigy in his hand, bringing out his own poppet and settling it in the middle of the square. Then he sent his magic spiraling from the poppet to the effigy, a soft pop punctuating the air as the spell began.

Effigest spells weren't flashy. That was the way Jack liked it. It was inconvenient in times like this, however, when he wanted a quick indication if it had been effective or not. But instead, he had to bide his time, his ears straining against the chorus of cicadas as he listened for human voices.

And then it began. Jack grinned, cracking his knuckles as he waited. Before long, the shadows of men and women became visible, running away from the camp, some of them jumping onto the backs of confused donkeys or mules in their haste to leave the area. Maybe casting Rising Dread on a large area wasn't sporting, but it was certainly entertaining.

<You're going to go to Perdition for that,> Zepheus commented.

Jack shrugged. *Yeah, going to Perdition for a lot of things.*

But he hadn't yet seen any sign that his spell on the mage tent had succeeded. He crossed his arms, having no choice but to wait it out a little longer.

Silhouettes stormed from the camp, making a beeline in his direction. Jack rose, standing lightly on the balls of his feet as the indentured mages closed in on him. Five in all—far fewer than he had hoped for— approached with a mix of wariness and outright hostility.

Weak sparks danced on the fingertips of one man while a tornado of sand blew around the legs of a woman in the lead. The sight of the fire piqued Jack's interest, though it quickly cooled. *Not Kittie.* He shelved his disappointment, cocking his head as they drew to a stop, some of them holding weapons that glinted in the moonlight. Jack approved of their precautions.

"Howdy," the outlaw drawled, dispelling his Obfuscation spell as he spoke. His tweak to Rising Dread had rendered them resistant to the fear portion, instead drawing them to the keystone.

The indentured mages startled as they noticed his presence. Guns clicked, an ominous warning. Jack was ready to draw if needed, figuring he was quicker than any of their lot. He hoped it wouldn't be necessary.

"Who are you?" the Pyromancer asked.

"A concerned citizen," Jack replied.

"*Outlaw,*" a woman murmured.

"Outlaw *mage,*" another corrected.

Jack shifted his weight from foot to foot. "You're not wrong. You can thank me for rescuing you later—"

"Rescuing us?" the Pyromancer spat, the sparks on his fingers spiking higher before settling. "You've ruined us! We'll never be free now."

Rather beef-headed, aren't you? Jack raised a brow. "You're free of your captors now, the way I see it." He gestured to the expansive darkness behind him. "You're in the *Gutter.* The Confederation has no claim to any mage here."

An Earthshaper shook her head, kicking grit toward Jack. "They'll come for us. They always do." Her voice rose with dismay.

Jack ground his teeth. He had forgotten the blinding terror that was ingrained into indentured mages. For so many of them, utter obedience was a way of life. It was how they survived from day to day. "We can protect you from that." *But can we?* He kept the doubt from creeping into his words.

"We know what happened here," another of the mages whispered. "It's not safe."

The outlaw scowled. "You don't have to come back to Fortitude with me. Not if you don't want." He jutted his chin toward the camp. "But it'll be a cold day in Perdition before I let an operation like that stay here." He pocketed his poppet. "Seems to me you have three choices: either come to Fortitude with me, set out for another town in the Untamed Territory where you can live free and clear, or go crawling back to your Saltie masters." He spat on the ground for emphasis.

<Someone's coming.>

A mage opened his mouth to speak, but Jack lifted a hand to command silence, focused on the sharp clatter of hooves arriving from the south. A moment later, Zepheus trotted in Clover's wake as she bolted toward Jack.

Clover was a Knossan, a race that looked like the result of an amorous pairing between human and bovine. She towered over him, a formidable seven feet tall and faster on two legs than an unspelled human. She slowed as she approached, ignoring the cluster of indentured mages who backed away at the sight of her. They hadn't planned on coming face-to-face with a Knossan, much less an agitated one.

"Clover?" Jack cocked his head as she came to a stiff-legged stop, her sides heaving. He didn't know if he wanted to find out what disaster had forced her to seek him out at this time of night.

"She's gone," Clover gasped, her eyes white-rimmed.

He blinked, slow to digest Clover's meaning. "Who?"

Clover gave him a forlorn look. "Emmaline. She's *gone.*"

"DON'T YOU COME IN HERE AND THREATEN MY SON, JACK," NADINE growled as he stalked up and down the aisle of the clinic, hemmed in by empty cots.

Upon Clover's announcement, he'd left the fate of the indentured mages in the Knossan's hands so he could high-tail it back to town. He had almost torn apart his own home in the search for clues but found no helpful letters left behind. Oberidon, Emmaline's pegasus, was missing from the stables, and none of the remaining good-for-nothing stallions had a clue where he'd gone except that the spotted stallion and his rider headed out sometime the previous afternoon.

That left Jack with only one other source for questioning: Reuben Collins. Nadine's son had worked with Emmaline extensively at the bakery, and over time, the two became close enough to earn Jack's disapproval. Reuben seemed to have a good head on his shoulders and recognized that Jack was a threat to his existence if he got too *friendly* with Emmaline, so the kid behaved. *So far.* But now, he wasn't telling Jack anything helpful. *Curse him to Perdition.*

"And *you're* not the one with the missing *child*," Jack spat in response. Tension crackled through the air as Nadine squared her shoulders, pulling on her own formidable magic. Jack usually had the common sense to not bait a life-sucking Healer, but at the moment, he didn't give a damn.

Reuben cleared his throat, ducking his head. He was about as magically inclined as a loaf of bread, but even without power, he knew how close the two outlaws were to violence. "Sir, she's *not* a child."

Jack's eyes narrowed, and he prepared a scathing retort, but Nadine beat him to it. She prowled over, poking him in the chest. "Before you nay-say that you *think* about it and you think *good*. That daughter of yours has been through trauma, and what have *you* done about it?"

The outlaw's jaw worked open in surprise, then snapped shut. Nadine's words were like a punch in the gut. After Emmaline's capture and imprisonment at Fort Courage, their relationship ran into a snarl. They'd had their share of troubles as she grew into her teenage years, and things had only gotten worse. After Courage, she'd grown more distant and refused to speak of what happened. And Jack hadn't known what to do to bridge the gap between them, thus had done nothing. Not a damned thing, because he was too afraid that he would sever whatever small connection they still shared.

But rather than say all that aloud, he crossed his arms. "That's neither here nor there. I need to find her. Before..." *Before I lose her like I lost her mother.* His heart squeezed in his chest. He swung his bleak gaze to Reuben. "What did she talk about with you? I need to know if she's put herself in danger." He failed to conceal the raw *need* in his voice.

Reuben swallowed, fidgeting with the buttons on his shirt as he debated his response. Jack tried not to glower but suspected he failed. "She's been talking about leaving Fortitude for a while now." He paused, looking up as if expecting Jack to have an irrational response. The outlaw almost did, but he mastered himself and motioned for the kid to continue. "Em's been upset about a lot of things. Blaise's capture. Whatever they did to her at Fort Courage…" He made a helpless gesture. "She's, um, mad at you, too." He whispered the last bit, cringing.

Jack sucked in a breath, stung. But that was fair. It was likely true. Emmaline had argued that they needed to get Blaise back—because he was her friend and had sacrificed everything. But the Breaker was far behind enemy lines, all the way in Izhadell from what Jack had gleaned. And he wasn't a starry-eyed greenhorn like Blaise. He was a wanted man, and going that deep into Confederation lands was a dangerous and foolhardy prospect. *Oh.* Emmaline wasn't a wanted outlaw, though. At least not the same way he was. *Blame it all, but it makes sense.*

"Has she gone to free Blaise?" Jack asked.

Reuben shrugged. "I…I don't know. Maybe she's just gone out to think? Clear her head?" He licked his lips, full of cautious hope. But the pegasi had seen Oberidon leave with full saddlebags (and *why* had none of those sugar-addled studs thought to ask about that?), which meant they weren't going out for an overnight jaunt.

Jack raked a hand through his hair. Reuben knew nothing. Emmaline hadn't told Clover, and she usually confided in the Knossan bartender. Which meant his daughter knew Clover wouldn't allow her to do whatever balderdash she had come up with. He blew out a frustrated breath. *If I were Emmaline, what would I do? Where would I go? I'd want information first…*

"I'm a bally fool," Jack growled.

Nadine frowned. "What?"

He waved a hand at her. "I'll tell you if I'm right." Without another word, he spun and stomped out the door of Nadine's clinic, jogging down the steps of the porch as he made a beeline across the ruins of the town to his home.

The door slammed in his wake as he stormed into his bedroom. *I'm a fiddlehead. I should have thought to check here earlier.* Jack studied the wood floor, noting that the dresser was an inch out of place, judging by a disturbed layer of dust. He shouldered it out of the way, revealing the hidden panel on the wall. *Not so secret anymore.*

He removed the box of letters contained within, flipping through them. He cursed, realizing that the most recent acquisitions were missing. Letters from Jefferson Cole, also known as Doyen Malcolm Wells of Ganland.

"You're as dead as a can of corned beef if she goes running to you, Cole," Jack snarled softly.

CHAPTER TWO

Magelover

Jefferson

"*Y*ou *lied* to me."

Blaise Hawthorne, the Breaker of Fort Courage and one of the greatest current threats against the might of the Salt-Iron Confederation, stared across the weathered expanse of the table, chewing on his lower lip. Unwashed tendrils of hair fell over his haunted blue eyes, the young man's gaze flitting to the cell door every few seconds as if expecting an attack.

Jefferson bit back his excuses because they came up short as far as Blaise was concerned. He owed the Breaker nothing less than the full truth, but that wasn't something to reveal here. Not in the prison wing of the Golden Citadel. It was far too dangerous. "I'm sorry," Jefferson murmured, painfully aware that it wouldn't be enough. "I never misrepresented who I am, though. There were matters I couldn't divulge to you." *Please don't ask me to say more than that. My position is delicate as it is.*

Blaise bowed his head, studying his hands. He seemed to withdraw from the conversation for a moment, as if willing himself to another place and time, his eyes unfocused. It worried Jefferson to see him like that, but all he could do was wait and hope that Blaise would return to the conversation.

The silence stretched on, and he longed to reach out and touch Blaise's arm. But that, too, would be unwelcome. "I never wanted to hurt you."

Those words stirred the Breaker from whatever thoughts he'd banished himself to. He lifted his head, his lower lip trembling. Fury rose in Jefferson, and he reined in the inclination to storm out and demand answers. What cruelty put Blaise in such a state? There was a time for that later, when he could play the game from a position of power. For now, he had to do his best for the man who sat before him, shattered.

"I thought..." Blaise started, then gave a shake of his head like a dog drying water from itself, leaving Jefferson to wonder what he had been about to say. He started on a different path. "You didn't come to see me for so long once they brought me here. I thought..."

Jefferson pursed his lips, able to fill in the rest of the unspoken words. *I thought you hated me. I thought you had* used *me after telling me you wouldn't. Maybe you think I'm less than a person.* "No," he said sharply. "It's nothing you may think. It's the rules of your predicament." *Predicament.* Yes, that was an apt word. It made it sound like something they could overcome. Jefferson hoped so, at any rate. He gave Blaise an earnest look, rewarded when the other man met his eyes, which he hadn't done until that moment. "They make it exceptionally difficult for someone like you to have visitors. My lawyers had to dig up some rather obscure legal precedents."

"War criminals like me," Blaise whispered, correcting him.

You did what needed to be done. Jefferson wanted to say the words aloud, but to do so here would be treason and he was on rocky footing as it was, being connected to Blaise. His lawyers, truth be told, were going through creative legal contortions just to keep him from facing a similar fate, which would prove quite inconvenient, all things considered.

"That's not who you are," Jefferson responded, insistent. He knew better. He knew the *real* Blaise, the person trapped behind this current troubled visage.

Blaise flinched, an echo of old pain crossing his face. "Funny you say that when I don't really know who *you* are." And then the spark of defiance receded as Blaise averted his eyes once again. "You told me you would explain."

Blast it all. Jefferson gave a gentle shake of his head. "I can't. Not here." The disappointment that flashed across Blaise's face spoke volumes, and Jefferson regretted it. Any trust Blaise had in him was eroding fast, and he was the only one within these walls on the young man's side.

"Why did you come?" Blaise asked, his voice little more than a rough whisper.

It stung that he had to ask. "I needed to make sure you were okay." But it was clear that he wasn't, not at all. Jefferson wished he could pull Blaise into an embrace and take him from this place, but that was outside the realm of his power. There were some things money couldn't buy.

"I'm not." The Breaker swallowed, staring hard at the table. He idly ran his thumbnail over the woodgrain, his hand shaking. "What's going to happen to me?"

"I don't know," Jefferson replied, spreading his hands. "It's in discussion among the Council."

"Oh." Blaise scrubbed at the side of his gaunt face, his beard shaggy and unkempt. Jefferson made a mental note to ensure that the prisoners had proper hygiene items. Blaise opened his mouth as if to say something else, then clamped it closed.

"We're going to get through this," Jefferson murmured, tapping his fingers atop the table. "I promise you."

Blaise shook his head. "Don't make promises you can't keep."

Gods, whatever they had done had stripped Blaise of the optimism he'd possessed. The young man had never been bold, but he had been persistent. And that was gone, wiped out by whatever the Confederation did to crush the will of a mage. Jefferson leaned over the table, fierce. "I told you once before I would fight the entire Confederation for you. *That*, I assure you, was no lie."

If the mage was about to say something else, a reverberating knock on the door to the visitation room squashed it. "Time's up!" the guard hollered, his brassy voice making Blaise tremble.

Three muscular guards strode into the room, two bearing salt-iron shackles for Blaise, and the third to escort Jefferson from the premises. It cut Jefferson to the core, watching Blaise offer his swollen, welt-covered wrists for the guards. They slapped the shackles on and dragged him from his seat before he even had a chance to stand.

"Mind yourself with him!" Jefferson snapped, bolting up from his chair and slamming a palm onto the table.

The closest guard sneered at him. "You're not the boss of us, *magelover*. Get a move on before we find a reason to keep *you* here."

I may not be the boss of you, but I know how things work. Jefferson composed himself, straightening his greatcoat as he rose, offering a disgruntled glare to the guard escorting him to the exit. He hoped he had more luck with the situation as his alter ego, Malcolm Wells.

———

Malcolm

Under the best circumstances, Salt-Iron Council sessions were exercises in patience and maintaining one's composure. Under the guise of his true-born self, Malcolm Wells discovered he was stretched to the brink when the topic up for debate was Blaise Hawthorne. He fiddled with the lapel pin that marked him as a Doyen to give his fractious hands something to do.

Doyens from each of the eight Confederation nations sat on the Council, accounting for twenty representatives in all. The older nations had three representatives, while the newer nations only held two positions. Malcolm was the youngest among the Council, one of its rising stars.

As with any gathering of opposing groups, the Council boasted factions who shared ideologies. Among them, he was one of the most outspoken for those on the Faedran faction who supported the idea of mage equality. Malcolm wasn't alone in that regard, but the Mossbacks, who preferred to keep the mages firmly under their thumb, outnumbered his faction. His best hope was that they could play on the sensibilities of the Moderates.

"There is no reason this man should draw another breath," Doyen Hollis Burrows of Canen said in response to something Malcolm had missed. Regardless, his words set Malcolm's teeth on edge. As if Blaise were a mad dog to be put down.

Predictably, Burrows's words caused an outburst among the group. Hollis enjoyed stirring the pot. But to Malcolm's surprise, Gregor Gaitwood of Phinora was the first to command the floor. "Let's not be hasty," Gregor cautioned, lifting his hands in a placating gesture. His gaze slid around the room, reminding Malcolm of a snake hunting for mice. "While I understand we have disposed of threatening mages in the past, we should explore *all* of our options."

Roberta Thayer of Argor consulted her notes, lifting a finger to get Gaitwood's attention. "According to the report, more than a hundred men and women died at Fort Courage. Is that not true?" She was the sort of Moderate who loved her facts and figures, using numbers to guide her vote.

Not all by Blaise's hand. Malcolm bit back the retort. He cleared his throat to draw their attention. At the time of the attack, Argor was so new to the Confederation it didn't have a Doyen sitting on the Council, so she wasn't privy to all the details. And the report, of course, neglected certain points. "If I may, Doyen Thayer, it's important to note that Breaker Hawthorne was *not* the only outlaw mage at Fort Courage that day."

"But he's the only one we have at hand," Burrows replied sourly. He pounded his desk with a fist. "I say we use this one as an example. The outlaws need a reminder not to cross the Confederation. Garus watch over us if they grow bolder."

"My dear colleague, may I remind you of the circumstances?" Doyen Leonora Peppers, also of Canen, asked as she rounded on her country-man. She held up a sheaf of papers. "If you like, I can read the first-hand accounts of our own soldiers who were present at the attack on the Gutter town, Itude. Confederation forces were the original aggressors." Leonora followed her words with a tepid smile.

"The Gutter isn't a recognized nation, and as such, has no protections," Burrows argued.

"All the same, it violates the Oscen Agreement." Malcolm looked up, eyes narrowed as the burr of an idea hooked into his mind. He would think more about that later.

Irving Dempcy, Gaitwood's crony from Phinora, snorted. "The OA doesn't cover mages."

Leonora shot a look at Malcolm. "Would you like to respond, or shall I?" Malcolm offered her a small *go ahead* bow, and she smiled like a hunter going in for the kill. Malcolm had always liked Leonora, and not only for their common ground regarding mage freedoms. She was as keen as a razor's edge and enjoyed using her words to eviscerate those who disagreed with her. "You are correct, Doyen Dempcy, regarding the lack of coverage for mages. However, it covers *human* civilians. Human civil-ians died at Itude. Quite a few of them."

Doyen Selma Dahen of Phinora, who usually counted among the Moderates, frowned. "I would say that's a consequence of associating with outlaws." She gave an elegant shrug. "Lay down with dogs and get fleas."

Malcolm couldn't allow that to stand. He shook his head, vehement. "Listen to yourselves. I know how most of you feel regarding the mages. You're *better* than they are." He hated every word that spilled from his mouth, but he had to play to the crowd. "That is the tenet most of you subscribe to: that the taint of magic makes them unstable and unreliable. Undeserving of trust. Incapable of being a true member of society, like a normal human." The heads of the Mossbacks nodded in agreement. His fellow Faedrans frowned as they waited to see what point he would make. *Wait for it.* "If we don't allow the OA to cover the human civilians of Itude and don't allow that to factor into the reason they attacked Fort Courage in the first place, it makes us no better than the mages."

Murmured conversation followed his revelation. Leonora gave him a small nod of agreement as she connected the dots. "As Doyen Wells has shown, Breaker Hawthorne and his group had justifiable cause to attack Fort Courage that day."

Gregor Gaitwood rose from his seat, seizing the floor. "Doyen Peppers speaks the truth. The Commander who led the misguided attack on the outlaw town has been disciplined."

Malcolm curled his lip at that. Leave it to Gregor to throw his own brother to the wolves, though it was true that Lamar Gaitwood had been the aggressor.

"And Doyens Cole and Peppers are correct: the fault lies with us." Gregor spread his hands, plaintive, as he continued. "Our forces failed to bring in the Breaker for proper *training* when the opportunity arose in Desina. This is our chance to amend this oversight."

You had better not suggest what I think you are. Malcolm narrowed his eyes, tension settling into his shoulders.

Leonora had the same thought, judging by the sudden tilt of her head. "Doyen Gaitwood, are you suggesting we apply the geasa to the Breaker? Assign a handler to him?"

"I am."

Her frown deepened. Knowledge of theurgists wasn't one of her strengths, however, and she deferred to one of the other Faedrans with more background on the topic. "Doyen Jennings, is there any record of a bound Breaker?"

Seward Jennings of Mella startled when she called his name. He coughed, fumbling through papers and scrambling to grab his pen. "Ahem. I would need to consult the archives." Round wire-frame glasses slipped down his nose, and he pushed them back into place. "Doyen Peppers, you are correct in noting that if we vote to apply the geasa to the Breaker, we must do so with caution."

"Why is that?" Doyen Vollie Musselman of Desina, one of the newest representatives, asked.

Jennings was an academic on mages and their history, taking great pride in that knowledge. He straightened, reminding Malcolm of a molting owl preening its feathers. "Certain strains of mages do not cooperate when bound to a handler. That is to say, effects can range from killing both parties to issues such as mental instability in one or both." He gained confidence as he spoke. "Interesting fact: did you know that binding to a Necromancer will instantly kill the handler?"

Vollie paled at that, cupping a hand over her mouth.

"Yes, thank you for that *interesting fact*, Doyen Jennings," Malcolm said quickly.

Gregor Gaitwood tilted his head, thoughtful. "Doyen Jennings, will you look into the matter so that we can hold a vote on this issue when we revisit the topic?"

Jennings's eyes went wide. It wasn't often they called on him for such duties. "It would be an honor, Doyen Gaitwood."

Settle down. You're on our *side, Seward.* Malcolm gritted his teeth. He bided his time as the discussion ended with an agreement to continue the topic in the next session. Malcolm was the last to leave the Council chamber, tussling with thc problem at hand. He would have to keep close tabs on Seward to see if he discovered anything about Breakers before the vote.

Malcolm sighed. He hoped Blaise wasn't right to advise him against making promises he couldn't keep. Because he desperately wanted to keep this one.

CHAPTER THREE

Selfish Piss Goblin

Jack

"There must be another way." Clover snuffled with worry as she paced up and down the short hall outside Jack's bedroom. She paused, hooves scuffing the hardwood floor. "We'll think of something."

Jack's back was to her as he methodically folded clothing on the bed and snugged them into a water-resistant bag. "There's no other way. No one else *can* go after her."

The Knossan sighed. Jack glanced over his shoulder when he heard the groan of wood. Clover leaned her bulk against the door-frame. "It's too dangerous."

At that, the outlaw grunted. "I'm no delicate flower."

She stomped, her hoof thundering against the floorboards. "You know very well that's not what I mean." She tossed her horns toward a wanted poster hanging on Jack's wall. Most people thought he kept the damned thing there as a bit of vanity, assuming he enjoyed the notoriety. And while that held a grain of truth, there was more to it. It also served as a reminder, a cautionary tale of what awaited if he dared too far into Confederation lands. "If you're caught, they'll *hang* you, and then it will all be for naught."

Jack frowned. "I'm aware." He had his own share of fears about going after Emmaline. Clover was right. If the Salties captured him, he was a dead man walking. Death was always an option when Jack did just about anything, but he worked to skew the odds in his favor. Dying didn't scare him. But it would be extremely inconvenient to die before getting his daughter to safety.

"Perhaps Hank can take a letter to Mr. Cole—" Clover started, but abruptly halted when Jack's lips peeled back over his teeth in rage.

"He's done *quite* enough," Jack growled.

She shook her horned head, confused. "You either need to explain yourself, or I will see to it you do not leave town."

He froze at the genuine threat in her voice. Jack narrowed his eyes. "Don't tangle with me. I don't have the patience for that."

Clover lashed her tail, crossing her arms. "I would not dare go up against your magic. But Nadine could."

Jack hissed out an irritated breath. He was being an unfair cuss, but the stress of Emmaline's disappearance had his patience stretched to the limits. And Clover was right. If anyone could put him in his place, it was the town Healer. Nadine didn't look like much, but she had sucked the life out of soldiers at the Battle of Itude to keep herself on this side of Perdition.

"What are you not telling me?" she asked.

He sealed the bag after slipping a final pair of socks inside, keeping his focus on the simple actions of preparing to leave the town he had built up and ultimately failed. "Cole's been sending me letters."

"About?"

Jack wrinkled his nose. "Guess."

"Blaise?"

"Yeah." Jack licked his lips, wishing he didn't have to discuss it. The first letter from the duplicitous entrepreneur had piqued his curiosity, but that interest transformed into anger when he realized Cole was asking for *help*. Help freeing Blaise. Emmaline had discovered the letter and demanded to know what they could do to free the Breaker.

Nothing. There was absolutely nothing to be done because Blaise was in Izhadell. It would be easier to set foot on the dusty path that led to Perdition and meet Nexarae, the goddess of life and death, for a whiskey than free Blaise from the Golden Citadel.

Predictably, Emmaline hadn't liked her father's answer. Not that Jack could blame her after Blaise had given up *everything* for them. And Jack repaid the debt by letting him rot in the Confederation's clutches.

No one knew how much Jack stewed over the conundrum. Rumor had it he still didn't like Blaise and was happy to see him gone. Yeah, the Breaker could be whiny, irritating, and priggish. But underneath that veneer of anxiety and flour, he had a lot of gumption Jack had come to admire.

"So you believe Emmaline has gone to help Cole free Blaise?" Clover asked.

"She went through my cache of letters," Jack said, spreading his hands. "Em didn't leave a note or anything else for me to go on, so that's all I can assume." Teenagers were damned frustrating. No wonder his instructors at the Golden Citadel had always been so angry with him.

Clover sighed. "You'll go to Jefferson Cole, then?"

"That's the plan." *And if he even so much as looks at me wrong or thinks to betray me, he dies.*

The Knossan rubbed her muzzle. "Will you send a coded letter when you arrive?"

At the worry in her voice, Jack hesitated. Blame it all, he had forgotten that he and Emmaline were the closest thing Clover had to family, too. Their situation terrified the Knossan just as much as it did Jack. "It's come to my attention that Hank knows how to contact Cole. So yes."

A hint of the tension left her frame, though Jack knew she wouldn't truly relax until the people she cared about were safe. "Thank you."

Jack shoved the bag of clothing into his saddlebag, buckling it closed. "Got something I need you to do for me until I get back."

At his change of topic, Clover made an interested noise. "What's that?"

Good. Maybe giving her a task would keep her occupied. "Help those new mages settle in. And work with Kur Agur to keep an eye on the Gutter for any new incursions."

Clover *hmm*-ed with thought. "We can't run them off as you can. Even with the new mages, I am uncertain about our chances. And we should not risk Nadine."

That was accurate enough. Among their original mages, the Confederation had stripped Raven, Vixen, and Butch of their magic at Fort Courage. Jack wasn't sure how long any of them would stick it out in the town. Raven and Vixen had telegraphed signs of being ready to move on with their lives and skip town for weeks now, and Jack didn't blame them. As for their other mages, they had either died in the attack or left Fortitude in the ensuing weeks.

Jack waved a hand, dismissive. "No need to do all that. Just watch them. I'll handle the rest when I'm back." Because he *would* be back.

His words offered the reassurance she needed, and Clover nodded. "We can do that." She tilted her head as he dropped his saddlebag on the floor by the door. "When do you intend to leave?"

"At first light."

"Mornin', Jack!"

Jack grunted at the chipper voice, squinting into the early morning sunlight. "You're up awful early for you, Vixen." He pulled the brim of his hat up, so he had a better view of the flame-haired outlaw standing outside the stables. The tap of boots on the hard-packed dirt announced Raven's arrival. He slipped up beside Vixen and put an arm around her. It hadn't escaped Jack's attention that since Fort Courage, the pair had become close, bound by the shared anguish of losing their magic.

"Word is you're going to Phinora after your daughter." Raven studied him with flinty eyes. "We want to go with you."

What in Perdition are you thinking, pup? You'll get eaten alive. Jack didn't say it aloud, though. It stung to be reminded that you didn't have a lick of magic. It was about the worst violation for a mage, having a part of yourself stripped away like that. "Nah."

Vixen blinked. "What do you mean, *nah?*"

Jack wheeled on her. "It means no. You're not going with me." Raven opened his mouth to speak, and Jack held up a hand to silence him. "I'll make better time alone. Be easier to lay low. Less risky."

Raven tensed, and Jack caught the glint of a knife in his hand. "You know why we want to go." His voice crackled with emotion.

Yeah, he did. "And that's why I can't let you go." Jack said it with more gentleness than he wanted, catching himself too late. Fortunately for him, the pair had their hackles up over his denial. He raised his hands to show he wasn't done speaking, not yet. "I've been in your boots. Don't you forget it. Why in Perdition do you think I stuck to the Gutter and Untamed Territory?"

They exchanged glances, and Jack realized that had never occurred to them. But then again, until his shameful secret had come out after the assault on the town, everyone assumed he'd had magic all along. None of them had realized it was all bluster and bad attitude until after the fact.

"Maybe we thought you had a lick of common sense," Vixen said at last, crossing her arms.

Jack couldn't help it. He laughed. "Here I thought you knew me better'n that." He shook his head. "Your mugs are still on wanted posters all across the Confederation. We go together, some Saltie is gonna figure us out. Magic or not, they'll be happy to hang you either way."

"We're not defenseless babes." Raven's knife winked, a dangerous reminder.

Jack cocked his head. Truth be told, he had a lot of respect for Raven and Vixen, with or without their magic. He wouldn't want to be in a dark alley with Raven getting the drop on him. Time to pull out the big guns. "You're not. But Fortitude is. The Gutter is." He gestured around, encompassing the buildings that had been gutted by fire. "And if I do say so myself, her best protector is about to be gone, so *y'all* might have to do." Jack crooked his index finger at the pair. He hoped they took it for the compliment he intended.

Vixen blew out a frustrated breath. "We love this place as much as you, but sitting here ain't gonna get our *magic* back." She rubbed her arms and added, "Or our friend."

Jack heard the guilt she failed to hide in her words. He knew a thing or three about guilt, having lumped the Breaker's situation squarely on himself. "You don't owe him a thing."

She gave him a sour look. "You're such a selfish piss goblin, Jack. And you think you're tougher than a chupacabra covered in salt-iron, but everybody knows we'd have been lost to the Salties at Fort Courage if not for him. We owe him. And I'm the one who helped him learn his magic."

Jack snorted. *Mentor's guilt.* That was a new one. He was damn sure the woman who taught him how to use his magic never suffered a day of guilt in her life for all his atrocities. The brief thought of his mentor was a shock to his system, and he curled his lips like he had just bit into a lemon. "Y'all are good, but there's no way you're getting into the Cit without magic. Especially if you're not familiar with the place."

"But *you* are," Raven pointed out.

"I am," Jack agreed.

"Did Em go to free him, do you reckon?" Vixen asked, her eyes glittering with hope.

The outlaw shrugged. "Don't know." And he fervently hoped Emmaline didn't get anywhere near the Golden Citadel. His gut clenched at the very idea. If things went well, he'd catch up to her before she even arrived in Phinora.

Vixen stepped up to him, staring him down. Jack wondered if it was an old habit from when she had magic. If she still had her Persuader abilities, then he would have had cause to worry. "You need to get him out."

He wanted to snarl back that he didn't *need* to do anything; that she wasn't the boss of him. But she was right. Instead, he ducked his head, his jaw tight. "Once I find Em and get her somewhere safe, I'll see what I can do about the Breaker."

His words almost surprised him, as much as they did Raven and Vixen. They stared at him. No doubt they expected him to rant and rage that he would do no such thing. But then Vixen's lips spread into a crimson grin. "And you'll bring him back here?"

Jack shrugged. "If I can get him out, that'll be up to him." He had little hope for the state Blaise might be in if he escaped the Cit. None of the other Ringleaders had been on the inside. And the Confederation did a bloody effective job of dispelling rumors about the conditions within. But Jack knew. The Blaise that walked out of the Cit might very well be a shadow of the man he had been.

"That's fair," Raven said after a moment. He rubbed the back of his head. "Fine. You go to Phinora and find your daughter and free Blaise. We'll do our best to keep things in line here."

"No more damned mining companies." Jack shook a finger at them. "You see any more, figure out a way to make the new mages earn their keep and run 'em off."

"They're not outlaws. Not yet," Vixen said with a shake of her head.

Jack pivoted on his heel, heading into the depths of the stables. "They're living in the Gutter. You better learn 'em, then." He waved a hand over his shoulder. "Now, if you'll excuse me, I need to be sure my good-for-nothin' pegasus has eaten and then be on our way."

CHAPTER FOUR

The Secret Appeal of Tragedies

Malcolm

Malcolm idly swirled the wine in his crystal goblet, studying the revelers dancing below the veranda. He was off his game. Flirting, wheeling, and dealing were his usual pastimes for such an occasion. He had spent much of the evening chatting up the Moderate Doyens in attendance, taking their figurative pulse on the issue of Blaise Hawthorne.

Nothing encouraging so far. Even those among Malcolm's own Faedran party, who were normally receptive to the idea of mage equality, *feared* the Breaker and had questions surrounding his powerful magic. Malcolm couldn't very well tell them that Blaise would be happier baking cookies than tearing apart a town. How could he explain away such intimate knowledge?

He didn't have nearly enough time before the vote. Malcolm and his fellow Faedrans were in an uphill battle. Already, one of his cohorts had suggested they cede Blaise to the geasa and refocus their attention on securing more rights for the mages who *hadn't* committed atrocities. The cold logic infuriated Malcolm. But he knew that for the goals he had been striving toward for years, it was the best path.

But he wasn't ready to give up on Blaise. Not now. *Not ever.*

"Can I tempt you with a nibble, sir?" A serving girl interrupted his thoughts, offering a silver tray with an assortment of tasty finger foods.

She nestled it close to her ample bosom, tilting her head coquettishly. She smiled, making it clear that she was serving up more than the goods on the tray.

"Thank you. This will do." He nodded to the girl, selecting a finger sandwich. She made a frustrated sound before striding off to either do the job they hired her for or to snag another high-profile bedfellow. Malcolm returned his attention to the task at hand, circulating through the crowd until he found his target. Doyen Seward Jennings completed a rousing dance with his wife, who was a stunning and talented actress Malcolm had seen grace many a prominent stage. At first glance, Malcolm thought it might be a marriage of convenience, but the intense heat between the pair made him reconsider that idea. *Lucky man, Seward.*

"Doyen Jennings, you and your lovely wife cut quite a figure on the dance floor," Malcolm commented, amiable as he approached them, raising his goblet in appreciation.

Seward blushed at the compliment. "I normally don't like to dance, but Lizzie insisted."

Lizzie patted his arm. "You *do* like to dance, just not in front of people."

Malcolm chuckled. *They're a cute couple. Something to aspire to.* "Then it stands to reason you may need a break from such social demands. Can I beg a moment of your time?"

Seward cocked his head. "Did you come to the gala with the express purpose of furthering your agenda?"

"Is there any other reason to attend?" Malcolm replied. Though truth be told, yes, there were plenty of reasons. He quite enjoyed them, for one. It was pleasing to be fawned over and admired. To be propositioned and coveted. But he knew Seward had only come out of a sense of duty (and probably at the behest of his wife).

"True enough," Seward agreed, blowing out a breath. He glanced at his wife. "Lizzie, will it bother you if we speak?"

She waved a hand. "Do what you must. Wait." She paused, her coils of dark hair bouncing as she turned to study Malcolm. "Ah! You're the one my Cuddle Bear told me about! You know the Breaker?"

Seward's eyes widened at the nickname, and Malcolm managed not to quirk a smile. Truth be told, he was more focused on Lizzie's question. "My cousin is well-acquainted with him."

Lizzie stepped forward, conspiratorial. "Have you seen this *dashing* rogue in person? I've heard he's as powerful as a hurricane and twice as scary." She shivered in delight.

A muscle in Malcolm's jaw twitched. Gods, he longed to correct whatever gossip she had gotten about Blaise, but for his purposes, Malcolm

Wells had never met him. Only Jefferson Cole had. "I have had little chance to speak with my cousin, madam. But from what we've been told, the Breaker is no different from any other mage."

She deflated with disappointment at his words. "That's unfortunate."

That caught Malcolm by surprise. "I beg your pardon?"

Lizzie shrugged. "It would make a better story if he were. His story has me inspired to write a play, and an *unusual* character always makes for a better tragedy."

This will be no tragedy. He met her gaze. "As much as I enjoy the theater, I don't believe that would be a good fit."

Lizzie waved a hand. "No, no, it absolutely would! Do you know the secret appeal of tragedies?"

Malcolm frowned. He hadn't expected to debate theater with anyone tonight, but here he was. "And that is?"

She offered a demure smile. "A masterfully presented tragedy is an elegy for someone who *matters.* Whose story is worth telling, even if they never achieve a happy ending or lose it all along the way. Even if they fail, they *mattered* to someone."

He blinked at her provocative description, heart squeezing. Yes, Blaise mattered, but if Malcolm had a say, there would be no tragedy. He dipped into a shallow bow. "I'll admit I've never thought of it that way. Best of luck with your endeavor."

Lizzie slipped over to chat with a cluster of other ladies, and once she had moved away Seward grimaced. "I apologize if her question came across as crass. She wants to help bring visibility to the issues we support but is figuring out the best way to go about it."

Malcolm shook his head. "It's not a problem. We need all the allies we can get." And Lizzie's excitement planted another seed of an idea. Something else for later, if ever there was a later. "I wanted to ask what you had discovered in the archives."

Seward blinked for a moment, then a smile broadened his face. "Ah! Yes, I was there earlier. Are you aware it's been over fifty years since the last record of a Breaker?"

"I wasn't aware," Malcolm replied truthfully. He paused, thoughtful. "But isn't magic hereditary?"

The other Doyen waggled his fingers. "It can be, but magic isn't a dominant trait passed down from parent to child." At Malcolm's raised brows, Seward ducked his head. "I have my own thoughts on how magic crops up in a family line, but it's quite difficult to prove." He cleared his throat. "As I was saying, we haven't seen a Breaker in a long time. I could not locate any references to any of them being bound to a handler via the geasa."

That was interesting. Malcolm took a sip of wine. "Why do you think that is?"

Seward glanced around, as if making sure no one was listening in. "I suspect it's because of what the magic can do. In an untrained Breaker, it's as dangerous to friend as it is to foe."

Malcolm swallowed, recalling what Blaise had told him of his past. But that was no longer the case. Blaise had mastered his magic. "Seward, in your opinion, what is the best course of action regarding Breaker Hawthorne?"

The other Doyen sighed. "Personally, I would love to see research done. However, that's unlikely to happen." And Malcolm was glad for that, at least. But Seward was right—the natural philosophers were eager to crack Blaise open like a walnut to see what made him tick. "I disagree with execution, so the next best option is the geasa."

Malcolm frowned. "Are you viewing it from the lens of a criminal case, then? Would you consider it differently if not for Fort Courage?"

Seward nodded. "It's hard to argue against the lives lost, Malcolm. I think the Breaker should face the consequences of his actions. If we do anything else, we risk looking like we favor mages regardless of their crimes, and that will damage our credibility."

Disappointing, but that made sense in a depressing way. "I see. I admit, I know very little of this business about the geasa and how it's done. Can you enlighten me?"

Seward's face became animated, and it was clear this was a topic he had taken pains to research. "Absolutely! It's really very interesting. It's the intersection of alchemy and magic. They use the mage's own blood as a base to create the Ink. It's a brilliant process."

Malcolm was proud that somehow, he maintained a neutral but interested expression. Inwardly, he seethed at the idea, suspecting there would be nothing kind about the process.

"The blood is delivered to the alchemists at the Arboretum, where it's mixed with reagents to create the Ink for the geasa. The mage in question already has a tattoo, applied when they were first registered. But if they don't, they're assigned a sigil and issued the tattoo. The person selected as their handler receives a matching tattoo, made from the mage-blood Ink." Seward beamed. "Isn't that interesting?"

"Quite," Malcolm lied. Awful was more like it. "Matching tattoos, hmm? What's the design look like?" Seward blinked, the question catching him off guard. Malcolm cleared his throat as he sought to cover his unusual question, lest Seward become suspicious of his prodding. "I've heard they're quite artistic." He'd heard no such thing, so hoped it was plausible.

Seward relaxed, taking on the posture of a man who enjoyed a good lecture. "Oh, each one is unique. That's the thing. Geasa tattoos cannot be repeated. The sigil is made of runes—specialized alphabet, you see. As unique as a fingerprint. One sigil, one mage, one handler."

That bit was interesting. Malcolm tipped his head. "What happens if two handlers bind to the same mage?"

Seward shrugged. "Intriguing question, but I've never come across mention of that. I would presume the first binding may block the second. There have been cases where a theurgist or handler was bound to a new partner in events where one or the other died, but that's the extent."

Malcolm nodded. That was good to know. He was about to speak again, but Lizzie trotted over, grabbing Seward's arm. "So sorry to interrupt! But Cuddle Bear, there's someone I must absolutely introduce you to." Her eyes were wide as she offered Malcolm an apologetic smile. "It's the one and only Edward Monroe. You know, star of *Angry Rainbows* and *Honor of the Eclipse?*"

Seward blinked, startled. Malcolm chuckled. He had to admit, he liked Lizzie and her enthusiasm. "I appreciate the time you gave me, Seward. Mrs. Jennings, I won't steal you away from your husband and the heartthrob that is Edward Monroe any longer." He gave her a good-natured wink.

<hr>

HE REMAINED AT THE GALA UNTIL THE GREY HOURS BEFORE DAWN. TO KEEP up appearances, once he finished his discussion with Seward, he entertained the company of anyone who caught his fancy. It involved dancing and conversation, though he had his share of amorous invitations. Had he been Jefferson, he might have taken them up on the offer because that was a very Jefferson thing to do. Malcolm was a little more restrained, though not by much. But thoughts of Blaise distracted him, keeping him from temptation.

With a contented sigh, he retired to his bedroom in the estate house. Malcolm drew open the drawer of the bedside table, opening a small velvet box and plucking out his cabochon ring. His mind was abuzz with everything he had learned at the gala, and he had discovered he slept better as Jefferson. But even though his body was tired, his mind clung to the information provided by Seward like a dog with a bone. By the time the pastel rays of sunlight painted the eastern sky, Jefferson was certain that the best course of action was to keep Blaise out of play. As far as the geasa went, he had an idea of how to circumvent it. But he needed help. It wasn't something he could do alone.

He rose from the bed and removed his ring, tucking it into the bedside drawer. Malcolm dressed, and after his breakfast, he sought Flora, his half-knocker acquaintance. It was early afternoon by the time he called her into his private study.

Flora narrowed her eyes, as if she detected he was up to something as soon as she settled into the armchair opposite him. "I see that look in your eye, boss. What are we doing?"

He grunted at her use of *boss*. It was a tease, since Malcolm much preferred to consider her a friend rather than an employee (though she was that, too). "I need you to steal something for me."

Flora hopped out of her chair, pushed a footstool in front of him, and climbed onto it, laying her hand across his forehead.

"What are you doing?" Malcolm asked.

She leaned over to peer into his eyes. "Checking your vitals because something is wrong with you. *I'm* supposed to be the one with that sort of idea." She jumped off the stool and climbed back into her seat. "What am I going after?"

He steeled himself because this would be audacious even by her standards. "A specific vial of Ink from the Arboretum."

Flora tilted her head, studying him as if expecting he might laugh and call it all off as a joke. When he didn't, she put her hands on her hips, giving him her best glare. Between her short stature and pink hair, she looked adorable—not that Malcolm would tell her that. "Mal, *no*. You can't be serious!"

Malcolm sighed, scrubbing at his face with one hand. "I don't know how else to help him. I can't break him out of the Cit." Tabris knew he and Flora had discussed it, but without more willing helpers, that was a non-starter.

Flora pulled out a butterfly knife and flipped it around. Anyone else might have found it an intimidating move, but Malcolm knew her too well. "I'm not great at being the voice of reason, so this is awkward, and I'm kinda mad you're putting me in this position." She scowled at him for good measure. "But have you thought this through? I mean *really* thought beyond this first step."

Malcolm managed a small smile. "I have. The Ink isn't the only thing I need you to get. I also need you to find out the sigil assigned to Blaise Hawthorne."

At that, she closed her knife and tucked it away. "That's not what I meant. Why are you so infatuated with him? It's not like you."

He winced at her question. It took him back to the time Blaise had asked the same. Malcolm wasn't sure if Flora would understand. "The

only thing he ever wanted from me was a chance to be himself. And I..."
He trailed off, swallowing as he struggled for the words to explain.

"And you want the same thing," Flora supplied.

Malcolm lifted his eyes, filled with gratitude that she understood. Flora had been his close friend for years, but even so, he had feared she wouldn't understand this. But maybe that had been short-sighted since Flora knew something about that, too. "Yes, and I think we could have that."

"Hmm." Flora pulled the knife back out, fidgeting with it. "Back to your scheme, then. There's only one reason you'd need that sigil. Are you sure about this?" She scrutinized him. "I can get away with shenanigans. I'm a *nobody*."

At that, Malcolm straightened. He loved Flora and thought the world of her. "You're *not* a nobody."

She shrugged. "My point is, I'm not *you*. Not a Doyen. You have responsibilities and all these wonderful plans. You want to change the world."

Malcolm sighed. "I can still do that."

Flora offered a sad smile. "I like your mettle, but I'm not so sure. Look, Mal, you've already got your hands full with your masquerade. Do you really want to add more to the load?"

As annoying as it was, she had a valid point. Maintenance of his two personas was exhausting. But this was *Blaise* they were talking about. "He doesn't deserve this."

"No," she agreed softly. "But you can't save everyone."

Malcolm swallowed, meeting her eyes. "No. Sometimes it's enough to save one."

Flora put her hands on her hips, staring back at him. "Saving him? Are you sure *this* is saving him and not *using* him?"

Malcolm dropped his gaze to the floor. In his mind, it seemed like such a good idea. The only one that might even work since nothing else had come to fruition. "They're going to use him. *You* threw your lot in with me. I don't use *you*."

Flora was quiet for a few minutes, no doubt reflecting on their own history. She pursed her lips. "I had a choice." And to that, he had no adequate response, so he continued to stare at floor. Finally, she sighed. "Right. Far be it from me to be a hypocrite. But I still don't know how you'll ever make things work out if you get him free. Especially if you're planning what I think you're planning. Not and still do what you want to do."

Malcolm glanced away, guilty. That was another cog in his plan he hadn't worked out yet. He hoped that by the time he got there, an answer would present itself. And that was funny because that wasn't usually the way he operated. Malcolm had the long game in mind. He hadn't expected Blaise Hawthorne's appearance on the board, however.

"I've been juggling things for years. Just one more ball in the air."

She snorted. "More like juggling a flaming chupacabra. This is going to make your masquerade seem boring by comparison."

He shrugged, rueful. "Never a dull moment with me, you know."

Flora laughed. "And I'm here for it." She took a deep breath, as if reaching a decision. "Okay. I'll do a little breaking and entering. Once I have the goods, what do you want me to do?" She raised her brows. "Because I should definitely not bring them back here."

Right. Malcolm massaged his forehead. He already had a good idea of where to go once he had the necessary items. "Do you have any dead drops around Faedra's Garden?"

Flora nodded. "I do. Two streets over." She rubbed her hands together. "Around the back of the Sour Eel Bar, there's a loose brick in the wall that I've used a few times. Do you know the place?"

Malcolm didn't, but he waved away the concern. "I'll figure it out. Can you get it by tonight?"

Flora glanced at the clock on the wall. It was almost two in the afternoon, and Malcolm knew she preferred to sneak around in darkness. Not ideal.

She shrugged, unbothered by the implications. "It's doable. I'll have it at the dead drop by seven."

Malcolm breathed a sigh of relief. He had suspected Flora might put up more of a fight. He was glad to see she was on board. "Thank you."

Flora leveled a finger at him. "You know I'm only doing this because if I don't, you'll find someone else who will."

Was he that obvious? He chuckled. "You're right."

She rose from her chair, stretching. "What are you going to be doing in the meantime?"

Malcolm smiled. "Paying someone a visit."

CHAPTER FIVE
Trust Issues

Jefferson

Blaise looked up for an instant before bowing his head again as Jefferson eased into the visitation cell. The younger man stayed in his seat as the guards ushered the entrepreneur inside. Jefferson pulled out the chair opposite Blaise and sat. The Breaker's hands were in his lap, but spatters of dried blood staining his sleeve didn't escape Jefferson's notice.

Jefferson half-rose in his chair as soon as the guards left them to their sham of privacy, hands braced against the table as he peered over to get a better look at Blaise's arm. "What is that? What happened?"

Blaise shook his head, silent.

Tabris grant me grace. Jefferson reined in his anger. Blaise experienced enough of that without him adding to it. "You can tell me."

For a moment, Jefferson thought Blaise had shut himself down again, refusing to speak or acknowledge him. But then the young mage shifted his left arm, resting it on the tabletop. A bandage made from dirty strips of cloth was wrapped around his forearm between his elbow and wrist, though blood had seeped through that, too. Blaise moved it with care, as if it bothered him. Malcolm imagined it did. "They took blood. That's how they do it."

"Oh," he murmured, heart squeezing at the sight. Curse them. They hadn't even sent for a Healer to attend to it. A simple matter. Even basic wound care and clean bandages from a physician would have been a good start. Gods, were they *trying* to kill Blaise from lack of effort or pure sloth? "One moment, please."

Blaise withdrew his arm back into his lap as Jefferson rose from the table, keeping his anger coiled within. He knocked on the door, and a guard opened it, allowing him to slip out.

"Done so soon?" The guard had the audacity to smirk.

Jefferson summoned up all the haughtiness he possessed. "I need to speak to your superior."

The guard blinked slowly. "What? Why?"

"*That* is not your concern." Every ounce of contempt he possessed oozed into his voice. *Magelover* he may be, but the power that wealth and affluence brought were in his corner. He was a genuine danger to this man's status as a guard if he didn't act, and soon. The guard realized this and scrambled away.

Jefferson hated to keep Blaise waiting and wondering, but he would not tolerate this any longer. After a brief wait, an older man ambled up the corridor to him, a perplexed look on his face.

"Mr. Cole, Grand Warden Kerney. I heard you had *concerns*?"

Jefferson heaved back his shoulders. "I do. Why has this man not had proper medical treatment?" He jerked a thumb toward the visitation cell where Blaise waited.

Kerney stared at him, uncomprehending. "What?" Then he realized who Jefferson meant, and he chuckled. "Oh. *Oh*, I follow. He's treated as is his due."

Jefferson clenched his fists. "I disagree. And I believe there are several accords being violated with this." He narrowed his eyes. "I have the ear of a Doyen."

The Grand Warden flinched at that, though he didn't let it cow him. "We're doing nothing wrong here." He frowned, lips curling with disdain. "If he wanted to be treated better, he should have thought about that before he did what he did." With that revelation, Kerney turned, waving him off as he trudged away.

Jefferson ground his teeth. He wished he could say aloud that it wasn't Blaise's fault. He motioned for the remaining guard to allow him back in, frustrated that the net gain had been absolutely nothing.

Blaise was stiff and aloof as Jefferson crossed the short distance and took his seat. "I told them it hurts. They won't help me."

Jefferson sighed. "You're right, they won't. But I want to."

The Breaker kept his blue eyes on Jefferson, his shoulders loosening. "They let you come visit me again." His tone was neutral, giving no indication of how he felt about it.

Jefferson nodded, relieved that Blaise had spoken at last. "You're allowed three visitors a week, per regulations." No doubt that would change if a handler was assigned to Blaise. So much would change in that case. No sense in dancing around the subject. "I've brought an update you deserve to hear."

Blaise swallowed, the muscles in his cheeks tightening. "What did you find out?"

"The Council plans to bind you to a handler."

As soon as the words left Jefferson's lips, outrage flared in Blaise's eyes. But as quickly as the anger appeared, it fled, and his demeanor changed. His gaze fell back to his lap as the news hit home. "Oh."

What have they done to you? Jefferson reached across and placed a hand over Blaise's. It was a gamble—he was very aware the other man was averse to unwelcome touch and might shrink away. Blaise's skin was icy, as if his gaunt frame could no longer hold its own heat. But he didn't withdraw his hand. "We'll figure something out, I promise."

The younger man's chin dipped against his chest. "You know how I feel about being used."

Jefferson leaned forward, heart pounding. "I know." And he had an idea for how to skate around this, but what would Blaise think of it? He warred with the idea of telling him. A large part of Jefferson wanted to. He wanted to be open and honest with Blaise because he deserved nothing less. But caution won out. He was sure they were being observed, and if anyone suspected Jefferson's plan, he was certain to be stopped. "I'm not done fighting for you."

Blaise shook his head. "Is it even worth it? If you continue, I'll only drag you down with me."

Jefferson narrowed his eyes. "You're worth it. And don't let anyone tell you otherwise."

At that, Blaise looked up at him again, quivering as if he were about to break. Gods, Jefferson wanted to know what they were doing to him in the Golden Citadel. Blaise's fingers twitched beneath his.

"I...I mean it." Blaise's hesitation showed the lie for what it was. "Now that they have me, they'll never let me be free. Never let me just...be me." He bowed his head again, and it cut Jefferson to the core.

Jefferson tightened his fingers around Blaise's wrist. "Do you trust me?"

The younger man blinked, surprised. He lifted his head, and it gratified Jefferson when Blaise met his eyes. "Yes."

"Then trust me when I tell you this is not the end. You will get to do what you love again." Jefferson prayed he wasn't lying to Blaise. "I'm doing everything I can to make it so."

Blaise sighed. "I want to believe you."

Sometimes, a spark of belief was all that was needed to ignite hope. Jefferson rubbed Blaise's hand. "Then *do*. I'm fighting for you." Blaise rewarded him with a small nod.

They spoke for a few more minutes before Jefferson was escorted out. He hated these brief visits, these glimpses of the way the young mage's spirit was cracking, the pain reflected in his eyes. And it was all Jefferson's fault.

He strode to the exit, absorbed in thoughts of his plan. There was a very real chance Blaise would hate him for it, but Jefferson believed it was the least of all the evils. Blaise was correct on the point that now that the Confederation had him, they were loath to let him go. Jefferson was still searching for a way to free him, but until he could make any headway on that, this was the only way he knew to stop Blaise from being bound.

They couldn't bind Blaise to someone else if Jefferson did it first.

<hr>

Flora

FLORA COULDN'T LOSE THE FEELING THAT SHE WAS BEING WATCHED. OVER the years, she'd developed keen instincts. She had to, or she wouldn't have made it this far. It was a simple thing to gain access to the Arboretum, the lovely parcel of land that had, in a former incarnation, once been a sprawling public park. But, as was typical, the Confederation claimed it as a place for the alchemists, with imposing walls constructed around it and buildings added to the complex. Flora supposed it was because of the variety of plants imported from all over Iphyria that grew across the grounds in neat, maintained beds. *Need a rare, plant-based reagent? We've got you covered.*

Getting into the Arboretum was simple for Flora, though she was thorough and made a full reconnaissance of the land. She liked to know all the entrances and where any sentries might be posted. Security was overall lax, with most of it concentrated at the main gate. It made sense, as none of the alchemists were mages or had a straightforward way up and over the walls without help. Barbed wire lined the top to dissuade anyone who might try to scale them.

Interesting. Were they trying to keep the alchemists in, the public out, or a combination of both?

Flora set that puzzle aside to think about more when she had the time. The sun was still high overhead, and she had to make her way around the grounds with care. She preferred nocturnal escapades—not only was it easier to stay hidden, but darkness improved her vision, too. Humans didn't realize that under normal daylight conditions, knockers were near-sighted. Thanks to Jefferson, Flora had glasses that corrected her problem. All the same, she preferred the night.

It took some doing, but she located the Ink storage area in a supply room. Even better, it was unattended because no one expected their supplies to up and run off. Flora slipped into the storage room, not bothering to turn on the mage-light. Her eyes quickly adjusted to the darkness, and she read the labels on the bottles one by one. She didn't like the idea of mages being bound any more than Malcolm did. She entertained the idea of fouling the whole lot out of spite. But Malcolm's instructions were clear. The Ink for Blaise Hawthorne *only*.

She picked up the vial with the Breaker's name on it. Flora frowned at it. "You had better be worth all this fuss."

Flora was certain she heard something behind her, perhaps the door opening. She spun, knife in hand. But the storage room was still dark. Flora scowled, scanning the area for signs of anything amiss. Nothing seemed unusual. She opened the pouch at her side and drew out some gauzy linen, wrapping it neatly around the precious bottle before depositing it back in the pouch and closing it securely.

She set her jaw. *Right.* Now time to figure out where they kept the list of sigils.

CHAPTER SIX

Something Off the Menu

Jefferson

Flora's dead drop was easy to find, thanks to Jefferson's many years of acquaintance with the half-knocker and figuring out how she worked. The loose brick was low to the ground, and it was a simple matter to tug it away when no one was around to see.

A thrill of victory surged through him as he pulled out a small leather sack containing a vial swathed in cloth and a folded square of paper. Jefferson tucked the vial into a pocket and opened the paper. Flora had scratched the sigil onto the slip with a charcoal pencil, nothing more. Jefferson hoped the Inker would understand what it meant.

Sometimes living two lives was a nuisance. There were so many intricacies to keep track of, and when he had settled on the idea at first, he hadn't realized how involved it would turn out to be. It was one of those things that seemed like a good idea, but over the years had lost some of its luster. This, however, was one of the times it was exceedingly helpful.

After all, it would have been odd for Doyen Malcolm Wells to be seen going to one of the seedier parts of Izhadell. Not unheard of for politicians to go there—oh, no, far from it—but he curated a certain persona for Malcolm that differed from Jefferson. Malcolm wasn't as adventurous and would turn up his nose at going to the red-light district. Jefferson, on the other hand, kept an open mind and would go just about anywhere if either a profit or a good time were sure to follow. Preference given to profit, of course.

As far as houses of ill repute went, Faedra's Garden was one of the more specialized among them. It catered to those with a certain taste—specifically, those who sought the thrill of rolling in the sheets with a mage.

If Malcolm had such inclinations, he would never have considered going to such a place since it warred with his beliefs. The mages who worked there were all serving out indentures, and from what he understood, they had a chance of paying them off, thanks in part to their affluent clientele. In his guise as Jefferson, he had gone to Faedra's Garden with associates a few times. It was an upscale club, offering dinner and a show besides the more carnal pleasures that resided within. All in all, a fun place, though Jefferson had never been one who hurt for willing partners.

Jefferson joined the loose line of men and women entering Faedra's Garden for the evening show. A buxom hostess approached to seat him, but he shook his head and pulled out a bronze chit, handing it to her. Jefferson had paid an exorbitant amount for the token that would grant him what was usually an amorous encounter with a mage. "I'm looking for a more *intimate* experience."

The hostess nodded at this part of their standard dealings. "Follow me." She turned and passed through a curtain of beads. "Itching for anything in particular?"

"An Inker."

The hostess paused. "You understand what you're getting into?"

"Absolutely."

She muttered something that sounded very much like, "Some men just get off on the pain."

She was right about that. But he had other plans.

The hostess led him down a long hallway, placards on each door listing the name of the occupants and their status. Many of them were otherwise engaged, and Jefferson was thankful that the resident Inker was unclaimed.

The hostess drew to a stop before a crimson door at the end of the hall, knocking crisply three times before holding it open to allow Jefferson to enter. "Lindsay, you've got a customer. Good luck." The last bit she addressed to Jefferson. And then she strode out, heels tapping as she receded.

A woman sat before a mirror, adding a trio of combs as the finishing touches to her flaxen hair. The Inker was dressed in a black and gold dress that was all lace and left her arms bare, displaying a colorful tapestry of tattoos. She aimed a coy glance over her shoulder, then back at her reflection as she added the final comb into place. "What do we have here? You want a new tattoo, a good time, or a little of both?"

Jefferson glanced around the room. "Something off the menu. I intend to pay you well for the effort."

The Inker pivoted on her chair, tilting her head so that her hair cascaded over one shoulder like a waterfall. "What are you interested in? I get asked to do lots of freaky things." She shrugged as if it were just another day on the job. Which it was.

Jefferson pushed aside the distaste he had for mages forced to serve out indentures. "I'm looking for a tattoo. It must be applied with specific Ink."

She crossed her arms, a smile playing on her lips. "I see. We have ourselves here someone who fancies dabbling in the mystical world of an Inker." She winked and laughed. "Leave it to the professionals, Mister..."

"Chisolm," Jefferson supplied, knowing very well that only fools offered their actual names in situations like this. Even if he weren't dabbling in something seditious, she could still use information about him as leverage or to earn favors of her own from others. Potentially pay off her indenture faster. Information was dangerous, and he had no illusions that even the amount of money he was about to offer her would help.

She narrowed her eyes. "Right. Chisolm, then. As I said, you're better off telling me what you're after and letting me apply the proper Inks." Her gaze flicked over him. "You're handsome enough, so I doubt you're looking for a tat to attract a lover. Hmm. Something to keep you virile, perhaps? I'd be happy to try that out with you." Lindsay rose from her chair and sashayed closer.

Malcolm snorted. "Lindsay—may I call you Lindsay? I know what I'm after and I don't need help in that area." He pulled out a promissory note and passed it to her.

Lindsay took it from him, puzzled as she read the terms. She raised her brows. "Is this real?"

"Every bit of it," Jefferson said.

She gave him a dubious look. "This would..." The Inker shook her head. "This can't be right. You must have written it wrong. This would pay off my indenture." She stared at him, the note quivering in her grasp.

Jefferson cocked his head, unable to hide the twitch of his mouth into a smile. "Oh, would it?"

Was it his imagination, or did she almost seem afraid at the prospect of her indenture being paid off? Her gaze shifted to the floor. "I can't accept that. I don't have anywhere to go."

Blast. He hadn't thought of that simple thing. Indentures were notoriously hard to pay off, and when they were, the mage in question was still something of a social outcast, excluded from basic rights like owning land, a residence, or a business. They relied on family members who were themselves non-mages. Otherwise, they entered service to someone who would pay them a wage and offer room and board—someone like Jefferson himself. He had a few such mages in his employ.

But another thought occurred to him. "Do you need to stay in Phinora?"

She shook her head.

There it was. "Pay off your indenture and go to the Gutter or the Untamed Territory."

Lindsay stared at him like he had lost his mind. "Are you kidding me? That's wild country. Outlaw lands. I wouldn't survive a day there. I'm better off staying here."

Jefferson smiled. This was an area of expertise. "To the contrary. I'll sweeten the deal. After you pay your indenture, I'll make sure you have safe passage on a steamer to Rainbow Flat, if you so desire. I think you'll find it more pleasant than Izhadell."

She blinked. "You're serious about this."

In reply, he inclined his head.

Lindsay took a shaky breath. "Right. What do you want from me, then?"

Jefferson slipped his hand into his front coat pocket and pulled out the tiny vial, carefully unwrapping it from its linen protections. "Are you familiar with the designs used for the geasa?"

The Inker froze, startled by the question. "You want a geasa tattoo? Why?"

"I have my reasons." He held up the vial. "This is the Ink you need to use."

Lindsay took the Ink from him, turning the vial over in her hands. "This is the real shit." She hissed out a breath. "What sort of mage does this belong to? Do you know what this would sell for in the shadows? This would pay the indenture of every single man and woman working in Faedra's Garden."

Jefferson's lips tightened. "I'm not at liberty to speak about the mage." He resisted the urge to snatch the vial back from her. He hadn't known how valuable the geasa Ink was, though he had assumed it was difficult to come by.

She shook her head. "My suggestion is forget whatever you were planning and sell this." Her tone turned urgent. "How did you even get it?"

He waved a hand. "You don't need to know how I got it. Will you do the tattoo or not?" Frustration tugged at Jefferson with each passing minute. He didn't know what he would do if Lindsay refused the task. One thing was certain: he couldn't allow her to stay in Izhadell with knowledge of what he possessed.

Lindsay's eyes flicked from the Ink to him. "Do I have a choice?"

As far as questions went, Jefferson despised that one. "Everyone has a choice."

The Inker laughed bitterly. "Spoken like someone with a dragonshit load of privilege." She took a deep breath, thinking. At last, she said, "I'll do it, but know that this is dangerous. There's a reason they only apply these at the Golden Citadel." Lindsay opened a drawer and pulled out a spool of thread and a needle.

Jefferson blinked. "I thought you were an Inker."

She placed the spool and needle on a silver tray, alongside a pair of shears and a handkerchief. "I am, but like other mages, each Inker works their craft differently. I'm a skin stitcher." She lifted her chin, a challenge. "Having second thoughts?"

"No," Jefferson replied, full of determination. "How does this work?"

Lindsay settled him in a sumptuous armchair, setting the tray down on a decorative table and pulling a stool over. She threaded the needle, then held it up between her thumb and index finger. "I dip the thread in the Ink and pull it through your skin with the needle. Simple."

Jefferson licked his lips. "I'm a human embroidery hoop, then?"

"Something like that," Lindsay agreed with a laugh as sharp as her needle.

He pursed his lips, glancing between the young woman and the Ink. Jefferson's gut clenched at the idea of the needle dancing in and out of his skin. But all he had to do was summon up a mental image of Blaise and his haunted gaze at the Cit. The Breaker was going through far worse. Jefferson could handle a little discomfort. "Fine. How long will it take?"

The Inker's eyes flicked to the vial of Ink. "Hmm. A couple of hours."

Lovely. Jefferson nodded, and she scooted closer. He watched as she dribbled a tiny amount of the precious Ink into a shallow bowl, leaving her thread to soak in it. Lindsay turned her attention to her human canvas, gripping his upper arm and frowning.

"You have a glamor." The Inker said it matter-of-factly, as if it weren't an unusual occurrence in her line of work. Perhaps it wasn't. "You'll have to remove it for this."

Damn. He hadn't been counting on that. "Why?"

"I have to see what I'm doing. Whatever you have going on there will obfuscate my view." She waved a hand in a broad gesture to encompass his entire body.

He stilled. "How do you know it's a glamor?"

She snorted with disdain. "Oh, please. You're not the first person to come here with some cheap glamor to hide your true identity, Mr. Chisolm. Whatever it is, drop it, or this won't work."

Jefferson gritted his teeth. He hadn't planned on that problem in all of this. And cheap glamor? It was most certainly not, though he knew what she was talking about. If one had the coin and the contacts, glamors of dubious quality were available for purchase. Though they were nowhere near as thorough as his ring. With a grimace, he pulled his ring off and pocketed it for safe keeping. The magic sluiced off him, his features melting into those of Malcolm Wells.

Lindsay nodded, cocking her head. "There we go. Hmm, not bad looking without the glamor either if I do say so myself. You certainly weren't trying to make yourself more handsome, that's for certain." She blew him a kiss. "Are you sure you don't want to do anything else before I get to work?"

"Only the tattoo," Malcolm answered, uncomfortable at his sudden vulnerability. But he was in a room with the shades drawn. No one would know.

"Right." The Inker nodded. "Do you have the sigil?" He withdrew the slip of paper from his pocket, unfolding it and handing it to her. She raised a perfectly arched eyebrow. "Huh. Okay, let's get to it." She rose and brought over a blank sheet of paper and a charcoal pencil, making room for them on a small side table. She tapped the pencil against the paper for a moment and then began to sketch.

"Is something amiss with the sigil?" Malcolm asked, worried that Flora had copied it incorrectly or nabbed the wrong one.

"No," Lindsay said as she drew. "It's more elaborate than the geasa tattoos I used to apply back in the days of my early training." She slanted her eyes at him. "The more elaborate the flourishes, the stronger the mage." An unspoken question hung in the air between them. Malcolm's blood chilled. He opened his mouth to spin a defense, but the Inker continued her musings. "Although I may be a humble worker at Faedra's Garden, my mama didn't raise a fool. No, she didn't. I know when my silence is being bought."

Malcolm clenched his jaw, frustrated at her insight. While that hadn't been his intent—not fully, at any rate—he understood why she perceived it in such a way. Any denials at this point would be fruitless and only make her more suspicious. "You'll honor it? Keep your silence?"

She nodded, brushing a lock of her hair back into place. "That's what we do at Faedra's Garden, Mr. Chisolm. We keep the secrets of our clients." A tight smile touched her lips, but no matching warmth filled her eyes. Her earlier flirtations had vanished, replaced by the professional veneer of someone wanting to complete a task and be done with it. Without a doubt, Malcolm had lost whatever esteem she may have had for him. As Lindsay had said, she wasn't a fool, and she realized the intent of the tattoo. She didn't approve.

"I appreciate your candor," Malcolm murmured, glancing at the silver needle. The thread gleamed wetly within the basin, and he had to tamp down the momentary squeamishness that rose when he thought about it being laced under his skin.

"I'm satisfied that the design is ready. We can begin if you like." Lindsay placed the finished drawing beside the bowl.

Malcolm nodded. "Please."

He fervently hoped he was making the right choice.

***

"Oh, my apologies," Malcolm murmured as he bumped into a dark-clad man outside Faedra's Garden. The stranger turned, and Malcolm squinted his bleary eyes into the gaslamp-lit gloom, startling because he *recognized* the face. A Gaitwood. The tattoo had taken hours to apply, and his tired brain stalled as he tried to recall the name. *He only has one arm. Lamar.* He staggered back and away as Lamar stared at him, and Malcolm quickened his step to hail a hackney cab to take him home.

As he settled onto the plush bench seat, Malcolm was frustrated with himself. He was off his game and had been sloppy with his failure to resume the façade of Jefferson before leaving Lindsay's room. But he had as much right as anyone else to carouse at Faedra's Garden. *It will be fine.*

Before allowing him to leave, the Inker covered the fresh tattoo with ointment and a bandage with strict instructions to keep it on for at least twenty-four hours. That was fine with Malcolm. It meant no one would see what he had done for at least a day. He rubbed idly at the bandage as the hackney arrived at his home.

His head felt like he had been kicked by a horse. Malcolm supposed it was maybe due to a lack of food. Lindsay had offered him refreshments, but he had declined. Perhaps he should have taken her up on them. He pushed his way inside, stopping by the dark kitchen to grab a snack and a drink before finding his bed. Aside from two security staff patrolling the outside, his estate was blessedly quiet. Malcolm enjoyed the peace the early hour offered, though the food and drink did nothing to relieve his headache.

Rest. Rest would set him right. It had been a very long day. With a yawn, he started up the steps to the master bedroom, his eyelids heavy with the need for sleep. Malcolm was barely undressed before collapsing in the welcoming comfort of his bed. Yes, sleep would solve everything.

CHAPTER SEVEN

Arboreal Annoyance

Jack

"Huh. Forgot it was that time of year already," Jack muttered at the sight of the gallows standing beside the road they were traveling down. A corpse hung from the gallows, the unfortunate man's body spiraling like a grotesque marionette at the end of a string. The stench of decay tinged the light breeze.

Zepheus tossed his head, ears flicking this way and that. He sashayed to the side as if he were a skittish yearling and not a battle-hardened warrior. But then, he hadn't expected such a sight to greet them at the limits of Izhadell. <Time of year for *what*?>

"Luminary Festival." Jack's lips were tight, his blue eyes hard. It was a stark reminder of what he was risking by coming here.

The palomino pranced down the road, tail swishing with his unease. <They celebrate with death? Why would they do such a thing?>

Jack chuckled without humor; his voice low so anyone who saw him speaking to his mount might assume he was keeping a fractious animal calm. "The highlight of the Luminary Festival is the execution of mages that they've declared criminals. *Outlaws*." Gods, not for the first time he hoped Emmaline was safe. "Though half the time, the poor sods you see like that don't have a lick of magic."

Zepheus snorted. <And they think mages are the monsters.>

Jack grunted. Yeah, Zepheus had the right of it. The outlaw was quiet as they continued onward, wondering how his life would have differed if he hadn't been brought into the fold as a theurgist so young. But that was a consideration for another time. "Let's get the lay of the land first."

Izhadell was every bit the eyesore Jack remembered. As far as he was concerned, Phinora as a whole was one big cesspit, with the capital city the worst of it. Izhadell sprawled for miles outside of the walls that had originally contained the city. Inns, saloons, homes, warehouses, factories, and every other sort of building imaginable cropped up wherever land was available, pushing farms out to the farthest reaches.

A group of children ran through the streets, playing chase and yelling at one another. One boy stopped, staring at the golden stallion with wide, wondering eyes. The others skidded to a stop, their clothing matted with grime and their hair unkempt. Orphans, by the looks of them. They probably survived by begging and stealing, and no doubt pegged Jack as a likely target, since he had taken to dressing as a merchant to better fit in. The outlaw tugged gently at the reins, asking Zepheus to stop so that he could dismount as the urchins gathered in a goggling clump.

<I'll keep an eye out for cut-purses.> The stallion relaxed nearby.

Jack kept his eyes on the children. He reached into the pouch at his waist, drawing out coins for each child. They watched with sharp-edged avarice, and as soon as a little girl received her coin, she ran off like a squirrel. Jack held up a finger to caution the remaining three from fleeing. "Got more for you. It's not much, but it's something."

He moved to Zepheus's saddlebags, pulling out dried corn husks, string, and bits of colorful rags. The children watched as he expertly crafted a trio of tiny dolls. For half a second, Jack considered spelling them, giving them a simple little working to grant the kids luck filling their bellies or protection. He had done that before, once upon a time. But he knew more now than he did back then, and doing so would put him in jeopardy. He figured the waifs would enjoy a toy even if it didn't have magic attached.

"For you," he said, crouching down and offering the dolls to them, along with a shiny coin. A hesitant girl crept forward first, claiming the largest of the poppets, before running off with a mad giggle. The remaining children, both boys, snagged the last pair and bolted.

<Good thing no one you know is around to see that. Might ruin your reputation,> Zepheus teased, though he sounded pleased by his rider's actions.

"You know I like kids," Jack muttered as he climbed back into the saddle. "It's everyone else that raises my dander."

The stallion bobbed his head and continued onward into the city. Zepheus blew out a snotty snort at the filth surrounding them, flicking his ears this way and that. A film of mud and dung lined the cobblestone streets, and a haze of persistent smoke veiled the air. <This place stinks. I don't like it here.>

Yeah, me either. Jack patted the stallion's neck in silent agreement. It didn't escape his notice that he received many a covetous look, due in part to Zepheus's golden coat. Most Phinoran steeds favored earth tones, so the palomino stood out more than Jack liked. But he knew better than to leave Zepheus behind. Not that the stallion would allow such nonsense.

While Zepheus stood out, Jack had gone to great pains to make sure that he himself did not. He wore brown trousers, a plain button-down shirt, and a frock coat that gave the illusion of a merchant and used a henna dye to darken his blond hair. He grudgingly traded his slouch hat for a checked tweed hat, though it did make him look more respectable, and that was ultimately what he required.

Zepheus threaded his way through the afternoon crowd. Jack didn't have a firm destination in mind, not yet. He had been away from Izhadell for so long he wanted to get the lay of the land. In his previous occupation as a theurgist, and during his time as an outlaw, he had discovered the value of familiarity with an area. And in a place like Izhadell, it often meant the difference between life and death.

It took the better part of the day for them to transcribe a circle around the city. By the time they finished, Jack had a better sense of the layout. They found an unassuming inn to spend the night, and after he settled Zepheus in the stable, Jack headed inside to claim a table in the common room and eat.

The outlaw was halfway through his meal when the first sign came that the respite would be short-lived. <There's a unicorn sniffing around here,> Zepheus advised, his voice distant.

Outwardly, Jack didn't so much as twitch at the news. He took a sip of whiskey, setting it down as he surveyed the room. As far as he could tell, there were no Trackers in the inn yet, but it might only be a matter of time. Jack weighed his options. Going to ground in the inn would cause problems—too many witnesses, too many potential things to go wrong. Not enough clear routes of escape. He rose from the table, pulling a handful of coins from his pouch and dropping them to cover his expenses.

He slipped out of the inn, debating his options. Jack considered using a spell, but the whole point of the unicorn was to sniff out a mage, and that would draw the beast to him like a pegasus to apple pie. No, his best bet was to confuse his trail.

<You can ride me bareback from the stables,> Zepheus offered.

Jack gave a mental headshake. That wouldn't do. It would make his need to escape too obvious, and then someone would call the guard on him simply for behaving suspiciously. Best to play it as if nothing were amiss.

He strode past the stables, heading to the unclaimed land beyond the inn. Whatever idiot had founded Izhadell had started the city beside a giant swamp. As Izhadell grew, the outer bounds of the city grew to encompass the muck. Architects and indentured mages had worked to raise much of the occupied areas up out of the wetlands, but that only meant bayous and soggy marshes existed beyond those bounds. Jack leaped down from the road onto the grassy bank lining the swamp.

The swamp had two things going for it: first, Jack knew the further he got into it, the more it would reek because of the Phinoran habit of dumping their refuse there. Unicorns sought magic users by scent, and the pungent aroma would interfere with that. And second, the unicorn would be less inclined to hunt him on the spongy ground. Unicorns were native to flatlands, not swamps.

He was out of range from Zepheus's telepathy, so could no longer rely on the pegasus for help. Jack strode through the grasses, listening to the croaking frogs and the occasional splash of an alligator slicing through the water. As far as critters went, he wasn't too concerned about gators. He'd tangled with worse. He'd take a gator over a chupacabra any day. A single shot from his sixgun would warn off the reptile. That just pissed off a chup.

Jack paused after slogging through the swamp for an estimated five minutes. A bird called a warning, and a sleepy heron swooped overhead, making Jack duck in surprise. He heard the telltale slop-sucking sound of hooves moving through the bog and the frustrated snort of a unicorn. Jack brushed his fingers against his holstered sixgun, hurrying onward.

Then he realized he could hear multiple sets of hooves. Damn, the Tracker and unicorn weren't working alone. This complicated things but didn't make them impossible. It meant he needed to shoot and kill the unicorn, which was a shame. The pegasi harbored a grudge against the unicorns for working for the Confederation. But Jack knew they were pawns as much as he had been. He would rather set the unicorn free if given half a chance.

Sometimes, Jack reasoned in his cold way, death was a sort of freedom. He pulled out his sixgun and sidled up against a cypress, waiting.

Dusk had fallen over the swamp, casting long shadows. His pursuers didn't follow him with mage-lights, which was a pity. It would have made them easy pickings. Jack bided his time, listening to the sucking movement of the unicorn and horses getting ever closer to his position. He hazarded a glance and spotted the shining unicorn's horn.

"May Faedra guide you to Perdition," Jack murmured, then sighted on the unicorn and fired.

The equine made a terrified scream as the bullet struck, the beast's rider lurching off in surprise. Jack couldn't see where he had hit, but he already knew it hadn't been a clean kill shot. Cursing to himself, he aimed again as men and women shouted in confusion. This time he was rewarded as his bullet carved a path squarely through the unicorn's head. It sank to the swamp, twitching as the life fled it.

"Mage!" The scream went up as they realized who was responsible.

Jack turned and bolted. Yeah, maybe he had only pissed them off further by killing the unicorn. But now, he could use his magic unfettered, and that gave him an advantage. Even with…he paused, making a quick mental count of the number of pursuers he had seen when he aimed at the unicorn. Counting the fallen rider, four. Even outnumbered, his magic gave him the upper hand. And no doubt they didn't realize they were on the trail of Wildfire Jack, Scourge of the Untamed Territory.

Oh, but they would regret that.

Jack holstered his sixgun and pulled out his personal poppet as he slogged through the swamp, sending frogs scattering in a hopping frenzy before him. He flipped through the mental catalog of spells he could try. Some of them he hadn't used in so long, they were a risk in this situation. Others required reagents—something he despised carrying around with him. Jack much preferred to get creative with his magic and improvise as needed.

Water breathing was the simplest, but Jack would rather not immerse himself in the swamp and get up close and personal with any inquisitive gators. He could try a speed spell, but it was likely to be fouled because of the terrain. Speed was only good if he didn't lose his boots to the sucking mud. No, maybe the best way was *up*.

Jack shimmied against another cypress, peeling off a strip of bark and touching it against the poppet. The effigy glowed for an instant as his spell charged it, and he hoped he wasn't about to suffer from a serious rebound. The Climber's Grace working required a nut of some sort to symbolize a squirrel or a hair from a cat, but Jack had neither. He chose the bark as a stand-in and reconfigured the spell accordingly.

And damn it, his improvisation failed. As soon as he pocketed the poppet and touched his hand to the tree, intending to scale it, instead the tree *grabbed* him. Jack yelped as he sank into the cypress, panic seizing him.

He couldn't move, and it was the scariest sensation he'd felt since Lamar Gaitwood had trapped him. But this time, it was his own fool doing. Jack forced himself to calm down and focus. He'd gotten himself into this mess, and he for damn sure could get out of it. None of his magic was permanent (unless it was something lethal). As long as he didn't continue to fuel the spell, it would fade in time. Jack could dispel it if only he could get his hands on the poppet, but that was an impossibility in his current state.

Once he was calm, he realized he wasn't trapped. The cypress was a living thing, and his spell had temporarily incorporated him into it. Jack could observe everything outside of it once he steadied enough to know he would (probably) be okay.

The Tracker limped through the swamp, accompanied by three others. With a start of surprise, Jack realized that one of them was none other than Lamar Gaitwood. Two thoughts rushed into the outlaw's mind. First, what in Perdition was Lamar doing searching for him in a swamp? And second, where was Blaise when he needed the Breaker around to drop a Jack-eating tree on top of Lamar?

Lamar turned in a slow circle, a scowl on his handsome face. As he moved, Jack noticed that his old friend was missing an arm. Leave it to Blaise to only wing someone with an entire airship. Jack wished he could grab his sixgun and send Lamar to Perdition. Sadly, cypress trees were piss-poor with sixguns, so instead, he watched in arboreal annoyance.

"He was just here, Commander," the Tracker said, shaking his head. "How does a maverick just disappear in this swamp?"

"This is no *maverick*," Lamar corrected him. The Commander's gaze scanned the area, but it had grown darker still, and Jack was certain Lamar was more likely to be half-jackass than half-cat, thus unable to see in the fading light. "I only know one person who would shoot a unicorn out from under you like that." As he spoke, he stared at the cypress tree.

C'mon, tree, fall on him. You can do it, Jack encouraged his current host. The cypress remained in place, unimpressed.

Lamar and his group cast around for what seemed like an interminable time before giving up and calling it a night. Jack remained within the tree until the first blushing rays of dawn touched the horizon, at which point, the tree expelled him out beside a startled young alligator that launched into the water as soon as he appeared.

Jack winced, slowly rising to his feet. Every muscle in his body felt wooden, and little wonder, since he had been motionless for so many hours. With a soft groan, he took a moment to stretch and limber himself, glad to be in command of his own body again. It wasn't often his spells went wrong, and that had been a humbling experience.

He made his way back to the inn, stopping by the stables first since Zepheus peppered him with questions as soon as he was close enough. The mother hen of a stallion hadn't slept all night, worried for his rider.

<Where were you? You were out of my range.> The pegasus shoved his soft nose into Jack's chest, nearly bowling him over.

Jack stroked the broad, white blaze down Zepheus's face. "Talk is for later. I just spent the night as a tree, and I need a few hours of shut-eye."

<You can't tell me you spent the night as a tree and expect to leave it at that,> Zepheus retorted, lipping at him.

"I can and I will," Jack rumbled. He needed to get some rest for the day before they did anything else. While Jack had discovered the cypress tree *slept* at night (who knew?), he hadn't had the same luxury. But the stallion's concern warmed him, and he left Zepheus contentedly chomping on a bucket of sweet feed. Jack groaned, stretching his arms as he plodded back to the inn. He was looking forward to peeling off his muck-encrusted boots and getting some much-needed sleep.

<What's it like being a tree?> Zepheus asked, glancing over his shoulder at his rider.

Jack grunted. He should never have breathed a word about his predicament last night, but he hadn't been thinking straight. "Trees know better than to ask stupid questions."

<So prickly. You sure you weren't a cactus?>

"I hate you." Jack tapped the stallion with his heels. He ignored Zepheus's amused snort. Truth be told, he was only mildly irritated. He felt better after several hours of sleep, secure in the knowledge he'd successfully evaded Lamar and his crew. Though Lamar sniffing around was bothersome.

After Jack tucked into some grub, they made their way through Izhadell to Doyen Malcolm Wells's residence. As far as things went, this was the straightforward part. In his doe-eyed madness, Jefferson Cole had sent Jack his address since the outlaw was aware of his two-faced ploy. That was helpful, since he had no desire to make inquiries around town that could draw suspicion.

Getting into the residence and securing an audience with him might be another issue, but Jack figured he'd tackle that once they arrived. After all, he was riding a pegasus, if it came down to it. Though Jack was a firm believer in leaving his ace in the hole.

By late afternoon, they found the Wells residence. A towering stone wall and thorny hedge stretching for the sky protected it from curious eyes. Sharply dressed security with rifles manned a shack at the front entry, which made sense as it was the home of a Doyen. Jack rode past, scanning the scene.

<How are we going to get in?> Zepheus asked.

Jack tilted his head, considering. After all the letters, he was certain if he approached the gate and identified himself, he would be allowed entry. But he would rather not have more people aware that Wildfire Jack Dewitt was in Izhadell. "Give me a minute. I'm thinking."

Zepheus started on a lap around the estate, but Jack pulled him up short, eyes narrowed. Something about the ground ahead didn't sit well with him, though he wasn't sure what. He slid out of the saddle, taking a few steps forward and then kneeling. A soft hiss and a pop served as Jack's only warning as a tiny knife shot through the air, grazing his shoulder. Another followed, though Jack had the sense to duck, and it claimed his derby, sending it whirling into the nearby hedge.

Zepheus shrilled a cry, and Jack cursed, spinning to search for attackers. Sixgun in one hand and poppet in the other, he was primed and ready for action.

"Trap," Jack growled, glancing down at the stripe of red across his shoulder. It stung, but it wasn't very deep and could wait. As long as the knife wasn't poisoned.

<Who puts traps around a place like this?>

Someone with secrets to hide. It made a heap of sense to Jack, based on his knowledge of the Doyen. "Someone smart."

<Someone who has people after them,> Zepheus added, nostrils distended as he sucked in stories from the air. <There's a body up ahead.>

"And if you're smart, you'll turn tail and get out of here," a familiar, high-pitched voice rang out.

Jack knew the speaker, and despite the threat, was glad to hear her. "Hello, Flora." He and Zepheus slowly turned until they were facing the short, fierce woman.

She had her pistol in one hand and a knife in the other, as if she hadn't quite decided which form of violence to choose. The half-knocker squinted at him through her glasses, gaze moving from Zepheus's unusual color to Jack. "Do I know you?"

"You do," Jack confirmed. "Can I show you?"

"Nope," Flora denied him with a quick shake of her head. "I'd rather you leave and not come back."

She was touchy about something, and that had Jack's interest piqued. But Flora looked ready to shoot him with little provocation, which normally he could understand, but right now, it would prove inconvenient. <I'll handle it,> Zepheus advised him, arching his neck.

What...? Jack didn't have time to ask. The palomino shook his mane, and with the movement, his wings unfurled into existence. He ruffled them before settling them at his sides like a bird going to roost in a tree. *Gods, I ride such a damn prissy peacock.*

Flora blinked, then holstered her pistol and shoved her knife back into some hidden sheath on her person. "Well, why didn't you just come out and say so?"

"Think I tried that, and you said no," Jack retorted.

"You're different." Flora walked closer, peering up at him. "I mean, you still look like someone I'd have a good time with, if you know what I mean, but you used to be blond, right?"

Jack shrugged. "Still am, under the dye."

Flora winked at him. "Oh yeah, that's smart." Then her countenance shifted, aloof. "What in Perdition are you doing here?"

"I'm here to see Cole."

Flora looked them over. "If you weren't a damned outlaw, I'd send you off and tell you to come back another day, but you can't exactly do that, can you?" Before Jack could speak, she answered herself. "No. Guess we'll have you as a guest, then. C'mon." She turned and waved for them to follow, as if moments earlier she hadn't thought about putting a bullet in Jack's skull or burying a knife in his back.

Zepheus concealed his wings again and plodded after her. Jack pulled a bandanna out and dabbed at the weeping gash on his shoulder. "What's the story with the traps around the perimeter?" he asked, as Flora guided them around various tripwires and pressure pads.

"Everybody needs a hobby," she replied, poking at a bit of soggy ground with a stick. A giant steel trap leaped out, crushing the stick between rusting teeth. "Go forward about ten feet and stop while I reset this."

"This seems a little extreme for a hobby. Even by my standards," Jack remarked, watching as Flora expertly wrestled the steel trap back into position. "But then I imagine politicians aren't popular."

"There are those who would be happy to see Malcolm dead, yes," Flora agreed, her voice shrill with annoyance. "And I do everything in my power to prevent that."

Flora looked like a brisk wind might blow her over, but she had a tenacity that Jack admired. He might not like or approve of her boss, but he could get behind her brand of grit. She finished resetting the trap and ushered them through a side gate. Flora showed them to the stables first.

<Jack,> Zepheus said, tossing his head and flaring his nostrils. <Emrys is here.>

The outlaw looked past the palomino, and sure enough, in a nearby paddock, a familiar black stallion napped beneath a shade tree. Zepheus whinnied, a command and a query. Emrys awoke, rolling to his feet with a snort and shaking his massive body, raising a cloud of dust. The ebony stallion paused at the sight of the palomino, though he whinnied when he caught Zepheus's scent.

"Oh yeah," Flora said, following their interaction. "Blaise's pegasus is here."

"How long?" Jack asked, his voice rasping.

The half-knocker shrugged. "Couple months."

<You should go talk to him,> Zepheus admonished Jack, shoving him with his nose.

Jack grumbled. There was no love lost between him and Emrys. The stallion held a deep grudge about the way Jack had treated Blaise when they had first met. And for reasons beyond that. With resignation, Jack climbed the fence and dropped to the other side, though Emrys laid his ears back when the outlaw approached.

"Emrys, what are you doing here?" Jack asked.

<I came to find someone who would help Blaise. What are *you* doing here?> Emrys snapped his teeth to emphasize his annoyance. <Did you decide to care about someone other than yourself?>

Jack clenched his jaw. There it was. Like Emmaline, after Blaise's capture, the black stallion had also told Jack to go after the Breaker—and he had refused. And what was Jack supposed to say to that? He hadn't come here expressly for Blaise, even though he harbored guilt about the situation.

When he didn't answer, Emrys swished his tail and turned away. <As I thought.>

Jack shook his head. "Yeah, I'm lower than a snake's belly, and I didn't come just for Blaise. I think Em ran off to Phinora and I have to find her."

That made the stallion hesitate. He swung his head around, one dark eye focused on Jack. <And Oby was with her?>

Jack nodded. "Yeah. You haven't seen them, have you?"

Emrys snorted. Before he had vanished from Fortitude, Emrys and Oberidon had been companions. <No, I have not. But I don't leave this place much.>

Just as well. The pegasus needed to keep a low profile for his own safety. Jack understood that. "Thanks anyway."

Emrys bobbed his head, walking over to a tree and leaning his rump against it, wiggling his hindquarters to scratch an itch. <I like Emmaline. I hope you find her.>

Jack turned away, heading to the enormous manor house behind Flora. He was accustomed to the disgustingly elaborate homes of the wealthy from his time as a theurgist and had no need to gawk at the sights. Flora called for a housekeeper to prepare a guest room, then took him into a parlor where a young woman brought in refreshments.

Jack eyed Flora. "I thought you worked for Cole, but this is Wells's home. Doesn't that cause problems?"

"Jefferson doesn't have a residence in Izhadell, so he stays with his *cousin* Malcolm," Flora clarified, testy. "It's perfectly reasonable for me to be here."

They enjoyed some refreshments in silence, waiting for Jefferson Cole or Malcolm Wells or whoever to make an appearance. Jack figured that had to be damned annoying, not knowing who to expect. At least the food was excellent.

A short time later, a staffer slipped into the parlor and murmured something in Flora's ear. The half-knocker looked alarmed, hopping out of her chair in a rush to the door. Before Jack could ask what the matter was, the door opened, and Malcolm Wells staggered in.

The first thing Jack noticed was the eerie brightness in his eyes—not the keen look he would have expected, but the glassy expression that often accompanied fever. His hair was damp and matted, too. Malcolm looked around the room, as if he was having a hard time focusing.

"Malcolm!" Flora snapped at him, grabbing his arm. "You don't look well. You need—"

"I need to talk to Jack." Malcolm's unfocused gaze finally found him. "Emrys told me he had come at last." His voice quivered, proof that he was unwell, but it held an edge of manic hope.

"Talk when you feel better." Flora's tone had a veneer of desperation. Jack narrowed his eyes. She was hiding something. What was it with this cursed politician and his penchant for concealing things?

Malcolm glanced in her direction, shaking his head. "My chair, Flora." He lurched over to an armchair, shivering all the while. He sank into it, his breath shallow. Flora stood nearby, furious, but apparently unwilling to go against his wishes. The Doyen opened his mouth to speak, but no words came. Instead, his head lolled to the side, and he went limp.

"Mal!" Flora cried, shaking his arm.

Jack sighed. It would be just his luck that Wells was going to die in front of him from a pox or something, before the man could be useful. "What in Faedra's name is wrong with him?"

Flora gritted her teeth. "That's not for me to say." She rubbed the side of her face, looking much older than she was, though Jack didn't rightly know how old that was. "When he's up to taking visitors, you can speak to him. But not until then."

Jack narrowed his eyes. He needed to get on Emmaline's trail. And figure out how to get Blaise out of that cursed Cit. "I don't have time to waste."

"And I'm out of patience for arguing with outlaws," Flora snarled. "You're a guest here for now, but not if you press your luck."

Jack crossed his arms, though she had a point. He aimed a finger at her. "I want to speak to him as soon as he's awake."

"You'll speak to him when I say you can." Flora turned her back on him, and that was that.

CHAPTER EIGHT

Dodgeball

Blaise

The stone wall of the cell was cool against Blaise's cheek. He sat on the rough stone bench, leaning against the wall with his eyes half-lidded. He was always tired, always hungry. His captors in the Golden Citadel did the bare minimum to ensure his continued existence, and little beyond that.

A tear trailed down his cheek, forging a path through the grime on his face. Blaise couldn't remember the last time he had felt clean. It probably aligned with the last time he hadn't been scared. Or hadn't felt hopeless. He scrubbed away the tear with the back of his hand, wincing as the movement aggravated the blisters on his wrist. His only solace was that within the cell, his captors removed the salt-iron shackles. There was no need when the walls surrounding him were reinforced with the metal. His proximity to the salt-iron caused a chronic throbbing at the base of his skull and soured his stomach so that even the limited food they offered him didn't sit well.

He missed his life. He missed Emrys and would have given anything in that moment to fly away on the stallion's back. Blaise missed his friends in Itude. He missed his family. And, gods help him, because it was such a *complicated* thing, but he missed Jefferson, even though he had visited recently. Magic rose as his anguish grew, and Blaise curled his fists at his side.

The harsh scrape of metal and wood announced he wasn't going to be alone much longer. He jerked upright, pulse racing. A silhouette darkened the doorway, and a deep laugh greeted him.

Oh no. Blaise had no love for this guard. None of the men and women who staffed the Cit were kind to him, but Heathcliff took it to another level. He fancied himself a mage-trainer, coaxing his charges to learn new tricks with their power. His practices were anything but gentle.

"Breaker, time to put you through your paces."

Blaise huffed out an unhappy breath, his eyes flicking to the damaged walls of his cell. Between a strange potion the guards plied him with and his constant state of unease, his control had become erratic, and cracks lined the walls, proof that he was just as dangerous as everyone said. He didn't want to go with this man, but by the same token it wasn't something he could avoid.

Slowly, his muscles complaining at the effort, he rose from the bench. He shuffled into the corridor, wincing at the bright mage-lights that lined its length. Heathcliff led him to the recreation yard, a salt-iron enclosed dirt lot that other imprisoned mages were allowed to use to stretch their legs and take in fresh air, enjoying a few moments of relief. Blaise wasn't afforded such liberties.

"Stand in the middle," Heathcliff directed.

Blaise licked his lips nervously, noticing the guard stood beside a ramshackle pile of stones and broken bricks. He moved to obey, his empty stomach lurching as Heathcliff picked up one of the stones, tossing it from one hand to the other.

"You familiar with dodgeball, Breaker?"

Blaise's mouth went dry, panic rising. He knew the childhood game. Had even played it a few times before he had been shunned for his magic. It was a game he'd never been good at, much too graceless and clumsy.

Heathcliff leered. "I see you are." He glanced at the smooth stone in his hand. "We're going to do something similar, except if this rock hits you, you'd better break it." He narrowed his eyes. "Or it's going to *hurt.*"

And then without so much as a warning, Heathcliff began to hurl the stones and chunks of brick at him. Blaise avoided the first few, but then one struck his leg, forcing him to his knees. He couldn't rise, not with the guard throwing more at him, all the while screaming at him to get up.

I'm going to die here. Hopelessness warred with panic for a few heartbeats but was quickly replaced by growing fury. Anger because he didn't deserve this. No one deserved this, no matter what they had done. *This is not going to be my end.*

A nub of brick grazed his cheek. Blaise yelped, raising a hand to probe the fresh wound. Blood slicked his fingers, but Heathcliff didn't offer him even a moment of peace to recover. Another brick flew, this one striking his shoulder.

His magic boiled, as angry as a disturbed hive of bees, demanding to be used. Blaise didn't understand what Heathcliff expected of him. He missed Vixen's lessons and the way she had always helped him figure out what to do. This...this was brutality disguised as education.

A flat, grey stone whistled toward him. Blaise saw it coming, and time seemed to slow, his world narrowing to only him and impending injury. It was going to hit his face, and it was going to *hurt*.

Blaise threw up a hand as a shield, preferring to break his fingers than lose an eye. He felt the itch of his magic swarming across his palm, coating his skin. His mind jogged backwards, to a time when he had been surrounded by people who had believed in him. Vixen, and her unrelenting assurance that he could do anything with his magic. Emrys, with his steady faith in his rider. And Jefferson, so certain that Blaise was all that had stood between the Confederation and the lives of thousands in the Untamed Territory.

Sweat beaded his brow. A prisoner he may be, but he didn't have to be a *victim*. Blaise gathered his magic, concentrating it in his raised hand. He didn't stop there, pushing it out. Other mages could build constructs with their magic—after all, that was what the cage of a Trapper was. Within the confines of the Cit, he'd had ample time to think about that. Blaise grunted with the exertion of forcing his magic out into a brief, shimmering shield reminiscent of a soap bubble. Then he closed his eyes, fearing the worst.

The stone never struck his flesh. He heard something that reminded him of the sound of gravel being smashed beneath strong hooves. He flinched, still expecting imminent impact.

Heathcliff whistled, followed by a colorful curse. Blaise uncurled from his defensive position, breathing a sigh of relief that the guard had eased his assault. Heathcliff's dark eyes gleamed with malevolent pride. "You did it, Breaker. I didn't think you would, but you *actually* did it. I might be able to forge you into a weapon after all."

Blaise swallowed, following the guard's gaze. A fine spray of gravel littered the ground nearby. No, not gravel, he realized. It was all that remained of the stone Heathcliff had hurled at him. His magical shield had worked.

CHAPTER NINE

Honor, of a Sort

Malcolm

Malcolm huddled in a chair by the fire, a thick blanket covering his lap and a cup of warm tea with honey close at hand. Marta, his cook, checked on him frequently, a frown creasing her face. Flora came and went, and once Malcolm tried to ask her about the dream where a man with Wildfire Jack's voice stood in the parlor. She told him to go to sleep.

He didn't know what illness gripped him, but he awoke with a fever and chills. Marta insisted on going for a skilled Healer, but Malcolm put his foot down. He feared a Healer would discover the tattoo, and then it would all have been for nothing. He didn't even allow his own staff Healer, Agnes, to check on him because out of all his staff, only Flora knew what he'd done. He couldn't trust anyone else with the dangerous choice he'd made.

So he sat in his chair, shivering and going through the mail that he hadn't attended to yet. He hoped Flora would return soon so he could ask what she knew about the effects of the tattoo. Perhaps a mild illness was normal. He had entertained the idea of sending a query to Seward, but that would have been a little too bold.

Malcolm heard a commotion outside the door. It had to be Flora. He set aside the correspondence he had been reading, so tired it was hard to keep his eyes open. He had thought the tattoo would hurt after it was applied, but the sudden illness outweighed whatever discomfort he'd expected. *Stay awake.* Malcolm took a sip of tea, wishing Flora would hurry.

The door to his study opened, and Flora traipsed in, followed by someone taller. Malcolm blinked as the stranger took off their hat, revealing a vaguely familiar face.

"Wells," the stranger's deep voice growled. The hair color didn't match, but he would recognize Wildfire Jack's sixgun-serious tone anywhere.

"Jack?" Malcolm asked, blinking in confusion. "You look different."

"You're not the only one in this room who can change their looks," the outlaw pointed out.

"He demanded to see you," Flora said with a sigh.

"Been waiting two days to talk to you. You sleep more than a bear in winter."

Malcolm shivered. Two days? He was now certain that Jack had tried to speak to him before he had gone to sleep—no, not sleep. He looked to Flora. "What happened to me? Oh no. I missed the vote." Malcolm raised a trembling hand to scrub at his face, mindful of Blaise's fate.

She crossed her arms. "I don't think the vote matters worth a hill of beans right now."

Jack glanced between the pair of them, suspicious. "What did I walk into?"

Flora huffed, jerking a thumb at Malcolm. "I'll tell you to save him some breath. He got a geasa tattoo to bind him to Blaise."

Malcolm's eyes widened as she spoke the words. He was too slow and weak to ask her to call them back. Jack's expression frosted over, and he turned to Malcolm with cold, calculating eyes. As if he were deciding exactly how he wanted to kill the man before him.

"Now, why would you go and do a thing like that?" Jack's voice was as dangerous as the promise of distant thunder.

Flora realized her tactical error and had her knives in hand. "Don't you *dare* threaten him."

Their threats were exhausting. Malcolm wished he had just stayed asleep. But it was important that Jack understand why he had done it—because even with Flora's protection, Malcolm didn't think he stood much chance against Wildfire Jack if he were truly angry. "Let me explain. *Please.* Flora, put your blades away."

"I'll only put them away if he agrees to not murder you."

Jack and Flora glared at one another.

Malcolm sighed. "I did it out of love, Jack."

Those words shook the outlaw, and he broke the staring contest to round on Malcolm instead. "Don't make excuses about *love* when you chose the route that bends someone to *your* will. To manipulate them."

Malcolm glanced down at his hands, fumbling with them beneath the blanket. "What else could I do? You wouldn't come or answer my letters. And I…" He bit his bottom lip, uncertain how to explain the sickening conclusion he had reached. Maybe it *was* greedy and manipulative to bind Blaise to him so no one else could have him. "I didn't see another way."

"There has to be another way." Jack's voice dripped with loathing. Of those in the room, Jack knew the most about the subject.

"That ship has sailed," Flora said. "Can't undo what he's done."

The outlaw looked Malcolm up and down. "I know exactly how to undo it."

If Malcolm hadn't already been chilled, Jack's brutal assessment would have done it. He was too tired for this. "Did you come all this way to kill me? That seems out of character, even for you."

Jack tilted his head, eyes flinty. "No, but I'm not one to take options off the table."

He talked big, but Malcolm suspected Jack had come for a purpose. Other than Blaise, at that. Even though the outlaw owed the young man so much. He set that frustrating thought aside for the time being. "Why are you here?"

Jack's blue eyes settled on him, cold as ice. "I'm looking for my daughter."

That caught Flora's attention, too. "What? Was she taken?"

The outlaw shook his head. "No. She ran off."

Ran away, more like. Malcolm had only been around Emmaline a few times in the bakery, but he knew Blaise thought well of her. They had become friends, so much so that Blaise was determined to get her back when Lamar's force kidnapped her and the other mages. Despite that, something didn't add up…

"And why did you come to me?"

Jack's jaw tightened. "Because she found the letters you sent me, asking for help."

Ah. That made more sense. "I'm sorry, but we haven't seen her." Though, just to be sure, Malcolm glanced at Flora. It was something she would be aware of.

She shook her head. "I'll keep an ear out."

That took some of the wind out of Jack's sails. He seemed to deflate, as if he had been hoping they had concealed his daughter somewhere on the estate. "I'd appreciate that."

Well, at least he was back to being decent to Flora. *Progress.* "Yes, we'll do anything we can to help you find her."

That earned him a suspicious look. "Would you?"

Malcolm rubbed his cheek. "Whatever you may think of me, I don't wish you or your child ill."

Jack crossed his arms, a mixture of relief and annoyance washing across his face. Malcolm assumed the outlaw had bridled against coming to ask for help at the doorstep of a Doyen of the Salt-Iron Confederation. Jack shifted his weight from one foot to the other, but only offered a slight nod in response.

Malcolm picked up his tea and sipped it, appreciative of the relief it brought. "I doubt I can do much in my current state, but we will help you."

"Yeah, about your current state," the outlaw said, his sharp gaze assessing Malcolm as if he were a practice target. "I'd check into it fast, if I were you."

"Why is that?" Malcolm asked.

Jack gestured to him. "I'm no Healer nor doctor, but just from what I know of history, seems to me like you have the symptoms of Manifestation Illness."

What? "That can't be right." Malcolm traded looks with Flora. Manifestation Illness was the disease that had spawned the first mages two hundred years prior. *How would I have contracted that?*

She patted his hand. "I'll look into it, Mal. You're going to be fine."

Jack snorted, as if he didn't quite believe that. Malcolm opened his mouth to say something, but darkness swam before his eyes and claimed him.

———

Jack

FLORA CURSED AS WELLS LOST CONSCIOUSNESS, MOVING TO SHIFT HIM SO he didn't fall out of the chair. She brushed the back of her hand against his forehead. "What makes you think it's Manifestation Illness?"

Jack glanced away. "Stories from when I was a theurgist."

The half-knocker gave him a cutting look. "Got any info you can give me? It's kind of important."

The outlaw shook his head. "I have no love for that man, but I won't feed you some old wives' tales. No, if I were you, I'd snoop around the source." When she made a *go on* gesture, he suggested, "Ask an alchemist."

Flora considered it, then nodded. "Not a bad idea. I'll do that tonight."

She halted their conversation, taking it upon herself to get the ill Doyen to his bed. Jack was rather impressed that she was ready to carry

Wells there all by herself. It was a bit like watching an ant carry something ten times its size. The outlaw helped her with the burden once she got Malcolm into the hallway, figuring it would reflect rather poorly on him if he followed in the wake of the tiny woman carrying around a grown man.

Flora got Malcolm settled on his bed and then turned back to Jack. "And what are you gonna do?"

"Search for my daughter."

Flora frowned. "So, I know you have the whole disguise thing going on, but you're still a wanted man."

"Don't care. I can't stay here sitting on my thumbs. I have to *do* something." Truth be told, he cared. Jack was aware that he wasn't invulnerable, and his magic and savvy wouldn't always save him. But this was his *child*, and she was all that he had left in the world to prove he was worth a damn.

Flora glanced at her boss tucked beneath the covers. "Why didn't you answer his letters?"

Jack frowned at her swift change of topic. "What does that have to do with—?"

"Answer the question." Her voice was as sharp and commanding as the crack of a whip.

Few people could get away with talking to Jack like that. Flora was one of them. He had seen what she was capable of firsthand. And she was stressed and upset about someone she cared about. Jack could relate. "Coming to Izhadell is an invitation to the gallows for someone like me."

"You should have given him the courtesy of a reply," Flora retorted. "And to be frank, your answer is dragonshit. You're here *now*."

Jack snorted. "I'm the first to admit I'm a damn hypocrite. But I have good reason."

The half-knocker pointed an index finger up at him. "Blaise gave up everything for you. And then you didn't lift a finger to help him."

Jack bristled at that. He wanted to snarl at Flora that she didn't understand. How dare she judge him? But he couldn't because he felt exactly the same. His shoulders rose in agitation, and his eyes narrowed. "Again, what does *that* have to do with *this*?" He waved a hand at Malcolm's prone form.

"Mal thought he was the only one who cared about Blaise. And he's probably right." Flora leaned against the foot of the bed. "The Council has been debating what they're going to do to your *friend*."

"I know that," Jack growled. He had heard that much through his intelligence channels. Not a blamed thing he could do about it.

"*They* decided to bind him. It wasn't all Mal coming up with the idea on his own."

Jack stilled at that. He had tried not to think about what was happening to Blaise behind the walls of the Golden Citadel. The Breaker was at the tail-end of the age where they could—and would—bend a young mage to the will of the Confederation. He hissed out a breath, staving off old memories of the screams he had heard from the corridor that led to the cells of the older mages. Jack had been one of the lucky ones. He had been young when the Confederation molded him into a theurgist.

"So don't hold it against him. He really saw no other choice. It was this or allow Blaise to bow to a new master in a few days." Flora turned away, scrubbing a hand over her face. She offered Jack a sympathetic look as she changed the subject again. "I meant what I said. If I hear anything about your daughter, I'll let you know. Come back here tonight. I'm sure he'd want you to be welcome." She nodded her head toward Malcolm.

Jack wanted to snarl and deny the hospitality just because he liked to be contrary most of the time, and he didn't like Malcolm Wells and whatever game he was playing with Blaise. But by the same token, he couldn't afford to be choosy. Wells had as much to hide as he did, so perhaps it was an ideal place to go to ground. "Much obliged. There a good angle for a pegasus to come in from after dark? Some way that the griffin riders won't see?"

Flora pursed her lips, thoughtful. "The griffin riders have been out of Phinora for a couple months now. Ever since Fort Courage, they've been deployed to the borders."

"That so?" Jack murmured. It sounded right. They had seen griffin riders when they had gone through Argor but couldn't recall spotting any since. That was odd. "They change protocol on that?"

Flora shrugged. "I don't know. I heard there was trouble around the Gutter, so they might send more to keep tabs. Don't suppose you'd know anything about that?"

Ah-ha. Jack had seen no griffin riders around the mine, but the eastern Confederation border was massive, and the few pegasi sentries left in Fortitude had reported seeing them occasionally. It pleased him to know that the trouble he had caused the mining companies bore fruit.

"I wouldn't know a thing," he said with a wink.

Flora laughed because she liked to cause trouble as much as he did. "If you approach from the north and fly over the fence, you should be able to come in unseen. I'll even do you a favor and disarm the traps I have there."

Jack touched the brim of his hat. "Kind of you." Then he paused, his gaze back on the Doyen's prone form. "You believe him? About his reason for doin' it?"

Flora ran a hand through one side of her pink hair. "Yeah. I don't understand it, but he has a good heart."

The outlaw scrunched his nose. He wouldn't go that far, but if the gritty half-knocker thought the story had a grain of truth, it probably did. Jack crossed his arms, considering. "I could stick around a couple hours before I head out on my search. If you need someone to play nanny."

"He's a very sick man, not an infant."

"I said what I said. And you're gonna be gone, too, so the way I see it you won't mind him having some extra protection."

Flora frowned. "A few minutes ago, you were threatening to kill him. That doesn't scream *trustworthy* to me."

Jack shrugged. "Got a better option?"

She didn't, and they both knew it. "We just can't let word get out about what Mal did."

Jack smirked. As much as he'd love for word to get out to see the politician squirm, he knew it meant things would go south for Blaise, fast. "On my honor as an outlaw mage."

She quirked a brow. "You have honor?"

"Of a sort."

CHAPTER TEN

Bone to Bone, Flesh to Flesh

Jack

Jack hadn't been forthright about his reasoning to stay behind and watch over the sick man. Once Flora left, he made it his business to go through the contents of the bedroom—books atop the short bookcase near the door, a notebook temptingly left on the dresser, and all the drawers. To his disappointment, nothing of interest presented itself.

"You're no blasted choir boy," Jack muttered to Malcolm. The Doyen didn't so much as twitch an eyelid at his comment. If not for the gentle rise and fall of his chest, the outlaw would have thought him dead. His skin was as pale as porcelain, his face glistening with sweat.

It was going to be damned problematic if the two-faced Doyen up and died before he could use his resources to help Jack free Blaise. Because even though he had been careful not to mention it in the earlier conversation, that remained one of his goals. Jack was skilled, but this was the Golden Citadel he was going up against. He needed any advantage he could get.

He drummed his fingers against the wood of the dresser. "Hmm." Jack was no Healer, but his magic was more flexible than most. He thought back to the time Emmaline had kept him from Perdition's gates with her magic, a plan coming to mind. It was a modification to another spell he had cast before—a working to keep infection of a wound at bay until a Healer tended to it. The more Jack thought about it, the more it seemed worthwhile.

Jack left to grab the items he needed, sneaking back into the master bedroom with no one any the wiser since his guest room was down the hall. He twisted a rudimentary poppet together—not his best work, but an effigy didn't have to be pretty to be effective. Strands of hair clung to a brush on the dresser, but since Jack had no way to confirm it belonged to the Doyen, he went straight to the source and plucked three hairs from Malcolm's head. He enjoyed pulling the frustrating peacock's hair out. He was disappointed Wells didn't so much as stir.

After securing the hairs to the poppet, Jack tightened his hand around the tiny form and called on his magic to activate it. He felt the soft pulse of power as the connection formed between Wells and the doll. Jack pulled a chair up beside the bed and plopped down. His mentor at the Cit had excelled at using magic to impact the human body, though mostly for ill. But she had ingrained in him the law of opposites—just as a working could rot a man's gut, so too could it cleanse. Or at the very least, hold off the rot.

Too bad Emmaline wasn't here. She was a natural at it. Jack shook away the thought. He focused on crafting the words for the charm. The outlaw preferred spells that didn't require chanting or reagents, but sometimes it was necessary. For a charm like this, the words held as much power as his intention. He was no poet or bard, but at least no one was around to judge his performance.

Jack cradled the figure in his hands. "Bone to bone, flesh to flesh. Blood to blood, marrow to marrow. Faedra, walk this one away from Perdition's gate."

The poppet looked the same as it had, though Jack's magical sense assured him that something was happening. If someone had asked him to explain, he wouldn't be able to. It was like the pressure in the air before a rainstorm, a rising tide of power. Jack tucked the poppet into his coat. Flora would probably lose her mind with rage if she found out he could hex her boss. Jack figured it was solid insurance to have on his side.

With the spell complete, the outlaw was restless. Since the manipulative peacock seemed stable, he decided the best recipe was to walk around the grounds, so Jack headed out to the barn. Zepheus grazed beside Emrys in the paddock. They raised their heads at his approach, and Emrys broke away first, approaching him with ground-eating strides. He pulled up short, just in front of the outlaw, tossing his head.

<What's wrong with Jefferson? Something is wrong.> The stallion's mental tone was ripe with worry, his eyes white-rimmed.

The stallion's use of the alter ego's name made Jack blink. It was odd for a pegasus to be concerned for anyone besides their rider. Zepheus had a soft spot for Emmaline, and that itself was unusual. "He's sick."

Emrys pranced in place, unsettled. <I've seen sick humans. I have brushed against their minds. Something is *wrong*.>

Jack squinted at the black pegasus, then turned to look at Zepheus as the palomino plodded over. "Zeph?"

<I don't know the man's mind enough to weigh in. But Emrys has been here for several weeks, and while Wells is not his rider, they have formed an alliance.> Zepheus said all of this privately to Jack, so that Emrys wouldn't catch his mental advice.

An alliance. Jack bet Emrys didn't know about the stunt the politician had pulled. And as Blaise's pegasus, he had a right to know. He laid a hand on Emrys's neck, which might invite snapping teeth if he wasn't careful. But the stallion was out of sorts, seeking comfort, and didn't fight it. "There's something you need to know." Jack explained the politician's ploy.

When he finished, Emrys flicked his ears, as if processing the information. Finally, he bobbed his great head, reaching a conclusion. <I approve.>

Of all the things Jack thought the stallion would say or do, that wasn't it. "*What?*"

<I understand what he's doing and why.>

Jack scratched his head because he sure didn't. All he saw was greed and abuse of power. "How do you see it?"

Zepheus traded a knowing look with Emrys, bobbing his head as if he had drawn the same conclusion.

<You see it as something like the relationship between a spirit-broken nag and an unkind master. But it is not that. No, he is approaching it like a pegasus and rider. A partnership.> Emrys sounded certain.

Jack frowned, not agreeing with any of that. "But Blaise is being exploited. He doesn't have a say."

Emrys shook his ample mane. <You're wrong. He already made a choice in his heart.>

For the Breaker's sake, Jack hoped Emrys was right. But that wasn't something to worry about, not now. He had done his due diligence. The outlaw turned to Zepheus. "Be ready. As soon as Flora gets back, we're going to start the search for Em."

CHAPTER ELEVEN

Just a Dream

Jefferson

Jefferson was no stranger to this dream.

The sun warmed his back as he stood on the outskirts of Fortitude. Or perhaps it was Itude, before the assault. The small town that stretched before him looked as empty as a ghost town, but curiously, the buildings appeared whole, which shouldn't have been the case. He strolled up the street, enjoying the brisk air.

Every building was just as he remembered it from his last visit, their façades unscarred by fire and battle. The Broken Horn Saloon stood on one side of the town square, welcoming anyone in need of a drink. The Jitterbug Diner sat beside the cheerful yellow bakery. Jefferson's breath caught at the sight of the bakery.

He walked up the street to the building, his strides long and purposeful. The bakery drew him like a magnet, his first connection to Blaise. Jefferson knew that if he walked into the bakery, he would find the young mage, and at least in his dreams, everything in their world would be *right*.

Jefferson trotted up the steps and tugged open the door. The hinges creaked, announcing his arrival. As expected, Blaise stood in the middle of the bakery, but something was off. Legs braced, arms curled into a protective stance as he glanced around with uncertainty. Blaise was never uncertain in the bakery. It was his domain, one of the few places he seemed sure of himself. This wasn't how Jefferson's dream went at all. "Blaise?"

The Breaker turned at his voice, but otherwise seemed rooted in place. "I was in a nightmare…" He swallowed as his words trailed off, and the fear in his eyes made Jefferson want to rush over, but he knew that would be the wrong move. As hard as it was, he waited at the threshold while Blaise gathered his thoughts. "I can't sleep. And when I *do* sleep, it's always the same nightmare. It's never…" He shook his head and sank down to his knees, as if the effort to finish the sentence was overwhelming.

Jefferson stared at him. This Blaise before him wasn't the one who usually existed in his dreams. This one had the hard edge of panic so prevalent in Jefferson's recent visits with the younger man. Had that bled into Jefferson's subconscious and become a part of his dreams? Or was something else going on here?

Blaise had never spoken to him about a lack of sleep—or anything else about the treatment he received. Jefferson leaned against the door-frame, thinking. What had he been doing before he fell asleep? Wait. He hadn't gone to sleep. He'd been talking to Jack and Flora.

What is going on? Jefferson swallowed. He recalled he had been ill but determined to speak with the outlaw. And then he remembered darkness overtaking him.

"Jefferson?" Blaise's voice was little more than a whisper.

"Sorry," Jefferson murmured. "I'm here."

"You're never in my nightmares." Blaise looked up at him, trembling.

But you're always in my dreams. Jefferson nodded. "This isn't a nightmare." At least he hoped it wasn't. He didn't know what it was or what was going on. "Mind if I come in?"

"I can't stop you."

Jefferson's stomach sank at Blaise's words. It seemed impossible, but he was becoming more certain by the moment that the real Blaise had bled into his dream. He took a step closer. "I'm not like that. I won't ever force anything with you." *Liar. You're bound to him with a—oh no, is that what's doing this?*

Ignorant of Jefferson's thoughts, Blaise blinked at him. "You can come in." He rose from the floor, reaching up to grab the counter to get to his feet, as if he didn't have the strength to do it otherwise.

As the Breaker rose, Jefferson got a better look at his condition. He was almost skeletal, arms spindly and cheeks sunken. Jefferson came closer and saw a crescent-shaped gash on the mage's cheek, surrounded by bruising. "Who did this to you?"

Blaise seemed to shrink into himself. "You can't do anything about it."

"I *am* doing something about it," Jefferson retorted with such ferocity that Blaise took a step back. He swallowed, lowering his voice. "I am."

The mage narrowed his eyes, suspicious. "Wait." Blaise closed the distance between them, surprising Jefferson by putting a hand on his arm, just below the fresh tattoo. The Breaker's fingers were like ice, just as they had been at their last visit. Jefferson felt the too-real tingle of magic against his skin. "What is this?"

"It's me."

Blaise stared at him, tears welling in the corners of his blue eyes. "I don't understand."

"I don't either. Not yet," Jefferson admitted. He would have to tell Blaise about the tattoo later. But not until he had figured out what was going on with this. "But it's *me*. Really."

"And we're in Itude?" Blaise glanced out the window, brow crinkling in confusion. "But the town..."

He didn't finish, but Jefferson knew. The last time Blaise had seen it, the town had been in ruins. "Fortitude. Your friends renamed it Fortitude after the battle." Jefferson licked his lips, uncertain. "I think it's just a dream, though."

Blaise's shoulders drooped. "Is it sad that I wish it were real?"

"No, not at all," Jefferson said. "You were happy here." Maybe it was the first place Blaise had been truly happy before everything had gone wrong.

Blaise nodded. "I was." Then his expression hardened.

"What's wrong?"

"I don't get to be that anymore. Happy."

Jefferson shook his head. "That's untrue. It may be a dream, but we're in *your* bakery. You can be happy here."

Blaise worried at his bottom lip. "It's just a dream. It doesn't help anything."

"I disagree. You spoke of nightmares. I think a pleasant dream is what you need." Jefferson gestured around them. "Tell me, if you could do anything right now in this dream, what would you do?"

The Breaker stared at him, then the corners of his mouth curled into the slightest of smiles. "You know what I would do."

Yes, Jefferson did. It was a relief to see any cheer on Blaise's face. Although it wouldn't have been Jefferson's choice of activities, he knew exactly what would bring Blaise the happiness he deserved. "I suppose I'm in the mood for dessert. So, tell me, cake or cookies?"

Blaise pulled out a set of mixing bowls, and the joy that replaced his earlier fear was all the reward Jefferson needed. "Why not both?"

"Both is good," Jefferson agreed. "I'll get the flour and you can tell me how to help."

As far as fever dreams went, it wasn't what Jefferson had expected. But he didn't mind it. Not one bit. And for the record, Blaise's dream cookies were every bit as good as the real thing.

Flora

MALCOLM WAS A ONE-TRACK-MINDED IDIOT SOMETIMES. FLORA SIGHED AS she skulked to the perimeter of the Arboretum. She considered the barbed wire lining the fence again. The half-knocker had never given much thought to the alchemists before and hadn't cared to learn about them. She knew they brewed some wicked potions besides those she found helpful in her line of work.

But now, she realized their plight was the same as the theurgists. If Malcolm found out, he would be furious and would no doubt plot ways to improve their conditions, as well.

She snorted at that. He had a good heart but was always busy thinking of things from a political angle. The problem was, he hadn't learned yet that he *couldn't* save the world. But he sure was going to try. Flora decided to keep the knowledge of the alchemists to herself, at least for now.

While they had designed the perimeter to keep the curious out, Flora wasn't most people. She had enough knocker blood in her to make it a non-issue. Flora sidled up against the wall, then closed her eyes as she concentrated on finding her attuned metal. Like full-blooded knockers who had an affinity for specific metals or precious stones, Flora could always locate hers. Then it was simply a matter of locking on and using her magic to pull herself to it. Malcolm was aware of her ability, but he didn't know what her metal was. No one did, and that was how Flora liked it.

If anyone learned salt-iron was her metal, she would be eyeball-deep in trouble. The Confederation would want to use her, as surely as they used the mages. Her fellow knockers would hate her because like all magical creatures, they despised the stuff. Flora didn't understand why she not only tolerated it but could *locate* it. Probably thanks to her human mother. But it was a dangerous ability to be graced with.

The Arboretum had little salt-iron, unlike the Golden Citadel. She got in and out of there easily and had done so many times. Hadn't told Malcolm about that either, but she liked Blaise and had checked on him. She felt sorry for the Breaker. No one deserved what he was going through. Flora thought Malcolm was out of his mind to be so obsessed with the younger man, but she would go along with his insane plans because Blaise deserved happiness and freedom. Not abuse.

There. It took some concentration, but she finally homed in on the bit of salt-iron within the Arboretum. Flora focused on it and hopped into the air, her magic activating with the movement. There was a moment of disorientation as the world grew dark and then brightened, and then Flora found herself by her target. And she wasn't alone this time.

The other person in the room threw something at Flora, a glass vial that smashed to bits at her feet. The contents hissed against the floor, rising in a thin veil of orange mist. Flora held her breath, something that she could do for a very long time thanks to her knocker heritage. But whatever the potion was didn't need to be inhaled. She felt her motions slowing even as she tried to go for her blades. *Oh schist!*

"Who are *you?*" the woman demanded, her voice equal parts afraid and angry. Maybe closer to angry, Flora reflected.

Actions spoke louder than words, though. The half-knocker dropped into a crouch—*slowly*, painfully slowly. Under the sway of whatever that concoction was, her natural speed had been banished. A herd of turtles could probably move faster than her now.

Flora didn't like losing the upper hand. At long last, her fingers tightened around the hilt of her knives, and she brought them out, though the woman didn't seem the least bit impressed. With the speed Flora was moving, all she had to do was take a step to the left to easily avoid any threat.

This is the worst. Flora glowered at the woman.

"Let me ask you again," the alchemist hissed. "Who are you?"

Flora cocked her head, assessing the situation. If not for that annoying bit of alchemy, she would have found a way to remove the woman from the equation. But that wasn't a possibility until the potion wore off or she was given a counter. She was in one dill of a pickle.

Sometimes she had to cut her losses. Fighting wasn't going to do her any favors here. "Name's Flora. I'd offer you my hand, but it would take five minutes to shake." She was glad the potion didn't seem to have an impact on her mouth, aside from a strange dryness that attacked her tongue. "And you are?"

"Wondering what you're doing in the Arboretum," the woman replied, hands on her hips. "Especially here." She gestured to the charred interior of the building where they stood.

To be fair, Flora had the same questions for the alchemist. Or at least, why was she in the burned-out building? Flora had thought it might be a safe place to appear, but clearly, that wasn't the case. "I'm here on business." It wasn't a lie. Not fully, anyway.

The woman raised her brows, skeptical. "I'm sure the gate guards appreciate you popping on by them."

Maybe it was a threat, but the flippant way the alchemist said the words made Flora think otherwise. "Oh, you know, I'm just making life easier on them."

"I'll bet you are," the alchemist replied. She reached into a hip bag, pulling out a blue vial. "I have the antidote for that potion, so long as you don't intend to gut me."

"I'll behave," Flora promised. "You can't blame me for taking offense when you throw a potion at me."

"I stand by what I did," the woman said, uncorking the blue vial and sprinkling the contents over Flora. Whatever it was, it dried almost the instant it touched her rough skin. But it did the job, breaking her free from the effects of the first potion. Flora wiggled her fingers with greater appreciation as the alchemist asked, "Something I can help you with?"

"Actually, yes." Flora wasn't one to look a gift horse in the mouth—or gift alchemist. "You know anything about the Ink used for the geasa?"

The alchemist went still. "What about it?" Then she narrowed her eyes, suspicious. "Wait. One of our Inkwells is missing. A very specific one." Something dangerous flickered in her eyes. "Would you know anything about that?"

So they had discovered Flora's theft. Not surprising. Flora widened her eyes, affecting a look of innocence. "Oh, that's awful. Who would do something like that?"

"Who, indeed?" the alchemist murmured. She paced the length of the room, pausing by one of the charred stone walls. "I'll answer your question if you do something for me."

Lovely. Flora didn't want it to come down to barter, but sometimes that was how life worked. "I won't kill anyone." No, she only did that for Malcolm. And even he didn't know about it most of the time.

The alchemist shook her head. "Nothing like that, I hope." Her expression turned hungry. "It's my family. They've kept me apart from them. I haven't heard..." She swallowed. "I need to know if they're okay. And you seem to be uniquely skilled to discover that."

Well, she was right about that. "I'll try. Who am I looking for?"

The woman hesitated, walking to the door and peering out. When she was satisfied, she turned back to Flora. "Daniel Hawthorne and my children, Lucienne and Brody."

Flora blinked. Hawthorne? It couldn't be a coincidence. She knew for a fact Blaise's mother was an alchemist... "Wait. Are you Marian Hawthorne?"

The alchemist tensed. "And if I am?"

Flora wasn't sure if she should squeal with glee at her good fortune or curse. Marian hadn't mentioned a thing about Blaise, and Flora wasn't sure what that meant for the situation. "I know your son."

Marian's face registered confusion. "Brody?"

"Blaise."

The alchemist took a step forward, her hands balled into fists. "Are *you* among those responsible for what's happened to him?"

Flora's eyes flicked as a new vial appeared in the alchemist's palm, lifting her hands in a gesture of placation. "*No.* No, I'm a friend."

Marian's chin jutted upward, the muscles in her neck taut. "How can I trust that?"

Well, it was now or never. "Because I work for someone who wants to free him."

The other woman crossed her arms. "That's imposs—wait, is this why you're asking about the Ink? *You* took it, didn't you?"

"I will neither confirm nor deny that accusation," Flora replied. "But the reason I'm asking is because of Blaise."

Marian licked her lips. "Ask."

"If someone were to hypothetically find themselves tattooed with an untested Ink, what are the side effects? What sort of reaction would you expect? Hypothetical reactions, of course." Flora cleared her throat, glancing away.

Marian almost dropped the vial in surprise. She tucked it back into the hip bag. "Side effects depend on the person and the mage. As far as reactions, since it's made from the blood of the mage being bound, it has trace amounts of the original Manifestation virus. In most cases, it's so small it has no impact on the handler. But *this* is not like most cases." Her face hardened.

Flora crossed her arms. "And why is that?"

The alchemist shut her eyes briefly, as if staving off a bad memory. "I told them they shouldn't try to bind him, but no one would listen to me. Because I'm only an *alchemist*." She nearly snarled the last word in her frustration. Flora understood—as far as she was concerned, alchemists were brilliant creatives. But alchemists were similar to mages in that those higher in the Confederation government didn't heed them. "I told them it was dangerous, but they're more focused on turning him into a weapon."

Flora nodded, trying to appear sympathetic despite not understanding. And she very much wanted to understand so that she could help Malcolm. "What makes it so dangerous?"

Marian's eyes settled on her; the corners crinkled with regret. "I shouldn't tell you. I need to share this information directly with whoever was misguided enough to bind to my son."

The half-knocker narrowed her eyes. "Wait. You can leave this place?"

The alchemist raised her brows. "You seem like the resourceful sort who could get me out."

Flora sighed. *Humans.* Sometimes they really were so annoying, but Marian's faith was also flattering. "I probably could. Would you be able to help, though? He's very sick."

Marian's mouth puckered with thought. "There's a potion I can make. I used it once before when…well, I'll get into that later. I'll trade the potion for my family's safety."

"Hey," Flora protested, "I'm already helping Blaise *and* getting you information about your family!"

"You're helping *your* friend, which, in turn, helps Blaise," Marian corrected.

Flora made a face. "Fine. Yes. I'll bring back information about your family tomorrow. And figure out a way to get them somewhere safe."

Marian smiled. "Then we have a deal."

CHAPTER TWELVE

Shut Your Piehole and Accept the Praise

Jack

Once Flora came back from her errand, Jack and Zepheus made a foray into Izhadell but came across no fruitful leads, forcing them to retire to the Wells estate again for the night. When Jack returned, he discovered the Doyen had awoken and was asking for him.

That was a good sign, and Jack pushed his way into the master bedroom at the insistence of a staffer. Malcolm was still abed, but he was more upright with a bevy of pillows at his back. He sipped something from a mug—soup, judging by the salty tang that filled the air.

"You're still this side of Perdition," Jack rumbled, leaning against the threshold.

Malcolm nodded, and he set the mug down on the bedside table. "Fortunately, yes."

The outlaw studied him. The man's skin was still too pale, and he shivered, but at least he was conscious. "What do you want?"

The Doyen chuckled. "Getting to the heart of the matter, I see."

"I'm a straight shooter," Jack agreed with a smirk. *In more ways than one.*

Malcolm nodded, and his normally handsome visage seemed more haggard than before. "You, ah…have more knowledge of theurgists and handlers than anyone else I can speak to right now. Would you mind if I asked you about that?"

Jack tensed. As a matter of fact, he minded. It was something he didn't like to think or talk about. And it still pissed him off that this man had the gall to do that to Blaise. Even if it was a way to help him, there was no way the Breaker would have agreed to it. But Jack knew the way to free a mage from a handler. All he needed was for Wells to help him get Blaise out...and how unfortunate if something happened to the Doyen after that. He patted a hand against his pocket to assure himself the poppet was still there.

"Please. I think it's important," Wells added in a whisper.

"I do enjoy hearing you beg," Jack drawled. "What's your question?"

"When you had a handler, what was the connection like?"

Jack frowned. Damn this man. He really was going to scratch Jack's old wounds like that. Maybe this would help him understand why what he had done was a violation, though. "You ever seen the way they break a unicorn?"

Malcolm looked puzzled but shook his head. "No. What does that have to do with this?"

"Everything," Jack snapped. "They force a salt-iron bit in its mouth, which blisters and burns their tender gums. The beast has no choice but to submit to ease the pain. That's their version of *this*." He shoved up his sleeve to display his old, dead tattoo. "A handler is like the unicorn's Tracker, imposing their will onto someone who can't do a damn thing against it."

Malcolm swallowed. "But it doesn't have to be like that."

"Doesn't it?" Jack asked. That ran counter to his experience.

"I'm asking because..." The Doyen sighed, seeming at a loss for how to explain himself. "Did you ever have dreams about your handler?"

Jack brayed a laugh. "That's the most gods-damned ridiculous thing I've ever heard. Sleep was my *escape* from that—" He cut himself off. For one thing, Reynolds had never come down with any illness when they were first bound. And for another, Wells regarded Blaise differently. There was a very real, if slim, possibility that something was afoot. "What are you saying? And this better not just be about you being hornier than a dragon."

The Doyen felt well enough to raise an eyebrow but didn't comment. "What I'm saying is that when I was asleep or unconscious—I honestly don't know which—I had a dream and Blaise was in it."

Jack shrugged. "So?" After all, it was no secret Wells was obsessed.

"That's not the unusual bit. I've dreamed about Blaise before, and he behaves a certain way in those dreams." He glanced away, leaving the gist of such dreams to Jack's imagination. The outlaw curled his lip. "This was more like the *real* Blaise. I mean, the one I've visited in the Cit." Malcolm rubbed his face. "Scared and damaged."

Jack narrowed his eyes. Yeah, he knew Blaise wouldn't get on well in the Golden Citadel. No one would, but especially not someone as fragile as him. "Let me make sure I follow. You think you had a dream, or perhaps a hallucination, with the *real* Blaise in it?"

"I would argue it can't be a hallucination if Blaise was real."

Jack waved a hand. "Whatever." He frowned. "Human minds are blamed good at fooling us, Wells. And you've been sicker than a three-legged dog."

"So, you don't think it's…"

"What?" Jack gave him a sharp-eyed look.

"Magic?"

The outlaw snorted. "Never have I ever heard of any sort of magic with dreams. Nah. Fever's been addling your brain. Probably just means you need more rest." He pointed a finger at him. "Which you should get now."

Jack headed to the door, shutting it behind him. He'd seen a lot of mages in his day, but this? Dream magic? He snorted. *Yeah, and a chupacabra's my uncle.*

———

The NEXT AFTERNOON, JACK AND ZEPHEUS PROWLED THE STREETS AROUND the Golden Citadel once again. The number of buildings that had sprouted up outside the Cit's walls was surprising. During Jack's time as a theurgist, the area surrounding the extensive complex had been open land. Time changed all things, he mused.

The first spot of luck happened when Zepheus caught a brief whiff of a familiar scent. According to the palomino, pegasi had a different scent bouquet than the average horse, though human senses weren't refined enough to process it. The stallion turned off the busy street and down a quieter avenue, finally drawing to a stop outside a saloon.

<Oby's around here somewhere,> Zepheus said, flicking his ears. <You want to go put your ear to the ground while I stay out here and see what I can discover?>

"May as well," Jack murmured to the pegasus, patting his shoulder. He made a show of loosely tying Zepheus to the hitching post outside the saloon. Jack always made certain that, if necessary, the stallion could free himself. It had benefited him countless times before.

The outlaw sauntered inside, listening to the familiar sounds of a saloon busy with the evening rush. A group in one corner sang bawdy songs off-key, much to the chagrin of the pianist. Billiard balls clacked against each other, though raucous laughter from a nearby table quickly drowned out the sound. Jack took it all in as he claimed a stool at the bar. This place, he understood. The rest of Izhadell, not so much.

The bartender took his drink order, and while Jack drank, he listened in to the surrounding conversations. He monitored the door, and before long, he saw a familiar face slip in and snag a table in the corner.

Jack fought the impulse to stalk over to Emmaline, grab her by the arm, and haul her out of there. She was his daughter—she would fight him if he did that. And he didn't want to draw undue attention to himself. Instead, he stayed where he was and watched her, wondering what she was up to. Was she meeting someone? That's what he would be doing in her shoes.

But time passed, and no one came. She nursed a drink and half-heartedly ate. Jack paid his tab and slowly rose from his stool, turning and ambling over to her table. Emmaline saw him coming and her eyes widened, but that lasted only a heartbeat as a sullen expression crossed her face, and she hunched over as he took a seat opposite her.

"You shouldn't be here," she said after a moment, her voice tight.

"No place else I should be," Jack replied, doing his best to keep his tone even. "Why'd you run off?"

Emmaline lifted her head, eyes alight with challenge. "You wouldn't understand."

Jack leaned forward. "Try me."

"You just want to drag me back to the Gutter. You want..." Emmaline shook her head as she trailed off.

Heavy footsteps clopped nearby. Jack glanced over his shoulder and saw the bartender looming close. "This man bothering you?"

Jack bristled, his right palm brushing against the holster at his side. Emmaline lifted a hand, and whether it was to quell him or her prospective rescuer, he couldn't say. "I'm fine." She shot a look from Jack to the bartender, and after a moment, the bartender drifted off, though he gave the outlaw a menacing glare for his trouble.

"How do you know what I want?" Jack asked once they were alone. "You've hardly said two words to me for the past few months."

"Your actions say plenty," Emmaline fired back. "Always watching me. Not wanting me to do this or that."

He frowned. "Of course I'm going to protect you after..." After he had failed her. He had failed his entire town.

"I can take care of myself, thank you very much." Emmaline said it with all the bravado of a sixteen-year-old. And maybe, just maybe, she was right. She was the product of an outlaw town. She had survived things that the townies of Izhadell could only imagine. But here she sat, in the middle of Izhadell, a maverick mage. And that was dangerous.

"You may think so, but you know shit about the pisspot of scumbaggery you're in right now," Jack retorted. "We should leave."

<Jack?> Zepheus tried to interrupt.

"*You* should leave, yes," Emmaline corrected, crossing her arms. "It's not safe for you here."

<Jack, I *really* need you to stop talking and listen.>

Jack narrowed his eyes. "You're coming with me. You came here to free Blaise—"

"What?" she snapped, scowling. "That's not the only reason I came."

<You need to *get out* of there. Lamar is coming!>

That got Jack's attention. "What?" The question came out as a growl, and Emmaline no doubt thought he was addressing her. He turned to glance at the door, and he and his daughter cursed in unison as tow-headed Lamar Gaitwood stepped inside.

Half of the lanterns in the saloon's interior were out, which meant that his nemesis wouldn't spot him immediately. Jack weighed his options. As much as he'd like to see Lamar dead, this wasn't the ideal place. Too many witnesses. And too deep in hostile territory. And Emmaline in the line of fire, though Jack had faith she could handle herself. But he didn't want to take the risk, and any ballsy move he made would endanger her, too.

"Lamar," Jack hissed at her. "I'm not here."

Her eyebrows rose in question at his statement, but he didn't have time to explain. Jack already had his poppet out, preparing his spell. Obfuscation was a tricky working. Anyone who knew where he started from would still see him. But anyone who didn't—for example, a Saltie asshole like Lamar—would have to physically run into Jack to find him. Unless he had a unicorn with him, in which case all bets were off. But Zepheus had made no mention of unicorns.

He felt the frisson of magic as it fell into place over him like a mantle. That done, he rose from the table. He had no desire to be caught in close quarters. Jack edged along the perimeter, careful to keep clear of anyone who might inadvertently run into him as Lamar stalked into the bar.

Emmaline was no fool. Her eyes followed her father's progress for the briefest of moments before she changed tactics. She pulled a small book out and flipped through it, pretending to pay studious attention to it. Jack found a good vantage point near the end of the bar that led to the kitchen. Lamar scanned the saloon, intent as only a man on the hunt would be. Jack had the unsettling feeling that Lamar truly was after him.

Jack didn't like being quarry. He much preferred the roles to be reversed. It was a shame that he didn't think his Obfuscation spell would stand against taking a shot at Lamar. *Too obvious.*

Lamar's gaze settled on Emmaline, and Jack reconsidered his stance on shooting his old friend then and there. The Commander strode over to her with quick, purposeful steps, moving to occupy the chair Jack had claimed only moments before.

Jack bit back the urge to walk over and plant a fist in Lamar's handsome mug. Or a bullet. Instead, he stayed where he was as his enemy leaned close to his daughter and said something. Emmaline offered him a baleful glare in response. *That's my girl. Now gut him under the table.*

Emmaline said something to Lamar, and Jack would have paid a mountain of gold to hear. Lamar's head jerked back, and he tightened his hand into a fist. He glanced around the bar again, and Jack wondered briefly if she had mentioned his presence.

Nearby, the same bartender who had approached Jack earlier studied the situation, a scowl on his face. He put down the pitcher he had been wiping dry, moving around the bar to head back to Emmaline's defense. Normally Jack had little love for the heroic ranger type, but since he couldn't intervene in this situation himself, he approved.

The bartender loomed over Lamar, all muscle and attitude, his eyes on Emmaline. His voice was a rumble that carried to Jack's position. "You need a hand?"

"This man is bothering me." Emmaline lifted her chin, eyes bright.

Lamar glared at the bartender. "This doesn't concern you."

"My bar, my property." The bartender cracked his knuckles for emphasis. "Get out and leave the girl alone."

Lamar straightened, annoyance etched on his face. He tapped one of the gaudy medals decorating the front of his uniform. "You're speaking to a Commander of the Salt-Iron Confederation."

"Don't care. You're harassing a paying customer. Get out."

Yeah, aside from the kerfuffle earlier, Jack liked this bartender. Now, if only he would follow that up with a punch to Lamar's face. That would be perfection.

Meanwhile, Lamar seemed to debate his next steps. But mage or not, it wouldn't be good for the Commander's image to haul off a young girl who was minding her own business. From what Jack had discovered, his old pal had been in hot water after the mess of Fort Courage, so he had to take it easy or risk more blow-back. Lamar frowned, lowering his voice to offer parting words to Emmaline before he rose and headed for the door.

Jack watched Lamar go, debating all the while which path to take. On the one hand, it was tempting to trail after his nemesis and end him at last. But on the other, he had found Emmaline, and he wasn't eager to let her slip away again. Because he knew she would. His daughter had lost track of him, courtesy of his spell, and he saw by the way she tensed her muscles she was preparing to make her own escape as soon as possible.

She bided her time, though, as if wanting to make sure that Gaitwood was gone. Jack supposed Oberidon might be in the vicinity and apprising her of the situation, as Zepheus had done for him. Not for the first time, Jack wished he could communicate directly with his pegasus. It would be handy at times like this.

After a half-hour had passed, she finally rose and slipped out of the bar. Jack followed in her wake, keeping his spell active so no one realized she had a tail. She made her way up the street to a grungy inn, where she let herself into a room on the third floor. No sign of Oberidon, but that didn't mean much of anything.

Jack put his boot into the door before she could close it. The solid wood hitting his foot shattered his Obfuscation spell, and Emmaline jumped in surprise as he shimmered into view on the other side of the door. She had a pistol in her hand quick as a rattlesnake, though thankfully, she didn't fire.

"Daddy!" she hissed, eyes narrowed.

"I wasn't going to give up that easy," Jack murmured, shouldering his way inside and shutting the door behind him.

Emmaline turned the bolt on the lock, slipping her pistol back into its holster and crossing her arms. "Your pig-headedness is going to get you killed one of these days."

"I'm only here because you ran off," he countered.

She threw up her hands. "You should be happy to hear I'm fine. Go back home. Go back to the Gutter and be the heartless outlaw I know you are."

He bristled at that. Was that all she thought he was now? When had he become that and stopped being her father? Jack tried to rally and think of something wise to say, but her words stung. Emmaline meant the world to him. And he meant so little to her?

It took Jack a moment to realize she was giving him a strange look. He hadn't given a hot-tempered reply, as was his usual mode of conversation. No, instead his mouth opened and closed, like a fish out of water, as he tried and failed to figure out how to repair things with her.

"Daddy?" Emmaline asked. Her voice was soft, having lost some of its righteous fury at his inability to respond.

Jack wasn't one to let his emotions show. And maybe, he realized, that was wrong in this case. He recalled, so many years ago, when their little family had first been torn asunder, there had been many a night when he and Emmaline would curl up and cry until they fell asleep, missing Kittie like she were a physical part of them that had been torn away. Over time, the place where Kittie had been scabbed over, and Jack tried to always keep a brave face on for his daughter as she grew. Tried to be the tough one. And now that was all she saw: the stone-faced, icy bastard of an outlaw.

"Do you know why I came looking for you?" Jack's voice trembled with uncharacteristic softness.

Emmaline pursed her lips. "Because you don't think I can take care of myself."

He shook his head. No, he had faith that she could do that. "The same reason I would fight a fort full of soldiers for you. You're my child. You're a piece of my heart walking around outside my body. I *love* you."

She gave him a mistrustful look. "Something's wrong with you. Are you drunk?"

"Am I—?" Jack sputtered, then snorted. "Gods, girl. I can't tell you I love you without you having to ask that?"

Emmaline glanced away. "It's not something I hear from you."

And that's my fault. "I know." He had thought that being there for her and showing her was enough, but it wasn't. Jack pulled her into an embrace, relieved when he felt her relax against him. "I *know* you can take care of yourself. You're my girl, so I'm pretty sure there ain't nothing you can't do if you put your mind to it."

"Really thinking you're not my father," she muttered into his shoulder.

"Shut your piehole and accept the praise."

Emmaline lifted her chin. "Okay, so maybe it is you." After a moment, she pulled away again. "Do you know why I came here?"

Jack allowed her to step away from him. "I assume you were hoping to free Blaise."

At that, she glanced away, as if shamed. "I…I thought about it. I came around here to see if I had a chance, but I don't think so." Emmaline worried at her bottom lip, and Jack knew she was regretting that she couldn't save her friend. "But really, this is why I came." She dug a hand into a pouch at her waist, carefully pulling out a doll.

Jack stared at it, swallowing. "Explain."

"I'm looking for Mom."

Her words shocked him to the core. How many years had he done the very same, and with nothing to show for it but more heartbreak? Jack shivered because with Emmaline's magic, she had a genuine chance of success. He exhaled softly, not even daring to hope. "And?"

"She's alive. Hiding." Emmaline's voice was soft, breathy, and victorious. "Made herself purposely hard to find. But *I can do it.*"

Jack's pulse raced. Then he paused, frowning. "Wait. Did you take hair from your mother's poppet without asking?"

"Um. Maybe?" She shot him a pleading look. "It's easier to beg forgiveness than ask permission."

He snorted. "Yeah." Another thing she'd learned from him. "For future reference, it's rude to steal a reagent from another mage."

Emmaline blinked. "But we're outlaws."

"Outlaw doesn't mean we're uncultured trash goblins, though." He crossed his arms, though he couldn't keep up the stern front for long. Not with knowledge of what she could do. "You're going to find her?"

His daughter gave a determined nod. "Yeah." Emmaline glanced away, as if suddenly embarrassed. "I was mad at you. I thought if I figured out where she was, I could live with her."

That almost ripped his heart right out. Gods, he was such a terrible father, to drive her to such thoughts. She cringed, as if expecting him to rail at her. And a part of him wanted to. But then he would fall into the same trap that was driving her away. He prided himself on being able to adapt and learn new tricks. This was no different.

Swallowing, he met her eyes. "I want you to know I hope you find her."

Emmaline stared at him, and he was sure she was going to make another retort that he couldn't possibly be her father. But maybe she saw he was desperately trying to make things work. She nodded. "Thanks. You can come along."

Oh, how he wanted to. But he shook his head, surprising her. "Nah. I have something else to take care of that you thought I should do. I'll catch up after."

Her face crinkled in confusion. "What?" Then after a beat, her eyes widened. "Oh. Daddy, are you going to get Blaise out?"

"I am," Jack whispered, the words a pledge. He gasped in surprise as she flung her arms around him again. He stroked her hair, breathing in her scent, content. For the moment, his daughter was safe, and things were a little better in his world. He might have to confront some of his old demons at the Golden Citadel, but for the moment, he allowed himself to just *be*.

CHAPTER THIRTEEN

Dream On

Jefferson

Metal and wood shrieked as they fractured under strain, clamorous and ghastly. A haze of smoke cloaked his view of the world as the floor he stood on bucked beneath his feet. No, not a floor —a *deck*, Jefferson realized as he absorbed the surrounding scene. He *knew* where he was. And at the same time, he wasn't certain how he knew that.

He was on board what had once been *his* airship before the Confederation had commandeered it and turned it into the warbird *Retribution*. Screams rose from the ground below as the ship bobbled again. Someone crouched on the deck ahead, back arched as his hands braced against the wood. Even with the young man's back to him, Jefferson knew who he was looking at.

"Blaise!" he called out above the bedlam. The Breaker didn't seem to hear him at first and remained where he was, trembling with effort. Jefferson strode closer. "Blaise!"

The mage jerked to attention at the new voice, glancing over his shoulder at Jefferson with an incredulous expression that swiftly shifted to one of horror. "*No.* You shouldn't be here."

The deck shuddered beneath them, so real and heart-stopping that Jefferson dropped into a crouch as well. "*I asked you to do this.*" Jefferson glanced around, stomach lurching as he realized the scope of what he had urged Blaise to do so many months ago. "What happened to you is my fault. There's no place else I should be."

The warbird listed to one side. Blaise yelped as he lost his balance and stumbled. Jefferson dove to him, wrapping his arms around the younger man. There was a soft pop, and the warbird shimmered out of existence, replaced by the floor of the bakery. Jefferson pulled himself away from Blaise, watching as the Breaker curled up, hugging his knees against his chest as he stared at the change of scenery, bewildered.

"You're safe now." Jefferson raised his hands in a calming gesture.

Blaise quivered. "What's happening? That's never happened in my nightmare before."

Your nightmare? Oh, Blaise. Jefferson got to his feet, leaning against a counter. The wood felt solid and so *real*, just as real as the airship had been. "You're not there anymore. You're safe."

Blaise rubbed his arms as if he were cold. "I'm not safe."

Jefferson cocked his head, trying to decide if it was better to stay put or move closer. *Nothing ventured, nothing gained.* He stepped over to Blaise again, slowly sitting on the floor opposite him. "May I talk to you about something?"

The question seemed to jar Blaise from whatever bleak thoughts had gripped him. He blinked. "What?"

"Do you remember the last time we were together?"

Blaise glanced away, his expression unreadable. "Rainbow Flat."

"No," Jefferson corrected, voice gentle. "*Here.* Your bakery. We made cookies."

Blaise shook his head. "That was just a dream."

"No. I mean, yes, it was, but..." Jefferson paused as Blaise looked at him with confusion. "I think this is *us*, Blaise. The real you. The real me. But in a...dream world." He felt silly even saying the words, but they somehow seemed right.

The Breaker pressed his lips together in thought. "How?"

Jefferson chuckled nervously, rubbing his chin. "I only want to help you. You know that, yes?"

Blaise stared at him. "What did you do?"

Jefferson flicked his gaze to the floor, guilty. Heart drumming so loud he fancied Blaise could hear it, he struggled to find the words. Why was it a simple matter to go toe to toe with the other Doyens, but so difficult to tell Blaise this one thing? *Because I care about him, that's why.* "I couldn't come up with any other way to save you. I'm sorry."

"*What did you do?*"

In answer, Jefferson rolled up his sleeve. His tattoo wasn't there at first, but he brushed his hand over the skin, and the ink swirled into existence like thin, living serpents. Blaise hiked up his own sleeve and watched as his geasa tattoo rose to visibility in response. His face falling, Blaise yanked the sleeve back down and turned away, his expression crumpling.

"It was the only way," Jefferson whispered, at a loss for how else to explain it.

Blaise's mouth shifted into a thin line and a muscle in his cheek twitched. "You *know* how I feel about being used."

Yes, he did. Jefferson sighed. He wanted to argue that he wouldn't allow anyone else to have Blaise, but he knew the mage would misunderstand. He didn't want to be seen as a possession. And he *wasn't*. Jefferson wanted his love and trust, nothing more. "I won't allow anyone else to use you. To be bound to you and..." Jefferson faltered, wilting beneath the spark of anger in the other man's eyes.

"I wish you hadn't." Blaise's voice was tight. "You didn't...gods, Jefferson. You didn't even *ask* me." He shook his head in frustration and levered to his feet, stalking the short distance to the other side of the bakery before whirling, his back against the counter. "Why didn't you ask?"

"I *couldn't*." Jefferson realized this wasn't one of those cases where it was better to beg forgiveness than ask permission. He knew Blaise would be angry, but he had been so confident that the result justified the terrible cost. "It's a poor defense, but the visitation room at the Cit isn't exactly a safe place for such a conversation."

Blaise turned, staring out the small window. The angle of his shoulders radiated his resentment. "You're smarter than that. You could have figured something out."

Jefferson rubbed his forehead. "Nothing else was working, and we were running out of time."

Blaise shook his head. "I *still* can't believe you didn't ask." He shifted to face Jefferson again, crossing his arms. Blaise was no longer the wild-eyed prisoner, righteous fury suffusing him. "I thought you *cared* about me."

Oof. That one hurt. Jefferson clenched his teeth. He could make fancy arguments with the other Doyens all day, but this...*this* was painful. He *did* care. Jefferson swallowed, tucking his chin against his chest. "I...made a mistake."

"Yeah, you did," Blaise agreed. When Jefferson looked up, the young man was running a hand through his hair. "But what's done is done, and I assume this is something we can't change?" At the slight shake of Jefferson's head, Blaise sighed. "I'm going to be mad at you for a while."

"You can. That's fair," Jefferson said. Anger could ebb, worn down by apologies and the healing of time. Hatred was not as easy a thing to die.

Blaise sucked in a deep breath, as if he were steadying himself. "Is that how *this* is possible?" He waved a hand to encompass the bakery.

Jefferson waggled his fingers in an indecisive gesture. "Maybe? I'm still figuring things out, so I can't answer that." He cleared his throat. "There were some unforeseen consequences brought about by being bound to you."

Blaise's brow furrowed. "What do you mean?"

"The tattoo made me quite ill," Jefferson murmured, rubbing absently at his bicep. "Manifestation Illness, if you can believe that."

Blaise stared at him, gaping.

Jefferson gave a rueful smile. "I probably had the same expression when I found out."

Head tilted, Blaise studied him. "Manifestation…wait, that's not good. It could kill you." His earlier anger fled, replaced by a rush of worry.

"I think I'm past that," Jefferson said. "Though I will admit, I've never been sicker in my life."

Blaise studied him, frowning as he thought. Jefferson wished he knew what was going on in that head of his. The younger man said nothing for several minutes as he digested the information. "Does that mean you're like me? A mage?"

"Something like that," Jefferson agreed. "But not a Breaker. I suspect I have some sort of magic that allows me to manipulate dreams. Do you know anything about magic like that?"

Shaking his head, Blaise sighed. "I'm not the person to ask. I didn't know a thing before getting to Itude." He rubbed his hands together, as if the mention of magic agitated his own. "What does this mean for you? You're a *Doyen*."

Jefferson coughed into his fist. That was something he would rather not think about, but it was a valid question. "It means I have to keep this new ability quiet."

Blaise frowned, his eyes frosting. "More secrets."

"But not from you," Jefferson replied, adamant. At the Breaker's raised eyebrows, he blew out a flustered breath. "Right, very well. You think I misled you, but that was *not* my intent."

Blaise crossed his arms, and strangely, it pleased Jefferson to see how focused the other man was on him. Jefferson was a source of frustration, which meant he distracted Blaise from other concerns—like his predicament in the Cit. *Minor victories.* "You didn't tell me who you *really* were, and you had the chance to do so in Rainbow Flat." Blaise held up a finger, ticking it off. "And then you do that." He gestured to his bicep, raising another finger for the tally.

Jefferson licked his lips. "May I tell you who I am, then?"

The Breaker nodded. "I've been waiting on this explanation for a while."

"We wouldn't have gotten along well at all when I was younger," Jefferson began, watching as the bakery melted away from around them, replaced by the parlor of his childhood home. Blaise rose and moved to stand beside him, glancing at the opulent brocade drapes, the gilded portraits hanging on the walls, and the grandiose carved furniture. Every facet of the room resonated with wealth and power.

"Some things seem to be the same, though," Blaise murmured at the splendor.

Jefferson gave an unapologetic shrug. "You can see why I'm accustomed to the finer things in life." He sobered, crossing the room to the door. Blaise remained where he was, so Jefferson beckoned him over. "Come on. This is your chance to learn more about who I am. Who I *really* am."

At that, Blaise followed. Jefferson headed down a hallway until they reached a door that led outside. The weather was fair, the temperature pleasant. The fragrance of jasmine clung heavily in the air from the nearby gardens. Jefferson paused, the ambiance taking him back. He didn't care much for that particular scent, not anymore. It reminded him of who he had been and where he came from.

Blaise noticed and glanced at him. "What?"

Jefferson rubbed the back of his neck. "I'm not a good person, Blaise. I'm trying to make up for things, but…"

The Breaker studied him. "I know a little about that."

Jefferson paused, shaking his head with regret. "I don't think you do, actually. You don't have an unkind bone in your body." He sighed, rallying himself. Blaise deserved to hear the truth. "In that respect, we're nothing alike."

The surrounding estate was pristine, kept that way by a legion of servants, some of them indentured mages. He led Blaise through the landscaped garden, the hedges so high they shrouded his family's dirty secret. Jefferson remembered a time when he hadn't thought twice about that. How many young women and men had he dallied with beneath the fragrant rose arches? He had lost count. His wandering subconscious made ghosts of his past romances appear, and by the way Blaise flinched, he saw them, too.

"They're all Malcolm," Blaise murmured, studying a frozen tableau where the man in question cradled an amorous redhead in his arms.

"We're on the Wells Estate, so yes," Jefferson agreed. He tilted his head, trying to remember the woman's name. She was the daughter of a dignitary. Rosalind? Raquel? Something like that. Didn't matter. She had been an amusement, nothing more. "You, ah, should know that I have a bit of a lascivious past."

Blaise raised his brows, shooting him an amused look. "Do you see my surprised face?"

Yes, well...Jefferson found himself embarrassed about confronting it with Blaise. He didn't want him to get the wrong idea. Blaise was *nothing* like the others. Jefferson had no intention of tossing him to the wayside. "Right. Well, this isn't even the worst thing about me. Rather tame, honestly. Come on."

He led Blaise deeper into the garden, examining his own sudden discomfiture over his past. Jefferson had never been embarrassed about his romantic exploits before, but now he found himself in the odd position of not wanting to scare Blaise away. His relationship with the Breaker was as delicate as the scales on a butterfly's wings, and Jefferson feared damaging it further than he already had.

They reached the massive stone fountain that occupied the center of the garden. Jefferson walked over to a nearby bench, tapping a rhythm into the bricks beneath it. Blaise watched him, perplexed, but then jumped as the flagstones around the fountain shifted with a grinding clatter, a wooden hatch concealing stairs that led down to a subterranean passage.

"What's this?" Blaise asked.

Jefferson pressed his lips together. "The actual way my family amassed our *shipping* fortune." He started down the steps. "Not *me*, mind you. I told you the truth about that. So please remember that."

Blaise followed him down, glancing up as the daylight vanished, replaced by the lambent glow of lanterns. Jefferson's pulse quickened at the cries and moans echoing against the stone walls. He heard Blaise's quick intake of breath when the sound carried to him. Jefferson pressed onward until they were in the holding area, surrounded by cells filled with humans and people of mystical races.

It was a dream, so Jefferson made the inhabitants ignore him and Blaise, but that didn't stop how real it was. The Breaker stared around him, face pale in the light. "What am I looking at?"

Jefferson rubbed his forehead. "My family invests in flesh. The Wells family is part of a thriving trafficking network that spans the entire Confederation." He cast a furtive look at Blaise, half expecting to see outrage reflected in his eyes. The Breaker's mouth twisted into a deep frown, and his blue eyes appeared more troubled than angry. Jefferson continued, "We—I mean *they*, I don't do this anymore—sell to a variety of clientele. Brothels. Menageries. Ritualists. Apothecaries. Alchemists." He ticked them off on his fingers one by one.

Blaise walked down the middle of the long, narrow room, studying the prisoners. He trailed his fingers along the dark metal bars. They were salt-iron, but in the dream world they were harmless. The metal crumbled at Blaise's touch, tumbling down like a satisfying rain. "I assume there's a lot of money to be had here."

"You have no idea," Jefferson murmured. Oh, and if his family knew he had access to a Breaker...gods, he didn't even want to think about that. He had burned his bridges thoroughly, but greed could pave over them.

"So what happened?" Blaise asked.

At the question, Jefferson licked his lips. "I have a sister. Younger than me—a little older than you." He sighed, and not for the first time, wondered if fate had put Blaise in his path as a reminder. "When she was ten, her magic manifested."

Blaise stared at him. "You have a mage in your family?"

"*Had*." Malcolm failed to keep his bitterness from bleeding through to his voice. "Our father prided himself on coming from a line without the taint of magic—his description, not mine. He blamed our mother." And looking back, Malcolm pinpointed that as the moment his mother went over the cliff of her addictions and never turned back. "Father sold my sister to the highest bidder."

Blaise hissed out a breath. "What became of her?"

"I should clarify: he sold her off as a bride, which I suppose isn't any better." Malcolm shook his head. "And I...I knew it was wrong, but the girl I grew up with went from being my sibling to something *other*." He winced. "I was raised to look down on mages."

"What changed?" Blaise asked, tentative. As if he were worried Malcolm had somehow misled him.

"Flora. I came across her, and she...showed me the error of my ways." He ran a hand through his hair, roughing it backward. "That's a long story for another time. But I wanted you to understand that once upon a time, I *would* have used someone like you."

Blaise glanced at him. "How can I be sure you won't now?"

The question made Jefferson's heart ache. He didn't know how he could make his intentions for Blaise any clearer without scaring him off. "I won't. And if I even think about it, I assume Flora will shank me."

"I could see that," Blaise agreed. He turned in a tight circle, thoughtful. "What will your family think of this?" He gestured from himself to Jefferson.

Jefferson sighed. That was something he didn't want to consider.

"We're not on speaking terms. I ended up being disinherited when I became a magelover. Had my engagement broken off and everything."

"Engagement?" Blaise squeaked.

Oh, are you jealous? Jefferson very much wanted to ask but decided to hold on to that question for another time. "Yes, to an heiress. If you care to take a gander, Cinna is the one I'm fadoodling by the unicorn topiary." He made a face. "That was a rather fortunate side effect of being disowned. Ending that engagement was a gift from the gods."

"*Fadoodling?*" Blaise shook his head, then pursed his lips. "Didn't she love you?"

Jefferson chuckled. Blaise was adorably naïve about the workings of elite society, and that was a blessing. "Few unions are based on love in the higher social echelons of the Confederation. But you're kind to think that."

Blaise quirked an eyebrow at him. "And you still haven't explained how *Jefferson* figures into all this. Flora told me it was so you could travel through the Untamed Territory without problems."

"Ah, that's true to a degree," Jefferson agreed. "That's my favorite use, yes." And he didn't know how to explain to Blaise that he just felt more at home in this skin. Less like the filth he associated with the Wells name. Maybe someday, he would figure out a way to explain it. "I purchased the ring before I met Flora but hadn't used it much. But then to do what needed to be done required Jefferson and not Malcolm."

"To do what?" Blaise asked.

Jefferson chuckled. "That's part of the story for another time. Flora taught me the important lesson that you can be magical and still a person."

"You don't say?" Blaise asked wryly.

"It was a very radical idea after my upbringing." Jefferson shook his head. "And after dealing with Flora, I wondered why mages and magical beasts were treated one way in the Confederation, but differently in places like Ravance or the Untamed Territory. That was something Jefferson could investigate more easily, as an unknown."

Blaise frowned. "Were you a Doyen then?"

Jefferson shook his head. "No, but I was a Wells, which made life difficult. I was reviled among my former cohorts for my inclinations, and elsewhere I was viewed as the enemy." He smiled. "Jefferson's goal was to travel, gather information, and make money. I discovered I enjoyed that. Jefferson was the person I decided I'd like to be if I had a choice. Nor did he have the legacy of a family built up on the suffering of others."

Blaise worried at his lower lip, and for a moment, Jefferson wondered if he had said something wrong. But the younger man shook his head.

"You said you were a bad person. Bad people don't care about becoming better."

Those words warmed Jefferson's heart, and he thought perhaps Blaise understood him, at least a bit more. "I'm not perfect."

"No. You're spoiled and entitled," Blaise agreed.

"Devilishly handsome."

"Egotistical." Blaise nodded.

Jefferson chuckled. "Forgive me for the deception?"

"I forgive you for the Malcolm and Jefferson thing. Still mad at you about the geasa." Blaise crossed his arms.

"But maybe a little less mad since I pulled you out of a nightmare?" Jefferson held his thumb and index finger a tiny bit apart.

That won a small smile from Blaise. "A little. I just wish I didn't have to go back."

Yes. Jefferson desperately wished the same.

CHAPTER FOURTEEN

Monsters

Malcolm

He awoke to the jarring sensation of someone forcing his mouth open to pour a concoction down his throat. His gag reflex took over, and Flora cursed, her strong hands forcing his head up.

"Oh, no, you don't," she growled.

He swallowed the potion, eyes snapping open at the bitter taste and oily feel of it sliding down his throat. To his surprise, Flora wasn't the only one in the room with him. A woman with curly brown hair stood on one side of the bed, arms crossed as she watched him.

"Ugh. What *is* that?" Malcolm moaned, casting a covetous look at the glass of water nearby. Flora handed it to him, and he drank, feeling slightly less vile as the water cleansed his palate.

"Something to help you survive," the unfamiliar woman replied. "So *you're* the one misguided enough to bind himself to my son."

"Yep, that's the blowhard you're looking for." Malcolm hadn't noticed Jack sitting in the corner.

He ignored the judgmental outlaw, focusing on the woman's harsh and confusing words. Malcolm thought that was rather unfair since he still wasn't feeling well enough to figure out what she meant. *Bind myself to... wait.* "You're Blaise's mother? Marian Hawthorne?" He was rather proud that her name came to mind, considering how disconnected he felt. "And before you rail at me for poor decisions, I was running out of options to help him."

Marian cocked her head. "I won't be the one to judge what you did." Apparently, she understood how Blaise would react, too. Her eyes were steely. "But you're a *Doyen*. Surely *you* could do more."

Oh, if only. "It's not that simple, and it's an uphill battle as far as mages are concerned." Especially Blaise, after the disaster at Fort Courage. He pursed his lips. "The Council was determined to bind him, and our side wouldn't have the votes to stop it."

She nodded, expression cool. "And so you took it upon yourself. Thinking that you were giving him a mercy." Jack snickered from his corner.

And here he thought she wasn't going to judge what he had done. He grimaced. "Better me than someone else. Someone who doesn't love him."

His words brought her up short. Marian raised her eyebrows, casting a quick glance at Flora, who nodded. "I see." Her tone softened. "Doyen Wells, I don't know if you can fully appreciate what you've sacrificed for Blaise."

Malcolm had some idea, but he wondered if he'd misunderstood the full scope. "And that is?" He didn't miss the way Jack stayed quiet the entire time, absorbing their conversation.

The alchemist paced the length of the room, as if debating her words. "The Ink used for the geasa originates from the blood of the mage being bound. It has trace amounts of the Manifestation virus. In most cases, it's so small it has no impact on the handler. But this is not like most cases." Her face hardened.

"And why is that?" Jack rumbled, leaning forward in a manner that reminded Malcolm of a hunting hound at the end of its leash.

Marian angled to address him. By the slash of her brow, Malcolm suspected she didn't know what to make of the outlaw. He presumed they had been introduced while he was knocked out. "Because there are too many unknowns surrounding my son, which makes it dangerous." Marian fidgeted with something in her hands, and Malcolm realized she was spinning a silver ring around one of her fingers. Whatever information she had, the alchemist was nervous about sharing it.

"We'll keep anything you have to say in our confidence," Malcolm said. He hoped Jack would, though he knew it was a gamble. The outlaw gave no indication one way or the other.

Marian nodded, the corners of her eyes crinkling with emotion. "Blaise wasn't born a mage. He was *made* into a mage."

Jack shot out of his seat, hands fisted at his side. "*Dragonshit.* That's not possible."

Malcolm was inclined to agree with the outlaw, but he didn't have much information on the topic. A glance at Flora proved she wanted to hear more before jumping to conclusions.

The alchemist fixed an impassive look at Jack. "The whole *point* of alchemy is to achieve the impossible. Transmute base metals into precious metals. Mix a panacea to cure any disease—"

"Bind one man's will to another. Block out all magical ability. Yeah, I know *all* about alchemy," Jack retorted, his entire body taut.

Blaise's mother was as placid as a lake, though Malcolm suspected she held back more information beneath the surface. "I won't argue with you, as it's the truth. One such pursuit years ago was an experiment to transmute our own mages."

Jack's mouth pressed into an angry line. Malcolm's gut lurched at her words. He suspected she spoke the truth because it was very much something the Confederation would do. But how could a mother do that to her child? Malcolm fought off a shiver, afraid that perhaps Blaise had grown up with his share of monsters, too.

The outlaw must have come to the same realization. His blue eyes glinted with a menacing chill, and Malcolm wondered if the alchemist knew the peril she was in.

Marian didn't quail at the heightening danger in the room. And perhaps she didn't need to—alchemists didn't look like much, but they were formidable. "Before you judge me, know this: I love Blaise with every bit of my being."

Jack's eyes smoldered like banked coals. He unfolded from the chair, rising slowly like a dragon on the prowl. Even though he hadn't crossed the room to be closer to the alchemist, he still seemed to loom over her. "How could a *parent* do that to a *child*?" The outlaw's voice was a low rumble, outrage and menace lacing every syllable.

To her credit, Marian averted her gaze under the storm of his words. "Even parents make mistakes."

Jack growled something unintelligible, crossing his arms and turning away in disgust. Malcolm's gut clenched as he realized Blaise had a history of people using him. And this...there was no way the young man knew this. Surely, he would have told Malcolm as much.

"What happened?" Malcolm asked.

Marian pressed her lips together, shaking her head. "That's not for me to tell you. Not when Blaise doesn't know." She took a tremulous breath.

Malcolm's brow knit, thoughtful. He wondered if the Council at the time was aware of this. But the Doyens of the past had a history of destroying records they didn't want discovered by others, so it would be hard to uncover. *To do this to a child, though...*

Jack uttered a raspy laugh. "And y'all think the *outlaw mages* are the monsters."

Marian lifted her chin. "I'm not proud of the things I did. Are you?" She met the outlaw's eyes, as if she were taking his measure.

He bared his teeth. "Not denying I'm a monster. Are *you?*"

She flinched and made the wise choice not to reply. "Blaise almost died from the process. I developed a potion that helped him pull through." Her lower lip quivered, her eyes glistening with unshed tears. Malcolm thought she might say more, but she released a shuddering sigh and wiped at one of her eyes.

"Why work for the Confederation?" Flora asked, her eyes owlish behind her glasses.

Marian glanced at Jack. "You assume I had a choice." The outlaw twitched at her words, and for an instant, understanding sparked between the pair. "When you're treated well, as the alchemists are, you don't question it. Don't misunderstand me—we're commodities as much as the theurgists are—but our egos are so coddled that it doesn't *matter.*" She combed her fingers through her curly hair. "At least, it didn't matter to me until Blaise. I took him, and I ran." Marian glanced away, clamming up. If there was more to the tale, they wouldn't hear it from her today.

"You ran," Jack repeated, grudging admiration in his voice.

Marian smiled, bitter. "I did. The first and only alchemist to do so. That's why the Arboretum is locked up tight now." She shook her head. "But it was all for nothing. The Confederation has Blaise. All I did was delay it."

"Not if I have a say in it," Malcolm replied. He ran his tongue over his teeth, which were still greasy from the potion. "So that potion…"

She glanced at the empty bottle on the bedside table. "The same one that helped Blaise pull through when he was sick."

That explained that. "Going back to the start of the discussion…you mentioned that binding to Blaise might be dangerous."

She nodded. "The Confederation has a brief memory. For the most part, they only know what Blaise *is* and not how he came about. And it's important it stays that way, or they'll uncover the true danger behind him."

"You mean beyond the whole *breaking things with a touch* magic he has going on?" Flora asked, eyebrows so high they brushed against the fringe of her bright hair.

Marian leveled a finger at Malcolm. "We had his blood at the Arboretum. I stole samples and studied it myself." She was quiet for a moment, though her heels tapped as she paced the floor again. "A mage's power is a biological part of them—it's literally in their blood. Blaise's magic tried to attack the virus, but that's the one thing it can't destroy." She sighed, pushing dark hair out of her eyes.

Malcolm cocked his head. He wasn't sure if he was following her train of thought very well in his present condition. "What happens, then?"

She gave him a wry look. "It ends up twisting the virus since it can't break it. My theory is that it spawns new types of magic."

"*Oh.*" Malcolm blinked, his mouth going dry. He gestured for the water, and Flora handed it to him.

Jack muttered a curse that no one else quite heard. Flora glanced between the two of them. "Something you're not sharing with the group?"

Malcolm rubbed his chin, recalling how he had grabbed Blaise and pulled him from the nightmare, and how his previous flings had appeared at a thought. "Maybe." He explained his experiences as best he could, though he suspected he sounded like he was raving.

Marian nodded and made a soft humming sound. "The fact that you actively manipulated the dream points to potential magic," she said. "Most people are at the mercy of their subconscious."

"Really?" Jack snorted, incredulous. "You think that's what this is? *Dream* magic?"

"Says the man who plays with dolls," Flora pointed out sweetly. Jack bristled.

The alchemist held up a hand to halt the brewing argument. "The point stands that Doyen Wells likely has a new type of magic if my theory holds true."

"I'm a mage," Malcolm murmured, though the words sounded strange to his ears. He had bandied around the idea with Blaise, but it struck him differently now that he was awake.

"And in typical *you* fashion, you have to be special." Flora crossed her arms. "But then you always were a dreamer."

Marian raised her eyebrows. "Dreamer. Yes, that fits. *Dreamer* is what you are." She studied Malcolm again. "We should be glad it's not a flashy magic."

"Just what we need. An untrained mage," Jack grumbled.

Malcolm swallowed. The outlaw was right—untrained mages were unpredictable and dangerous. And factoring in that he had a new type of magic, it was a recipe for disaster.

"If only there were a freeloading mage around who could earn his keep," Flora taunted, earning a glare from Jack. "Oh wait, *there is.*" She waggled a finger in the air. "Though I suppose maybe you'd rather not, since from what I heard you didn't have the balls to train Blaise, either."

Malcolm groaned. Flora had just thrown down the gauntlet, and he didn't think this would end well.

Jack strode over to the half-knocker, glowering as he towered over her. "I had a *damned* good reason for not training him. First and foremost, I would have likely killed him if we were in the same room for too long." Then he froze, glancing at Marian with an air of chagrin. "No offense to present company. Just speakin' the truth."

Marian raised her brows and didn't comment on that, at least. "It's right that a new mage needs training. Especially since it's vital we keep this quiet. We can't let it get out that Blaise's blood can spawn new mages. Much less new strains of magic."

A range of emotions flickered over Jack's face. Finally, he crossed his arms. "Fine. I'll see what I can do."

Why did Malcolm think that sounded like a veiled threat to punch him in the face?

A FEW HOURS LATER, MALCOLM FOUND HIMSELF IN THE DUBIOUS POSITION of being Jack's student. Flora had taken Marian Hawthorne back to the Arboretum, which left the outlaw alone with him.

"No time like the present," Jack commented as he swept into the room where Malcolm sat up in bed, going through correspondences he had missed.

"Oh." Malcolm shuffled the envelopes to the bedside table. "I thought you might need to search for your daughter."

The outlaw gave him a sideways look. "Don't need to. Found her."

Malcolm blinked at that. "Oh. That's good?" He wondered why Jack was still here if that was the case.

Jack frowned, assessing the room. "Now I have to focus on my promise to free Blaise. Which means you need to know a thing or three about magic, so you don't hinder us."

His words gave Malcolm pause. "You want to free Blaise?"

The outlaw stared at him as if he were daft.

Malcolm waved a hand. "Right. That's fine. Magic, yes. I'm listening."

Jack grabbed the wingback chair and dragged it closer. He settled down into it. "Good. 'Cause I'm not one to repeat myself." He put his booted feet up on the cushioned stool, which made Malcolm cringe, but he said nothing. "And we're gonna start with the basics since I figure you can't tell skunks from house cats as far as magic goes."

Malcolm clamped his mouth shut. The outlaw wasn't wrong. While he supported the mages, he was aware there were mechanics of their power he might not fully grasp. And he wanted to.

"First, gotta start off with resources. Magic exists everywhere, in anything that lives, whether it's plant or animal. It's a form of energy that we can tap." Jack held up a leather pouch that Malcolm hadn't previously noticed. He displayed a handful of items: feathers, a beeswax candle, a fang as long as his index finger. "It's even in the reagents some of us use. And most importantly, every mage has a reservoir of magic we tap into to manipulate the world around us."

Malcolm nodded. That was the longest non-threatening discussion he'd heard from Jack so far. "So magic is a part of every living thing? Even non-mages?"

"Harder to make magic sound frightening if it's so ingrained in the world around you, ain't it?" Jack mused. "But yeah, that's why my magic works on people without power. Sympathetic magic." He shrugged. "That's a more advanced topic."

Malcolm shook his head, bemused. *It seems magic has as many nuances as politics.*

"Next thing to know," the Effigest continued, "is magic is neutral. It's like this." He uncurled his left hand to reveal a bullet nestled in his palm.

Malcolm frowned in confusion. Leave it to the outlaw to compare magic to his preferred form of mayhem, which didn't seem very neutral at all. "Bullets aren't neutral."

"Aren't they?" Jack asked, tossing it into the air and catching it. "By itself, it does nothing. Give it to me, and I can take a life. Give it to a wrangler defending his herd from a murder of chupacabras, and it offers protection."

Now Malcolm saw what he meant. "Give it to a hunter with a starving family, and he can feed them."

Jack aimed a finger at him, and the outlaw looked almost pleased. "The goal is to turn you into that hunter. Just gotta learn how to wield your magic to make it serve you."

"But I *have* been wielding it," Malcolm said, then paused. Or he *thought* he had.

The Effigest rolled the bullet between his thumb and index finger. "Every greenhorn mage says that until they learn better." He gave Malcolm a long, considering look. "Without training, a maverick mage is likely to draw attention, through misuse or accident. Nothing brings a Tracker 'round faster than that."

Malcolm winced. "I see." The last thing he needed was a Tracker and unicorn on his tail. Affluence and position would only shield him from so much. "How are you able to help me learn, if our magics are so different?"

"Back in the day, it was easier to lose a Tracker. The Confederation didn't have unicorns and there were entire hidden villages of mavericks," Jack said. Malcolm pursed his lips, wondering how this was going to answer his question. The outlaw smirked at his expression. "Sometimes magic is inherited in families, like to like. But not always. There's ways to figure out basic magic theory, and to apply it to other types." He tapped his temple with meaning.

Malcolm nodded, interested. "And how do we do that?"

Jack narrowed his eyes, studying him. He removed his boots from the stool and leaned forward, vaguely predatory. "That's what we need to figure out, you and I, *Dreamer.*"

CHAPTER FIFTEEN

Light in the Darkness

Blaise

Each morning, when Blaise awoke from whatever paltry sleep his nightmares allowed, he did his best to forget everything from the day before. Maybe it wasn't the best strategy for dealing with the trauma of his current situation, but he had few options. Banishing the memories to a far corner of his mind and pretending they had happened to someone else was the only way he had come up with to get through this.

And then Jefferson had appeared in his dreams, and as crazy as it was, he didn't want to forget that. Even if he was mad at the man. *Is it real?* Out of reflex, he rubbed at the tattoo on his upper arm. He didn't think they could be real—probably just a figment of his shattering mind, desperate to hold on to something, *anything*, that might offer hope. And above all, that was what he needed. Hope, and to know that he wasn't alone. That there was a light in the darkness.

A key scraped against the lock, and he tensed before scooting away from the door. Blaise hated when the guards came in. It never ended well for him—or for the guards. But that wasn't his fault, not really. The pair of guards threw the door open and stepped inside, the woman on the left training her revolver on Blaise as her counterpart moved closer—and gods, he realized it was his tormenter, Heathcliff, bearing salt-iron shackles.

The pair moved cautiously around him, as if he were a rabid animal that might strike out at any moment. Obedient as ever, he held up his arms so that they could clap the shackles around his wrists. He was almost tempted to make a snarky comment about the futility of the restraints, but he didn't know what they had in mind for him today and didn't want another beating.

"Get up," Heathcliff barked, as the female guard motioned toward the open door with the muzzle of her revolver.

Easier said than done. Blaise rose slowly, his muscles complaining for a variety of reasons—lack of exercise and use, inadequate nutrition, abuse. When he finally got to his feet, it took him a moment to keep his balance and get them to cooperate. Blaise took a shaky breath. He hated the Confederation for what they had done to him.

Once he got moving, it was a little easier to walk. He kept his head down, staring at his feet as the guards guided him through the halls. He had stopped trying to speak to them weeks ago. They considered him little more than an animal. It wasn't worth the expended energy to engage with them.

Heathcliff led him to a room he had been in several times before. Blaise swallowed, planting his feet firmly. *No. I don't want to go in there.* Old memories reared up like monsters, and he banished them with a shake of his head as his pulse raced.

"C'mon," Heathcliff growled, grabbing his arm. "Move it."

Blaise's magic swelled, boiling up like a thunderhead on a sultry summer afternoon. Panic seized him as he heard the other guard readying her weapon. His magic sizzled against the salt-iron fetters, the sound reminding him of grease in a too-hot frying pan. Both guards escorting him knew that somehow, over the course of his time in the Cit, his magic had grown resistant to salt-iron. Blaise didn't know if it was the potion he was administered or the fact that he had gone up against the metal before. The shackles irritated his skin but did *nothing* to his well of power.

The female guard jigged aside as Heathcliff cursed. Blaise's power assaulted him, and with a howl he sank to his knees as magic broke the small bones in his wrist. Blaise squeezed his eyes closed, frantic to pull back the reflexive surge of magic. His heart pounded and he cringed, expecting the next sound to be the roar of the revolver ending his life.

There was a click, but the blast never came. Instead, he heard a frustrated sigh. "Get that man to a Healer. Garus grant us wisdom, is everyone around here *incompetent?*"

Blaise bit his lower lip, opening his eyes to look at the speaker. An older man stood in the doorway, scowling at Heathcliff as a guard arrived to help him away. Another guard slipped up to replace him, offering a crisp salute. Whoever the man was, he wore authority as easily as the charcoal-colored, tailored greatcoat on his shoulders.

"Bring him in," the man said, jerking his head to indicate the room.

Blaise balked at the command. He didn't want to go in there. Nothing good ever happened in that room. He quivered but allowed them to lead him inside and sat down in the chair in its center, watching as they fastened leather straps to hold him in place. It wouldn't take much for him to break out of those bonds, as he had proven on multiple occasions.

He closed his eyes, focusing on keeping his magic under wraps as he listened to the authoritative man consulting with someone Blaise knew to be an Inker. No one bothered to introduce him to anyone because why would they? He was nothing to them, even though they were honing him into something that could tear down the very building around them. It would be very much like talking to a revolver the way they saw it.

"We applied the geasa to the handler yesterday. Why is it not taking?" the older man demanded of the Inker.

At that, the Inker sighed and walked over to Blaise, tugging up his sleeve without asking. Blaise's eyes flew open in alarm. The Inker brushed his thumb over Blaise's tattoo, eying the design with a critical eye. "I'm unsure, Doyen Gaitwood. Any other mage would be compliant by now, but there are so many factors with this one."

Gaitwood? Blaise blinked at that, studying the man. Come to think of it, his voice had a similar ring to it, like Lamar's. This was the man who had wanted him all along. *Why?*

Gregor Gaitwood's eyes flicked to Blaise before going back to the Inker. "You need to make it work."

The Inker stared at him, mouth dropping open with disbelief. "Ah, with all due respect, we're trying but no one on record has bound a Breaker." He hesitated. "And one of our alchemists strongly suggested we not do this."

"Alchemists work for *us*, not the other way around," Gregor retorted. "Find a way to make it happen. I want this mage." He pointed a finger at Blaise, as if it weren't obvious who he meant.

Blaise narrowed his eyes. What if his dreams with Jefferson were real, and he really *was* bound to the other man? What if that was what was fouling their attempt to bind him to someone else? Those thoughts rallied his spirit, and he lifted his chin. "I don't belong to you."

Gregor spun, glaring at him for daring to speak up. "You'll be mine, or you'll *die*, Breaker. Precious little is keeping you from the second option right now."

But he wasn't dead, not yet. Gregor wanted him for something, and no doubt, that was one of the few things keeping Blaise alive at the moment.

He fantasized about unleashing his magic and watching the carnage of the Golden Citadel falling to pieces around them. Nothing about that scenario was survivable for him, but that didn't stop him from considering it. But the idea made him heartsick because that wasn't who he was.

"I want to try binding him again this afternoon," Gaitwood declared.

The Inker winced. "That won't be possible, sir. The alchemists need more time to prepare a fresh batch of Ink."

Gregor froze. "What happened to the rest of the first batch?"

"It…ah…went missing."

Went missing. Blaise's thrill at the news was short-lived. Gregor's face twisted in rage, and he swept an arm across the Inker's table. Glass vials and other implements Blaise was unfamiliar with crashed to the stone floor. The Doyen whirled on the Inker. "Inexcusable. Make another batch."

Blaise's heart raced. There was still a chance the dreams were just figments of his tortured mind. But there was also a chance they weren't. And if that was so, maybe Jefferson, in his misguided, selfish way, really *had* bound himself to Blaise. In which case, he was *still* going to be mad at Jefferson. But why else would the Ink have gone missing?

"Sir, we'll be starting over from scratch," the Inker clarified, hesitant. "We'll need more blood."

Gregor's gaze settled on Blaise. "Drain as much as you need. Call in a Healer if his condition becomes too precarious."

Blaise swallowed, and he thought about breaking the restraints and fighting back. But he knew that wouldn't end well. Instead, he focused on the one thought that gave him hope: he had an ally.

CHAPTER SIXTEEN
Unlikely Alliance

Lamar

The most insulting thing about the aftermath of Fort Courage was Lamar's requirement to report to his brother on a regular basis. Perhaps he should have been grateful since the agreement allowed him to keep his title of Commander, even though many of his direct reports were shuffled to others.

He paused outside the door to Gregor's office, gathering his thoughts before lifting his fist to knock on the door. Lamar waited, pounding again when several minutes passed and no one answered.

"I know you're in there, you addled snollygoster," Lamar muttered, digging out a key. Gregor had been adamant that he had to be invited in, but at this point his brother was just being rude. He shoved the door open, striding into the empty reception area and through the open door that led to the office where Gregor sat, frowning at him. "You seemed to not hear me knock."

"That's because I didn't want to be disturbed." Gregor turned away. "I'm busy."

"It's my assigned day to report to you, *dear* brother, so here I am." Lamar made an ironic bow, flourishing his single arm knowing the sight would disturb his sibling. Gregor made no effort to mask his disgust at his brother's disfigurement. "And I have news."

That, at least, piqued Gregor's interest. He set aside the papers he was reviewing. "Then tell me your news and leave."

"Wildfire Jack is in Izhadell. His daughter, too."

Gregor blinked, his mouth screwing up with thought. No doubt trying to recall just who Wildfire Jack was and why he mattered. "And?"

Lamar clenched his jaw. "He's the outlaw traitor who worked with the Breaker."

Recognition flared in Gregor's eyes. "Is he, now?" His voice held an edge of annoyance. "Did you capture him?"

Lamar's gaze slid to the floor in humiliation. He had been so close. He knew he had been close in that swamp, and still didn't understand how the blasted outlaw had escaped him. "I lost the trail. But he's *here*. One of my informants told me as much." Recruiting the urchins to keep an eye on the city borders had been one of his brilliant ideas. He had been more than happy to pay the lad who had brought news of the man riding the palomino stallion. Jack had even been fool enough to give the child a handmade doll. Lamar had recognized his style immediately.

Gregor scowled. "Can't let him get anywhere near that Breaker. For whatever reason, that causes no end of trouble for you. Find him."

"That's the goal," Lamar replied, keeping his voice even.

Gregor picked up a pen, tapping it against a blank sheet of paper. "He can't be skulking around Izhadell without help. Didn't you tell me you took his magic?"

"I did." Lamar narrowed his eyes because that bothered him. The only way Jack could have evaded him was with magic. He couldn't possibly have it back. "And I received a report from another operative of a sighting."

Gregor nodded. "Where did they see him?"

"Near Doyen Wells's property."

At mention of his adversary, Gregor's teeth ground together. Lamar didn't mind dropping that name one bit. He knew Wells got under his brother's skin. Not only did the men have opposing views, but they vied for the same donors. "What news is there from his property?"

Lamar shook his head. "Not much. It's a hard place for spies to get into. A deathtrap."

Gregor made a dismissive sound.

Lamar quirked a smile. "When I say *deathtrap*, I'm not exaggerating. I believe he's hired Jefferson Cole's vile little woman to place traps around it."

Gregor crossed his arms. "She's another to kill when the chance presents itself. Dirty half-breed."

Lamar curled his upper lip. "Yes, well, if you can help me do that without creating an international incident, I'd be appreciative." He had no love for Flora Strop, either.

Gregor doodled on the paper before him, contemplative. "They're all connected. They must be. Wells. Cole. Your outlaw. The Breaker."

Lamar wondered what his brother was getting at. The Breaker was held in the Golden Citadel. And while he knew a thing or two about Wells and Cole, he wasn't ready to enlighten Gregor. "He won't matter once he's bound."

Judging by the twitch of Gregor's eyelid, that was the wrong thing to say. "And therein lies my problem." Gregor pursed his lips. "What could prevent a mage from being bound?"

Lamar blinked. That was a question he hadn't expected. He frowned, dredging his thoughts, but couldn't come up with an answer. There were types of mages that were unwise to bind, but it was still possible (although fatal). "Nothing, as far as I know. That's…unprecedented."

"*Frustrating*, that's what it is." The Doyen rose from his chair to stalk the length of the room. "All my work for nothing. The annoyance of a tattoo for *nothing*."

Lamar swung his head around at that, eyes narrowed. "Tattoo?"

"He was to be *mine*," Gregor muttered, and it would have reminded Lamar of a petulant child if the words weren't so chilling. "*Mine* to reshape the Confederation with, as I like. *Mine* to remove the obstructions of the other Doyens and leaders."

The Commander stood very still, analyzing that sentence with great care. *Dangerous* words. *Treasonous* words. Heart pounding in his chest, he considered what he would say next with caution. "I wasn't aware of these aspirations." Lamar kept his voice neutral, feigning mild interest and nothing more.

Gregor made a contemptuous snort. "It wasn't something I'd make known to *you*."

"Why do you do so now?"

Gregor smiled at him. "When you were an esteemed, decorated Commander, it would have been dangerous to tell you my plans. I know how you think. You would have gone running with the information and been my ruin." His brother prowled around him, transcribing a broad circle. "But now you're in *my* debt—I'm the reason *you're* not ruined—and you will keep my secret. For that matter, you'll *help* me."

Lamar swallowed. He wanted to deny it, but Gregor was right. His brother the Doyen had been the only thing standing between him and a career in shambles after Fort Courage. While his situation wasn't the rosiest, he wasn't a beggar on a street corner or behind salt-iron bars like he might have been otherwise. What else could he do? He nodded.

"Excellent." Gregor chuckled. "Stick with me, and you'll be justly rewarded. If we find that outlaw of yours, I'll even let you kill him."

"You're too kind," Lamar rumbled, though his mind was already whirring. He had no wife or children—he had dedicated himself to the ideals of the Confederation. It was a way of life for him. Gregor was his brother in blood and name, but his loyalty to the Confederation overshadowed their tumultuous relationship. And Lamar wouldn't see it brought down by anyone. Even his own brother.

Gregor was right. He was shamed, and no one with any clout would listen to him. But he knew someone *without* clout who might.

Flora

FLORA HOPED THAT JEFFERSON APPRECIATED THE LENGTHS SHE WAS GOING to for him and his mancrush. She had no problems with snooping around on his behalf for political or financial reasons, but this was uncharted territory. Throw in a guilt-ridden alchemist and an unstable outlaw, and it was a powder keg.

She did like Marian Hawthorne, though. The woman had a keen mind and a healthy mistrust of anyone she didn't know. Flora had earned a small measure of her trust once she brought back news of her family. Turned out the Confederation was treating them better than anyone else in the Hawthorne family, housing them on a secured estate but allowing them more freedom than the alchemist or Breaker.

Flora had just escorted Marian back to the Arboretum after another visit to check on Malcolm's condition. Security had been brought up a notch, though the alchemist made no mention to Flora if it was because they had discovered her jaunts outside the walls. Whatever the reason, Flora found a way around it.

Some of Flora's knocker brethren could take passengers when they transported to their metal of choice, but that was beyond her capabilities. However, she was accustomed to coming up with new and creative ways to circumvent problems. Elaborate distractions at the main gate made getting Marian in and out through a service entrance a snap.

She was resecuring the door when she heard the heavy crunch of boots behind her. Flora considered using her magic to vanish and be done with it, but she wanted to know what sort of threat she might have to deal with. She turned and frowned when she recognized the one-armed man walking up to her.

"Look who's here to single-handedly ruin my day," Flora commented, nonchalant.

Lamar Gaitwood froze at the cut of her words, his face scrunching in irritation. Was it nice? No, but Flora didn't care. Gaitwoods were trouble, and she was happy to make him feel unwelcome. Maybe it wasn't wise to bait the man, but Flora had a deep and abiding dislike for him. Lamar was aware she worked for Jefferson and had ties to Malcolm.

The Commander paused, and she had the sense that he was counting to ten to keep himself calm. Nice that he had some anger control mechanisms. He might need them if he continued talking to her. "I came to speak with you," he said when he regained his composure.

"Congratulations, you just did. And now we're done."

"Why are you at the Arboretum?" Gaitwood asked.

She narrowed her eyes. "Can't a girl take a walk around a pretty garden without being all suspicious?"

Lamar stared at her. "The Arboretum isn't open to the public."

"I know. I'm not the public." Flora dimpled at him. "I'm not *human*, so I didn't think it applied to me." Yeah, she was half-human, so she was fudging a bit. But she let enough vitriol leak into her tone to lend it credence.

Something about her words struck him, and for once Lamar seemed to falter. But he had magic, so maybe he understood not being considered human by others. Though *she* definitely considered him human. A big, especially dumb human. Magic or not, if it looked like a duck and quacked like a duck, it was a duck. Or a human, in this case.

Lamar shifted in place, glancing up at the rising moon overhead as he gathered his thoughts. Flora hoped he hurried it up. She had places to be and things to do. "I can't believe I'm telling you this," Gaitwood muttered with a shake of his head, which piqued her interest.

If he was fishing, it was a fine hook. "Telling me what?"

The Commander shuffled in a nervous circle, and Flora wondered if it was an act or if he was really this agitated. If he had two hands, she was certain he would have wrung them together in distress. As it was, he had his sole fist clenched by his side. "My brother is trying to bind the Breaker to *himself*."

Flora almost gaped at the announcement, but she kept her jaw locked and played it cool. As far as declarations went, this was right up there with Malcolm's preposterous idea to bind Blaise first. She made a *so what* gesture. "Okay?"

Lamar stared at her. "You can't allow him to do that."

She laughed. "Oh, I can't, can I?" Flora made a grand flourish to encompass herself. "So you came to the mighty Flora Strop, hero for hire, to solve the problems of a big, strapping man?"

Gaitwood clenched his jaw. "No, I came to Flora Strop, minion of Jefferson Cole, dandy with more money than sense."

He probably thought she'd take offense at being called a minion, but there were worse disparagements out there. "Yeah, well, this may come as a surprise to you, but his line of credit isn't good for buying war criminals on the free market." She shrugged. "Nothing we can do about it."

He watched her, eyes glittering. It was several heartbeats before he spoke, and when he did, his voice was low and soft. "That's not true. I know about the tattoo on Malcolm Wells's arm. In fact, I know he and Jeffer—"

Flora was on him *fastfastfast*, knife out as she leaped at him like a poxed squirrel scaling a tree. She scrambled up his chest and held the knife at his throat, keeping purchase on him by grasping his collar with her other hand. "Give me one good reason not to end you right now and dump your corpse into the swamp for the gators."

Lamar's eyes bugged out, which was gratifying. The tip of the knife nuzzled against his neck. "I didn't come here to get into a fight with you, Strop."

"This is no *fight*. For it to be a fight, you'd have to stand a chance," Flora scoffed.

He swallowed, the movement scraping his skin against the blade. A bead of blood appeared. "I came because I don't want my brother to have his way."

Now that was interesting. Flora cocked her head but didn't withdraw her knife. "No? Why's that?"

"Would you put away your weapon so we can speak like normal people?"

"I'm not a *normal people*, so I decline." Flora stared at him. "Keep talking."

Lamar sighed, a rivulet of sweat streaking down his forehead. "My position in the Confederation—"

"Yeah, rather strained after Fort Courage, so I hear."

He made a frustrated sound at her interruption. "As I was saying, I serve the *Confederation*. My brother seeks to destabilize it and take control of the whole thing."

Okay, maybe she needed to let him keep talking. She wished she had popcorn because this was getting *good*. Truth rang in his words, and as much as she hated him, she had to grant him that. In one smooth movement, she sheathed her knife and released her grip, dropping to the ground. "I'm listening."

Lamar's shoulders drooped with relief. He rubbed at the scrape on his throat. "Just because I'm privy to the secrets I mentioned, doesn't mean I'll divulge them. In return for my silence, I request an alliance."

Flora raised her eyebrows. She didn't like that Lamar knew some of Malcolm's secrets, not one bit. But it cost nothing to hear him out. "Yeah? What do you want?"

The Salt-Iron Commander straightened. "I want the Breaker out of the Cit and as far from Confederation lands as possible. Do that, and the secret will remain safe with me."

Yeah, that was about as safe as using a chupacabra as a sheepdog. But the way she saw it, she or Jack could take care of that later. She definitely liked the first part, though. "That won't be easy."

He smiled. "No, it's not. But it will be much easier with the help of a Commander, don't you think?"

"Well, when you put it that way…" Flora nodded. Then a thought occurred to her. Two birds, one stone. "I'll work with you if you do one thing for me."

Gaitwood's face blanked. "But I'm getting your friend out and keeping those secrets—"

Flora waved a hand. "Nuh-uh. That's all stuff to benefit my employer. This is a little something for *me*. You can help my hero for hire service that you seem to think I have going on. You agree to this, or I don't pass on any information to my boss."

His brows knit at that. "You would betray him like that?" His voice was a sneer, as if he could think of nothing lower.

Flora shrugged. Lamar didn't know her, didn't know that she would do just about anything for Jefferson and that this was all a bluff. "He's just a payday."

The Commander studied her, as if searching for the lie and not finding it. "What is it?"

Flora glanced at the Arboretum. "I need you to use your position to get Alchemist Hawthorne's family out of Phinora."

Lamar's eyes hardened. "Why?"

"'Cause I made someone a promise, and now you have me haring off to save a Breaker with you." She gave a dramatic sigh to demonstrate how inconvenienced she was by this. After a beat, he nodded agreement, and she offered her hand. He took it awkwardly, and Flora crushed his hand a little in hers, just because she could. "It's a deal."

Lamar nodded. "Oh, and Strop?" She glanced up at him. "I meant what

I said about the secret. I'm a man of my word, and I will keep it. But in the event I have an untimely demise, it's included in sealed letters to my lieutenants with instructions to open after my death. And at that point, all the world will find out."

She swallowed but nodded. *Keep the rattlesnake alive, got it.*

CHAPTER SEVENTEEN
Bitter End

Emmaline

Emmaline's back was ramrod straight in the saddle. She knew she was being watched. It was a sense she'd developed early. It didn't worry her, though—not really. To all appearances she might look like an easy mark: a young woman riding alone. But she prided herself on being more than met the eye. *Pegasus, sixgun, magic.* Yeah, she wasn't her father, and she wasn't sure she'd ever be in his league of sheer menace, but she could hold her own.

At least, that was what she told herself. It was a struggle to have such confidence after Fort Courage.

<Someone at three o'clock. Keeping their distance,> Oberidon informed her, flicking a speckled ear to the side in question.

Emmaline patted his shoulder in thanks. She held the reins loosely with her left hand, only doing so for show. A tiny poppet rested in the curl of her palm, the leather of the reins rubbing against it with each step Oberidon took. If someone asked how her magic worked to find someone, there was no way to describe it. When Emmaline held her mother's poppet, she felt a tug in her belly that told her if she was going in the right direction or not. If she went the wrong way, her stomach soured as if she had eaten something bad. Whatever this magic was, it was ingrained in her and likely not something she could teach another Effigest.

Oberidon kept to the trail that wound to the northwest, though as they continued through the area known as the Uplands, the forest surrounding them became dense, sometimes blocking the path. Every time he diverted from the trail, her gut twisted and didn't settle until they headed the right way again.

<Are we close?> Oberidon asked, turning his head to look back at her.

This spell worried her pegasus. It cost her a lot to maintain the working, but she wasn't about to let it falter. "Not much farther." And the words felt right to say, although she couldn't put a finger on the *why*.

The pegasus bobbed his head, continuing onward. Emmaline used her free hand to take a swig from her canteen and was mid-sip when a peculiar sensation shoved against her. She screwed the lid on the canteen and dropped it back into place, alarmed. "Oby?"

<I felt it, too. Magic of some sort.> He stopped in his tracks, pinning his ears and taking a few strides backward. <We shouldn't go this way.>

Emmaline's stomach roiled as her pegasus moved counter to the demands of her magic. She clenched her teeth, clamping her right hand over her stomach as her back arched in pain. "No. Keep going. *Please.*"

Oberidon froze beneath her, quivering. <I can't.>

Son of a bat-eared harpy. Emmaline sucked in a breath to quell the pain. Gods, she would have thought it was her monthlies if she didn't know better. But they no longer came—not after what had been done to her at Fort Courage. Gingerly, she dismounted, standing beside the spotted stallion as she considered their options. "Why can't you go forward?" There was no physical barrier stopping them.

Oberidon fluttered his nostrils. <Because I *can't.*>

Emmaline frowned. Sometimes Oberidon was a goof, like the time he submerged himself up to his eyes in a pond and swam around, munching on lily pads. But he knew how important this mission was to her. Oberidon wouldn't fool around, not for this. Pegasi were intelligent—smarter than a lot of humans, in fact. But sometimes, people—or pegasi—could be misled into believing something was true, even when it wasn't. The magic continued its insistent push against her, but the beckoning of the effigy overrode it.

"You stay put," Emmaline murmured, rubbing his velvety nose.

Oberidon's ears flopped sideways, miserable that he was letting her down. She turned away from him, but before soldiering onward, she had an idea. Emmaline turned back and snagged his reins. Oberidon couldn't take *her* forward, but perhaps *she* could lead *him*. He snorted and doggedly trailed after her.

It took ten steps before reaching whatever was pushing magic against them. It was a sort of invisible barrier, pulsing before her with the looming command to run in the opposite direction. Emmaline gritted her teeth as it assaulted them.

"I didn't come this far to turn back now." Head down and trembling with exertion, she powered through the magical bulwark. Oberidon followed in her wake, snorting and skittish.

Emmaline hadn't realized the cost of breaking through. She stumbled to her hands and knees, the poppet falling away from her. But her stomach didn't sour, and she knew she was still going the right way. Distantly, she was aware of the sounds of feet slapping against the ground as people made their way toward her. It alarmed the outlaw part of her, the part that was always on edge and alert. But she had other priorities. She scrabbled a hand through the grass, searching for the poppet. She *needed* it.

<Em! We're outnumbered!> Oberidon's panic bled into her mind, and Emmaline lifted her head to stare at the semi-circle of men and women a dozen paces ahead of them, many with rifles and revolvers out and ready.

"*How* did you break through those wards?" an older man with a shiny bald head demanded from the crowd.

"I was tailing her! She just walked on through," a young man piped up, pushing his way through the underbrush to join the group.

Emmaline licked her lips, surveying the group. *Defenders. Maybe sentries. I think we stumbled onto some sort of hidden settlement.* Yeah, that sounded right. Like Fortitude before the battle. Except this place had some sort of fancy ward, which was a marvelous idea. She blinked as she realized she hadn't answered them yet. Gods, she hadn't realized how bad the fatigue from magic drain could be. "Um, magic?"

Someone shoved past the man who had posed the question, booted feet carrying them to Emmaline's side. Oberidon made a querying nicker, uncertain. The stranger knelt in front of Emmaline, helping her into a sitting position. Emmaline quivered at the odd flutter in her stomach. She looked up and into a face that could have been her own in a decade or two.

"Katherine, who *is* this? Who broke through our wards?" another of the gathered mages demanded.

"My daughter," the strange woman whispered, her voice afire with emotion. "My *daughter* broke the wards."

Emmaline blinked as the words registered. She shook her head, vision clearing with the effort. "*Mom.*" That accounted for the flutter. She had found her target. Completed her mission.

Her mother pulled her close, and Emmaline was so tired her mind drifted to the last time she had been curled against this woman when she was three years old. The stale scent of alcohol wafted off her mother's clothes and breath, but all Emmaline focused on was the *rightness* and security of their embrace. Something scratchy bit into the palm of her hand—*oh, the poppet.* Magic coursed through it, still draining her.

Her mother tensed, as if she felt the power, too. She angled to peer at the poppet, though she wobbled with the movement. She placed her hand over the tiny doll in Emmaline's grasp. "Cancel your spell, baby. I don't know how you did it, but you're done."

Emmaline tightened her fist around the poppet and ended the spell, relief settling over her as the ongoing draw on her limited magic ended. "I found you. I can't believe I found you."

"She broke our wards," the older man from earlier complained again.

"Shut your stupid mouth, Basil," her mother snapped, unsteadily getting to her feet. She offered a hand to Emmaline, who declined because, as tired as she was, she didn't want to topple her mother. "You act like you don't know the first thing about repairing it."

"But if she did it then—"

Emmaline blinked as a ball of flame appeared in her mother's upturned palm. "*Not. Another. Word.*"

Basil's mouth was wide and gasping, like a fish out of water. "Katherine, you're drunk. You wouldn't—"

"Don't tell me what I wouldn't do," she retorted. She closed her hand, quenching the flame so the smoke wisped away to nothing. She put an arm around her daughter. "Come on. We'll speak more after we get grub in you and some rest." Her mother tottered a few steps. "And maybe I need to sober up a little more."

Emmaline glanced back at Oberidon, who followed along, obedient. The other defenders parted to allow them to pass, and a short distance later, signs of civilization appeared. Small homes and even what looked like businesses clustered in a clearing. "What is this place?"

Kittie smiled. "Welcome to Bitter End."

———

Kittie

KITTIE BRUSHED BACK AN ERRANT LOCK OF HER DAUGHTER'S GOLDEN HAIR, the simple motion taking her back more than a decade. She swallowed, fighting back the tears that threatened to spring from her eyes unbidden. Not now. She needed to be strong, even if all she wanted to do was curl around her exhausted child and protect her from the world.

Effigest. Emmaline was an Effigest like her father. Kittie set aside that information for later—she had so many questions, but they would wait. She had her own battles to fight first. Starting with her allies.

She steeled herself, head high, as she opened the door of the small cottage she shared with her husband, who was away. As expected, a small throng awaited her. Leander Benton, sentry chief for Bitter End, led the group with his arms crossed. "You've got some explaining to do, Katherine."

Kittie studied him. Leander was taller and bulkier than her—than anyone else in town, in fact. He liked to think that his sheer size gave him an advantage, and maybe against others, it did. But she'd gone toe to toe with better men.

Stanley Cavin, who fancied himself the mayor of their idyllic little band of misfits, stepped around Leander, putting an arm in front of him. "What he means, of course, is that we're curious how that slip of a girl breached the wards like a hot knife through butter."

Kittie glanced at the closed door behind her, debating how much to tell them. None of them knew anything about her life before her arrival at Bitter End. "I already told you: she's my daughter."

Stanley frowned, shifting his weight from foot to foot as if her explanation bothered him. It probably did, in the grand scheme of things. He glanced at her hands like they were coiled rattlesnakes. "What else haven't you told us, Katherine? Does Hugh know?"

She scoffed at that. As if she would have told her husband anything of who she was. Of who she had been. Of the life she believed lost to her forever. No, she wasn't willing to bare those wounds to anyone here. "He doesn't know. I'll tell him when he returns." Even though he would be furious. But she could take the heat.

Stanley and Leander traded glances. "She's a mage?" Stanley asked.

Kittie nodded. She hadn't been able to speak to Emmaline much since she burst through the barrier, her daughter had been so worn out. But there was no doubt she had magic.

"What is she?" Leander asked.

Kittie smiled. "A maverick. That's all I can tell you right now."

Leander scowled. Stanley licked his lips. "We need to know if anyone followed her. That's all we ask."

"And all you need to know is that if she was followed, I'll turn anyone on her trail to ash." Kittie turned on her heel and strode back into her house.

CHAPTER EIGHTEEN
Unconventional Teaching Methods

Malcolm

"Up and at 'em," Jack declared as he threw open the door to Malcolm's room.

Malcolm blinked from where he reclined on the bed, supported by a flock of goose-down pillows. He had been going through the notes of the recent Council sessions he had missed, staying up-to-date with political events. "What?"

The outlaw jerked a thumb at the open hallway behind him. "We're going to practice. And you're not gonna laze around here all day to do it."

Malcolm frowned. *That's unfair.* "I'm not lazing around. And I'm in the middle of something, thank you very much."

Too late, he realized that was the wrong tack to take with Jack. The outlaw crossed his arms. "That so? Guess you got all your sleepwalking magic figured out then." His eyes glinted. "And if I came at you now, you could stop me, is that right?"

"Wait, what?" Malcolm asked with growing alarm. Surely he had misheard the volatile mage. "*Stop* you?"

Jack grinned. "If I were to attack you, could you stop me in my tracks?" At Malcolm's blank look, he added, "Using your magic."

Brow scrunching in confusion, Malcolm shook his head. "But my magic isn't offensive. Or defensive, for that matter." At least, he didn't think so. The disapproving crinkles in the skin around Jack's eyes told a different tale, however.

"Thinking like that is gonna get you in trouble," the Effigest rebuked him, leaning against the door-frame like a languid cat.

With a frustrated sigh, Malcolm folded up the meeting minutes and shoved them into a folder, which he set aside. "Fine, but you already know the answer. Why even ask?"

"Because," the outlaw rumbled, studying him, "you're gonna learn."

Defend himself with magic? Dream magic, at that. Malcolm rubbed his chin, thoughtful. Jack worked with him a few times a day. Jefferson had made a little progress and could now call up the dreamscape without falling asleep. He had a better idea about how to manipulate his power, but it still felt like rowing in a rain-swollen river: he was more likely to go with the flow than direct the current. He wanted to respond that he couldn't do it, but the outlaw would be sure to argue against it. Which meant that Jack had devised tactics he could use already.

Malcolm shifted upright and tossed the sheets back, freeing himself to swing his legs out of bed. "If you were me, what would you do?"

Jack jabbed an index finger at him. "By the grace of the gods, I'm *not* you because that would be damned annoying. And that's for you to figure out. C'mon."

"But I'm not even dressed—"

The outlaw aimed a contemptuous look at him. "You're dressed enough. We're not going to a gods-forsaken gala."

That was true. Malcolm winced as he took in his disheveled state. His current shirt was rumpled and unkempt, and the trousers he had on were a comfortable pair from five seasons previous. But the outlaw had little patience, so Malcolm gingerly pulled out a pair of shoes and crammed his feet into them, following Jack out.

The Effigest headed out to the stables. Malcolm cocked his head, curious, but didn't ask. Square hay bales crouched outside the two stalls used by the pegasi, though someone had draped saddle blankets over them to serve as cushions. Emrys and Zepheus peered over their stall doors, curious.

"What are we doing?" Malcolm asked.

The outlaw sat on one of the covered bales, elbows on his knees. "We're taking the training up a notch. You been in your fancy dreamscape every night?"

Malcolm swallowed, the mention of the dreamscape turning his mind to Blaise. "Yes."

Maybe Jack detected the twinge of emotion in his voice. He narrowed his eyes but didn't comment. "Good. Means you're using your magic regularly, so you may know more about it than you think. Long as you're not terrified of your magic, it's possible to learn how to wrangle it naturally."

Malcolm nodded, knowing Jack was referring to Blaise before he had wrestled his power under control. Little wonder the young man's dangerous magic had intimidated him.

Jack glanced back at the pegasi, then to Malcolm. "I want you to make Emrys sleep."

"Excuse me?" Malcolm was sure he'd misheard.

The outlaw smirked. "You heard me."

The black stallion bobbed his head. <I volunteered. It is fine.>

Malcolm pursed his lips, uncertain. "I've never—"

Jack held up a hand. "Stop your caterwauling and do it."

Right. It was clear the outlaw wouldn't relent until he tried. And *succeeded*. Malcolm winced, glad Jack hadn't been the one to train Blaise. That would have ended poorly for everyone involved. Malcolm took a deep breath to center himself. His magic was easiest to manipulate when he was asleep, but Jack was training him to use it while he was awake, too. He wasn't very good at it, though. It was an uncomfortable feeling, being so clumsy at something like this.

He imagined the magic was within him like a lump of clay, ready to be formed. *No, I don't like that analogy.* Perhaps it was more like the words of a script, to be acted upon. *Yes, I like that.* He was no playwright, but at the theater he knew what to expect. He was the director. Malcolm smiled, enjoying the idea.

"Stop fooling around," Jack reminded him.

Malcolm wrinkled his nose at the interruption, then imagined he was directing the script—his magic—to his actor, Emrys. He held the stallion's proximity in his mind, and there was a sensation like static when his power found its target. *Sleep.*

Jack's sharp intake of breath was all the proof of success he needed. But just to be sure, Malcolm opened his eyes and turned to the stall behind him. Emrys was still upright, but his head was low, eyes closed. One hoof was cocked in a relaxed posture.

"Don't stop now. Give 'im a dream," Jack ordered.

Give him a dream? Malcolm frowned. "I don't—" He stopped himself before Jack could interrupt. "Wait, I think I can." It couldn't be that much different from what he had done on instinct with Blaise. Except now he had to do it while he was awake and Emrys was asleep.

Malcolm closed his eyes, concentrating. He focused on the stallion's presence, finding him. There was no way he could tell if the pegasus was still asleep, but he hoped that was the case. Malcolm imagined the dreamscape unwinding before him. It was a vast, grey space, ready to be formed. Itude was easiest, so he called the town up. But this was Emrys, and he deserved something special. Malcolm recalled the broad tables that had covered the town square at the Feast of Flight, and they appeared before him.

"Hmm, yes," he murmured, another idea coming to him. Every imaginable sort of dessert popped into existence on the tables.

Pleased, he sought Emrys and pulled the stallion into the dreamscape. The pegasus trotted along as if all were normal, though he came to a stiff-legged halt at the sight of the heavily-laden tables. His ears pricked forward with interest.

<Is that what I think it is?> Emrys quivered with delight.

Malcolm grinned. "Every sort of treat Blaise ever made? Yes."

<For me?> The stallion arched his neck, nostrils flared.

"And only you."

Emrys bolted over to the tables, thrusting his muzzle into a decadent cake, nearly toppling it onto a nearby pie. He took a chomping bite from each one, going down the line as if he hadn't eaten in weeks. Malcolm was glad it was a dream because he would have felt terrible if he colicked Blaise's pegasus.

Something—no, someone—grabbed Malcolm by the shirt collar, hoisting him up. With a gasp, he opened his eyes and found Jack glaring at him. The outlaw levered back an arm, and Malcolm was certain he was about to take a punch. *Not my face.* He tried to writhe away, but the outlaw was stronger and better prepared. Jack snaked a foot behind Malcolm's ankle, jerking his leg out from under him so he stumbled to the ground with frantic, pinwheeling arms.

The outlaw stood over him, a foreboding shadow. Panic gripped Malcolm. After all this, Jack had become untethered and was going to kill him. *No.*

Malcolm pulled at his dream magic, hurling it at the outlaw. *Sleep, you bastard!*

Jack slumped to the ground, landing on a saddle pad that had been moved to cushion his fall.

"What?" Malcolm gasped, pushing into a sitting position as he panted for breath. He glanced back at Zepheus. Jack's palomino was the only other witness who was awake. "What is *wrong* with him?"

<It was a test,> the pegasus answered, chewing thoughtfully on a wisp of hay.

A test. Malcolm made a face. "Why didn't he—oh." Jack had, in fact, given him ample warning. He leaned back against the prickly hay bale, his heart pounding like a runaway horse. Gods, that had been terrifying. To think Jack had only been *play-acting*. Malcolm didn't want to ever fight him in earnest.

He sat there for another half hour until the outlaw stirred with a yawn. Jack rubbed at his face, sitting up slowly. "You did it, huh?"

Malcolm crossed his arms. "You really need to work on your teaching methods."

The outlaw grinned. "My methods may be unconventional, but I'm a very effective teacher, I'll have you know." He clambered to his feet, stretching as if he'd had a nice cat nap. "It worked?"

Malcolm massaged his forehead. "Yes."

"Then why are you mad?"

"I *thought* you were going to kill me!"

Jack laughed. "If I wanted to kill you, you'd be gettin' dressed for the bone orchard already." He turned and headed for the stable door, waving a hand over his shoulder. "Keep practicing, Sleepwalker."

CHAPTER NINETEEN

Breaker Unleashed

Blaise

Sleep didn't come easily to Blaise, not in his current circumstances, but he was exhausted and weak from the day, his body bruised and tender. Previously he had been afraid to sleep because nightmares greeted him as soon as he drifted off. But now he welcomed the dreams that he knew would rescue him from the darkness.

He was back in Itude, his body hale and clean. Blaise glanced down, self-conscious. He didn't think Jefferson would care what he looked like, but all the same, he worried about being a disappointment.

Jefferson was nowhere to be seen. Blaise walked through the empty town, reveling in the simple joy of his body working as it should. No aches and pains. No cuts or bruises. He shaded his eyes as he caught a strange shimmer of movement. Blaise glanced down and noticed a gleaming thread of magic stretching from himself to the distant horizon. He'd never seen that before—but then again, he'd been distracted. Gently, he touched it with a finger, mindful of his magic. Something about the thread was comforting. It reminded him of Jefferson.

"Is this the geasa?" Blaise murmured, studying it. Such a fragile thing, easily sheared apart by his magic. If the Confederation bound anyone else to him, he was confident he could break free.

"You can do it if you want," a familiar voice said. Jefferson strode up, resplendent in a tan frock coat. Blaise couldn't remember ever seeing him in such a light color before, and it brought out the gold in Jefferson's hair. "Break it, I mean. I wouldn't blame you."

Blaise looked over his shoulder. "Are you reading my mind?"

Jefferson chuckled. "I don't think so. But I know how you feel about this." He tilted his head, shoving his hands in his pockets. "May I ask you something?"

Curiosity tempered Jefferson's tone. Blaise nodded. "Sure."

"Why haven't you tried to escape?" Concern lined Jefferson's green eyes.

Blaise dropped his gaze, recalling that Jefferson hadn't seen him recently. Didn't know that each day he was weaker than the previous. "It's not as easy as breaking down a door or a wall and walking out of here." He rubbed the back of his neck. "I could probably do that, yeah. But after that? There's all the guards I would face. They have guns, and we already know what a bullet can do to me." As if summoned by the memory, the old wound in his arm twinged. At the same time, Blaise recalled the short-lived shield of magic he had created. He shook his head, dismissing it. "Magic doesn't solve everything."

"No, I suppose it doesn't," Jefferson agreed. Then a smile curled his lips, and he took a step closer. "What if I told you we're going to get you out?"

The words came as such a surprise that Blaise was certain he'd misheard. "What?"

"We're going to get you out. Soon. Within a few days, I hope," Jefferson said, the words coming in a rush of excitement. He flapped his hands around as if he couldn't control them. "You'll be free."

Blaise stared at him. Freedom. That seemed like such an elusive concept right now. His mouth went dry. "How? Where will I go?" He looked down, eyes welling with tears. "You haven't seen me...the *real* me...for a while. I'll have a hard time getting out. I'm too weak."

Jefferson studied him. The corners of his eyes crinkled with worry. "All the more reason to get you out."

Blaise swallowed, overcome with emotion. He couldn't help it; the idea was so overwhelming all he could do was sit down where he was, which was in the middle of one of the dusty streets. He put his face in his hands.

He heard the scuff of Jefferson crouching down beside him. "What's wrong?"

How could he explain? Blaise shook his head. He didn't know how to express the mixed sense of relief and renewed hope, but also the anxiety that he had forgotten how to fit in. Or worse, that no one would want him. That they would free him and see him for the broken thing that he was. And he didn't want to say any of those things because then Jefferson might decide to leave him behind.

An arm slung around his shoulders, warm and comforting. The spearmint scent of Jefferson's aftershave wafted to Blaise. "Hey. Come back to me."

The words were almost a plea, and they were what Blaise needed to hear in that moment. "I'm here."

Jefferson gave him a sideways glance, as if he feared Blaise would spook away from beneath his arm like a skittish horse. But Blaise didn't— it was kinder than any touch he'd experienced recently. "This is our time. What do you want to do?"

"Talk," Blaise said softly. "No one talks to me like I'm..." He shook his head. "Like I'm a person."

Jefferson's eyebrows slashed together before relaxing. "We can talk. Whatever you like."

Blaise nodded, thankful, and got back to his feet with care. They walked together through the town, passing by the bakery. He glanced at it for a moment, reconsidering. *Another time*, he promised himself. Right now, he needed to be heard.

"I'm going to tell you some things because I don't think I'll be brave enough to tell you outside of a dream," Blaise whispered. "It's just too much."

Jefferson took his hand. "I understand. I'm listening."

Blaise bowed his head, and with the wind of the dreamscape whistling overhead, he told Jefferson of the things he had endured. The beatings and the experimentation. How they sometimes bled him until he was too weak to move. The way the guards and staff treated him as if he were nothing.

Jefferson listened, intent, never interrupting, his expression open as he nodded, somehow knowing that all Blaise needed was to be listened to. Blaise felt like he was talking about someone else—it was difficult to recognize that all those things had happened to *him*. It was good to tell someone, to have someone listen and simply be there.

He finished, tears streaming down his face and his shoulders sagging with exhaustion, and he didn't fight it when Jefferson pulled him into an embrace that offered comfort, strength, and love. "I'm sorry. Gods, I'm *so* sorry," Jefferson said after a few minutes, his voice taut with suppressed anger.

Blaise swiped at his runny nose. "Why is my nose snotty when I cry in a dream?"

"So I can do this," Jefferson said, pulling out a handkerchief and offering it to him. "But I don't know. I guess we expect it, and it happens."

Blaise nodded, dabbing at his nose with the handkerchief. "I'm sorry I'm a mess."

Jefferson shook his head. "You're not a mess, and there's no need to apologize. I just wish I could do more."

Blaise glanced away, rubbing at the tattoo on his bicep. He felt a little better for having told someone what he had endured. It was cleansing to have validation, even if he was still in the situation. But that wasn't the only thing weighing heavily on his mind. "I'm not like the others."

Jefferson drew away, blinking at him in bewilderment. "What? Not like who?"

With chagrin, Blaise realized there was no way the other man could have followed the wild path his thoughts went down. "The people you were with in the dream garden."

"*Oh.*" A cringe flashed across Jefferson's face. Then he clasped his hands, shaking his head. "I don't expect you to be." He shifted until he was shoulder to shoulder with Blaise again.

"Doesn't that bother you?"

Jefferson raised a brow. "Why would that bother me?"

Blaise pursed his lips, uncertain if this was a conversation he even wanted to have. But they had dabbled with the topic previously in Rainbow Flat—and gods, that felt like a thousand years ago. "I don't know if that's something we would ever do."

He expected to see hurt or anger on Jefferson's face. Instead, he merely nodded his head. "There's more to love than sex."

Blaise rubbed the back of his neck. Unschooled as he was in that topic, he was quickly becoming out of his depth. "Is there?"

"Of course." Jefferson's voice turned soft. "Intimacy is amazing, but if that's all that exists, then it's purely lust." His gaze flicked to Blaise, green eyes assessing. "It's also being accepted by someone else for *who* you are."

Odd as it was, Blaise realized Jefferson was speaking about himself, not Blaise. How strange, since Blaise had never stopped to think the other man sought acceptance, too. Jefferson had given Blaise a glimpse of his past life, one that had been bereft of caring. He'd been a commodity, something to be bartered and used.

"And it's being there for someone you care about, come what may," Jefferson continued, unaware of Blaise's thoughts. He ran a hand along the ridge of his jaw. "Granted, if we had this conversation ten years ago, I would give you a very different answer. And that's what you saw in the garden." Jefferson ended the statement with a self-deprecating shrug.

Blaise nodded. He appreciated Jefferson's words, though he was uncertain if the other man truly understood him. "And if I never...want to be like the people in the garden?" Blaise inwardly winced. Why was it so hard, so uncomfortable, to talk about sex? It was a part of life, but one that he didn't want to think about.

Jefferson cocked his head, lips pursed as if he were trying to figure out why Blaise was so adamant about this discussion. "I won't mislead you. I was hoping for that with you. But if you listened to anything I just said, that's not what I *need*." And then, as if he wanted to make certain that Blaise didn't misunderstand, he added, "You. *You* are all I need in whatever way you're willing to grant me that."

"You realize I have boundaries. Things I may never be comfortable doing." Blaise wanted nothing less than certainty.

Jefferson chuckled. "I'm aware. Sort of like your preference for switchel over wine." He gave an exaggerated sigh, then grew serious again. "I know that. And believe it or not after the garden, I *respect* that."

Blaise swallowed, shaken by the intensity in Jefferson's voice. *He understands. And he doesn't mind.* That could change with time, Blaise feared. But that was something to worry about if it came down to it. He released a heavy breath, then put an arm around Jefferson, resting his head against the other man's shoulder.

They talked for as long as they could, until the wakefulness of early morning tugged Blaise away, returning him to his stark reality. The ragged blanket he laid on was a far cry from the safety of Jefferson's bulk, and the cell was foreign after the sun on his skin in the dreamscape. But he felt more hopeful than he had in the past. The memory of Jefferson's face bathed in the sun's glow, watching him with compassion and affection, was a balm for his soul. He felt wanted. He felt human.

And that was all he needed to hold on until rescue came.

———————————

GREGOR PACED BEFORE BLAISE LIKE AN AGITATED GRASSCAT, PEPPERING THE Inker with questions on why yet another attempt to bind him had failed. Blaise tuned out most of the Doyen's rant. At this point, it wasn't anything he hadn't heard before. He allowed his mind to wander from the hopelessness of his situation. There was nothing he could do at this point to change his predicament.

He often thought of Jefferson and his sandy brown hair. Jefferson, who came to him each night, lighting the darkness with stars and dreams that Blaise knew were real.

"*Look at me when I speak to you!*" a voice raged in front of him, sharp as the crack of a whip. Gregor Gaitwood was inches from his face.

Blaise jumped, though he was fastened tightly to his customary seat, and he didn't move far. But his magic reacted, rising to the surface and breaking free like a stampede. He didn't care to call it back, but let it loose. It snapped the binds that held him in place, the leather flaking and falling to the floor in chunks. The salt-iron shackles on his wrists groaned and grated under the magical assault. Metal shavings drifted down as his power slowly, inexorably did the unthinkable.

The Inker shrank back. "He's breaking the *salt-iron*."

"Of course he is. He's unlike anything we've seen before," Gregor said, his focus still on Blaise. *"Why can't we break you, boy?"*

Blaise met his eyes, something he rarely did anymore, and smiled. Days ago, he wouldn't have dared to do it. But Jefferson had renewed his sense of self and his shattered confidence. They could do everything in their power to beat him and keep him down, but they weren't going to win. Not while he had people fighting for him.

"Because *I'm* the Breaker, and that's what *I* do," Blaise answered, his voice little more than a raw whisper as his power chewed through the shackles. They fell to the floor with a clatter.

Guards rushed in and swarmed him. Maybe he would regret his words later, but in this moment, he didn't. His words had sown doubt in Gregor Gaitwood, and that was all Blaise needed to feel empowered at last.

But Gaitwood wasn't about to let him have the upper hand. The guards crushed Blaise's face against the stone floor as the Doyen announced, "Give him the potion. I'll make use of him before it's too late."

CHAPTER TWENTY

How to Save a Life

Flora

No one thought anything amiss when a courier brought Flora a coded letter. It was a frequent occurrence, and not a single one of Malcolm's staffers so much as batted an eye as she withdrew, tucking it beneath her arm. Just as well. It would have been awkward to explain away a letter from Lamar Gaitwood.

Maybe she should have told Malcolm and Jack that the Commander was throwing in his lot with them. Flora didn't know Jack well, but she knew enough to understand that he was capricious and bore a grudge against Lamar. In fact, a crashing airship had almost smashed the fool to a pulp because of that grudge. She couldn't fault him since Lamar was the walking equivalent to skunk stank. Flora wasn't above using every tool at hand. And Lamar may disagree, but he was definitely a tool.

Flora considered passing the information to Malcolm, but he had enough on his plate. And besides, this wouldn't be the first time she quietly took care of something on his behalf. That was her job. The information that Lamar had on her employer concerned her—*how did he find out?*—but she would figure out how to scrub that dangerous information out of existence. It was delicate and would take longer, but if Lamar kept his end of the bargain, she would fix it.

She found a quiet room and tore the correspondence open. Flora hissed out a frustrated sigh at the simple code the Commander had used.

Amateur. Her Uncle Jasper could've figured it out, and he didn't have a mind for such things.

The precious cargo you requested for transfer is headed to Rainbow Flat. Other target must move tomorrow. Meet me tonight at the Sour Eel. 22:00. Alone.

Flora frowned at the note. On the one hand, if he could be believed, then Marian's family was on their way to safety, and that was promising. But on the other...they weren't quite ready to free Blaise. They were close, but this was too soon. She wondered if this was some sort of double-cross. If Jack got wind of it, he would think so. But it wouldn't hurt to meet the good Commander tonight to see what he had to say and feel things out.

Jack

JACK SHOT A GLANCE AT FLORA. THE HALF-KNOCKER SEEMED JUMPIER THAN usual, which maybe was to be expected when planning a jailbreak from a place like the Cit. But he'd witnessed the casual carnage she wrought at Fort Courage, and that seemed more in line with what he knew of her. Something was up, and he didn't like it.

But all the same, he was glad for the change of pace. He had spent the last several days lurking around Wells's fancy-pants estate, his training sessions with the pretty boy his only entertainment. It was high time for action.

Now, they clustered in the broad center aisle of the stables so that the pegasi could plot along with them. Flora had produced a map of the Golden Citadel and the surrounding area, spreading it out on a crate in the middle of their huddle. When asked how she acquired it, she simply replied that she had connections. *Strop's blowing a bunch of corral dust at us, but why?*

"Getting in is going to be the challenge," Jack murmured, running his fingers over the entrance on the map. "Won't be able to use my magic."

"What, you can't use your hexing to look like someone else?" Flora asked.

A muscle in Jack's cheek twitched in annoyance. "*First of all,* hexing is harmful; charming is helpful. I go both ways."

"You do, huh?" Flora's brows rose.

"Shut your piehole before I hex *you,*" the outlaw growled. "I'm an *Effigest,* not a Hexxer or a Charmer. And besides, you're thinking of an

Illusionist. My workings can't change how someone looks." He shrugged. "And even if I could, it wouldn't help me get in."

Malcolm frowned. "Why not?"

"Because," Jack said, tracing the perimeter of the Cit on the map, "there's a ward in place all the way around that detects magic."

The Doyen blinked in surprise. "But I'm able to enter as Jefferson with no fuss."

Yeah, and Jack wondered how that was. "And no one's ever questioned you?"

Malcolm shrugged. "I mean, not yet..."

"How *do* you keep that two-faced guise of yours?" Jack asked, leaning forward. He didn't care if the question was insensitive. In fact, he kinda liked the way the other man winced at the words.

Malcolm traded a glance with Flora, appearing to debate the wisdom of divulging his secret. She crossed her arms, then gave a small nod. Malcolm pulled a gaudy ring into view. "This ring is spelled with a glamor."

An item. That was sort of what Jack expected. He tapped his fingers against the map, considering. "A glamor from an enchanted item is different. Remember our little chat about magic?" Jack lifted a hand to gesture to the world around them.

"About it being everywhere?" Jefferson asked.

"In anything that *lives*," Jack corrected. He jerked his chin to indicate the ring. "Not alive."

Flora canted her head, thoughtful. "Kinda major oversight by whoever designed the ward."

"Not all theurgists care to be thorough," Jack said with a shrug. He had known the designer. The mage was long dead, but the magic remained intact. The odds of the Confederation upgrading it were slim. Why change something that worked?

"If I had another enchanted item, we could get you in easily!" Jefferson said as he caught on to the intricacies of the ward. Then he scratched his chin, deflating. "But there's no time. So how do we get Jack in? Disguised as a guard, perhaps?"

Jack snorted. "That's not gonna work. You can bet the gate guards can identify everyone who works the grounds by sight." Absently, he rubbed at his shoulder as old memories stirred. "Too bad we can't wait 'til nightfall."

Flora snagged Malcolm's watch from his breast pocket, flipping it open to check the time. It was after midnight, and none of them were under any illusions to go haring off without a solid plan. "We'll miss our window if we wait. And Mal still has to contact Blaise."

The outlaw blew out a frustrated breath. "Well, not sure how far y'all would get inside the Cit without me."

"No, we need you," Malcolm agreed.

Flora shifted, scratching at her stone-colored forehead as she reached a conclusion. "I have an idea, but Jack won't like it."

Jack tilted his head. "Try me."

The half-knocker gave a nervous laugh. "Full disclosure, I got the map we're looking at from Lamar Gaitwood." Malcolm's jaw dropped, and Jack stilled. "Also, he's the one that told me about Gregor's plan to move Blaise tomorrow."

At Lamar's name, fury flooded through Jack's veins. Flora Strop was a damned traitor. He launched at her, but she expected his move and dodged out of the way with unnatural alacrity. Jack twisted, pulling on the magic of his own poppet to grant him speed as he went after the half-knocker. He was so pissed off he forgot Malcolm was there. And that he had magic of his own.

Jack awoke an hour later, flat on his back. Zepheus's muzzle hovered over him, blowing equine breath into his face. <You should let people explain things first before you try to murder them,> the pegasus advised.

The outlaw grunted, sitting up. Something scratched against his head, and he reached up and plucked straw from his hair. He glared at Flora and Malcolm. The Doyen was watching him like he was a dangerous beast. Flora didn't so much as glance his way, poring over the map.

He leveled a finger at Malcolm. "Don't you *ever* do that to me again."

Curse him to Perdition, but Malcolm *smirked* at him. "I was just making sure I could stop you in your tracks."

Jack grunted, getting to his feet. "There better be a damned good reason Strop's thrown in her lot with Lamar."

"We discussed it while you napped." Malcolm nodded. "Long story short, Gregor is betraying the Confederation, and Lamar doesn't like it."

"Hmm." Jack rubbed his chin. From his history with Lamar, that was likely. "Explain."

He listened as Malcolm recounted Flora's information. Gregor wanted to take out the other members of the Salt-Iron Council? As far as goals went, Jack thought that was a pretty good one. But it would leave Gregor the sole surviving member, and it sounded like he was keen to make a power grab. Yeah, that checked out for Lamar's motivation. Didn't mean Jack liked it, though.

"My idea is that Lamar can take you into the Cit," Flora said once Malcolm finished. She held up a hand before Jack protested. "Don't tell me he's going to betray us. He's on our side for the time being. He wants Blaise as far from Izhadell as we can take him so Gregor can't use him."

Jack pursed his lips, glancing at Malcolm. "You trust this?"

The Doyen sighed. "I don't know what other choice we have. Either we assume the information is good and act on it, or we mistrust it and don't. If we don't..." He looked away, shaking his head.

It would be the end of the line for Blaise, and maybe for all the mages in Phinora if Gregor succeeded at killing the Council. Jack bared his teeth. Yeah, Gregor would start a war. There would be a genocide of anyone with magic.

Dread tickled his spine. Emmaline was still in Phinora, going after Kittie. He closed his eyes briefly. They would be at risk, too. "Fine. We'll do it, but if Lamar betrays us, I'm killing him."

"Yeah, I know how you operate," Flora said with a roll of her eyes. "So we're doing this?"

Jack didn't want to. Every instinct screamed *wrong, wrong, wrong*. But if he was honest with himself, it was more than Lamar's presence setting him off. It was the Cit itself.

<I will be outside the walls. It will not be like the last time you were there,> Zepheus assured him, bumping him gently with his muzzle.

The outlaw nodded. "Yeah, we're doing this." He yawned. "Time to get some shut-eye for real while I can. Sleepwalker, tell Blaise we're coming for him."

"It's *Dreamer*," Malcolm muttered with a shake of his head. "And I would love to."

CHAPTER TWENTY-ONE

Hurricane

Jefferson

The dreamscape was a discordant nightmare.

Falling asleep after finalizing their plans to free Blaise hadn't been easy. It was the second glass of wine that eased him into slumber. At first Jefferson thought it was the wine that had forced the dream into a confusing jumble.

It was difficult to make heads or tails of what he was looking at—warped skeletons of buildings existed and then faded away, the landscape shifting from the Gutter to a forest and then to a prison cell. An unnatural wind whipped against Jefferson, screaming with unrelenting fury, making it impossible to walk forward.

It had never been like this before, and he didn't understand what was happening. He was supposed to be the master of his magic. Jefferson froze, tapping into his power. It rose to his summons, and he sent it out against the nightmare dreamscape, struggling to bend it to his will. In the distance, something shattered with the brittle tinkling of broken glass.

Jefferson gritted his teeth and glanced down at his feet. With a start, he realized that the dreaming world around him was fracturing. The ground beneath him grew into a crack that yawned wider and wider, threatening to swallow him whole. He dodged aside, breaking into a clumsy jog against the biting wind.

"Blaise!" Jefferson called, stumbling as he suffered an annoying moment of not being able to run in his dream. It took everything he had to break free and bolt onward. "Where are you?"

He knew Blaise was there. Jefferson sensed his presence through their bond. But it was as if he were everywhere, all around him. And with a shock, he realized Blaise *was* all around him, in a way. Breaker magic was assaulting the dreamscape, ripping it asunder. But that made little sense. This was a safe place for Blaise, a haven. *Something has changed.*

Metal crunched, and Jefferson had the sickening suspicion that it was a memory of the destroyed airship. Screams sounded in the distance. The pressure inside the dreamscape built until Jefferson feared that he, too, might end up cracked like an egg. He needed to *do* something, but what? The wrath reminded him of the hurricanes that swept ashore in Ganland. The magic swirled around him, inexorably tearing at everything in his dreamscape, destroying it bit by bit.

Blaise was doing this. The power was like a building flood, wild and lethal. Jefferson had the uncomfortable thought that it might be possible for Blaise to kill him here. But no, he wouldn't intend this destruction. Blaise's magic might be a hurricane, but Jefferson could find the eye of the storm.

He focused on the bond through the geasa. Surely Blaise wouldn't fault him for using it, not right now. *There.* Jefferson found him, and he truly *was* everywhere. It was like he was coming apart at the seams. A profound sense of despair coursed through the link.

"Oh, Blaise," Jefferson murmured. Gods, he needed to plan a strategy, but there wasn't time. Breaker magic battered all around him, though Jefferson pushed back with his own to keep it at bay. *Think. The geasa means I can exert my influence on Blaise.* He had promised never to do that. But this was an extreme circumstance. "I'm sorry. You have my permission to be mad at me about this later."

Gritting his teeth, Jefferson fumbled with the geasa, searching for the thread that connected them. *There. Got it.* It reminded him of reins attached to a bridle, though he had kept them slack all this time. He reached out with his mind and imagined himself giving them a light tug—nothing harsh, just enough to draw attention. And mercy of mercies, it worked. The magical onslaught around him abated.

"Good, I have your attention. I know you don't want to do this, so let's see if I can figure out how to curb that magic of yours." Jefferson was uncertain if Blaise could hear him, but speaking didn't hurt anything. It made *him* feel better about the situation, at any rate. He kept a firm grasp on the geasa, assessing the howling storm of Breaker power that whipped around him but which blessedly had stopped tearing at him.

Where had all this unleashed magic come from? Jefferson wished he could shove it back where it originated from. He didn't see any way to do that, though.

Take some. Please.

The voice in his head surprised Jefferson. It wasn't his own. It was weak and desperate. *Blaise.* Jefferson swallowed. Take some of his magic? Was that even possible? He had never heard about anything like that between a theurgist and a handler, but—oh, he wasn't just a handler. He was a mage, too.

"All right, if you insist," Jefferson murmured.

Blaise must have been waiting for his assent. As soon as he gave it, the hurricane of magic came again, but this time, rather than trying to shred him, it flowed into him. He gritted his teeth against the torrent of power, standing his ground. It stung at first, as if his whole body were on fire. Then his reservoir, which had been sapped from its earlier use against Jack, claimed the incoming power.

Once, when he was a young child, Jefferson's family had gone out for a pleasure cruise with another family. The water in the Bay of Stars had been choppy, but none of the adults had paid any heed. Jefferson, always curious, had ventured too near the side of the boat, hoping to spy a dolphin. He was perched atop the railing and never had a chance when a swell dumped him into the bay. Foam-capped waters surged over his head and the current tried to drag him down. Blaise's magic flowing into him was just as overwhelming as the tide had been.

But then, a crewman had gone over to rescue him. Jefferson didn't have that now. All he could do was set his feet, hold his breath, and hope this wasn't his undoing.

After either an eternity or a few seconds the magical storm around him died down to nothing. The dream sky overhead cleared, leaving Jefferson in a grassy meadow. He felt a strange mix of exhausted and sated, as if he'd run a race and promptly stuffed himself with a fine meal during a solstice celebration. He flopped down on his back, staring at the azure expanse.

Jefferson heard a soft exhalation next to him. He turned and found Blaise nearby with his eyes screwed shut, trembling. "There you are. Are you okay?"

The Breaker's eyes flashed open. His breath huffed a few times as he calmed, but he seemed to come back to himself remarkably well for all that had just happened. "Maybe."

Maybe? Well, Jefferson would take a maybe. "What was that all about? You've never been like that before." He couldn't hide the concern in his voice.

Blaise was quiet for a moment, and while he gathered his thoughts,

Jefferson shimmied closer to him. "Gaitwood is determined to make me into a weapon." He didn't shrink back from Jefferson's proximity but instead seemed to gain confidence from it. "They gave me a potion, and it did that." He gestured with one hand to the dreamscape. "Made my magic volatile."

"Not volatile," Jefferson corrected, thoughtful. "I mean, it was fierce, but there was *so much* of it. Like you were overflowing."

Blaise nodded. "That's how it felt until I gave some of it away." He sucked in a shaky breath. "I still have a lot—more than usual—but I can handle this. Barely." The Breaker angled a guilty look at Jefferson. "I'm sorry if giving you my magic hurt."

"It was...an experience," Jefferson said. If he had felt like he was drowning, then what had it been like for Blaise? Beside him, the Breaker was shaking with either exhaustion or fear. Perhaps both. "I'm fine, though, really. We're in the dreamscape. Everything's under control."

"I almost destroyed it. And you."

Jefferson schooled his expression to hide the fact that he'd shared a similar sentiment moments earlier. "But you didn't. I'm fine."

Blaise ran his fingers along the sides of his nose, following his mustache down into his beard, as if he were trying to soothe himself. "I don't want to hurt anyone I care about."

Jefferson swallowed, growing still at Blaise's soft admission. The younger man wasn't free with his feelings, not like Jefferson. He guarded them closely, as if he feared being rejected by the world. And with good reason, Jefferson reflected. There were no other assurances he could offer to Blaise—the fact of the matter was, his magic *could* hurt the people he cared about, if given another chance with whatever Gregor had planned. And that reminded Jefferson why he had come to the dreamscape in the first place.

With a groan, he sat up, eyes alight. "We're getting you out. Today."

Blaise stared at him for a moment, his mouth agape. "Really?"

"Really."

The Breaker's body slacked with relief. "I thought that would never happen."

"Hey." Jefferson slipped his fingers beneath Blaise's chin. "I keep my promises."

Blaise nodded. "It's just...after the potion they gave me, I think I'm running out of time." His voice cracked, and he took a shaky breath.

Jefferson realized Blaise had not only worried about *Jefferson's* mortality, but his own. *Absolutely heartbreaking.* All it did was reaffirm Jefferson's drive to free him. "We're coming for you. You're going to be okay. You're going to be *free.*"

Blaise stared skyward, the skin at the corners of his eyes crinkling with skepticism. "That sounds like a distant dream."

Jefferson chuckled. "Perhaps not so distant. We're in a dream right now, after all."

At the reminder, Blaise sat up gingerly, as if the overload of magic had bruised him. He met Jefferson's gaze and smiled. "I'll be waiting."

CHAPTER TWENTY-TWO

Impending Betrayal

Jack

Jack glared at Lamar. Lamar glared back.

"Would you two kiss already?" Flora demanded from her position beside the back of the unoccupied jail wagon.

Jack's lips curled into a snarl at the half-knocker's words. He patted the sixgun at his side. "Pucker up, Lamar."

The Commander sighed, rubbing his forehead as if he were second-guessing his agreement to their plan. "You can't carry a revolver into the Golden Citadel."

Jack crossed his arms. He didn't care if he looked like a petulant child. Lamar's inclusion in this had him riled up, and every fiber of his being screamed for blood before his former friend betrayed them. Sometimes Jack was impulsive, and at others, he was methodical and calculating. As much as he wanted to go with his gut instinct, he reined it in. He would wait like an ambush predator.

His eyes snapped to the revolver at Lamar's waist. "Fine." Jack turned and strode over to Zepheus, removing his gun belt and securing it to the saddle.

<Don't do anything stupid,> the palomino reminded him, nipping at Jack's sleeve.

The outlaw paused, pulling the palomino's head up so he could press his forehead against the equine's. Zepheus knew the storm of emotions that boiled within his rider. "Not making any promises I can't keep."

Zepheus's hide quivered as he shooed away a fly. <I'm serious. I can't bolt into the Cit and rescue you.>

A tiny smile tugged at the corners of Jack's mouth. Zepheus, loyal asshole that he was, would come after him if it came down to it, and they both knew it. But he was right—that wouldn't end well for him, not this deep in Confederation territory. "Yeah, I'm serious, too." He stalked back over, though he disliked the vulnerability of not having his sixguns. "Better?"

"Much," Lamar agreed, though his spine was stiff. Jack studied his old friend. Lamar was nervous about what they were going to do. Did his nerves point to an impending betrayal?

Well, if they did, Jack already had plans to derail it. He stepped up into the back of the jail wagon, relieved to discover the bars were the normal variety of iron. He flicked a finger against them experimentally. "Couldn't spring for the real thing, eh?"

"I didn't think you warranted it," Lamar replied. He had a last-minute discussion with Flora, then climbed into the driver's seat. The half-knocker vanished, using her own abilities to travel to the Golden Citadel.

Jack sat down on the floor of the wagon as Lamar got the mule team moving. He smiled. Lamar didn't realize he had his magic back. Or if he somehow did, he hadn't been able to arrange for one of the reinforced salt-iron jail wagons. That was fine. This worked for Jack.

As they traveled the short distance to the Cit, he readied his effigies and went over the plan. Malcolm should already be on the grounds, in the guise of Jefferson. Zepheus and Emrys were waiting a mile outside the Cit's walls, ready to come when called. Flora was...well, Jack wasn't certain about the half-knocker. She assured them she had her own ways of getting in. Lamar was the only unknown in the plan, and Jack figured out how to handle that.

The wagon trundled to the grimy courtyard where prisoners were regularly unloaded. Jack peered out through the bars, watching as guards approached to speak with Lamar. The Commander jumped down from the driver's box, gesturing to his captive as he spoke. A moment later, Lamar turned and unlocked the gate. The guards stood nearby, rifles out in case Jack got any ideas.

Oh, he had lots of ideas. He smirked as he came closer, allowing Lamar to clap shackles onto his wrists. Mundane iron shackles. But Jack kept his eyes averted, lest the guards suspect anything.

"Come on," Lamar directed, guiding Jack to the entrance.

As if the outlaw didn't know where he was going. He bit back a retort since that didn't fit with the image he needed to present until they got deeper into the Cit. Jack went through the motions of allowing Lamar to record his information with the registrar. Yeah, word was going to get out that the Scourge of the Untamed Territory had been brought in. Once the Salties figured out who was responsible for getting the Breaker out, they were going to be mad as a nest of hornets. But that was fine. Jack didn't mind adding more deeds to his legendary reputation.

Lamar grabbed his arm to urge him onward. Jack growled, staving off the urge to call up his magic and show the Commander exactly how helpless he was. *Wait. Stay focused.* But it was so damned hard with Lamar right there.

"Surprised you came back for the Breaker," Lamar murmured once they were away from anyone who might overhear.

Jack glanced at him. Did he detect jealousy? Disbelief? Interesting. "I'm not here to make nice-nice with you."

"That's obvious," the Commander agreed. "I want the Breaker gone from here." He glanced at Jack. "Though I'm curious to see how you'll manage it."

"I'm always full of surprises," the outlaw said.

They continued in a stormy silence until they stood outside the hulking prison wing. Jack didn't need to touch the walls to feel the oppressive presence of salt-iron incorporated into the façade. He had forgotten about that. It meant this building wouldn't work for his purpose. Jack slanted a look across the courtyard. *The dorms might work.* "C'mon." He took a step forward, pausing for Lamar to follow.

"That's the theurgist dorms, not the prison," Lamar pointed out as Jack changed their course.

"Yep," Jack agreed with a smirk. Theurgist or prisoner, it didn't matter. He could work with that.

"What are you doing?" Lamar asked, suspicious, as Jack dug several effigies out of the pouch at his side. It was a challenge with the shackles, but he managed.

Jack chuckled. "And here I thought you weren't stupid."

The Commander cocked his head, his eyes troubled. "But you don't have magic."

He sounded baffled, and Jack enjoyed that. The outlaw said nothing, figuring a demonstration would be more informative. He pulled out four poppets—Jack had attuned three of them to targets already, but the last was not. "Unlock these cuffs, and then give me a strand of your hair."

Lamar's face clouded. "I will *not* remove those cuffs. You'll have to do whatever it is with them on."

He fears me. Because he's just now realizing he doesn't know what I'm capable of. Good. Jack smiled. "Have it your way. But I still need the hair unless you want to be caught up in my working."

"You don't have magic," Lamar repeated.

"That so?" Jack murmured.

"I was there when you were dosed with the potion," Lamar mused as he tried to figure out how Jack could possibly have magic now. He blinked. "How did you get it back?"

Lamar knew him well enough to know he wouldn't lie about his magic. Not after everything he'd endured. "That's on a need-to-know basis, and you don't need to know," Jack drawled. No way in Perdition was he going to tell Lamar that the *Breaker* had fixed him.

The Commander stared at him, then plucked a hair from his crown and offered it to Jack. The outlaw accepted and attached it to the fourth poppet, though it was a challenge with the shackles. He had doubted Lamar would agree to it. *You're mine now.*

"For the record, I don't like giving you that," Lamar said.

Jack shrugged. "I don't give a damn. The other option is to have you under the sway of *this* effigy." He hefted one of the diamond-shaped effigies for Lamar's benefit. "Now come on, I need to get these into place."

Lamar sighed but followed along. "What are you crafting?"

Jack ignored the question, reaching down to place the first effigy at the northernmost wall of the dormitory. He leaned down, whispering the words to prime it with a violent twist to his Rising Dread spell.

"*Jack.* Answer me." Lamar's voice was rife with warning.

The outlaw rose, the cuffs rattling with his movement. "Something to give us plenty of cover to get in and out."

Jefferson

JEFFERSON PRIDED HIMSELF ON HIS CALM AND PATIENCE, BUT HE HAD precious little of either while he sat in Grand Warden Kerney's office. Especially since the man was refusing to provide any information.

"I don't answer to you," Kerney said, not for the first time in their conversation. He sat on the other side of a broad desk, beefy arms crossed over his potbelly. "It doesn't matter that you know people on the Council."

Maybe if he had come as Malcolm, he would have received a different reaction. But Jefferson had an established history with Blaise's welfare, and he'd decided it was in his best interest to continue with this guise. It would spare Malcolm Wells from suspicion, especially since he had arranged for his impersonator to attend that day's Council session. He had confidence that actor Rex Godfrey would do an admirable job in his place.

And it was possible Malcolm wouldn't have had a better reception. As the public face of the Faedran faction, he certainly had no friends among those who ran the Golden Citadel. Because, of course, if Malcolm had his way, the Cit would no longer have reason to exist.

Flora stood nearby, ostensibly playing the role of diligent assistant for this encounter. She had dressed for the part in a tailored blouse and skirt, her pink hair pulled back into a severe bun that drew less attention to her. The half-knocker looked like a very short woman who didn't get enough sunlight, which meant that the Grand Warden ignored her presence.

"And as I said, I came to open a dialogue with you regarding the methods used on the mages here to see if any accords are being violated." Jefferson crossed his arms, matching Kerney's defiance.

The Grand Warden scoffed. "No accords are being violated. These are *mages* we're talking about."

Jefferson ground his teeth. Kerney said *mages* as if he were speaking of roaches or vermin. He would never understand how so many Phinorans refused to accept that those with magic were just as human as they. Unfortunately, he knew it wasn't a problem exclusive to Phinora. "And they're—"

"Stop." Kerney cut him off, lifting a hand. The Grand Warden tilted his head as if he were listening to something.

"Is something wrong?" Jefferson raised his eyebrows at the faint shouts echoing down the corridor.

The Grand Warden rose from his seat, striding with purpose to the door. He opened it and exchanged words with a guard who awaited him outside before glancing back to his visitor. "Mr. Cole, something has come up, and we'll need to revisit this topic at a later time."

Jefferson narrowed his eyes. While he suspected he knew what had come up, he wouldn't let the atrocities here off so easily. Especially after his encounter with Blaise last night. "My time is a precious commodity, Grand Warden. I expect you or one of your aides to compile the relevant files. I will send my staffer to retrieve them for review in three days' time." He gestured to indicate Flora, who gave a pert nod.

Distracted, Kerney flapped a hand at him. "Fine, yes. There are matters I need to attend to now."

"Then you won't mind if I take a look around."

Kerney's mouth worked as if he were struggling to find a response. He cut a look toward the door and seemed to reach a decision. Whatever was going on, Kerney was loath to tell a *magelover* like Jefferson. No doubt it would reflect poorly on the Grand Warden. He stalked across his office, picking up a paper from a tray on his desk. Kerney snatched up a pencil and circled something before turning to thrust it at Jefferson. "The Golden Citadel is, as always, open and welcoming to approved visitors. However, we have an incident near the dorms. I've circled the wings where you are free to travel, but for your own safety I ask that you not visit that wing."

Jefferson raised his eyebrows. That was much more than he had expected. He accepted the paper with a gracious nod. "I appreciate your concern for my welfare." And then, to maintain his role, he added, "I assume these wings will have your guards on hand in case I run into any problems?"

"Yes, of course, though there may be fewer as some will have adjusted to address our other issue." Kerney turned away. "Now, I must leave you, Mr. Cole."

"Thank you for your time," Jefferson said, and realized he meant it. Kerney had given him valuable information.

He stepped into the hallway after Kerney, watching as the Grand Warden took purposeful strides down the corridor. Jefferson turned and walked the other way, glancing down at the map. Raised voices echoed down the hall, but he ignored them, instead focusing on the plan. *I'm coming, Blaise. Hang on.*

"That man is shiftier than a greased basilisk," Flora muttered. "I don't like him."

"He's hiding a lot," Jefferson agreed, voice soft. "Come on."

It was difficult to maintain a leisurely pace. Jefferson wanted to charge down the corridors of the Cit until he found Blaise and got him out. But instead, he walked as if he were observing. He pulled a small note-pad from his pocket, pausing from time to time to jot down notes before continuing onward. Flora trailed in his wake like an obedient aide. Once, a woman in a crisp uniform asked if he needed an escort to the exit, but he declined, telling her he was making observations and recommendations. It was accurate enough. There was a lot he would change about the Cit.

Jefferson's pulse raced as he finally reached the area that housed the older mages. The cacophony of a fight met their ears—crashes, shouts, and the solid thump of fists against flesh. He felt the insidious slither of something washing over his skin, like raindrops trailing down water-resistant canvas. Jack's spell, turned away by the protections the Effigest had afforded them.

Flora swallowed, taking a deep breath. "Phew. Sounds like they're having a good time." She pushed her glasses up the bridge of her nose, shifting from one foot to the other as if the magic were trying to influence her, too.

"I don't know if I'd call it *that*," Jefferson murmured. He glanced at the sign identifying the building as the dormitory. According to the map in his hands, the prison wing wasn't far. And then, at last, they would free Blaise. "Let's go."

As they passed by the last entrance to the dormitory, an armed guard rushed out of the door to stop them. "Identify yourselves!" His service revolver was out, though it quaked in his grasp. Jack's magic had him close to violence.

Before Jefferson could say a word, Flora stepped forward. She held up a finger to forestall him from using his magic. Their goal was for no one to discover that Jefferson Cole was a mage.

Flora batted her eyelashes at the guard, her voice dripping with honey-sweetness. "Oh sugar, I'd *love* to identify myself."

The guard stared at her, puzzled. Then something shifted in his expression, and Jefferson realized that lust was another flip of the coin of violence. The guard released a long, whistling breath as Flora minced closer. Jefferson rubbed the side of his face, debating if he should just leave Flora there with her prey and continue to look for Blaise or stay and watch her back.

When the guard was close enough to loom over her, Flora swept into motion. Her knee flew up into his groin in a brutal move that made Jefferson cringe in sympathy. The guard howled, dropping his revolver. Flora neatly kicked his knee out from under him, sending her victim crashing to the ground. She picked up the revolver and tucked it into her waist, then stripped off the guard's uniform jacket.

"Can I ask what you're doing?" Malcolm blinked as she ripped a sleeve off the uniform.

"Making sure he can't come after us." Flora was efficient as she tore a strip off the sleeve, using it as a gag that she stuffed into the guard's mouth. She used the other sleeve to create binds for his hands and feet, then used her considerable strength to shove him back into the dormitory. "That was fun."

"I'm a little concerned at how good you are at that," Jefferson said as they continued onward.

She favored him with a wide-eyed, innocent look. "I'm a woman of many talents."

He supposed that was true. Jefferson consulted the map, feeling a rush of victory at their proximity to the prison wing. He quickened his strides, but as he drew closer, a sudden ache developed in the back of his neck.

Jefferson gnashed his teeth against the pain. "Gods, what *is* that?" he muttered.

"It's the salt-iron," Flora said, patting his arm with sympathy. "Keeps the prisoners compliant."

"Charming." Jefferson winced. No wonder mages hated the stuff. He didn't like the dull throb in his head, nor the way he could feel traces of his magic seeping away like water from a cracked cup. Minor things, he told himself, compared to whatever Blaise had endured here.

Flora skipped ahead as if she were out on a lark. She dragged open the heavy door to the prison, poking inside to check for any resistance. Flora waved him inside with an exuberant grin. "The coast is clear."

Jefferson slipped inside. A small desk crouched beside another door, the chair rocked back against the wall as if the prior occupant had left in a hurry. And no doubt they had if the guard had responded to Jack's distraction.

"This one's locked," Flora grumbled as she tugged at the door. Unwilling to relent, she planted her feet and gave the handle another jerk. Metal groaned from the strain, but otherwise didn't give.

"Suppose I'm already going to be in enough trouble," Jefferson reasoned, moving behind the desk. He pulled open the various drawers, sifting through the contents. Half-eaten apple. A wooden box filled with broken charcoal pencils. An envelope full of love letters. A deck of playing cards and a bag of dice. "Blast it. No keys."

"That's because I have them."

Flora whirled, her readiness for violence telegraphed in every muscle. Jefferson, too, was on alert, though he quickly calmed when he realized the speaker was Lamar. The Commander strode into the reception area, swinging a ring of keys on the index finger of his remaining hand.

"That's handy," Flora quipped, earning a scowl from Lamar.

"That wasn't very nice," Jefferson said.

"Nah, but I enjoyed it," Jack smirked as he came up behind them, the shackles on his wrists rattling as he walked.

Lamar ignored them with great dignity, turning to slip a key into the lock. There was a grating sound and then the mechanism within gave. Flora sprang forward, hauling the door open with renewed enthusiasm. Lamar pocketed the key ring.

The Commander led the way into the corridor, followed closely by the outlaw. Jefferson hurried along in their wake, struggling to fight off the effects of the salt-iron. Lamar and Jack seemed unbothered by it.

"Do you not feel the salt-iron?" Jefferson asked them.

Lamar shrugged. "I'm around it all the time."

Jack said nothing, though his eyes glittered dangerously. If the metal irritated him, he was hiding it well. The Effigest's chilling gaze flicked to Lamar, as if the Commander's presence was a distraction from the discomfort. Lamar paid no heed to Jack's vengeful look, instead focusing on each door as they strode down the long corridor.

"This one," Lamar said, stopping in front of a cell. The Salt-Iron Commander glanced up the hallway as he produced the key ring from his pocket.

Jefferson's attention snapped to the Commander. "This is Blaise's cell?"

"Yeah," Jack muttered, all the violence bleeding away for a moment. He pointed to the walls. "Didn't notice that, eh?"

Jefferson blinked in surprise as he saw what Jack meant. Someone had reinforced the stone walls with wood planks and salt-iron, but the whole thing was deteriorating. The wood was rotted and chipped. Sections of the stone wall had long, spider web-shaped cracks. Even the salt-iron had crumbled in some places, leaving shavings on the floor. Jefferson's mouth went dry. *Blaise did this?*

Jefferson swallowed, recalling the nightmare. "But…he can control his magic." He hadn't told them about last night. There hadn't been time.

Lamar finally found the proper key for the door and shoved it home into the lock. The cell door creaked open. Jefferson rushed over, peering inside.

He had prepared himself for many things, but not for this.

"Where in Perdition *is* he?" Jack snarled, giving voice to Jefferson's thoughts.

Lamar clenched his jaw. "We must be too late. Gregor must have moved him early."

"But moved him where?" Flora asked.

"To the Council."

CHAPTER TWENTY-THREE
Empty

Jack

This mess was supposed to go differently. Blaise was *supposed* to be there. They were going to drag him out of this overgrown outhouse and get out. And then Jack would take his revenge on Lamar. He tightened his fists, staring into the cell as Jefferson stepped inside, snooping around as if hoping beyond hope that a grown man was hidden out of view in the small space. *Futile. Stupid.* But Jack was almost tempted to do the same.

"*No.* No, this can't be." Jefferson's voice was dull as his gaze swept the vacant cell.

Lamar shook himself like a wet dog, appearing as troubled as the rest of them. Maybe he *was* on their side. Or just a damned convincing turncoat. "The Council. They took him to the Council." He, too, sounded hollow.

Jefferson pivoted. His eyes were wild, as if he knew something he hadn't told the others. "They're going to use Blaise to kill the Council. We have to get him before he reaches the chambers." He consulted his pocket watch for the time.

What in Perdition? "How do you know this?" Jack snapped.

The Dreamer scrubbed at his face with a hand. "Last night. He was in a bad way in the dreamscape." Nearby, Lamar shifted, his eyes widening as he listened.

"Stop talking," Flora warned Jefferson, who blinked as he realized that perhaps he'd said too much.

Jack hid a smirk. *Don't you worry. I'll cover your tracks.* "You have an idea what route they'll take?"

Jefferson took a ragged breath, then nodded. "I do, yes."

Jack aimed a finger at him. "Good. Y'all start after him. I need to gather my poppets, and then I'll follow."

"No, absolutely not." Lamar shook his head. "I have to stay with you."

Please do. "Aw, didn't know your black heart cared so much."

Jefferson cast another forlorn look into the empty cell. "Yes, I'll start after him."

He sounded shaky and uncertain, shell-shocked. That wouldn't do. The dandy needed to *focus.* Jack stepped up to him, snapping his fingers. "Hey. You know what to do. You can do it."

Jefferson nodded, swallowing. "Right. Yes. Come on, Flora, let's go."

The half-knocker cast a suspicious glance at Jack over her shoulder but followed Jefferson after a moment. The outlaw watched her go, then pivoted to head down the hallway. Shouts and fighting still reverberated through the building, proof that his working was still in full force.

"What spell was that?" Lamar asked, keeping pace beside him.

Eh, at this point what did it hurt to tell him? "Modified Rising Dread." Jack shoved open the outer door, breathing a sigh of relief as he put a little more distance between himself and all that salt-iron. He needed to retain whatever magic he could before it bled away.

"I don't remember that one," Lamar remarked.

"You wouldn't." Jack had never used it around Lamar in his theurgist days. He made a beeline for the rear of the theurgist dormitory, scanning for the place he'd tucked an effigy. *There, behind that bush.* He picked it up, returning it to his pouch. As he started for the next one, he asked, "Where's my wife?"

The Commander hesitated at the steel in Jack's voice. "Your wife?"

"Kittie Dewitt. Don't play stupid like you don't know who she is."

Lamar blew out a breath as they walked. "I know who you mean. I was…surprised that you asked, is all. I don't know where she is."

Jack slowed. He had long suspected Lamar was part of the group that had tracked her down and taken her, but he had no proof. The outlaw chewed on Lamar's assertion as he picked up the next two effigies. As they walked toward the final effigy, Jack palmed a poppet from his pouch.

The last effigy lay just ahead, concealed by the branches of a bush in dire need of trimming. The protection afforded by the shrub would work in the outlaw's favor. The effigy was still draining some of his magic, so Jack needed to time things right. He plucked it from where he had hidden it, canceling the working. As soon as he sensed the magic wane, he flipped his attention to the poppet he had assigned to Lamar.

The Commander froze in place as Jack settled a paralysis spell over him. The outlaw smirked, content as a tomcat with a mouse beneath his paw. He had waited so long for this day. Jack cast a spell of strength onto his personal poppet. Strength was a huge magic drain, so he used it only briefly to rip the cuffs from his wrists. All the while, Lamar stared at him with growing horror as he realized the severity of his predicament.

"That's right. Trapped, like *you* trapped *me*," Jack crooned. "But I'm not bitter about *that*. Oh, no." He stepped closer to Lamar, liberating the revolver from the Commander's holster. "Nah, you see, I've been holding a grudge about you taking my *magic*. Stealing my *wife*." Jack's heart raced as his fury mounted. "Destroying my *town*. Kidnapping my *daughter*." He stalked in a circle around Lamar, hoping the other man felt every bit of the despair and terror Jack had endured.

A bead of sweat trailed down Lamar's forehead. Jack adjusted the paralysis spell enough to allow the Commander to speak. "*Jack*. Jack, *please*. Can't you see I'm *helping* you?"

"I *do* like hearing you beg," Jack said. "But if you think I believe your song and dance, you're a damned fool."

Lamar's eyes widened. "I'm telling the truth. We were friends once. Why won't you believe me? You *know* me."

"And that's why I don't believe you," the outlaw replied coldly.

"Jack, think about this. We have about two minutes before this area is crawling with soldiers. You won't be able to take all of them, and this will all have been for nothing."

As far as arguments went, it wasn't a bad one. Already, he heard the distant sound of soldiers arriving to bolster the guards, who must have been overwhelmed by the berserking mages. Jack glanced down at the revolver in his hand. It wasn't as familiar as his own sixgun, but it was serviceable. He hoisted it, pointing it at the Commander's forehead.

"No!" Lamar yelped, his protest silenced as Jack pulled the trigger. The world narrowed until it was only Jack, Lamar, and the sharp report of a bullet flying true.

The paralysis spell lost its grip, unable to work on a dying man. Lamar slumped to the ground, limp as a rag doll. Jack shoved the revolver into his waistband, staring down at the Commander's body. He had thought he would feel a sense of victory and justice, but instead, a hollow emptiness settled over him.

There was no time to analyze that now. Time to get out of the Cit while the getting was good.

CHAPTER TWENTY-FOUR
Damage Control

Jefferson had difficulty maintaining a sedate pace as he and Flora headed out of the Citadel grounds. Luckily, the place was in complete chaos, and no one paid attention to their exit. Once they left the walls of the compound, they broke into a jog. Jefferson whistled every few steps, hoping to catch the pegasi's attention.

The pegasi trotted out of the nearby forest, ears pricked forward. Emrys studied the pair, dark eyes worried. <Where is Blaise?>

"We were too late," Jefferson sighed as he hurried up to the stallion.

The pegasus's hide quivered. <What do you mean?>

"I mean, he's on the move, and we have to catch up." Jefferson glanced at Zepheus. "Jack will come behind us. Emrys, can you carry Flora and I?"

<I will,> the stallion agreed gamely.

Flora waved a hand. "Nah, don't worry about me. I'll be able to find them."

Jefferson stilled. "What do you mean?" She had already kept Lamar's involvement a secret until the last moment. What else had she not divulged? The half-knocker shifted under his focused gaze. "If it relates to finding Blaise, *tell me*." Emrys loomed nearby, snorting his agreement.

Flora's shoulders tensed and her face fell. "I'll tell you, but..." She rubbed her face. "Promise me you won't tell anyone else."

Jefferson had never heard her so serious or worried before. "Yes, of course."

"I'm attuned to salt-iron."

He stared. Jefferson wouldn't have been more surprised if she'd turned into a tap-dancing jackalope. It was the last thing he had expected from her. "*What?*"

"You heard me." She frowned. "If they have him in a salt-iron jail wagon—which they will if they're smart—then he's that way." Flora pointed to the southwest.

Jefferson ran a hand through his hair. "That confirms they are taking him to the Council. Let's go." He climbed into Emrys's saddle, the stallion prancing in anticipation. Flora nodded, vanishing to follow the salt-iron trail.

The pegasus surged forward into a fluid canter, ears tipped back for Jefferson's guidance. The scenery sped by. Jefferson felt the nervous energy of the pegasus beneath him, and he wished they could take to the air to hunt for Blaise. But that would invite too much trouble. He had to trust that he was on the right track.

<Can you find him with your geasa too?> Emrys asked as they raced along.

Oh, if only it were that easy. "I don't think it works like that."

<Understood. I should be able to sense him when I'm in range.> Emrys plowed onward, lengthening his strides.

A few moments later, his ears flicked forward, slowing as his nostrils flared. The pegasus arched his neck, tail flagging behind him with joy. <I found him.>

Jefferson patted the stallion's neck. "Let's get him."

The pegasus charged up the road, and over the next hill, the jail wagon dawdled into view, pulled by a pair of mules lumbering along at a glacial pace. To Jefferson's dismay, he realized the wagon was under guard. *I suppose it makes sense. High-value prisoner and all.* Two armed outriders accompanied it, along with a sharpshooter perched atop the wagon beside the driver. He quailed as he realized they were about to attack Confederation defenders.

Emrys sensed his dismay, drawing to a stop. <Choose. Blaise or your Confederation.>

Blaise. He would pick Blaise every time, without hesitation. But he didn't know how they were going to do this. Flora appeared nearby, her eyes on the distant wagon.

"I don't think I can handle them all," Jefferson admitted. "They're armed."

The half-knocker rubbed her hands together in anticipation. "I can stop the wagon. I can even take out all of them if you want. But it's going to be bloody."

None of it was bluster. Flora was preternaturally strong and fast, with skin tough enough to deflect a knife, though bullets could still wound her. Yet here she was, offering to take on some of the Confederation's best on his behalf.

"Get the wagon to stop and distract the guards however you can. I'll do my part," Jefferson said. When her grin widened, he added, "But for Tabris's sake, don't kill anyone!"

"That all depends on you, boss," Flora replied, giving him an ironic salute. "You ready?"

Jefferson swallowed, patting Emrys's neck. The stallion bowed his neck, sidestepping as he awaited the command. "No time like the present."

Flora disappeared with a pop of displaced air. Emrys peered back at his rider. <Do whatever you need to prepare. I'll be ready.>

Jefferson took a deep breath, closing his eyes to calm himself. He summoned his magic and found it ready to heed his call. At least he wouldn't have to fumble for it. Jefferson was aware of the pegasus slowing to a walk, then he felt Emrys's muscles bunch beneath him in surprise as a metallic crunch rang out.

"Shit!" a guard called.

"That the Breaker's magic?" another asked, voice loud and wary. Jefferson's eyes flashed open when he heard a gun being readied.

Jefferson swallowed. "Get me closer, Emrys." *Hope I don't fall asleep in the saddle because that would make for an awkward rescue.*

Emrys surged forward. Ahead, the wagon ground to a halt, pitched at an awkward angle. A dark, circular shape spun up the road—a wagon wheel, rolling free of the axle. Jefferson realized Flora's ploy inadvertently put Blaise in danger as his escort assumed the Breaker was responsible for the damage that had befallen the wagon.

The escort riders were focused on their current problem, ignoring the drum of hoofbeats as Emrys approached. Jefferson clung to the saddle for all he was worth, summoning his magic and focusing it forward. This had been so much easier when he had used his power against Jack or Emrys. He was more familiar with them, and they were easy to target. This was like trying to reach into a stream and grab a fish with bare hands. Jefferson missed his first attempt as the stallion drew closer to the wagon. And then he missed two more.

On his fourth try, he found the sharpshooter. Jefferson wasn't sure which of them was more surprised. He felt the soldier's presence and hastily summoned up the dreamscape, pulling him into it. One of his fellows, an outrider with a bushy mustache, made a cry of dismay as the slumbering sharpshooter slumped against the wagon.

"Smith! Are you dead?" Bushy Mustache demanded.

"Nah, he's snoring," the other outrider replied, rubbing his nearly nonexistent chin in bewilderment.

Jefferson sought Bushy Mustache but found Tiny Chin instead. *Doesn't matter.* He shoved the outrider into the dreamscape.

Bushy Mustache was even easier, as Jefferson gained a knack for snagging his targets. Moments later, he had the driver ensnared as well. The man had gone to retrieve the errant wheel, collapsing to the road with a yawn as if he were seeking his bed.

Flora clapped her hands, impressed. "That was fun! You made it look easy."

"It wasn't." Jefferson's heart raced from the magical exertion. He dismounted, though as soon as his feet hit the ground, his knees nearly buckled beneath him. Emrys snorted, sidestepping to keep him from falling.

"You okay over there?" Flora asked as she tied one of the outrider's horses to the wagon.

"I've been better. Can you look for a key and get Blaise out?" Jefferson leaned heavily against Emrys, grateful for the support. "I need to do more than just dump them in the dream." He glanced at the nearest sleeping outrider.

"Why?" Flora asked as she perused the saddlebags.

He winced. Flora had already admitted her secret, so he supposed he might as well tell her what he thought he could do. He didn't like it because it was unethical and seemed like a violation. Just thinking of it made him understand why some of the populace feared mages and didn't want them to have a voice in government. "You know how sometimes a dream seems so real, you could swear it really happened? I think I may be able to influence their memories within the dreamscape."

<I can still taste the food from the Feast of Flight dream.> Emrys smacked his lips in agreement.

Flora whistled. "Give it a shot." She returned to her search for the key.

Jefferson nodded. He had done unethical things before. Why did this feel so different? He wrapped a hand around Emrys's mane to keep himself upright, steadying his breathing as he slipped back to the dreamscape. The men were still where he had left them, though he felt them trying to stir. Jefferson lulled them into a deeper sleep with his magic. They stopped struggling, content. Jefferson smiled. Their minds were malleable. Impressionable.

"Got it!" Flora crowed. Jefferson cracked one eye open to see her brandish a key and skip around to the back of the wagon to unlock the door.

Jefferson swallowed, splitting his attention between his dream and reality. Sweat beaded on his forehead with the effort, and the dull throb at the base of his neck reminded him that he was closer to salt-iron than he liked. Flora scuttled into the wagon and appeared a moment later with her arm around Blaise's midsection. Jefferson's heart broke when he saw the young man's scarecrow-thin frame and haggard face. Blaise's body shook violently, as if he were cold—*no*, that wasn't it at all. As if he were struggling to hold back an impossible amount of magic.

He let go of Emrys, abandoning the dreamscape for the moment. "Flora, step away." Jefferson slung his arm around Blaise, bothered by how feather-light he was. Emrys crowded close, nickering softly and sniffing Blaise all over.

The Breaker sagged against Jefferson, whimpering. "I can't. I can't…"

<What did they do to him?> Emrys's voice vibrated with cold fury.

"The outrider with the keys had a potion." Flora held the small amber bottle aloft. "Why did someone write '*administer on Council grounds*'?"

Jefferson shook his head. He didn't have time to explain, not right now. No time to tell them that little bottle was probably the last bit of an alchemical potion designed to send Blaise beyond the limits of magic he could contain. "Blaise, I'm here. It's okay. Give me some of that."

Blaise blinked, as if finally registering his presence. Jefferson felt a pulse of immense relief through their bond, followed by a frisson of fear. "It's too much. Too dangerous. Don't want to hurt you."

"Shh, you won't," Jefferson whispered, fervently hoping it was the truth. "Just like last night. *Remember?*"

The Breaker's lips twisted in a rictus of anguish, his entire body shaking so badly that Jefferson knew without a doubt how Gregor meant for Blaise to destroy the Council. He was a living bomb, about to shatter himself and everything around him. If he didn't siphon off some of that magic, they wouldn't last much longer.

"Jefferson?" Flora asked, concern in her voice.

He shook his head. Didn't have time for her right now. "Come on, Blaise. You don't have to bear it alone. And I can use the magic, anyway." Jefferson hazarded a glance at the guards. The sharpshooter was stirring. *Blast.* Spreading his power among multiple targets made it not as potent. Jack had slept much longer.

Blaise gave him a desolate look. "Don't want to kill you."

Gods, he doesn't realize he may do that no matter what. They were running out of time. If Blaise's magic didn't do them in, one of the waking guards might. "I trust you," Jefferson murmured, leaning in to kiss Blaise. If this was their end, he wouldn't die without doing that once more.

Blaise melted against him, something about their closeness breaking down whatever barrier he had up. A flood of magic swept through the geasa, pouring into Jefferson like a rising tide.

So much power. Jefferson had felt like he was drowning last night. That was nothing compared to this. He was drowning with every nerve ending on fire, every bone threatening to crack beneath the strain. Lungs crushing beneath the sheer might of the magic sweeping into him. Jefferson's vision swam, and he felt Emrys's muzzle shove against his spine to keep him upright.

How had Blaise contained it for even two minutes? Jefferson struggled against it, gathering the magic as best he could and lugging it to the dreamscape. It was difficult, almost impossible, to ignore the way the unfettered magic attacked his very being. But he had to, or he and Blaise would both be lost. Jefferson gritted his teeth, latching onto the sharpshooter and dragging him back into slumber.

Jefferson had a vague sense that Blaise was observing him somehow, but he was too busy constructing a new lie to replace their reality. He didn't have time to think it through, so made them believe that after the axle on their wagon broke, another wagon took their prisoner away. It was better than the reality of a well-known entrepreneur taking them down with magic.

When he finished, it took him a moment to realize Blaise was supporting *him*. The younger man's blue eyes were clouded with worry. "Are you okay?"

"I'm supposed to be asking you that," Jefferson replied, though he nodded. Exhaustion dogged him and he felt raw from the burn of magic, but Blaise was *free*. That was worth celebrating—once they reached safety. "Emrys? Can you carry the both of us?"

The stallion nuzzled Blaise. <I would normally say no, but Blaise weighs next to nothing. He's going to need to eat a lot of cake to fill out.>

"Maybe after he can keep down nourishing food," Jefferson muttered as the pegasus knelt so he could help Blaise into the saddle.

A few moments later, he was atop Emrys, with Blaise nestled behind him, the young man's arms around his waist. Thrilling as it was, Jefferson had no illusions about the severity of their situation. But they would focus on that later.

Blaise was free.

Malcolm

Agnes bent over Blaise. The Breaker sat in the coziest chair in the study, one of his arms propped on a pillow as the Healer applied an ointment to the gash that ran the length of his forearm. She had been nervous of the young man at first, but her countenance changed to professional concern when she took in his ragged condition.

"I used a little of my magic on him, but he's been through a lot. I fear pouring too much into him and shocking his body," Agnes informed Malcolm once she had finished her ministrations. "I'll need to check that arm twice a day, if he'll allow it." She hadn't missed how Blaise had shrunk from her touch, though he was too tired to do more.

"Thank you," Malcolm told her, moving to sit near Blaise. Once Agnes left, he leaned forward. "Blaise? How are you?"

Blaise hadn't spoken since they'd arrived at the estate, and Jefferson had to change his appearance. He trembled, and Malcolm knew from their bond that it wasn't because of his magic, at least. The Breaker closed his eyes. "I don't know."

Malcolm pursed his lips. He wasn't sure how to make Blaise feel better. Perhaps it was something only time and distance from the trauma would heal. Or perhaps, Malcolm thought with regret, he might never heal. "It's okay to not know. But you're free."

Blaise shook his head and was about to say something when Flora and Jack boiled into the house like a pair of tussling gamecocks. The outlaw had never caught up to them, and the half-knocker had gone out to find out what had become of him while Malcolm got Blaise settled.

Flora screeched and Jack growled terse responses littered with creative expletives. Malcolm considered knocking them both out, but that would only delay their row. Blaise stared at the arguing pair, bewildered and worn.

"Stop this at once!" Malcolm commanded, pulling on his authoritative Doyen voice.

Flora and Jack paused, and the outlaw stopped short when he realized Blaise was there. His eyes narrowed to outraged slits as he took in the Breaker's rough condition.

"Care to explain what all this is about?" Malcolm gestured to the general madness of the pair. "Were you carrying on like that the whole way here from the Cit?"

"No. Found him on the road to your estate." Flora gave Jack her best death-glare. "What is *wrong* with you?"

"*Vengeance*," Jack rumbled, his hands fisted at his sides.

Flora whirled with an exasperated look, focusing on Malcolm. "We have problems because of this spawn of a syphilitic swamp rat." Jack lunged at her, but she was too fast and dodged out of the way, claiming a place on a chair beside Blaise. She focused on him for a moment, shooting him an encouraging smile. "Hey sugar, you've looked better."

"Don't call me that," Blaise said, staring at the ceiling as if he couldn't handle their drama right now.

Malcolm decided, all things considered, Blaise was taking whatever they were going on about very well. He, on the other hand, wanted to focus on anything else but their theatrics. Malcolm rubbed his forehead. "Either tell me what's going on or go kill each other outside so we can have a little calm. I just committed yet another act of treason, and I have other things on my mind."

"He," Flora declared, waving a finger at Jack, "killed Lamar Gaitwood."

Malcolm blinked in surprise. While that didn't sound like a *good* scenario in the grand scheme of things, it hardly sounded like the *worst* thing. Lamar had caused so many problems for Blaise that Malcolm didn't have any charitable feelings toward the man. But he had also helped to get Blaise out. Or at least tried to.

Blaise leaned forward, eyes on Jack. He looked like he wanted to say something, and his mouth opened slightly before he shut it again.

"I had *reason*. A *just* cause," Jack said, his shoulders tense. It sounded as if he'd been repeating the phrase over and over like a mantra. And like he didn't fully believe it anymore.

Malcolm didn't want to unpack whatever baggage went along with that right now. He looked at Flora. "Right. I agree that this is not the best ending for someone who was helping us. But it sounds like there's more to it than that?"

Beside Blaise, Flora straightened. She waved her hands around. "Just so you know, I didn't tell you because I was going to take care of the problem. *Quietly.*" She shot a disgruntled glare at Jack.

Blaise slowly rose from his seat, rubbing at his chin. He gave Malcolm an apologetic look. "I'm going out to the stables. This is…too much for me right now." The Breaker paused beside the outlaw before he made his way to the door. "Good to see you, Jack." The outlaw gave him a curt nod.

Malcolm watched him leave, frustrated that he couldn't follow and had to deal with this ridiculousness instead. But it was for the best. Blaise had been through so much. Emrys would keep tabs on the Breaker until Malcolm could check on him again. He rounded on Flora. "Continue."

The half-knocker put her hands on her hips, unapologetic. "Lamar discovered you were bound to Blaise. And I'm pretty sure he figured out you're also Jefferson. That information was surety for his life."

Jack's eyes narrowed, and his mouth moved with something that might have been a silent curse. A chill raced down Malcolm's spine. "Lamar arranged it so if something happened to him, that secret comes out?"

Flora nodded.

"We could have avoided this if you'd told us from the *start*," Jack growled.

"Is that so?" Flora challenged. "I should never have trusted that you could behave any better than a rabid chupacabra."

"Yeah, well, that's on you," Jack agreed, crossing his arms.

Malcolm rubbed the bridge of his nose. "This isn't the time to argue. The fact of the matter is that now, not only has Gregor lost the mage he wanted to use for his plot, but he *also* has prime ammunition to use against me."

"*Your* fault," Flora hissed at Jack. The outlaw's shoulders tensed, fire in his eyes.

Malcolm shook his head. "We can't worry about who's to blame. It doesn't matter." He held up a hand to count off their issues. "One, they will accuse Jefferson in the plot to free Blaise. Two, Wildfire Jack will take blame as well—now not only for Blaise's escape but the death of Commander Gaitwood. And three, word will soon get out that I bound myself to Blaise." He paced the length of the parlor.

"I don't care about my reputation," Jack said. "I need to leave anyway."

Malcolm studied him, and he might have misread it, but he thought he saw a shadow of regret on the outlaw's face. Rather than comment on it, he nodded. "Just as well, since we'll present too big a target with all of us here."

"Oh sure, abandon us after *you* cause all the problems," Flora groused. "Where are you going, anyway?"

"None of your gods-damned business." Jack turned on his heel and stalked to the door, slamming it in his wake.

"Right," Malcolm sighed. "So we'll have to do some damage control." He tried not to think about how *much* damage control. Maybe if he feigned calm, it would be true. Or maybe he could hop on a steamer with Blaise, get new identities for them both, and start a new life in Thorn or Highhorse. Never mind that leaving Phinora right now would take nothing short of a miracle.

Flora eased back into her chair. "What do you have in mind?"

Malcolm sank down into the seat Blaise had occupied and put a hand over his face. "You flatter me by thinking I've gotten that far. No. I think this is going to be a late night. Call in my attorney—disasters like this are what I pay him for. Wait." Malcolm straightened, removing his hand as he snapped his fingers. A kernel of a plan was forming. "Get me Seledora, too."

Flora frowned. "But she's all the way in Rainbow Flat. That'll take time. And she's—"

"Doesn't matter. You heard me." Malcolm pursed his lips. "I think we can buy a little time. They can't just force their way onto my estate and drag Blaise and I out." That was one of the small perks of being a Doyen. His home was, effectively, an embassy. "Oh, and reach out to Doyen Jennings's wife."

Flora studied him. "Thirty seconds ago, you didn't have an idea, but I suspect you do now. What is it?"

Malcolm smiled. He was tired, a little panicked, but he felt better now that an idea was fermenting in his mind. "We're going to get ahead of the narrative."

CHAPTER TWENTY-FIVE

Impulsive as a Weasel in a Hen House

Jack

Jack stormed out of Wells's overstuffed temple of opulence, stalking to the stables. Circumstances forced him to make an abrupt pivot when he realized that in his anger, he had forgotten his saddlebag of clothing and supplies. He avoided Malcolm and Flora as he traipsed to the guest quarters, irritated as a flea-bitten manticore. Once he had the bag slung over his shoulder, he made his way back out to the stables.

He blazed a path to Zepheus, although the pegasus was pissed at him, too. The stallion called Jack *rash* and *impulsive as a weasel in a hen house*. "I wasn't *rash*. I'd been planning this for years," the outlaw grumbled to no one in particular.

"I understand," a soft voice said from a nearby stall.

The outlaw tensed. *Blaise.* He had forgotten the Breaker had fled before the rising tide of his argument with Flora. Blaise rested his forearms against the top of Emrys's stall, peering at him with haunted eyes.

Blaise was the last person he expected to understand, but then again, Blaise had been imprisoned in the Cit for months. Jack knew firsthand how the treatment foisted upon mages could twist and blacken a person's soul. Jack had hoped Blaise would prove more resilient. "Do you?"

The Breaker lowered his head until his chin rested atop the wood of the stall. "I understand, but I don't agree with what you did."

Jack didn't let the relief that flickered through him show on his face. Maybe they hadn't broken Blaise to the core as he had feared. "Didn't expect you would."

Emrys walked up beside Blaise, thrusting his head out and snorting at Jack, as if to emphasize that Blaise was a better person than him in every way. The stallion wasn't wrong.

"Did you come for me?" Blaise asked.

Jack frowned. Damn it, of course Blaise would ask that, all the while looking like a kicked puppy.

"It's okay if you didn't. That would be a stupid move on your part, and you're not usually stupid."

Jack set his jaw, then realized that the Breaker had sassed him on purpose. Even fresh from the torture of the Cit, he was trying to help someone else. That was good. He wasn't broken. Jack was tempted not to let the barb go uncontested, but he wasn't foolish. Blaise was a Breaker, and after the abuse of the Cit there was no way to know how he might respond. So Jack held his tongue. He went the route of the truth because if anything Blaise would appreciate that. "I came because Emmaline ran off."

That caught the Breaker's attention. He straightened, the corners of his eyes creased with concern. "Then why are you *here?*"

Jack couldn't help it. He chuckled because Blaise had the right of it. "I found her. And she humbled me." He rubbed his forehead. "Here I thought she ran off to free you. She wanted to, by the way."

Blaise smiled, though the corners of his mouth quivered with the effort. "I was afraid she might. She's brave."

"I was going to go with *overly confident teenager* but then the apple doesn't fall far from the tree," Jack said dryly. "Anyway, she's tracking down her mother." He couldn't help it; his voice cracked on the last word. He'd tried to keep his mind off Kittie so he could focus on the task at hand, but now that he had kept his promise and Blaise was free, the thought of her dug into his brain like spurs.

"That's all you ever wanted," Blaise observed, getting to the core. "You going after them?"

"Yeah."

"Good luck," Blaise said. "I hope you can finally be happy."

Jack nodded, turning away from the Breaker before hesitating and spinning around again. "Something I need to tell you. You restored my magic."

Blaise's brow knit in confusion. "I did?"

"You did," Jack confirmed. "When you freed me from Lamar's trap.

You're like a gods-damned miracle worker." He shifted in place. What he wanted to say next didn't come naturally. "Thank you."

The Breaker straightened, rubbing his chin. "You're welcome." He swallowed. "And…thank you. For helping to free me."

Jack was about as used to being thanked for a good deed as he was returning the favor. He touched two fingers to the brim of his hat and inclined his head. "I better get."

Jack had just opened Zepheus's stall door when the young man spoke again. "What's going to happen to me?"

The outlaw pursed his lips, urging the palomino out into the broad aisle so he could recheck his equipment. "Don't know, kid. But Wells seems less of a self-absorbed peacock than I thought, and he might actually have your best interest in mind."

Blaise twitched at his use of *kid* but didn't protest. "I want to go to Itude." He paused, shaking his head. "I mean, Fortitude."

So Wells had told him about the town's name change. Jack pulled a burr out of his pegasus's mane, tossing it aside. "If you can get there, you'd be welcome back. The Gutter needs more mages like you." Blaise stared after him as Jack ambled out the door, Zepheus's hooves ringing on the hard-packed dirt.

CHAPTER TWENTY-SIX

Machinations

Gregor

Gregor picked up the ladder-back chair, flinging it against the wall with a resounding crash. *Unbelievable.* He had been so close, and they had stolen the Breaker from his clutches at the last instant. Fists curling at his side, he stared at the broken ruins of the chair.

One of the miscreants involved had to be Lamar's hated outlaw. The Effigest's name had been recorded in the Cit's logs that day, but now the man was nowhere to be found. And then some of Gregor's best men had been discovered asleep along the road, beside a broken-down jail wagon empty of the Breaker. None of them remembered how they had fallen asleep, but they were certain they had transferred the Breaker to another wagon. Except there *was* no other wagon.

Gregor didn't believe a word they said. Just in case they were in league with either the outlaw or one of those bleeding-heart Faedrans, he made certain the failed guards were flogged.

The most curious, mind-boggling part of the entire thing was Lamar's involvement. He had been the one to turn the outlaw mage in to the Cit. And then he had been found dead, slain by his own revolver. Had he somehow played a role in the bid to free the Breaker?

Perhaps he should have felt a pang of sadness, an emptiness from the death of his brother. But Lamar was a mage. Gregor's only regret that he could no longer take advantage of his sibling's position as Commander.

A knock sounded on his office door. Gregor hunched his shoulders, sneering at the idea of answering it. He was in no mood to deal with anyone else. The knock came again. "Go away!"

And yet, it came a third time. Gregor growled to himself, stalking over and slinging it open, prepared to berate whoever dared interrupt his brooding. He stopped when he came face to face with a woman in the uniform of a Confederation soldier. The pin on her chest marked her as one of Lamar's lieutenants.

"Pardon the interruption, Doyen Gaitwood, but I have something you'll want to see." She inclined her head, deferential, though she otherwise maintained her perfect posture.

He studied her, frowning. "I'll allow it. Come in."

The soldier slipped inside, glancing at the destroyed chair but wisely keeping any comments to herself. She revealed a carry pouch at her side, opening it to pull out an envelope wrapped in crinkling wax paper. "To protect it from the elements," she murmured, offering it to him. Gregor noted a glistening dew on her clothing. In his preoccupation, he hadn't noticed it had started to mist outside.

He nodded sharply, taking it from her and opening it. He chewed on his bottom lip, thoughtful, as his eyes took in Lamar's cramped handwriting. When he reached the end of the missive, a smile curved onto his lips. His one-armed sibling wasn't so useless in the end. Gregor met the soldier's gaze. "Do you know anything about the contents of this letter?"

She shook her head, her expression stony. "No, sir. But I presume it's related to our Commander's murderer?"

"It is." At his words, she tensed, rage growing in her eyes. Rage was something he could work with. "Lieutenant...I apologize, I didn't catch your name."

"Lieutenant Davis."

Gregor offered her a hesitant smile. "Thank you, Lieutenant Davis. Can I count on your support to bring the perpetrators to justice?"

"Yes, sir. And those I command. Say the word and we are yours."

Perfect. Yes, Lamar's death was proving to be infinitely useful. "Our first step will be to bring in Doyen Wells. He's the mastermind of this plot." He crumpled the letter meaningfully in his hand.

Davis frowned. "That will be difficult if he's gone to ground at his residence."

Blast, she was right. But maybe Malcolm would slip up. "Send a contingent to surround his estate, in that case. If he so much as sticks his nose out, grab him. He can't stay in there forever." She nodded. Gregor took the opportunity to sift through the papers on his desk. He had a stack of *Wanted* handbills somewhere...ah, there. Wildfire Jack Dewitt's mean eyes stared up at him from the topmost paper. "And I want this man. Do you recognize him?"

Her eyes flickered with suppressed anger. "He was at Fort Courage. I was there."

Good. That would offer her ample motivation. "I want him, too."

CHAPTER TWENTY-SEVEN
Blaise Bloody Hawthorne

Blaise

Blaise rested his cheek against Emrys's warm neck, eyes closed as he inhaled the comforting scent of equine, hay, and dust. The stallion said nothing, simply offered his bulk as a much-needed anchor from the whirlwind of emotions and thoughts swirling through Blaise's mind. He was a confusing mix of relieved, frightened, angry, and smitten. That last one was, strangely enough, the hardest to cope with. There were so many complications.

It had been easier to grasp in prison. Jefferson's dream visits were a respite, a balm after his hours of mistreatment. And while they were so very real, they were still a dream, which made them safe. But now he was here in reality, in Jefferson's—no, Malcolm's—home. That made things real and a little frightening in a way that differed from the terrors of his time in the Cit.

He realized, when he came face to face with Malcolm, that he was nervous around the man. Which made little sense because he was *also* Jefferson. At the same time, he *wasn't*. It was stupid to think of it like that. But since when had his thoughts ever made any sense? He sighed into Emrys's mane.

<He's coming,> the stallion advised him. No need to specify who.

Blaise heard the grate of wood as the stall door opened. "How are you doing?" Malcolm's voice was like sunshine on a winter day, welcome warmth in the bitter cold.

"I'm here," Blaise said with a shrug, turning to face him, though he stayed close to his pegasus, hungry for reassurance and Emrys's protection.

"That's not an answer, you know." Malcolm leaned against the feed trough, studying him. "Agnes wants to check your arm again. But it can wait."

Blaise nodded but didn't say anything.

Malcolm adjusted his posture so that he met Blaise's lowered eyes. "Are we okay?"

And that was the real question. The one Blaise didn't know the answer to, and it was frustrating. "I don't know."

Malcolm's chin dimpled with concern. "Why not?"

Why not? Blaise shook his head, then regretted it when the move made him dizzy. He had to be more careful. "Because...because just *look* at us." For emphasis, he gestured between them. "You're a *Doyen*. I'm...I'm a..." He squeezed his eyes shut. Blaise didn't want to say *prisoner* or *war criminal*, even though they both described him. *Breaker. Sorcerer.* "I'm *me*. You're my handler."

Malcolm blinked at him, and it was clear from his startled expression he hadn't seen it as such. "Is this because I had to use the geasa to stop you last night?"

Blaise shivered at the mention, his gut clenching as he staved off the reminder of the dark alchemy surging through him. He didn't want to think about that ever again. But maybe that was a part of it. Jefferson had made it clear he could use the geasa, if he chose. "You have *power* over me."

"But it's not like that," Malcolm protested.

Blaise crossed his arms. "Isn't it? Because that's how it seems."

Malcolm took a tentative step closer. "But that's not how it is *here*." He slapped a hand against his chest, over his heart. His big brown eyes pleaded with Blaise, full of so much emotion that the Breaker couldn't help but uncross his arms, some of his tension bleeding away.

Emrys bumped Blaise with his nose. <He doesn't look like Jefferson, but his heart is the same.>

Blaise glanced back at the stallion, lips pursed. The pegasus always had keen insight into people, and it was clear Emrys not only liked Malcolm but had worked with him. *Trusted* him, even.

"I didn't know how else to get your attention. To save you," Malcolm whispered.

Blaise sighed. "You won't use the geasa against me again?"

Hurt flashed through Malcolm's eyes, but he shook his head. "I didn't use it *against* you, I used it to *help* you. To help *us*."

Blaise raked a hand through his unruly hair. He needed a haircut, a shave, and a bath—probably not in that order. A change of clothes, too. He was a walking disaster.

"Blaise?" Malcolm roused him from his thoughts. "I promise you. My position...the geasa. I would *never* use any of it against you. I'm sorry if you think I did. That was not my intent. I just want to be *me* with you." His voice was tinged with such raw distress that it shook Blaise. He met Malcolm's eyes again, momentarily surprised by the veiled pain he read in their depths.

Maybe Blaise wasn't the only one with old wounds. He thought back to the glimpse of Malcolm's old life revealed in the dreamscape. He nodded, understanding. "You can be you."

Relief reflected in Malcolm's eyes, and he took another step closer. Something about the tilt of his head reminded Blaise of Jefferson, and the very thought stirred his core. Malcolm brushed a hand against the healing wound on Blaise's cheek, his touch tender. The corners of his eyes crinkled, and Blaise thought he was about to speak, but he didn't.

Blaise knew what he wanted to ask, though. He answered the unvoiced question, because after all he'd endured, he *needed* to feel wanted. He leaned into Malcolm, breathing out a soft sigh as warm and welcoming arms wrapped around him.

Salty tears ran down Blaise's face, dampening Malcolm's shoulder. Malcolm pulled back. "What's wrong?"

Blaise shook his head. He didn't know how to answer that. How could he explain that for the first time in what felt like forever, he felt safe? And loved? He closed his eyes, breathing in Malcolm's minty fragrance. Then his wandering mind recalled why he had left the house in the first place. *Jack and Flora.* "Why was Flora so angry at Jack for killing Lamar? I mean, I generally frown on that sort of thing but...again, *Lamar*."

Malcolm made a face. "Can we not talk about that?"

Blaise shook his head, his worries swooping back into place. "I couldn't stay in there to hear their yelling. But I want to know. I don't want to be left out." Because at the heart of it, he felt like he was the reason this had all happened. Whatever bad thing had transpired wouldn't be so if not for him.

Reluctantly, Malcolm explained the issue. Emrys listened too, ears pricked with interest but keeping his thoughts to himself as the Doyen outlined the situation.

Blaise chewed on his bottom lip. "What's going to happen to you? You're a Doyen. And I'm..." He winced. He was a war criminal. A *murderer.* And Malcolm had so many plans to help the mages throughout the Confederation. All his plans were going to be shattered, another casualty of Blaise's destruction.

"You're *Blaise bloody Hawthorne,* and you're amazing and kind and literally the best person I have *ever* met," Malcolm said with conviction. "Don't worry about me."

Blaise crossed his arms. "You don't know me very well if you think I won't worry about you. Anxiety should be my middle name."

Malcolm chuckled. "Fine, fine. I should have said I'm coming up with a plan."

Blaise cocked his head. "What can I do to help?" Mention of a plan put him at ease.

"First things first, focus on getting well." Malcolm brushed a hand against Blaise's too-thin chest. "You worry about that. I'm buying us some time before my plan comes to fruition."

"Are you going to tell me this plan?"

Malcolm smiled. "Once I have it all figured out, absolutely."

"I thought you had it figured out."

"I said I'm coming up with a plan. Though I appreciate the amount of faith you have in me, even I need a little time to work in my wondrous ways," Malcolm clarified with a grin.

⸻

Malcolm

"Mr. Wells!" Marta wailed, indignant, as she burst into Malcolm's study. One of Marta's many charms was that, like Flora, she was overly comfortable around him and discarded the usual social niceties like knocking. "The Breaker is in my *kitchen!*"

Her appearance and level of upset momentarily alarmed Malcolm, but as he absorbed her words, he leaned back in his chair, a grin spreading across his face. "Oh. Is that so?" That was excellent news. Something to take his mind off the fact that the Confederation had his home surrounded, eager to snap him or Blaise up if they so much as stuck a toe beyond the gate.

Marta marched up to his desk. "Sir, with all due respect, *that is my kitchen.*"

He chuckled. She was protective of her domain, and he would have supported her under other circumstances, but not this time. Malcolm eased forward, folding his hands atop the desk. "Marta, please allow me to explain something. I know you think he's dangerous."

She gave a sharp nod, her eyes catching the slew of newspapers arrayed on his desk. She scowled at the headlines: *Traitor Jefferson Cole Missing. Breaker on the Run: Soldiers Surround Wells Estate.* Malcolm shuffled the papers away. He didn't want Blaise to see those, either.

He aimed a winning smile at Marta. Malcolm appreciated that she had held her tongue against Blaise, but he knew her, and read the unease in her body whenever Blaise was around. "He's a *Breaker*, Mr. Wells. *A Breaker in my kitchen.*"

"No harm will come to anything in there, I assure you." Malcolm rose from the desk. "That may be the safest place for him." She glowered at him, dubious. "He loves to bake, Marta. It calms him."

At that, her brow furrowed with thought. Then she nodded. "I can understand that."

"To put you at ease, I'll check on him to be sure all is well." Malcolm headed to the door. Little by little, Blaise was creeping out of the shadow cast over him by the Golden Citadel. Venturing into the kitchen had to be a positive sign, by Malcolm's judgment. He edged past Marta and hurried down the hall, ignoring her *hrmph* of annoyance. She didn't like others going into her kitchen—including him.

As Marta reported, Blaise was there. The young man was a sight to behold, his hair cut and slicked back, his beard neat, and skin clean. He wore a set of Malcolm's clothes from years ago, and they hung baggy on his slender frame, but all the same, it was a happy improvement from his garments of the previous day. He had sugar and flour stationed on a nearby counter, bowls and pans surrounding him. Fragrant, freshly-washed berries and a bowl of cream loomed near tins of spices. Blaise moved more slowly than Malcolm was accustomed to seeing when he was at work doing what he loved, but it was to be expected. Blaise glanced over his shoulder when he heard the door open, a guilty look crossing his face.

"I think your cook is mad at me."

Malcolm smiled, waving a hand in dismissal. "Marta's not used to sharing her space. She'll get over it." *Probably.* "What are you making?"

"Cookies." He gestured to the other assortment of ingredients. "And a berry cream cake."

Oh, that was promising. Marta had a sweet tooth to rival a pegasus. "If you give her a cookie, she'll definitely get over it." Malcolm eased over to a section of the counter that wasn't covered in supplies and leaned against it. "How are you feeling?"

Blaise closed his eyes for a moment, taking a deep breath and then exhaling slowly, as if centering himself. He was having a tough time adjusting to life outside the Golden Citadel. Malcolm was glad for the high walls around his home—it shielded Blaise from the fact that the Confederation knew he was there. Malcolm was gambling they would respect his position as a Doyen and the sanctity of his estate. It was also very possible they wouldn't.

"Feeling like I needed to come and do this," Blaise answered after a moment, jutting his chin toward the ingredients. "I needed to take my mind off things. Sometimes it's like I'm drowning in my thoughts and in my magic. Or like they're both eating me alive." He scrubbed at his face, leaving a trail of flour along one cheek and dusting his beard. "And Emrys said that while you have been very nice and given him sweets, they're not up to the quality he prefers."

Malcolm studied Blaise, wanting to turn him back to the discussion about how he was faring. It had become difficult to read anything through the geasa, as if Blaise had discovered a way to avoid broadcasting through it. But poking too deeply at the question might force him away, and Malcolm was unwilling to take that risk. "Yes, well, I'm sorry that my award-winning chef is not up to your stallion's standards." If Blaise wanted to keep things light, Malcolm would match him.

The younger man set back to work, though his movements lacked the certainty and precision they'd held before. His hands trembled as he poured ingredients, a sign of how much he was struggling. "Thank you for taking care of Emrys, by the way."

What else could Malcolm have done? Emrys had become an ally, wanting Blaise free as much as he did. "You're welcome. He's a good pegasus. And a good friend."

Blaise looked down at the flour, which he had been about to measure when Malcolm came in. "He is." He picked up a tin measuring cup and gave it a contemplative look, as if he had lost his train of thought.

"You're going to be okay." Blaise's quailing uncertainty thrummed through their bond, the first thing Malcolm had detected in a while. "I know it."

"Maybe," Blaise whispered, dubious.

"No maybes," Malcolm corrected. He straightened, stepping closer to rest a hand gently on Blaise's shoulder. "Want me to ask Marta if she has chocolate around here somewhere?"

Blaise blinked, surprised by the question. Then he nodded. "Semisweet. Not baking chocolate."

"There's a difference?"

"*Of course* there's a difference."

Malcolm hid his smile as he turned away. One way or the other, he was going to make sure Blaise was okay.

Flora

THE ARBORETUM WAS ON HIGH ALERT AFTER THE SHENANIGANS AT THE Golden Citadel, but that wasn't about to stop Flora. She was on a mission of compassion. After all the things that had been botched, she decided that Marian, at least, deserved to know Blaise was free. And she had a troubling question for the alchemist—one that hadn't occurred to the others yet.

It took some doing, but she found Marian in the small quarters that served as her room. The alchemist was playing cards to pass the time, though she looked up abruptly as soon as the half-knocker made her appearance. She gathered the cards up and set them aside, her shoulders tense. "Well?"

Flora grinned. "We got him. He's safe."

"Blaise won't be safe until he's off Confederation lands," Marian replied, though her shoulders relaxed at the news. She swallowed. "I wish I could see him."

Flora gave a sad shake of her head. "Too risky. This place is being watched closely, and things didn't go according to plan."

Marian's back straightened, steel glinting in her eyes. "Where is he? They can't get him again." The alchemist fisted her hands, bony knuckles standing out like the spines of a dragon.

"The estate," Flora answered. "He'll be safe there for a time." Marian's brow knit, as if the response wasn't to her satisfaction. But there was little to be done. When the alchemist didn't give voice to her concerns, Flora addressed her own. "You said that Blaise's blood can spawn new mages."

Marian nodded, weary. "Yes."

"How likely is it that Gregor Gaitwood will have magic?" Flora steeled herself for an answer she wouldn't like.

To her surprise, Marian started laughing. Flora wondered if maybe the stress had gotten to her, but after a full minute of mirth, the alchemist quieted with a savage grin. "Doyen Gaitwood is as magical as a boar going to market."

Flora's eyes widened as she caught on to what the woman was implying. "You switched the Ink?" *With pig's blood of all things. Oh, that's grand.*

"The second batch, yes. You nabbed the first batch before I could complete the swap." Annoyance crossed Marian's face for a moment before evaporating. Flora wondered if Marian had been the presence she'd sensed that day. "No one would listen to me about Blaise, so I took matters into my own hands." The alchemist licked her lips. "If there is *anything* I can do in the future to help keep him safe, let me know." She met Flora's eyes.

The half-knocker nodded. "And is there anything I can do for you?" Because blast it all, Flora *liked* this gutsy woman.

Marian offered a sad, reflective smile. "You've already done it."

CHAPTER TWENTY-EIGHT

Echoes of Jack

Kittie

"What is this place?" Emmaline asked as she walked beside her mother. They strode down the main street (the only street) to the corral on the outskirts of the town, where Emmaline's pegasus awaited her. The overuse of magic had drained the girl, and she slept for days once she had gotten settled.

"The only bolt-hole for mages in the Confederation," Kittie answered, tamping down her impatience. She brimmed with questions she was eager to ask, but her daughter had just as many. Maybe more. "You sure stirred up the fire ants by punching through our wards like you did."

Emmaline gave an unapologetic shrug, a move that reminded Kittie almost painfully of Jack. "Didn't know what I was going against, but I'd do it again if I had to."

You even sound like your father. "I'm glad you did." *Ugh. Blasted headache.* Kittie licked her lips, struggling against the urge to take a swig from the flask at her side. It was a losing battle. The hazy comfort of liquor had been her solace for too long. Emmaline frowned as she took a sip of brandy.

And then they arrived at the corral, Emmaline's attention drawn by the striking spotted pegasus who trotted to the fence, thrusting his head over the railing. Kittie would be the first to say the stallion was handsome, and she was fiercely proud that her daughter was the one who rode him. She watched as Emmaline fussed over the pegasus, climbing the fence and dropping down to the other side.

A gaggle of children raced over, eyes wide and curious. They climbed on the fence nearby, though they all had enough sense not to go into the corral. Kittie watched them out of the corner of her eye.

"Miss! Miss!" A freckled girl with red hair waved a carrot in her hand. "My ma said that's a pegasus! But I thought they had wings?"

Emmaline put an arm around her stallion's neck, turning to the curious group. "Your ma is right." She combed her fingers through Oberidon's mane, whispering something to him, and a moment later, a pair of long, speckled wings unfurled from his shoulders. Even Kittie sucked in a breath of wonder, captivated by the magnificent sight. The spotted stallion ruffled his wings, twisting his neck to preen a feather in place before folding them neatly at his sides.

"Oooooh," the children chorused.

"Can I give him a carrot? What's his name?" the red-head asked, her face scrunched in delight.

Emmaline grinned, the pegasus following as she walked closer to their audience. "Sure. You can call him Oby."

"Here, Oby!" the girl dangled the carrot in her hand.

Oberidon's lips curled daintily around the vegetable, tugging it into his mouth with a crunch. <Thank you. It's delicious. Do you know what I like even more?>

The children squealed in unison as the pegasus's voice resonated in their minds. Kittie smiled. She had forgotten that the equines could do that.

"What?" the girl squeaked, rapt.

"Oby, don't be greedy," Emmaline corrected the stallion, bonking him on the muzzle. He lipped at her in mock retaliation, and their interplay made Kittie's heart sing. "He's going to tell you to bring cookies, and then he's going to get so fat and sassy he won't be able to fly."

The children howled with laughter. Oberidon laid his ears back. <One cookie never hurt.>

Kittie watched as Emmaline bantered with the children a little longer. A boy broke away from the group, returning a few moments later bearing a cookie like a hard-won prize. Emmaline allowed them to break it into tiny pieces and take turns feeding the pegasus, and afterward, the children drifted off, happy.

Emmaline's interaction with the children was another heartrending echo of Jack. She couldn't hold her questions back any longer. Once the children were out of earshot, Kittie climbed onto the top rail. "Em, I have to ask. Only because..." She drifted off, shaking her head as she fought back the emotions she had bricked away so many years ago. "I thought you were dead. I was *told* you were dead." The yawning emptiness of those words opened a deep gulf between them, and Kittie trembled. She took another drink from her flask to settle her nerves.

Emmaline flinched, her mouth dropping open. "*Oh*. What do you want to ask? Ask me anything." She scurried up the fence and sat beside her mother, rubbing Oberidon's forehead.

"What happened to your father? Is he…?"

Emmaline blinked. "Daddy's alive. At least the last I knew." She looked chagrined. "He…well, it's a long story. After you got stolen away from us, he kept me safe." Emmaline scraped at the wood with a fingernail, thoughtful. "Daddy never stopped trying to find you."

Something inside Kittie crumbled to ash. *Jack tried to find me. He wasn't dead. He just couldn't get here.* She swallowed. "How did you find me when he couldn't? And where is he now?"

Her daughter pulled the tiny doll-like figure from her pocket. "My magic is better at finding people than his. I'm an Effigest. Like *him*." Something about the way Emmaline emphasized the last word told Kittie that there had been strife between the pair. Not surprising in the least. "And Daddy…he's helping a friend of ours. He let me look for you by myself." Her voice softened as she pulled back some of the vitriol.

A smile tugged at Kittie's mouth. "And you succeeded. Now what?"

Emmaline chewed on her lower lip. "I should find him once my magic's replenished. Let him know I found you." She fixed an imploring look on her mother. "And maybe you'll come back to the Gutter with us?"

Kittie blinked. Jack had settled in the Gutter? She tightened her grip on the top rail. "There are some things I need to take care of here."

"Please, Mom. I…I missed you." Emmaline's voice cracked, crestfallen.

As if Kittie hadn't missed her child and husband with every fragment of her being. As if the easiest path hadn't been to drown her sorrows. "I missed you, too. That doesn't mean I won't go. I only need time to handle something."

"What?" Emmaline asked.

Kittie studied the churned dirt in the paddock. Would Emmaline hate her? "I have to tell my husband."

Emmaline stared at her, and Oberidon snorted. "What…what do you mean? What about Daddy?"

Kittie jumped down from the fence, stumbling and almost fell her knees. She straightened, trying to preserve her dignity. "What else was I supposed to do? I thought he was *dead*. That *you* were dead." She gestured to herself. "Was I to just wither away and die?" There had been a time when she'd wished for that—the time before she had cured her grief with liquor and the first comforting arms she fell into.

Her daughter sighed. "No. it's just that…" She shook her head. "Daddy's a jackass but he waited for you."

Of course, he had. Jack was far from perfect, and Kittie wouldn't have blamed him if he sought comfort from the soiled doves of the Untamed Territory. But that wasn't his way. He would only fall into bed with someone he had an emotional connection to. "That's why I need time, Em. Just a little." Kittie swallowed. "I love your father." But would Jack feel, as Emmaline did, that Kittie had betrayed them? It was impossible to know. Was he still the man he had been, or had he changed as much as Kittie herself?

Emmaline nodded. "We don't have much time. I left him in Izhadell." She stuck her hand into a pocket, pulling out a tiny doll. "And he's on the move."

Izhadell. Kittie tensed. Jack was in Phinora? She seldom left the limits of Bitter End's wards, but she knew very well that he would be a wanted man. Jack was no innocent, and she couldn't imagine the years doing anything to change that. "Why is he in Izhadell?"

Emmaline licked her lips. "It's kind of a long story. But it's about that friend I told you about."

Kittie nodded. "I have all afternoon. Tell me."

CHAPTER TWENTY-NINE
Puppeteer

Jack

Soldiers and guards patrolled Izhadell like a murder of chupacabras on the hunt. Maybe killing Lamar had been a miscalculation, but Jack didn't regret it. Not really. Zepheus reminded him that the increased presence of guards and soldiers in the streets of the capital city was a direct result of his actions.

"Not as if freeing a war criminal from the Cit played a part or anything," Jack muttered.

<Doesn't help that the murderer of a Salt-Iron Commander is running around free.>

The outlaw huffed out a breath, fingers tight on the reins. The last few days had been rough, requiring the use of Obfuscation more frequently than he liked. By night he bunked in abandoned buildings and by day he skulked through the outskirts of Izhadell, searching for leads.

He had exchanged his usual clothing for the nondescript, professional clothing of a merchant again. Though the hair dye had washed out, a check in his small hand mirror proved he had cleaned up well and only bore a passing resemblance to his Wanted posters. Those always somehow made him look meaner.

<You *are* a mean son of a plucked griffin,> Zepheus reminded him.

Jack shrugged, not about to deny the truth of the statement. He nudged the palomino onward, heading to a tavern. Wells probably hadn't noticed it with his concern over Blaise, but Jack had relieved him of some of his wealth. Just enough to get some jaws yapping so that he could find out what he needed.

The customers in the tavern were on edge, alarmed by the heightened presence of guards and the rumors racing through the streets about the Breaker holed up at the Doyen's estate. Jack grabbed a barstool and listened in. Their fear of Blaise was damned annoying. Not that they used his name. No, to the public at large, he was the Breaker. The outlaw who had single-handedly destroyed Fort Courage and injured or killed scores of Confederation men and women. *I never get any credit.*

But the mysterious murder of Commander Gaitwood was also a hot topic for debate. The only problem was that the idiots suspected Blaise of that, too. Jack nearly slapped a hand to his forehead. *Bunch of beef-headed coots.*

<You're on your own if you correct them.> He could imagine Zepheus pinning his ears back in annoyance.

No, Jack wouldn't correct them. His current guise wouldn't have such knowledge. *Unfortunately.* Instead, he flagged over the bartender. "Any young, blonde girls come in here?"

The bartender, a stocky, middle-aged woman with her hair pinned into buns, glowered at him. "We don't cater to such appetites here, you blighter."

Jack tilted his head. "If that's the case, you're one of the few."

She glared at him, baring her teeth in an unfriendly smile. "If that's what you're after, then you'd best be on your way."

The outlaw tapped a finger against the bar, taking a moment to decide how he wanted to play it. *Figures I'd walk into the one place in all Phinora that isn't happy to offer innocents up for the taking.* "I apologize, but you misunderstand. I'm looking for the girl for *other* reasons."

At that, the bartender gave him an assessing look. She had probably heard all the lies before. "And?"

"She has a horse—a particular one I'm interested in." Yeah, maybe focusing on Oberidon was the smarter way to play it. "I run a breeding operation."

The bartender studied him, then nodded. "Right. Anything particular?"

"Spots. Unusual for a Phinoran-bred."

The bartender licked her lips. "The sort with the blanket patterns on their hind end, like the Mellan Spotted? Or the piebald type like the Petrian Trotter?"

Jack shook his head. "Not like either of those." He racked his brain for the name of the spotted breed native to Oscen and the northern Untamed Territory.

"Pelushan?"

The outlaw snapped his fingers. That was it. "Yes, spots all over the body like a Pelushan. The particular one I had my eye on had liver brown spots."

The bartender gave a small smile. "There's someone I can ask." She rubbed her fingers together with meaning.

Jack reached into his coin purse and drew out two golden eagles, sliding them across the bar. She dropped them into a pocket, holding up her index finger in a *wait* gesture. She saw to another customer, then slipped into a room behind the bar. Jack took another sip of his drink as he waited.

<You've got guards incoming.>

Jack stayed on the barstool, though he turned just enough to have an eye on the door. True to Zepheus's warning, a trio of guards entered, surveying the tavern. The common area grew quiet, save for a rowdy group at the billiards table too absorbed with their game to notice. Jack ignored the guards when they approached the bar. The bartender returned, frowning at the newcomers.

"Don't want any trouble from you lot," she warned the leader.

The man shrugged. "Answer my questions, and we'll be on our way. You seen any mavericks or strange doings around here?"

Jack took another sip of his beer. Technically, he wasn't a maverick.

The bartender rolled her eyes. "I work with the public. There are always strange doings." One of the newcomers snickered, though he stopped when his neighbor elbowed him. "You need to be more specific."

The lead guard sighed. "I don't know the name of 'em. The sort that messes with dolls and stick figures?"

"Puppeteer?" one of his cronies guessed.

"No, those are the ones who do the plays for children. They're entertainers, not mages," the guard who had snickered corrected.

Gods. I'm surrounded by half-wits that couldn't teach a hen to cluck, and I don't dare correct them. Jack sighed and took another swig.

"Eff...effer...oh thunderation, I don't know." The lead guard spread his hands in exasperation.

"Effigest," Jack muttered.

The guards brightened. "Right! Yes, that. What this fine man said." The leader gave Jack a grateful nod before returning his attention to the bartender. "We're looking for one of those. But a girl, long blonde hair. We think she's the one who killed the Commander. Found one of the little doodads at the scene."

It's a poppet, you fiddlehead. Jack stared at his mug, troubled because he didn't think he'd left any evidence behind. And he knew for a fact the Cit had a record of his alleged capture. Unless they were dumber than he thought, they would also know he was no longer on the grounds. So why look for Emmaline? She hadn't been at the Cit.

Oh. Then he realized why. As far as the Confederation knew, Jack had no magic. It was documented that Lamar had Jack's magic stripped. And Emmaline had been in their custody for a time. They had a record of her magic. And she, like Jack, had a compelling reason for wanting Lamar dead. Lamar had seen her in Izhadell. *Damn it.* Now it was even more urgent that he track her down before the Salties did.

The bartender gave a noncommittal shrug. "Lots of girls on the streets around here. Gonna need more than that."

The lead guard nodded. "She rides a spotted horse. Like one of them Pelushans."

The bartender smiled, canting her head. "That so? Boys, then I have somebody you should meet. This gentleman here is looking for that horse. Perhaps you can work together."

All eyes turned to Jack. He took another drink as the lead guard shifted to face him. *To Perdition with this bartender!* And here Jack had thought she might be a reasonable person.

"Is that so?" the leader asked, suspicious.

Jack rolled his shoulders in what they might construe as a lazy shrug. "Maybe. Got an eye out for interesting horseflesh."

"And why is that?"

The outlaw met the guard's eyes. Jack wanted to plant a fist in the man's face, but that wasn't something his current persona would do. At least not without good reason. Jack himself needed little cause. "Breeding stock."

"How did you know about this horse?"

Jack rolled his eyes. "Because I'm not blind or stupid like you boys." Maybe he shouldn't have said that. The guards tightened up their ring around him. Yeah, he definitely shouldn't have said that.

<I can hear you being stupid. I'm around the back if you can get out.>

"You must be new in town. No one insults the guard around here," the leader growled. "We keep the peace, though we're not afraid to remind rabble like you of what we can do."

<Oh, they're going to regret that,> Zepheus commented.

Jack ignored the stallion, lifting his chin in defiance at the young man's words. Judging by their youth, Jack estimated he had between fifteen and twenty years of age on them. They were all young and eager to prove themselves. No doubt they saw him as a man past his prime.

None of them knew they were dealing with an outlaw, much less a mage.

"I think it would be in your best interest to leave me alone to finish my drink," Jack advised them, turning away. As much as he was spoiling for a fight, the odds weren't in his favor in these close-quarters, outnumbered as he was. At least without using magic or a sixgun. But those would give him away. *Please show you have the common sense of a drunk goblin and don't poke the monster.*

They chose violence. A hand clamped on Jack's shoulder. "That's quite enough from you. A night in a cell will teach you some respect." The guards laughed, foreshadowing that getting Jack to the aforementioned cell would include some roughing up first.

Jack sighed. He met the bartender's eyes. "This is on you."

She shrugged. "I have no regrets."

Yeah, well, she was going to regret the clean-up that her tavern would require. He glanced back at the guard, palming his personal poppet as he attempted to shrug his shoulder free. "This is your last warning. Get your Garus-besotted *Saltie* hands off me."

The guard's mouth opened to make a retort, then snapped shut as he and his cohorts digested the insult Jack had hurled at them. The bartender goggled at him, too. No fine, upstanding Confederation citizen would call another a *Saltie* or disparage Garus, their precious god of wisdom. Which meant that he wasn't a fine, upstanding Confederation citizen. Jack smiled as they connected the dots.

Fingers tightened on pistols. A handful of customers who sensed trouble brewing skulked out, but others were now on alert, eager at the promise of bloodshed. "You're coming with us, outlaw."

"Nah." Jack took a last sip of his drink, simultaneously pulling on the magic of his primed poppet for a burst of strength and speed.

He rammed his mug into the leader's face, his hand a blur as it smashed into the man's nose. The guard sprawled backward into one of his fellows.

The remaining guard dodged out of the way, aiming his pistol at Jack. For half a second the outlaw thought the guard might hesitate and not shoot, but by the determined slant of the man's brow, he realized that was an incorrect assumption. He had the advantage and whipped his leg out, kicking the guard's knee so that his shot fouled, the bullet slamming into a wall.

And just like that, fights boiled out across the room. The remaining customers, out of boredom or inebriation, started a melee of their own. Billiard balls flew across the common area like cannonballs, a cue ball sailing past Jack's nose. Beer bottles shattered as enthusiastic brawlers broke them on the edge of tables. A giggling dancehall girl jumped off the bar and landed on the back of the guard who had tried to shoot Jack, whooping as if she were astride a half-broke unicorn.

Jack slid beneath a table, avoiding a guard who had recovered and lunged after him. He leaped up on the other side, hurling the table into his pursuer and, in the process, taking out a burly man who howled with rage. Jack was distracted, trying to track the other guards.

He didn't realize until too late that the burly man had jumped to his feet and was barreling at him like an angry bull. Jack turned when he caught a glimpse of a shadow in his peripheral vision.

A beefy fist smashed into his right cheek and eye. Jack's head cracked backward, and he saw stars. It wasn't the first time he'd taken a punch, but this one had poor timing. His eyes watered as he staggered away from his new assailant. The punch served as a great comeuppance, smacking Jack right in the pride—where it hurt the most.

Jack pulled out his sixgun, sighting it on the big man who had his hand cocked back for another punch. His vision blurred, but this close Jack wouldn't miss. "Try that again." The man backed off, realizing his brawn was no match for a bullet.

The outlaw turned, slipping out into the streets while the guards were distracted by the chaos, skirting around the building to the back where Zepheus was waiting. The palomino eyed his shiner as he mounted. <What happened to the guards?>

"They tested the Scourge of the Untamed Territory and failed," Jack growled, rubbing at his tender cheek. "Now let's get out of here before more arrive."

<Where to?>

"Anywhere but here."

CHAPTER THIRTY
The Power of Baked Goods

Malcolm

Sunlight filtered through the window, chastising Malcolm for his lateness. He shifted in his bed, pausing when he noticed the contours of a dark shape on the other side, curled up. Blaise's eyes were closed, his face slack and hair a wild nest from whatever restlessness had possessed him. But he was peaceful in his slumber, and all Malcolm wanted to do was stare at him and try to figure out how he had snuck in here during the night without him realizing.

In the days since Blaise's release, Malcolm had kept himself away from the dreamscape at night, giving the Breaker the space he needed. Or at least, the space Malcolm suspected he needed. Blaise didn't talk about it and had closed himself off, spending most of his time with Emrys. But maybe Malcolm had been wrong. He frowned, considering his options. *Nothing ventured, nothing gained.*

Malcolm rolled over to face him, the mattress jarring with the movement. It shook Blaise awake, as was his sneaky intent. Blaise's eyes flashed open, and Malcolm detected a shiver of panic and embarrassment through the geasa.

"Um, howdy," Blaise murmured. "Sorry."

Why are you apologizing? Malcolm would gladly wake up like this for the rest of eternity. "Nothing to be sorry about."

Blaise relaxed at his words. "I just...being alone...I..." He faltered, shaking his head against the pillow.

Not for the first time, Malcolm had to rein in his anger at what the Cit had done to Blaise. He reminded himself that this was part of his gambit. It was a systemic problem he was going to address and correct. But for the moment, Blaise was the priority. "Hey, you never have to be alone here. Not when I'm around. You know that, don't you?"

Blaise swallowed. "Yes, but..." He closed his eyes. "I know the Confederation is outside your walls. Waiting. For *me*."

"Not just for you, love." Malcolm hid a secret smile when Blaise's eyes flew open at the endearment. "You give yourself too much credit. They want me, too. And I have business to attend to regarding that issue today."

Blaise adjusted, braced upright on his elbow. His hair was still an adorable mess, which Malcolm wanted to point out but didn't want to risk embarrassing him. "Did you come up with a plan?"

Malcolm nodded. "Mostly. I had some parts of it confirmed late last night. Very late." Technically, it had been morning. Blaise must have come in once Malcolm collapsed from exhaustion. He read the hunger for information on the Breaker's face, so he sat up. "I'll tell you, if you like."

"Please do."

There was a knock at the door, followed by Flora's voice. "Hey, Mal! You better get your tail down here because company's coming in a half hour!"

Malcolm groaned. "Change of plans. Let's get dressed and I'll update you as we choke down a quick breakfast." He swung his legs over the side of the bed, glancing over at Blaise. As much as he adored that man, he had no taste for clothing. "I'll pick something out for you." Malcolm had splurged and bought a small wardrobe of clothing he hoped might fit Blaise. "Come on. To the closet in your guest room!"

Blaise raised his brows but dutifully trailed behind him out the door.

Flora saw the pair exit the master bedroom and whooped. "It's about time, you two!" She blew air kisses at them.

Blaise's cheeks flamed, and Malcolm scowled at her. If it were anyone else, he wouldn't have cared what Flora thought about their nocturnal activities. But with Blaise he cared very much. "It's not like that."

Flora snorted, favoring them with a skeptical look. "If you say so, boss."

Malcolm clenched his jaw, hoping Flora hadn't dimmed the spark of Blaise that had shone through this morning. He hazarded a glance at the Breaker, who hung back a step behind him. Something flickered in Blaise's eyes that Malcolm couldn't read, and then he ducked his head and whispered, "Thank you."

"Of course," Malcolm said, voice soft. Flora was right, though. He wanted more, *longed* for more. But he cared for Blaise too much to force the issue. Malcolm clung to the hope that perhaps some day, Blaise might change his mind. Until then, he would wait. And dream.

He laid a gentle hand on the younger man's shoulder, guiding him to the neighboring guest room so that Malcolm could peruse the array of clothing.

A short time later, Blaise stared at his reflection, dressed in fresh, well-tailored clothes. Malcolm had helped him tame the mess of his hair with a comb and scented oils. The Breaker didn't say a word but shook his head at himself in disbelief. Malcolm smiled, rather pleased with the results.

Once Malcolm himself was dressed, he met Blaise downstairs for breakfast and laid out the plan. Which, predictably, Blaise was dubious of. "How sure are you this will work?"

"Not sure at all," Malcolm replied, trying to stay upbeat. It was an audacious gamble, but it was all he could come up with. "My back-up plan is that we sneak out, get on a steamer, move to Theilia and start a new life as goat herders."

"No offense, but you would last less than five minutes as a goat herder," Blaise said seriously.

"Yes, and this is why it's the back-up plan." Malcolm nodded, pleased that Blaise was willing and able to banter.

"But I don't like the part where I have to, you know, *meet people*." Blaise worried at his bottom lip.

Malcolm gave a pained sigh. "My darling little introvert, you know meeting people is one of my favorite things to do, right?"

"You can do that, and I'll stand in a corner and pretend not to be there."

Malcolm chuckled. Blaise had no idea he would be the star attraction. But he would never think that of himself. "It's going to be fine. You'll be great."

Blaise

IT WAS NOT, IN FACT, FINE OR GREAT. IT HAD BEEN EASY TO BELIEVE Malcolm when he spoke with such confidence, but quite another thing when Blaise faced the reality. He knew from Emrys about the Confederation forces amassed outside Malcolm's gates. Malcolm pretended like it was nothing to worry about. Anxiety clawed at Blaise's insides.

Blaise braced himself for some sort of sneak attack or ambush from the Confederation ranks when the front gates opened to allow entry to Malcolm's guests. Nothing more threatening than staffers with dour faces accompanied the carriage that came up the drive. Blaise relaxed as he watched Malcolm greet the new arrivals. He had found a corner to skulk in (he hadn't been kidding about that), and Flora was nearby, though she said that she would have to duck out soon. She didn't want to be seen.

Blaise wished he could do the same.

He slipped into the parlor, noticing that Malcolm's staff had laid refreshments out on a table. Finger sandwiches and fresh-squeezed lemonade. "No cookies? Everything's better with cookies." Not to mention the berry cream cake. He huffed in annoyance.

Malcolm was still greeting their guests outside. Blaise hurried to the kitchen and grabbed a tray, arranging an assortment of cookies. He was afraid of running out of time, so discarded the idea of bringing the cake to the parlor. Cookies would have to do. He couldn't help his satisfied smile at the sweets.

A few moments later, Malcolm led his guests inside. When they entered the parlor, Blaise was already seated in a chair in the farthest corner. Maybe Malcolm would realize he hadn't been joking.

Malcolm's eyes slid to Blaise as he entered, making a little *get over here* gesture with one hand as he and his guests swept into the room. Blaise frowned and shook his head.

"There he is, just as I said!" Malcolm's voice rang with false cheer, and he stepped over to Blaise, leaning down. He lowered his voice. "Please. We need all the allies we can get."

The sincerity and worry in Malcolm's brown eyes won Blaise over. With a soft sigh, he nodded and rose from the chair, rewarded by the Doyen's relieved smile. Malcolm turned back to their guests.

"Doyen Seward Jennings and Mrs. Lizzie Jennings, it's my pleasure to introduce you to Blaise Hawthorne."

Blaise had to admit it warmed his soul that Malcolm hadn't mentioned his magic at all. Even though he knew it was going to be discussed. It was just a tiny, precious nod to the fact that his magic didn't define him, and Malcolm believed that. It was a part of who he was, but not the sum.

Doyen Jennings was shorter than Malcolm, and he beamed as he stared at Blaise. He extended a hand, then grunted as he corrected himself. "Oh, my apologies, I don't know what's proper."

That was a little surprising, since aside from Malcolm, everyone with any power in the Confederation assumed Blaise's touch would destroy them. They weren't wrong. "We can shake. If you like." Blaise focused on keeping his magic under wraps and calm, though he was anything but. He extended his hand, and Jennings took it with a clammy and cool hand, as if he were a little nervous, too.

The woman at Jennings's side watched Blaise with rapt attention, thoughtful. She glanced at Malcolm. "He's easy on the eyes. I think we can work with this." She tilted her head, dark ringlets cascading to one side.

Easy on the eyes? Blaise glanced at Malcolm, whose lips twitched at her assessment. He couldn't offer a comment, however, as Doyen Jennings interceded. His gaze flitted between Blaise and Malcolm with keen interest.

"I will admit, Mal, the revelation shocked me. You, the figurehead of the Faedrans, betraying us to bind to a mage?" The words surprised Blaise. He hadn't thought of it from their political perspective. He was about to speak up, but the Doyen continued. "But now I see your argument. You're right. He wasn't treated well, and not even a prisoner deserves that."

Blaise had put on a little weight, but his cheekbones were still prominent, and the stone bruise on his cheek stubbornly refused to retreat. Self-conscious, Blaise rubbed at the underside of his arm, though the wicked, still-healing gash was concealed by his long sleeve.

Jennings didn't even know about Gregor's plans for him. Didn't know anything about the potion that turned him into a destructive force. Malcolm had said that was something they couldn't reveal, not yet. Baby steps.

"Still," the Doyen mused after a moment, "surely you could have gone about it a better way than binding to a mage?"

"Not while obtaining actual evidence," Malcolm lied.

Meanwhile, Mrs. Jennings snatched a cookie and nibbled at it, walking around Blaise in contemplative circles. He might have found it annoying, but her first bite elicited an *ooh* of pleasure, and he did like when people enjoyed his baking. "You said this was a two-pronged attack, Doyen Wells. What's *my* role?"

Malcolm smiled. "Excellent question, Lizzie! As you heard, I'm going to demand an Inquiry into the conditions of the mages at the Cit."

"Going to be difficult with Gregor leveraging an Inquiry against *you* for binding to a mage," Doyen Jennings pointed out. "As the rumor mill predicts will happen."

Malcolm waved a hand as if this were inconsequential, keeping his focus on Lizzie. "Play the sympathy angle. Seed whatever rumors you can to buy our plight as much favor as you can."

"Only rumors, or can I…be more creative?" Her eyes flashed, eager.

"What did you have in mind?" Malcolm's voice rose with interest.

Blaise slunk a few feet away so he would no longer be the literal center of attention.

"Remember when I told you I was interested in penning a play about him?" She gestured to Blaise with the remains of her cookie. *Wait, what?* Before he could catch up, she plowed onward. "I have a draft ready. I can rewrite the third act however you like."

"Er," Blaise protested. *A play? About me?* "What in the blueberry muffins are you talking about?"

Lizzie snapped her fingers, trotting across the parlor to pick up a napkin. She pulled out a pen and started writing. "I love that expression! Let me jot it down."

Malcolm was doing a poor job of hiding an amused smile. "I didn't agree to this," Blaise hissed.

"Come on," Malcolm said, sidling up beside him, voice soft. "We need every advantage. Even the smallest bits of propaganda will help."

"I think we need to brush up on your goat-herding skills." Yes, that sounded more and more tempting.

Malcolm put a companionable arm around him. Blaise almost shrugged it off but he liked it, much to his own chagrin. "My goat-herding skills will remain woeful. What if I promise to never drag you to the play about yourself?"

Blaise sighed. He wasn't sure why a play about himself would be anything but a terrible idea, but Malcolm seemed to think it was worthwhile. And Malcolm was doing so much to help him, he couldn't be a heel and fight everything. "I might live with that."

"Thank you," Malcolm whispered, his breath warm as he leaned close to Blaise's ear. He turned back to Lizzie. "Madame, if you'd like to discuss this with Blaise, I'll go over strategy with Seward."

"Wait, I have to *discuss* it?" Blaise fought back a wave of panic. He wanted to go out to the stables and bury his face in Emrys's mane and not be here.

Malcolm paused in front of him, meeting his eyes. "Lizzie is here to help. It's going to be okay. You can do this." Then he added a wink for good measure before abandoning Blaise to the playwright while he and Seward retired to the study.

Oh well. At least he still had cookies.

***

"What did you *do*?" As soon as the Jenningses left, Malcolm rounded on Blaise, his eyebrows raised so high they brushed against a curl of his dark hair. "Lizzie was *purring* with joy when they left."

Blaise offered the last cookie to him. "Cookie."

Malcolm eyed it, tempted but undeterred. "Later."

"No, I mean, you asked what I did, and that's the answer." Blaise waved the cookie with meaning. "You're not the only one who can come up with ideas, you know."

Malcolm's expression softened. "That's true. But you were supposed to talk to her so she can finish her play about you to gain support."

"Did that, too." Blaise couldn't help the pride that bloomed in his voice.

Malcolm glanced from the cookie to Blaise, giving in to temptation. He snagged it and took a bite. "So it went well?"

Blaise winced. He wasn't good at reading people, and Lizzie Jennings was no exception. "Probably? She asked a lot of questions. Including who made the cookies, and it surprised her when I said I did. Then we got off topic for a while, and she tried to get me to come work for her until she remembered that was a bad idea."

Malcolm blinked. "Are you seriously telling me Lizzie Jennings tried to steal you away from me for your *baked goods*?"

"You'll be happy to hear I told her no."

Malcolm snorted at that. "I should hope so. Why does it seem as if you're leaving out a *but*?"

There it was. Blaise was rather proud of this next bit. Malcolm was so much savvier than him at this political business, but Lizzie had given him an irresistible opening. "That's what I was trying to tell you. The Jenningses are hosting a party in a few days."

"Gala," Malcolm corrected absently. "Yes, Seward mentioned that to me in passing. But we can't go. If you leave the grounds of my estate before the Inquiry, we'll be right back where we started."

Blaise grinned. "I have no intention of leaving this estate until it's safe for me to do so. My desserts, on the other hand…"

Malcolm slanted a wily look at him. "Wait. I see where you're going with this. That's…that's *brilliant*."

"You once told me my cakes could stand up against the best of the best in Ganland." Blaise hoped that was still true. He was out of practice, and that worried him.

"I meant every word." Malcolm sounded fiercely proud. He rubbed his hands together as he considered the idea. "That's quite the coup. I wish I had thought of it myself."

"You've had a lot on your mind," Blaise murmured. Then he paused, thinking back to something Malcolm had said. "Hold on. You think I would willingly go to someone's fancy party? You're familiar with the fact I'd rather hide in a corner, right?"

Malcolm chuckled. "It's a *gala*. And I may have a long-term goal of taking you to one."

Blaise snorted. "Did you miss my failed attempt at invisibility earlier?"

"And aren't we lucky that's not your magic?" Malcolm grinned.

"It's a pity. Would be so useful." Blaise shook his head, then rubbed his hands together as he turned his attention back to his new goal. "I need to take an inventory of your kitchen. Do you mind?"

Malcolm studied him, a tiny smile curling his lips. "Do what you need to do."

Turning, Blaise strode to the kitchen, and for the first time in a long time, he felt more like himself. He had a purpose, and it was something he could *do*. Now he just had to hope Marta would allow it.

CHAPTER THIRTY-ONE
Not All Monsters Are Alike

Jack

Jack spent days lying low, though he bridled against the delay this put in his search for Emmaline. He considered doubling back to Wells's place, but that wouldn't solve anything. Not to mention the estate's perimeter was crawling with guards. The Doyen and Blaise had enough on their hands without his added complications. While he waited, he did everything he could think of to aid his search. Emmaline herself had a knack for finding people with her Effigest magic. Jack figured if she could do it, maybe he could, too. He tried, but nothing did the trick. His poppet for her only told him she was out there somewhere, with no sense of direction. It was damned frustrating.

"And I'm the fool who didn't plan far enough ahead to figure out a rendezvous," Jack groused to himself. Although he had half-expected Emmaline to track him down by now. It made him worry that something had gone wrong. That she had been captured or hadn't found Kittie.

Besides the guards and soldiers Jack originally encountered, bounty hunters had taken up his trail. The fools were eager to cash his head in for gold and fame, though they were more an inconvenience than a threat. At first, he had worried the Confederation might send out a pair of theurgists, but he soon realized most of those coming after him were norms, without a lick of magic. They had youth and weapons, but those didn't hold a candle to a seasoned outlaw mage partnered with a pegasus.

In other circumstances, Jack might have found the constant interruptions entertaining. As it was, they were pissing him off, so he decided at last to see if he could make them *useful*.

He stood over the latest bounty hunter, a spirited young woman with red hair who reminded him of Vixen Valerie. Maybe the resemblance was why he didn't kill her outright, like the rest. *Nah, not really.* He hoped she had information. She lay sprawled in the boggy clearing, panting through the pain of a broken arm, Jack's sixgun trained on her.

"May as well shoot me, you bastard," she spat.

Jack canted his head, amused. "Mighty rude of you. You attacked me first, after all." And it was true. He wasn't a dunderhead, and he played the innocent traveler card until the hunters came at him.

The huntress glared at him. If she had magic, he would have recruited her for the Gutter in a heartbeat. He liked her spunk. "Of course, I attacked you. Who wouldn't? Your mug is plastered on *Wanted* posters all over the place."

"Yep," Jack agreed, spinning his revolver for show. "So you know I have no qualms with putting a bullet in someone's brain. That's enough to make you wonder why you're still alive, eh?"

"Because you're a monster. You probably want to force yourself on me." She struggled into a sitting position, whimpering when she jarred her arm.

The outlaw spat in the dirt, jaw jutting as he holstered his sixgun. He knelt beside her, meeting her eyes. "I'm not gonna argue that I'm a monster. But not all monsters are alike."

Zepheus stood nearby, wings mantled and ears flattened. <Not sure how that's going to convince her of anything.>

Yeah, he was getting to it. Jack kept his focus on the huntress. "Ask yourself what the Scourge of the Untamed Territory is doing this deep in Confederation lands."

"Assassinating good Confederation men and women, I assume," she shot back.

<I mean, she's not *wrong*.>

Annoying pegasus. Jack frowned. "I'm trying to find my *daughter*."

She blinked, taken by surprise at his admission. Then her face shifted to suspicion. "How do I know that's true?"

"Because you're still alive." Jack shifted to sit down cross-legged nearby. His sixgun was still handy if needed. "What's your name?"

"Lauren."

He nodded, accepting it at face value. Might not be her real name, but it was something. "Well, Lauren, pleased to make your acquaintance. I'll make you a deal. You tell me anything you know that might help me find my daughter, and you get to live."

"How generous," she muttered.

He smirked. "I have my own code of honor, thank you kindly. Now, tell me if you have any information on a girl with blonde hair who rides a spotted stallion."

Lauren twitched at the description. "I know she's *Wanted*, same as you." She licked her lips, some of the fight leaving her as she asked, "That your daughter?"

Jack tilted his head. "You're a smart woman and can probably figure that out. Where was she last sighted?"

The huntress stared at him, as if considering whether she would answer. She glanced down at her limp arm. "I can do you one better, if you let me live."

"How's that?"

"I can give you the handbill."

Jack's pulse quickened. When the Confederation really wanted someone, they distributed individual handbills to bounty hunters. Often the handbills included information not found on a general *Wanted* poster. "Deal. Where is it?"

"If you can find my horse, it's in the pannier."

<Just a moment.> Zepheus trotted off, returning shortly with the reins of the woman's bay gelding between his teeth as he led the steed back. The gelding smacked his lips as he walked, incriminating evidence that he had fled the scene not out of fear but greed for the surrounding foliage.

Jack rose and rifled through Lauren's saddlebags, nodding with satisfaction as he found the missive. He slipped it into his own saddlebag, then shoved his boot into the stirrup to mount. "It's your lucky day, Huntress Lauren. You get to live to tell the tale of how you survived an encounter with Wildfire Jack."

"You're an arrogant bastard, and you can go straight to Perdition."

He smiled, giving her a little salute. "All in good time, darlin'. Thanks for the help." And with that, he rode off.

CHAPTER THIRTY-TWO

Rekindled

Kittie

Kittie glanced at the calendar on the table. *He's due back today.* She hadn't told Emmaline much about Hugh Fasig, the man she had married. What was there to say, besides he had served the purpose of distracting her from past pain with his own sort? She didn't love him, and it wasn't something she was proud of.

After she and Emmaline shared a quiet breakfast, they set into the cadence of their day. Kittie served as one of the town laundresses, cleaning and mending clothing for the other citizens. Not a glorious occupation, but it had given her something to do. And it ensured she always had a full flask and needn't rely on her husband for that.

Emmaline plucked a sock in need of mending out of the nearby basket, holding it up as if it were offensive. "Mom, why?"

Kittie selected a needle from her sewing kit. "Why what?"

Her daughter gestured to the domestic scene around them, tossing the sock onto the top of the basket. "I don't understand this. You're a *mage*. A Pyromancer, even. Aren't you meant for more than this?"

Kittie swallowed at the question. She didn't want to answer it, instead focusing on threading her needle. "I don't know what you mean."

"This...this isn't *you*." Emmaline frowned.

"I don't know what you expect of me," Kittie replied, picking up the discarded sock. She found the hole in the toe and set to work mending it.

Emmaline rose from her chair, pacing the small laundry room. Even the way she hunched her shoulders reminded Kittie of Jack. "Daddy told me stories about you when I was little. Before he..." She turned away, toeing a pile of dirty laundry thoughtfully. "Before it hurt him too much to talk about you. He called you a firebrand. Said you wanted to change things. Change everything for mages. Find a way to lead them to freedom."

Kittie bowed her head. That felt like it had been a lifetime ago; dreams that had belonged to someone else. "That was another time, Em."

"What changed?"

"*I* changed." Kittie sighed. She focused on finishing the sock, then found its mate. "I discovered it was futile. One person can't take on something as big as the Confederation and win."

Kittie couldn't bear to go into detail about how her time in the Golden Citadel had hammered that message home. They had made certain she knew that it was because of her fight against the Confederation that her loved ones were gone. That was all it took to snuff out her fire. *What use is magic if it can't protect the ones you love?* Why fight, only to face more pain?

Emmaline pursed her lips and said nothing for a few minutes. Kittie kept to her work, though she sipped from the flask to bolster her nerves.

"What if it wasn't just one person, though?" Emmaline asked at last.

Kittie glanced at her, shaking her head. "I wouldn't do that again." Not now that she had her daughter back. It wasn't worth the risk, especially if they found somewhere they could live in peace.

"Why not?" Emmaline asked, challenge ripening her voice. "What if you had something worth fighting for?"

The needle stabbed into Kittie's index finger, so distracted was she by Emmaline's question. With a hiss, she drew it back and set the sock aside. "I had something worth fighting for, and I lost it *all*." Kittie swallowed, focusing on the tiny blossom of red on her fingertip. "I don't think I could survive that happening a second time." Sometimes she wasn't so sure she had survived the first occurrence. Maybe she was a banshee, cursed to walk the land, not knowing her soul was already in Perdition.

"Daddy would keep fighting," Emmaline pointed out.

That made Kittie smile. Gods, but she missed that man. "Faedra didn't grant him the sense to know when to quit."

Emmaline pursed her lips. She still struggled to speak well of her father, bothered by something she hadn't divulged yet. But she shook her head. "Nah. He'd change his strategy. That's what he would do."

Kittie thought about that as she took up the troublesome sock again. "What are you wanting me to do?"

"To be *you*." Emmaline's voice was a whisper, and something about it reminded Kittie of quiet voices on warm summer nights. Sitting on a porch watching fireflies with a wide-eyed toddler on her knee. "To be my mother and the firebrand I *know* you can be."

"I never stopped being your mother," Kittie said. And that was true, even when she had mourned her daughter as lost. But the *firebrand*...she was dead and gone. She had no more illusions of leading the mavericks to freedom as she had as a starry-eyed young woman. Foolish.

Emmaline settled down, getting to work on the laundry. Their conversation died, and Kittie lost herself in the routine. But shortly before their lunch break, a voice shattered the peace.

"Katherine!"

Kittie dropped the pants she was patching, hands trembling. Gods, this day was taking a toll on her. She took a swig from her flask, returning it to her side. Beside her, Emmaline shot her a questioning look. "Mom?"

"It's my husband," Kittie said, putting a hand on Emmaline's shoulder. Her daughter glanced at her quaking fingers, frowning. Kittie pulled her hand away, hurrying to the door. "Wait here. *Please.*"

Hugh Fasig was ten paces from the door to the laundry, closing the distance like a fast-moving squall line. "Katherine! What's this rumor I hear about your *daughter* showing up?" His voice was like a peal of thunder. "How in Perdition do *you* have a daughter?"

Kittie lifted her chin. She wasn't proud of the fact that she had omitted mention of her past, but there it was. She needed to do better, even if it hurt. But maybe, just maybe, things would hurt a little less now that she knew her family hadn't made the long walk to Perdition. "Welcome back, Hugh. Surprise, I have a daughter. I thought she was dead." Kittie laughed humorlessly. "Turns out my first husband isn't dead, either."

Hugh stared at her, stunned by her announcement. "What do you mean?"

"It means we're done."

He was many things, but Hugh was not a compassionate man. Selfish and mean-spirited were better descriptors. His lips curled into a snarl. "I don't see what claim he has to you. *He's* not the one who's been here with you all these years."

Claim. Jack had no claim to her, but he was the fire of her heart. "This topic isn't open for debate. I'm only doing my part to let you know, as a kindness." She wouldn't cower before him as she had in the past. She wasn't going back to the old ways, the ways of *Katherine*—vulnerable, seeking comfort in the bottle and in his arms. In Bitter End, she was Katherine Larue, too heartbroken to bear the name Kittie Dewitt.

Hugh scowled. "You're not going anywhere. You're *mine.*"

"I don't belong to anyone."

His face became thunderous, and he was upon her faster than she could react. Hugh's fingers dug into her shoulders, and Kittie yelped. Her magic roared up, demanding release. She held it back, writhing against him as he wrapped a hand around her throat, spitting obscenities into her face.

And then his shout turned into a scream of agony as he released her. Kittie staggered away, massaging her neck with one hand. She stumbled against the wall, gasping for breath.

"Mom! Are you okay?" Emmaline asked, sliding to a stop beside her. Something small was in her hand, but Kittie was too distracted to figure out what it was.

"I will be," Kittie rasped after a moment, mopping at her forehead. She stared at Hugh. He was squealing like a hog going to slaughter, his hands clasped to his groin as he rolled around on the ground. "Did you do something to him?"

"Yep." Emmaline didn't sound apologetic at all. She hefted the thing in her hand, and Kittie realized her crafty daughter had made a poppet out of a pair of socks. Three sewing needles pierced the tiny doll's lower abdomen. "When I heard what you called him, I remembered seeing a basket with his name on it, and I pulled the socks out. Didn't have time to do much more than a simple hex."

A simple hex. Kittie was shaking from her close encounter with Hugh, but *she* had almost done more than a simple hex. She whooshed out a breath. "Release him so I can speak to him, please."

Emmaline frowned. "You sure?"

"*Please.* He won't try to hurt me again." At least Kittie hoped he wouldn't be that stupid. Hugh was a coward at heart.

The young Effigest sauntered over, arms crossed. She loomed over the downed man, removing the needles one by one. When she finished, he lurched into a sitting position, bracing his arms behind him in preparation to vault to his feet.

"*No sir,*" Emmaline snapped, her braid whipping as she planted a boot firmly in his chest, pinning him back down. She held up the makeshift poppet. "Next time it'll be more than a prick for your little prick." Emmaline stared at him until he looked away, then removed her foot.

Hugh scrambled to his feet, hands curled into fists. "You little—" He doubled over as Emmaline rammed a needle into the poppet's stomach.

"*Ah, ah, ah.*" Kittie shook a finger at him, flames dancing on the tip of her fingernail. "I would choose your next words with care if I were you." Emmaline pulled the needle out, allowing Hugh to straighten.

He glared between the pair, eyes alight with fury. He wasn't stupid, and while Hugh was a mage, his ability to change eye color had him at a disadvantage. But he was a fair shot with a pistol, which Kittie was glad to see he kept holstered. "I'm leaving town this afternoon for another sales trip, Katherine. When I return, you best be out of *my* house."

Kittie met his gaze, unblinking. She had no claim to the home and didn't plan to fight him on it. "That won't be a problem."

"Just remember, you were *nothing* without me, Katherine Larue!" He jabbed a finger in her direction.

"When you found me, I was nothing but ash. But even ashes can be rekindled with a spark," Kittie replied. She had a staring match with him for another minute before he turned on his heel and stalked off. Kittie shook her fingers, dismissing the flame. She wiped her face with one hand, exhaustion tugging at her after the tense standoff. "Thank you, Em."

Emmaline watched until Hugh was out of sight, then turned away. Her shoulders slumped, and Kittie noticed her daughter was shaking. "I thought he was going to kill you. Why would you be with someone like that?"

Kittie shook her head. "Sometimes, when we're hurting, we do stupid things."

Emmaline followed her mother back inside the laundry. The Effigest stuck the needles back into Kittie's pincushion and untwisted the sock poppet, tossing them back into the basket they originated from. "Daddy's the king of doing stupid things, then."

Kittie wondered about that. Emmaline seemed to be at war with her feelings about Jack, vacillating between love and disdain. Maybe that was typical for her age. Kittie picked up a pair of pants in need of hemming and found her seam ripper. "We all make mistakes."

Her daughter snorted. "He'd never admit to that."

It sounded like, in some ways, Jack hadn't changed. Kittie tore out the seam. "Want to tell me what has you so mad at him? I see he's taught you some of his magic, so it can't be that."

Emmaline rubbed her arms, frowning. "It all started with Fort Courage..."

CHAPTER THIRTY-THREE
Razzle-Dazzle

Blaise

<Blaise!> At first, Blaise thought he detected alarm in Emrys's voice, but he realized it was excitement. <You won't believe this! There's a pegasus *mare* here.>

Blaise turned over, jostling the bed so that beside him, Malcolm jerked awake. It was still early, the window untouched by dawn's fingertips. Malcolm's hand brushed against his arm, only a brief touch to reassure each other.

"Something wrong?" Malcolm mumbled, drowsy.

"Emrys says there's a pegasus mare here."

Malcolm yawned. "Oh. Is that all? That's Seledora. Smart of her to fly in during the night." He rolled over and pulled the blanket up over his shoulders.

That Malcolm knew about a pegasus mare's impending arrival was enough to shake the last vestiges of sleep from Blaise's mind. He tugged at the blanket. "You can't just pass this off like it's normal for a pegasus mare to be here. Even *I* know that's not normal."

"Can we talk about it at breakfast?" Malcolm dragged the blanket back into place, snuggling into its soft depths.

They both had stayed up far too late the previous evening, each working on their separate projects. Malcolm busied himself with the voluminous amount of paperwork he needed for his Inquiry. Blaise had been hard at work on the desserts for Lizzie Jennings's gala. But Blaise was awake, and sleep wasn't going to revisit him soon. Maybe he should have let Malcolm sleep, but he wanted answers.

He shifted closer, leaning over until he was near the other man's ear. "I need you to tell me about it now."

Malcolm yawned, then unwound from his blanket cocoon. "Should have left it at the first three words of that sentence."

Blaise snorted. He nudged Malcolm's shoulder, ignoring the flirtation. "Why is there a pegasus mare here?"

Malcolm rolled onto his back, reaching over to flick the mage-light on the bedside table. "Seledora is one of my attorneys. She flew in from Rainbow Flat."

Blaise blinked. "You have…a pegasus attorney?"

"I'm rather progressive that way." A slow smile slid across his face. "She handles affairs for Jefferson, but I saw no harm in calling her in to represent us. She's the one who approved all of our original paperwork for our business agreement."

Blaise sat up, frowning, as he tried to work this out. "There's such a thing as pegasus attorneys?"

Malcolm rubbed his eyes. "I believe she is the only one, but yes, that means there is such a thing. And Seledora is here because she's part of my strategy."

"And that is?"

Malcolm sat up, coming to the realization Blaise wouldn't let him get back to sleep anytime soon. They had both been so absorbed with their work, they hadn't taken the time to discuss the details of their joint campaigns. "Razzle-dazzle. Part of the gamble I'm making. If this goes wrong, this may be the last big impact I can make on my long-term goals."

Blaise nodded, understanding. He hated being the reason that Malcolm might have to abandon his ambitions.

"Don't you blame yourself for that," Malcolm said quickly, leaning over to peck Blaise on the cheek. "I decided that for this effort, I'm going all-in. Turn this Inquiry into such a circus that anything they believe we've done wrong is minor by comparison."

Blaise mulled that over. "I guess that's one way to do it."

Malcolm grinned. "I'm going to hit them with everything I've got. Turn the world on its head if I can."

And that, right there, was why Blaise found himself falling for this man. His fervent desire to create meaningful change, to make the world a better place. And it had started with his determination to love Blaise, no matter who he was.

"I THOUGHT YOU WERE BRILLIANT, BUT NOW I'M HAVING MY REGRETS," Malcolm commented to Blaise from across the kitchen. He had two bowls in front of him: one containing pear he had already peeled and sliced, and another with fruit he still needed to attend to.

Blaise grinned at him. "You were the one who told Marta we didn't need any help." He couldn't help ribbing him on that bit. Malcolm had blatantly done it as a bid to give them more alone time, which Blaise appreciated. Malcolm had made an unfortunate miscalculation, however. Blaise was determined to make a good showing for Lizzie's gala. As much as he loved the unfettered joy that baking brought him, he was also serious about it.

"Yes, and that's one of the stupider things I've said in my life. I'm not cut out for this." Malcolm added another slice of pear to his completed bowl.

Blaise slipped over to him, peering into the bowl. "You'll be ecstatic to hear that you don't need to peel or slice any more pears, then."

"Overjoyed," Malcolm agreed, setting the knife aside. "What next?"

"Hmm." Blaise gave him a contemplative look. "Want to try your hand at decorating?"

Malcolm brightened at that. Blaise had hoped he might—he had a keen eye for detail, and while he wasn't as enthusiastic about basic tasks like slicing fruit, this would play to his strengths. "Show me what to do and I'll try it."

As he suspected, Malcolm was a quick study, and before long, he was piping frosting onto one of the cooled cakes. Blaise focused his attention on the audacious bread monstrosity he was wrangling into shape.

"Blessed Tabris, what are you *doing* over there?" Malcolm asked when he took a break to select a new food coloring to mix into his frosting.

"Eight-strand plaited loaf," Blaise murmured, concentrating on weaving the long tendrils of dough together. It looked, he decided with a little chagrin, like he was trying to wrestle an octopus into shape. "Who's Tabris? I've heard you say that before."

Malcolm kept his attention on the cake he was working on. "Oh, I suppose he's not as known in Desina, hmm? Tabris is the Gannish god of wealth and fortune."

"That makes a lot of sense," Blaise said, then paused, frowning at the array of dough before him. Oops, had he lost track? "Seven under six and over one." He untangled the tentacles and corrected the braid.

"I think I underestimated your enthusiasm for this." Malcolm glanced over at his squid-like loaf. "But I have to say, this haul is going to be impressive."

Blaise coaxed the last tendrils into place. He studied the loaf before him, then tucked the ends beneath it to give it a tidy look. *Not too bad.* "That's the goal. Win them over like a sugar-starved pegasus."

Malcolm paused, watching him. "I wish everyone could see you like this. Doing what you love."

Blaise was quiet for a moment. He knew what Malcolm meant, but it turned his thoughts to the upcoming Inquiry. Malcolm had told him what to expect, and Blaise wasn't confident of their chances. He would have to attend and speak. Answer questions in front of *people*. Feel the judgment of a thousand eyes on him. Everything he had endured, all his wounds and flaws, would be unveiled and on display. And they would no doubt bring up Fort Courage. *I'm a killer. A threat.*

Blaise swallowed, pushing away that thought, and instead, stared at the plaited loaf. "I'm kind of glad that only a few people see this side of me."

"Why is that?"

Blaise shook his head. "Because I don't want to share this with everyone." And he couldn't help it, but the grin that lit Malcolm's face made his stomach flop. He cleared his throat. "Now, back to the serious business of baking."

"Stick to the strategy," Malcolm agreed with a wink.

CHAPTER THIRTY-FOUR
Overdue Credit

Jack

Jack should have known things were going too well. Things always had a way of getting mucked up sideways to Perdition, but he had been hopeful. The handbill, enchanted by a Confederation Scryer, displayed the latest information on the target. It even included a perfect image of Emmaline, so lifelike he couldn't help the tears that stung the corners of his eyes. Crisp text laid out the pertinent information: her name, approximate age, magic type, and last known location. It terrified him to see his daughter as the subject of a bounty. Her life wasn't meant to be like this.

But, he supposed, it was inevitable. She was his daughter, after all.

He and Zepheus set off to the northwest, the direction the handbill suggested. As helpful as the handbill was, something about it rubbed him the wrong way. He and Lamar had never used them in their work, but then again, they'd had no need. The handbills were helpful to the mundane bounty hunters without magic to call on or unicorns to stalk their prey.

<Are you forgetting the Confederation had an airship wrapped in magical protections?> Zepheus pointed out when Jack mulled it over with him as they stopped for a drink at a creek.

The outlaw shook his head. "Not gonna forget that anytime soon."

Emmaline's face peered up at him from the parchment surface. "This reminds me of some of the books in the Archive at Highhorse."

The pegasus tilted his head to peer at the handbill. <I've been to Ravance with you. I think they would consider that inferior work.>

Jack snorted, amused. "You're probably right. They'd have a little map on there, enchanted by a Scryer, showing exactly where—" He stopped short, jaw agape as he folded the handbill up and threw it into the creek. It splashed, floating for a few seconds before sinking below the surface, curious tadpoles darting over to investigate.

Zepheus snorted, lowering his head to watch it sink. <What was that for?>

Shaking his head, Jack rose and put a foot in the stirrup. "I was a fiddlehead to take that."

The pegasus danced in place as Jack settled in the saddle. <Why?>

As Zepheus broke into a steady trot, Jack shook his head, mentally kicking himself. "Because it's magic. Can't believe she bamboozled me."

The palomino's ears pitched back, listening. <Are you saying...*oh*. I see.> And at that, Zepheus said no more, instead, shifting into an urgent lope to put more distance between themselves and any pursuers.

Jack balanced in the saddle, trusting Zepheus to continue onward as he scanned their surroundings. He had a poppet primed and ready to go if needed, but he didn't have any beneficial spells for the stallion. It had never occurred to him to try a working on the pegasus before. He thought about it as they continued, and after a few miles, he asked Zepheus to stop.

<You seriously want to stop now?> Zepheus asked as Jack slipped down from the saddle, striding over to the perimeter of a marsh.

"It won't take long, and it may be worthwhile." Jack stooped over, breaking off several stems of tall grass. He plucked a handful of willowy sticks from the spongy ground. The pegasus watched, puzzled, as he used the grass to tie together a very rough semblance of a stick horse. Jack held it up for the stallion's assessment.

<Is that...is that a poppet of *me*?> He sounded flattered.

"Yep," Jack replied. "I just need a bit of hair or a feather, if you don't mind."

<Feather,> Zepheus said, craning his neck around. The hide over his shoulders twitched as wings popped back into existence. Zepheus turned and nuzzled a loose covert feather. He wrapped his lips around the quill, plucking it out and presenting it to the outlaw. <Here.>

Jack accepted, attaching it to the equine poppet as Zepheus dismissed his wings from sight. He ran a hand over it to prime the unusual poppet, grinning as magic flooded through it.

Zepheus prodded the likeness with his nose. <What are you planning?>

"Salties were probably tracking us with that spelled handbill. We need stealth," Jack said, reaching up to balance the poppet on the pommel of the saddle. "I think I can muffle the sound of your hooves to give us the advantage. Sort of like a poor man's Dampener." Nowhere near as good as a Dampener, since they were experts at shutting down whatever was their specialty—sound or vision, sometimes both. But it was worth a try.

It took a few tries to get the spell right. Each time he attempted the working, he had Zepheus walk in a circle around him. The first two times, it had no impact on the sound—instead, Jack himself was muffled, a classic case of (luckily harmless) spell misfire. That was a hazard of devising a brand-new spell. The third time made Zepheus's hooves louder, which was jarring, but at least now the magic wasn't bouncing back to Jack.

The fourth time was the charm. He grinned, satisfied as Zepheus moved around him, hooves whisper-light. "I still got it," Jack murmured, mounting.

<If you mean an ego, then yes, you certainly do.>

The outlaw grunted a reply, but he couldn't hide his pleasure with the result. He'd have to remember that spell. Might be handy in the future. A sort of modified Obfuscation. *Maybe it would work with a sixgun.* Yeah, that would be handy.

They started on their way again. Jack grimaced as the afternoon wore on, and he discovered the magical toll of the new spell. Perhaps it was because of Zepheus's sheer size, but it packed a wallop and drained him fast. By comparison, his own Obfuscation was cheap. Jack held the line as best he could, not wanting to relinquish the advantage this gave them. But by the time dusk fell and a small town came into view, he was ready to call it a day.

Jack dropped the spell on the outskirts. It would be telling for him to ride in on a "horse" that made no noise. Relief washed over him as the magic dissipated. Jack flipped open a saddlebag and stuffed the poppet inside for safe keeping. Zepheus plodded to the livery, where Jack rented a stall for the night and untacked the stallion.

"Gonna grab a bite and see if I can learn anything new. Then I'll be back here for the evening," Jack murmured as he rubbed Zepheus's forehead. Sleeping in stables wasn't glamorous. Or comfortable. But Jack was on edge this deep in Saltie territory, and he stood a better chance with his pegasus. Not that he would say that aloud.

But Zepheus understood. He leaned into the caress, blowing out a hay-scented sigh. <But first, feed me. *Priorities*, mage.>

"Priorities," Jack agreed with derision. But he saw to it, going out and bartering for a bucket of sweet feed which he delivered to the stallion.

<And stop by the mercantile and get a bag of sugar for the water bucket?> Zepheus bumped his nose against it. Jack had carried a little with them, but it was all used up.

"You're a blasted hummingbird," Jack griped, good-natured. They both knew he would.

But first he had to see to himself. Jack needed fuel to keep his own fires burning, and he was spent from the new spell. He strode into the lone tavern, pausing at the entry to assess the room. He saw nothing that meant trouble. Well, trouble aside from the normal variety that haunted a place full of inebriated blowhards.

Men and women laughed uproariously over a card game in the corner. Billiards balls clanked together. A pianist played a tune on a piano in sore need of tuning as a woman with a voice like warm honey did her best against the odds. Jack ambled toward the bar since his preference was to chat up the barkeeps first—even though that hadn't worked out the best for him last time.

He paused halfway to the bar as a customer sitting alone at a table caught his eye. It took every bit of discipline he had to not turn and race over to her. Emmaline sat at the table, hunched over as if trying to avoid notice. But he recognized the sweep of her hair and the angle of her cheeks. Jack faltered. He corrected his course, heading for the table.

Jack stood behind the chair opposite her. "Anyone sitting here?"

Emmaline lifted her head, eyes widening in surprise. She bit her bottom lip for a moment, then shook her head. "All yours."

Jack claimed the seat, putting his elbows on the table. *Why is she acting guilty?* "Any luck?"

A server slipped over, and Emmaline wisely said nothing. "Welcome, traveler! Here's our menu. Can I get you a drink?" She thrust a menu at the new arrival.

Really, Jack wanted nothing more than for the server to vanish into a pit. He accepted the menu, though, knowing there were certain social niceties he needed to uphold. "I'm good for the moment." The server gave a bright smile and walked off.

"How—?" Emmaline started.

"Answer me first." Jack couldn't rein in his tension. The handbill had him unnerved. He wanted answers, and then to get Emmaline out of here and to safety.

"Any luck with what, Father?"

Jack stilled. *Father?* Since when did Emmaline call him that? *Since never.* Jack's mind raced as he took stock of the situation. No spotted stallions in the livery. It was possible Oby might be hiding outside town, seeing as he stood out like a sore thumb. He wanted to be damn sure before he made his next move.

He pulled on the last dregs of his magic, drawing his sixgun lightning-fast. "Maybe you should tell me, *daughter*. What were you supposed to be doing?" Alarm bells were ringing in his head. *This isn't her. Can't be her. This is wrong. She would know.*

She swallowed. "What are you doing? We're in *public*."

Yeah, perhaps she had a point. All around the tavern, eyes shifted to their tableau. Interest and menace. Jack weighed the options: 1) shoot her, 2) keep the sixgun aimed at her until he had some gods-damned answers, 3) holster the sixgun.

"Put it away, Papa," Not-Emmaline urged, holding her hands up in a placating move, eyes pleading.

That decided it for him. *A liar wears her face.* He pulled the trigger, the muzzle flashing as the bullet tore through Not-Emmaline's skull. She hadn't been expecting his volatile response and only made a soft exhalation as he snuffed out her life. No, *his* life, Jack corrected as the Illusionist's guise melted away, dispelled as the theurgist could no longer maintain it in death, revealing a young man.

Across the room, someone shrieked as if pained by the loss. *The handler.* He whipped around, trying to find the Illusionist's handler, but instead was greeted by the sight of half the occupants of the tavern turning on him. Too late, he realized it was a trap. Power rippled through the air, proof that some of those surrounding him were theurgists. And Jack was on their shit list for killing one of their own.

<I heard a shot. I'm coming!> Zepheus called.

Jack couldn't focus on the stallion. He swung his gaze around, tugging at his magic again, but that damn spell he had used all afternoon left him hung out to dry. He had gotten out of similar scrapes before, though.

Jack rolled his shoulders. Sixgun in hand and another at his back. Knife in his boot. He grinned. "If you wanna start a fight, you better throw the first punch," Jack advised them, making a rude gesture with one hand. Then he didn't give them a chance as he charged.

The melee was a blur, and that was by Jack's design. Most theurgists required concentration and space to work, and he wasn't about to give them any advantage. The problem was the handlers on the scene, who were trained for combat against mages. Jack focused on the theurgists first, or at least the ones he pegged for theurgists. It was hard to tell without them using their magic. They were the ones more likely to flinch when he came at them, and he took out three in quick succession with a mix of bullets and fists to the face. Jack dove beneath tables and hurled chairs to keep the handlers away, though he knew that risked giving the theurgists an opportunity to work.

And he was right to be concerned. They must have had a Telekinetic, which spoke volumes for how wanted a man Jack was. A table jerked up from the floor and flew right at his chest, slamming the outlaw against the wall. Jack hissed out an agonized breath, then shook off the sensation. He couldn't afford to let pain be a distraction.

Jack ducked as the Telekinetic sent a bottle at him, the quick motion shooting sparks of agony through his chest. He was too disoriented by the pain to avoid the chair that battered him next. It worked in his favor—or so he thought—because it shoved him closer to the door. Gritting his teeth, poppet curled in his fist, Jack tried to call on his magic to stave off the pain, but he had nothing left.

Gotta do this the old-fashioned way, then. He staggered to the threshold, his spare sixgun in hand as he brandished it at the menacing knot of assailants. "I didn't start this," Jack snarled at them. "But now you know why *I'm* the Scourge of the Untamed Territory."

"You killed our *Commander*," a theurgist spat, eyes blazing.

"And you killed more of our number at Fort Courage," another added, stepping forward with hands that crackled with power. The Telekinetic.

Sure, now *they give me overdue credit.* Jack narrowed his eyes. So his pursuers had been under that jackass Lamar's command at Courage. Their ferocity and determination to take him down made that much more sense.

<I can't get out. And they have salt-iron!> Zepheus punctuated his fear with a piercing whinny.

Shit. They knew about Zepheus, too. Jack tucked one arm against his aching chest to stanch the stabbing pain, spinning on his heel to sprint for the stables to help his pegasus. He drew up short, a gleaming brass muzzle pointed at him.

Gregor Gaitwood studied him, eyes full of disdain. "You're the one Lamar went on about for years? You don't look so impressive." He pulled the trigger of the hexgun.

That was the last thing Jack had been expecting. He was so surprised he didn't even flinch as the pellet splattered against him, releasing the spell housed in the casing. Sleep tugged at him, darkening his vision, and Jack collapsed.

HE AWOKE TO THE GENTLE SWAYING OF A WAGON BENEATH HIM, THE STEADY clop of hooves and the rumble of wheels on the road the best clues to his fate. Jack kept his eyes closed, suspicious of being watched. His wrists itched, and he felt the oppressive weight of salt-iron shackles on them. *Blast them all.* That was something he'd hoped to never experience again.

While he waited, he cataloged his condition. Aside from the hives on his wrists caused by the shackles, his midsection was tender. And his magic was as dry as the Gutter in a drought. *Let's look on the bright side. I'm not taking the long walk to Perdition. Look at me, being all optimistic and shit.*

After several more minutes passed, he cautiously opened the eye pressed against the floorboards. He didn't spy any boots or other potential signs of watchers, so he opened his other eye and discovered he was alone in a jail wagon. *Yeah, that's not surprising.* Jack eased into a sitting position, trying to push away the grogginess caused by the sleep spell. He cursed his luck that Gregor Gaitwood had somehow gotten his slimy hands on a hexgun. Probably one of Jack's missing hexguns at that. *Insulting.*

He idly rubbed at the inflamed skin beneath the shackles, bridling against the salt-iron. They were taking no chances with him this time, he noted. They had figured out he had his magic back and were responding in kind.

Jack sighed as he braced a hand against the wall and rose, moving to peer out the tiny window. Gods, but his chest hurt. Cracked ribs, probably. He closed his eyes as the very act of breathing stabbed at his innards. Maybe not just cracked. He needed a Healer after the abuse the Telekinetic had hit him with, but that didn't seem likely to happen anytime soon. The outlaw forced his eyes open to figure out where he was.

They were trundling into Izhadell already, which meant that he had been out for quite a while. Maybe that accounted for why he had foolishly thought he wasn't hurt as badly as he was, too.

Where was Zepheus? If the pegasus was free, he had half a chance of getting out of this mess. But if the stud was captured... Jack swallowed, refusing to think the worst. *This isn't the first terrible scrape we've been through. And I'll be damned if it's the last.*

Colorful lanterns and banners for the Luminary Festival still decorated the businesses and homes they passed. *Huh. With everything else going on, I forgot it's still that time of year. How lucky.* No doubt he'd end up the finale in the hangman's noose.

As he stared at the column of theurgists riding behind the jail wagon, Jack's stomach soured when he saw a familiar flash of gold at the end. *Zepheus.* Beaded salt-iron rope looped the stallion's neck, blocking his mental speech and effectively clipping his wings. There would be no help from the pegasus. Jack's only remaining solace was that, as far as he knew,

Emmaline was still free. Jack hoped fortune favored her and that she found her mother. *Alive.*

The outlaw settled back on the floor with a grunt, probing at his chest with one hand. *Yeah, that's tender.* He wasn't willing to admit defeat. Not yet. As long as he was alive and kicking, he was going to fight.

To his surprise, the jail wagon didn't take him to the Cit. Jack expected to be taken there and reintroduced to the maximum-security wing. Instead, the wagon continued, rolling through the city and to the other side, eventually coming to a stop in the driveway of a sprawling plantation.

Jack rose with a grunt, biting the inside of his cheek to distract from the intense pain caused by the movement. Armed men and women approached the wagon, and he took a step backward into the dark depths. No sense giving up any advantage he had.

With a click and a grating of metal, they threw the door open, flooding the interior with light. Jack entertained the idea of launching himself at them, but without access to magic or weapons, they outmatched him. He could probably strangle one with his shackles, but that would leave him vulnerable to attacks from the others. He took a step forward, and his ribs promptly reminded him that he'd be doing no such thing.

"Get out," a familiar voice snapped. "I see you in there analyzing how to murder the guards."

Jack allowed himself a savage grin as he fought off the pain. "Can't blame a man for trying." He took another step closer, the grin shifting to a snarl when a pair of guards reached out and grabbed his arms to drag him out.

Their harsh handling sent waves of anguish through him, and as they stood him before Gregor Gaitwood, it was all he could do to remain upright and not whimper. Every whistling breath was agony. Through slitted eyes, he saw a pair of theurgists lead Zepheus away. The pegasus balked, but after shouts and the slash of a whip from his handlers, the stallion plunged forward.

Gregor Gaitwood stood ten paces away, the hexgun holstered at his side. "Oh, are you hurt? That's unfortunate." He clucked his tongue, looking to one of the men who stood nearby. "Call the Healer. This state won't do for him."

A wizened older woman arrived on the scene, favoring him with a deep scowl as she assessed his injuries and muttered about idiot men. She turned to Gregor. "Two broken ribs." She uttered a wheezing laugh. "It would be a simple thing to pierce his lung with a bit of bone. Do you want this man alive or dead?"

Good question. Jack tried to take a deeper breath to test her assessment concerning his ribs, and his vision swam with the effort.

"He's worth more to me alive. Do what you need," Gregor commanded the Healer.

Why does he want me alive? Jack didn't have long to wonder before the soldiers were in motion, removing the shackles to allow the woman to work her magic. She laid her hands on him, and nothing about her power was gentle. Maybe he was too used to Nadine, who had awe-inspiring command of her magic. This Healer's power was like being dragged behind a runaway wagon. It seared over his entire body, assaulting his aches and pains as she repaired the damage that had been done.

It was painful but effective. When she pulled her magic away he felt raw and achy, but could fill his lungs with sweet air again. He choked out a curse. "Gods-damn you. Your Healing is the worst ever."

"But did you die?" she asked, giving him a rude gesture before striding away.

Gregor watched her go, then waved a hand. The soldiers replaced the shackles on Jack's wrists. "Come along without a fight. Easier to have you walk than drag you if you're asleep."

Or a corpse? The fact that he was still alive was concerning. To be sure, he was thankful for it and shouldn't look a gift pegasus in the mouth, but it was odd. The theurgists who had ambushed him had been furious. No one would have faulted them for killing him, especially after he had taken out some of their number. But they acted with discipline and had kept him alive, which meant they had orders from someone on high to do so. Someone like Doyen Gregor Gaitwood.

He trailed along with the guards as they followed Gregor up the winding alabaster staircase and into the manor. They made their way to a parlor where an afternoon repast awaited. Jack frowned, wondering what was going on as a guard pushed him down into a chair. Gregor sat nearby, picking up a glass of iced tea and taking a sip. He didn't offer Jack anything, but that was no surprise.

The outlaw studied the parlor. They must be at Gregor's home, which was interesting. A pity he didn't know the layout of the place, but he would pay close attention now that he was feeling more like himself. "What do you want, Gaitwood?"

Gregor set the glass of tea down, his gaze venomous. "I *wanted* the Breaker, but I suppose you'll have to do." A calculating smile slid across his face. "But there's a certain brand of justice in my brother's killer being brought to heel. Though I appreciate you taking care of that familial embarrassment, seeing how he was ready to betray me."

Pin prickles of regret bit into the back of Jack's neck. Lamar had been telling the truth. But he shook away his misgivings. He couldn't bring back the dead, even if he wanted to. He focused on Gregor. Jack didn't trust anyone who celebrated the death of a family member. Even if that family member was scum like Lamar. And he didn't like the wording of *being brought to heel,* either. "So hang me and get it done with."

The Doyen smirked. "That's too simple. No, I'd rather use you until you've been run into the ground. But cheer up. I know how much you enjoy killing members of the Confederation. You'll get to try your hand at the other Doyens."

"I'm not an assassin," Jack shot back.

"You were once, and you will be again." Gregor rose, pacing around the parlor with fluid strides. He paused to cast a contemplative look at Jack, lips curling with glee. "It's going to be poetic when word gets out that a Gutter rat has slain most of the Council. Especially those starry-eyed Faedrans."

Jack stared at him, his mouth going dry. Gregor was right. There was a time when that would have pleased Jack to no end, and he would have slept well at night after doing the deed. And under the right conditions, he still might do that now. But not at Gregor's behest. "You're crazier than a drunk Knossan if you think I'll do that for you."

"I'm not asking." Gregor rolled up his sleeve, revealing a tattoo. He tapped it with a finger. "I meant this for your friend, but as I understand it, we can make it work for you, instead."

How? Jack narrowed his eyes. He wouldn't have suspected that Gaitwood himself would attempt to become a handler, but maybe after Malcolm's stupid move, he shouldn't have been surprised. The Doyens were a spectacularly egotistical lot. "Good luck binding to me when you already have a tattoo keyed to someone else."

Gregor smiled. "Alchemy has made strides since you were last a theurgist. I don't need luck." He snapped his fingers to get the guards' attention. "Please, escort our *guest* to his quarters and call for the alchemist."

CHAPTER THIRTY-FIVE
Words Matter

Blaise

<I don't think she even knows I exist.> Emrys sighed heavily as Blaise loosened clumps of dirt from around the frog of the stallion's left hoof.

The *she* he referred to was Seledora. Blaise was still figuring things out for himself regarding relationships, but it was apparent Emrys wanted a mate. Seledora was an eye-catching mare, a dark dapple grey with wings that reminded him of a dove (when she showed her wings, which wasn't often at their current location). She spent much of her time in a box stall that had been repurposed into an office, either consulting with Malcolm or reading over texts and drafting documents with the help of one of Malcolm's staffers who served as her hands.

"To be fair, she's kind of busy right now," Blaise pointed out. "Did you forget she's here to help with my, er, situation?"

"Speaking of that!" Malcolm piped up, peering into the stall and grinning at Blaise. "When you're done, would you join me in the house? I have something to show you."

Blaise released Emrys's hoof from between his knees, setting it down on the ground. He tucked the hoof pick into his back pocket. "I hope you're more serious than the last time you wanted to show me something." Emrys snorted with amusement.

Malcolm chuckled. "I assure you I was serious then, too. But no, I want you to see the fruits of our efforts so far."

The fruits of...oh. The propaganda. He followed the other man up to the house and into the study, newspapers and magazines stacked on the desk.

"Look! Every newspaper Flora could get her hands on from the last several days. Some are more sensational than others." Malcolm pulled one off the top to display the headline *Mages: Misunderstood and Mistreated.* He shuffled it to the bottom and held up another, featuring an article titled, *BREAKER to Debut at the Legend Theater.*

Blaise narrowed his eyes at the title. "Um, is that the play Lizzie was writing?"

Malcolm grinned. "It is."

"And she named it *Breaker?*" Blaise rubbed the bridge of his nose.

"She had to name it *something* to attract attention," Malcolm pointed out, infuriatingly reasonable. His eyes softened when he saw Blaise's tension. "Look, I know you hate being called that. But trust the process."

"Trust the process," Blaise repeated, unconvinced. "Okay. What else?" Malcolm still had a large stack of papers.

"Now, before you lose your mind, these next few headlines are from some of the yellow papers." Malcolm brandished the next one. *The Doyen and the Breaker: Secret Love Affair Revealed.*

Blaise cupped a hand over his mouth. "What is *that?*"

Malcolm coughed. "I warned you some of them are...sensational."

Blaise snagged the paper from his hands, reading over the article. It *was* sensational, citing details that weren't true. Except maybe for the bit about them being in love, though he was still figuring out how he felt about that. His stomach flopped with nerves. "It's ridiculous," Blaise muttered, folding it up and slapping it down on the desk. "Is this the sort of thing you have to deal with as a Doyen?"

Malcolm laughed, then mulled his question over. "I'll let you in on a little secret. When I became the youngest Doyen to hold a seat, one of the papers reported it was due to my charms as a half-dragon."

Blaise blinked. "Wait, what? You're not half-dragon." His face scrunched, uncertain. "There's no such thing...right?"

"I'm not an expert, but I think that would be biologically impossible." Malcolm snickered. "But yes, this is something I've dealt with before. Jefferson's had his share as well. The yellow journalists love *all* of me."

"Of course they do." Blaise sighed. He plucked another paper from the pile, making a face. *Doyen Seduced by War Criminal Breaker.* "Oh, come on. That's unfair." He glared at *Love Triangle: The Breaker, the Doyen, and the Entrepreneur.* His cheeks warmed at how close to the truth *that* particular rag came.

"Alas, too bad Jefferson's on the run himself," Malcolm shook his head at the headline. "He'd have been quite flattered. You know, there used to be rumors about Jefferson and I having a thing."

That brought Blaise up short, and he stared at Malcolm. "How would that even work?"

Malcolm's eyes danced. "Oh, that's right. You haven't been introduced to Rex."

"Rex?"

"Rex Godfrey. He's an actor I have on retainer to portray Malcolm when needed. Sometimes Jefferson and Malcolm are invited to the same events, and it would be suspicious if they never appeared together, don't you think?"

That made a fair amount of sense, and leave it to Malcolm to have it all figured out. Blaise folded up the paper with the bold love triangle headline and shuffled it to the bottom of the stack.

"Don't let that one get to you. They're not all that bad." Malcolm flipped through, demonstrating that many headlines kept the romantic inclination but read more favorably.

"Bad enough that I may just die of embarrassment," Blaise muttered, tugging at his collar. Already his face was hot, and he wished the ground would open up and swallow him, never to be seen again.

Malcolm studied him, sympathy in his eyes. "I know. I'm sorry—I should have realized that the more sensational journalists might take the rumors Lizzie planted in this direction. But what's done is done. On the positive side, I think this only supports one of my arguments for the Inquiry."

Blaise glanced at the stack, wondering how the sordid headlines could possibly help. "And that is?"

Malcolm smiled. "That mages are every bit as human as non-mages. Look, most of those articles read like absolute trash, but here's the thing: you will never see an article like that written about a mage or a theurgist. They're not considered worth writing about. But *you* are."

"Lucky me." Blaise blew out a sigh.

Malcolm put an arm around him. "I know this is so far outside your comfort zone it's like you've gone to the moon, but I promise it will be okay."

Blaise's gaze fell on the stack of papers. All those things printed about him. About *them*. Some of them were true, but so many were skewed. Some outright lies. But really, was it any change from the rumors that had plagued his life before? He picked up one of the newspapers, eyes flicking over the article. It made very little mention of his magic or the dangers associated with him. That was a difference from the rumors of the past.

"I don't think I'll ever get used to this," Blaise admitted.

Malcolm bumped against his shoulder gently. "I don't expect you to. And I promise to shield you from it in the future when I can. But for now, this is just another tool that we can use to our advantage." He paused. "There's one more to show you. I saved the best for last."

Blaise gave him a skeptical look. "Why am I filled with dread when you say those words?"

"Trust me," Malcolm said, digging out something that didn't look quite like the other newspapers. A magazine. "This is an advanced copy, but it will be in homes across Izhadell tomorrow." He flourished the cover, showing that the magazine was *Hale's Ladies' Book*. Blaise had never heard of it, but from the cover he gleaned it was aimed at women. "Look at this." Malcolm tapped an article with his forefinger.

Breaking Bread: Desserts by Talented Mage the Star of Gala. Blaise snatched the issue from Malcolm, his excitement growing as he read. His desserts and breads had been the breakout stars of Lizzie's gala, with many high-profile women in attendance demanding to know who had crafted the treats.

"They called me *talented*," Blaise said, staring at the glossy paper. "There were so many other words they could have used, and they chose that one." Words mattered. He traced it with his fingertip, almost afraid it wasn't real.

Malcolm gave him a fond look. "Of all the things I just showed you, that is the one with the most truth." He picked up the papers and tucked them under his arm.

"I'm keeping this one." Blaise held the magazine protectively.

Malcolm chuckled. "I thought you might. That's fine, you more than earned it. Between Lizzie's gala, the rumors, the play, and the actual evidence we'll bring to the Inquiry, I think we can win the court of public opinion."

Blaise rubbed his chin. "Is that what matters, or will it matter more how the other Doyens vote?"

"Both matter," Malcolm answered. "But with the public in our favor, it will make it that much harder for anyone to vote against us."

Blaise glanced down at the magazine, hope kindling in his heart. Maybe, just maybe, they stood a chance.

CHAPTER THIRTY-SIX
The Talk of the Town

Malcolm

Having Seledora around gave Malcolm an unfair advantage. The walls of his estate were under constant observation by Confederation troops, eager for him to slip up and set foot outside his gates. They failed to appreciate the fact that they should watch the sky, too.

And so it was that Malcolm made an early start to the day, heading out on the mare's back before the sun was even a casual suggestion on the horizon. It had been hard to get out of bed with Blaise in a contented slumber so close to him. It still amazed him every morning when he woke up and found the younger man there. Blaise kept space between them as he grappled with whatever was going on in that head of his, but he was *there*, and that was what mattered.

<Not very observant, are they?> Seledora remarked as she touched down on the road a mile from the estate, briskly hiding her wings as she continued at a trot.

"And for that, I'm grateful," Malcolm replied. For him to demand his Inquiry, he had to get to the Council chambers in person. Council rules stated he couldn't use a surrogate or correspondence. It had to be him, and Gaitwood and his fellow Mossbacks were doing everything they could to prevent it. He reached around to check the straps on the carry satchel on his back. *Still secure.*

He kept an eye out as they trotted along. Malcolm wished he could ride into town in the guise of Jefferson Cole, but his alter ego was in just as much trouble. He missed being Jefferson for so many reasons. Not only was he more comfortable in his second skin, but Blaise had always seemed more at ease with Jefferson. But for now, he had to sustain the narrative that Cole wasn't around. He hoped that none of the guards would recognize him. It would be a simple thing for them to arrest him outside of the diplomatic immunity provided by his residence as a Doyen, and then this would be all for naught. Unless he used his magic...

<That's something we need to avoid,> Seledora mentioned, as if she had been monitoring his train of thought. Which was likely. She didn't miss much.

The mare had noticed the change in him when she arrived. She had been quick to ask about the circumstances, citing that she needed all the information on hand about her client. He had told her, and she hadn't outright judged him, but he got the sense from the way her ears pitched back that she didn't approve. But what was done was done, even if it made life more challenging. It pleased her that very few others knew, at least.

"That's the plan," Malcolm agreed. He still had conflicted feelings about his use of power to free Blaise. Would he do it again in a heartbeat? Absolutely. But as a Doyen, it bothered him.

Seledora kept a sedate pace, and they arrived in the city proper at mid-morning. It wasn't until they neared the complex where the Council met that someone recognized him.

"It's him! It's Doyen *Malcolm Wells!*" The voice of a female admirer rang out, the elated pitch both flattering and worrisome.

"Oh my gods, it *is* him!" another called out.

<This is *ridiculous*. Is this because of those absurd newspapers?> Seledora demanded, lengthening her strides to carry them closer to their goal

"Either that or because I was voted the Confederation's most eligible bachelor for two years in a row," Malcolm said, wincing as a cry went up and a nearby patrol went on alert.

Up ahead, he saw another group of guards on the move, attempting to block the path to the complex. If Malcolm set foot on the Council chamber grounds, he had authority there, and the guards couldn't hold him. But out here, it was a different story.

Seledora slowed, her head high with uncertainty as she spied the looming blockade. <Is there another route?>

Malcolm smiled. There was. "Up and over, my lovely."

<First, *never* call me that again. Second, are you certain?> Her black-tipped silver ears flicked back.

Everything he had done for the last several days was an enormous gamble, so what was one more? And besides, her nature was going to be revealed at the Inquiry, regardless. "Yes. Let's make a flashy entrance."

Seledora arched her neck, nostrils cupped as she snorted with determination. Malcolm blinked as her wings flowed out from her shoulders, silvery dust wafting off her wingtips. The bystanders cried out with a mix of wonder and fear. No one knew what to make of a pegasus in their midst. Seledora tore toward the guard formation, Malcolm leaning low over her neck.

The guards had their rifles up, ready to fire.

Malcolm didn't think they would shoot, unless it appeared she was going to strike them. He hoped she saw that, too. They were moving too quickly for him to point it out.

He felt the muscles in her hindquarters bunch as she surged skyward, wings spreading to catch the air. She tucked her forelegs neatly beneath her as she sailed over the blockade with twenty feet to spare. The guards yelled something unintelligible, and then Seledora coasted to the ground to land delicately, tail arched behind her.

That was magnificent. Not for the first time, Malcolm wondered why Blaise disliked flying on his pegasus. It certainly got the blood pumping. "Nicely done!" He patted her neck as she pranced in a tight circle, staffers flooding out of the hall to see what the commotion was all about. It wasn't long before the Doyens on-site joined them.

Seward had a huge grin on his face as he strode out, pounding Doyen Aaron Thatcher, Malcolm's cohort from Ganland, on the back. "I told you that scoundrel was up to something! See? Didn't I?"

Leonora Peppers studied the scene as Malcolm dropped out of the saddle, allowing the reins to dangle. "You've been the talk of the town for the past week, Malcolm, and now you're treating us to more of the show. To what do we owe the pleasure?"

Malcolm unstrapped the satchel from his back and pulled it around, opening it to remove a folder stuffed with documents. "I'm here to lodge a formal Inquiry into the treatment of mages at the Golden Citadel." He presented the folder to Leonora, who accepted it as the senior-most Doyen present.

She tucked the folder beneath her arm. "Accepted. Do you have counsel?"

<He does.> Seledora stepped forward to stand beside him as an equal. The mare tipped her head in amusement as people all around them gaped at her mental speech.

Seward's jaw seemed to nearly unhinge, eyes bugging at the spectacle of pegasus telepathy. Malcolm had forgotten how shocking it could be to "hear" one of the equines for the first time. "Did she just speak?" Seward shook his head, remembering to shut his mouth.

<She did,> Seledora confirmed for the startled Doyen, her dark eyes glinting. The mare arched her neck, legs squared neatly beneath her. <I am Seledora, attorney-at-law. I shall represent Doyen Wells for this Inquiry, so long as Senior Doyen Peppers finds it permissible.>

Leonora didn't bat an eye. It took more than a talking pegasus lawyer to fluster her. Moreover, she seemed pleased that Seledora had identified her as the one in charge of the proceedings. "It is, Counselor Seledora. Thank you. We'll start—"

"Hold!" an imperious voice called out. Malcolm turned, annoyance growing as Gregor Gaitwood stalked in. "I, too, wish to lodge a formal Inquiry—into Doyen Wells and his corruption by fraternizing with a criminal."

Leonora's gaze cut to Malcolm, expecting a rebuttal. She appeared surprised when he merely nodded. "Very well. While it's highly unusual to invoke two Inquiries at once, we'll accept them. However, as Doyen Wells brought his about first, it will have priority."

Gaitwood clenched his jaw. "Priority? There is higher priority than corruption of an elected official? This is an outrage."

"No, it's the rule," Seward piped up. "Should have lodged yours sooner, Gregor. Better luck next time."

Malcolm aimed a brilliant smile at Gaitwood. "Yes, it's unfortunate."

The glare Gregor aimed at him would have stripped the paint off a building. Gregor wasn't going to like Malcolm's show at the Inquiry one bit. He smiled at Gaitwood, touching two fingers to his forehead in a cheery salute.

CHAPTER THIRTY-SEVEN

Voice for the Voiceless

Blaise

"Are you *sure* I can leave?" Blaise asked, not for the first time, as he stared at his reflection in the mirror. Now that the day of the Inquiry had arrived, his stomach churned at the thought of going. Public opinion of him might be favorable, but he was painfully aware there were still a chunk of people out there who hated him and what he was.

"Of course, I'm sure," Malcolm reassured him, slipping closer to adjust his collar. "The soldiers are gone. Nothing can happen until the Inquiry is complete."

Depending on if it ended in their favor. Blaise rubbed the back of his neck, worried. "And what happens if we lose?"

He expected Malcolm to declare that they wouldn't lose, but he didn't. The Doyen shook his head, and his voice was raw when he spoke. "I'm trying very hard not to think about that."

Malcolm's admission brought Blaise up short. It was so easy to assume Malcolm thought everything would work out somehow because he pressed onward as if it would. It was the face he showed to the world, but in that moment, he made himself vulnerable to Blaise, his own fear bright in his brown eyes.

"I've done some audacious things in my life, but this tops them. And I don't know if it's going to work. I promised I would fight the Confederation for you." Malcolm's voice was apologetic.

You promised to fight. You never promised to win because we both know that might be impossible. Blaise licked his lips. "I didn't mean to bring you down. It's just...this is a lot. And it's only going to get harder today."

Malcolm took his hand, though his grasp was loose, allowing Blaise to escape if needed. Blaise tightened his grip as the Doyen spoke. "I know. But you can do this. You're not the only one hurt by the Cit. Be the voice for the voiceless."

And how could Blaise refute that? He knew in his heart that others had been through the same. And were still going through the same. He studied his reflection in the mirror again. His face had filled out a little since he'd gone to ground at Malcolm's estate. He looked less haggard and more like the person he had been. Blaise wanted to pretend that everything in the Golden Citadel had happened to someone else. But that wasn't being true to himself.

"I'm sure we could find someone to teach you the finer points of goatherding in Theilia," Blaise hazarded.

Malcolm chuckled. "That ship has quite literally sailed. We're committed to this course now." He studied his reflection, rubbing his chin. "Besides, Theilia is difficult to get to. It would make more sense to start a new life in the Untamed Territory. Maybe I could learn how to hustle billiards and card games."

"To think I assumed you'd prefer to start your own dancehall," Blaise commented.

Malcolm winked. "Jefferson already has one of those." He cleared his throat and flashed a reassuring smile. "Back to the matter at hand. The Inquiry will host *more* than the Salt-Iron Council. This is a big event, and I have it on good authority that many a high-profile lady will be in attendance to see the magical baker who created those scrumptious desserts for Lizzie Jennings. You're going to have people rooting for you."

Blaise ducked his head. That was overwhelming in a different way. So many eyes on him. Watching his every move. Judging him. "I don't think I can do this."

Malcolm bumped against his shoulder, eyes mischievous. "You can absolutely do this. And if you get nervous..."

Oh gods. Blaise frowned at him. "Don't say what I think you're about to say."

"Just imagine that everyone in the crowd is naked."

Blaise blew out a frustrated breath. "Not helping."

"Fine. Then just imagine that *I'm* naked." Malcolm spun in place, spreading his arms with a flourish and a tempting grin.

Blaise's face flamed. "This is the exact opposite of helping."

Malcolm raised his brows, looking quite satisfied with himself. "Are you sure? Because now you're not thinking about being in front of all those people. You're thinking about *me*." The fact that he was right was downright annoying. Blaise crossed his arms. Malcolm licked his lips, his countenance softening again. "I promise that you're going to be fine. You're not doing this alone. And I *know* you can do it."

It was reassuring to hear the conviction in Malcolm's voice. Blaise relaxed a little. "Really?"

"Indeed. Now come on, you're as ready as you'll ever be. Let's go make history."

———

SOMEHOW BLAISE SURVIVED THE FIRST DAY OF THE INQUIRY. HE TREATED IT like his time at the Golden Citadel, confining it as an experience separate from himself. He didn't recall any of the questions they asked him, though he knew he answered them in as much depth as he could, reliving painful memories he wanted to keep buried. Even the now-healed scar on his forearm burned with remembered pain when he had discussed it.

They asked, too, about the fateful day at Fort Courage that had led to all this. That was another topic Blaise preferred to shy away from. The mere thought of it made him queasy and light-headed. But it was relevant to the discussion as most of the Doyens demanded to know why he'd chosen to destroy the airship. And Blaise told them, because Malcolm was right about one thing: they were asking him questions and treating him like a human, as well as a mage.

The stresses of the day took their toll, and he was bone-tired and done with being around humans by the time they arrived back at the estate that night. He had ridden on Emrys, who was pleased to appear, wings and all, beside the lovely Seledora. Emrys quickly keyed into the mood of his rider, refocusing his attention to keep Blaise from mentally falling apart.

Now Blaise leaned against the stallion in the stable, having already untacked and groomed him. He knew he should go up to the house, but he couldn't bring himself to do it. Malcolm was already there, no doubt waiting for him. Wondering about him. Maybe even worried about him.

Emrys huffed out a comforting breath scented by sweet feed. Blaise didn't know if Emrys had been close enough to scrape the details of his ordeal from his mind as he spoke. If he did, the pegasus didn't remark on it. He simply offered himself to Blaise as a balm for a wounded soul. <You should go up soon. He cares about you,> Emrys said.

"I know," Blaise whispered. "But he might want to talk about it. And I don't want to talk about it."

<Give him more credit than that,> Emrys rebuked. <And if he asks, then tell him you don't wish to discuss it. He'll respect that.>

It was solid advice. Blaise's gut knew it, but his mind disagreed. Ever since he had been freed from the Cit, Jefferson no longer visited his dreams. A nagging part of Blaise suggested it was because Malcolm finally realized how neurotic and broken he was. And today had bared his problems to the entire audience of the Council chamber. No one would want anything to do with that.

Emrys froze, ears flicking as something caught his attention. He moved away from Blaise, trilling a whinny.

"What is it?" Blaise asked

<Zepheus.> Emrys nosed him aside, using his nimble lips to manipulate the bolt on his stall door and striding out with purpose. Blaise blinked and then followed along.

They found the golden pegasus in the stable courtyard, limping and riderless. His wings were bedraggled, as if he had been in a fight, and his eyes were white-rimmed. He was bare of saddle and hackamore.

All thoughts of the day's events fled from Blaise. He rushed over to the pegasus. "Zeph! What happened? Where's Jack?" Blaise's mind raced. Jack had gone after Emmaline and his wife...

<They have him.> Zepheus hung his head. His coat was dark with sweat, and he trembled from exertion.

"Who has him?"

<Gregor Gaitwood. They had me, too, but I escaped.>

Blaise rubbed his forehead. He recalled Gaitwood sitting in the Council chamber earlier, though he had made every effort not to look at the man. Bad enough he had felt the searing heat of the Doyen's eyes on him all day. Why did Gregor Gaitwood have Jack? This didn't bode well.

First things first. Blaise focused on the stallion. "Come on. Let's take care of you, then I'll go tell Malcolm, and we'll figure something out."

<I'm worried about Jack.> Zepheus's voice was weary with defeat.

Blaise urged the pegasus into the stables. "He's a fighter. Whatever's going on, we'll figure something out." At least he hoped so. He settled Zepheus into a stall and saw to his needs before steeling himself to head to the house and alert Malcolm to this new problem.

Malcolm

HE HAD NEARLY GIVEN UP HOPE THAT BLAISE WOULD COME UP FOR THE night. It had been an arduous day for him. The younger man's blue eyes were haunted from reliving his hardships and misuse. Malcolm knew he didn't want to talk about it, and he understood. All the same, it stung that

Blaise hadn't even come up so they could spend time together. Malcolm reminded himself that Blaise was still working through things, and he would come up when he was ready. But it was hard. Malcolm wanted to be a part of the healing process.

And then Blaise pushed open the door to the master bedroom, striding in with a resolve he'd lacked earlier in the day. There was a spark in his eyes again. Something had him worked up. Malcolm straightened. "What is it?"

"Jack. I mean, Zepheus came back. Without Jack." He made a circular gesture with one hand. "They were ambushed, and Zeph says Gregor has him."

"Gregor?" Malcolm frowned. That made little sense. While it wasn't by any means good that someone had caught the outlaw, logic and protocol dictated he would have gone to the Golden Citadel to be held and eventually hung. "Are you sure about that?"

"Zeph was sure," Blaise answered. "I believe him."

Malcolm studied Blaise, thoughtful. The Breaker had come up to him for a purpose. "Right. What are you thinking?"

Blaise looked him in the eye. "Do you think we could find Jack in his dreams? The same way you found me?"

At that, Malcolm blinked. It wasn't something he had thought about—didn't even know if it was possible. But Blaise was so earnest and hopeful that Malcolm didn't want to disappoint him. "I could try," Malcolm agreed after a moment. "But I'm not as good with my magic as you are with yours."

Blaise raised his brows, incredulous.

"What?" Malcolm asked.

"Sorry. I thought you were joking. I don't consider myself *good* with magic." Blaise shrugged.

Well, at least he had shaken off the haze of his recounted trauma. Malcolm was content with that. "I know you're good with it." Blaise was something the Confederation hadn't seen in living memory: a Breaker in control of his power, not the other way around. "I'm still figuring mine out. Some parts, like the dreamscape, just naturally developed."

Blaise stepped closer and grabbed his hand, which was a welcome surprise. "We'll figure it out together, then. We need to find Jack, if we can, and figure out what's going on."

Mmm, pushy. I like this. Malcolm kept that to himself. Didn't want to scare off this feisty side of the Breaker. "What's the plan?" He quite enjoyed the way Blaise tugged him over to the bed.

"What do you think?" Blaise asked.

Malcolm bit his lip to keep from saying aloud what he really wanted to say. Blaise was on a mission, and it wouldn't be welcome. So he settled for quirking a brow suggestively.

"You're hopeless," Blaise grumbled, but he said it with fondness.

"Hope*ful*, you mean," Malcolm corrected softly, meaning it. He sat on the edge of the bed and peeled his shoes off, tucking them below. He unbuttoned his shirt, pleased when Blaise cast a furtive glance his way. "Are you proposing we go to the dreamscape and search from there, or what? I've not done anything like this before." *Though, I'm always up to try new things with you.* Should he tell Blaise that? No, that would be too much.

"I'm a Breaker, not a Dreamer." Blaise sat down on the opposite side of the bed, his back to Malcolm. There was a soft thump as he took off his boots, dropping them on the floor. "But that would be my guess. How did you do whatever it was when you found me in the dreamscape?"

Malcolm frowned with thought. "I think I found you because of our connection through the geasa. Though I think even without it, I had plenty of motivation to find you." He glanced back and found Blaise watching him, so he threw in a wink for good measure.

"I'm motivated to find Jack, so that will have to do," Blaise said, a hint of a smile curling his lips.

Malcolm flopped down on the bed. "Sugar, I'll do just about anything you ask me to." He patted the space on the bed beside him.

Blaise studied him, and Malcolm was certain the young mage was going to chide him about the nickname. Instead, he dropped onto the bed. "I'm going to remember you said that."

Malcolm grinned, pleased. *I hope you do.* He rolled onto his side, facing Blaise. "Very well. Let's do this." Blaise shifted to face him, and the sight of those blue eyes watching him made his heart race.

"Do I have to be asleep? How does your dreamscape work?" Blaise asked. The Breaker adjusted his pillow. "I think I'll have a hard time falling asleep after..." He squeezed his eyes shut, and Malcolm caught the glimmer of a tear in one eye.

Nightmares. Blaise feared being consumed by nightmares after revisiting his memories. Malcolm found his hand beneath the covers. "You don't have to be asleep. I've learned that I can make people sleep. I can pull you to the dreamscape."

Blaise's fingers relaxed. "And you said you weren't good with your magic."

Malcolm's heart soared at the compliment. "Are you ready?"

"Yes."

"Sweet dreams," Malcolm murmured, pulling on his magic.

It was easy to focus it on Blaise. *So* easy. His Dreamer magic settled over the young man like a blanket, lulling him into a peaceful sleep. Malcolm smiled, watching as Blaise's face slackened. He reached over to brush back an errant coil of hair that had fallen across Blaise's forehead. Malcolm sighed with contentment, then burrowed into his pillow as he sent himself to slumber.

The dreamscape swelled around them, and Malcolm—no, he was *Jefferson* here, he corrected himself—discovered Blaise by his side, where he belonged. The world around them was different, a grey void. Blaise turned in a circle, inspecting their surroundings.

"Why does it look different?"

"The Itude dreamscape is *ours*." Jefferson didn't want anyone else intruding on that particular space. "Besides, it takes magic to build all of that and I don't know how much it will take to find Jack."

Blaise slanted him a look. "If you run low, I can share."

Jefferson swallowed. He tried not to let Blaise see how much he would like that. He coughed and then realized the corners of Blaise's mouth had tugged upward. "You said that *on purpose*."

"I said what I said." Blaise's tone was flat.

"You're being quite unfair," Jefferson complained. Then he realized something. "Hold on. You flirt with Jefferson and not Malcolm. Why is that?"

Blaise blinked. "Wait, what?"

"Just an observation," Jefferson murmured, coy.

Blaise cleared his throat, crossing his arms. "I don't know *how* to flirt."

"Trust me, you've figured it out." Jefferson couldn't help the grin on his face. He rubbed his hands together, refocusing. "All right, let me figure out how to find Jack."

CHAPTER THIRTY-EIGHT

Hypocrites

Jack

Of all the things to dream about, that pompous peacock Jefferson Cole was the last thing Jack wanted. His waking life was terrible enough without his dreams being plagued, too. But there he was, sauntering out of a grey mist like some damned fashion icon, greatcoat slung over one shoulder.

"I found him, Blaise!" Jefferson called.

The Breaker appeared through the mist, and Jack set his jaw, narrowed his eyes, and glared at them. Blaise spotted him and hurried through the strange nothingness, stopping when he was ten feet away. "Jack?"

"Get out of my dreams," the outlaw growled. "It's the only place I can catch a damned break." And then, because it was a dream and he figured why not, he lunged at Jefferson. And stopped in his tracks.

He couldn't move. Gods, he hated the sensation of trying to run or move and being immobile in a dream. Jack writhed against the invisible force that held him in place, furious.

"Saying this will only make you hate me more, but my world, my rules," Jefferson said, his hands clasped behind his back.

"Jack, it's *us*," Blaise added, daring to come closer. "Zepheus found me and told me what happened. That you were captured. This was the only way we could think of to help."

Jack stared at him. He had thought—really thought—that this was all a frustrating trick of his subconscious. But maybe it wasn't. For Blaise to know those details and to speak them aloud…he swallowed, his fists uncurling. As his tension left him, the invisible bonds slackened, and he was free. "Zeph got loose? This is real?"

"Yes, and sort of?" Blaise shrugged.

"It's complicated." Jefferson lagged back, keeping Blaise between them. "Is it true that Gregor Gaitwood has you?"

Gaitwood. The name set Jack's blood afire. "Yes."

Jefferson pursed his lips. "What does he want with you? I thought an outlaw like you would go straight to the Golden Citadel."

Jack crossed his arms. "Especially this time of year." He shifted his weight, shaking his head. "Nah. He has more games afoot. He's pissed that Blaise slipped his grasp."

Blaise paled and stared down at the ground, as if the kid felt guilty. "Sorry."

The outlaw snorted. "Nothing to be sorry about. I don't regret my part in freeing you." He meant it. Blaise lifted his chin, surprise shining in his eyes.

"What does he intend with you?" Jefferson asked.

Jack pinched his lips together. He angled away, shoulders tense again. Really, he didn't want to say it because to speak it was to make it true. And the truth hurt. "Gaitwood bound me with the geasa."

Soft footsteps approached behind him. A hand settled on his shoulder. "I'm sorry." Blaise's voice was soft, and even in the dream, his hand trembled. Jack wondered what it had cost him to reach out to make that contact. The outlaw wasn't normally one for softness, but in that moment, it meant the world to him.

"*No*," Jack insisted, his voice gruff. "You don't apologize for that, damn it. It wasn't *your* fault."

The Breaker pulled his hand away, as if he expected Jack to whirl around and attack him. Like he would have done before. Jack longed to lash out at a more deserving target. Preferably Gregor Gaitwood. "Gaitwood's a damned hypocrite." Jack eased around to face them again, allowing his eyes to fall on Jefferson. The other hypocrite among them.

"He is that," Jefferson agreed, his tone even. "And I'll ask again, what does he intend to use you for?"

Jack shifted his weight from foot to foot, absently rubbing at his throat. In his waking hours, the geasa controlled his words and actions. It didn't seem to impact his functions in the dream, though. Would he be able to warn them? "Same thing he was planning to use Blaise for, I reckon. Kill the other Doyens. Probably the Luminary, too. I don't know squat beyond that. A man like Gaitwood won't tell me everything. I'm nothing. A tool." None of the normal geasa restrictions came into play. He was unfettered in the dream. Maybe the Dreamer was worth a damn after all.

"A weapon." Blaise's voice was little more than a whisper, but somehow it reverberated through the surrounding grey expanse.

"Yeah," Jack agreed, dour. Gods, he hated the geasa. The only time he felt like he had any freedom at all was when he slept. *Freedom.* He pointed a finger at Cole. "And he wants you in the bone orchard. The *other* you, I mean."

Blaise's jaw tightened, hands clenching. Jefferson only nodded, as if that hadn't surprised him. "There's no love lost between us. He disliked me before my stunt with Blaise, and the Inquiry has only made it worse." He paced in a small circle. "Is there any way we can free you?"

Jack stared at him. Did he hear that right? Jefferson Cole wanted to free *him*, an outlaw? He glowered, not about to show that it made him feel a little less hopeless, a little less forsaken. Yeah, he had warmed up to Blaise, but he wasn't about to call that dandy a friend. Regardless, Jack had analyzed the situation, looking for every possible way out of it. "You couldn't get Blaise out of the Cit without me."

"But now I'm in the mix," Blaise said, his blue eyes meeting Jack's.

The outlaw should have realized Blaise would pony up. He wasn't a fighter, but he wasn't a coward, either. Jack shook his head. "Gaitwood knows I have my magic back. I'm locked up with salt-iron."

Jefferson wrinkled his nose at that. "Vile stuff." He ran a hand through his hair. Jack had seen him enough recently to know the gesture for what it was: a tell for unhappiness. It genuinely bothered him he couldn't help Jack. That was...strange.

The outlaw made a dismissive gesture. Curse them for giving him all these feelings in a damned dream. "Blaise is free. That was always the goal. I'm an old man. Not as if I matter." *Lie, lie, lie.*

Jefferson raised a brow. "I have it on good authority you're ten years my senior. That's hardly old."

"By outlaw standards, it is," Jack muttered, hoping they would take his meaning. Damn them. He liked Blaise, and he didn't want the idealistic kid to wander into something and end up trapped. Again. He seemed to have a penchant for that. Although maybe Jack shouldn't point that out since he didn't have a sterling record, either.

Blaise's eyes were troubled. "But you *do* matter. What about Em? And Kittie?"

He had hoped his family would escape mention. The outlaw whirled away so that neither of them saw the way his face crumpled at the thought that he had been *so close*, and ultimately so far, from what he had always wanted. The people he had made himself vulnerable for. "If you come across them, tell them what happened to me." *Tell them I'm sorry. Tell them I love them. That they're my entire world.* His throat constricted, and even in the gods-cursed dream, the words wouldn't come. It was like the geasa, choking his words back. But it wasn't the geasa. It was him.

Behind him, Blaise's boots scuffed the hazy ground. "We'll come for you."

The outlaw spun, shaking his head. "No. *No.*" His voice was almost hoarse with emotion. "Don't be stupid. Gregor still wants you. Both of you."

The Breaker smiled. "I'm not stupid. But I *am* your friend."

Jack sighed. Yeah, Blaise was stupid.

CHAPTER THIRTY-NINE

Pour Some Sugar On Me

Blaise

Blaise hadn't realized that the Inquiry was going to last as long as it did. He had expected that it would be over in a day or two. Never would he have imagined that they would draw it out over several weeks, but to his dismay it did. Every staffer or guard who served at the Cit was called in to speak and examined at length. Weeks of traveling to the Council building each morning with Malcolm to see what awaited them. Weeks of being on the alert, not knowing when Gaitwood might try to use Jack against them.

"He's probably waiting things out to see how the first Inquiry ends," Malcolm advised Blaise. It made a little sense, but Blaise couldn't help but be on edge. He spent every minute within the chamber tensed for danger, not knowing what Jack might be capable of with his magic restored. The outlaw was a merciless killer without magic. Blaise assumed he would only improve with his special brand of power.

Malcolm (as Jefferson) and Blaise reached out through the dreamscape almost every night, though Jack was either contrary in his typical fashion or had no additional information for them. Blaise pitied the outlaw. He had escaped from this before, and his gloom over his predicament shrouded the dreamscape with thunderheads as Jefferson subconsciously drew on the outlaw's mood.

Despite Jack's situation, the nights in the dreamscape helped Blaise more than anyone else would ever know. Not only was it a much-needed distraction from the Inquiry, but it served as a surefire way to chase away the nightmares that were certain to follow. It was also much more than that for Blaise. It gave him the opportunity to reconcile Malcolm and Jefferson as the same person in his mind. Blaise came to grips with the fact that he loved that very confusing man.

Three weeks into the Inquiry, Blaise was almost accustomed to the spectacle. Seledora transformed from a fantastical to an ordinary sight (which, he supposed, was Malcolm's point all along) and the pegasus lawyer was as sharp as any of the humans in the chamber.

Blaise himself had gained a steady flow of curious admirers, which would never cease to amaze him. They came and asked him questions during recesses, with topics ranging from his relationship with Malcolm (*awkward*), to his magic (*even more awkward*), to baking (*best topic ever*). When his fans (that was what Malcolm called them) left, their whispers didn't escape his hearing. They were witnessing history, they said. They had met a living legend. Blaise didn't feel like a legend, though. He was afraid, and stressed, and in the grand scheme of things, he felt tiny and insignificant.

After a final long day of arguments, witnesses, and stacks of documents taller than Seledora, Malcolm's cohorts from the Faedran faction invited them out to a celebratory dinner. The next day was a scheduled break for everyone involved, with the Doyens reconvening the day after that to deliberate and reach a verdict. The end was near, and everyone was relieved.

And that was how Blaise found himself in the private room at a posh restaurant, being toasted as some sort of hero. As glasses tinkled, he certainly didn't *feel* like a hero. Blaise said as much to Malcolm, who was at his side.

"But you are," Malcolm insisted, raising his chalice in yet another toast. There had been many toasts already, and the Doyen appeared pleasantly sloshed. "You think you're nothing. A zero. But you're wrong." He took a long swig before settling the crystal goblet on the table. Blaise sighed. Malcolm usually unwound with a glass of wine in the evenings. But not *this* much.

"He's right, you know," Lizzie agreed with an emphatic nod. She sat across from Blaise, declaring that it was only right as she had done so much for their cause. "And oh, you should come to opening night at the Legend tomorrow!"

"Opening night?" Blaise asked, puzzled. He sipped his blackberry ginger switchel, enjoying the rich flavor.

"For *Breaker*, of course!" Lizzie announced with pride, her dark eyes dancing. "The timing couldn't be better, especially with the Inquiry ending this week! Anyone who's *anyone* is going to be there, and you simply must come. It would be an absolute windfall for you to attend." She aimed an endearing smile his way. "You *will* come, won't you?"

In all the frenzy of emotions surrounding the Inquiries, Blaise had forgotten about the play. He was certain he didn't want to see whatever fantastical fiction she had created about his unfortunate life.

"Nah, he won' go," Malcolm said, slurring uncharacteristically. Blaise froze beside him, alarmed. He'd never seen Malcolm drunk before—he held his wine well, but certainly never had this much. "Too embarrassed, even though there's not a *damn* thing to be embarrassed about."

Blaise rubbed the bridge of his nose. "I'm not embarrassed." Maybe if he said it out loud, it would become true.

"Are so."

"Am not."

"You are. E'rything embarrasses you. Even *me*." Malcolm's voice dipped into an octave of sadness Blaise didn't know he was capable of. "And I put all of myself out there for you. I've risked everything for you."

Blaise swallowed, something inside of him torn by Malcolm's drunken words. He had been hesitant to divulge his changing feelings, distracted as he was by the Inquiry. *Later,* he had thought. *When things are settled. When I'm more certain.*

But Malcolm's words also stirred something deep within, his old hurt regarding the geasa. "I never asked you to do that."

Malcolm stared at him, eyes bleary. "I couldn't leave you there. Couldn't allow someone *else* to have you."

Lizzie's eyes were owlish at the conversation. Her mouth dropped open as if she were trying to come up with something to say to turn the tide, but Blaise wouldn't have any of it. *Stupid, drunk Malcolm.* "I'm *not* a charity case. *Not* property. *Not* a commodity to be bought or sold."

Hurt flashed across Malcolm's face, as if Blaise had wounded him. Perhaps he had. The Doyen averted his gaze. *Shame.* That was shame etched across Malcolm's handsome face. It only riled Blaise's agitation further, validating his words.

Blaise's palms itched, his magic rising. He shoved it down. The last thing he needed was for his power to break loose here, in front of all the Faedran Doyens. He rose from his seat. "I need some air."

If anyone spoke to him as he beat a quick retreat, he didn't hear it. Blaise found an exit that led to a back alley and walked into a darkness only punctuated by the light coming from windows and the stars overhead. He shut his eyes, releasing a whistling breath as he leaned against the restaurant's wall. He stayed that way for several minutes until he felt his magic unwind and seep back to his core.

"You know he wouldn't have said any of that if he were sober," a familiar voice pointed out. Flora dropped to the ground from the roof.

Blaise pushed away from the wall. "And that's what makes it worse."

The half-knocker studied him for a moment. He wondered how well she saw in the dark. All he could see was her face angled to look at him, her pink hair nothing more than a darkly gleaming curl in the night. "You know he's stupidly, madly in love with you, right? I can see you're dense about the whole courting thing, so I thought maybe I should spell it out for you."

Blaise snorted. "You're not wrong about the dense part, but...yeah, I know how he feels about me." He rubbed the back of his neck. "What would you do if you were me?"

Flora laughed. "That's the wrong question to ask. I would have shagged him back in Itude."

Blaise cringed. He had forgotten that Flora wasn't shy about her emotions and drives. Well, and she actually *had* drives. "Okay, that was a stupid question. I deserved that answer. What do *I* do?"

"Him, obviously." Flora bleated a laugh at her own joke, then stepped closer to pat his arm. "Sorry, I don't have filters sometimes, and you have to admit, you were asking for it. How do *you* feel about him?"

Blaise sighed. "I don't know." *Lie. Liar.* Why was it so hard to admit aloud that he loved Jefferson?

Flora was quiet for a moment, and Blaise shifted uneasily in the silence that hung between them. After a bit, she said, "If that's true, that's fine. But don't go breaking a good man's heart because you're afraid of the unknown. Nothing about you has *ever* scared him. He's never thought for two seconds about turning away from you. Even when it was in his best interest to do so. That's a rare and precious thing." She patted his arm again, this time more forcefully, as if she were trying to hammer some sense into him, before letting go and scaling the side of the restaurant to perch on the roof.

Oh, biscuits. She was right. Why did emotions and relationships have to be so messy? Life had been simpler when he thought he had no prospects. But his existence then had lacked the color and verve it had now. Flora was right. *Rare and precious thing*, indeed. He steeled himself and started back toward the restaurant.

He took a quick step back as the door opened, and Malcolm stumbled out. The Doyen didn't seem to see him, instead wobbling unsteadily before bracing an arm against the wall.

"Malcolm? Are you okay?" Blaise wished he could see better in the darkness.

"Dandy. Was lookin' fer the quincy. Need to vomit." It was followed by the sound of splatter as he made good on his words. Blaise winced in sympathy. And hoped that none of it had gotten on his boots.

"Well, this is certainly not that," Blaise advised him. Overhead, the moon peeked out from behind a cloud, revealing that Malcolm had aimed beside a trash can. Inside would have been better, but sometimes close counted. Blaise's boots had survived, at least. "Do you need help? Can I get you something?" What helped someone when they were drunk? He had absolutely no idea.

"I nee'…I nee'…" Malcolm fumbled over the words, then retched again. "I nee' to go back in time and tell my idiot self to not drink so much after you left. And before that, too." He wiped his mouth on his sleeve, an appalling move he would never have done sober. "But you know what? I love you. Like, *love*-love you. So much." He took a step closer and would have fallen had Blaise not swooped in to keep him upright. Malcolm giggled.

Blaise sighed. "I love you, too."

Somewhere above them, Flora cackled. "I *knew* it!"

"Not fair," the drunk Doyen complained, ignoring the hidden half-knocker. "Not fair sayin' that right now."

Blaise paused, trying to figure out where the stables were from their current position. Silent as a wraith, Flora hopped down and pulled out a mage-light, crooking a finger. Blaise steered Malcolm in her wake, wondering if Seledora could keep an unsteady rider on board. They would cross that bridge when they got there.

"Shut up," Blaise muttered as they walked. "I do love you, idiot. I just don't show it like you do."

"If you love me, then kiss me. Wait, no. My mouth tastes like warm garbage right now." Malcolm grumbled with disappointment.

"I *have* kissed you before," Blaise pointed out, patient.

"That's all, though." Malcolm's voice reflected a small measure of his earlier hurt—and his longing. "You don't know how much I want *more* of your attention. *More* of you." He wove on his feet, leaning heavily against Blaise. "Do I need to let you pour some sugar on me? 'Cause I will, you know."

"Oh my *gods*," Blaise muttered. "Just when I thought one conversation was the most embarrassing in my life, another appears."

"Kinda like cutting the head off a hydra." Flora spun, the mage-light dancing in her palm tinting her grey skin with a bluish haze. "I don't know what's going on between you. Or what you've said to one another in the past. But you both need to figure this out. *Soon.*"

I thought I had more time. "We will," Blaise promised, because there was no other answer. She was right. They needed to figure out what they were to one another. They both deserved that much.

Relief washed through him when they reached the stables. Emrys snorted, reading his rider's tension. But the stallion didn't comment, though his ears flicked whenever Malcolm giggled. That was happening far more frequently now, along with the formerly dignified Doyen murmuring terms of endearment.

<I'll keep my client on-board,> Seledora assured Blaise, even though Malcolm almost faceplanted twice just getting into the saddle. At least someone in their haphazard group had confidence.

By some miracle, they reached Malcolm's estate without disaster. Flora found a groom to tend to the pegasi, and Blaise helped Malcolm into the house. He was still giggling, muttering something about royal icing. Blaise eased him down on the bed, prying off his shoes so that he would be comfortable. Malcolm flopped backward onto the bed, eyelids drifting closed.

Blaise worked the sheet and blanket out from beneath him, then pulled them up so he wouldn't get cold. Malcolm snored softly—another unusual trait brought about by his current state—and for a moment, Blaise considered leaving him alone for the night so he could sleep in peace. But he thought about how Malcolm had already given up so much for him. The least he could do was sacrifice a night of sleep. Blaise prepared for bed and then settled down beside the sleeping Doyen.

"I do love you. But I love Jefferson more," Blaise whispered, touching Malcolm's slack cheek. That was the source of his true embarrassment: he realized that, even though they were the same person, he had a preference. He didn't want to hurt Malcolm with the revelation. But he needed to be honest, so he resolved to find a way.

But first, he had to wait for Malcolm to sober up. He closed his eyes and went to sleep, disappointed to discover that a hungover Malcolm was incapable of summoning his Dreamer magic.

***

Jack

JACK REFUSED TO ADMIT IT TO JEFFERSON OR BLAISE, BUT HE LOOKED forward to their intrusions into his dreams. They didn't happen every night, and he was fine with that, but their appearance gave him hope. Hope was all that he had left. Hope was *everything*.

And now he didn't just want to see them, he *needed* to see them. He had actual information. Gregor Gaitwood had realized that the tide of the first Inquiry was against him, and he was ready to remove pieces from the game board. From what Jack gleaned, there was going to be a week-long break before the new Inquiry began, and Gaitwood was justifiably concerned about Wells continuing to work his political magic.

"Where in Perdition *are* you?" Jack stared at the dark ceiling. He picked up a poppet he had left on the bedside table, tossing it from hand to hand. Malcolm's poppet. He wanted to destroy it, but the geasa wouldn't allow him to act against something connected to his magic. And the poppet was still active, tied to the Doyen.

Jack was thankful Gaitwood was ignorant in the ways of his power. Real handlers learned the ins and outs of their theurgist's magic, so they could unleash it to the best of their ability. It was like the working relationship Jack had observed between wranglers and their ponies, where the rider had an almost innate ability to guide their steed's movements with the pressure of a knee or the flick of a rein. The ponies knew their job, and the cowboy let them do it, within reason.

Gregor was nothing like that. He treated Jack, and therefore the geasa, like a servant. He had a set of commands, and that was it. Much of it was left up to Jack's interpretation, which was all the free will he had. Gregor didn't care if he used bullets or magic. They were all the same to him. He had no clue about the depths of the outlaw's magical potential.

He stared at the poppet. "Means you're lucky, you feckless dandy." Jack dropped it onto the table again, rolling onto his side to stare across the darkened room. He kept waiting for the sudden pull of sleep, the insistent tug of Jefferson drawing him into the dreamscape. The Dreamer had lulled him into it before, and Jack hoped against hope that he would do so now.

The dreams never came.

CHAPTER FORTY
The Most Confusing Person Ever

Blaise

"I'm feeling personally attacked right now by the fact that the sun is up." Malcolm winced, raising a hand to shield his eyes from the offensive ray of sunlight that slipped through the curtains.

Blaise glanced over from where he sat in an armchair in the corner, reading a book. He marked his page and placed the book on the bedside table, then clasped his hands in front of him as he studied Malcolm, whose hair was mussed and face pale. "How are you feeling?"

Malcolm winced. "Like I made a very poor life choice last night. Fortunes of Tabris, I haven't drunk like that for years. And definitely not as *me*." He rolled onto his side with a groan. "I think I need to vomit."

"Wouldn't be the first time," Blaise remarked, rising from the chair to help.

Malcolm appreciated his aid and, from what Blaise could tell, had very little memory of the previous night. He asked how the festivities with the other Doyens had gone, and Blaise danced around the topic, saying that it went well. He wanted—no, *needed*—to get to the heart of their fight last night. Because that's what he realized it had been, and it didn't sit well with him—even if Malcolm didn't remember it.

Marta brought up breakfast for them—though the food she provided for Malcolm was bland: toast, bananas, and ginger tea, which she told Blaise would help him recover from the nasty effects of the hangover.

Malcolm sat cross-legged on the bed, sipping the tea and nibbling toast, muttering that he didn't want to see any other company until his head stopped pounding. It was a little disconcerting to see the sophisticated Doyen sitting in bed with toast crumbs raining down beside him, but Blaise decided he liked how it made him more *real*.

"Apologies if I was awful last night. I haven't drunk like that in a very long time," Malcolm said once he polished off the first piece. He wiped his fingertips on a linen napkin, frowning at the crumbs. He busied himself sweeping them into the napkin with one hand.

Malcolm's not stupid. He knows something happened but doesn't know what. Blaise wished the other man knew, to prevent the need for explanation. But this was something Blaise couldn't hide from—not if he really cared about the other man. And he did. Or he thought he did, anyway. Blaise hadn't slept at all last night, too busy examining how he felt about Jefferson and Malcolm and where to go from there.

"There *is* something we need to talk about," Blaise said after a beat, trying to keep his tone neutral. "Last night you said some things that made me think." Malcolm opened his mouth to interject, but Blaise held up a hand. "Let me finish, please. It's important. You put yourself out there for me and you show me constantly how you feel. And that's harder for me..."

Malcolm nodded. "I know. It's okay."

"No, it's really not." Blaise rubbed at his face. Everything made more sense in his head, but suddenly he was at a loss for the right words. He wished he could just throw his jumbled thoughts at Malcolm so he would understand. Sadly, it wasn't that simple. "We need to decide what we are to each other."

Malcolm reached for his cup of tea and took a sip, though Blaise saw it for what it was: a delaying tactic to allow him a moment's thought. His forehead puckered. "What did I say that brought this about?"

"That you wanted more than kisses."

"*Oh.*" The single word held the sharp edge of regret and truth. Malcolm swallowed, and he gave an abrupt nod. "I remember what you told me before—how you feel about that. That doesn't stop how *I* feel about *you*. When you're near, you're all I can think about. But not *only* because of how I want you. You make me feel *loved*. Something I never had with...with anyone before." He raked a hand through his hair, mussing it further.

He's afraid of losing that. Blaise studied Malcolm from the tendrils of black hair standing at attention atop his head down to his legs curled on the mattress. His stockinged toes poked out from beneath the sheets. "I love you, too. But..."

A range of emotions flickered over Malcolm's face, and Blaise's stomach cramped. The Doyen had years of practice at schooling his expression, and his face briskly turned neutral, though the corners of his eyes crinkled with uncertainty. "But what?" His voice was soft and a little husky, as if he were afraid of something but denying the fear.

Blaise rubbed the back of his neck. "I'm *attracted* to Jefferson."

Malcolm's eye-crinkle disappeared, replaced by confusion. "You realize *I'm* Jefferson, right?" He sounded more amused than hurt. "Quite literally two sides of the same coin."

"I know it's stupid." Blaise swallowed, tension creeping into the base of his neck. He shouldn't have said anything. Why couldn't he be normal? "But I wanted you to know."

Malcolm licked his lips. "It's not stupid. As they say, the heart knows what it wants."

"Who says that?" Blaise had never heard such a thing, but that didn't mean much.

"Heard it at the theater," Malcolm said, rolling his shoulders in a casual shrug. He gave Blaise a curious look. "May I ask how you came to that conclusion?"

"I just..." Blaise faltered. He didn't want to tell Malcolm he'd been thinking about him—and Jefferson—all night. Puzzling through his feelings. Struggling to identify what separated Jefferson from Malcolm in his mind. "I don't know."

"We can test your theory, if you like." Malcolm reached over, opening the drawer of the bedside table, and pulling out a velvet box. His ring nestled inside, the scarlet stone glinting in the morning light. He plucked it from the velvet and held it between his thumb and index finger, an invitation. "What do you think?"

"I thought you were trying to keep up the image that Jefferson is in Ganland right now. You know, since he's a wanted man," Blaise said, though his pulse raced. For weeks he had only seen Jefferson in the dreamscape, where he was Malcolm's preference, too.

"A wanted man, you say?" Malcolm's mouth twitched, teasing.

"You know what I mean," Blaise muttered, though he only feigned his annoyance. And judging by the way Malcolm's eyes danced, he was aware. "Isn't this inviting trouble?"

"No one's going to know." Malcolm slipped the ring onto his finger, magic sluicing over him as he changed. Obsidian hair brightened to tawny brown, and his five o'clock shadow faded away. Brown eyes shifted into an intense green. Jefferson aimed a crooked smile at him. "Better?"

Blaise swallowed. "Um, I think so."

"Gods, you are the most confusing person ever."

That was accurate. Even Blaise knew that. He couldn't take his eyes off Jefferson, and even though logically he *knew* he was still the same person, he couldn't deny the draw. Because Jefferson had been the one to first show interest in him back in Itude. Jefferson had been kind and talked to him. "Oh. It was Jefferson first," Blaise murmured to himself.

"What?"

Blaise shook his head, sitting down on the bed, close enough so that his shoulder brushed Jefferson's. "If you thought I was confusing thirty seconds ago, please don't ask me to explain what just went through my head."

"If your thoughts were about me, then no explanation necessary," Jefferson replied, a rumble in his voice.

The heat in his tone made Blaise feel giddy, like the prospect of trying a new and challenging recipe. He thought back to Flora's words. *Rare and precious.* This man loved and treasured him, not caring that he was a walking mess of a human being. No matter his magic. There was no judgment. Jefferson didn't ask him to be anyone else but who he was. And that was...liberating.

He turned, leaning in, until his lips met Jefferson's. Their arms entangled, and for an instant, Blaise fought back against the old panic of someone so close. *This is okay. This is safe.* Jefferson's hands were as tender as his lips were demanding. He ran a finger along Blaise's jaw, scuffing the edge of his beard with his nails. His touch was bliss, a kindness that Blaise hadn't felt in the Cit outside of the dreamscape.

Blaise quivered, pulling away with a soft sigh. He closed his eyes as Jefferson stroked the short hair at the nape of his neck.

"Are you okay?" Jefferson asked, his hand light on Blaise's neck.

"Yes," Blaise murmured, meeting the other man's eyes. Did he know what he was doing? No. But he was with Jefferson, and that meant things would be all right. Blaise traced a hand up Jefferson's chest until he reached the top button of his shirt, still rumpled and unchanged from the previous evening.

Jefferson rested a hand atop his, green eyes pensive. "What are we to each other?"

Blaise paused beneath his touch. He had been so focused on Jefferson's presence that he'd forgotten his earlier hesitation. "Safety. Acceptance." The words felt right as he said them, ringing with truth. "I *do* love you."

A shiver swept through Jefferson, one that Blaise felt beneath his hand. "And I love you. But this..." Jefferson curled his hand around Blaise's. "Is this what you want?"

Is it? Blaise swallowed. He knew he was standing on the edge of a cliff. This had the potential to change things between them, and his inexperience with relationships was a detriment. He cared about Jefferson—when they were together, he felt whole. Someone who made him the man he wanted to be, not the man everyone else thought he was. "I want you to know how I feel about you." He toyed with the top button.

Jefferson swallowed. "You just told me. That's a treasure in itself. As much as I want you, I'm afraid I'll drive you away if we do anything more." The skin on his brow puckered with indecision.

Blaise touched Jefferson's cheek, smooth as if he had just shaved. Jefferson shuddered, leaning into the caress. "You won't drive me away. Not with this."

Jefferson froze beneath his touch, though Blaise suspected he was like a coiled spring, ready to be released in an instant. "You were crystal clear about your stance on sex before. What changed?"

How could a question be both difficult and easy to answer? Blaise tipped his head as he thought. "I realized that when you care about someone, you want to make the other person happy."

Conflicting emotions warred on Jefferson's face, a mixture of anticipation and uncertainty. "Not at the sacrifice of *your* happiness, though."

"Who says I won't be happy?"

Jefferson hissed out a breath, studying him. "Gods, Blaise. You certainly know how to tie me in knots. I—"

Blaise crushed his mouth against Jefferson's, cutting off whatever protest he was about to make. The Dreamer tensed for a heartbeat before melting against Blaise with a low moan. Jefferson's hand found the back of Blaise's neck again, fingers winding around a lock of his hair.

Blaise looped his arms over Jefferson's shoulders when they parted. "You were saying?"

"I have no idea what I was saying," Jefferson murmured, resting his forehead against Blaise's. He closed his eyes for a moment. "Wait, I remember now." Jefferson's eyes flashed open again. "This. *Us.*" He shook his head, as if annoyed that his usual eloquence had fled. "What I mean to say is, I think I can make you happy, too."

Blaise smiled. "I'm counting on it."

BLAISE'S BACK NESTLED AGAINST JEFFERSON'S CHEST, WARM AND welcoming. He breathed out a soft, contented sigh, turning over when a familiar hand brushed against his arm.

Green eyes flashed a greeting as a satisfied smile slid across Jefferson's face. He had shed his earlier fears, emboldened by Blaise's change of heart. "I must say, all that kneading bread does wonders. The way you rubbed my—"

Blaise touched a finger to his lips. *Great, now he's downright cheeky.* "Don't ruin this."

"I was going to say *back*," Jefferson replied, eyebrows raised, the very picture of innocence. "Why? What did *you* think I was going to say?"

Blaise couldn't help it. He laughed because everything about this was ridiculous and wonderful. Jefferson grinned, his expression one of unfettered delight.

"No, really. What did you think? I'm genuinely curious." Jefferson rested his chin on one hand, inviting an answer.

"I won't dignify that with a response," Blaise mumbled, shaking his head. He couldn't even be annoyed at the question. Jefferson was nearly effervescent in his joy, and it was infectious.

Jefferson planted a gentle kiss on his cheek. "I was only teasing. And trust me, it was a compliment."

Blaise's cheeks heated for a new reason at that. "Oh." He swallowed as Jefferson draped an arm over his bare side, pinning him with a serious look.

"Are we okay?" Jefferson asked, his voice soft. "Because as much as I've wanted this, I don't want to harm what we have."

What we have. Blaise turned those words over in his mind, enjoying them. They had something he'd never expected to have in his life. It was new, and a little frightening, but it was *his*. Blaise discovered it was something he wanted to protect, this love he had found.

Blaise realized he hadn't given Jefferson any sort of response, lost in his thoughts. "I'll be honest. I'm still figuring things out, but I think we're going to be okay."

CHAPTER FORTY-ONE

Breaker: The Musical

Blaise

"I can't believe you actually agreed to this." Malcolm's voice reverberated with excitement as he and Blaise found their seats in the Legend Theater. A grin lit his handsome face as his eyes feasted on the sights and sounds all around them.

Blaise gave a small shrug, tolerating the hubbub because it made Malcolm happy. After the revelation that the Doyen had forgotten most of the previous evening, Blaise had, much to his surprise, reminded him of their invitation to the debut of Lizzie's play. "I know you enjoy this sort of thing."

"I do," Malcolm agreed, grasping Blaise's hand and giving it a quick squeeze.

They were both in a pleasant haze. With the Inquiry recessed for the day, there was no need to hurry anywhere. Malcolm's staff cleared his schedule so that Jefferson and Blaise spent most of the day together. The more time they were together, simply *being*, the more certain he was that they would be okay. Blaise hadn't felt like he would be okay for a very long time.

An usher seated them in a private box along with Doyen Jennings and his wife. Lizzie was radiant, beaming with pride. Blaise couldn't help but smile as people stopped by to chat with her. It was a bonus that the admirers focused on her rather than him. As the titular Breaker, he was interesting but not as influential for the sycophants as the talented Lizzie Jennings. Blaise was fine with that.

The house lights dimmed as orchestral chords wafted through the theater. An *orchestra*. They had an entire orchestra. Blaise shook his head, overwhelmed at the opulence. Lizzie's admirers retreated to their own seats as the lights came up on the stage, illuminating a young man strutting to the center. Music swelled as a chorus dressed in scarlet filed onto the right side of the stage.

Blaise groaned. "Wait. Is this a musical?"

Malcolm chuckled. "Yes. Did you miss that part on the program?" He held it up for Blaise's inspection. "Look, none other than *Edward Monroe* is playing you."

"I don't even know who that is." Blaise wondered if he could burrow so deeply into his seat that no one would see him. The seats in the theater were exceptionally plush.

"All you need to know is that you should be flattered," Malcolm assured him. He craned his neck to get a better look at Blaise's face. "What's wrong? Afraid the songs will be so catchy that you'll hear people singing about you?"

"Actually, yes." Blaise rubbed the side of his face as the young man on stage belted out a song about his life. "Do you think it's possible to die of embarrassment?"

Malcolm glanced at him but otherwise kept his attention focused on the stage. "Don't be ridiculous."

"All I'm saying is we might find out if it's possible."

In the darkness, a hand pressed against his, warm and reassuring. Malcolm eased closer. "If you're truly upset, we can leave."

Oh. Blaise hadn't meant that. "We can stay. Um, sometimes I just like to complain about things." Though he thought this was a valid complaint. Sweet Faedra, had the actor just sung the line *A stalwart Breaker, who would rather be a baker?* The chorus echoed it a moment later, so yes, he absolutely had.

The reflected stage lights illuminated the hint of a smile on Malcolm's face. "Noted." His hand roved to Blaise's knee, settling there like a comforting weight.

The worst part was the fact that the songs *were* catchy. And fun. Did it divert from reality? It did, to the point where Blaise sometimes forgot it was about him. Which, all things told, made it more palatable. The musical's storyline was engaging and often over-the-top.

A few minutes before the intermission, an usher delivered a note to Malcolm. He unfolded it and read it, brow furrowed. He leaned over to whisper, "I'll be back in a few moments."

Blaise nodded, though he didn't want to be left alone. Well, he supposed he wasn't alone. Seward and Lizzie were nearby, watching the production. They had become sort-of friends, so he had the reassurance of their combined presence until Malcolm returned. He nibbled on his bottom lip, keeping his attention on the current musical number in which the actress playing Vixen was helping to train actor-Blaise's magic. Lovely aerialists swung around on billowing silks in the background. Blaise couldn't figure out what they had to do with anything, but they made for a striking scene.

Intermission came and went, and still Malcolm hadn't returned. Blaise clasped his hands in his lap, constant worry distracting him. He licked his lips, glancing around for any sign of the Doyen. A few more minutes passed, and he poked at the geasa bond between them, but it was quiet. And quiet was unusual. Wrong. He should have felt something there, Malcolm's steady presence as sure as the beating of his own heart.

Blaise closed his eyes, swallowing. Just because he didn't feel Malcolm didn't mean that the worst had happened. His hands itched with his rising anxiety. All he had to do was find Malcolm and assure himself that he was fine. No big deal. He rose from his seat, giving Seward a small nod as he exited the box.

Blaise peered down the long corridor, trying to decide which way Malcolm might have gone. Was Flora around? She had a penchant for lurking near Malcolm when he was in public. Blaise wouldn't have been surprised to discover her somewhere nearby. That thought made him feel better.

He walked along the concourse, almost wandering behind the scenes to where the actors and actresses did whatever it was they did behind the curtain. Still, there was no sign of Malcolm. What had been in the note that had drawn him away? Blaise should have asked more questions. He rubbed the back of his neck, torn about what to do next. Maybe he had gone outside? That was the only other place he hadn't checked.

Gas-powered lamps lit the streets outside the Legend Theater, fending off the encroaching darkness. Blaise peered up and down the street, unsettled that he found no sign of Malcolm. He started a loop around the theater complex.

The chill of danger tickled Blaise's spine as he stepped into a back alley, and he knew without turning around who made him feel that sense of impending doom. Blaise froze, swallowing. "Howdy, Jack."

Boots scuffed the ground as Blaise pivoted, slow and careful. The outlaw stood at the other end of the alley, his sixgun holstered. He somehow looked older than his years, as if the geasa had sapped the fight out of him. Blaise couldn't imagine that Jack, who seemed to exist on pure spite alone, would lose any of his fighting spirit. But Jack was being *used*, and Blaise knew that was one of his greatest fears. A part of him had wanted to deny Jack's situation in the dreamscape, but now it stared him in the face.

Jack didn't speak, simply touched a finger to his broad-brimmed hat.

"I'm going to guess you're why I can't find Malcolm?" Blaise asked, somehow keeping his voice calm.

The outlaw stared at the ground at Blaise's feet, then gave a sharp nod. "He's not dead." Jack's voice was a pained rasp, as if it had cost him to even say that much.

Somehow, Blaise knew there was a *yet* attached to that. There was no guarantee for Malcolm's safety at this point. He stood still, thinking. Jack was a man of action. If he were here to fight, Blaise would already be a bloody pulp. But instead, the outlaw remained in place, like a reluctant marionette. He had an idea. "Jack, what if I broke the geasa?"

Cold blue eyes snapped up to Blaise's face. "*No,*" the outlaw choked out. One of his hands reached out like a claw, and he shook his head, adamant. "Wells."

Oh. The geasa shackled Jack's tongue, but he'd bought enough slack to warn Blaise. The Breaker trembled, his magic swarming as fear swept over him. Jack had done something with Malcolm but couldn't tell him what. Malcolm was in danger. Jack was trapped. And there wasn't a thing Blaise could do about it.

"You have to come with me," Jack said finally, resigned. As if he had been hoping that Blaise would somehow come up with a plan to save them all. "It's the only way anyone gets out of this alive."

Blaise froze, trembling. He was about to speak when Flora rained down on them like a rabid goblin. She landed on Jack's back, knocking the outlaw down with surprising force. Blaise stumbled backward as they fell in a cursing, spitting tussle. Flora screamed with such enthusiasm Blaise thought his eardrums might burst, and he wondered why the city guard didn't come running. Though if Gregor were behind all this, he had likely arranged for them to either not be around or ignore whatever they heard.

Jack was not at the top of his game or full of fight. Their battle was short and ended with the outlaw flat on his back, Flora perched atop his chest with her knives at his throat. "Where's Malcolm, you cold-hearted bastard?"

"Flora, stop," Blaise called, walking closer with caution. Jack was breathing hard, eyes closed. "He can't help it. He's under Gaitwood's control."

She glanced up at him. "Hrmph." Flora put away her knives and crossed her arms, maintaining her position over Jack. "Can I just stab him a little?" Jack's eyes flew open, and he bucked beneath her with a furious growl.

"Please don't," Blaise said quickly. He ran a hand through his hair, tugging at it. "Let him up. I have to go with him."

The half-knocker shook her head. "No. How will I ever explain to Malcolm that I let you go with Killhappy Murderface here? There has to be another way." She climbed down from her position atop Jack's chest, though she brought her blades back out.

"Gaitwood wants Blaise," Jack said, groaning as he adjusted into a sitting position. He winced as he moved, a thin trail of blood seeping from a gash on his forehead. He didn't seem to notice it.

Flora's pink ponytail whipped around as she shook her head. "Exactly! This is what you were trying to avoid. What *Malcolm* fought so hard to avoid."

Oh, Blaise knew. And he didn't like it, but he couldn't go on if he became the reason Malcolm no longer drew breath. And besides... "I trust Jack. We'll figure something out."

"Okay, let me point out that putting your trust in someone under the sway of the geasa is a poor life choice." Flora put her hands on her hips. "He's already got Malcolm! You want Gregor to collect the whole set?"

If Jack had input, he was quiet, unable to voice it under his current compulsion.

Flora was right. It was stupid. Blaise didn't have any sort of plan besides the drive to know that Malcolm was okay. But maybe... "Jack, Flora can leave here with no harm done?"

"Long as she doesn't come at me again. Might have to kill her then."

"I'd like to see you try!" Her knives glinted in the gas-lamp light.

Blaise sighed, holding up a hand. "Wait." He approached Jack, who stood as still as a statue. Blaise reached up and plucked a hair from beneath the outlaw's hat, receiving no response aside from frigid eyes watching him. Blaise plucked a few hairs from his own head for good measure, then wrapped them in a bandanna before handing the strange package to Flora. He knelt down close to her and whispered in her ear, "Can you find Emmaline? She can help."

The half-knocker scowled, then pocketed the precious bandanna. "I'll try. Stall for as long as you can." She stepped back, glancing between Blaise and Jack. "Outlaw, if anything happens to Malcolm, I'll be the last thing you'll ever see." Jack made no response, further proof that the man wasn't in control.

Blaise rose, turning to face the outlaw as Flora hurried off. "All right. Let's go."

Jack escorted Blaise to a dark carriage waiting nearby. Once the outlaw opened the door, Malcolm was visible, slumped across one of the bench seats. Blaise gasped, vaulting inside to check for a pulse.

"Told you he wasn't dead," Jack grunted, climbing up and closing the door behind him. The outlaw claimed the seat opposite the Doyen, crossing his arms as he waited for Blaise to finish his assessment.

Malcolm's eyes were open, but he was motionless aside from involuntary blinking. Blaise chewed his bottom lip with worry, brushing a hand across Malcolm's cheek. Magic pulsed through the downed man.

"Don't," Jack urged, though his voice was neutral.

"What did you do to him?" Blaise drew back from Malcolm, taking a seat next to Jack.

"Paralysis spell." Jack pulled a poppet from his customary pocket, turning it over in his hands. "He's fine." The muscles in his jaw worked, as if he wanted to say more. Instead, he shook his head, eyes burning with frustration.

Blaise nodded, rubbing the side of his face as he shot another glance at Malcolm. As tempting as it was to ignore Jack's command and break the spell, Blaise figured that wouldn't end well. Magic against magic, he could probably beat the outlaw in a fight. But he wasn't a fighter. Besides, Jack was armed and had a lifetime of experience. Blaise sat, fervently wishing he and Malcolm were watching the ridiculous musical instead of this.

"Why haven't you done that to me?" Blaise asked, shifting his eyes from Malcolm to Jack.

The Effigest was quiet for so long that Blaise didn't expect an answer from him. After several long moments had passed, Jack finally said, "There's no need."

Blaise nodded, since Jack had the right of it. While Malcolm was at risk, he would behave. Blaise was more likely to fight if Jack used his magic against him. The outlaw respected the power of a Breaker.

The carriage rolled into the night. Jack glanced out the window, a resigned expression on his face. He touched his throat, as if testing his limits. "How was the play?"

That wasn't a question Blaise had been expecting. Jack clearly had directions for topics he could and couldn't discuss. This one must not have been off-limits. He shrugged. "It's not a play, it's a musical. And the part I saw wasn't bad, considering that I had to watch a bunch of people singing and dancing about me."

"Musical, huh?" Jack sounded almost normal for a moment. "Am I in it?"

Weird conversations with Jack weren't unusual, but this ranked up there among the strangest. "Um, yeah. There's an entire number about you punching me in the face, in fact."

"Is that so? I might have to check that out." Then a silent sneer curled his lips. No doubt he was thinking, *If I ever get free.*

"It was a distressingly catchy tune," Blaise agreed, which turned Jack's sneer into an almost-amused smile.

They grew quiet, watching the dark scenery scroll past their windows. Blaise frowned, wondering where they were going. He considered asking Jack, but he figured the outlaw wouldn't be able to answer, even if he knew. So he waited, and a half-hour later his question was answered by their arrival at a train station.

Blaise had never seen a train in person before, and the size of the hulking metal leviathan crouched on the tracks at the head of a dozen railway cars was surprising. The station house was lit by pools of golden gas lanterns arrayed around it, casting it in a haunting light. The carriage bypassed the station house, and the horses drew to a halt near the last passenger car.

There was a scrape and thump as the driver got down from the box. A moment later, the door opened. Jack glanced from Blaise to Malcolm. "I'm going to remove the working. Don't try anything. My instructions are clear if you do."

"Got it," Blaise whispered.

Jack cupped the poppet in his palm. Blaise couldn't quite make out if he did anything special or said something, but Malcolm made a great gasp and struggled upright, shaking. He sagged against the velvet seatback for a moment, rubbing his forehead. Blaise wanted to rush to him, but he wasn't sure if that would set Jack off, so he froze where he was. "Are you okay?"

Malcolm offered Blaise a brave smile. "I'm functional, so we'll leave it at that."

"Let's go," Jack ordered, jutting his chin toward the door.

Blaise reached out and helped Malcolm up. The bond between them shivered at the touch, and he relished Malcolm's presence again. The Doyen flashed a grateful smile and together they stepped down from the carriage, goaded by Jack toward one of the passenger cars.

They mounted the steps into the rail car. It was lavish, all polished dark woods, beautiful draperies on the windows, and paisley-patterned, velvet-covered seating. Voluminous rugs with a floral design cushioned the floors, and the coach had the look of a fabric shop that had vomited its contents into a train car. He was so busy gawking he didn't realize they weren't alone until Malcolm growled.

"Good to see you again, Doyen Wells," Gregor Gaitwood said from his seat on a couch, camouflaged among the ridiculous patterns like Iphyria's gaudiest predator. "How was the show?"

"What are you *doing*, Gregor?" Malcolm demanded, furious. For a moment, Blaise thought he might rush across the car and attack the other man. He wouldn't have blamed him.

Gregor smirked. "Winning." He glanced at Jack and must have issued some sort of silent command because the outlaw took out his poppet, and Malcolm froze, staggering before Jack grabbed him and eased him down to a safe spot on one of the awful rugs.

Blaise balled his fists at his sides, magic swimming beneath his skin. He wanted to do or say something, but not if it risked Malcolm. He settled for glaring at their smug captor.

Gaitwood rose from his seat, moving to what Blaise guessed was a mini-bar set up at the other end. He pulled something out and poured it into a glass, then ambled over and offered it to him. "Drink up."

Blaise curled his lips, turning away. "I don't drink."

"You'll drink *this*," Gregor replied, holding it out again. "I'm not stupid enough to risk being in a locomotive with a Breaker after what you did to the *Retribution*."

Blaise took the glass and peered at its contents. He didn't want whatever it was, but he didn't see any other options. "I'll drink it, but I think I deserve to know what it'll do."

Gregor stared at him. "You deserve *nothing*."

Was that so? Blaise tapped a tiny vein of his magic, shooting it through the glass. A spider web-thin crack shimmied up one side. "You're threatening me and someone I care about. It's not unreasonable for me to ask. Because if I think this is going to kill me, I may just decide to take you out with me."

The Doyen glared at him, then heaved a put-upon sigh, relenting. "It won't kill you. It's a sleep potion."

Sleep? Blaise cast a glance at Malcolm. He didn't know where they were headed, but maybe, just maybe, they still had a chance. He drank.

CHAPTER FORTY-TWO

Boss Mares

Kittie

Cursing and the sounds of a skirmish carried across the short expanse of Bitter End. Kittie's head jerked up from the work shirt she had been mending as Emmaline packed their meager belongings. Jack hadn't come to find them, and whether it was from lack of ability or something else, they didn't know. She and her daughter had resolved to find him, instead.

Emmaline traded looks with her. "Are we under attack?" Her hands tremored, a tell that made Kittie frown. Her daughter had spoken of the assault on Itude, and it was evident she hadn't forgotten the trauma.

"Let's find out." Kittie slipped her needle into the shirt she had been working on, placing it in a nearby basket for safe-keeping. She rose, heading for the door.

"Hang on, don't you want a pistol or something?" Emmaline called as she grabbed her revolver and stuck it into her waistband.

Kittie shook her head. "I don't need it." Not now, with the incentive to have full control of her fire. But it was nice to know that her daughter was armed. That would allow Kittie the chance to focus.

They followed the sounds of fighting to a copse of trees bordering the wards. Other citizens of Bitter End had heard the commotion as well, though they elected to retreat, guiding children away from town. A furious screech echoed through the woods, causing birds and squirrels to burst away, and both women broke into a jog. Through the branches, Kittie spotted a shock of bright pink hair weaving between the trio of men struggling to fight off the invader. An invader, Kittie realized, who couldn't be over four feet tall. *A child?*

Emmaline's eyes widened, and she accelerated into a run. "Wait! I know her!"

Kittie raised her brows. *Must be something related to Jack, then.* The sentries hadn't heard Emmaline's revelation, too embroiled in their frantic fight against a surprisingly agile and slippery foe. It was unlikely they would cave to Emmaline's command, anyway. Kittie strode forward, tucking her chin and rolling her shoulders. She didn't know if a young Effigest could stop a brawl, but as a Pyromancer, she had a few compelling tricks up her sleeve. Kittie rubbed her hands together in anticipation, glancing at her daughter. "Stay back."

"But—"

"*Do as I say.*" Kittie's urgency ended Emmaline's protest, allowing her to turn her attention to the combatants. The pink-haired terror was holding her own against the men, faster and tougher than they were. It was as if they were trying to capture a greased pig. Kittie snapped her fingers, and a line of flame sprung up from the ground, forming a dancing wreath around the group. Emmaline gasped, taking a hesitant step backward, but Kittie ignored her. Everything around them was very, very flammable, and it took all her concentration to restrain the fire's drive to consume.

The primordial force roaring around them got their attention. Few creatures alive would ignore flames in their vicinity, even in the fever of battle. The pink-haired woman untangled from the melee, edging a few paces back from the men who clustered together, sweaty, bruised, and bleeding. Kittie had the distinct impression the invader had been doing her best to neutralize the sentries and nothing more.

"Who is she?" Kittie barked to Emmaline, glancing over her shoulder.

"Flora," Emmaline answered as the little woman waggled her fingers in greeting.

"*How* did she get past the wards?" Basil panted, stomping the ground. He flashed an angry look at Emmaline, no doubt blaming her for this.

"Honey, it's gonna take more than a little hocus pocus to contain me." Flora winked, then turned her attention to Kittie and Emmaline. "Hey kid, is Sparky there your mom?"

"Howdy, Flora," Emmaline drawled. "You bet she is. What are you doing here?"

Flora twirled her knives and sheathed them, ignoring the humiliated sentries glowering at her. Kittie dropped her wall of flames with another snap of her fingers, allowing the small woman to cross to them.

"We need—" Basil started.

Flora held up a hand, all four feet of her rigid and commanding. "Don't care. Not listening." She looked to Kittie and Emmaline. "We need to talk, but I've got some friends on the outside who need to come in. Can someone drop that ward?"

Kittie blew out a breath. She looked to Basil. He was going to be delighted. "Can you?"

He stared at them as if they had lost their minds. Maybe they had. "What?"

"Listen, there're three annoyed pegasi out there. I'd do it quick-like if I were you," Flora advised.

"Pegasi?" Emmaline asked, on alert.

Flora frowned, giving a tiny shake of her head. Her eyes were on the menfolk, who she clearly didn't trust.

Basil scowled. "I would need to check with the mayor—"

"Faedra's tits, I hate bureaucracy sometimes," Flora muttered.

Kittie decided she liked this woman. "Basil, it's *pegasi*. Not humans. Do it quickly and bring the wards up again. No fuss, no muss."

Basil complied, though he grumbled the entire time, and a few moments later, three equines trotted in. Kittie assumed they were pegasi with their wings hidden. Emmaline had told her about Jack's pegasus, and she recognized the palomino stallion immediately.

He froze as he entered the clearing, nostrils quivering as he picked up her scent. Then he released a soft, throaty nicker and trotted over to her, shoving his exquisite head against her chest.

<You are my rider's mate.> The stallion's voice resonated in her mind, part declaration and part reassurance. <I am called Zepheus, and I am honored to finally meet you.> He blew out a warm breath, tickling her chest.

"And I'm honored to meet you," Kittie murmured, marveling at the magnificent stallion. The scars that laced his coat might have made him unappealing to others, but Kittie knew an old warrior when she saw one. He was a good match for Jack. But if the palomino was here without his rider, what did that mean? Her heart squeezed in her chest. "Where's Jack?"

Zepheus flattened his ears. <We will explain.>

"We need to go somewhere to talk," Flora announced as Basil sealed the wards again. "Privately." She gestured to indicate that the pegasi were to be included as well, leaving Kittie to wonder how that would even work.

Emmaline studied the trio of pegasi and made connections that Kittie could only guess. "What happened? It's not right for Emrys and Zeph to be here without…"

Flora's face turned more serious than it had been moments ago. "That's what we need to talk about. They need help." Her gaze shifted to include Kittie. "From both of you."

JACK SHOULD HAVE BEEN THE ONE SITTING ON ZEPHEUS'S BACK. KITTIE imagined that astride the pegasus, he would look like a legendary warrior, rough and ready. A smile touched her lips as she thought about how his blond hair would be gilded by the setting sun, Zepheus's coat shining like a newly-minted coin.

Her smile evaporated as her mind turned back to the information they had brought. The news that Jack had been bound by the geasa again settled in the pit of her stomach like a rotten meal, and the way she saw it, no one would fault her for the flask she had at her side. She took a swig of liquid courage.

They were an odd group. A washed-up Pyromancer, a pink-haired half-knocker, a teenager looking to prove her mettle, and four ornery pegasi. After their strategy session, they had decided it would be wisest to travel at night, when the equines could reveal their wings and take to the skies, as long as they had moonlight to navigate by. But first, Flora suggested they make a brief stop in Izhadell.

"What for?" Emmaline asked, fidgeting with Oberidon's reins.

"Got one more ally to pick up," Flora answered, and didn't elaborate. She simply encouraged Emrys to surge forward with an exuberant shout.

As they neared the outskirts of Izhadell, Kittie realized they were headed for the Arboretum. She liked alchemists about as much as goats liked chupacabras. Kittie treated herself to another draw from the flask as the pegasi fluttered to a ground halt a half-mile outside the walls of the garden.

Flora dropped down from the huge black stallion's back, landing nimbly. "I need to go in and have a word with someone. I won't be long."

"No. We're going with you." Kittie shook her head.

The half-knocker frowned. "That's not a good idea. I'll have an easier time going in unseen. This," she gestured to their group, "is a circus."

"We can handle ourselves." Kittie slid down from Zepheus's back, cursing at the shock of her boots hitting the ground. She nearly stumbled but caught herself at the last moment and covered it with a smile that promised more confidence than she had. Emmaline raised her eyebrows, dubious, but followed suit with a much more graceful dismount.

<We'll stay nearby and keep an ear out in case you need us.> The palomino pegasus arched his neck, ambling off a few strides.

Flora shrugged and pivoted, heading for the Arboretum. "Fine. I was trying to avoid going in the big dumb human way, but we'll figure something out."

"I could just burn a hole in the wall," Kittie offered.

Flora aimed an index finger at her as they walked. "I like that energy, I do. But that would announce our presence and hinder our ability to find who I'm looking for."

"Who *are* we looking for?" Emmaline asked.

The half-knocker pursed her lips, reluctant to respond as she studied the wall in front of them. Flora laid a hand against the bricks before continuing. "Blaise's mother is here."

Emmaline's eyes widened. Kittie glanced between them. All she knew of this Blaise was that he had been a friend of Emmaline's and was a powerful and rare breed of mage. "This place is for *alchemists*."

"Yep." Flora found whatever she was searching for. "Be right back." She vanished in a way Kittie thought must be particular to knockers, then reappeared a moment later, opening a rusting gate twenty feet ahead. "C'mon. The coast is clear."

Kittie wrinkled her nose in distaste, thinking of the ill effects of alchemy. But for whatever reason, the pegasi trusted Flora, so Kittie followed along and hoped that their faith wasn't misplaced. Emmaline trailed after the smaller woman without hesitation, though as soon as they made it to the other side of the fence, her head swiveled as she took in the sights.

"You know, it's really more of a botanical garden than an arboretum," Flora commented as they passed a stand of moonlit maples with darkened beds of flowers planted around them.

"It was just an arboretum, years ago." Kittie couldn't help but admire the pearly white flowers on a nearby magnolia tree, illuminated beneath the nearly full moon.

"Before the Salties got all grabby." Flora nodded. She paused outside what looked like a storage area. "Okay, I know you're big on following me, but I need you to wait here a moment." She opened the door and gestured to the interior of the room. Shelves lined with neat rows of vials holding liquids and jars containing powders filled the room.

Kittie nodded, summoning a tiny flame in her palm to light the area while Flora went off in search of their mysterious ally. It danced across her skin, cheerful and obedient as she read the labels on the containers.

"What are these?" Emmaline asked.

"Months, if not years, of work," Kittie murmured. She narrowed her eyes when she came to the Inkwells, organized alphabetically by surname. Her pulse sped as she brought her light closer to read the cramped script on the labels. None of them bore her husband's name, but that meant very little. The door opened, and Kittie spun, the flame flaring as she went on the defensive.

"Just me, Sparky," Flora said, holding up her hands. A curly-haired brunette loomed behind her, rubbing sleep from her eyes. The half-knocker grinned at them. "Quick introductions! This is Marian Hawthorne, Blaise's mother. Also a scary-effective alchemist. The walking fire hazard is Kittie Dewitt, Pyromancer, wife of blowhard outlaw Wildfire Jack, and an all-around badass." Kittie raised her brows, deciding to take the litany as a compliment as Flora turned to her daughter. "Emmaline Dewitt, Effigest-in-training, the daughter of the badass and the blowhard, and friend to Blaise. Are we all good?"

Kittie licked her lips, trading hesitant looks with Marian. She didn't want to trust an alchemist. They had harmed too many mages. Emmaline glanced between them, uncertain.

Flora blew out a breath. "Make nice, boss mares. The clock is ticking."

Emmaline was the one who broke the standoff. "She's Blaise's *mom*." Her voice trembled with emotion.

Marian nodded. "I am. And I'll do anything to protect him." Her eyes were haunted by old regrets that Kittie understood on a primal level, even if she didn't know exactly what they were.

Kittie cocked her head, releasing a pent-up breath. "An alchemist working with mages. Will wonders never cease?"

"Gonna be a lot of ceasing if we don't get to your manly men in time," Flora commented. "Let's go."

"Wait." Marian's command froze them in place. Kittie turned to face her slowly, ready to pull on her magic if needed. Something gleamed in the alchemist's eyes. *Tears.* "I need to do something first. I failed at it the last time I escaped from this place."

Escaped? Years ago, Kittie heard rumors of an alchemist who had escaped the Confederation. All information about the topic was quashed as quickly as it appeared. Maybe there was a grain of truth to the rumors. Marian squared her shoulders with determination, studying the contents of the nearest shelf.

The half-knocker sighed. "How long is this gonna take?"

Marian continued reading the labels, pulling a handful of tiny bottles from the shelves. "Not long. I'm just going to make sure they can't use any of my discoveries again."

That caught Kittie's attention. She stepped closer. "What do you mean by that?"

The alchemist didn't look at her. "I don't want my work to hurt anyone. I've done enough harm." Her expression was stricken. A mother would only wear an expression that wounded if she thought she had harmed her own child.

"Need a drink?" Kittie offered her flask, commiseration from one mother to another.

Marian blinked, surprised. Then she laughed. "I don't drink, but after all this I should consider it." She focused on Kittie, thoughtful. "How would you feel about turning all this to ash?" Marian made a sweeping gesture to encompass the room they were in—and presumably the entire Arboretum. She glanced at the half-knocker. "Do we have time for that?"

"I like arson as much as the next person, so I guess it depends on how fast it is." Flora considered the laden shelves around them. "But first let me gather a few—"

Marian caught her hand before she touched any of the potions on the shelves. "No. I made the mistake of not being thorough the last time I left. I won't be sloppy again. *Everything burns.*"

The half-knocker's eyes widened with understanding, and though it had to be difficult for her, she stepped away from the temptations. "Gotcha."

A thought occurred to Kittie, and she held up a hand. "Wait. Is there anything in here that *breaks* a geasa?"

Marian narrowed her eyes, crossing her arms. "None of these potions leave here."

Kittie met her eyes. "Please. The geasa has snared my husband. I know how to break it, but…" What if his handler wasn't around to be burned to a crisp? What if he was protected, and she failed to get to him? Failure had so many ways to rear its head.

The alchemist matched her stare for stare but was the first to turn away. Marian sighed, drifting across the room to scour the shelves. She picked up a vial, turning it over in her hands. "It's rare and expensive. No records exist documenting how to make it. Except here." She tapped her temple. "*I* will carry it. *I* will use it. This doesn't leave my possession."

Kittie wanted to argue, but Marian had drawn her line in the sand. She nodded. "Thank you. Now what?"

"Now," Marian said as she wrapped the precious potion in a cotton wrap, tucking it into a pouch at her belt, "we burn this place to the ground." Her tone went flat.

Kittie swallowed. She had no qualms with attacking the Confederation, not after everything the Salties had taken from her. "What about the other alchemists?"

Marian grimaced. "I may regret it later, but we should only take out anyone who tries to stop us." She stepped over to the small window, peering out into the darkness.

Kittie nodded, hiding her relief. She didn't like to use her magic to kill, but she wouldn't hesitate if it was necessary. She glanced at Emmaline. *My child, who witnessed the destruction of her town. Her home. She doesn't need to see this.* "You should go back to the pegasi."

Emmaline shook her head, adamant. "I'm staying with you." She straightened with determination. "This isn't my first fight."

Kittie wanted to argue, wanted to protect her daughter from the horrors of the world. But it was too late for that. Emmaline had as much as told her so. Sometimes it was hard to reconcile this Emmaline with Kittie's last memory of her child, little more than a wide-eyed toddler chasing butterflies. The child was gone, replaced by a woman hardened by the hand life had dealt her. Kittie inclined her head in acquiescence.

Flora nodded. "Back up isn't a bad idea. I suspect fire is going to cause a swarm of testy folks."

Kittie cracked her knuckles, striding to the door. All things considered, support was welcome. Pyromancy on this scale was a massive power drain, and it wouldn't be long before she was defenseless. She took a drink from the flask to fortify herself, capping it with a sigh. "Time to release the dragon."

CHAPTER FORTY-THREE

Welcome to the Dreamscape

Blaise

"I thought you'd never fall asleep," Jack griped as the dreamscape swirled into life.

Blaise breathed a sigh of relief as Jefferson and Jack walked toward him from different paths. The surrounding land shimmered into an endless field full of brilliant wildflowers.

"You try falling asleep when your body has been paralyzed for hours," Jefferson replied, massaging his arms, as if doing so while dreaming might help his physical body. He paused when he saw Blaise, a smile curling his lips. He quickened his pace until he was mere inches away. "There you are."

"Howdy," Blaise said, breathless, as he studied Jefferson's face. He closed his eyes for a moment, recalling the shelter of his embrace. He felt arms wrap around him, and then Jefferson's forehead gently pressed against his.

"Are you okay?" Jefferson whispered.

"I should be the one asking you that," Blaise murmured, opening his eyes. His pulse raced at the memory of Malcolm helpless, caught in the web of Jack's spell. *Jack.* He turned toward the outlaw, though he didn't shrug out of Jefferson's embrace. "What's going on?"

Jack's arms were crossed, shoulders tensed with false bravado. "We're prigged, that's what." Disappointment shone in his eyes. "If you'd come in a gods-blasted dream the other night, none of this would have happened. You bother me every other night but not the one that counts."

Jefferson coughed, releasing Blaise. "Oh. That was my fault."

Blaise shook his head. "No, it was my fault."

Jack glared at them. "I'm more than happy to blame both of you, but that won't do shit to help us. And that's what I would rather focus on."

"You're insightful when you're angry," Jefferson observed, earning another glare. He put an arm around Blaise. "And you're right. We missed the opportunity to prevent this. Now we need to figure out what to do about the situation."

Blaise studied the distant horizon—bluebonnets, primroses, and paintbrush flowers spread as far as the eye could see. It was easy to ignore reality in this idyllic dream. "Can someone update me on our situation? I don't know anything beyond when Gaitwood forced me to sleep."

The outlaw paced in a circle, trampling wildflowers beneath his boots. "I caught a look at Gregor's schedule. I think we're bound for Ganland. By train, in case you forgot that detail." When Blaise nodded, he continued, "I don't know what we can do. At least not yet. It was smart of you to send Flora to look for Em, but I don't know how they'll catch up to us in time."

"Ganland," Jefferson repeated. "With stops, it'll take us a week and a half to get there. If Flora can find Emmaline and they come after us with the pegasi, we may have a chance."

"*If* Flora can find Em," Jack pointed out.

"A lot of ifs." Blaise rubbed his chin, thinking.

"Don't doubt Flora. She'll come through. Always does." Jefferson was unshakeable in his confidence.

Something occurred to Blaise. "Jefferson, can you pull her into a dream, too?"

"Hmm." His face scrunched in thought. "If I can find her. I've never had reason to visit her dreams, so it's a bit like trying to catch a specific fish in a big pond." Jefferson rubbed his cheek. "She would be easy to locate if she were close. But I've known her for years, so perhaps she won't be as difficult to find as Jack."

"I do enjoy being difficult," Jack agreed. Blaise noticed he had relaxed a little more over the past few minutes, letting some of his agitated guard down.

Jefferson excused himself, wandering off to one side of the meadow, leaving Blaise and Jack alone. The Breaker shifted where he stood, glancing at the outlaw. "How are you holding up?"

Jack shot him a stony look. "I'm not."

Blaise rubbed the back of his neck. Guilt roiled over him, even though he wasn't responsible for Jack's predicament. "Hey, if you need someone to talk to, I'm here."

"You think I want to talk about any of this?" Jack gestured to his head, and Blaise knew he was referring to the geasa and the control it wielded over him.

"And I'd rather not talk about what I endured in the Cit. So if you ever want to not talk about it together, I'm here."

The outlaw snorted. "How can you make no sense and a great deal of sense at the same time?"

Blaise managed a small smile. He was about to reply when they heard Flora's indignant yell as she appeared in the dreamscape. The half-knocker came in on the defensive, knives out (how did she have knives?). She crouched a few yards from Jefferson, then straightened as she recognized him, regarding him with suspicion. Flora narrowed her eyes, scanning the area before turning back to Jefferson. "Is this your magic, or is my subconscious giving me a guilt trip for napping during our break?"

Jefferson chuckled. "Welcome to the dreamscape, Flora."

She put her knives away—or rather, they vanished from existence. She relaxed, giving Blaise a nod and sticking her tongue out at Jack. "Well, this is handy." Flora held out her hand, and a box of popcorn appeared. Blaise wondered how she managed that, or if Jefferson made it appear for her. Too much was happening to worry about the weird details.

"We certainly hope so," Jefferson agreed. "I heard what you were asked to do. Any luck?"

Flora grinned, gulping down a mouthful of popcorn before speaking. "Actually, yeah." She angled an index finger at Blaise. "You're cleverer than I gave you credit for, so good for you. I found Emmaline." At her declaration, Jack lifted his chin, relief flooding his face. Flora turned to focus on the outlaw. "And she was with someone else." Jack froze, his body atremble. Blaise knew who he was hoping for. "You know someone named Kittie?" Flora asked, coy.

Blaise had not expected Flora's words to drive Jack to his knees. But they did. He went down, his face slack with disbelief and eyes crimped shut. He made a sound that was half-whimper and half-sob. Blaise didn't know if he was relieved or upset. Maybe both.

The half-knocker grinned, enjoying the impact she was having. She glanced at Blaise. "And that's not all. I've got someone else with me that'll particularly interest you."

Blaise swallowed. What? "Who?" He couldn't imagine who it could be.

"Marian Hawthorne."

CHAPTER FORTY-FOUR

Meet the Parents

Malcolm

For Malcolm, it was not the luxurious train ride he was accustomed to when traveling from Izhadell to his homeland. Gregor had Jack keep him paralyzed most of the time, though he was allowed short breaks three times a day to see to his bodily needs. Each time Jack released him, Malcolm looked for some way to gain advantage of the situation, but Gregor had the outlaw in line like a well-trained hound. He always loomed nearby, a tangible menace.

Malcolm worried about Blaise as they traveled. Because of the sleep potion, he drowsed most of the time, and Gregor compelled Jack to help see to the young man's needs. But Blaise drank and ate very little, and by day Malcolm couldn't help but fret about his condition. He wasn't sure how he would have made it through the interminable days without the ability to check in with the Breaker through the dreamscape.

"I've been through worse," Blaise admitted quietly one night.

"That doesn't make it right," Malcolm responded, remembering the scarecrow of a man he'd rescued from the Cit. Blaise had only recently filled out again. Malcolm didn't know how much malnutrition a body could take.

Malcolm lost track of the days, but it didn't surprise him when the train pulled up to a station and Gregor prepared to disembark. The Doyen barked at Jack to release Malcolm, and the next thing he knew, they'd hustled him into a carriage. His legs nearly gave out from under him as he tried to negotiate the steps, and Jack growled with irritation as he thrust him onto the bench seat. Malcolm knew what was coming next. He sighed as his muscles locked up, and he lost command of his body again.

Jack brought Blaise to the carriage next, gentler, as he guided the groggy young man inside. Blaise blinked owlishly at Malcolm, struggling to stay awake, but the potion won out, and he curled up on the floor. Jack shook his head and sat down, soon followed by Gregor.

Malcolm had a thousand questions he wanted to ask the other Doyen. But they remained trapped within, locked away as he stared at Gregor's knees, which were the sum of his field of vision with his body paralyzed. Unremarkable scenery, as far as he was concerned.

Gregor said nothing as the carriage started forward. Malcolm wished he would say something. It was surprising, as he would have assumed Gregor was the gloating sort. But he seemed content knowing that *he* had won and Malcolm had lost. The Inquiries didn't matter one lick in their current situation.

If not for poor Blaise nestled on the floor, Malcolm wouldn't have been able to withstand the uncertainty. Even Jack's sullen presence, puppet that he was, helped. They were a team—a hamstrung, ineffective team, but a team nevertheless.

They traveled for another hour or two, the fabric of the seat chafing his cheek. The carriage turned down a road, and the horses slowed. Gregor's knees moved, as if he anticipated rising soon. They must be near their destination. Malcolm patiently waited. What other choice did he have?

The carriage ground to a halt. Gregor rose and exited, leaving Jack to watch them. Malcolm heard Jack shift and curse softly. The dull vibration of male voices carried through the shell of the carriage, but Malcolm couldn't identify them.

A few moments later, the door to the carriage opened. "Bring out Malcolm," Gregor ordered.

Jack obeyed without comment, releasing the spell. Malcolm gasped with relief, bracing an elbow beneath him to lurch into a sitting position. The next thing he knew, Jack clamped a hand onto his shoulder, launching him past Blaise's prone form and toward the exit. Malcolm stumbled down the stairs, falling to his knees when he reached the ground, as his legs revolted from lack of use.

"Up," Jack growled, hoisting Malcolm to his feet.

His mouth dried as he realized where he was, the discomfort all but forgotten. Horror and panic vied for his attention. Malcolm looked over his shoulder, trembling at the sight of the backward wrought-iron letters that spelled out *Wells Estate*. Ahead, the villa loomed at the end of the manicured drive, the stately columns guarding the entry covered in creeping ivy. To their right, fanciful topiaries reared up, bringing back dreadful memories. "No," he whispered, hoarse.

"Home sweet home, hmm?" Gregor asked, smirking.

That was why Gregor had been careful to withhold any information. He wanted to see Malcolm fall to pieces when faced with his past. The past he had resolved to turn his back on. And it was tempting. Nausea roiled in his stomach at the very thought that not only was *he* here, but *so was Blaise*.

"And here I assumed you wanted Blaise just so you could murder all the upper echelons of the Confederation in one go," Malcolm commented, narrowing his eyes. He wouldn't let Gregor see him wilt, not here. No, he would leave all the panic and worry for later.

Gregor scowled at him. "The *Breaker* told you, didn't he?" He realized he had admitted too much and gritted his teeth. After a beat, his lips twisted into a smile. "Never mind, that doesn't matter. That was the original goal, yes. But then you and that outlaw interfered and ruined my plan." Gregor paused, and Malcolm feared he would stop talking. He wanted to know what had motivated this change. The other Doyen shrugged. "I thought all was lost, but my dear brother's death brought me gifts I hadn't expected." He chuckled.

Nearby, Jack tensed, anger radiating from the lines of his body.

Gregor studied Malcolm. "I didn't know we were so alike. I would never have guessed that *you* would be one to use a mage."

Malcolm swallowed, lifting his chin. Gaitwood was baiting him. He pressed his lips together, refusing to react.

He waited a moment, but Gregor gave up on his bait and continued. "I'll admit, your Inquiry had me worried. But then my men delivered the outlaw to me and..." Gregor scuffed a heel against the cobblestones. "And then someone made me an offer that was hard to refuse." He glanced ahead to the house with meaning. "Let's go meet the parents, shall we?" Gregor's eyes glittered with malice, his gaze sliding back to the carriage where they'd left Blaise. "What will they think of you prigging a *sorcerer*?"

"*Do not*," Malcolm rumbled, trembling with fury, "*ever* speak of Blaise like that." As soon as he spoke, he realized he had taken the bait like a foolish pegasus colt stepping into a sugar-snare.

Gregor chuckled. "You really *are* a magelover, aren't you? I thought maybe those rumors you had Jennings's wife spread were just that. But I suppose not." He licked his lips, as if savoring a fine meal. "Undoing everything you fought for is going to be so gratifying."

And he would, Malcolm realized. He swallowed, wanting to say something else, to fight back. But there was no way he could win this, not right now.

Gregor turned to Jack. The outlaw waited nearby, his shoulders rigid. "See that the Breaker is secured, then join us inside." Jack's eyes narrowed, but he moved to obey.

There would be no help from Jack. Malcolm sighed, ducking his head as he followed Gregor up to the villa, resigned that the ghosts of his past were about to haunt his present.

By the time they reached the elegant, curved staircase leading to the entry, Malcolm's muscles were more or less compliant to his commands. At least he wouldn't stagger in front of his parents like a drunken sailor. A grey-haired butler opened the door, inclining his head to Gregor and not at all surprised to see either of them. Malcolm didn't recognize the man, but that wasn't unusual. His parents had always gone through the hired help as if they were expendable.

"Doyen Gaitwood, what a pleasure to see you again." Malcolm's father, Stafford Wells, posed in the middle of the foyer. He nodded towards the grand room behind him. "Come and be welcome."

Stafford didn't so much as acknowledge his son's presence. Malcolm had expected nothing less. Gregor gave him a meaningful look, so Malcolm turned and preceded him into the grand room, as obedient as a child. It looked much the same as he remembered, wallpapered in an awful salmon-pink floral design with matching furniture. Not for the first time, Malcolm wondered if he was adopted because there was no way he would have picked such a hideous design. He consoled himself with the knowledge that, since he had left home, the offensive area rug had been removed, exposing lovely hardwood floors.

Malcolm realized belatedly that his father was staring at him, as if aware that his son was judging his beloved decor and finding it detestable. Malcolm hoped he did.

"Have a seat," Stafford invited, speaking more to Gregor than to Malcolm.

Gregor claimed a place on the pink sofa. Malcolm glanced around before settling upon a wingback chair that gave him a little distance from his father and the Doyen. Gaitwood made himself at home, leaning forward to pick up a finger sandwich from a tray laid out before them. As hungry as Malcolm was, he would rather eat charcoal than anything from his parents' house.

Stafford and Gregor exchanged benign pleasantries, as was customary during a business transaction. Malcolm knew the song and dance. He sat and waited, stoic, and thankful that at least Gregor hadn't had Jack paralyze him again. The outlaw had joined them after presumably seeing to Blaise and now waited nearby, a silent sentinel. The hate rolling off him was almost palpable. If Jack ever slipped the chain of the geasa, Gregor was in serious trouble.

Stafford nodded to his son. "I see you brought him as we agreed. Do you still believe he can be coerced to our side?"

What? Malcolm glanced from Gregor to his father, uncertain where this was going. He wanted to speak up, but until he knew more about the game they were playing, anything he said or did could jeopardize not only himself but Blaise.

Gregor smiled. "I think with the proper persuasion, anything is possible."

Stafford's eyes shifted to Malcolm. He hadn't been beneath that gaze for years, and he had forgotten how his father assessed everyone as if he were studying a price tag. Even his own flesh and blood weren't immune to the look. "Is that so?"

"You know I will *never* support the cruelty you engage in." Malcolm met those calculating eyes, unflinching.

The way his father smiled reminded him of the alligators that called the swamps of Phinora home. "Fine words for someone who has *bound* a mage to him. But then you always were a hypocrite."

Anger surged through Malcolm again, and even his magic took notice. For a breath he thought about using it, but he didn't know what had become of Blaise. He pushed the magic back down, the thought of his father discovering it a new aspect of horror. Malcolm trembled with rage. His father laughed, sonorous and mocking.

Gregor took a sip of iced tea, for all the world looking like he was enjoying the entertainment. "You have all the coercion you need to encourage your son to work with you, Mr. Wells." He raised his glass in a salute.

Stafford raised a brow. "Do I?"

Gregor smirked. "I think he would do just about anything to keep that Breaker of his safe. Treason, for one." He spoke casually, as if they were discussing an innocuous topic like the weather. But somehow, Malcolm suspected Gregor knew just how deep in the mire he was.

Stafford studied his son, revulsion spreading across his expression. "Really, Malcolm? You could have done so much better than that. We could have paired you with a *normal* man or woman—whoever you desired." Before Malcolm could respond, his father plowed onward. "The regulations and laws that you and your Faedrans have squeaked through the Council ever since you took your seat have caused no end of problems for my bottom line. You're going to set things right and change them back."

Malcolm gaped. "But…no! There is no way I will do that. Absolutely *not*." His father referred to all the trafficking legislation he had worked on tirelessly. Malcolm knew very well the impact it had had on his family's *shipping business*. "And even if I could, the other Doyens wouldn't allow it."

"They have to be alive for that," Gregor murmured, a reminder and warning.

His father leveled a stern look at him. "You've run roughshod over the family business long enough. You're going to step back into line *or else*."

There was no need to ask what he meant. Stafford had ways of bending others to his will. And now that he knew the strings to pull for his son, Malcolm would have no choice but to dance to his tune. *But Flora is coming*. She had never failed him before, and she was bringing help. All he had to do was stall. Malcolm bowed his head. He met his father's gaze. "I understand."

———————

MALCOLM STARED AT THE CHARTREUSE CEILING OF HIS ROOM, HIS MOUTH A thin line. His parents had left it much the same as the day he had left. They had not allowed him to express his own tastes and interests in the interior, so there were no touches that made the room his. And in the current circumstances, he was fine with that. He laced his fingers over his midsection, a vain attempt to quell the sickening ache spreading through him.

To say dinner that night was awkward was an exaggeration. His mother had been there in body, but not in mind. Malcolm couldn't remember a time when she hadn't depended on drink or her favorite hallucinogenic herb to make it through the day. Once, he had felt sorry for her, knowing it was a crutch to survive married life. But she had never fought against her dependencies to rally for her children, and there came a time when Malcolm realized the nanny who raised him was the closest thing to a mother he'd ever had.

Belinda Wells hadn't acknowledged her eldest child's presence, either. But then, she didn't seem cognizant of much of anything. Not for the first time, Malcolm wondered how his father could allow his wife to just wither away beside him. Likely his father didn't care. Belinda was just another possession.

None of that had been the worst of it. No, the worst came during the humiliating dessert course, when everyone else chose from an array of fine desserts. But not Malcolm. Instead, his father rose from the table and strode to his bar, pulling out a small amber bottle. At first, Malcolm thought it might be some sort of liquor, but the savage smile his father aimed at him forced him to reconsider. Stafford pulled out a bottle of bourbon, pouring it into a glass before adding the contents of the amber bottle. He brought it over to Malcolm and set it before him on the table.

"Only time I'll ever fix you a drink."

Malcolm stared at it, fighting down panic because he knew this was not a gesture of kindness. It was one of dominance. "I'm fine, thank you."

His father took his seat and stared at him. "You'll drink every last drop. That potion costs more than the finest racing unicorn."

Malcolm stilled. *A potion?* He was so troubled by the significance of the potion, he hadn't noticed some of his father's muscle slip into the parlor. "I think not."

Stafford's visage turned stormy. "I won't have my son bound to a mage. Makes the both of you worthless."

What? Fresh fear blossomed at his father's words. He intended to break the geasa. "No!" Malcolm lunged at the glass, hoping to spill it and render it useless, but the thugs were quicker. They were on top of him in an instant, as if Stafford had warned them what to do if he refused. Malcolm thrashed against them as they hauled him down to the floor. A part of him wondered why Gregor didn't have Jack paralyze him, but that wasn't how Stafford worked. Malcolm's father preferred to dominate as physically as possible.

Malcolm panted as he struggled against them. He wasn't a brawler, but he knew where a man's tender bits were. He scored a strike against the groin of an assailant, not feeling the least pang of sympathy at the howl that followed. Then someone smashed his face against the cold wood floor, and he couldn't move. Malcolm's vision swam, and as a last-ditch effort, he tried to call on his magic. He didn't care if they discovered he was a mage. They weren't going to take Blaise away from him.

But the magic shied from him, like trying to catch an eel with his bare hands. Malcolm couldn't focus on it, not like this. He cried out as they held him down. Someone forced his mouth open. Malcolm tried to shake his head, but they braced him, so he couldn't even do that as they poured the concoction down his throat.

It burned as it went down, leaving a cloying taste like oil and copper. Malcolm nearly vomited it right back up, desperately hoping to do so. Restrained as he was, they didn't give him the option. Woozy and miserable, the thugs held him down for what felt like an eternity.

"The first part of our deal is complete," he heard Gregor say. "Is it to your satisfaction?"

The heavy sound of footfalls nearby belonged to Stafford. He peered down at Malcolm, who regarded him with bleary eyes. "I believe so. As agreed, I'll give you half of the payment now. The other half will be deposited to your account in Thorn once Malcolm has done his part on the Council."

Thorn? Gregor had accounts in the Untamed Territory? Malcolm moaned, struggling into a sitting position as his father's goons released him. "What makes you think I'd ever help you after you've done this?" It was difficult to speak. His tongue felt fuzzy and strange.

Gregor smiled. "Because you've already proven you would do anything for the Breaker."

Malcolm clambered to his feet, swaying. "Blaise won't let you get away with this."

Stafford regarded him with a stony expression. "The jeopardy is mutual, son. If he misbehaves, *you* will be the one to suffer."

"I don't think we need the geasa to control either of you." Gregor's smile was downright predatory. And blast it all, but the greasy Doyen was right.

They escorted him to his room after that, locking him inside. Now he was alone—truly alone because he didn't even have the geasa. The alchemical potion churned against his insides, and he thought he was being torn in two. He curled into a ball on the bed, eyes watering against the pain. Malcolm agonized at the knowledge of everything he had ever fought for coming undone. Including his scheme to save Blaise.

CHAPTER FORTY-FIVE

Weakness and Strength

Blaise

Blaise's head throbbed. He swiped a hand across his closed eyes, groaning as he tried to figure out where he was and what he last remembered. His mind was foggy, and as he sat up, he realized he had been lying on a dirty blanket that someone had charitably thrown on the floor beneath him. Wherever he was, it was dimly lit and surrounded by salt-iron. He felt it in his bones.

He rolled onto his back, staring at the ceiling. Something about the place tickled the recesses of his brain, though it was strange, like a memory that didn't belong to him. *Where have I seen this place before?* Blaise slowly rose into a sitting position as his eyes adjusted to the gloom. Swallowing, he recalled why it was familiar. He had seen it in Jefferson's dreamscape. It was the holding area beneath the Wells family gardens.

But was this a dream or reality? Blaise took stock of the situation. Based on the hunger gnawing at his stomach and his pounding headache, he assumed it was reality. Jefferson never allowed his dreams to harm him. If it wasn't a dream, then where was Malcolm? He was nowhere in sight.

He shut his eyes, taking a calming breath. A new prison was not something he wanted to wake up to, and it would take very little for him to give in to the depths of despair. Blaise rubbed at the long scar on the tender skin of his forearm. He didn't want to use the geasa, but he knew

Malcolm had used it before to check on him. And that wasn't an abuse. He pushed against the geasa, trying to get a sense of Malcolm's condition. Nothing was there but a yawning emptiness, like a string that had lost its kite.

Blaise trembled, hugging himself as he tried to look at the situation logically. A lot of things could cause that, probably. Maybe the salt-iron was interfering? He quickly discarded the idea since all the salt-iron in the Cit had never touched the geasa. All he knew was he was alone, afraid, and worried. None of those were good things for a Breaker. His magic rose as his anxiety grew, his palms itching as he rubbed them together. The dungeon was reinforced with salt-iron, but the Golden Citadel had been, too. Salt-iron was no match for a motivated and distressed Breaker. He got to his feet, stretching a hand toward the bars.

"I wouldn't do that if I were you." Jack stepped into the single pool of light, his tone resigned. "I got sent to babysit you in case you pulled something."

Blaise quelled his power. The outlaw was still under Gregor's thrall, but at least Blaise didn't feel alone anymore. And maybe, just maybe, Jack could provide some information. "Where's Malcolm?"

"Alive," Jack growled.

Blaise cocked his head, pursing his lips. Something had Jack's hackles raised, and it wasn't Malcolm. Maybe something related to him, though. "Are we at the Wells Estate in Ganland?"

Jack gave a curt nod. Whatever restrictions Gregor had placed on him, he could discuss this. "Yeah. How did you know that?"

"That's an explanation for later." Blaise rubbed his cheek. "Do you know what they're planning?"

The outlaw licked his lips, as if trying to figure out how much he could say. Blaise wondered if Jack had more rein now because Gregor was distracted elsewhere. "Bad business all around." He tried to say more but instead looked as if he were gagging on the words, shaking his head with frustration.

"It's okay," Blaise said softly, not wanting Jack to suffer any more than he already was. "What time is it? For that matter, what day is it?"

Jack relaxed. He pulled out his pocket watch. "I don't even know what day it is anymore. Whatever day it is, it's just after noon."

Blaise nodded in thanks. He couldn't recall the last time he had spoken to Jefferson. Certainly not since they had arrived at the Wells Estate. Why was that? He had been a constant, reassuring presence before. "Do you know why I can't feel Malcolm through the geasa? Is it the salt-iron or...something else?"

The outlaw twitched at the question, and for a moment, Blaise thought he might be unable to answer it. Then Jack tilted his head, eyes narrowed. "Not salt-iron. Only reason would be if the handler was dead, but that ain't the case." He frowned, shaking his head as if a fly were annoying him.

Blaise waited to see if Jack would finish the explanation, but he never did. The outlaw paced the length of the dungeon, then found a bucket and turned it upside down, sitting atop it, lost in whatever thoughts he was allowed. Blaise sat down on the dirty blanket, making a silent vow that if anything had happened to Malcolm, he would tear this place down brick by brick.

With only a leashed theurgist for company, the afternoon and evening lasted an eternity. Relief washed over Blaise when Jack announced it was time to get shut-eye. The blanket provided little protection from the hard ground and negligible warmth, but Blaise had grown accustomed to dozing in terrible conditions.

The dreamscape curled in around him like a cat snuggling against its master. As the grey took shape, Blaise realized two things: first, it was only him and Jefferson for the moment, and second, they were in what looked like Malcolm's home in Izhadell.

They were in the master bedroom, which was one of their last happy memories together. Jefferson sat on the edge of the bed, head down and shoulders hunched. He looked up, green eyes latching onto Blaise. Then he shoved up from the bed, crossing the room in a handful of long strides as he pulled Blaise close against him as if he would never let go. Jefferson's chin rested against Blaise's shoulder, fitting like a missing puzzle piece.

"Jefferson?" Blaise returned the embrace, needing it just as much. "What happened?"

Jefferson's heart thumped against Blaise a dozen times before he answered. "It's gone."

Swallowing, Blaise pulled back just enough to see Jefferson's face. A single tear slid down one of his cheeks, leaving behind a luminous trail. He wasn't used to seeing Jefferson fall apart. He was the sturdy one, the one who had everything figured out. Blaise licked his lips. "What's gone?" Though he had an idea. It would explain his inability to detect Malcolm through the bond. "The geasa?"

Jefferson nodded, then sagged against him, lifting a hand to scrub at one eye. "I tried to fight them, but it was too much. They overpowered me."

A jolt of protective anger shot through Blaise. "Are you hurt?"

Jefferson slipped out of the embrace, moving back to the bed and sitting down on its edge. Blaise followed, determined to stay close. "In the only way that matters. My father gave me some sort of potion that took away the geasa."

His father. Blaise had suspected something like that, based on where he had awoken. That was alarming, but something to face later. Right now, he needed to mend Jefferson however he could. He didn't know what to say. Blaise wanted the joyful, ebullient Jefferson back. How could they have gone from so happy, so victorious, to this? He put an arm around Jefferson, resting his head on his shoulder.

Jefferson glanced at him, sniffling. "I don't want to lose what we have. Our connection."

"The geasa is *not* our connection," Blaise pointed out gently. "It never was."

Jefferson sighed, scrubbing at his face with his free hand. "That may be so, but..." He trailed off, angling to face Blaise better. "You were right about me, before. I treated you like a possession. I wanted you to be mine, to belong to me." Jefferson laughed, but it was hollow and devoid of humor. "Look at me. I'm more like my father than I care to admit. I was foolish to think I could escape his influence."

"*No*," Blaise said, shaking his head, surprised at the sudden ferocity in his own voice. "If even half of what you told me about Stafford Wells is true, you're nothing like him. You *care* about people. You love me for *who* I am, and not because of *what* I am." Jefferson was staring at him now, like a man seeking rescue. "And if I'm yours, then *you* are mine. There's no geasa or power in this world that can take that away."

Blaise backed up his words with action, pulling Jefferson into a proprietary embrace. Their lips crushed together, Blaise tasting the salt of his love's tears. Jefferson shuddered against him. After a moment, the tension in his muscles ebbed at Blaise's touch.

"For someone not keen on intimacy, you certainly enjoy kissing," Jefferson remarked.

"I enjoy kissing *you*," Blaise corrected. He loosened his grip on Jefferson. "Every word I said was true."

"Thank you for that." Jefferson rubbed at the tattoo on his bicep as if it bothered him. It had faded a little, perhaps as an effect of the potion. "I forgot how much power he could wield over me. My father, I mean." He shook his head. "And now he has you, and it's all my fault."

Blaise kissed his cheek. He wished there was something he could say, but he didn't fully grasp their situation yet, aside from knowing the outlook was grim. So he took Jefferson's hand in his, because that felt right.

Jefferson glanced down at their entwined fingers. "My father plans to use us. Both of us. Not just you."

Blaise frowned. "Why would he use—oh, *Malcolm*." The Doyen. The man with political power.

"My father and Gregor are going to force me to undo everything I've ever fought for." Jefferson rubbed at the bridge of his nose.

"How?" Blaise asked. Jefferson angled his head to look at him, and Blaise suddenly knew what would force his hand. "Oh." He wasn't sure how he felt, being Jefferson's weakness. He met Jefferson's eyes. "You can't do that."

A sad smile flickered across Jefferson's lips. "I don't want to, no. But I would, for you."

Blaise shook his head. "But your legacy..." All of those innocent people who would suffer if the changes Malcolm Wells had fought for were removed. The Confederation was far from perfect, and it needed more people like Malcolm fighting for the right path.

"My legacy means *nothing* without you." Jefferson exhaled an unsteady breath. He shook his head. "Stafford Wells has never loved anyone in his life, but he knows how to use it against others. Against *me*."

Malcolm never stood a chance with a father like that. Blaise wrapped one arm around Jefferson, their shoulders bumping with the motion. "Does he know about your magic?"

Jefferson managed a wan smile. "No. That's one of the few things in our favor."

"Then we'll figure something out," Blaise said. "Have you tried contacting Flora? Is that why you didn't come to me last night?"

Jefferson grimaced, looking embarrassed. "No. I...I didn't call up any dreams last night. I was too upset." He glanced downward, swallowing hard. "And afraid."

It was difficult to imagine Jefferson afraid of anything. Blaise only thought of him as bold and charismatic. But everyone had something that would make them come undone. Blaise was going to have to pretend to be the strong one. "Even more reason you should have." He leaned over and gently kissed Jefferson, a token of affection and support.

Jefferson relaxed, sighing when they parted. "I'm sorry. It's hard to think sensibly right now. I feel like my father and Gregor have stripped me of all my authority, all I've ever worked for and earned. I'm just the child expected to grow into my father's shadow again. To become a thing I don't want to be."

"I won't allow that," Blaise replied, and it was true. He didn't like to fight. Didn't *want* to fight. But he would fight for that.

"SO THIS IS THE BREAKER?" STAFFORD WELLS PEERED AT BLAISE THROUGH the salt-iron bars as if he were assessing livestock at a sale.

And perhaps, Blaise thought with annoyance, that was how he felt. When the elder Wells had arrived in the dungeon, his silhouette lit by a lantern, Blaise mistook him for Malcolm. As he drew closer, Blaise realized his error. Stafford Wells possessed the same athletic build and chiseled face, and without a doubt, he was what Malcolm would look like in another thirty years. But there was not so much as an ember of kindness in his eyes, only cold calculation. Blaise understood why Malcolm was uncomfortable staring at that face in the mirror and preferred to be someone else.

"Yes," Gregor answered, sounding bored. Jack stood nearby, eyes downcast. Malcolm was nowhere to be seen, and if not for the dreams, Blaise would have fretted over his absence.

"Doesn't look like much," Wells observed. "I doubt this scrawny slip of a boy could break a twig in two."

Blaise's head snapped up at that. He smirked, stepping up to the bars. "Come closer and find out." At his words, Jack lifted his chin, surprise registering in his eyes. *See, Jack? I've learned a thing or two from you.*

Gregor's head whipped in Blaise's direction. "Don't make me reconsider dosing you with the sleep potion."

Blaise was tired of bullies. This place was full of them, and it was even worse with Malcolm and Jack hanging in the balance. He bit his tongue because he really wanted to invite Gregor to try that. But he would send Jack, and Blaise had no desire to fight the outlaw. Instead, he met Gregor's challenging gaze. Every impulse within tore at him, telling him to look away, but he couldn't help the thrill of satisfaction when the Doyen dropped his gaze first.

"He cracked a salt-iron-reinforced airship like an egg. Don't let his unremarkable looks fool you." Gregor's voice was sour as he turned his back on Blaise.

Stafford continued to study him, as if Blaise were a puzzle he couldn't figure out. "Normally, I would prefer to use a mage such as this. Or better still, sell to the highest bidder." He rubbed his chin as he mused.

"The more fruitful long-term option is to use Malcolm first." Gregor's greedy eyes slid to Blaise. "Once he's done his part, I'll take care of him, and you can do as you like with this one."

His words set Blaise's nerves on edge, but he remained still, listening. Malcolm's father nodded in agreement. "You're right. That is best for the bottom line. And that will give me ample time to grow interest in the purchase of a Breaker."

That was too much. Blaise crossed the cell in three quick steps, wrapping his hands around the bars, his magic boiling at their callous words. The salt-iron bit into his palms, but he didn't care. His power roared up and crackled through him, crashing against the barrier. A high-pitched, eerie squeal assaulted their ears as Breaker magic corroded the metal.

"Tabris help us!" Stafford leaped backward. Gregor, too, was shaken and stumbled away, though he recovered quickly. With resignation, Jack pulled his sixgun and stepped closer, his piercing eyes pleading for Blaise to stop.

Blaise relented, pulling his magic back as he unwrapped his hands from the bars. Metal flaked away. He dusted his hands together, not regretting his show of force.

"He *is* a monster, isn't he?" Stafford murmured, though he sounded awestruck. And greedy.

A year ago, Blaise would have shrunk back at being called a monster. But he knew now that there was strength in being misperceived. He stood his ground, unmoving, hoping that he looked intimidating and not like the frightened ball of anxiety he truly was. Stafford and Gregor considered him for another few minutes before turning to leave him alone. Night couldn't fall soon enough.

CHAPTER FORTY-SIX

Where There's Smoke, There's Fire

Malcolm

Sleep eluded Malcolm. Frustrated, he paced the length of his room, pausing with each pass before the bay window to stare out into the darkness. He wanted—no, *needed*—to sleep. He'd had no luck contacting Flora through his dreams over the past few evenings. If it was because of some failing of his magic, he didn't know. But with each passing day that he and Blaise were in his father's custody, his hopes for their escape diminished.

Blaise wouldn't speak about his conditions in their dreams, but Malcolm knew he wasn't treated well here, either. If Stafford Wells was smart—and he was when it came to dealing with the precious commodity of mages—he would keep Blaise weak and vulnerable. Minimal food and salt-iron would do it. Malcolm put his face in his hands, distraught. At least he knew they wouldn't physically harm Blaise. As long as Malcolm cooperated, anyway.

He settled onto the seat of the bay window, back against the wall and legs folded as he gazed at the twinkling stars. And that was the thing, wasn't it? For Blaise, he would absolutely walk back all the changes he had fostered in the Confederation. And they would revile him for it. If it meant that Blaise lived…well, then it would be worthwhile. He thumped his head against the wall. But what sort of life would that be for either of them?

Malcolm wished he could at least fall asleep. Maybe he could talk to Blaise more about their limited options. Or maybe Jack had information. Restlessness and worry still seized him, and he knew that his mind wouldn't rest.

He yawned, rubbing at his eyes. When his vision cleared, he thought he saw something in the distant darkness. A strange disruption in the starry sky. Malcolm squinted, not daring to hope. A multitude of large birds called this part of Ganland home. Seaside, where the Wells estate was located, was near the coast, and those faraway shapes might be herons or pelicans. Except he didn't think those birds were active at night.

On the horizon, a wing clipped the edge of the full moon, followed by an unmistakable equine shape. Malcolm whistled out a breath, blinking in surprise. *Am I really seeing that?* A pegasus. No, not just one. *Four.*

"Flora Strop, you beautiful little miscreant," Malcolm murmured to himself, hope surging.

Blaise

"Get up. Blaise, wake up."

Blaise grunted, rubbing at his bleary eyes. He had been asleep, but not in the dreamscape. *Disappointing.* He sat up on the thin blanket. Something in Jack's voice was borderline frantic, and he couldn't figure out why. "Huh?"

"Smoke. I smell smoke." The outlaw stood at the base of the staircase that led to the surface, peering up. He braced one hand against the wall, as if he wanted to go up to investigate.

Smoke? That got Blaise's attention, and he rose. There was a tremor of excitement in Jack's voice. And Blaise suspected he knew why. He knew about the type of magic wielded by Jack's wife.

"Definitely smoke," Jack whispered, shifting his weight from foot to foot. For a moment, Blaise almost forgot that the geasa bound him. Then a change flowed over him, his muscles tensing as Gregor put his call out. The outlaw growled with frustration, blue eyes wild and angry. Blaise winced in sympathy as Jack bowed his head and trod up the stairs, boot heels slapping a resentful cadence against each stone step.

"Oh good, I don't have to kill him."

Blaise jumped, heart pounding, and defensive magic crackled beneath his palms. His terror was short-lived, though, when he recognized the voice. Flora somehow stood in the cell with him, face creased with disgust. Her gaze fell on the bars he had damaged, and she walked over, poking them with a finger.

"You do that?"

"Um, yeah," Blaise answered, rubbing the back of his neck. "I wasn't expecting you. How did you even get in here?" Knockers were mystical creatures, and he was in a salt-iron cell. There was no logical explanation unless… His eyes widened.

She put a finger to her lips. "Our little secret. I mean that, got me?"

He nodded. "I understand." Gods, if anyone knew of her attunement to salt-iron, of all things…she would never be safe. Or free. Flora risked everything by coming here, and gratitude flooded through him. "I'm glad to see you."

Flora beamed. "Now that's what I like to hear. Where does that grass-bellied sidewinder have Mal?" Her visage skewed dangerously with each word, and a knife was in her hand by the end of the question.

Blaise shook his head. "I…I don't know. All I know is he's on the estate somewhere. They don't let us see each other."

"Of course not." Flora sighed. She licked her lips, eyeing the damaged salt-iron bars. "Can you get yourself out? I need to find Mal. Going to be disappointing if we come all this way for him to burn up in friendly fire."

Her words spurred his panic. "Fire? So there *is* a fire?"

Flora nodded. "Jack's wife. I swear, I think he married a blasted dragon. It's impressive." She bounced on her heels. "Anyway, are you good? Because if so, I should hop out."

Blaise swallowed, glancing at the bars of his prison. He was weary and not at his best, but there was no one else to save him unless someone nabbed the key from Stafford Wells. Blaise nodded, cracking his knuckles. "I'll be fine."

The half-knocker raised her eyebrows, detecting his uncertainty. She blew him a kiss and vanished.

Blaise closed his eyes for a moment. Help had come. His palms still stung from his display of force, but that was something that could be tended to later. He had to get out. Blaise moved over to the bars he had assaulted earlier, grimacing as his raw skin met the detestable metal. His magic roared up, defensive against his pain. He poured it into the bars, grimacing against the combination of his magic being leeched away and the force it took to shatter salt-iron.

Gods, the potion they'd given him in the Cit was awful, but the amount of sheer power it gave him would have made this child's play. He didn't have that now, but maybe he didn't need it. Blaise was the Breaker of Fort Courage. He had taken out an airship reinforced with magic and salt-iron. *I can do this.* He hunched his shoulders as the salt-iron grated away at him, hollowing him out.

The metal fractured beneath the onslaught of his magic. He heaved a ragged sigh as the two bars shattered to the point where he could kick the remnants out with his booted foot. Blaise angled his body and slipped out through the opening. He reached the other side, shutting his eyes with relief for an instant. He wasn't out of the woods yet, but now he could do his part. *I'm coming, Jefferson.*

Blaise took the stairs two at a time, though he revised that to one at a time when he stumbled and almost fell face-first. He had enough enemies without his own feet betraying him. At the top, a small landing crouched beneath the trap door that led to freedom. Blaise pushed against it, discovering that it was locked from the outside. It was going to take more than some old wood to stop him now. He rested the flat of one hand against the panel, ramming his magic into it. Wood cracked and whined as it shattered before him.

He climbed out, grime and dust clinging to his clothing. *Hard to believe I once looked presentable enough to go to the theater.* Blaise winced as a splinter bit into his arm, but that was a minor complaint. Smoke drifted across the garden, choking the air. In the moonlit haze, fire ravaged a beautiful estate home. Shouts rang out in the chaos, the silhouettes of men and women shifting like grotesque specters. A few fled, but most of them were involved in fighting the fire or—

Mages. They were fighting mages. And pegasi.

<Blaise!> A desperate voice slammed into his mind. Emrys landed in the garden, his wings clipping a pair of topiary dragons. The stallion surged over to him, his massive hooves ripping up the turf, shoving his muzzle against Blaise's chest. <Get on my back. Let's go. *Please.*>

Blaise bit his lip, glancing at the temptation of the saddle on Emrys's back. Every instinct clamored for him to climb aboard and go. Emrys's own panic and guilt at having left him behind at Fort Courage were clear in the stallion's white-rimmed eyes. Blaise wrapped his arms around Emrys's thick neck. "I can't. Not yet. I'm sorry. I have to find Jefferson."

<I understand,> Emrys said with resignation, hanging his head. <But I will not leave you.>

Blaise smiled, warmed by the pegasus's devotion. "Thanks. I—"

"Blaise!"

The unexpected voice made him freeze, and he turned slowly, not believing his own ears. He trembled as his mother strode over and swept him into a hug, alternately laughing and crying. Blaise understood since he felt the same. He had forgotten that Flora had mentioned she was coming, too. Or maybe he hadn't dared to hope. It was ridiculous and made no sense, but he couldn't help the feeling that his mother was there and everything would be okay. Because that was how Marian Hawthorne worked.

"Mom, I..." Blaise faltered. He wanted to tell her so many things, but they would have to wait. "I have to go help."

She smiled at him, pressing her forehead against his. "I know. So do I."

Emrys snorted, arching his neck. Blaise knew the stallion still wanted to whisk him away to safety. When his mother released him, he turned to the pegasus. "This isn't Fort Courage, Emrys."

"No way in Perdition," Marian agreed, surprising Blaise with the ferocity in her voice. She squared her shoulders, glancing at him. "I'm so proud of you. Of the man you've become." Marian licked her lips, as if she wanted to say more, but she shook her head and stared at the burning house.

He rubbed the back of his neck, shrugging. "Thanks." Blaise patted Emrys's shoulder. "Come on, let's see what we can do." He had a boyfriend to find.

CHAPTER FORTY-SEVEN

The Dragon

Jack

Kittie wasn't anywhere in sight, but Jack felt her presence in the marrow of his bones. How could he not, when she'd left her signature so clearly across the battlefield?

The flames that clawed at the house shifted and swelled, sometimes taking on the shape of a massive reptilian head and at others a whip-like barbed tail. Kittie had once told him that among Pyromancers, she was a dragon. As ever, Jack believed every word. His geasa-trapped heart rattled at the bars of his cage. His wife was here, and there was nothing he could do about it.

Except fight her if it came down to it.

He took a silent mental count. *Kittie, Emmaline, Marian Hawthorne, and probably Flora.* Four brave women against Gregor's minions, himself included. And some of the elder Wells' servants, he added with chagrin, as he recognized them among the armed defenders.

A fluting scream split the air, followed by the crunch of hooves colliding with an unyielding body. *And the pegasi.* Zepheus's golden form strafed overhead. The stallion circled around, coming to ground nearby. He trotted toward Jack, tail flagging like a banner, nostrils wide and questing.

Jack suspected he was trying to communicate, but the geasa allowed nothing through. The outlaw shook his head. Sometimes Zepheus was a pain in the ass, but he loved that stallion and missed his meddlesome ways.

A command seared against his brain. Jack winced, closing his eyes before snapping them open. He strode past Zepheus with determination, ignoring the stallion's querying whinny. Gregor wanted his guard dog by his side. Gunshots rang out, testament to the genuine threat. *Good*. He hoped Gregor was so scared he pissed his pants.

"Daddy!" Emmaline's voice was like a shot to the heart. He slowed. Gregor's new command bade him to fight anything that was identified as a threat. And gods, Emmaline was a threat.

She stood twenty feet away, her hair crimson in the firelight. Smoke curled from the muzzle of the sixgun in her hand, a fallen combatant groaning nearby. The girl who had run away from Fortitude was gone, replaced by a competent warrior woman. A gust of hot wind tousled her hair, her brow slanted with determination. She strode toward him, every step deliberate, her head held high.

Sweat trickled down Jack's brow. He didn't want to fight her, but if she came any closer, he would be forced to. Emmaline crossed whatever invisible threshold he had, and Jack pulled his sixgun.

His brilliant daughter, Faedra bless her, was ready. She holstered her sixgun, swapping it out for a poppet. Emmaline was nowhere near as practiced as he was, and he regretted that they hadn't added more to her repertoire. His finger caressed the trigger of his sixgun as she cast her spell. He stumbled, losing his target as his left arm pinwheeled to keep his balance.

But the geasa wouldn't let him back down, and Jack was too wily for a simple hex to undo him. He straightened, adjusting his grip as he squinted at Emmaline through the sights.

A gust of wind unbalanced him as Zepheus swooped in, the stallion skidding to a halt inches from the outlaw. The pegasus slammed his wings into Jack, long primary feathers gusting the revolver from his grip. It went spinning toward Emmaline, who lunged and snagged it from the ground before Jack could react.

The stallion backed off, folding his wings and loping away to another part of the battle where he was needed. Emmaline stared at her father, tucking his precious sixgun into the small of her back.

Jack gritted his teeth. Though she'd claimed his sixgun, it wasn't his only weapon. The geasa was out for blood, and he had a knife in his boot. His fingers twitched, and he almost reached for it. But instead, his fingers found her poppet.

Emmaline knew it on sight. "Daddy, no!"

He struggled against the geasa, mentally rifling through the catalog of spells it would allow. It was fortunate Gregor didn't know his full potential, or they would be in dire straits. Jack was capable of some spells he wasn't proud of. Breathing hard, he settled on one that was benign but would keep her out of the action.

Sorry, sweetheart. She collapsed with a gasp as he invoked the paralysis spell.

Somewhere nearby, Oberidon screamed, bolting away from his own battle to come to her aid. The spotted stallion saw him, ears pricking forward as he debated if Jack was friend or foe. His ears swept flat against his skull an instant later as he realized Jack wasn't on their side, not right now. The pegasus stood over Emmaline, stiff-legged and teeth bared, a threat to anyone who came too close. Jack backed off, able to give the stallion room since Oberidon hadn't attacked him.

At least someone would watch over Emmaline. Not for the first time, Jack hated himself. He pivoted, the geasa reminding him of the command to get to Gregor. A new voice stopped him in his tracks, his heart pounding.

"Jack Arthur Dewitt."

Kittie

THE SMOKE AND THE CRACKLING OF THE SURROUNDING BLAZE MUFFLED Kittie's voice. But it still made her husband quiver like he'd heard the primal bellow of a dragon. If she was less of a realist, she might have thought that the sound of her voice, absent from his life for so many years, was all it took to shatter the alchemy that ensnared him. His face contorted as if he were grappling against the geasa. And maybe he was. But they both knew it was a losing battle. The will of a human—even a stubborn mule of a man like Jack—was no match for alchemy.

"Jack," Kittie tried again, though this time her voice faltered. Exhaustion from keeping her flames compliant tugged at her. Charred corpses littered the ground in her wake, a testament to the amount of power she had already spent. Fire was a simple thing to call, but took an incredible amount of will to keep leashed and obedient. This inferno was no exception. Sweat trickled down the side of her face as she walked toward him.

He made a strangled sound, as if trying to warn her off. His eyes—oh, she had forgotten how beautiful his blue eyes were, like a placid lake in winter—met hers, pleading. Kittie wouldn't let him warn her away. She wasn't going to back down. Licking her lips, she cast a glance at Emmaline, torn between worry for their daughter and annoyance at her husband. He had almost shot their child, and would have, if not for Zepheus. As much as she loved Jack, Kittie hated to think of what she might have done if Jack had pulled the trigger. At least whatever spell he had cast seemed harmless. Emmaline's pegasus stood vigil over her, and Kittie was confident she could count on him.

Jack's full attention was on her. He stood so still it was almost possible to think that he was a magnificent statue, bathed in the glow of her inferno. Kittie spared a glance to ensure that her husband was her only opponent. Somewhere nearby, the little half-knocker had rejoined the battle, shrieking as she moved with frightening speed and ferocity. The grey mare was a looming shadow in the smoke, striking out with wicked hooves, battering with her wings, and harrying her attackers with snapping teeth.

Kittie knew Marian was out there somewhere, too. She had seen evidence of the alchemist's handiwork: a man with a face melted from a caustic potion, sobbing as he struggled to breathe, and a woman screaming that she couldn't *see* as she ran into the fire, clawing at her eyes. Kittie decided perhaps alchemists weren't so bad when they were on *her* side.

"Oh, Jack. I never thought I'd see you again." Kittie drew back the flames threatening the stables. She didn't know if there were animals within, but if there were, they didn't deserve a fiery tomb. Then she returned her attention to Jack, taking another step. "Emmaline told me that you never gave up. You never stopped believing that you would find me." Another step. And another.

Jack stared at her, breathing hard, as if he were in the fight of his life. Maybe he was. Kittie swallowed at the thought, her resolve flagging. Her hand found the flask at her side, and she took a quick swig to renew her courage. "It doesn't have to be like this." Kittie clipped the flask back onto her belt. "Do you want to be free?"

He couldn't speak because the dark alchemy that bound him had its hooks in too deep. But those eyes she had lost herself in before tracked her every move, and Kittie was almost certain she saw him tremble.

"Who do I have to kill to free you, Jack?" Kittie asked, raising her hands as the flames leaped skyward behind her, fanning out like wings. *Come on, Marian. Where are you?*

She took another step, and combined with her question, it set off whatever trigger he had to launch an offensive. With a roar, all recognition vanished from his eyes, replaced by the fury of a monster. He lunged forward and attacked.

CHAPTER FORTY-EIGHT
The Death of Malcolm Wells

Malcolm

Glass exploded as Malcolm slammed a ladder-back chair into the window. He tossed it aside, grabbing a throw pillow and using it to brush away shards of glass that had landed on the windowsill. The night air carried the telltale sounds of fighting and the threatening crackle of flames, accompanied by acrid smoke. He wrapped his hands around the bars on the outside of the window, rattling them. They weren't salt-iron, so didn't hurt or leech his magic, but that didn't matter a bit if he died from smoke or flame.

"Damn." The bars were secure, and he had little hope of getting them to budge. He ran a hand through his hair, laughing at the hopelessness of the situation. The Confederation feared the might of mages, and here he was—a *mage*—utterly helpless. What good was his magic?

Frustrated, he shook his head, weighing his other options. The door that led to the hallway was locked. Malcolm sized it up, wishing that his education had included helpful topics such as escaping dire circumstances. He gave it an experimental kick, driving the heel of his shoe into the unrelenting wood. The door shuddered slightly but otherwise didn't give. "Why does the theater make that look like such a good idea?"

Malcolm paced back over to the window, peering out. The pegasi were engaged in the battle below, their shadows distorted by the flames. Maybe one of them could help? He clutched the bars, watching as two of the equines coordinated their attacks. "Help! I'm up here!" In the dancing firelight, he spotted his attorney's telltale dappling. He whistled. "Seledora! Help me!"

The mare was amid her own battle with an attacker, hooves flying and teeth raking. One of her black-tipped ears flicked his way, and she squealed. Maybe she had heard him? Malcolm rubbed his face, sweat dripping down into his collar.

The door rattled, and he spun, thinking that surely rescue had come. He gasped when his father entered, a little sooty but otherwise uninjured. Stafford glanced around the room, then motioned to Malcolm. "Come on, son. We need to get out of here."

His father hadn't come to rescue him out of the kindness of his heart. No, it was all self-serving. He still saw Malcolm as the key to removing political roadblocks for his business. "I'm not going anywhere with you." Malcolm crossed his arms, taking a step back.

A scrape outside the window distracted Malcolm for an instant, but his father was speaking, and he couldn't split his attention. "Then you'll *die* here," Stafford stormed. "Set aside your foolish pride and come with me."

Foolish pride. Malcolm might be guilty of that in other areas, but not here. Not when it concerned the family business. He shook his head, backing closer to the bay window.

The jarring clang of breaking metal startled both father and son. Malcolm thought for a moment the fire had eaten away another crucial part of the home, further dooming him. But no. He turned and realized the metal bars were gone. A familiar form climbed through the wreckage, a phantom in the haze. The heavy flap of departing wings signaled the fly-by of a pegasus. Blaise yelped as a shard of glass slashed the palm of his hand.

"Blaise!" Malcolm shouted. At the same time his father cursed, taking a step back and glaring at the Breaker as if he were a fiery demon. Malcolm glanced from his boyfriend to his father, shock chilling him when he saw the gleaming pistol aimed at Blaise. "No!" Malcolm screamed, lunging at his father, but it was too late.

Someone else was faster. Stafford reeled wildly, his shot striking the ceiling. The pistol fell from his grip, dropping to the bed as he wheeled in confusion and pain. A pearl-handled knife was lodged in his back, blood already soaking his shirt. Flora stood in the doorway, panting.

"Guess you found him first," Flora said with a wave to Blaise, leaning against the threshold. "I got distracted."

Stafford groaned. "Help me, Malcolm!" He stumbled closer to the bed, shaking as he sat, spatters of blood on the floor marking his path.

"Want me to finish what I started?" Flora asked casually, pulling out her other knife. She twirled it in her hand, meaning every word. Not that Malcolm had ever doubted.

Malcolm stared at his father. Blaise came up beside him, slinging an arm around him. The Breaker held his injured hand tight against his chest, blood seeping between his fingers. The younger man stared at Stafford, swallowing.

Malcolm glanced at him, uncertain. "What should I do?" Stafford was a horrible human, but he was still Malcolm's father.

Blaise was quiet for a moment. Regret clouded his eyes. "I don't know what to tell you. I prefer not to hurt anyone, but he had no issues with hurting me. Or you." His eyes turned stony at that. "He signed off your death. After you changed whatever laws they needed, the plan was to kill you and sell me."

Flora's grip tightened on her knife. "Mal?" She had no qualms with this brand of justice.

Malcolm swallowed. He knew his father was callous, but this…this was unbelievable. Or was it? He shook his head. No, he had known the depths of his family's depravity from the day they had sold his sister. His father would never change. Greed and the hunger for power burned brighter in his heart than anything else, including love. Flora shifted her weight, waiting for the verdict.

He crossed the room to where his dirty, discarded greatcoat was folded atop the dresser. He picked it up and removed the lapel pin that represented his status as Doyen. Malcolm dropped the pin on the bed beside his father, who gave a damp cough as his son drew near. He met his father's eyes. "The Wells legacy dies today."

"You can't be serious," his father rasped.

"I am. I no longer wish to be a part of this family. Goodbye, Father." Malcolm fumbled in his pocket as he turned to face Blaise.

The younger mage peered at him with concern. "What do you mean?"

"Traitor to your bloodline!" Stafford roared.

Somehow, the old man had steadied enough to pick up the pistol from the bed. Malcolm had missed it, consumed with other worries. Blaise tugged him close as the weapon discharged. The Breaker grunted and rocked on his feet, and Malcolm panicked. "No, no, *no!*" He pulled Blaise aside as another gun boomed, punctuated by a soft cry from Stafford.

Malcolm sat Blaise on the bench of the bay window and glanced over his shoulder. His mother stood in the doorway, her arm braced against the frame. A tiny pistol was in her hand, and she cackled as she brandished it before dropping it to the floor. Flora scooped it up and took a dozen cautious steps backward.

"*Worthless bastard,*" Belinda spat, the pupils of her eyes dilated as she stared at her dying husband. Her gaze drifted to Malcolm. "My son. I'm sorry. So sorry. Couldn't protect you until now." She blinked, and her moment of lucidity vanished. Belinda stared at him as if he were a stranger before wandering into the smoke-filled corridor, muttering to herself.

Blaise sagged against Malcolm, returning him to the reality of what had just happened. "Oh gods, are you hurt?"

The Breaker shook his head, though he trembled. "No."

Malcolm stared down at a smear of red on his sleeve, pursing his lips at a matching drip from Blaise's hand. "What do you *mean, no?* You're bleeding!"

"Oh. I guess I'm hurt, but I wasn't *shot,* which is a noteworthy difference." Blaise gingerly lifted his hand, blood welling from a jagged slash across his palm. "I haven't had much luck with stairs or windows tonight."

Malcolm allowed himself a near-hysterical laugh. "I don't know how you weren't shot. Fortunes of Tabris." *My father was going to shoot me. He almost did. And he almost killed Blaise.*

Blaise licked his lips. "I thought he was going to kill you. I didn't know if it would work, but I had to try."

Malcolm blinked, almost afraid to find out what he meant. "What did you do?"

They both made it a point not to look at the gasping, dying man on the bed. Blaise pointed at something that looked like metal shavings littering the floor, along with a worrying amount of the young man's blood. "Um, I did that."

Blaise had shattered a *bullet.* Malcolm didn't even know that was possible. Didn't care. They could worry about the implications later. "Thank you."

Flora poked at the ruined shrapnel with the toe of her boot. "You stopped a *bullet.*"

Blaise shrugged, bowing his head and curling his injured hand against his chest.

"You. Stopped. A. Bullet," Flora repeated, her eyes wide.

Malcolm clapped Blaise on the shoulder, deciding to change the topic. He took a shaky breath. "Malcolm Wells dies today."

Flora had moved to use a blanket to clean her gore-covered blade, and she froze, scowling. "Come again?"

Blaise stared at him, swallowing. "What do you mean?"

Malcolm revealed the cabochon ring he held in the palm of his hand. "The masquerade is over." He slipped it onto his finger, the magic settling over him like a mantle as his features shifted.

Blaise's brows rose with understanding. He nodded. "What about your mother? Should we go after her?"

Flora waved a hand before Jefferson could even consider answering. "Parts of the house are starting to fall in. Too dangerous. As far as I'm concerned, she made amends for her wrongs and can go to Perdition in peace now."

Jefferson sighed. It was harsh, but Flora was right. He nodded, but still felt the yawning pit of emptiness within. It was heart-rending that his mother hadn't stepped up for him until the end. "We should get out while we can." He paused, alarmed by the amount of blood seeping into Blaise's shirt from his hand. "We need to do something about that."

The young mage shook his head. "After we get out of here." He jerked his chin to the open window. "Come on. Emrys and Seledora are on standby."

Jefferson turned to Flora, trying to keep his father's body—no, *Malcolm's* father's body—out of his field of view. "Can you get out safely?"

"I'm dandy. You're the one I'm worried about." She gave an ironic salute, then stuck her tongue out at Stafford's corpse.

Blaise had already moved over to the window, whistling for Emrys. Jefferson came up behind him, peering over his shoulder. "Wait. Is that Jack?" A shadowy figure faced off against a woman and a pegasus, the trio wreathed by flames.

"Yeah," Blaise rubbed at his forehead, smearing blood and soot across it. "I need to get down there."

Jefferson put a hand on his shoulder. "I would expect nothing less."

CHAPTER FORTY-NINE
Fury of the Ghost Riders

Jack

Jack decided that a quick death was too much of a mercy, *too kind*, for Gregor Gaitwood.

The cowardly Doyen had called off his summons, instead making the deliberate choice to engage the outlaw in a pitched battle so he could make his escape. Jack found himself fighting against his long-lost wife and his pegasus, internally cursing Gaitwood with every passing moment. The utter loss of free will was bad enough, but as he fought them, he was little more than a spectator within his own body. He couldn't stop it. He was glad that Zepheus had disarmed him earlier—otherwise he would have already taken them down, and he couldn't have lived with that.

All he had was a knife, his brawling skills, and magic. Against most other opponents, he would still have the upper hand. But Zepheus knew him well, and the stallion was as much a fighter as his rider. And Kittie… well, he knew immediately that she had lost her fighting trim, and maybe she was a little drunk. But she was a Pyromancer, and until the flames died, she was a threat. Fire was a merciless destroyer. There was a reason most sensible creatures fled before its fury.

He assessed the situation, calculating. The charred corpses gave him a solid idea of the amount of raw magic she had expended to control the burn. Her attention was split between fending off Jack and watching for any new attackers so that she and Zepheus weren't caught unawares. Kittie was flagging, between the enormous amount of power and her careful sallies against Jack. She hadn't come to kill him.

But Jack, with the geasa in command, had no such compunctions.

She danced through the flames, deceptively light-footed as she hid the drag of her magic. Jack was thankful he didn't have a poppet to represent Kittie with him. His primary was tucked away safely at home in the Gutter. As it was, he had to use his magic in a more general way, which made her more challenging to target. And Gregor didn't know shit about Effigests to coerce him to use the magic properly.

Something about the way Kittie and Zepheus coordinated their attacks made Jack suspect they were herding him somewhere. He didn't know where—or care, for that matter. That meant they had a plan, which meant there was hope. He knew hope was as fragile as a dandelion, blown away by the slightest breeze. Jack couldn't help it. He clung to the glimmer of hope because it was all he had left. It was a buffer against the horror of the things the geasa was making him do.

Jack lunged at Kittie when he saw an opening. A corona of flame surrounded her, but the geasa forced him to ignore it as he wrapped his hands around her neck, crashing down to the ground with her. Kittie kicked him in the groin—and oh gods, but that *hurt*, and he wanted to curl up into a ball, but the damned geasa wouldn't allow it, overriding the pain with the drive to kill. Kittie's flames extinguished with a surprised hiss as he tightened his grip.

His world exploded into blinding stars. Jack tumbled away from Kittie, his fingers scrabbling for purchase and only finding empty air. The air whooshed out of his lungs as he hit the ground, and his right arm and shoulder screamed with pain. He caught a glimpse of gold. Damn, Zepheus had kicked him. Jack staggered to his feet, even though his body was ready to give in. The geasa wouldn't stop until he was dead...or they were. He charged.

Something—no, someone—smashed into him from the side, sending him spinning off his path and down to the ground again. Jack snarled as his attacker's hands fumbled against his upper arms, outstretched fingers clawing at his sleeve. He spun, catching the other person in the stomach with a brutal kick, sending him hurtling. A distant part of him realized it was Blaise. He had just kicked away his best chance at breaking the geasa. *Damn it.*

More reinforcements had arrived. Two newcomers dogpiled onto him, flattening him to the ground as they pinned his upper body and legs. Pink hair gleamed in the eerie light. Flora. Jack writhed beneath them, howling as someone rammed something between his lips. His teeth clanked against the glass lip of a bottle, and an oily liquid dribbled into his mouth. Jack tried to turn his head, but they wouldn't let him. He swallowed the concoction down, gagging at the sensation of it oozing down his throat like a slug.

The potion hit his stomach with a twisting, stabbing sensation. Jack gasped as something within him seemed to loosen and snap, like a chain breaking. No, like a *geasa* breaking. Jack's heart pounded as the fetters fell away from his mind. His eyes widened as he searched for any lingering remnants of his leash. It was gone. He was alone with his own thoughts and drives again.

Well, not really alone. Jefferson sat on his chest, breathing hard as he glared down at the prone outlaw. Flora had her long arms wrapped around his legs.

"Get off me before I punch you in the face," Jack growled at Jefferson.

"You're sounding more like your charming self," Jefferson remarked, though he didn't budge. He shifted his gaze, concern etched on his face. "Blaise, are you okay?"

A short distance away, the Breaker pulled himself into a sitting position, clutching at his midsection. In the firelight, his face was pale. "Great. Never better." He shook his head. "I didn't get to break the geasa, though."

There had been a time when Jack would have enjoyed kicking the young man, but that time had passed. Now he just felt bad about it. Blaise had been trying to help him, and Jack had kicked him in the stomach for his troubles.

"It doesn't matter because I did." Marian Hawthorne strode over to her son, kneeling beside him to check his injuries. She licked her thumb and rubbed a smudge of soot from his cheek before glancing back at Jack. "It should have worked." The alchemist pulled something out of her hip bag, gently taking her son's hand and sprinkling a powder onto his bloody palm.

"It did," Jack agreed, staring at the smoke wafting overhead as his actions during the battle caught up with him. He needed to get up, to break Emmaline free of the paralysis. And Kittie...gods, he had fought her. Something he never wanted to do. "*Get off.*"

<He's free. I can speak to him again.> Zepheus's voice was a welcome addition after so long. Jefferson gave Jack a dubious look but climbed off. Flora followed suit, eyes twinkling with mischief.

"Not a *word*," Jack warned the half-knocker, though doing so only made her giggle.

His body hurt in places he didn't know could hurt. Jack cataloged his injuries to make sure it was safe to move. His shoulder and upper arm were going to be one massive bruise, but Zepheus hadn't broken anything. One of his hands was blackened, but he thought it was more from soot than a burn. Or so he hoped. Jack didn't feel fully connected to his body. He was bleeding in several places, and his head felt like it was wrapped in cotton, but he was alive. It was more than he had expected.

With a ragged sigh, he pulled out Emmaline's poppet and dropped the paralysis hex. Jack didn't look at Kittie. He couldn't. She had seen the monster he was, and there was no coming back from that. Tears prickled the corners of his eyes as Emmaline rose and dusted herself off, grimacing.

"I'm sorry," Jack muttered to her, eyes downcast. He had almost shot her. *Gods, I almost killed my daughter. And my wife.* He shook his head.

"Daddy." Emmaline's voice was soft, and she came closer, taking his hand. She shifted her position until he couldn't avoid looking at her. "I know that wasn't you. All you ever wanted is to protect me because you're like a dragon with a hoard." He swallowed at her words, nodding. His daughter opened her palm, revealing a poppet. "But you can make it up to me by teaching me that hex."

He blinked, relief washing over him at her forgiveness. "I will."

She smiled. "Now there's somebody you need to see. She came a long way for this." Emmaline turned, looking expectantly at her mother.

Jack followed her gaze. Kittie stood a dozen paces away, bleeding from a few gashes and scrapes she had picked up during all the fighting and rubbing at the red lines on her throat. Soot smeared her right cheek, and her brown hair hung in bedraggled hanks as the inferno calmed behind her. She was the most glorious and welcome sight he had ever beheld. Jack strode over to her before he even realized he was in motion, a moth to her flame.

His mouth went dry as he stared into her eyes, all the things he longed to tell her dying on his lips. But his lost words didn't matter as her face drew close to his and their lips met, seeking and exploring.

Kittie smelled of hickory smoke, a scent that clung to her even when her magic was quiet. It was part of her and gods, how he had missed it. He melted against his wife, pulling her close. She burned against him with the fire of her love and forgiveness. It made him temporarily forget about all his new aches and pains.

"So you want me to kill Doyen Sleazypants while you make out or what?" Flora asked from somewhere nearby, interrupting an otherwise legendary kiss. She held a mage-light in her hands that bathed the area with its glow now that the fire had died.

Jack pulled away from Kittie with regret, glancing over his sore shoulder. Emmaline stood nearby, her smile grim. Blaise and Jefferson were watching as well, supporting each other. As were four pegasi. Jack had forgotten they might have an audience. And did he care? Not really. He was going to savor this moment, though the half-knocker was right. They had unfinished business.

"He's mine." It was Jefferson who spoke, his tone brooking no arguments.

The outlaw wanted to ask what business the entrepreneur had, but the answer was in his eyes. Deep-seated anger burned in their depths, a fury that demanded justice. Jack almost felt sorry for Gaitwood because he suspected Jefferson didn't deal in merciful death.

"I'll stand in your place, if you need," Jack offered. He could make the Doyen suffer, too.

Jefferson blew out an angry breath. "He has done nothing but turn the lives of those I care about into a living nightmare. I intend to do the same to him." His shoulders tensed, and even Blaise looked at him with uncertainty.

Could he do that? Jack wondered if it was just righteous bluster. But he didn't know the full capabilities of the man's magic. And honestly, it was a little disturbing if that was the case. And fitting. Jack nodded, pulling out a poppet. It had taken some doing, but he had snagged a napkin Gregor used once and incorporated it into a doll. He whistled to get Emmaline's attention and then tossed it to her. "Hunt him down."

She blinked at the tiny form, then nodded. Emmaline leaned over the doll, whispering words of power to activate it. A moment later, she narrowed her eyes, pointing to the northwest. "That way." Oberidon trotted over to her, snorting.

<We will join the hunt. He can't be far,> Zepheus announced, rearing and pawing at the air. Emrys and Seledora snapped to attention, nostrils dilated and muscles quivering. The palomino whinnied a challenge.

The grey mare trotted over to Jefferson, prancing in place. She must have said something to him because a moment later, he climbed into the saddle.

Blaise limped over to Emrys, tender from Jack's kick. It took him longer to get into the saddle, but when he finally settled, he pinned Jefferson with an insistent look. "Not letting you go without me."

Zepheus's haunting cry split the air as he bolted into the starlit sky. In a flurry of wings, the other pegasi took to the air, the moonlight reflecting off their glossy feathers and sweaty coats. Jack smiled, savage. Surely Gregor had never imagined that his foolishness would end with him being hunted down by a herd of bloodthirsty pegasi, an enraged dandy, a liberated Breaker, and a teenage Effigest.

Jack turned back to Kittie, satisfied that Gregor was going to be taken care of. "Wanna go for a walk in the moonlight?"

She choked out a ragged laugh, glancing behind her at the smoldering estate. "Is that what you call fleeing this?"

"I was trying to be romantic." Jack attempted a charming smile, though he supposed it was probably ghastly, covered as he was in soot and blood, stinking of sweat and death.

"I didn't know you did romantic. I thought you only did surly or arrogant and there weren't other options," Flora commented from nearby, watching them with intense interest. Marian stood beside the diminutive woman, looking weary but amused.

Kittie looped her arm through his, ignoring their audience and mindful of his injuries. "I would love to go for a moonlit walk with you."

Jefferson

CHILDREN THROUGHOUT IPHYRIA GREW UP HEARING STORIES OF THE GHOST Riders. Legend had it that the revenants and their dragon-winged equines served the goddess Nexarae, rounding up the souls of the guilty and dragging them to Perdition to face justice.

As Seledora flitted through the star-dappled sky in Oberidon's wake, the pegasi trumpeting their fury with every wingbeat, Jefferson fancied their group looked like the living equivalent. He hoped so. He wanted Gregor to know fear when they descended upon him.

Jefferson tightened his grip on Seledora as the mare changed course to follow the spotted pegasus. Who was he to have these savage thoughts? A quick glance at Blaise, off to his right on Emrys, was the only reminder he needed. Jefferson wasn't doing this out of vengeance, even if it felt like it. No, he was doing it out of the need to protect those he cared about. Blaise, most definitely. But he was just the tip of the iceberg. If Gregor remained unchecked, he would do more damage to the vulnerable. And Malcolm Wells was no longer around to block him.

Emmaline shouted something, but her words were lost to the wind. <We are close,> Seledora informed him, descending. Her ears were flat against her head, and the tight bow of her neck radiated anger.

The first grey rays of dawn tempered the sky at their backs as the pegasi crashed through the underbrush, squealing challenges. Sleepy birds and a family of deer fled before them. Jefferson peered straight through the arc of Seledora's ears, though in the dim light he couldn't see as well as their mounts. Emrys plowed along beside the mare, Blaise's face unreadable in the grey light.

Zepheus and Oberidon broke off to either side. <He is near,> Seledora reported, and Jefferson wondered at the bloodthirsty note in her mental voice. The mare might be for law and order in her profession by day, but now that was not on her mind. She was as furious as the stallions. A distant part of Jefferson knew that might be a problem for her later, if anyone could prove she was complicit.

"*No.* No, no! Get back!"

A dozen yards away, a beautyberry shrub thrashed as Gregor bolted around it. Zepheus and Oberidon slipped around behind him, cutting off his only escape route. Gregor stood in the ring of irate pegasi, his hands up as he frantically searched for a way out. Emrys mantled his wings in a threat, the ground quaking beneath the force of his great hooves. Zepheus half-reared, forelegs slashing the air.

Gaitwood swallowed, turning in a slow circle as the sunlight broke through the clearing. He realized the pegasi had riders, and his face slackened with relief, especially when he saw Jefferson. "Mr. Cole, thank Garus you're here! Please, tell the mages to call off their monsters."

"I only see one monster here," Jefferson replied from his seat on Seledora's back.

Blaise remained on Emrys, face impassive, though his stallion snorted at Gregor's insult. Jefferson dismounted, his hands behind his back as he approached the Doyen. He made a show of smoothing his bedraggled greatcoat. He canted his head, regarding Gaitwood coolly. Jefferson smiled as Gregor took in the state of his clothing, connecting that it was the same as Malcolm Wells had worn.

"What…? I don't understand…" Gregor sputtered.

Jefferson studied him. "There's nothing to understand. By all rights, this should be your end." Hooves drummed behind him, and Seledora snaked her neck for emphasis. "But that would be too simple. Too merciful after what you put us through. After what you did to *him.*" His voice shook with emotion as he glanced back at Blaise.

Gregor shrank back. "I'll give you whatever you want, Cole. *Anything.* Name it, and it's yours."

Jefferson's green eyes glinted with barely suppressed anger. He shook his head. "You can't give me anything I want." Trembling, he balled his fists at his side. Boots crunched through dry leaves and grass, and a hand rested on his shoulder. Blaise arrived to steady him.

Another pair of boots hit the ground. Emmaline, dismounting from Oberidon. Jefferson glanced back and saw her crouching low, rubbing the poppet's legs into the dirt. "He ain't gonna move till I let him. Do what you need."

"What? No!" Gregor protested, struggling where he stood. He tugged his right leg, but his foot refused to budge from the ground. With a cry, he sat down, trying to pull off his shoes. "Wicked sorcery! To Perdition with you, b—"

Blaise closed the distance to him so quickly, Jefferson hadn't registered he was in motion. He held his hands up, palms aglow with magic the color of moonlight. "Not another word." His shoulders squared, chin tucked. The Breaker had reached the limit of his tolerance.

Jefferson stepped beside Blaise, and the young man relaxed. Gregor was fortunate that even when angry, Blaise had incredible restraint. But he might wish otherwise once Jefferson was done with him. The trapped Doyen stared at him as he found a clear place to sit down, crossing his legs.

"What are you doing?" Gregor asked.

Rather than answer, Jefferson shook his head. Gregor would find out soon enough. Blaise sat down beside him, and even Emmaline moved to join their small group, lending her own assurance.

Jefferson closed his eyes, drawing in a deep breath. He needed to find a place of calm to control his magic, and his previous failures daunted him. A warm hand found his, and he smiled. And then, to his surprise, he felt magic surge from Blaise and into himself, granting him a wealth of power. It wasn't the wild, painful torrent Malcolm had helped Blaise ease from the alchemical potion. This was a gentle lending of strength. The geasa was gone, but Blaise was right. They didn't need it.

"Do what you need to do," Blaise murmured, though the Breaker didn't know Jefferson's intentions. But he believed in him, nevertheless.

Jefferson squeezed his hand in gratitude, calling up his Dreamer magic. Gregor had made Blaise's life a nightmare. It was time to return the favor.

CHAPTER FIFTY

New Beginnings

Jack

Jack closed his eyes, savoring the warmth of Kittie's body tucked against his. It had been so long since he'd shared a bed with anyone; he had forgotten how comforting it was. How it made him feel human and wanted. He wouldn't admit it to anyone—aside from maybe Kittie if she asked—but that was something he sorely needed after his time in Gaitwood's thrall.

It had been a rough few days since the Wells estate had gone up in flames, and Cole had left Gaitwood a gibbering shell of a man, tortured by nightmares. A little concerning to know the Dreamer was capable of that, but he had been utterly drained after the effort and good for little else besides using his name and connections to smooth things over when local officials became involved. He had the connections to bring in a Healer to tend to the worst of Jack's wounds. He was still bruised and sore, but he could work with that.

Before long, their dogged little group made their way to the entrepreneur's home outside the Gannish capital to recover and assess their options. Jack especially enjoyed it because, at long last, he had his wife all to himself, with no prying eyes or listening ears.

Kittie shifted beside him, rolling onto her back. Something made sleep elude her, and he knew it wasn't guilt for the lives she had snuffed out with her gift of flame. She could be as fierce and merciless as he. With a soft exhalation, she turned to face him.

"What is it?" Jack murmured, stroking her lustrous chestnut hair.

Kittie propped herself up on one elbow, hazel eyes searching his. She traced a hand over his bare chest, caressing the scar of the wound that had almost claimed his life the previous year. "You waited for me all those years. But I didn't wait for you."

Her voice was ripe with guilt, and it sent a shiver down his spine. This was something he had feared; he had been out of her life for so long, it was reasonable for her to move on. Even if he couldn't. He knew the basics of her life after the Confederation had stolen her away—those had been things they could discuss openly as they traveled. But this was more private. Personal.

"Do you love him?" Jack asked, his voice a growl. He couldn't help it. This was his wife, the woman he had relentlessly searched for.

Kittie frowned at the question, as if it were the most ridiculous thing she had ever heard. "No. I said I didn't wait for you. That doesn't mean I loved someone else. There's a difference."

The outlaw held his peace because he didn't know what to say to that. In his mind, love and intimacy were as tightly bound as a vine climbing around a tree. And he feared that if he said the wrong thing, he would lose her forever. After all he had endured, that would unmake him. So rather than trust his words, he curled her closer against him, her hand hovering over his beating heart.

"I thought you were dead," Kittie continued when she realized he was holding his silence. "You and Em both. I...I was in a bad spot when I escaped from the Cit."

"I was in a piss-poor spot when I got back and found you taken," Jack whispered, trailing kisses along her shoulder. He didn't know where the information she was laying out would lead them, so he made the most of the opportunity.

Kittie sighed softly and shivered at the gentle brush of his lips. "I found a lover and I was fool enough to marry him, but that's all it was. I was hurting and needed comfort." She shook her head. "He was an asshole."

Jack raised a brow. "How fortunate that I'm not." Kittie snorted in derision. They both knew that was a lie. He chuckled; he couldn't help it.

"You're a lot of things," Kittie pointed out after a moment. "Look at you. You made something of yourself. All I did was tuck my tail and run to the first safe harbor I could find."

He couldn't blame her for that, not really. All he had to do was think about the Golden Citadel...Jack suppressed a shiver, deciding to keep the conversation light. He gave a lazy shrug. "Won't deny it. You *are* fadoo-dling the Scourge of the Untamed Territory, after all."

"Jackass," Kittie muttered at him, but it pleased him that his flippancy distracted her. "Here I am trying to be serious, and you're showing off your big ego."

He propped his head up with one hand. "That's not the only big thing I'm showing off." He added a leer for good measure.

Kittie smacked him on the shoulder with her fist, annoyed. Jack winced when she found the remnants of the deep bruise Zepheus's hooves had inflicted. He didn't mind, though. Not really. This banter was gloriously like old times. It was *right*. He wanted this back.

"I hate you sometimes," she growled.

"No, you don't."

Kittie surged against him, pinning him down so she was on top with her hands to either side of his head. He grinned up at her. She made a frustrated sound.

"I'll behave," Jack drawled, though he hoped she kept her current vantage point. She disappointed him by drawing back to a sitting position, arms crossed.

"I'm trying to tell you I'm not proud of what I became." She blew a tendril of hair away from her face. "I started drinking and...I felt so empty. Why have all this magic if it's worthless to protect the people I love?" Kittie shook her head, a single tear trailing down her cheek. He reached out and brushed it away. "I was desperate for something to fill that void, and I found someone."

He fiddled with the edge of the sheet, thoughtful. Was it so different from the approach he had taken? Jack had filled the hole in his heart in other ways. Searching for her. Picking fights. He nodded. "You sure you don't love him?"

The face she made was all the answer he needed. "Gods, no. He really *was* a piss goblin. Ended things with him as soon as I could."

"Good," Jack murmured, pulling her close again. "Means I don't have to hunt him down." He paused, mischief in his eyes. "Though if you have any of his personal effects and want me to work my particular brand of magic..."

Kittie snorted. "Hugh's an ass, but I think he's below the notice of the Scourge of the Untamed Territory." Her nails rasped against his skin as she ran a hand up his arm. "Besides, Emmaline terrorized him enough."

Jack nestled into the pillow, pleased. "Did she now? That's music to my ears. I reckon this means you might come back to the Gutter with me?" He hoped he kept the raw need out of his voice. But even if he failed, it didn't matter. He needed her, and that's all there was to it.

Kittie beamed at him, and it was like the sun had come out after a never-ending winter. He basked in the glow. "I was going to, whether you asked or not, Wildfire Jack Dewitt. A herd of pegasi couldn't keep me away."

Jack's pulse raced, and he feared his heart might explode like a misfiring sixgun. He pulled her close, and their lips met. Unbound joy poured through Jack—he couldn't recall the last time he had felt like this.

Their kiss began tame, like a candle, but in moments it scorched them both, spreading like an inferno. His fingers curled against her soft skin, exploring her with wild abandon. She was his, and he was hers. It reminded him of their first night together, only better. Now they were firmly rooted in one another. More mature. More grateful for the gift of each other.

After another interlude of exploration, Kittie snuggled up against him. "Wildfire Jack, hmm?"

"Huh?" he murmured, drowsy and sated.

She poked his chest. "Your outlaw name. You picked it because of me, didn't you?"

Oh, that. He rolled onto his side. "Sounds tough. Impressive. Like someone you don't wanna mess with." Jack flopped onto his back again. "Wildfire Jack."

Predictably, she saw through his dragonshit. "It sounds to me like a man who was pining for his flame-calling wife."

"Does it?" he asked with a wink. "Guess the world will never know."

Jefferson

It wasn't a simple task to find Jack on his own, but Jefferson was no stranger to getting someone alone so he could discuss delicate political dealings. All it took was a word to Flora, and she was on the job. His only regret was that he had to make up an excuse to keep Blaise away. That didn't sit well with him. Once he had more of the details worked out, he would go over them with Blaise. No sense in getting his hopes up.

The echo of boots on Eskelan tile announced the outlaw's arrival. Jefferson leaned against the balustrade of his veranda, smiling a greeting.

"Should have known it was you," Jack commented, though he said it with no real rancor. His wife's presence was reformative for him. He had lost some of the jagged edges that defined him, though Jefferson suspected if he said as much, the outlaw wouldn't appreciate it.

"I know I'm not your favorite person, but there's something I wanted to discuss without distraction." Jefferson pulled back from the edge of the veranda, crossing to a grouping of wicker furniture. He gestured to one of the chairs as he sat, and the outlaw followed him over. "I've been thinking about the Gutter."

Jack stiffened at his words. "What about it?"

Jefferson watched him for a moment, wondering what had set him off. "That's where Blaise wants to go," he explained after a beat, to which Jack nodded. "But it's already proven to be vulnerable to the Confederation."

The outlaw's expression turned stormy, and Jefferson regretted his phrasing. "Only *vulnerable* because—"

He held up a hand to quell the outburst. "Hold on, I apologize. But you know what I mean." Jack's frosty eyes met his, though that was the only agreement Jefferson received. "The Gutter is vulnerable because it's wild land, belonging to no one."

Jack's hackles were up. "What are you playing at?"

Jefferson was walking on eggshells, and he hoped the outlaw didn't take his next words poorly. He suspected Jack still had a poppet of him and could make his life miserable. "What I'm trying to say is that the Gutter should be its own nation."

The outlaw's jaw dropped, but he snapped it shut an instant later. His eyes narrowed, cynical. "What is this, a ploy so we'll join the Confederation?"

Jefferson almost laughed. That was…ridiculous. He shook his head. "Have you forgotten what I *am* now?"

Jack studied him. "No, I haven't, *Dreamer*." Somehow he made it both an insult and an honorific.

The wicker furniture creaked as Jefferson leaned forward. "Look, all it takes is a single established nation to recognize it. Well, that and all the other trappings of a new nation, but we can work that out."

"No nation in the Confederation is going to recognize the Gutter," Jack said, crossing his arms.

"Ganland might," Jefferson persisted, ignoring the dubious shake of the outlaw's head. "I promise you, it's true. I may not be Malcolm Wells anymore, but Jefferson Cole has just as many connections." He smiled as Jack's brows raised in tentative interest. "I only need the go-ahead to approach the Gannish leadership about it."

Jack rose from his chair, striding over to the edge of the veranda and staring out at the distant Gulf of Stars. Gulls called overhead, riding on the sea breeze. "What's in it for us?"

That was the opening he'd hoped for. Jefferson seized it. "Trade. Mutual protection."

The outlaw snorted. "I see why Ganland would have an interest in trade. Mutual protection, though?"

Jefferson crooked a finger. "Don't think of the Gutter as it is now. Think of it as it *will be*." He grinned. "A nation of free mages."

Jack shot him a sharp look, and Jefferson knew the idea had hooked him. "Like Ravance." The outlaw ran his hands over the balustrade, thoughtful. "You realize I'm only a single Ringleader of Fortitude. I can't speak for the entire Gutter."

"I'm aware, and I don't expect you to. But the spark of a fire has to start somewhere." The outlaw's eyes cut to him at the metaphor, and Jefferson smiled. "Talk to the other Ringleaders, see what they think. If you can, send a query to Asylum. I can test the waters of Rainbow Flat."

Jack canted his head, eyes narrowed. "You're thinking to claim that much land?"

"*I'm* not claiming anything. This is for..." Jefferson hesitated. He wanted to say *us*, but Jack would argue the point that Jefferson wasn't an outlaw. Not yet, anyway. "This is for people like Blaise and Emmaline."

Jack studied him, then gave a curt nod as he accepted the answer. "We were planning to head out to the Gutter soon, anyhow. I'll broach the topic with the others when I arrive and have Hank deliver our response." He paused, angling a shrewd look at Jefferson. "What's in it for *you?*"

He frowned. "Does it have to be self-serving?"

To his annoyance, the outlaw smirked. "With you, it normally is."

Jefferson tilted his head. He couldn't argue. On the surface, it was mostly true. "I admit, it hits several of my goals. A place where mages can be free, for one." And he wanted a place where Blaise would be happy and safe, but that was too private to share. He suspected Jack already knew, though.

"As long as we're honest," the outlaw drawled, ironic. He rubbed his hands together. "Let's do this."

"There's one more thing I want," Jefferson said, earning a disgruntled look. "But I think you know what that is."

Jack studied him, and for a few heartbeats, Jefferson feared the outlaw would deny him. But instead, Jack asked, "It's not really for you, is it?"

"Not this time."

CHAPTER FIFTY-ONE
Revelations

Blaise

The last few weeks had been strange, but compared to the circus that had been the Inquiry, it was sedate. Blaise didn't mind hunkering down at Jefferson's estate outside Nera. He was far from Izhadell and surrounded by people he was comfortable with. Jack, Kittie, and Emmaline had headed back to Fortitude. But Blaise still had Jefferson, his mother, and Flora—though by day Jefferson was busy, absorbed in a task he assured Blaise he would tell him about soon.

One afternoon, his mother sought him out in the massive kitchen, where he was cutting a small pumpkin in half. The oven was already warm, awaiting the sliced gourd that Blaise planned to set inside to roast. Emrys had asked for a treat, and Blaise had all the time in the world to make a delicious pumpkin pie happen. He glanced up at Marian's arrival but otherwise kept working, scooping seeds into a bowl. "Howdy."

His mother assessed the nearby collection of spices. Cinnamon, ground ginger, nutmeg, and cloves. "I'm glad to see you haven't lost your passion."

Blaise placed the pumpkin halves in the oven, checking the time on his pocket watch. *Take them out in an hour.* "Baking still relaxes me." Though his first few baking sessions had been hard. He banished the memories of those early, difficult days of freedom, turning to face his mother. Marian had been distant, lost in thought over the past few days. "I don't think you came to ask after my baking."

Something flitted across her face, a lightning-quick expression he couldn't identify. Regret? Pain? Fear? Marian shook her head, and she crossed the kitchen to stand beside him. "No. I'm glad to see you're happy with someone."

Blaise allowed himself a small smile. Jefferson had revealed the secret of his dual identity to Marian, insistent that she knew *Malcolm* had cared about Blaise, and he didn't want her to have any misgivings about *Jefferson*. As Blaise predicted, the news made her suspicious. She had been displeased that Malcolm had bound Blaise in the first place, and the duplicity only made things worse. Blaise thought perhaps she had spent the last few days reconciling her son's relationship. Blaise had argued on Jefferson's behalf, assuring his mother that he'd shared her concerns in the past, but no longer did.

"I *am* happy with him," Blaise agreed, enjoying the aroma of roasting pumpkin. He crossed his arms, studying her. Marian lifted her chin high, reminding him of a high-strung horse. Something was on her mind, and it wasn't Jefferson. "You have that look."

She raised her brows, questioning. "What look?"

"The same look you had on your face the day you were told I couldn't go to school anymore." Blaise recalled how difficult that day had been. She'd had the look of someone who knew she was about to lose a fight then, and the same expression was stamped across her face now.

Marian licked her lips, her shoulders drooping. "There's something I need to talk to you about."

He nodded, though old fears tried to take root. It was a difficult thing, shedding the memory of being a shunned outcast. He had friends—*real* friends—now. Someone who loved him. *None of this will be taken away from me.* "What is it?"

Marian rested her forearms against the counter, locking her gaze on the assortment of spices carefully arranged in their tins. "I should have told you long ago, but I..." She took a deep breath, lifting a hand to her face. "I've never pretended to be the perfect mother. I know I'm not. I tried to make up for my mistakes, to do the best for you."

Her words sowed nothing but confusion in Blaise. He couldn't even act like he understood. None of it made sense. "And you did." It was the only thing he could think of to say, and he knew his uncertainty bled into his voice.

His mother shook her head. "No, I didn't. I was foolish to think anything could ever make up for what I'd done to you." Her words were tremulous, and the sheen of tears in her eyes startled Blaise.

What she'd done to me? "Mom, I don't understand." He picked up the tin of cinnamon, if only to give him something familiar to cling to.

"I'm not your mother."

Blaise stared at her, the world around him seeming to slow down, everything contracting to that single, devastating sentence. He dropped the cinnamon, the metal clattering as it struck the counter and rolled against the cloves. Blaise wanted to deny it, to insist what she said simply wasn't true. But the regret reflecting in her eyes spoke the truth.

He blew out a long breath, as if he'd been punched in the stomach by the news. There had to be a reasonable explanation. Marian Hawthorne had raised him as her *son*, for Faedra's sake. "I'm adopted?"

His mother—he refused to think of her as anything else, because she *was* his mother—swallowed a lump in her throat. "Not quite." She glanced toward the small table in the corner of the kitchen. A tray of muffins sat in the middle—one of his earlier projects. Marian moved to the table and pulled out a chair.

Blaise followed, sitting on the opposite side. He plucked a muffin from the tray. He wasn't particularly hungry, but he suspected he might eat his emotions before too long. "If I'm not adopted, then what am I?"

"An experiment."

Blaise felt light-headed, like he couldn't breathe. This couldn't be. But at the same time, he knew it *could* be. *It's what alchemists do. Transmute. Transform.* Mixed components to do the impossible. His magic, stirred by his agitation, flowed up like a protective wave. The muffin crumbled in his hand, raining down on the table. "Tell me what that *means*."

Marian bit her bottom lip. "You know by now that I was a Confederation alchemist. I was full of myself, thinking I could tackle any challenge. Solve any problem with alchemy." She sighed, rubbing her cheek. Marian suddenly looked older than her years. "They tasked me with creating mages."

"Mages are *born*. You can't—" He stopped, realization hitting him. *Jefferson* hadn't been born a mage. That had been attributed to...what? Blaise frowned, struggling to put the pieces together. *Alchemists create the geasa tattoo with blood.* He idly rubbed at the long, pale scar on the soft underside of his arm.

"I can, and I did." Marian's voice was soft. "You were one of the orphans in a test group." She wet her lips, as if the very act of speaking her truth parched them instantly. "You were the only one to survive."

"I wasn't born a Breaker?"

The question hung in the air between them. Marian shook her head. The only sounds punctuating the silence were the ambient noises of the oven, soft pops and crackles. It didn't seem fair, the way that the kitchen was redolent with the warm, comforting scent of roasting pumpkin. Not when Blaise was learning that his life was a lie. His shoulders shook as he braced his arms against the table, his head sinking down until his forehead thudded against the surface.

"I'm not your mother, but I've always loved you as my own," Marian whispered. "Never doubt my love for you."

Blaise squeezed his eyes shut. He wanted to lash out, to yell...*something*. Instead, he felt hollow, like he didn't know who he *was*. He heard the scrape of Marian's chair and then she was there, her arms around him. Blaise thought about shrugging her away. He *hurt*, and *she* had caused this pain. One of the people he thought he could trust.

"Blaise?" she asked.

He shook his head. It was impossible to find the words to say what he wanted to say. Blaise didn't even *know* what he wanted to express. Nothing was adequate to describe the soul-shattering revelation. He lifted his head, rubbing at his eyes.

Marian was watching him, tears glistening on her cheeks. "I'm sorry."

Apologies changed nothing. Didn't change the fact that his life could have—*should have*—been different. He blew out a ragged breath. He wasn't willing to accept her apology, not with this wound so fresh. "Who *are* my parents, then?"

Marian shook her head. "All I know is that they died from the redrot pox going around Izhadell. We had easy pickings among the surviving children." She sighed. "I *am* sorry, Blaise. And I *do* love you, even if you don't believe me right now."

He swallowed, meeting her gaze. "I believe you." *And that's why it hurts so much.*

"I'm sorry I was away longer than expected today," Jefferson apologized as he stepped out onto the veranda. "How have things been here?"

Blaise reclined on a wicker settee, staring up at the twinkling stars overhead. "Just peachy."

Jefferson's green eyes flicked over him, narrowing with concern. "Flora tells me your mother set out to rejoin your family in Rainbow Flat." His inflection at the end almost made it a question.

My family. Were they ever really my family? Blaise levered into a sitting position, running a hand through his hair. It was a mess, but he didn't care. "Did you know?"

Jefferson walked over and sat down beside him, perplexed. "Know what?"

Blaise gestured to himself. "About me. I was born without magic. I could have been *normal*." He put his face in his hands. *I could have avoided so much pain. So much suffering.* Marian had been right. The knowledge stung. He still loved her, but he was allowed to ache from the news she brought.

Jefferson made a soft sound of understanding, and a hand settled on his arm. "Your mother told me after Flora enlisted her help. And I'm sorry I didn't tell you, but it was not my secret to share."

Blaise looked up at Jefferson. "She's not my mother, either." Somehow, he said the words without breaking.

"Oh." The settee creaked as Jefferson settled onto it. His eyes never left Blaise, brimming with so much love and...shared grief? "I had wondered how..." He paused, composing himself. Jefferson started again, his tone neutral. "I had wondered how a mother could do that to her child. I suppose that explains it."

Blaise nodded. He was glad Jefferson was here, glad that he had someone to talk to who knew what it meant to be betrayed by a parent. *But, unlike Malcolm's situation...* "She said she loves me. And I believe her."

"I think she does, too." Jefferson's voice was soft, though also protective. "People can change. However, you're also allowed to be angry."

"I don't want to be angry, but I am." Blaise mopped at his warming face with one hand. "I wasn't supposed to *be* this."

Jefferson wrapped an arm around him. He was quiet for a moment, and Blaise drew comfort from his presence. "Forgive me, but that's where I disagree." He pressed a kiss against Blaise's forehead. "I think you are *exactly* who you need to be."

"The world doesn't need a Breaker."

"Maybe not. But it *does* need you." Jefferson met his eyes. "It's made you who you are today. And for that, I am thankful."

Lips pursed, Blaise wanted to argue, but then he realized what Jefferson was getting at. His life had been riddled with pain, but the brilliance of his best times outshined the shadows of darkness. The friends he had made and the love he had found.

He rubbed at his nose, nodding. Blaise wasn't sure how to respond. *Thank you* seemed too small, so instead, he squeezed Jefferson's hand, earning a smile in response. Blaise straightened, deciding to change the subject. He didn't want to think about what might have been anymore. "Are you going to tell me what you've been up to?"

Jefferson smiled. "Actually, yes." The breeze rolling in from the Gulf of Stars tousled his hair. "I finished tying up Malcolm's loose ends."

Blaise winced. It was easy to forget that as far as they were concerned, Malcolm was dead. He thought it must feel strange to have such a large part of your life *gone*. "I'm sorry." It was more condolence than apology.

Jefferson put an arm around him again. "Don't be. It must be done, and I'm content with who I am now. Happy, even." And he was, that much was clear. It had been no lie when Malcolm claimed he was happier in the guise of Jefferson. It provided a clean slate without the sordid family affairs of the past. "Seledora is executing the will. Oh, and be aware that you now have a house in Izhadell."

"I *what* now?" Blaise stared at him.

Jefferson flashed a mischievous grin. "Malcolm bequeathed the house to you. Seledora found an archaic loophole to take advantage of to make you a very rare land-owning mage in Phinora."

Was that so? Blaise wasn't sure how he felt about that. "But...I don't want it."

Jefferson shrugged. "You can sell it if you like. We rather enjoyed upsetting the apple cart one last time." He winked, his good humor restored by the prospect of defying Phinora's policies.

Blaise shook his head. "No, I won't sell it." He didn't think he could ever sell something like that. But he didn't want to live there, either. How was he going to take care of a place so far away?

Jefferson read the question on his face. "You also were granted a large sum of money for its upkeep."

Blaise relaxed. "Okay. Is that all you're taking care of then?"

"No." Jefferson shifted on the cushioned seat, turning to face Blaise. "Madame Boss Clayton asked if I would put my name in for consideration to replace Malcolm as Doyen for Ganland."

Blaise swallowed. He hadn't even thought about who might fill the empty seat on the Council. Hadn't cared, really. "Oh?"

"I told her no," Jefferson said softly, fiddling with the cabochon ring on his finger. "But I had her ear for something else."

Blaise raised his brows. "And that is?"

Jefferson rose from the chair, moving to lean against the balustrade. Blaise watched him, lips pursed. "Thought I might try my hand at an ambassadorship. Specifically, to the Gutter."

The Gutter? Blaise's face scrunched as he tried to figure out what Jefferson meant. "But the Gutter isn't a country."

"It will be soon. I hope." Jefferson chuckled. "Boss Clayton will certainly agree—she's eager to forge a strong relationship with the Gutter. You're looking at Ambassador Cole." He canted his head to one side. "I mean, I *will* be, at any rate."

Well, then. Blaise rose, closing the distance between them again. "I'm not even going to pretend to know what goes into that. Tell me what it means for us." He was afraid to find out. After his mother's revelation, he was waiting for the other shoe to drop.

Jefferson licked his lips, and Blaise realized he was nervous. "Do you still want there to be an *us*? You've been through a lot and…" He shifted his gaze to the horizon. "I know I come across as too much sometimes."

"You can be *overwhelmingly* intense," Blaise agreed, his stomach fluttering. "If you can handle me and all of my oddities, I can handle you."

Jefferson's shoulders sagged with relief. "I wouldn't have it any other way."

Blaise clasped his hands together. "So, the Gutter? Would we go there?" Excitement laced his voice.

The future Ambassador bumped his shoulder against Blaise. "Yes. As Ambassador, I'm expected to live where I'm assigned. You know, so I can learn the customs. Become better acquainted with the people." He waggled his eyebrows suggestively.

"As long as I'm the only one you're getting *acquainted* with," Blaise muttered.

Jefferson grinned. "Ooh, you *do* get jealous." His eyes twinkled at the glare his words earned him. "I assure you, my life of debauchery is behind me." With all the practice of a politician, he flipped the conversation. "I was hoping to settle in Fortitude. What do you think?"

Blaise swallowed. He had hoped for that, but he wasn't sure. Until this conversation, he hadn't known what prospects he might have. His voice was husky with emotion as he said, "I'd like that a lot."

"I hoped you would," Jefferson murmured, his face close to Blaise's.

They stared into each other's eyes. Blaise's heart thundered in his chest. He was still awkward when it came to love, and intimacy would never be a simple thing for him. But Jefferson accepted that, and it was all he could ask. Blaise grinned, leaning in to close the gap between them.

Jefferson's green eyes sparked with joy as their lips brushed. *Maybe he's right*, Blaise thought as he lost himself in Jefferson's embrace. *I'm exactly who I need to be.*

CHAPTER FIFTY-TWO

Something to Fight For

Blaise

Formerly Itude, Fortitude perched on the canyon wall overlooking the Deadwood River. From Blaise's vantage point on pegasus-back, it looked to have recovered in the time since the attack launched by Lamar Gaitwood. He scratched his head as he tried to think of when that had been. After last year's Feast of Flight. They had missed this year's celebration, still in Ganland at the time while Jefferson finished his final arrangements.

Emrys and Seledora touched down outside the town. The last time he had been here—outside of Jefferson's dreamscape—the town had been in ruins. Blaise swallowed a lump that formed in his throat as he took in the sight. The town was whole and beautiful, the wind-pump towering over the smaller buildings with its long blades spinning lazily in the afternoon breeze.

"Home sweet home, hmm?" Jefferson asked, grinning as he lifted his flight goggles and snapped them against his forehead. He had taken to pegasus flight like it was in his blood, reveling in the opportunity. Blaise was still content to keep his feet on the ground, but everything seemed more palatable with Jefferson by his side.

"Something like that," Blaise agreed, patting Emrys's sweaty shoulder. The stallion folded his wings, the feathers whispering against his rider's legs. A handful of unfamiliar buildings had sprung up along the main streets of the town, and in the distance, frames of new homes were visible. He pulled his own flight goggles off, hanging them on the saddle horn. "Is this a dream? I feel like I'm dreaming."

<If it is, then I'd like to eat my weight in cherry pie,> Emrys suggested, his enormous pink tongue slurping out at the thought.

Jefferson laughed. "Not a dream, so let's not founder any of the pegasi."

<One cherry pie, then. That's reasonable.> The stallion glanced over his shoulder at Blaise. <Oh. We have something to show you.> A zing of delight accompanied his mental words as he flowed forward at a ground-eating trot. Seledora burst after him.

Blaise shot a furtive look at Jefferson, but the other man kept his eyes straight ahead. They were up to something. Emrys nickered with amusement, neck arched as they paraded into the town.

The black stallion drew to a dusty halt in front of a familiar building. The exterior, previously gutted by fire, had been repaired and painted a cheerful yellow. A handful of people stood outside, watching their approach. Jack leaned against a post that supported the porch shade. Emmaline stood nearby, bouncing on the balls of her feet. Clover's forearms rested against the porch railing, her tail flicking at their approach. Vixen whooped a greeting.

Seledora sidled alongside Emrys. Jefferson crossed his wrists over the pommel of his saddle, grinning at Blaise. "It's all yours."

"What?"

<Look up,> Emrys advised.

"Up here!" Emmaline couldn't help adding, gesturing to the name painted above the awning.

Blaise's Bakery.

He stared at it, wondering if he was reading it right. The former building only had the word *Bakery* painted overhead. It was Jack's building. He couldn't imagine the outlaw liking this one bit. Blaise glanced at the Effigest for confirmation.

"It's yours now. If you want it," Jack said with a nonchalant shrug, as if he didn't care one way or the other.

Did he want it? What sort of question was that? Blaise slid out of the saddle, marching up the steps and peering inside the window. A key clinked in the lock, and Emmaline pushed the door open. "Go on in."

Blaise stepped inside, trembling as he took in the interior. Everything had been restored and even improved. The original oven still stood in place, though care had been taken to make sure it was in proper working order. Blaise opened the cabinets, finding new bakeware and utensils. It was too much. He leaned against the island workspace in the middle, face in his hands.

"Is something wrong?" Jefferson's voice was soft as he stepped inside.

Blaise lifted his head, wiping away a tear from one eye. "No. It's...I can't believe it's *mine*. Is it because of our contract?"

Jefferson moved around the island, a puzzled expression on his face. "The contract...oh, *no*. Believe it or not, with all that's gone on, I forgot about that. No, this is because it makes you happy."

<Also because we require delicious treats,> Emrys added, ever helpful.

The stallion must have broadcast to Jefferson as well. The other man gave a small shake of his head and sighed. "Does it make you happy?"

Blaise smiled. "It does." He bowed his head, almost at a loss for words. Everything he had ever wanted—but thought he would never have. It was here, and it was his. All because someone cared about him. He met Jefferson's eyes. "But you know what? *You* make me even happier."

Jefferson stared at him, tapping his fingers against the countertop. "That's music to my ears." He drew closer, heat in his gaze.

<Excuse me, but your pegasi still have full saddlebags and haven't been compensated with cookies yet,> Emrys reminded them.

<You're contractually obligated to provide cookies upon arrival,> Seledora added.

With a laugh, Jefferson pulled away from Blaise, rubbing at the bridge of his nose. "I suppose it's in our best interest to keep my attorney happy."

<Always,> Seledora agreed.

"I'll get them settled if you want to look around a little more," Jefferson offered, putting an arm around Blaise. "Are the leftovers you made in Ganland still in your saddlebag?"

Blaise nodded. "Yes. And...Jefferson? Thank you. For everything." His voice broke at the last. *A bakery.* He had a bakery again, and it was *his*. He ran a hand over the cool smoothness of the counter, already imaging how it would look when he was back at work. Errant crumbs and escaped dustings of flour scattered across the surface.

Jefferson walked to the door, pausing to touch two fingers to his forehead in a salute. He looked as if he wanted to say something but gave a small shake of his head and hurried out to tend to the pegasi. Sometimes no words were necessary.

Jack

JACK SAT ON A SANDSTONE OUTCROPPING OVERLOOKING THE DEADWOOD River as the setting sun painted the horizon like a dazzling canvas. Gold and ochre rays pierced the feathery clouds dappled with violet and crimson. Zepheus grazed nearby, the stallion snorting a warning as someone approached.

"What are you doing brooding over here?" Kittie settled down beside him.

He chuckled. "Not brooding."

She raised her brows. "Are you sure? You certainly look the part, with the thunderous expression on your face."

Had it really looked like that? Jack shook his head. "Nah. Just thinking."

Kittie pressed something cold and flat against his palm. He glanced down, spotting a coin. "Golden eagle for your thoughts?"

Oh, that was a loaded question. He grunted. "I'm thinking about the future. About this thing we want to do." Jack gestured to the yawning canyon before them.

"Your outlaw nation?" Kittie asked.

"*Our* outlaw nation," Jack corrected. He might butt heads with Jefferson, but the dandy was right about who it was for. Folks like Blaise and Emmaline—yeah, they were outlaws in their own right. That couldn't be denied. But they needed a place that would allow them to just *be*. "Even if Ganland has the balls to recognize us, nothing about this is gonna be easy."

Kittie gently lifted the coin from his hand, tucking it into the pouch at her belt. "Since when does *Wildfire Jack* do easy?"

She liked to tease him about his nickname. He didn't regret selecting it, though. No, it had kept her alive to him all those years. Jack crossed his arms. "Easy would be nice for a change of pace."

Kittie unhooked the flask from her belt, offering it to him. He shook his head, and she took a swig. Kittie hadn't drunk like this, not before...everything. Jack figured even a near-sighted knocker could see that alcohol had become her crutch. This was another thing that he knew wouldn't be easy for them. Which was why it would be so *damned nice* if the Confederation didn't have a blasted tantrum over the Gutter.

"Nothing worth fighting for is easy," Kittie mused, though she, too, sounded tired.

The thunder of wings echoed against the canyon walls below. A sentry pegasus flew into view, the brilliant sunset glinting on the outstretched feathers of the sorrel tobiano mare. She was one of the new pegasi mares who had arrived at Fortitude recently, excited by the prospect of a livelihood. Lured to the rebuilt town by Jefferson's smooth-talking Seledora, much to the delight of the resident stallions.

Things in their world were changing. A smile touched Jack's lips. He leaned over and pressed a kiss to Kittie's forehead, enjoying the scent of smoke that wafted from her hair. "Not gonna be easy, no. But we're gonna make it happen."

They had to. The only other option was the Confederation crushing them, and Jack wouldn't allow that. He pushed those thoughts to the wayside, though, as Kittie leaned against him. She was solid and warm, and Jack almost felt as if he were dreaming as he watched the setting sun paint the walls of the canyon in new, darker hues.

This. This peace, this love, is something to fight for. He smiled.

The adventure continues in *Dreamer*.

Stay In the Know!

Thank you for reading Breaker and Effigest!
    Sign up to my newsletter for sneak peeks, short stories, and more!
www.amycampbell.info

And for exclusive early access to books and to join my reader community,
head over to Ream! https://reamstories.com/amycampbell

ABOUT THE AUTHOR

Amy Campbell is an independent author based in her hometown of Houston, Texas. With a passion for unusual fantasy adventures, she crafts novels that celebrate individuals unapologetically embracing their true selves. Adding a touch of enchantment, Amy weaves tales of captivating creatures like dragons and pegasi. Amy's dedication to writing has led her to pursue a full-time career as an author. When she's not immersed in the creative process, she spends time with her children.